The Monsieur Lecoq of the Sûreté Mysteries

Volume 3

The Monsieur Lecoq of the Sûreté Mysteries

Volume 3

Two volumes in One Edition

The Slaves of Paris

Émile Gaboriau

LEONAUR

The Monsieur Lecoq of the Sûreté Mysteries
Volume 3
Two Volumes in One Edition
The Slaves of Paris
by Émile Gaboriau

First published under the title
The Slaves of Paris volumes 1 & 2

Leonaur is an imprint of Oakpast Ltd

ISBN: 978-1-78282-802-0 (hardcover)
ISBN: 978-1-78282-803-7 (softcover)

http://www.leonaur.com

Publisher's Notes

The views expressed in this book are not necessarily
those of the publisher.

Contents

Chapter 1: Putting On the Screw

The cold on the 8th of February, 186-, was more intense than the Parisians had experienced during the whole of the severe winter which had preceded it, for at twelve o'clock on that day Chevalier's thermometer, so well known by the denizens of Paris, registered three degrees below zero. The sky was overcast and full of threatening signs of snow, while the moisture on the pavement and roads had frozen hard, rendering traffic of all kinds exceedingly hazardous. The whole great city wore an air of dreariness and desolation, for even when a thin crust of ice covers the waters of the Seine, the mind involuntarily turns to those who have neither food, shelter, nor fuel.

This bitterly cold day actually made the landlady of the Hotel de Perou, though she was a hard, grasping woman of Auvergne, gave a thought to the condition of her lodgers, and one quite different from her usual idea of obtaining the maximum of rent for the minimum of accommodation.

"The cold," remarked she to her husband, who was busily engaged in replenishing the stove with fuel, "is enough to frighten the wits out of a Polar bear. In this kind of weather I always feel very anxious, for it was during a winter like this that one of our lodgers hung himself, a trick which cost us fifty *francs*, in good, honest money, besides giving us a bad name in the neighbourhood. The fact is, one never knows what lodgers are capable of doing. You should go up to the top floor, and see how they are getting on there."

"Pooh, pooh!" replied her husband, M. Loupins; "they will do well enough."

"Is that really your opinion?"

"I know that I am right. Daddy Tantaine went out as soon as it was light, and a short time afterward Paul Violaine came down. There is no one upstairs now but little Rose, and I expect that she has been wise enough to stick to her bed."

"Ah!" answered the landlady rather spitefully. "I have made up my mind regarding that young lady some time ago; she is a sight too pretty for this house, and so I tell you."

The Hotel de Perou stands in the Rue de la Hachette, not twenty steps from the Place de Petit Pont; and no more cruelly sarcastic title could ever have been conferred on a building. The extreme shabbiness of the exterior of the house, the narrow, muddy street in which it stood, the dingy windows covered with mud, and repaired with every variety of patch,—all seemed to cry out to the passers by: "This is the chosen abode of misery and destitution."

The observer might have fancied it a robbers' den, but he would have been wrong; for the inhabitants were fairly honest. The Hotel de Perou was one of those refuges, growing scarcer and more scarce every day, where unhappy men and women, who had been worsted in the battle of life, could find a shelter in return for the change remaining from the last five-*franc* piece. They treat it as the shipwrecked mariner uses the rock upon which he climbs from the whirl of the angry waters, and breathes a deep sigh of relief as he collects his forces for a fresh effort. However wretched existence may be, a protracted sojourn in such a shelter as the Hotel de Perou would be out of the question. The chambers in every floor of the house are divided into small slips by partitions, covered with canvas and paper, and pleasantly termed rooms by M. Loupins.

The partitions were in a terrible condition, rickety and unstable, and the paper with which they were covered torn and hanging down in tatters; but the state of the attics was even more deplorable, the ceilings of which were so low that the occupants had to stoop continually, while the dormer windows admitted but a small amount of light. A bedstead, with a straw mattress, a rickety table, and two broken chairs, formed the sole furniture of these rooms. Miserable as these dormitories were, the landlady asked and obtained twenty-two *francs* for them by the month, as there was a fireplace in each, which she always pointed out to intending tenants.

The young woman whom M. Loupins alluded to by the name of Rose was seated in one of these dreary dens on this bitter winter's day. Rose was an exquisitely beautiful girl about eighteen years of age. She was very fair; her long lashes partially concealed a pair of steely blue eyes, and to a certain extent relieved their hard expression. Her ripe, red lips, which seemed formed for love and kisses, permitted a glimpse of a row of pearly teeth. Her bright waving hair grew low down upon her forehead, and such of it as had escaped from the bondage of a cheap comb, with which it was fastened, hung in wild luxuriance over her exquisitely shaped neck and shoulders.

She had thrown over her ragged print gown the patched coverlet of the bed, and, crouched upon the tattered hearthrug before the hearth, upon which a few sticks smouldered, giving out hardly a particle of heat, she was telling her fortune with a dirty pack of cards, endeavouring to console herself for the privations of the day by the promise of future prosperity. She had spread those arbiters of her destiny in a half circle before her, and divided them into threes, each of which had a peculiar meaning, and her breast rose and fell as she turned them up and read upon their faces good fortune or ill-luck. Absorbed in this task, she paid but little attention to the icy chilliness of the atmosphere, which made her fingers stiff, and dyed her white hands purple.

"One, two, three," she murmured in a low voice. "A fair man, that's sure to be Paul. One, two, three, money to the house. One, two, three, troubles and vexations. One, two, three, the nine of spades; ah, dear! more hardships and misery,—always that wretched card turning up with its sad story!"

Rose seemed utterly downcast at the sight of the little piece of painted cardboard, as though she had received certain intelligence of a coming misfortune. She soon, however, recovered herself, and was again shuffling the pack,—cut it, taking care to do so with her left hand, spread them out before her, and again commenced counting: one, two, three. This time the cards appeared to be more propitious, and held out promises of success for the future.

"I am loved," read she, as she gazed anxiously upon them,—"very much loved! Here is rejoicing, and a letter from a dark man! See, here he is,—the knave of clubs. Always the same," she continued; "I cannot strive against fate."

Then, rising to her feet, she drew from a crack in the wall, which formed a safe hiding-place for her secrets, a soiled and crumpled letter, and, unfolding it, she read for perhaps the hundredth time these words:

Mademoiselle,—
To see you is to love you. I give you my word of honour that this is true. The wretched hovel where your charms are hidden is no fit abode for you. A home, worthy in every way to receive you, is at your service—Rue de Douai. It has been taken in your name, as I am straightforward in these matters. Think of my proposal, and make what inquiries you like concerning

me. I have not yet attained my majority, but shall do so in five months and three days, when I shall inherit my mother's fortune. My father is wealthy, but old and infirm. From four to six in the afternoon of the next few days I will be in a carriage at the corner of the Place de Petit Pont.

Gaston De Gandelu

The cynical insolence of the letter, together with its entire want of form, was a perfect example of the style affected by those loiterers about town, known to the Parisians as "mashers;" and yet Rose did not appear at all disgusted by the reception of such an unworthily worded proposal, but, on the contrary, rather pleased by its contents. "If I only dared," mused she, with a sigh,—"ah, if I only dared!" For a time she sat deeply immersed in thought, with her face buried in her hands, until she was aroused from her meditations by the sound of an active and youthful step upon the creaking stairs. "He has come back," she gasped; and with the agile movement of a cat she again concealed the letter in its hiding-place, and she had scarcely done so, when Paul Violaine entered the miserable room. He was a young man of twenty-three, of slender figure, but admirably proportioned.

His face was a perfect oval, and his complexion of just that slight olive tint which betrays the native of the south of France. A slight, silky moustache concealed his upper lip, and gave his features that air of manliness in which they would have otherwise been deficient. His curly chestnut hair fell gracefully over a brow upon which an expression of pride was visible, and enhanced the peculiar, restless glance of his large dark eyes. His physical beauty, which was fully equal to that of Rose, was increased by an aristocratic air, popularly believed to be only found in the scions of noble families. The landlady, in her moments of good humour, used to assert her belief that her lodger was a disguised prince; but if this were the case, he was certainly one that had been overtaken by poverty. His dress, to which the closest attention had been paid, revealed the state of destitution in which he was,—not the destitution which openly asks for alms, but the hidden poverty which shuns communication and blushes at a single glance of pity.

In this almost Arctic winter he wore clothes rendered thin by the constant friction of the clothes brush, over which was a light overcoat about as thick as the web of a spider. His shoes were well blacked, but their condition told the piteous tale of long walks in search of employment, or of that good luck which seems to evade its pursuer.

Paul was holding a roll of manuscript in his hand, and as he entered the room he threw it on the bed with a despairing gesture. "A failure again!" exclaimed he, in accents of the utmost depression. "Nothing else but failures!"

The young woman rose hastily to her feet; she appeared to have forgotten the cards completely; the smile of satisfaction faded from her face and her features, and an expression of utter weariness took its place.

"What! no success?" she cried, affecting a surprise which was evidently assumed. "No success, after all your promises when you left me this morning?"

"This morning, Rose, a ray of hope had penetrated my heart; but I have been deceived, or rather I deceived myself, and I took my ardent desires for so many promises which were certain to be fulfilled. The people that I have been to have not even the kindness to say 'No' plain and flat; they listen to all you have to say, and as soon as your back is turned they forget your existence. The coin that passes around in this infernal town is indeed nothing but idle words, and that is all that poverty-stricken talent can expect."

A silence of some duration ensued, and Paul was too much absorbed in his own thoughts to notice the look of contempt with which Rose was regarding him. His helpless resignation to adverse circumstances appeared to have turned her to stone.

"A nice position we are in!" said she at last. "What do you think will become of us?"

"Alas! I do not know."

"Nor I. Yesterday Madame Loupins came to me and asked for the eleven *francs* we owe here; and told me plainly that if within three days we did not settle our account, she would turn us out; and I know enough of her to be sure that she will keep her word. The detestable old hag would do anything for the pleasure of seeing me on the streets."

"Alone and friendless in the world," muttered Paul, paying but little attention to the young girl's words, "without a creature or a relative to care for you, or to lend you a helping hand."

"We have not a copper in the world," continued Rose with cruel persistency; "I have sold everything that I had, to preserve the rags that I am wearing. Not a scrap of wood remains, and we have not tasted food since yesterday morning."

To these words, which were uttered in a tone of the most bitter re-

11

proach, the young man made no reply, but clasped his icily cold hands against his forehead, as though in utter despair.

"Yes, that is a true picture of our position," resumed Rose coldly, her accents growing more and more contemptuous. "And I tell you that something must be done at once, some means discovered, I care not what, to relieve us from our present miserable state."

Paul tore off his overcoat, and held it toward her.

"Take it, and pawn it," exclaimed he; but the girl made no move.

"Is that all that you have to propose?" asked she, in the same glacial tone.

"They will lend you three *francs* upon it, and with that we can get bread and fuel."

"And after that is gone?"

"After that—oh, we will think of our next step, and shall have time to hit upon some plan. Time, a little time, is all that I require, Rose, to break asunder the bonds which seem to fetter me. Some day success must crown my efforts; and with success, Rose, dear, will come afflu-ence, but in the meantime we must learn to wait."

"And where are the means to enable us to wait?"

"No matter; they will come. Only do what I tell you, and who can say what tomorrow—"

Paul was still too much absorbed in his own thoughts to notice the expression upon the young girl's face; for had he done so, he would at once have perceived that she was not in the humour to permit the matter to be shelved in this manner.

"Tomorrow!" she broke in sarcastically. "Tomorrow,—always the same pitiful cry. For months past we seem to have lived upon the word. Look you here, Paul, you are no longer a child, and ought to be able to look things straight in the face. What can I get on that thread-bare coat of yours? Perhaps three *francs* at the outside. How many days will that last us? We will say three. And then, what then? Besides, can you not understand that your dress is too shabby for you to make an impression on the people you go to see? Well-dressed applicants only have attention, and to obtain money, you must appear not to need it; and, pray, what will people think of you if you have no overcoat? Without one you will look ridiculous, and can hardly venture into the streets."

"Hush!" cried Paul, "for pity's sake, hush! for your words only prove to me more plainly that you are like the rest of the world, and that want of success is a pernicious crime in your eyes. You once had

12

confidence in me, and then you spoke in a very different strain."

"Once indeed! but then I did not know—"

"No, Rose, it was not what you were then ignorant of; but it was that in those days you loved me."

"Great heavens! I ask you, have I left one stone unturned? Have I not gone from publisher to publisher to sell those songs of my own composing—those songs that you sing so well? I have endeavoured to get pupils. What fresh efforts can I try? What would *you* do, were you in my place? Tell me, I beg you."

And as Paul spoke, he grew more and more excited, while Rose still maintained her manner of exasperating coolness.

"I know not," she replied, after a brief pause; "but if I were a man, I do not think I would permit the woman, for whom I pretended that I had the most sincere affection, to be in want of the actual necessities of life. I would strain every effort to obtain them."

"I have no trade; I am no mechanic," broke in Paul passionately.

"Then I would learn one. Pray how much does a man earn who climbs the ladder with a bricklayer's hod upon his shoulders? It may be hard work, I know, but surely the business is not difficult to learn. You have, or say you have, great musical talents. I say nothing about them; but had I any vocal powers and if there was not a morsel to eat in the house, I would go and sing in the taverns or even in the public streets, and would earn money, and care little for the means by which I made it."

"When you say those things, you seem to forget that I am an honest man."

"One would really suppose that I had suggested some questionable act to you. Your reply, Paul, plainly proves to me that you are one of those who, for want of determination, fall, helpless, by the wayside in the journey of life. They flaunt their rags and tatters in the eyes of the world, and with saddened hearts and empty stomachs utter the boast, 'I am an honest man.' Do you think that, in order to be rich, you must perforce be a rogue? This is simple imbecility."

She uttered this tirade in clear and vibrant accents, and her eyes gleamed with the fire of savage resolution. Her nature was one of those cruel and energetic ones, which lead a woman to hurl a man from the brink of the abyss to which she had conducted him, and to forget him before he has ever reached the bottom.

This torrent of sarcasm brought out Paul's real nature. His face flushed, and rage began to gain the mastery over him. "Can you not work?" he asked. "Why do you not do something instead of talking so much?"

"That is not at all the same thing," answered she coolly. "I was not made for work."

Paul made a threatening gesture. "You wretch!" exclaimed he.

"You are wrong," she replied. "I am not a wretch; I am simply hungry."

There seemed every prospect of an angry scene, when a slight sound attracted the attention of the disputants, and, turning round, they saw an old man standing upon the threshold of their open door. He was tall, but stooped a good deal. He had high, thick brows, and a red nose; a long, thick, grizzly beard covered the rest of his countenance. He wore a pair of spectacles with coloured glasses, which, to a great extent, concealed the expression of his face. His whole attire indicated extreme poverty. He wore a greasy coat, much frayed and torn at the pockets, and which had carried away with it marks of all the walls against which it had been rubbed when he had indulged a little too freely in the cheerful glass. He seemed to belong to that class who consider it a work of supererogation to disrobe before going to bed, and who just turn in on such spot as the fancy of the moment may dictate. Paul and Rose both recognised the old man from having continually met him when ascending or descending the staircase, and knew that he rented the back attic, and was called Daddy Tantaine. In an instant the idea flashed across Paul's mind that the dilapidated state of the partition permitted every word spoken in one attic to be overheard in the other, and this did not tend to soothe his exasperated feelings.

"What do you want here, sir?" asked he angrily. "And, pray, who gave you permission to enter my room without leave?"

The old man did not seem at all put out by the threatening language of his questioner. "I should be telling a fib," answered he calmly, "if I were to tell you that, being in my own room and hearing you quarrelling, I did not hear every word of what you have been saying."

"Sir!"

"Stop a bit, and don't be in such a hurry, my young friend. You seem disposed to quarrel, and, on my faith, I am not surprised; for when there is no corn in the manger, the best tempered horse will bite and kick."

He uttered these words in the most soothing accents, and appeared utterly unconscious of having committed any breach of etiquette in entering the room.

"Well, sir," said Paul, a flush of shame passing across his face, "you see now how poverty can drag a man down. Are you satisfied?"

"Come, come, my young friend," answered Daddy Tantaine, "you should not get angry; and if I did step in without any notice, it was because, as a neighbour, I find I might venture on such a liberty; for when I heard how embarrassed you were, I said to myself, 'Tantaine, perhaps you can help this pretty pair out of the scrape they have got into.'"

The promise of assistance from a person who had not certainly the outward appearance of a capitalist seemed so ludicrous to Rose that she could not restrain a smile, for she fancied that if their old neighbour was to present them with half his fortune, it might possibly amount to twenty *centimes* or thereabouts.

Paul had formed a somewhat similar idea, but he was a little touched by this act of friendliness on the part of a man who doubtless knew that money lent under similar circumstances was but seldom returned.

"Ah, sir!" said he, and this time he spoke in softer accents, "what can you possibly do for us?"

"Who can say?"

"You can see how hard we are pushed. We are in want of almost everything. Have we not reached the *acme* of misery?"

The old man raised his hand to heaven, as if to seek for aid from above.

"You have indeed come to a terrible pass," murmured he; "but all is not yet lost. The pearl which lies in the depths of the ocean is not lost for ever; for may not some skilful diver bring it to the surface? A fisherman may not be able to do much with it, but he knows something of its value, and hands it over to the dealer in precious stones."

He intensified his speech by a little significant laugh, the meaning of which was lost upon the two young people who, though their evil instincts led them to be greedy and covetous, were yet unskilled in the world's ways.

"I should," remarked Paul, "be a fool if I did not accept the offer of your kind assistance."

"There, then, that is right; and now the first thing to do is to have a really good feed. You must get in some wood too, for it is frightfully cold. My old bones are half frozen; and afterward we will talk of a fresh rig out for you both."

"Yes," remarked Rose with a faint sigh; "but to do all that, we want a lot of money."

"Well, how do you know that I can't find it?"

Daddy Tantaine unbuttoned his great coat with grave deliberation, and drew from an inner pocket a small scrap of paper which had been fastened to the lining by a pin. This he unfolded with the greatest of care and laid upon the table.

"A banknote for five hundred *francs!*" exclaimed Rose, with extreme surprise. Paul did not utter a word. Had he seen the woodwork of the chair upon which he was leaning burst into flower and leaf, he could not have looked more surprised. Who could have expected to find such a sum concealed beneath the old man's tatters, and how could he have obtained so much money? The idea that some robbery had been committed at once occurred to both the young people, and they exchanged a meaning glance, which, however, did not escape the observation of their visitor.

"Pooh, pooh!" said he, without appearing in the slightest degree annoyed. "You must not give way to evil thoughts or suspicions. It is a fact that banknotes for five hundred *francs* don't often grow out of a ragged pocket like mine. But I got this fellow honestly,—that I can guarantee."

Rose paid no attention to his words; indeed, she took no interest in them. The note was there, and that was enough for her. She took it up and smoothed it out as though the crisp paper communicated a pleasant sensation to her fingers.

"I must tell you," resumed Daddy Tantaine, "that I am employed by a sheriff's officer, and that, in addition, I do a little bill collecting for various persons. By these means I have often comparatively large sums in my possession, and I can lend you five hundred *francs* for a short time without any inconvenience to myself."

Paul's necessities and conscience were fighting a hard battle, and he remained silent, as a person generally does before arriving at a momentous decision.

At length he broke the silence. "No," said he, "your offer is one that I cannot accept, for I feel—"

"This is no time, my dear Paul, to talk of feelings," interrupted Rose; "besides, can you not see that our refusal to accept the loan annoys this worthy gentleman?"

"The young lady is quite right," returned Daddy Tantaine. "Come, let us say that the matter is settled. Go out and get in something to eat, sharp, for it has struck four some time ago."

At these words, Rose started, and a scarlet flush spread over her cheek. "Four o'clock," repeated she, thinking of her letter; but after a moment's reflection she stepped up to the cracked mirror, and arranging her tattered skirts, took up the banknote and left the room.

"She is a rare beauty," remarked Daddy Tantaine with the air of one who was an authority in such matters, "and as clever as they make them. Ah! if she had only someone to give her a hint, she might rise to any height."

Paul's ideas were in such a wild state of confusion, that he could make no reply; and, now that he was no longer held in thrall by Rose's presence, he began to be terrified at what had taken place, for he imagined that he caught a sinister expression in the old man's face which made him very suspicious of the wisdom of the course he had been persuaded to pursue. Was there ever such an unheard-of event as an old man of such a poverty-stricken appearance showering banknotes upon the heads of perfect strangers? There was certainly something mysterious in the affair, and Paul made up his mind that he would do his utmost to avoid being compromised.

"I have thought the matter over," said he resolutely; "and it is impossible for me to accept the loan of a sum which it would be difficult for me to repay."

"My dear young friend, that is not the way to talk. If you do not have a good opinion of yourself, all the world will judge you according to your own estimation. Your inexperience has, up to this time, been the sole cause of your failure. Poverty soon changes a boy into a man as straw ripens fruit; but the first thing you must do is to put all confidence in me. You can repay the five hundred *francs* at your convenience, but I must have six *per cent.* for my money and your note of hand."

"But really—," began Paul.

"I am looking at the matter in a purely business light, so we can drop sentiment."

Paul had so little experience in the ways of the world, that the mere fact of giving his acceptance for the money borrowed put him at once at his ease, though he knew well that his name was not a very valuable addition to the slip of paper.

Daddy Tantaine, after a short search through his pockets, discovered a bill stamp, and, placing it on the table, said, "Write as I shall dictate:—

17

On the 8th of June, 188-, I promise to pay to M. Tantaine or order the sum of five hundred *francs* for value received, such sum to bear interest at the rate of six *per cent. per annum.*
Frs. 500.

Paul Violaine.

The young man had just completed his signature when Rose made her appearance, bearing a plentiful stock of provisions in her arms. Her eyes had a strange radiance in them, which Paul, however, did not notice, as he was engaged in watching the old man, who, after carefully inspecting the document, secured it in one of the pockets of his ragged coat.

"You will, of course, understand, sir," remarked Paul, "that there is not much chance of my being able to save sufficient to meet this bill in four months, so that the date is a mere form."

A smile of benevolence passed over Daddy Tantaine's features. "And suppose," said he, "that I, the lender, was to put the borrower in a position to repay the advance before a month had passed?"

"Ah! but that is not possible."

"I do not say, my young friend, that I could do this myself; but I have a good friend whose hand reaches a long way. If I had only listened to his advice when I was younger, you would not have caught me today in the Hotel de Perou. Shall I introduce you to him?"

"Am I a perfect fool, to throw away such a chance?"

"Good! I shall see him this evening, and will mention your name to him. Call on him at noon tomorrow, and if he takes a fancy to you,—decides to push you, your future is assured, and you will have no doubts as to getting on."

He took out a card from his pocket and handed it to Paul, adding, "The name of my friend is Mascarin."

Meanwhile Rose, with a true Parisian's handiness, had contrived to restore order from chaos, and had arranged the table, with its one or two pieces of broken crockery, with scraps of brown paper instead of plates. A fresh supply of wood crackled bravely on the hearth, and two candles, one of which was placed in a chipped bottle, and the other in a tarnished candlestick belonging to the porter of the hotel. In the eyes of both the young people the spectacle was a truly delightful one, and Paul's heart swelled with triumph. The business had been satisfactorily concluded, and all his misgivings were at an end.

"Come, let us gather round the festive board," said he joyously.

"This is breakfast and dinner in one. Rose, be seated; and you, my dear friend, will surely share with us the repast we owe to you?"

With many protestations of regret, however, Daddy Tantaine pleaded an important engagement at the other end of Paris. "And," added he, "it is absolutely necessary that I should see Mascarin this evening, for I must try my best to make him look on you with a favourable eye."

Rose was very glad when the old man took his departure, for his ugliness, the shabbiness of his dress, and his general aspect of dirt, drove away all the feelings of gratitude she ought to have evinced, and inspired in her loathing and repugnance; and she fancied that his eyes, though veiled by his coloured glasses, could detect the minutest secrets of her heart; but still this did not prevent her putting on a sweet smile and entreating him to remain.

But Daddy Tantaine was resolute; and after impressing upon Paul the necessity of punctuality, he went away, repeating, as he passed through the door, "May good appetite be present at your little feast, my dears."

As soon, however, as the door was closed he bent down and listened. The young people were as merry as larks, and their laughter filled the bare attic of the Hotel de Perou. Why should not Paul have been in good spirits? He had in his pocket the address of the man who was to make his fortune, and on the chimney-piece was the balance of the banknote, which seemed to him an inexhaustible sum. Rose, too, was delighted, and could not refrain from jeering at their benefactor, whom she stigmatized as "an old idiot."

"Laugh while you can, my dears!" muttered Daddy Tantaine; "for this may be the last time you will do so."

With these words he crept down the dark staircase, which was only lighted up on Sundays, owing to the high price of gas, and, peeping through the glass door of the porter's lodge, saw Madame Loupins engaged in cooking; and, with the timid knock of a man who has learned his lesson in poverty's grammar, he entered.

"Here is my rent, *madame*," said he, placing on the table ten *francs* and twenty *centimes*. Then, as the woman was scribbling a receipt, he launched into a statement of his own affairs, and told her that he had come into a little property which would enable him to live in comfort during his few remaining years on earth; and—evidently fearing that his well-known poverty might cause Madame Loupins to discredit his assertions—drew out his pocketbook and exhibited several banknotes.

This exhibition of wealth so surprised the landlady, that when the old man left she insisted on lighting him to the door. He turned eastward as soon as he had left the house, and, glancing at the names of the shops, entered a grocer's establishment at the corner of the Rue de Petit Pont. This grocer, thanks to a certain cheap wine, manufactured for him by a chemist at Bercy, had achieved a certain notoriety in that quarter. He was very stout and pompous, a widower, and a sergeant in the National Guard. His name was Melusin.

In all poor districts five o'clock is a busy hour for the shopkeepers, for the workmen are returning from their labours, and their wives are busy in their preparations for their evening meal. M. Melusin was so busily engaged, giving orders and seeing that they were executed, that he did not even notice the entrance of Daddy Tantaine; but had he done so, he would not have put himself out for so poorly dressed a customer. But the old man had left behind him in the Hotel de Perou every sign of humility and servility, and, making his way to the least crowded portion of the shop, he called out in imperative accents, "M. Melusin!"

Very much surprised, the grocer ceased his avocation and hastened to obey the summons. "How the deuce does the man know me?" muttered he, forgetting that his name was over the door in gilt letters fully six inches long.

"Sir," said Daddy Tantaine, without giving the grocer time to speak, "did not a young woman come here about half an hour ago and change a note for five hundred *francs*?"

"Most certainly," answered M. Melusin; "but how did you know that? Ah, I have it!" he added, striking his forehead; "there has been a robbery, and you are in pursuit of the criminal. I must confess that the girl looked so poor, that I guessed there was something wrong. I saw her fingers tremble."

"Pardon me," returned Daddy Tantaine. "I have said nothing about a robbery. I only wished to ask you if you would know the girl again?"

"Perfectly—a really splendid girl, with hair that you do not see every day. I have reason to believe that she lives in the Rue Hachette. The police are not very popular with the shopkeeping class; but the latter, desirous of keeping down crime, generally afford plenty of information, and in the interests of virtue will even risk losing customers, who go off in a huff at not being attended to while they are talking to the officers of justice. Shall I," continued the grocer, "send one of the errand boys to the nearest police station?"

"No, thank you," replied Daddy Tantaine. "I should prefer your keeping the matter quiet until I communicate with you once more."

"Yes, yes, I see; a false step just now would put them on their guard."

"Just so. Now, will you let me have the number of the note, if you still have it? I wish you also to make a note of the date as well as the number."

"Yes, yes, I see," returned the grocer. "You may require my books as corroborative evidence; that is often the way. Excuse me; I will be back directly."

All that Daddy Tantaine had desired was executed with the greatest rapidity, and he and the grocer parted on the best terms, and the tradesman watched his visitor's departure, perfectly satisfied that he had been assisting a police officer who had deemed it fit to assume a disguise. Daddy Tantaine cared little what he thought, and, gaining the Place de Petit Pont, stopped and gazed around as if he was waiting for someone. Twice he walked round it in vain; but in his third circuit he came to a halt with an exclamation of satisfaction, for he had seen the person of whom he had been in search, who was a detestable looking youth of about eighteen years of age, though so thin and stunted that he hardly appeared to be fifteen.

The lad was leaning against the wall of the Quay St. Michel, openly asking alms, but keeping a sharp lookout for the police. At the first glance it was easy to detect in him the hideous outgrowth of the great city, the regular young rough of Paris, who, at eight years of age, smokes the butt ends of cigars picked up at the tavern doors and gets tipsy on coarse spirits. He had a thin crop of sandy hair, his complexion was dull and colourless, and a sneer curled the corners of his mouth, which had a thick, hanging underlip, and his eyes had an expression in them of revolting cynicism. His dress was tattered and dirty, and he had rolled up the sleeve of his right arm, exhibiting a deformed limb, sufficiently repulsive to excite the pity of the passers by. He was repeating a monotonous whine, in which the words "poor workman, arm destroyed by machinery, aged mother to support," occurred continually.

Daddy Tantaine walked straight up to the youth, and with a sound cuff sent his hat flying.

The lad turned sharply round, evidently in a terrible rage; but, recognising his assailant, shrank back, and muttered to himself, "Landed!" In an instant he restored his arm to its originally healthy condition, and, picking up his cap, replaced it on his head, and humbly waited for fresh orders.

"Is this the way you execute your errands?" asked Daddy Tantaine, snarling.

"What errands? I have heard of none!"

"Never you mind that. Did not M. Mascarin, on my recommendation, put you in the way of earning your livelihood? and did you not promise to give up begging?"

"Beg pardon, guv'nor, I meant to be on the square, but I didn't like to waste time while I was a-waiting. I don't like a-being idle and I have copped seven browns."

"Toto Chupin," said the old man, with great severity, "you will certainly come to a bad end. But come, give your report. What have you seen?"

During this conversation they were walking slowly along the quay, and had passed the Hotel Dieu.

"Well, guv'nor," replied the young rogue, "I just saw what you said I should. At four sharp, a carriage drove into the Place, and pulled up bang opposite the wigmaker's. Dash me, if it weren't a swell turn-out!—horse, coachman, and all, in real slap-up style. It waited so long that I thought it had taken root there."

"Come, get on! Was there anyone inside?"

"I should think there was! I twigged him at once, by the description you gave me. I never see a cove togged out as he was,—tall hat, light sit-down-upons, and a short coat—wasn't it cut short! but in really bang-up style. To be certain, I went right up to him, for it was getting dark, and had a good look at him. He had got out of the trap, and was marching up and down the pavement, with an unlighted cigar stuck in his mouth. I took a match, and said, 'Have a light, my noble swell?' and hanged if he didn't give me ten *centimes*! My! ain't he ugly!—short, shrivelled up, and knock-kneed, with a glass in his eye, and altogether precious like a monkey."

Daddy Tantaine began to grow impatient with all this rigmarole. "Come, tell me what took place," said he angrily.

"Precious little. The young swell didn't seem to care about dirtying his trotter-cases; he kept slashing about with his cane, and staring at all the gals. What an ass that masher is! Wouldn't I have liked to have punched his head! If you ever want to hide him, daddy, please think of yours truly. He wouldn't stand up to me for five minutes."

"Go on, my lad; go on."

"Well, we had waited half an hour, when all at once a woman came sharp round the corner, and stops before the masher. Wasn't she a fine gal! and hadn't she a pair of sparklers! but she had awfully seedy togs on. But they spoke in whispers."

"So you did not hear what they said?"

"Do you take me for a flat? The gal said, 'Do you understand?—tomorrow.' Then the swell chap, says he, 'Do you promise?' and the gal, she answers back, 'Yes, at noon.' Then they parted. She went off to the Rue Hachette, and the masher tumbled into his wheel box. The *jarvey* cracked his whip, and off they went in a brace of shakes. Now hand over them five *francs*."

Daddy Tantaine did not seem surprised at this request, and he gave over the money to the young loafer, with the words, "When I promise, I pay down on the nail; but remember Toto Chupin, you'll come to grief one day. Goodnight. Our ways lie in different directions."

The old man, however, lingered until he had seen the lad go off toward the Jardin des Plantes, and then, turning round, went back by the way he had come. "I have not lost my day," murmured he. "All the improbabilities have turned out certainties, and matters are going straight. Won't Flavia be awfully pleased?"

Chapter 2: A Registry Office

The establishment of the influential friend of Daddy Tantaine was situated in the Rue Montorgeuil, not far from the Passage de la Reine Hortense. M. B. Mascarin has a registry office for the engagement of both male and female servants. Two boards fastened upon each side of the door announce the hours of opening and closing, and give a list of those whose names are on the books; they further inform the public that the establishment was founded in 1844, and is still in the same hands. It was the long existence of M. Mascarin in a business which is usually very short-lived that had obtained for him a great amount of confidence, not only in the quarter in which he resided, but throughout the whole of Paris. Employers say that he sends them the best of servants, and the domestics in their turn assert that he only despatches them to good places.

But M. Mascarin has still further claims on the public esteem; for it was he who, in 1845, founded and carried out a project which had for its aim and end the securing of a shelter for servants out of place. The better to carry out this, Mascarin took a partner, and gave him the charge of a furnished house close to the office. Worthy as these projects were, Mascarin contrived to draw considerable profit from them, and was the owner of the house before which, in the noon of the day following the events we have described, Paul Violaine might have been seen standing. The five hundred *francs* of old Tantaine, or at any rate a portion of them, had been well spent, and his clothes did credit to his own taste and the skill of his tailor. Indeed, in his fine feathers he looked so handsome, that many women turned to gaze after him. He however took but little notice of this, for he was too full of anxiety, having grave doubts as to the power of the man whom Tantaine had asserted could, if he liked, make his fortune. "A registry office!" muttered he scornfully. "Is he going to propose a berth of a hundred *francs* a month to me?" He was much agitated at the thoughts of the impending interview, and, before entering the house, gazed upon its exterior with great interest. The house much resembled its neighbours. The entrances to the Registry Office and the Servants' Home were in the courtyard, at the arched entrance to which stood a vendor of roast chestnuts.

"There is no use in remaining here," said Paul. Summoning, therefore, all his resolution, he crossed the courtyard, and, ascending a flight of stairs, paused before a door upon which "OFFICE" was written. "Come in!" responded at once to his knock. He pushed open the door, and entered a room, which closely resembled all other similar offices. There were seats all round the room, polished by frequent use. At the end was a sort of compartment shut in by a green baize curtain, jestingly termed "the Confessional" by the frequenters of the office. Between the windows was a tin plate, with the words, "All fees to be paid in advance," in large letters upon it. In one corner a gentleman was seated at a writing table, who, as he made entries in a ledger, was talking to a woman who stood beside him.

"M. Mascarin?" asked Paul hesitatingly.

"What do you want with him?" asked the man, without looking up from his work. "Do you wish to enter your name? We have now vacancies for three bookkeepers, a cashier, a confidential clerk—six other good situations. Can you give good references?"

These words seemed to be uttered by rote.

"I beg your pardon," returned Paul; "but I should like to see M. Mascarin. One of his friends sent me here."

This statement evidently impressed the official, and he replied almost politely, "M. Mascarin is much occupied at present, sir; but he will soon be disengaged. Pray be seated."

24

Paul sat down on a bench, and examined the man who had just spoken with some curiosity. M. Mascarin's partner was a tall and athletic man, evidently enjoying the best of health, and wearing a large moustache elaborately waxed and pointed. His whole appearance betokened the old soldier. He had, so he asserted, served in the cavalry, and it was there that he had acquired the *soubriquet* by which he was known—Beaumarchef, his original name being David. He was about forty-five, but was still considered a very good-looking fellow. The entries that he was making in the ledger did not prevent him from keeping up a conversation with the woman standing by him. The woman, who seemed to be a cross between a cook and a market-woman, might be described as a thoroughly jovial soul. She seasoned her conversation with pinches of snuff, and spoke with a strong Alsatian brogue.

"Now, look here," said Beaumarchef; "do you really mean to say that you want a place?"

"I do that."

"You said that six months ago. We got you a splendid one, and three days afterward you chucked up the whole concern."

"And why shouldn't I? There was no need to work then; but now it is another pair of shoes, for I have spent nearly all I had saved."

Beaumarchef laid down his pen, and eyed her curiously for a second or two; then he said,—

"You've been making a fool of yourself somehow, I expect."

She half turned away her head, and began to complain of the hardness of the terms and of the meanness of the mistresses, who, instead of allowing their cooks to do the marketing, did it themselves, and so cheated their servants out of their commissions.

Beaumarchef nodded, just as he had done half an hour before to a lady who had complained bitterly of the misconduct of her servants. He was compelled by his position to sympathize with both sides.

The woman had now finished her tirade, and drawing the amount of the fee from a well-filled purse, placed it on the table, saying,—

"Please, M. Beaumarchef, register my name as Caroline Scheumal, and get me a real good place. It must be a cook, you understand, and I want to do the marketing without the missus dodging around."

"Well, I'll do my best."

"Try and find me a wealthy widower, or a young woman married to a very old fellow. Now, do look round; I'll drop in again tomorrow;" and with a farewell pinch of snuff, she left the office.

25

Paul listened to this conversation with feelings of anger and humiliation, and in his heart cursed old Tantaine for having introduced him into such company. He was seeking for some plausible excuse for withdrawal, when the door at the end of the room was thrown open, and two men came in, talking as they did so. The one was young and well dressed, with an easy, swaggering manner, which ignorant people mistake for good breeding. He had a many-coloured rosette at his buttonhole, showing that he was the knight of more than one foreign order. The other was an elderly man, with an unmistakable legal air about him. He was dressed in a quilted dressing-gown, fur-lined shoes, and had on his head an embroidered cap, most likely the work of the hands of someone dear to him. He wore a white cravat, and his sight compelled him to use coloured glasses.

"Then, my dear sir," said the younger man, "I may venture to entertain hopes?"

"Remember, *marquis*," returned the other, "that if I were acting alone, what you require would be at once at your disposal. Unfortunately, I have others to consult."

"I place myself entirely in your hands," replied the *marquis*.

The appearance of the fashionably dressed young man reconciled Paul to the place in which he was.

"A *marquis*!" he murmured; "and the other swell-looking fellow must be M. Mascarin."

Paul was about to step forward, when Beaumarchef respectfully accosted the last comer,—

"Who do you think, sir," said he, "I have just seen?"

"Tell me quickly," was the impatient reply.

"Caroline Schimmel; you know who I mean."

"What! the woman who was in the service of the Duchess of Champdoce?"

"Exactly so."

M. Mascarin uttered an exclamation of delight.

"Where is she living now?"

Beaumarchef was utterly overwhelmed by this simple question. For the first time in his life he had omitted to take a client's address. This omission made Mascarin so angry that he forgot all his good manners, and broke out with an oath that would have shamed a London cabman,—

"How could you be such an infernal fool? We have been hunting for this woman for five months. You knew this as well as I did, and yet, when chance brings her to you, you let her slip through your fingers and vanish again."

"She'll be back again, sir; never fear. She won't fling away the money that she had paid for fees."

"And what do you think that she cares for ten *sous* or ten *francs*? She'll be back when she thinks she will; but a woman who drinks and is off her head nearly all the year round—"

Inspired by a sudden thought, Beaumarchef made a clutch at his hat.

"She has only just gone," said he; "I can easily overtake her."

But Mascarin arrested his progress.

"You are not a good bloodhound. Take Toto Chupin with you; he is outside with his chestnuts, and is as fly as they make them. If you catch her up, don't say a word, but follow her up, and see where she goes. I want to know her whole daily life. Remember that no item, however unimportant it may seem, is not of consequence."

Beaumarchef disappeared in an instant, and Mascarin continued to grumble.

"What a fool!" he murmured. "If I could only do everything myself. I worried my life out for months, trying to find the clue to the mystery which this woman holds, and now she has again escaped me." Paul, who saw that his presence was not remarked, coughed to draw attention to it. In an instant Mascarin turned quickly round.

"Excuse me," said Paul; but the set smile had already resumed its place upon Mascarin's countenance.

"You are," remarked he, civilly, "Paul Violaine, are you not?"

The young man bowed in assent.

"Forgive my absence for an instant. I will be back directly," said Mascarin.

He passed through the door, and in another instant Paul heard his name called.

Compared to the outer chamber, Mascarin's office was quite a luxurious apartment, for the windows were bright, the paper on the walls fresh, and the floor carpeted. But few of the visitors to the office could boast of having been admitted into this sanctum; for generally business was conducted at Beaumarchef's table in the outer room. Paul, however, who was unacquainted with the prevailing rule, was not aware of the distinction with which he had been received. Mascarin, on his visitor's entrance, was comfortably seated in an armchair before the fire, with his elbow on his desk—and what a spectacle did

27

that desk present! It was a perfect world in itself, and indicated that its proprietor was a man of many trades. It was piled with books and documents, while a great deal of the space was occupied by square pieces of cardboard, upon each of which was a name in large letters, while underneath was writing in very minute characters.

With a benevolent gesture, Mascarin pointed to an armchair, and in encouraging tones said, "And now let us talk."

It was plain to Paul that Mascarin was not acting, but that the kind and patriarchal expression upon his face was natural to it, and the young man felt that he could safely entrust his whole future to him.

"I have heard," commenced Mascarin, "that your means of livelihood are very precarious, or rather that you have none, and are ready to take the first one that offers you a means of subsistence. That, at least, is what I hear from my poor friend Tantaine."

"He has explained my case exactly."

"Good; only before proceeding to the future, let us speak of the past."

Paul gave a start, which Mascarin noticed, for he added,—

"You will excuse the freedom I am taking; but it is absolutely necessary that I should know to what I am binding myself. Tantaine tells me that you are a charming young man, strictly honest, and well educated; and now that I have had the pleasure of meeting you, I am sure that he is right; but I can only deal with proofs, and must be quite certain before I act on your behalf with third parties."

"I have nothing to conceal, sir, and am ready to answer any questions," responded Paul.

A slight smile, which Paul did not detect, played round the corners of Mascarin's mouth, and, with a gesture, with which all who knew him were familiar, he pushed back his glasses on his nose.

"I thank you," answered he; "it is not so easy as you may suppose to hide anything from me." He took one of the packets of pasteboard slips form his desk, and shuffling them like a pack of cards, continued, "Your name is Marie Paul Violaine. You were born at Poitiers, in the Rue des Vignes, on the 5th of January, 1843, and are therefore in your twenty-fourth year."

"That is quite correct, sir."

"You are an illegitimate child?"

The first question had surprised Paul; the second absolutely astounded him.

"Quite true, sir," replied he, not attempting to hide his surprise;

28

"but I had no idea that M. Tantaine was so well informed; the partition which divided our rooms must have been thinner than I thought."

Mascarin took no notice of this remark, but continued to shuffle and examine his pieces of cardboard. Had Paul caught a clear glimpse of these, he would have seen his initials in the corner of each.

"Your mother," went on Mascarin, "kept, for the last fifteen years of her life, a little haberdasher's shop."

"Just so."

"But a business of that description in a town like Poitiers, does not bring in very remunerative results, and luckily she received for your support and education a sum of one thousand *francs* per year."

This time Paul started from his seat, for he was sure that Tantaine could not have learned this secret at the Hotel de Perou.

"Merciful powers, sir!" cried he; "who could have told you a thing that has never passed my lips since my arrival in Paris, and of which even Rose is entirely ignorant?"

Mascarin raised his shoulders.

"You can easily comprehend," remarked he, "that a man in my line of business has to learn many things. If I did not take the greatest precautions, I should be deceived daily, and so lead others into error."

Paul had not been more than an hour in the office, but the directions given to Beaumarchef had already taught him how many of these events were arranged.

"Though I may be curious," went on Mascarin, "I am the symbol of discretion; so answer me frankly: How did your mother receive this annuity?"

"Through a Parisian solicitor."

"Do you know him?"

"Not at all," answered Paul, who had begun to grow uneasy under this questioning, for a kind of vague apprehension was aroused in his mind, and he could not see the utility of any of these interrogations. There was, however, nothing in Mascarin's manner to justify the misgivings of the young man, for he appeared to ask all these questions in quite a matter-of-course way, as if they were purely affairs of business.

After a protracted silence, Mascarin resumed,—

"I am half inclined to believe that the solicitor sent the money on his own account."

"No, sir," answered Paul. "I am sure you are mistaken."

"Why are you so certain?"

"Because my mother, who was the incarnation of truth, often as-

29

sured me that my father died before my birth. Poor mother! I loved and respected her too much to question her on these matters. One day, however, impelled by an unworthy feeling of curiosity, I dared to ask her the name of our protector. She burst into tears, and then I felt how mean and cruel I had been. I never learned his name but I know that he was not my father."

Mascarin affected not to notice the emotion of his young client.

"Did the allowance cease at your mother's death?" continued he.

"No; it was stopped when I came of age. My mother told me that this would be the case; but it seems only yesterday that she spoke to me of it. It was on my birthday, and she had prepared a little treat for my supper; for in spite of the affliction my birth had caused her, she loved me fondly. Poor mother! 'Paul,' said she, 'at your birth a genuine friend promised to help me to bring up and educate you, and he kept his word. But you are now twenty-one, and must expect nothing more from him. My son, you are a man now, and I have only you to look to. Work and earn an honest livelihood—'"

Paul could proceed no farther, for his emotions choked him.

"My mother died suddenly some ten months after this conversation—without time to communicate anything to me, and I was left perfectly alone in the world; and were I to die tomorrow, there would not be a soul to follow me to my grave."

Mascarin put on a sympathetic look.

"Not quite so bad as that, my young friend; I trust that you have one now."

Mascarin rose from his seat, and for a few minutes paced up and down the room, and then halted, with his arms folded, before the young man.

"You have heard me," said he, "and I will not put any further questions which it will but pain you to reply to, for I only wished to take your measure, and to judge of your truth from your replies. You will ask why? Ah, that is a question I cannot answer today, but you shall know later on. Be assured, however, that I know everything about you, but I cannot tell you by what means. Say it has all happened by chance. Chance has broad shoulders, and can bear a great deal."

This ambiguous speech caused a thrill of terror to pass through Paul, which was plainly visible on his expressive features.

"Are you alarmed?" asked Mascarin, readjusting his spectacles.

"I am much surprised, sir," stammered Paul.

"Come, come! what can a man in your circumstances have to fear?

There is no use racking your brain; you will find out all you want quickly enough, and had best make up your mind to place yourself in my hands without reserve, for my sole desire is to be of service to you."

These words were uttered in the most benevolent manner; and as he resumed his seat, he added,—

"Now let us talk of myself. Your mother, whom you justly say was a thoroughly good woman, pinched herself in order to keep you at college at Poitiers. You entered a solicitor's office at eighteen, I think?"

"Yes, sir."

"But your mother's desire was to see you established at Loudon or Cevray. Perhaps she hoped that her wealthy friend would aid you still further. Unluckily, however, you had no inclination for the law."

Paul smiled, but Mascarin went on with some little severity.

"I repeat, unfortunately; and I think that by this time you have gone through enough to be of my opinion. What did you do instead of studying law? You did—what? You wasted your time over music, and composed songs, and, I know, an opera, and thought yourself a perfect genius."

Paul had listened up to this time with patience, but at this sarcasm he endeavoured to protest; but it was in vain, for Mascarin went on pitilessly,—

"One day you abandoned the study of the law, and told your mother that until you had made your name as a musical composer you would give lessons on the piano; but you could obtain no pupils, and—well, just look in the glass yourself, and say if you think that your age and appearance would justify parents in intrusting their daughters to your tuition?"

Mascarin stopped for a moment and consulted his notes afresh.

"Your departure from Poitiers," he went on, "was your last act of folly. The very day after your poor mother's death you collected together all her scanty savings, and took the train to Paris."

"Then, sir, I had hoped—"

"What, to arrive at fortune by the road of talent? Foolish boy! Every year a thousand poor wretches have been thus intoxicated by their provincial celebrity, and have started for Paris, buoyed up by similar hopes. Do you know the end of them? At the end of ten years—I give them no longer—nine out of ten die of starvation and disappointment, and the other joins the criminal army."

Paul had often repeated this to himself, and could, therefore, make no reply.

"But," went on Mascarin, "you did not leave Poitiers alone; you carried off with you a young girl named Rose Pigoreau."

"Pray, let me explain."

"It would be useless. The fact speaks for itself. In six months your little store had disappeared; then came poverty and starvation, and at last, in the Hotel de Perou, your thoughts turned to suicide, and you were only saved by my old friend Tantaine."

Paul felt his temper rising, for these plain truths were hard to bear; but fear lest he should lose his protector kept him silent.

"I admit everything, sir," said he calmly. "I was a fool, and almost mad, but experience has taught me a bitter lesson. I am here today, and this fact should tell you that I have given up all my vain hallucinations."

"Will you give up Rose Pigoreau?"

As this abrupt question was put to him, Paul turned pale with anger.

"I love Rose," answered he coldly; "she believes in me, and has shared my troubles with courage, and one day she shall be my wife."

Raising his velvet cap from his head, Mascarin bowed with an ironical air, saying, "Is that so? Then I beg a thousand pardons. It is urgent that you should have immediate employment. Pray, what can you do? Not much of anything, I fancy;—like most college bred boys, you can do a little of everything, and nothing well. Had I a son, and an enormous income, I would have him taught a trade."

Paul bit his lip; but he knew the portrait was a true one.

"And now," continued Mascarin, "I have come to your aid, and what do you say to a situation with a salary of twelve thousand *francs*?"

This sum was so much greater than Paul had dared to hope, that he believed Mascarin was amusing himself at his expense.

"It is not kind of you to laugh at me, under the present circumstances," remarked he.

Mascarin was not laughing at him; but it was fully half an hour before he could prove this to Paul.

"You would like more proof of what I say," said he, after a long conversation. "Very well, then; shall I advance your first month's salary?" And as he spoke, he took a thousand-*franc* note from his desk, and offered it to Paul. The young man rejected the note; but the force of the argument struck him; and he asked if he was capable of carrying out the duties which such a salary doubtless demanded.

"Were I not certain of your abilities, I should not offer it to you," replied Mascarin. "I am in a hurry now, or I would explain the whole affair; but I must defer doing so until tomorrow, when please come at the same hour as you did today."

Even in his state of surprise and stupefaction, Paul felt that this was a signal for him to depart.

"A moment more," said Mascarin. "You understand that you can no longer remain at the Hotel de Perou? Try and find a room in this neighbourhood; and when you have done so, leave the address at the office. Goodbye, my young friend, until tomorrow, and learn to bear good fortune."

For a few minutes Mascarin stood at the door of the office watching Paul, who departed almost staggering beneath the burden of so many conflicting emotions; and when he saw him disappear round the corner, he ran to a glazed door which led to his bed chamber, and in a loud whisper called, "Come in, Hortebise. He has gone."

A man obeyed the summons at once, and hurriedly drew up a chair to the fire. "My feet are almost frozen," exclaimed he; "I should not know it if anyone was to chop them off. Your room, my dear Baptiste, is a perfect refrigerator. Another time, please, have a fire lighted in it."

This speech, however, did not disturb Mascarin's line of thought. "Did you hear all?" asked he.

"I saw and heard all that you did."

"And what do you think of the lad?"

"I think that Daddy Tantaine is a man of observation and powerful will, and that he will mould this child between his fingers like wax."

Chapter 3: The Opinion of Dr. Hortebise

Dr. Hortebise, who had addressed Mascarin so familiarly by his Christian name of Baptiste, was about fifty-six years of age, but he carried his years so well, that he always passed for forty-nine. He had a heavy pair of red, sensual-looking lips, his hair was untinted by gray, and his eyes still lustrous. A man who moved in the best society, eloquent in manner, a brilliant conversationalist, and vivid in his perceptions, he concealed under the veil of good-humoured sarcasm the utmost cynicism of mind. He was very popular and much sought after. He had but few faults, but quite a catalogue of appalling vices. Under this Epicurean exterior lurked, it was reported, the man of talent and the celebrated physician. He was not a hard-working man, simply because he achieved the same results without toil or labour. He had recently taken to homoeopathy, and started a medical journal, which he named *The Globule*, which died at its fifth number. His conversation made all society laugh, and he joined in the ridicule, thus showing the sincerity of his views, for he was never able to take the round of life seriously. Today, however, Mascarin, well as he knew his friend, seemed piqued at his air of levity.

"When I asked you to come here today," said he, "and when I begged you to conceal yourself in my bedroom—"

"Where I was half frozen," broke in Hortebise.

"It was," went on Mascarin, "because I desired your advice. We have started on a serious undertaking,—an undertaking full of peril both to you and to myself."

"Pooh! I have perfect confidence in you,—whatever you do is done well, and you are not the man to fling away your trump cards."

"True; but I may lose the game, after all, and then—"

The doctor merely shook a large gold locket that depended from his watch chain.

This movement seemed to annoy Mascarin a great deal. "Why do you flash that trinket at me?" asked he. "We have known each other for five and twenty years,—what do you mean to imply? Do you mean that the locket contains the likeness of someone that you intend to make use of later on? I think that you might render such a step unnecessary by giving me your present advice and attention."

Hortebise threw himself back in his chair with an expression of resignation. "If you want advice," remarked he, "why not apply to our worthy friend Catenac?—he knows something of business, as he is a lawyer."

The name of Catenac seemed to irritate Mascarin so much, that calm, and self-contained as he usually was, he pulled off his cap and dashed it on his desk.

"Are you speaking seriously?" said he angrily.

"Why should I not be in earnest?"

Mascarin removed his glasses, as though without them he could the more easily peer into the depths of the soul of the man before him.

"Because," replied he slowly, "both you and I distrust Catenac. When did you see him last?"

"More than three months ago."

"True, and I allow that he seems to be acting fairly toward his old associates; but you will admit that, in keeping away thus, his conduct is without excuse, for he has made his fortune; and though he pretends to be poor, he is certainly a man of wealth."

"Do you really think so?"

"Were he here, I would force him to acknowledge that he is worth a million, at least."

"A million!" exclaimed the doctor, with sudden animation.

"Yes, certainly. You and I, Hortebise, have indulged our every whim, and have spent gold like water, while our friend garnered his harvest and stored it away. But poor Catenac has no expensive tastes, nor does he care for women or the pleasures of the table. While we indulged in every pleasure, he lent out his money at usurious interest. But, stop,—how much do you spend per annum?"

"That is a hard question to answer; but, say, forty thousand *francs*."

"More, a great deal more; but calculate what a capital sum that would amount to during the twenty years we have done business together."

The doctor was not clever at figures; he made several vain attempts to solve the problem, and at last gave it up in despair. "Forty and forty," muttered he, tapping the tips of his fingers, "are eighty, then forty—"

"Call it eight hundred thousand *francs*," broke in Mascarin. "Say I drew the same amount as you did. We have spent ours, and Catenac has saved his, and grown rich; hence my distrust. Our interests are no longer identical. He certainly comes here every month, but it is only to claim his share; he consents to take his share of the profits, but shirks the risks. It is fully ten years since he brought in any business. I don't trust him at all. He always declines to join in any scheme that we propose, and sees danger in everything."

"He would not betray us, however."

Mascarin took a few moments for reflection. "I think," said he, "that Catenac is afraid of us. He knows that the ruin of me would entail the destruction of the other two. This is our only safeguard; but if he dare not injure us openly, he is quite capable of working against us in secret. Do you remember what he said the last time he was here? That we ought to close our business and retire. How should *we* live? for he is rich and we are poor. What on earth are you doing, Hortebise?" he added, for the physician, who had the reputation of being worth an enormous amount, had taken out his purse, and was going over the contents.

"I have scarcely three hundred and twenty-seven *francs*!" answered he with a laugh. "What is the state of your finances?"

Mascarin made a grimace. "I am not so well off as you; and besides," he continued in a low voice, as though speaking to himself, "I have certain ties which you do not possess."

For the first time during this interview a cloud spread over the doctor's countenance.

"Great Heavens!" said he, "and I was depending on you for three thousand *francs*, which I require urgently."

Mascarin smiled slyly at the doctor's uneasiness. "Don't worry," he answered. "You can have that; there ought to be some six or eight thousand *francs* in the safe. But that is all, and that is the last of our common capital,—this after twenty years of toil, danger, and anxiety, and we have not twenty years before us to make a fresh fortune in."

"Yes," continued Mascarin, "we are getting old, and therefore have the greater reason for making one grand stroke to assure our fortune. Were I to fall ill tomorrow, all would go to smash."

"Quite true," returned the doctor, with a slight shudder.

"We must, and that is certain, venture on a bold stroke. I have said this for years, and woven a web of gigantic proportions. Do you now know why at this last moment I appeal to you, and not to Catenac for assistance? If only one out of two operations that I have fully explained to you succeeds, our fortune is made."

"I follow you exactly."

"The question now is whether the chance of success is sufficiently great to warrant our going on with these undertakings. Think it over and let me have your opinion."

An acute observer could easily have seen that the doctor was a man of resource, and a thoroughly competent adviser, for the reason that his coolness never deserted him. Compelled to choose between the use of the contents of his locket, or the continuance of a life of luxurious ease, the smile vanished from the doctor's face, and he began to reflect profoundly. Leaning back in his chair, with his feet resting on the fender, he carefully studied every combination in the undertaking, as a general inspects the position taken up by the enemy, when a battle is impending, upon which the fate of an empire may hinge. That this analysis took a favourable turn, was evident, for Mascarin soon saw a smile appear upon the doctor's lips. "We must make the attack at once," said he; "but make no mistake; the projects you propose are most dangerous, and a single error upon our side would entail destruction; but we must take some risk. The odds are against us, but still we may win. Under these circumstances, and as necessity cheers us on, I say, *Forward!*" As he said this, he rose to his feet, and extending his hand toward his friend, exclaimed, "I am entirely at your disposal."

Mascarin seemed relieved by the doctor's decision, for he was in that frame of mind when, however self-reliant a man may be, he has a disinclination to be left alone, and the aid of a stout ally is of the utmost service.

"Have you considered every point carefully?" asked he. "You know that we can only act at present upon one of the undertakings, and that is the one of which the Marquis de Croisenois—"

"I know that."

"With reference to the affair of the Duke de Champdoce, I have still to gather together certain things necessary for the ultimate success of the scheme. There is a mystery in the lives of the duke and duchess,—of this there is no doubt,—but what is this secret? I would lay my life that I have hit upon the correct solution; but I want no suspicions, no probabilities; I want absolute certainties. And now," continued he, "this brings us back to the first question. What do you think of Paul Violaine?"

Hortebise walked up and down the room two or three times, and finally stopped opposite to his friend. "I think," said he, "that the lad has many of the qualities we want, and we might find it hard to discover one better suited for our purpose. Besides, he is a bastard, knows nothing of his father, and therefore leaves a wide field for conjecture; for every natural son has the right to consider himself, if he likes, the offspring of a monarch. He has no family or anyone to look after him, which assures us that whatever may happen, there is no one to call us to account. He is not over-wise, but has a certain amount of talent, and any quantity of ridiculous self-conceit. He is wonderfully handsome, which will make matters easier, but—"

"Ah, there is a 'but' then?"

"More than one," answered the doctor, "for there are three for certain. First, there is Rose Pigoreau, whose beauty has so captivated our old friend Tantaine,—she certainly appears to be a danger in the future."

"Be easy," returned Mascarin; "we will quickly remove this young woman from our road."

"Good; but do not be too confident," answered Hortebise, in his usual tone. "The danger from her is not the one you think, and which you are trying to avoid. You think Paul loves her. You are wrong. He would drop her tomorrow, so that he could please his self-indulgence. But the woman who thinks that she hates her lover often deceives

37

herself; and Rose is simply tired of poverty. Give her a little amount of comfort, good living, and luxury, and you will see her give them all up to come back to Paul. Yes, I tell you, she will harass and annoy him, as women of her class who have nothing to love always do. She will even go to Flavia to claim him."

"She had better not," retorted Mascarin, in threatening accents.

"Why, how could you prevent it? She has known Paul from his infancy. She knew his mother; she was perhaps brought up by her, perhaps even lived in the same street. Look out, I say, for danger from that quarter."

"You may be right, and I will take my precautions."

It was sufficient for Mascarin to be assured of a danger to find means of warding it off.

"My second 'but,'" continued Hortebise, "is the idea of the mysterious protector of whom the young man spoke. His mother, he says, has reason to know that his father is dead, and I believe in the truth of the statement. In this case, what has become of the person who paid Madame Violaine her allowance?"

"You are right, quite right; these are the crevices in our armour; but I keep my eyes open, and nothing escapes me."

The doctor was growing rather weary, but he still went on courageously. "My third 'but'" said he, "is perhaps the strongest. We must see the young fellow at once. It may be tomorrow, without even having prepared him or taught him his part. Suppose we found that he was honest! Imagine—if he returned a firm negative to all your dazzling offers!"

Mascarin rose to his feet in his turn. "I do not think that there is any chance of that," said he.

"Why not, pray?"

"Because when Tantaine brought him to me, he had studied him carefully. He is as weak as a woman, and as vain as a journalist. Besides, he is ashamed at being poor. No; I can mould him like wax into any shape I like. He will be just what we wish."

"Are you sure," asked Hortebise, "that Flavia will have nothing to say in this matter?"

"I had rather, with your permission, say nothing on that head," returned Mascarin. He broke off his speech and listened eagerly. "There is someone listening," said he. "Hark!"

The sound was repeated, and the doctor was about to seek refuge in the inner room, when Mascarin laid a detaining hand upon his arm.

"Stay," observed he, "it is only Beaumarchef;" and as he spoke, he struck a gilded bell that stood on his desk. In another instant Beaumarchef appeared, and with an air in which familiarity was mingled with respect, he saluted in military fashion.

"Ah," said the doctor pleasantly, "do you take your nips of brandy regularly?"

"Only occasionally, sir," stammered the man.

"Too often, too often, my good fellow. Do you think that your nose and eyelids are not real telltales?"

"But I assure you, sir—"

"Do you not remember I told you that you had asthmatic symptoms? Why, the movement of your pectoral muscles shows that your lungs are affected."

"But I have been running, sir."

Mascarin broke in upon this conversation, which he considered frivolous. "If he is out of breath," remarked he, "it is because he has been endeavouring to repair a great act of carelessness that he has committed. Well, Beaumarchef, how did you get on?"

"All right, sir," returned he, with a look of triumph. "Good!"

"What are you talking about?" asked the doctor.

Mascarin gave his friend a meaning glance, and then, in a careless manner, replied, "Caroline Schimmel, a former servant of the Champdoce family, also patronizes our office. How did you find her, Beaumarchef?"

"Well, an idea occurred to me."

"Pooh! do you have ideas at your time of life?"

Beaumarchef put on an air of importance. "My idea was this," he went on: "as I left the office with Toto Chupin, I said to myself, the woman would certainly drop in at some pub before she reached the boulevard."

"A sound argument," remarked the doctor.

"Therefore Toto and I took a squint into everyone we passed, and before we got to the Rue Carreau we saw her in one, sure enough."

"And Toto is after her now?"

"Yes, sir; he said he would follow her like her shadow, and will bring in a report every day."

"I am very pleased with you, Beaumarchef," said Mascarin, rubbing his hands joyously.

Beaumarchef seemed highly flattered, but continued,—

"This is not all."

"What else is there to tell?"

"I met La Candele on his way from the Place de Petit Pont, and he has just seen that young girl—you know whom I mean—driving off in a two-horse Victoria. He followed it, of course. She has been placed in a gorgeous apartment in the Rue Douai; and from what the porter says, she must be a rare beauty; and La Candele raved about her, and says that she has the most magnificent eyes in the world."

"Ah," remarked Hortebise, "then Tantaine was right in his description of her."

"Of course he was," answered Mascarin with a slight frown, "and this proves the justice of the objection you made a little time back. A girl possessed of such dazzling beauty may even influence the fool who has carried her off to become dangerous."

Beaumarchef touched his master's arm kindly. "If you wish to get rid of the masher," said he, "I can show you a way;" and throwing himself into the position of a fencer, he made a lunge with his right arm, exclaiming, "One, two!"

"A Prussian quarrel," remarked Mascarin. "No; a duel would do us no good. We should still have the girl on our hands, and violent measures are always to be avoided." He took off his glasses, wiped them, and looking at the doctor intently, said, "Suppose we take an epidemic as our ally. If the girl had the smallpox, she would lose her beauty."

Cynical and hardened as the doctor was, he drew back in horror at this proposal. "Under certain circumstances," remarked he, "science might aid us; but Rose, even without her beauty, would be just as dangerous as she is now. It is *her* affection for Paul that we have to check, and not *his* for her; and the uglier a woman is, the more she clings to her lover."

"All this is worthy of consideration," returned Mascarin; "meanwhile we must take steps to guard ourselves from the impending danger. Have you finished that report on Gandelu, Beaumarchef? What is his position?"

"Head over ears in debt, sir, but not harassed by his creditors because of his future prospects."

"Surely among these creditors there are some that we could influence?" said Mascarin. "Find this out, and report to me this evening; and farewell for the present."

When again alone, the two confederates remained silent for some time. The decisive moment had arrived. As yet they were not compromised; but if they intended to carry out their plans, they must no longer remain inactive; and both of these men had sufficient experience to know that they must look at the position boldly, and make up their minds at once. The pleasant smile upon the doctor's face faded away, and his fingers played nervously with his locket. Mascarin was the first to break the silence.

"Let us no longer hesitate," said he; "let us shut our eyes to the danger and advance steadily. You heard the promises made by the Marquis de Croisenois. He will do as we wish, but under certain conditions. Mademoiselle de Mussidan must be his bride."

"That will be impossible."

"Not so, if we desire it: and the proof of this is, that before two o'clock the engagement between Mademoiselle Sabine and the Baron de Breulh-Faverlay will be broken off."

The doctor heaved a deep sigh. "I can understand Catenac's scruples. Ah! if, like him, I had a million!"

During this brief conversation Mascarin had gone into his sleeping room and was busily engaged in changing his dress.

"If you are ready," remarked the doctor, "we will make a start."

In reply, Mascarin opened the door leading into the office. "Get a cab, Beaumarchef," said he.

Chapter 4: A Trustworthy Servant

In the city of Paris it is impossible to find a more fashionable quarter than the one which is bounded on the one side by the Rue Faubourg Saint Honore and on the other by the Seine, and commences at the Place de la Concorde and ends at the Avenue de l'Imperatrice. In this favoured spot millionaires seem to bloom like the rhododendron in the sunny south. There are the magnificent palaces which they have erected for their accommodation, where the turf is ever verdant, and where the flowers bloom perennially; but the most gorgeous of all these mansions was the Hotel de Mussidan, the last *chef d'oeuvre* of Sevair, that skilful architect who died just as the world was beginning to recognise his talents. With a spacious courtyard in front and a magnificent garden in the rear, the Hotel de Mussidan is as elegant as it is commodious.

The exterior was extremely plain, and not disfigured by florid ornamentation. White marble steps, with a light and elegant railing at the sides, lead to the wide doors which open into the hall. The busy hum of the servants at work at an early hour in the yard tells that an ample establishment is kept up. There can be seen luxurious carriages, for occasions of ceremony, and the park phaeton, and the simple brougham which the countess uses when she goes out shopping; and that carefully groomed thoroughbred is Mirette, the favourite riding horse of Mademoiselle Sabine. Mascarin and his confederate descended from their cab a little distance at the corner of the Avenue Matignon. Mascarin, in his dark suit, with his spotless white cravat and glittering spectacles, looked like some highly respectable functionary of State. Hortebise wore his usual smile, though his cheek was pale.

"Now," remarked Mascarin, "let me see,—on what footing do you stand with the Mussidans? Do they look upon you as a friend?"

"No, no; a poor doctor, whose ancestors were not among the Crusades, could not be the intimate friend of such haughty nobles as the Mussidans."

"But the countess knows you, and will not refuse to receive you, nor have you turned out as soon as you begin to speak; for, taking shelter behind some rogue without a name, you can shelter your own reputation. I will see the count."

"Take care of him," said Hortebise thoughtfully. "He has a reputation for being a man of ungovernable temper, and, at the first word from you that he objects to, would throw you out of the window as soon as look at you."

Mascarin shrugged his shoulders. "I can bring him to reason," answered he.

The two confederates walked a little past the Hotel de Mussidan, and the doctor explained the interior arrangements of the house.

"I," continued Mascarin, "will insist upon the count's breaking off his daughter's engagement with M. de Breulh-Faverlay, but shall not say a word about the Marquis de Croisenois, while you will take the opportunity of putting his pretensions before the countess, and will not say a word of M. de Breulh-Faverlay."

"I have learned my lesson, and shall not forget it."

"You see, doctor, the beauty of the whole affair is, that the countess will wonder how her husband will take her interference, while he will be at a loss how to break the news to his wife. How surprised they will be when they find that they have both the same end in view!"

There was something so droll in the whole affair, that the doctor burst into a loud laugh.

"We go by such different roads," said he, "that they will never suspect that we are working together. Faith! my dear Baptiste, you are much more clever than I thought."

42

"Don't praise me until you see that I am successful."

Mascarin stopped opposite to a *café* in the Faubourg Saint Honore.

"Wait here for me, doctor," said he, "while I make a little call. If all is all right; I will come for you again; then I will see the count, and twenty minutes later do you go to the house and ask for the countess."

The clock struck four as the worthy confederates parted, and Mascarin continued his way along the Faubourg Saint Honore, and again stopped before a public house, which he entered, the master of which, Father Canon, was so well known in the neighbourhood that he had not thought it worth while to have his name painted over the door. He did not profess to serve his best wine to casual customers, but for regular frequenters of his house, chiefly the servants of noble families, he kept a better brand of wine. Mascarin's respectable appearance inclined the landlord to step forward. Among Frenchmen, who are always full of gayety, a serious exterior is ever an excellent passport.

"What can I do for you, sir?" asked he with great politeness.

"Can I see Florestan?"

"In Count de Mussidan's service, I believe?"

"Just so; I have an appointment with him here."

"He is downstairs in the band-room," replied the landlord. "I will send for him."

"Don't trouble; I will go down," and, without waiting for permission, Mascarin descended some steps that apparently led to a cellar.

"It appears to me," murmured Father Canon, "that I have seen this cove's face before."

Mascarin pushed open a door at the bottom of the flight of stairs, and a strange and appalling noise issued from within (but this neither surprised nor alarmed him), and entered a vaulted room arranged like a *café*, with seats and tables, filled with customers. In the centre, two men, in their shirt sleeves, with crimson faces, were performing upon horns; while an old man, with leather gaiters, buttoning to the knee, and a broad leather belt, was whistling the air the horn players were executing. As Mascarin politely took off his hat, the performers ceased, and the old man discontinued his whistling, while a well-built young fellow, with pumps and stockings, and wearing a fashionable moustache, exclaimed,—

"Aha, it is that good old Mascarin. I was expecting you; will you drink?"

Without waiting for further invitation Mascarin helped himself from a bottle that stood near.

"Did Father Canon tell you that I was here?" asked the young man, who was the Florestan Mascarin had been inquiring for. "You see," continued he, "that the police will not permit us to practise the horn; so, you observe, Father Canon has arranged this underground studio, from whence no sound reaches the upper world."

The horn players had now resumed their lessons, and Florestan was compelled to place both hands to the side of his mouth, in order to render himself audible, and to shout with all his might.

"That old fellow there is a huntsman in the service of the Duke de Champdoce, and is the finest horn player going. I have only had twenty lessons from him, and am getting on wonderfully."

"Ah!" exclaimed Mascarin, "when I have more time I must hear your performance; but today I am in a hurry, and want to say a few words to you in private."

"Certainly, but suppose we go upstairs and ask for a private room." The rooms he referred to were not very luxuriously furnished, but were admirably suited for confidential communications; and had the walls been able to speak, they could have told many a strange tale.

Florestan and Mascarin seated themselves in one of these before a small table, upon which Father Canon placed a bottle of wine and two glasses.

"I asked you to meet me here, Florestan," began Mascarin, "because you can do me a little favour."

"Anything that is in my power I will do," said the young man.

"First, a few words regarding yourself. How do you get on with Count de Mussidan?"

Mascarin had adopted an air of familiarity which he knew would please his companion.

"I don't care about the place," replied Florestan, "and I am going to ask Beaumarchef to look out another one for me."

"I am surprised at that; all your predecessors said that the count was a perfect gentleman—"

"Just try him yourself," broke in the valet. "In the first place he is as fickle as the wind, and awfully suspicious. He never leaves anything about,—no letters, no cigars, and no money. He spends half his time in locking things up, and goes to bed with his keys under his pillow."

"I allow that such suspicion on his part is most unpleasant."

"It is indeed, and besides he is awfully violent. He gets in a rage about nothing, and half a dozen times in the day he looks ready to murder you. On my word, I am really frightened at him."

This account, coupled with what he had heard from Hortebise seemed to render Mascarin very thoughtful.

"Is he always like this, or only at intervals?"

"He is always a beast, but he is worse after drink or losing at cards. He is never home until after four in the morning."

"And what does his wife say?"

The query made Florestan laugh.

"*Madame* does not bother herself about her lord and master, I can assure you. Sometimes they don't meet for weeks. All she wants is plenty of money. And ain't we just dunned!"

"But the Mussidans are wealthy?"

"Tremendously so, but at times there is not the value of a *franc* in the house. Then *Madame* is like a tigress, and would sent to borrow from all her friends."

"But she must feel much humiliated?"

"Not a bit; when she wants a heavy amount, she sends off to the Duke de Champdoce, and he always parts; but she doesn't mince matters with him."

"It would seem as if you had known the contents of your mistress's letters?" remarked Mascarin with a smile.

"Of course I have; I like to know what is in the letters I carry about. She only says, 'My good friend, I want so much,' and back comes the money without a word. Of course it is easy to see that there has been something between them."

"Yes, evidently."

"And when master and missus do meet they only have rows, and such rows! When the working man has had a drop too much, he beats his wife, she screams, then they kiss and make it up; but the Mussidans say things to each other in cold blood that neither can ever forgive."

From the air with which Mascarin listened to these details, it almost seemed as if he had been aware of them before.

"Then," said he, "Mademoiselle Sabine is the only nice one in the house?"

"Yes, she is always gentle and considerate."

"Then you think that M. de Breulh-Faverlay will be a happy man?"

"Oh, yes; but perhaps this marriage will—" but here Florestan interrupted himself and assumed an air of extreme caution. After looking carefully round, he lowered his voice, and continued, "Mademoiselle Sabine has been left so much to herself that she acts just as she thinks fit."

"Do you mean," asked Mascarin, "that the young lady has a lover?"

"Just so."

"But that must be wrong; and let me tell you that you ought not to repeat such a story."

The man grew quite excited.

"Story," repeated he; "I know what I know. If I spoke of a lover, it is because I have seen him with my own eyes, not once, but twice."

From the manner in which Mascarin received this intelligence, Florestan saw that he was interested in the highest degree.

"I'll tell you all about it," continued he. "The first time was when she went to mass; it came on to rain suddenly, and Modeste, her maid, begged me to go for an umbrella. As soon as I came back I went in and saw Mademoiselle Sabine standing by the receptacle for holy water, talking to a young fellow. Of course I dodged behind a pillar, and kept a watch on the pair—"

"But you don't found all your story on this?"

"I think you would, had you seen the way they looked into each other's eyes."

"What was he like?"

"Very good looking, about my height, with an aristocratic air."

"How about the second time?"

"Ah, that is a longer story. I went one day with *Mademoiselle* when she was going to see a friend in the Rue Marboeuf. She waited at a corner of the street, and beckoned me to her. 'Florestan,' said she, 'I forgot to post this letter; go and do so; I will wait here for you.'"

"Of course you read it?"

"No. I thought there was something wrong. She wants to get rid of you, so, instead of posting it, I slunk behind a tree and waited. I had hardly done so, when the young fellow I had seen at the chapel came round the corner; but I scarcely knew him. He was dressed just like a working man, in a blouse all over plaster. They talked for about ten minutes, and Mademoiselle Sabine gave him what looked like a photograph."

By this time the bottle was empty, and Florestan was about to call for another, when Mascarin checked him, saying—

"Not today; it is growing late, and I must tell you what I want you to do for me. Is the count at home now?"

"Of course he is; he has not left his room for two days, owing to having slipped going downstairs."

"Well, my lad, I must see your master; and if I sent up my card, the odds are he would not see me, so I rely upon you to show me up without announcing me."

Florestan remained silent for a few minutes.

"It is no easy job," he muttered, "for the count does not like unexpected visitors, and the countess is with him just now. However, as I am not going to stay, I'll chance it."

Mascarin rose from his seat.

"We must not be seen together," said he; "I'll settle the score; do you go on, and I will follow in five minutes. Remember we don't know each other."

"I am fly; and mind you look out a good place for me."

Mascarin paid the bill, and then looked into the *café* to inform the doctor of his movements, and a few minutes later, Florestan in his most sonorous voice, threw open the door of his master's room and announced,—

"M. Mascarin."

Chapter 5: A Forgotten Crime

Baptiste Mascarin had been in so many strange situations, from which he had extricated himself with safety and credit, that he had the fullest self-confidence, but as he ascended the wide staircase of the Hotel de Mussidan, he felt his heart beat quicker in anticipation of the struggle that was before him. It was twilight out of doors, but all within was a blaze of light. The library into which he was ushered was a vast apartment, furnished in severe taste. At the sound of the unaristocratic name of Mascarin, which seemed as much out of place as a drunkard's oath in the chamber of sleeping innocence, M. de Mussidan raised his head in sudden surprise. The count was seated at the other end of the room, reading by the light of four candles placed in a magnificently wrought candelabra. He threw down his paper, and raising his glasses, gazed with astonishment at Mascarin, who, with his hat in his hand and his heart in his mouth, slowly crossed the room, muttering a few unintelligible apologies. He could make nothing, however, of his visitor, and said, "Whom do you wish to see, sir?"

"The Count de Mussidan," stuttered Mascarin; "and I hope that you will forgive this intrusion."

The count cut his excuse short with a haughty wave of his hand. "Wait," said he imperiously. He then with evident pain rose from his seat, and crossing the room, rang the bell violently, and then re-seated himself. Mascarin, who still remained in the centre of the room, inwardly wondered if after all he was to be turned out of the house. In another second the door opened, and the figure of the faithful Florestan appeared.

"Florestan," said the count, angrily, "this is the first time that you have permitted anyone to enter this room without my permission; if this occurs again, you leave my service."

"I assure your lordship," began the man.

"Enough! I have spoken; you know what to expect."

During this brief colloquy, Mascarin studied the count with the deepest attention.

The Count Octave de Mussidan in no way resembled the man sketched by Florestan. Since the time of Montaigne, a servant's portrait of his employer should always be distrusted. The count looked fully sixty, though he was but fifty years of age; he was undersized, and he looked shrunk and shrivelled; he was nearly bald, and his long whiskers were perfectly white. The cares of life had imprinted deep furrows on his brow, and told too plainly the story of a man who, having drained the chalice of life to the bottom, was now ready to shiver the goblet. As Florestan left the room the count turned to Mascarin, and in the same glacial tone observed, "And now, sir, explain this intrusion."

Mascarin had often been rebuffed, but never so cruelly as this. His vanity was sorely wounded, for he was vain, as all are who think that they possess some hidden influence, and he felt his temper giving way.

"Pompous idiot!" thought he; "we will see how he looks in a short time;" but his face did not betray this, and his manner remained cringing and obsequious. "You have heard my name, my lord, and I am a general business agent."

The count was deceived by the honest accents which long practice had taught Mascarin to use, and he had neither a suspicion nor a presentiment.

"Ah!" said he majestically, "a business agent, are you? I presume you come on behalf of one of my creditors. Well, sir, as I have before told these people, your errand is a futile one. Why do they worry me when I unhesitatingly pay the extravagant interest they are pleased to demand? They know that they are all knaves. They are aware that I am rich, for I have inherited a great fortune, which is certainly without encumbrance; for though I could raise a million tomorrow upon my estates in Poitiers, I have up to this time not chosen to do so."

Mascarin had at length so recovered his self-command that he listened to this speech without a word, hoping to gain some information from it.

"You may tell this," continued the count, "to those by whom you are employed."

"Excuse me, my lord—"

"But what?"

"I cannot allow—"

"I have nothing more to say; all will be settled as I promised, when I pay my daughter's dowry. You are aware that she will shortly be united to M. de Breulh-Faverlay."

There was no mistaking the order to go, contained in these words, but Mascarin did not offer to do so, but readjusting his spectacles, remarked in a perfectly calm voice,—

"It is this marriage that has brought me here."

The count thought that his ears had deceived him. "What are you saying?" said he.

"I say," repeated the agent, "that I am sent to you in connection with this same marriage."

Neither the doctor nor Florestan had exaggerated the violence of the count's temper. Upon hearing his daughter's name and marriage mentioned by this man, his face grew crimson and his eyes gleamed with a lurid fire.

"Get out of this!" cried he, angrily.

But this was an order that Mascarin had no intention of obeying.

"I assure you that what I have to say is of the utmost importance," said he.

This speech put the finishing touch to the count's fury.

"You won't go, won't you?" said he; and in spite of the pain that at the moment evidently oppressed him, he stepped to the bell, but was arrested by Mascarin, uttering in a warning voice the words,—

"Take care; if you ring that bell, you will regret it to the last day of your life."

This was too much for the count's patience, and letting go the bell rope, he snatched up a walking cane that was leaning against the chimneypiece, and made a rush toward his visitor. But Mascarin did not move or lift his hand in self-defence, contenting himself with saying calmly,—

"No violence, count; remember Montlouis."

At this name the count grew livid, and dropping the cane from his nerveless hand staggered back a pace or two. Had a spectre suddenly

49

stood up before him with threatening hand, he could not have been more horrified.

"Montlouis!" he murmured; "Montlouis!"

But now Mascarin, thoroughly assured of the value of his weapon, had resumed all his humbleness of demeanour.

"Believe me, my lord," said he, "that I only mentioned this name on account of the immediate danger that threatens you."

The count hardly seemed to pay attention to his visitor's words.

"It was not I," continued Mascarin, "who devised the project of bringing against you an act which was perhaps a mere accident. I am only a plenipotentiary from persons I despise, to you, for whom I entertain the very highest respect."

By this time the count had somewhat recovered himself.

"I really do not understand you," said he, in a tone he vainly endeavoured to render calm. "My sudden emotion is only too easily explained. I had a sad misfortune. I accidentally shot my secretary, and the poor young man bore the name you just now mentioned; but the court acquitted me of all blame in the matter."

The smile upon Mascarin's face was so full of sarcasm that the count broke off.

"Those who sent me here," remarked the agent, slowly, "are well acquainted with the evidence produced in court; but unfortunately, they know the real facts, which certain honourable gentlemen had sense to conceal at any risk."

Again the count started, but Mascarin went on implacably,—

"But reassure yourself, your friend did not betray you voluntarily. Providence, in her inscrutable decrees—"

The count shuddered.

"In short, sir, in short—"

Up to this time Mascarin had remained standing, but now that he saw that his position was fully established, he drew up a chair and sat down. The count grew more livid at this insolent act, but made no comment, and this entirely removed any doubts from the agent's mind.

"The event to which I have alluded has two eye-witnesses, the Baron de Clinchain, and a servant, named Ludovic Trofin, now in the employ of the Count de Commarin."

"I did not know what had become of Trofin."

"Perhaps not, but my people do. When he swore to keep the matter secret, he was unmarried, but a few years later, having entered the bonds of matrimony, he told all to his young wife. This woman turned out badly; she had several lovers, and through one of them the matter came to my employer's ears."

"And it was on the word of a lackey, and the gossip of a dissolute woman, that they have dared to accuse me."

No word of direct accusation had passed, and yet the count sought to defend himself.

Mascarin saw all this, and smiled inwardly, as he replied, "We have other evidence than that of Ludovic."

"But," said the count, who was sure of the fidelity of his friend, "you do not, I suppose, pretend that the Baron de Clinchain has deceived me?"

The state of mental anxiety and perturbation into which this man of the world had been thrown must have been very intense for him not to have perceived that every word he uttered put a fresh weapon in his adversary's hands.

"He has not denounced you by word of mouth," replied the agent. "He has done far more; he has written his testimony."

"It is a lie," exclaimed the count.

Mascarin was not disturbed by this insult.

"The baron has written," repeated he, "though he never thought that any eye save his own would read what he had penned. As you are aware, the Baron de Clinchain is a most methodical man, and punctilious to a degree."

"I allow that; continue."

"Consequently you will not be surprised to learn that from his earliest years he has kept a diary, and each day he puts down in the most minute manner everything that has occurred, even to the different conditions of his bodily health."

The count knew of his friend's foible, and remembered that when they were young many a practical joke had been played upon his friend on this account, and now he began to perceive the dangerous ground upon which he stood.

"On hearing the facts of the case from Ludovic's wife's lover," continued Mascarin, "my employers decided that if the tale was a true one, some mention of it would be found in the baron's diary; and thanks to the ingenuity and skill of certain parties, they have had in their possession for twenty-four hours the volume for the year 1842."

"Scoundrels!" muttered the count.

"They find not only one, but three distinct statements relating to

51

the affair in question."

The count started again to his feet with so menacing a look, that the worthy Mascarin pushed back his chair in anticipation of an immediate assault.

"Proofs!" gasped the count. "Give me proofs."

"Everything has been provided for, and the three leaves by which you are so deeply compromised have been cut from the book."

"Where are these pages?"

Mascarin at once put on an air of injured innocence.

"I have not seen them, but the leaves have been photographed, and a print has been entrusted to me, in order to enable you to recognise the writing."

As he spoke he produced three specimens of the photographic art, wonderfully clear and full of fidelity. The count examined them with the utmost attention, and then in a voice which trembled with emotion, he said, "True enough, it is his handwriting."

Not a line upon Mascarin's face indicated the delight with which he received this admission.

"Before continuing the subject," he observed placidly, "I consider it necessary for you to understand the position taken up by the Baron de Clinchain. Do you wish, my lord, to read these extracts, or shall I do so for you?"

"Read," answered the count, adding in a lower voice, "I cannot see to do so."

Mascarin drew his chair nearer to the lights on the table. "I perceive," said he, "that the first entry was made on the evening after the—well, the accident. This is it: 'October 26, 1842. Early this morning went out shooting with Octave de Mussidan. We were accompanied by Ludovic, a groom, and by a young man named Montlouis, whom Octave intends one day to make his steward. It was a splendid day, and by twelve o'clock I had killed a leash of hares. Octave was in excellent spirits, and by one o'clock we were in a thick cover not far from Bevron. I and Ludovic were a few yards in front of the others, when angry voices behind attracted our attention. Octave and Montlouis were arguing violently, and all at once the count struck his future steward a violent blow. In another moment Montlouis came up to me. 'What is the matter?' cried I. Instead of replying to my question, the unhappy young man turned back to his master, uttering a series of threats. Octave had evidently been reproaching him for some low intrigue he had been engaged in, and was reflecting upon the character of the woman. 'At any rate,' cried Montlouis, 'she is quite as virtuous as Madame de Mussidan was before her marriage.'"

"'As Octave heard these words, he raised the loaded gun he held in his hand and fired. Montlouis fell to the ground, bathed in blood. We all ran up to him, but he was quite dead, for the charge of shot had penetrated his heart. I was almost beside myself, but Octave's despair was terrible to witness. Tearing his hair, he knelt beside the dead man. Ludovic, however, maintained his calmness. "We must say that it was an accident," observed he quickly. "Thinking that Montlouis was not near, my master fired into cover."

"'This was agreed to, and we carefully arranged what we should say. It was I who went before the magistrate and made a deposition, which was unhesitatingly received. But, oh, what a fearful day! My pulse is at eighty, and I feel I shall not sleep all night. Octave is half mad, and Heaven knows what will become of him.'"

The count, from the depths of his armchair, listened without apparent emotion to this terrible revelation. He was quite crushed, and was searching for some means to exorcise the green spectre of the past, which had so suddenly confronted him. Mascarin never took his eyes off him. All at once the count roused himself from his prostration, as a man awakes from a hideous dream. "This is sheer folly," cried he.

"It is folly," answered Mascarin, "that would carry much weight with it."

"And suppose I were to show you," returned the count, "that all these entries are the offspring of a diseased mind?"

Mascarin shook his head with an air of affected grief. "There is no use, my lord, in indulging in vain hopes. We," he continued, wishing to associate himself with the count, "we might of course admit that the Baron de Clinchain had made this entry in his diary in a moment of temporary insanity, were it not for the painful fact that there were others. Le me read them."

"Go on; I am all attention."

"We find the following, three days later:

Oct. 29th, 1842. I am most uneasy about my health. I feel shooting pains in all my joints. The derangement of my system arises entirely from this business of Octave's. I had to run the gauntlet of a second court, and the judge's eyes seemed to look me through and through. I also saw with much alarm that my second statement differs somewhat from the first one, so I have

53

now learned it by heart. Ludovic is a sharp fellow, and quite self-possessed. I would like to have him in my household. I keep myself shut up in my house for fear of meeting friends who want to hear all the details of the accident. I believe I may say that I have repeated the story more than a couple of dozen times.

"Now, my lord," added Mascarin, "what do you say to this?"
"Continue the reading of the extracts."
"The third allusion, though it is short, is still very important:

November 3rd, 1842. Thank Heaven! all is over. I have just returned from the court. Octave has been acquitted. Ludovic had behaved wonderfully. He explained the reason of the misadventure in a way that was really surprising in an uneducated man, and there was not an atom of suspicion among judge, jury, or spectators. I have changed my mind; I would not have a fellow like Ludovic in my service; he is much too sharp. When I had been duly sworn, I gave my evidence. Though I was much agitated, I went through it all right; but when I got home I felt very ill, and discovered that my pulse was down to fifty. Ah, me! what terrible misfortunes are wrought by a momentary burst of anger. I now write this sentence in my diary: *Never give way to first impulses.*

"These words," continued Mascarin, "were inscribed on every one of the pages following,—at least so those who examined the entries informed me."

Mascarin persisted in representing himself as the agent of others, but still the count made no allusion to the persons in the background.

After a few moments the count rose and limped up and down, as though he hoped by this means to collect his ideas, or perhaps in order to prevent his visitor from scanning his face too closely.

"Have you done?" asked he, all at once.
"Yes, my lord."
"Have you thought what an impartial judge would say?"
"I think I have."
"He would say," broke in the count, "that no sane man would have written such things down, for there are certain secrets which we do not whisper even to ourselves, and it is hardly likely that any man would make such compromising entries in a diary which might be lost or stolen, and which would certainly be read by his heir. Do you

think that a man of high position would record his perjury, which is a crime that would send him to penal servitude?"

Mascarin gazed upon the count with an air of pity.

"You are not going the right way, my lord, to get out of your trouble. No lawyer would adopt your theory. If the remaining volumes of M. de Clinchain's diaries were produced in court, I imagine that other equally startling entries would be found in them."

The count now appeared to have arrived at some decision, and to continue the conversation simply for the purpose of gaining time.

"Well," said he, "I will give up this idea; but how do I know that these documents are not forgeries? Nowadays, handwritings are easily facsimiled, when even bankers find it hard to distinguish between their own notes and counterfeit ones."

"That can be settled by seeing if certain leaves are missing from the baron's diary."

"That does not prove much."

"Pardon me, it proves a great deal. This new line of argument, I assure you, will avail you as little as the other. I am perfectly aware that the Baron de Clinchain will utter whatever words you may place in his mouth. Let us suppose that the leaves which have been torn out should fit into the book exactly. Would not that be a strong point?"

The count smiled ironically, as though he had a crushing reply in reserve.

"And so this is your opinion, is it?" said he.

"It is indeed."

"Then all I have to do is to plead guilty. I did kill Montlouis, just as Clinchain describes, but—" and as he spoke he took a heavy volume from a shelf, and opening it at a certain place laid it before Mascarin, remarking,—"this is the criminal code; read. 'All proceedings in criminal law shall be cancelled after a lapse of ten years.'"

The Count de Mussidan evidently thought that he had crushed his adversary by this shattering blow; but it was not so, for instead of exhibiting any surprise, Mascarin's smile was as bland as ever.

"I, too, know a little of the law," said he. "The very first day this matter was brought to me, I turned to this page and read what you have just shown me to my employers."

"And what did they say?"

"That they knew all this, but that you would be glad to compromise the affair, even at the expense of half your fortune."

The agent's manner was so confident that the count felt they had discovered some means of turning this crime of his early days to advantage; but he was still sufficiently master of himself to show no emotion.

"No," replied he, "it is not such an easy matter as you think to get hold of half my fortune. I fancy that your friends' demands will assume a more modest tone, the more so when I repeat that these morsels of paper, stolen from my friend's diary, are absolutely worthless."

"Do you think so?"

"Certainly, for the law on this matter speaks plainly enough."

Mascarin readjusted his glasses, a sure indication that he was going to make an important reply.

"You are quite right, my lord," said he, slowly. "There is no intention of taking you before any court, for there is no penalty now for a crime committed twenty-three years ago; but the miserable wretches whom I blush to act for have arranged a plan which will be disagreeable in the highest degree both for you and the baron."

"Pray tell me what this clever plan is."

"Most certainly. I came here today for this very purpose. Let us first conclude that you have rejected the request with which I approached you."

"Do you call this style of thing a request?"

"What is the use of quarrelling over words. Well, tomorrow, my clients—though I am ashamed to speak of them as such—will send to a well known morning paper a tale, with the title, 'Story of a Day's Shooting.' Of course only initials will be used for the names, but no doubt will exist as to the identity of the actors in the tragedy."

"You forget that in actions for libel proofs are not admitted."

Mascarin shrugged his shoulders.

"My employers forget nothing," remarked he; "and it is upon this very point that they have based their plans For this reason they introduce into the matter a fifth party, of course an accomplice, whose name is introduced into the story in the paper. Upon the day of its appearance, this man lodges a complaint against the journal, and insists on proving in a court of justice, that he did not form one of the shooting-party."

"Well, what happens then?"

"Then, my lord, this man insists that the journal should give a retraction of the injurious statement and summons as witnesses both yourself and the Baron de Clinchain, and as a conclusion, Ludovic; and as he claims damages, he employs a lawyer, who is one of the confederates and behind the scenes. The lawyer will speak something to this effect: 'That the Count de Mussidan is clearly a murderer; that the Baron de Clinchain is a perjurer, as proved by his own handwriting; Ludovic has been tampered with, but my client, an honourable man, must not be classed with these, etc., etc.' Have I made myself understood?"

Indeed, he had, and with such cold and merciless logic that it seemed hopeless to expect to escape from the net that had been spread.

As these thoughts passed through the count's brain, he saw at a glance the whole terrible notoriety that the case would cause, and society gloating over the details. Yet such was the obstinacy of his disposition, and so impatient was he of control, that the more desperate his position seemed, the fiercer was his resistance. He knew the world well, and he also knew that the cutthroats who demanded his money with threats had every reason to dread the lynx eye of the law. If he refused to listen to them, as his heart urged him, perhaps they would not dare to carry out their threats.

Had he alone been concerned in the matter, he would have resisted to the last, and fought it out to the last drop of his blood, and as a preliminary, would have beaten the sneering rogue before him to a jelly; but how dared he expose his friend Clinchain, who had already braved so much for him? As he paced up and down the library, these and many other thoughts swept across his brain, and he was undecided whether to submit to these extortions or throw the agent out of the window. His excited demeanour and the occasional interjections that burst from his lips showed Mascarin that the account of him was not exaggerated, and that when led by passion he would as soon shoot a fellow-creature as a rabbit. And yet, though he knew not whether he should make his exit by the door or the window, he sat twirling his fingers with the most unconcerned air imaginable. At last the count gave ear to prudence. He stopped in front of the agent, and, taking no pains to hide his contempt, said,—

"Come, let us make an end of this. How much do you want for these papers?"

"Oh, my lord!" exclaimed Mascarin; "surely you do not think that I could be guilty—?"

M. de Mussidan shrugged his shoulders. "Pray, do not take me for a fool," said he, "but name your sum."

Mascarin seemed a little embarrassed, and hesitated. "We don't want money," answered he at length.

"Not money!" replied the count.

"We want something that is of no importance to you, but of the utmost value to those who despatched me here. I am commissioned to inform you that my clients desire that you should break off the engagement between your daughter and M. de Breulh-Faverlay, and that the missing paper will be handed to you on the completion of her marriage with any else whom you may deem worthy of such an honour."

This demand, which was utterly unexpected, so astonished the count that he could only exclaim, "Why, this is absolute madness!"

"No; it is plain, good sense, and a *bona fide* offer."

An idea suddenly flashed across the count's mind. "Is it your intention," asked he, "to furnish me with a son-in-law too?"

"I am sure, my lord," answered Mascarin, looking the picture of disinterested honesty, "that, even to save yourself, you would never sacrifice your daughter."

"But—"

"You are entirely mistaken; it is M. de Breulh-Faverlay whom my clients wish to strike at, for they have taken an oath that he shall never wed a lady with a million for her dowry."

So surprised was the count, that the whole aspect of the interview seemed to have changed, and he now combated his own objections instead of those of his unwelcome visitor. "M. de Breulh-Faverlay has my promise," remarked he; "but of course it is easy to find a pretext. The countess, however, is in favour of the match, and the chief opposition to any change will come from her."

Mascarin did not think it wise to make any reply, and the count continued, "My daughter also may not view this rupture with satisfaction."

Thanks to the information he had received from Florestan, Mascarin knew how much importance to attach to this. "*Mademoiselle*, at her age and with her tastes, is not likely to have her heart seriously engaged." For fully a quarter of an hour the count still hesitated. He knew that he was entirely at the mercy of those miscreants, and his pride revolted at the idea of submission; but at length he yielded.

"I agree," said he. "My daughter shall not marry M. de Breulh-Faverlay."

Even in his hour of triumph, Mascarin's face did not change. He bowed profoundly, and left the room; but as he descended the stairs, he rubbed his hands, exclaiming, "If the doctor has made as good a job of it as I have, success is certain."

Chapter 6: A Medical Adviser

Doctor Hortebise did not find it necessary to resort to any of those expedients which Mascarin had found it advisable to use in order to reach Madame de Mussidan. As soon as he presented himself—that is, after a brief interval of five minutes—he was introduced into the presence of the countess. He rather wondered at this, for Madame de Mussidan was one of those restless spirits that are seldom found at home, but are to be met with at exhibitions, on race-courses, at the *salons*, restaurants, shops, or theatres; or at the studio of some famous artist; or at the rooms of some musical professor who had discovered a new tenor; anywhere and everywhere, in fact, except at home.

Hers was one of those restless natures constantly craving for excitement; and husband, home, and child were mere secondary objects in her eyes. She had many avocations; she was a patroness of half a dozen charitable institutions, but the chief thing that she did was to spend money. Gold seemed to melt in her grasp like so much snow, and she never knew what became of the sums she lavished so profusely. Husband and wife had long been almost totally estranged, and led almost separate existences. Dr. Hortebise was well aware of this, in common with others who moved in society. Upon the appearance of the doctor, the countess dropped the book she had been perusing, and gave vent to an exclamation of delight. "Ah, doctor, this is really very kind of you;" and at the same time signed to the servant to place a chair for the visitor.

The countess was tall and slender, and at forty-five had the figure of a girl. She had an abundance of fair hair, the colour of which concealed the silver threads which plentifully interspersed it. A subtle perfume hung about her, and her pale blue eyes were full of pride and cold disdain.

"You know how to time your visits so well, doctor!" said she. "I am thoroughly bored, and am utterly weary of books, for it always seems to me, when I read, that I had perused the same thing before somewhere or other. You have arrived at so opportune a moment, that you appear to be a favourite of timely chance."

The doctor was indeed a favourite of chance; but the name of the chance was Baptiste Mascarin.

"I see so few visitors," continued Madame de Mussidan, "that hardly anyone comes to see me. I must really set aside one day in the week for my at home; for when I do happen to stay at home, I feel fearfully dull and lonely. For two mortal hours I have been in this room. I have been nursing the count."

The doctor knew better than this; but he smiled pleasantly, and said, "Perfectly so," exactly at the right moment.

"Yes," continued the countess, "my husband slipped on the stairs, and hurt himself very much. Our doctor says it is nothing; but then I put little faith in what doctors say."

"I know that by experience, *madame*," replied Hortebise.

"Present company of course always excepted; but, do you know, I once really believed in you; but your sudden conversion to homeopathy quite frightened me."

The doctor smiled. "It is as safe a mode of practice as any other."

"Do you really think so?"

"I am perfectly sure of it."

"Well, now that you *are* here, I am half inclined to ask your advice."

"I trust that you are not suffering."

"No, thank heaven; I have never any cause to complain of my health; but I am very anxious about Sabine's state."

Her affection of maternal solicitude was a charming pendant to her display of conjugal affection, and again the doctor's expression of assent came in in the right place.

"Yes, for a month, doctor, I have hardly seen Sabine, I have been so much engaged; but yesterday I met her, and was quite shocked at the change in her appearance."

"Did you ask her what ailed her?"

"Of course, and she said, 'Nothing,' adding that she was perfectly well."

"Perhaps something had vexed her?"

"She,—why, don't you know that everyone likes her, and that she is one of the happiest girls in Paris; but I want you to see her in spite of that." She rang the bell as she spoke, and as soon as the footman made his appearance, said, "Lubin, ask *Mademoiselle* to have the goodness to step downstairs."

"*Mademoiselle* has gone out, *madame*."

"Indeed! how long ago?"

"About three o'clock, *madame*."

"Who went with her?"

"Her maid, Modeste."

"Did *Mademoiselle* say where she was going to?"

"No, *madame*."

"Very well, you can go."

Even the imperturbable doctor was rather surprised at a girl of eighteen being permitted so much freedom.

"It is most annoying," said the countess. "However, let us hope that the trifling indisposition, regarding which I wished to consult you, will not prevent her marriage."

Here was the opening that Hortebise desired.

"Is *Mademoiselle* going to be married?" asked he with an air of respectful curiosity.

"Hush!" replied Madame de Mussidan, placing her finger on her lips; "this is a profound secret, and there is nothing definitely arranged; but you, as a doctor, are a perfect father confessor, and I feel that I can trust you. Let me whisper to you that it is quite possible that Sabine will be Madame de Breulh-Faverlay before the close of the year."

Hortebise had not Mascarin's courage; indeed, he was frequently terrified at his confederate's projects; but having once given in his adherence, he was to be relied on, and did not hesitate for a moment. "I confess, *madame*, that I heard that mentioned before;" returned he cautiously.

"And, pray, who was your informant?"

"Oh, I have had it from many sources; and let me say at once that it was this marriage, and no mere chance, that brought me here today."

Madame de Mussidan liked the doctor and his pleasant and witty conversation very much, and was always charmed to see him; but it was intolerable that he should venture to interfere in her daughter's marriage. "Really, sir, you confer a great honour upon the count and myself," answered she haughtily.

Her severe manner, however, did not cause the doctor to lose his temper. He had come to say certain things in a certain manner. He had learned his part, and nothing that the countess could say would prevent his playing it.

"I assure you, *madame*," returned he, "that when I accepted the mission with which I am charged, I only did so from my feelings of respect to you and yours."

"You are really very kind," answered the countess superciliously.

"And I am sure, *madame*, that after you have heard what I have to say, you will have even more reason to agree with me." His manner as he said this was so peculiar, that the countess started as though she had received a galvanic shock. "For more than twenty-five years," pursued the doctor, "I have been the constant depository of strange family secrets, and some of them have been very terrible ones. I have often found myself in a very delicate position, but never in such an embarrassing one as I am now."

"You alarm me," said the countess, dropping her impatient manner.

"If, *madame*, what I have come to relate to you are the mere ravings of a lunatic, I will offer my most sincere apologies; but if, on the contrary, his statements are true—and he has irrefragable proofs in his possession,—then, *madame*—"

"What then, doctor?"

"Then, *madame*, I can only say, make every use of me, for I will willingly place my life at your disposal."

The countess uttered a laugh as artificial as the tears of long-expectant heirs. "Really," said she, "your solemn air and tones almost kill me with laughter."

"She laughs too heartily, and at the wrong time. Mascarin is right," thought the doctor. "I trust, *madame*," continued he, "that I too may laugh at my own imaginary fears; but whatever may be the result, permit me to remind you that a little time back you said that a doctor was a father confessor; for, like a priest, the physician only hears secrets in order to forget them. He is also more fitted to console and advise, for, as his profession brings him into contact with the frailties and passions of the world, he can comprehend and excuse."

"And you must not forget, doctor, that like the priest also, he preaches very long sermons."

As she uttered this sarcasm, there was a jesting look upon her features, but it elicited no smile from Hortebise, who, as he proceeded, grew more grave.

"I may be foolish," he said; "but I had better be that than reopen some old wound."

"Do not be afraid, doctor; speak out."

"Then, I will begin by asking if you have any remembrance of a young man in your own sphere of society, who, at the time of your marriage, was well known in every Parisian *salon*. I speak of the Marquis de Croisenois."

The countess leaned back in her chair, and contracted her brow, and pursed up her lips, as though vainly endeavouring to remember the name.

"The Marquis de Croisenois?" repeated she. "It seems as if—no—wait a moment. No; I cannot say that I can call any such person to mind."

The doctor felt that he must give the spur to this rebellious memory.

"Yes, Croisenois," he repeated. "His Christian name was George, and he had a brother Henry, whom you certainly must know, for this winter I saw him at the Duchess de Laumeuse's, dancing with your daughter."

"You are right; I remember the name now."

Her manner was indifferent and careless as she said this.

"Then perhaps you also recollect that some twenty-three years ago, George de Croisenois vanished suddenly. This disappearance caused a terrible commotion at the time, and was one of the chief topics of society."

"Ah! indeed?" mused the countess.

"He was last seen at the Café de Paris, where he dined with some friends. About nine he got up to leave. One of his friends proposed to go with him, but he begged him not to do so, saying, 'Perhaps I shall see you later on at the opera, but do not count on me.' The general impression was that he was going to some love tryst."

"His friends thought that, I suppose."

"Yes, for he was attired with more care than usual, though he was always one of the best dressed men in Paris. He went out alone, and was never seen again."

"Never again," repeated the countess, a slight shade passing across her brow.

"Never again," echoed the unmoved doctor. "At first his friends merely thought his absence strange; but at the end of a week they grew anxious."

"You go very much into details."

"I heard them all at the time, *madame,* and they were only brought back to my memory this morning. All are to be found in the records of a minute search that the authorities caused to be made into the affair. The friends of De Croisenois had commenced the search; but when they found their efforts useless, they called in the aid of the police. The first idea was suicide: George might have gone into some lonely spot and blown out his brains. There was no reason for this; he had ample means, and always appeared contented and happy. Then it was believed that a murder had been committed, and fresh inquiries were instituted, but nothing could be discovered—nothing."

The countess affected to stifle a yawn, and repeated like an echo, "Nothing."

"Three months later, when the police had given up the matter in despair, one of George de Croisenois' friends received a letter from him."

"He was not dead then, after all?"

Dr. Hortebise made a mental note of the tone and manner of the countess, to consider over at his leisure.

"Who can say?" returned he. "The envelope bore the Cairo postmark. In it George declared that, bored with Parisian life, he was going to start on an exploring expedition to Central Africa, and that no one need be anxious about him. People thought this letter highly suspicious. A man does not start upon such an expedition as this without money; and it was conclusively proved that on the day of De Croisenois' disappearance he had not more than a thousand *francs* about him, half of which was in Spanish *doubloons*, won at whist before dinner. The letter was therefore regarded as a trick to turn the police off the scent; but the best experts asserted that the handwriting was George's own. Two detectives were at once despatched to Cairo, but neither there nor anywhere on the road were any traces of the missing man discovered."

As the doctor spoke, he kept his eyes riveted on the countess, but her face was impassable.

"Is that all?" asked she.

Dr. Hortebise paused a few moments before he replied, and then answered slowly,—

"A man came to me yesterday, and asserts that you can tell me what has become of George de Croisenois."

A man could not have displayed the nerve evinced by this frail and tender woman, for however callous he may be, some feature will betray the torture he is enduring; but a woman can often turn a smiling face upon the person who is racking her very soul. At the mere name of Montlouis the count had staggered, as though crushed down by a blow from a sledge hammer; but at this accusation of Hortebise the countess burst into a peal of laughter, apparently perfectly frank and natural, which utterly prevented her from replying.

"My dear doctor," said she at length, as soon as she could manage to speak, "your tale is highly sensational and amusing, but I really think that you ought to consult a clairvoyant, and not a matter-of-fact person like me, about the fate of George de Croisenois."

But the doctor, who was ready with his retort, and, not at all disconcerted by the cachinnations of the countess, heaved a deep sigh, as though a great load had been removed from his heart, and, with an air of extreme delight, exclaimed, "Thank Heaven! then I was deceived."

He uttered these words with an affectation of such sincerity that the countess fell into the trap.

"Come," said she, with a winning smile, "tell me who it is that says I know so much."

"Pooh! pooh!" returned Hortebise. "What good would that do? He has made a fool of me, and caused me to risk losing your good opinion. Is not that enough? Tomorrow, when he comes to my house, my servants will refuse to admit him; but if I were to do as my inclinations lead me, I should hand him over to the police."

"That would never do," returned the countess, "for that would change a mere nothing into a matter of importance. Tell me the name of your mysterious informer. Do I know him?"

"It is impossible that you could do so, *madame*, for he is far below you in the social grade. You would learn nothing from his name. He is a man I once helped, and is called Daddy Tantaine."

"A mere nickname, of course."

"He is miserably poor, a cynic, philosopher, but as sharp as a needle; and this last fact causes me great uneasiness, for at first I thought that he had been sent to me by someone far above him in position, but—"

"But, doctor," interposed the countess, "you spoke to me of proofs, of threats, of certain mysterious persons."

"I simply repeated Daddy Tantaine's words. The old idiot said to me, 'Madame de Mussidan knows all about the fate of the *marquis*, and this is clearly proved by letters that she has received from him, as well as from the Duke de Champdoce.'"

This time the arrow went home. She grew deadly pale, and started to her feet with her eyes dilated with horror.

"My letters!" exclaimed she hoarsely.

Hortebise appeared utterly overwhelmed by this display of consternation, of which he was the innocent cause.

"Your letters, *madame*," replied he with evident hesitation, "this double-dyed scoundrel declares he has in his possession."

With a cry like that of a wounded lioness, the countess, taking no notice of the doctor's presence, rushed from the room. Her rapid footfall could be heard on the stairs, and the rustle of her silken skirts against the banisters. As soon as he was left alone, the doctor rose from his seat with a cynical smile upon his face.

"You may search," mused he, "but you will find that the birds have flown." He walked up to one of the windows, and drummed on the glass with his fingers. "People say," remarked he, "that Mascarin never makes a mistake. One cannot help admiring his diabolical sagacity and unfailing logic. From the most trivial event he forges a long chain of evidence, as the botanist is able, as he picks up a withered leaf, to describe in detail the tree it came from. A pity, almost, that he did not turn his talents to some nobler end; but no; he is now upstairs putting the count on the rack, while I am inflicting tortures on the countess. What a shameful business we are carrying on! There are moments when I think that I have paid dearly for my life of luxury, for I know well," he added, half consciously fingering his locket, "that some day we shall meet someone stronger than ourselves, and then the inevitable will ensue."

The reappearance of the countess broke the chain of his thoughts. Her hair was disturbed, her eyes had a wild look in them, and everything about her betrayed the state of agitation she was in.

"Robbed! robbed!" cried she, as she entered the room. Her excitement was so extreme that she spoke aloud, forgetting that the door was open, and that the lackey in the ante-room could hear all she said. Luckily Hortebise did not lose his presence of mind, and, with the ease of a leading actor repairing the error of a subordinate, he closed the door.

"What have you lost?" asked he.

"My letters; they are all gone."

She staggered on to a couch, and in broken accents went on. "And yet these letters were in an iron casket closed by a secret spring; that casket was in a drawer, the key of which never leaves me."

"Good heavens!" exclaimed Hortebise in affected tones, "then Tantaine spoke the truth."

"He did," answered the countess hoarsely. "Yes," she continued, "I am the bond-slave to people whose names I do not even know, who can control my every movement and action."

She hid her face in her hands as though her pride sought to conceal her despair.

"Are these letters, then, so terribly compromising?" asked the doctor.

"I am utterly lost," cried she. "In my younger days I had no experience; I only thought of vengeance, and lately the weapons I forged myself have been turned against me. I dug a pitfall for my adversaries and have fallen into it myself."

Hortebise did not attempt to stay the torrent of her words, for the countess was in one of those moods of utter despair when the inner feelings of the soul are made manifest, as during a violent tempest the weeds of ocean are hurled up to the surface of the troubled waters.

"I would sooner be lying in my grave a thousand times," wailed she, "than see these letters in my husband's hands. Poor Octave! have I not caused him sufficient annoyance already without this crowning sorrow? Well, Dr. Hortebise, I am menaced with the production of these letters, and they will be handed to my husband unless I agree to certain terms. What are they? Of course money is required; tell me to what amount."

The doctor shook his head.

"Not money?" cried the countess; "what, then, do they require? Speak, and do not torture me more."

Sometimes Hortebise confessed to Mascarin that, putting his interests on one side, he pitied his victims; but he showed no sign of this feeling, and went on,—

"The value of what they require, *madame*, is best estimated by yourself."

"Tell me what it is; I can bear anything now."

"These compromising letters will be placed in your hands upon the day on which your daughter marries Henry de Croisenois, the brother of George."

Madame de Mussidan's astonishment was so great that she stood as though petrified into a statue.

"I am commissioned to inform you, *madame*, that every delay necessary for altering any arrangements that may exist will be accorded you; but, remember, if your daughter marries anyone else than Henry de Croisenois, the letters will be at once placed in your husband's hands."

As he spoke the doctor watched her narrowly. The countess crossed the room, faint and dizzy, and rested her head on the mantelpiece.

"And that is all?" asked she. "What you ask me to do is utterly impossible: and perhaps it is for the best, for I shall have no long agony of suspense to endure. Go, doctor, and tell the villain who holds my letters that he can take them to the count at once."

The countess spoke in such a decided tone that Hortebise was a little puzzled.

"Can it be true," she continued, "that scoundrels exist in our country who are viler than the most cowardly murderers,—men who trade in the shameful secrets that they have learned, and batten upon the money they earn by their odious trade? I heard of such creatures before, but declined to believe it; for I said to myself that such an idea only existed in the unhealthy imaginations of novel writers. It seems, however that I was in error; but do not let these villains rejoice too soon; they will reap but a scanty harvest. There is one asylum left for me where they cannot molest me."

"Ah, *madame!*" exclaimed the doctor in imploring accents; but she paid no attention to his remonstrances, and went on with increasing violence,—

"Do the miserable wretches think that I fear death? For years I have prayed for it as a final mercy from the heaven I have so deeply offended. I long for the quiet of the sepulchre. You are surprised at hearing one like me speak in this way,—one who has all her life been admired and flattered,—I, Diana de Laurebourg, Countess de Mussidan. Even in the hours of my greatest triumphs my soul shuddered at the thought of the grim spectre hidden away in the past; and I wished that death would come and relieve my sufferings. My eccentricities have often surprised my friends, who asked if sometimes I were not a little mad. Mad? Yes, I am mad! They do not know that I seek oblivion in excitement, and that I dare not be alone. But I have learned by this time that I must stifle the voice of conscience."

She spoke like a woman utterly bereft of hope, who had resolved on the final sacrifice. Her clear voice rang through the room, and Hortebise turned pale as he heard the footsteps of the servants pacing to and fro outside the door, as they made preparations for dinner.

"All my life has been one continual struggle," resumed she,—"a struggle which has cost me sore; but now all is over, and tonight, for the first time for many years, Diana de Mussidan will sleep a calm and untroubled sleep."

The excitement of the countess had risen to so high a pitch that the doctor asked himself how he could allay a tempest which he had not foreseen; for her loud tones would certainly alarm the servants, who would hasten to acquaint the count, who was himself stretched upon the rack; then the entire plot would be laid bare, and all would be lost.

Madame de Mussidan was about to rush from the room, when the doctor, perceiving that he must act decisively, seized her by both wrists, and, almost by force, caused her to resume her seat.

"In Heaven's name, *madame*," he whispered, "for your daughter's sake, listen to me. Do not throw up all; am not I here ready to do your bidding, whatever it may be? Rely upon me,—rely upon the knowledge of a man of the world, and of one who still possesses some portion of what is called a heart. Cannot we form an alliance to ward off this attack?"

The doctor continued in this strain, endeavouring to reassure the countess as much as he had previously endeavoured to terrify her, and soon had the satisfaction of seeing his efforts crowned with success; for Madame de Mussidan listened to his flow of language, hardly comprehending its import, but feeling calmer as he went on; and in a quarter of an hour he had persuaded her to look the situation boldly in the face. Then Hortebise breathed more freely, and, wiping the perspiration from his brow, felt that he had gained the victory.

"It is a nefarious plot," said the countess.

"So it is, *madame*; but the facts remain. Only tell me one thing, have you any special objection to M. de Croisenois paying his addresses to your daughter?"

"Certainly not."

"He comes from a good family, is well educated, handsome, popular, and only thirty-four. If you remember, George was his senior by fifteen years. Why, then, is not the marriage a suitable one? Certainly, he has led rather a fast life; but what young man is immaculate? They say that he is deeply in debt; but then your daughter has enough for both. Besides, his brother left him a considerable fortune, not far short of two millions, I believe; and to this, of course Henry will eventually succeed."

Madame de Mussidan was too overwhelmed by what she had already gone through to offer any further exposition of her feelings on the subject.

"All this is very well," answered she; "but the count has decided that Sabine is to become the wife of M. de Breulh-Faverlay, and I have no voice in the matter."

"But if you exert your influence?"

The countess shook her head. "Once on a time," said she sadly, "I reigned supreme over Octave's heart; I was the leading spirit of his existence. Then he loved me; but I was insensible to the depths of his affection, and wore out a love that would have lasted as long as life itself. Yes, in my folly I slew it, and now—" She paused for a moment as if to collect her ideas, and then added more slowly: "and now our lives are separate ones. I do not complain; it is all my own fault; he is just and generous."

"But surely you can make the effort?"

"But suppose Sabine loves M. de Breulh-Faverlay?"

"But, *madame*, a mother can always influence her daughter."

The countess seized the doctor's hand, and grasped it so tightly that he could hardly bear the pain.

"I must," said she in a hoarse whisper, "divulge to you the whole extent of my unhappiness. I am estranged from my husband, and my daughter dislikes and despises me. Some people think that life can be divided into two portions, one consecrated to pleasure and excitement, and the other to domestic peace and happiness; but the idea is a false one. As youth has been, so will be age, either a reward or an expiation."

Dr. Hortebise did not care to follow this train of argument—for the count might enter at any moment, or a servant might come in to announce dinner—and only sought to soothe the excited feelings of Madame de Mussidan, and to prove to her that she was frightened by shadows, and that in reality she was not estranged from her husband, nor did her daughter dislike her; and finally a ray of hope illuminated the saddened heart of the unfortunate lady.

"Ah, doctor!" said she, "it is only misfortune that teaches us to know our true friends."

The countess, like her husband, had now laid down her arms; she had made a longer fight of it, but in both cases the result had been the same. She promised that she would commence operations the next day, and do her utmost to break off the present engagement.

Hortebise then took his leave, quite worn out with the severe conflict he had waged during his two hours' interview with the countess. In spite of the extreme cold, the air outside seemed to refresh him considerably, and he inhaled it with the happy feeling that he had performed his duty in a manner worthy of all praise. He walked up the Rue de Faubourg Saint Honore, and again entered the *café* where he and his worthy confederate had agreed to meet. Mascarin was there, an untasted cutlet before him, and his face hidden by a newspaper which his anxiety would not permit him to peruse. His suspense was terrible. Had Hortebise failed? had he encountered one of those unforeseen obstacles which, like a minute grain of sand, utterly hinders the working of a piece of delicate machinery?

"Well, what news?" said he eagerly, as soon as he caught sight of the doctor.

"Success, perfect success!" said Hortebise gaily. "But," added he, as he sank exhausted upon a seat, "the battle has been a hard one."

Chapter 7: In the Studio

Staggering like a drunken man, Paul Violaine descended the stairs when his interview with Mascarin had been concluded. The sudden and unexpected good fortune which had fallen so opportunely at his feet had for the moment absolutely stunned him. He was now removed from a position which had caused him to gaze with longing upon the still waters of the Seine, to one of comparative affluence. "Mascarin," said he to himself, "has offered me an appointment bringing in twelve thousand *francs* per annum, and proposed to give me the first month's salary in advance."

Certainly it was enough to bewilder any man, and Paul was utterly dazed. He went over all the events that had occurred during the day— the sudden appearance of old Tantaine, with his loan of five hundred *francs*, and the strange man who knew the whole history of his life, and who, without making any conditions, had offered him a valuable situation. Paul was in no particular hurry to get back to the Hotel de Perou, for he said to himself that Rose could wait. A feeling of restlessness had seized upon him. He wanted to squander money, and to have the sympathy of some companions,—but where should he go, for he had no friends? Searching the records of his memory, he remembered that, when poverty had first overtaken him, he had borrowed twenty *francs* from a young fellow of his own age, named Andre.

Some gold coins still jingled in his pocket, and he could have a thousand *francs* for the asking. Would it not add to his importance if he were to go and pay this debt? Unluckily his creditor lived a long distance off in the Rue de la Tour d'Auvergne. He, however, hailed a passing cab, and was driven to Andre's address. This young man was only a casual acquaintance, whom Paul had picked up one day in a small wine-shop to which he used to take Rose when he first arrived in Paris. Andre, with whose other name Paul was unacquainted, was an artist, and, in addition, was an ornamental sculptor, and executed those wonderful decorations on the outside of houses in which builders delight. The trade is not a pleasant one, for it necessitates working at dizzy heights, on scaffolds that vibrate with every footstep, and exposes you to the heat of summer and the frosts of winter.

The business, however, is well paid, and Andre got a good price for

71

his stone figures and wreaths. But all the money he earned went in the study of the painter's art, which was the secret desire of his soul. He had taken a studio, and twice his pictures had been exhibited at the *salon*, and orders began to come in. Many of his brother artists predicted a glorious future for him. When the cab stopped, Paul threw the fare to the driver, and asked the clean-looking portress, who was polishing the brass work on the door, if M. Andre was at home.

"He is, sir," replied the old woman, adding, with much volubility, "and you are likely to find him in, for he has so much work; but he is such a good and quiet young man, and so regular in his habits! I don't believe he owes a penny in the world; and as for drink, why he is a perfect Anchorite. Then he has very few acquaintances,—one young lady, whose face for a month past I have tried to see, but failed, because she wears a veil, comes to see him, accompanied by her maid."

"Good heavens, woman!" cried Paul impatiently, "will you tell me where to find M. Andre?"

"Fourth floor, first door to the right," answered the portress, angry at being interrupted; and as Paul ran up the stairs, she muttered, "A young chap with no manners, taking the words out of a body's mouth like that! Next time he comes, I'll serve him out somehow."

Paul found the door, with a card with the word "Andre" marked upon it nailed up, and rapped on the panel. He heard the sound of a piece of furniture being moved, and the jingle of rings being passed along a rod; then a clear, youthful voice answered, "Come in!"

Paul entered, and found himself in a large, airy room, lighted by a skylight, and exquisitely clean and orderly. Sketches and drawings were suspended on the walls; there was a handsome carpet from Tunis, and a comfortable lounge; a mirror in a carved frame, which would have gladdened the heart of a connoisseur, stood upon the mantelpiece. An easel with a picture upon it, covered with a green baize curtain, stood in one corner. The young painter was in the centre of his studio, brush and palette in hand. He was a dark, handsome young man, well built and proportioned, with close-cut hair, and a curling beard flowing down over his chest. His face was full of expression, and the energy and vigour imprinted upon it formed a marked contrast to the appearance of Mascarin's *protégé*. Paul noticed that he did not wear the usual painter's blouse, but was carefully dressed in the prevailing fashion. As soon as he recognised Paul, Andre came forward with extended hand. "Ah," said he, "I am pleased to see you, for I often wondered what had become of you."

Paul was offended at this familiar greeting. "I have had many worries and disappointments," said he.

"And Rose," said Andre, "how is she—as pretty as ever, I suppose?"

"Yes, yes," answered Paul negligently; "but you must forgive me for having vanished so suddenly. I have come to repay your loan, with many thanks."

"Pshaw!" returned the painter, "I never thought of the matter again; pray, do not inconvenience yourself."

Again Paul felt annoyed, for he fancied that under the cloak of assumed generosity the painter meant to humiliate him; and the opportunity of airing his newly-found grandeur occurred to him.

"It was a convenience to me, certainly," said he, "but I am all right now, having a salary of twelve thousand *francs*."

He thought that the artist would be dazzled, and that the mention of this sum would draw from him some exclamations of surprise and envy. Andre, however, made no reply, and Paul was obliged to wind up with the lame conclusion, "And at my age that is not so bad."

"I should call it superb. Should I be indiscreet in asking what you are doing?"

The question was a most natural one, but Paul could not reply to it, as he was entirely ignorant as to what his employment was to be, and he felt as angry as if the painter had wantonly insulted him.

"I work for it," said he, drawing himself up with such a strange expression of voice and feature that Andre could not fail to notice it.

"I work too," remarked he; "I am never idle."

"But I have to work very hard," returned Paul, "for I have not, like you, a friend or protector to interest himself in me."

Paul, who had not a particle of gratitude in his disposition, had entirely forgotten Mascarin.

The artist was much amused by this speech. "And where do you think that a foundling, as I am, would find a protector?"

Paul opened his eyes. "What," said he, "are you one of those?"

"I am; I make no secret of it, hoping that there is no occasion for me to feel shame, though there may be for grief. All my friends know this; and I am surprised that you are not aware that I am simply a foundling from the Hopital de Vendome. Up to twelve years of age I was perfectly happy, and the master praised me for the knack I had of acquiring knowledge. I used to work in the garden by day, and in the evening I wasted reams of paper; for I had made up my mind to be an artist. But nothing goes easily in this world, and one day the lady superintendent conceived the idea of apprenticing me to a tanner."

Paul, who had taken a seat on the divan in order to listen, here commenced making a cigarette; but Andre stopped him. "Excuse me; but will you oblige me by not smoking?"

Paul tossed the cigarette aside, though he was a little surprised, as the painter was an inveterate smoker. "All right," said he, "but continue your story."

"I will; it is a long one. I hated the tanner's business from the very beginning. Almost the first day an awkward workman scalded me so severely that the traces still remain." As he spoke he rolled up his shirt sleeve, and exhibited a scar that covered nearly all one side of his arm. "Horrified at such a commencement, I entreated the lady superintendent, a hideous old woman in spectacles, to apprentice me to some other trade, but she sternly refused. She had made up her mind that I should be a tanner."

"That was very nasty of her," remarked Paul.

"It was, indeed; but from that day I made up my mind, and I determined to run away as soon as I could get a little money together. I therefore stuck steadily to the business, and by the end of the year, by means of the strictest economy, I found myself master of thirty *francs*. This, I thought, would do, and, with a bundle containing a change of linen, I started on foot for Paris. I was only thirteen, but I had been gifted by Providence with plenty of that strong will called by many obstinacy. I had made up my mind to be a painter."

"And you kept your vow?"

"But with the greatest difficulty. Ah! I can close my eyes and see the place where I slept that first night I came to Paris. I was so exhausted that I did not awake for twelve hours. I ordered a good breakfast; and finding funds at a very low ebb, I started in search of work."

Paul smiled. He, too, remembered *his* first day in Paris. He was twenty-two years of age, and had forty *francs* in his pocket.

"I wanted to make money—for I felt I needed it—to enable me to pursue my studies. A stout man was seated near me at breakfast, and to him I addressed myself.

"'Look here,' said I, 'I am thirteen, and much stronger than I look. I can read and write. Tell me how I can earn a living.'

"He looked steadily at me, and in a rough voice answered, 'Go to the market tomorrow morning, and try if one of the master masons, who are on the lookout for hands, will employ you.'"

"And you went?"

"I did; and was eagerly watching the head masons, when I perceived my stout friend coming toward me.

"'I like the looks of you, my lad,' he said; 'I am an ornamental sculptor. Do you care to learn my trade?'

"When I heard this proposal, it seemed as if Paradise was opening before me, and I agreed with enthusiasm."

"And how about your painting?"

"That came later on. I worked hard at it in all my hours of leisure. I attended the evening schools, and worked steadily at my art and other branches of education. It was a very long time before I ventured to indulge in a glass of beer. 'No, no, Andre,' I would say to myself, 'beer costs six *sous*; lay the money by.' Finally, when I was earning from eighty to a hundred *francs* a week, I was able to give more time to the brush."

The recital of this life of toil and self-denial, so different from his own selfish and idle career, was inexpressibly mortifying to Paul; but he felt that he was called upon to say something.

"When one has talents like yours," said he, "success follows as a matter of course."

He rose to his feet, and affected to examine the sketches on the walls, though his attention was attracted to the covered picture on the easel. He remembered what the garrulous old portress had said about the veiled lady who sometimes visited the painter, and that there had been some delay in admitting him when he first knocked. Then he considered, for whom had the painter dressed himself with such care? and why had he requested him not to smoke? From all these facts Paul came to the conclusion that Andre was expecting the lady's visit, and that the veiled picture was her portrait. He therefore determined to see it; and with this end in view, he walked round the studio, admiring all the paintings on the walls, manoeuvring in such a manner as to imperceptibly draw nearer to the easel.

"And this," said he, suddenly extending his hand toward the cover, "is, I presume, the gem of your studio?"

But Andre was by no means dull, and had divined Paul's intention, and grasped the young man's outstretched hand just as it touched the curtain.

"If I veil this picture," said he, "it is because I do not wish it to be seen."

"Excuse me," answered Paul, trying to pass over the matter as a jest, though in reality he was boiling over with rage at the manner and tone of the painter, and considered his caution utterly ridiculous.

"At any rate," said he to himself, "I will lengthen out my visit, and have a glimpse of the original instead of her picture;" and, with this amiable resolution, he sat down by the artist's table, and commenced an apparently interminable story, resolved not to attend to any hints his friend might throw out, who was glancing at the clock with the utmost anxiety, comparing it every now and then with his watch.

As Paul talked on, he saw close to him on the table the photograph of a young lady, and, taking advantage of the artist's preoccupation, looked at it.

"Pretty, very pretty!" remarked he.

At these words the painter flushed crimson, and snatching away the photograph with some little degree of violence, thrust it between the leaves of a book.

Andre was so evidently in a patina, that Paul rose to his feet, and for a second or two the men looked into each other's eyes as two adversaries do when about to engage in a mortal duel. They knew but little of each other, and the same chance which had brought them together might separate them again at any moment, but each felt that the other exercised some influence over his life.

Andre was the first to recover himself.

"You must excuse me; but I was wrong to leave so precious an article about."

Paul bowed with the air of a man who accepts an apology which he considers his due; and Andre went on,—

"I very rarely receive anyone except my friends; but today I have broken through my rule."

Paul interrupted him with a magniloquent wave of the hand.

"Believe me, sir," said he, in a voice which he endeavoured to render cutting and sarcastic, "had it not been for the imperative duty I before alluded to, I should not have intruded."

And with these words he left the room, slamming the door behind him.

"The deuce take the impudent fool!" muttered Andre. "I was strongly tempted to pitch him out of the window."

Paul was in a furious rage for having visited the studio with the kindly desire of humiliating the painter. He could not but feel that the tables had been turned upon himself.

"He shall not have it all his own way," muttered he; "for I will see the lady," and not reflecting on the meanness of his conduct, he crossed the street, and took up a position from which he could obtain a good view of the house where Andre resided. It was snowing; but Paul disregarded the inclemency of the weather in his eagerness to act the spy.

He had waited for fully half an hour, when a cab drove up. Two women alighted from it. The one was eminently aristocratic in appearance, while the other looked like a respectable servant. Paul drew closer; and, in spite of a thick veil, recognised the features he had seen in the photograph.

"Ah!" said he, "after all, Rose is more to my taste, and I will get back to her. We will pay up Loupins, and get out of his horrible den."

Chapter 8: Mademoiselle De Mussidan

Paul had not been the only watcher; for at the sound of the carriage wheels the ancient portress took up her position in the doorway, with her eyes fixed on the face of the young lady. When the two women had ascended the stairs, a sudden inspiration seized her, and she went out and spoke to the cabman.

"Nasty night," remarked she; "I don't envy you in such weather as this."

"You may well say that," replied the driver; "my feet are like lumps of ice."

"Have you come far?"

"Rather; I picked them up in the Champs Elysees, near the Avenue de Matignon."

"That is a distance." "Yes; and only five *sous* for drink money. Hang your respectable women!"

"Oh! they are respectable, are they?"

"I'll answer for that. The other lot are far more open-handed. I know both of them."

And with these words and a knowing wink, he touched up his horse and drove away; and the portress, only half satisfied, went back to her lodge.

"Why that is the quarter where all the swells live," murmured she. "I'll tip the maid next time, and she'll let out everything."

After Paul's departure, Andre could not remain quiet; for it appeared to him as if each second was a century. He had thrown open the door of his studio, and ran to the head of the stairs at every sound.

At last their footsteps really sounded on the steps. The sweetest music in the world is the rustle of the beloved one's dress. Leaning

77

over the banisters, he gazed fondly down. Soon she appeared, and in a short time had gained the open door of the studio.

"You see, Andre," said she, extending her hand, "you see that I am true to my time."

Pale, and trembling with emotion, Andre pressed the little hand to his lips.

"Ah! Mademoiselle Sabine, how kind you are! Thanks, a thousand thanks."

Yes, it was indeed Sabine, the scion of the lordly house of Mussidan, who had come to visit the poor foundling of the Hotel de Vendome in his studio, and who thus risked all that was most precious to her in the world, her honour and her reputation. Yes, regardless of the conventionalities among which she had been reared, dared to cross that social abyss which separates the Avenue de Matignon from the Rue de la Tour d'Auvergne. Cold reason finds no excuse for such a step, but the heart can easily solve this seeming riddle. Sabine and Andre had been lovers for more than two years. Their first acquaintance had commenced at the Château de Mussidan. At the end of the summer of 1865, Andre, whose constant application to work had told upon his health, determined to take a change, when his master, Jean Lanier, called him, and said,—

"If you wish for a change, and at the same time to earn three or four hundred *francs*, now is your time. An architect has written to me, asking me for a skilled stone carver, to do some work in the country at a magnificent mansion in the midst of the most superb scenery. Would you care about undertaking this?"

The proposal was a most acceptable one to Andre, and in a week's time he was on his way to his work with a prospect of living for a month in pure country air. Upon his arrival at the *château*, he made a thorough examination of the work with which he had been entrusted. He saw that he could finish it with perfect ease, for it was only to restore the carved work on a balcony, which would not take more than a fortnight. He did not, however, press on the work, for the beautiful scenery enchanted him.

He made many exquisite sketches, and his health began to return to him. But there was another reason why he was in no haste to complete his task, one which he hardly ventured even to confess to himself: he had caught a glimpse of a young girl in the park of the *château* who had caused a new feeling to spring up in his heart. It was Sabine de Mussidan. The count, as the season came on, had gone to Germany, the countess had flitted away to Luzon, and the daughter was sent to the dull old country mansion in charge of her old aunt. It was the old, old story; two young hearts loving with all the truth and energy of their natures. They had exchanged a few words on their first meeting, and on the next Sabine went on to the balcony and watched the rapid play of Andre's chisel with childish delight.

For a long time they conversed, and Sabine was surprised at the education and refinement of the young workman. Utterly fresh, and without experience, Sabine could not understand her new sensations. Andre held, one night, a long converse with himself, and was at last obliged to confess that he loved her fondly. He ran the extent of his folly and madness, and recognised the barrier of birth and wealth that stood between them, and was overwhelmed with consternation.

The Château of Mussidan stands in a very lonely spot, and one of the roads leading to it passes through a dense forest, and therefore it had been arranged that Andre was to take his meals in the house. After a time Sabine began to feel that this isolation was a needless humiliation.

"Why can't M. Andre take his meals with us?" asked she of her aunt. "He is certainly more gentlemanlike than many of those who visit us, and I think that his conversation would entertain you."

The old lady was easily persuaded to adopt this suggestion, though at first it seemed an odd kind of thing to admit a mere working man to her table; but she was so bored with the loneliness of the place that she hailed with delight anything that would break its monotony. Andre at once accepted the proposal, and the old lady would hardly believe her eyes when her guest entered the room with the dress and manners of a highbred gentleman. "It is hardly to be believed," said she, as she was preparing to go to bed, "that a mere carver of stone should be so like a gentleman. It seems to me that all distinctions of social rank have vanished. It is time for me to die, or we are rapidly approaching a state of anarchy."

In spite of her prejudices, however, Andre contrived to win the old lady's heart, and won a complete victory by painting her portrait in full gala costume. From that moment he was treated as one of the family, and, having no fear of a rebuff, was witty and sprightly in his manner. Once he told the old lady the true story of his life. Sabine was deeply interested, and marvelled at his energy and endurance, which had won for him a place on the ladder that leads to future eminence. She saw in him the realization of all her girlish dreams, and finally confessed to herself that she loved him. Both her father and mother had their own pleasures and pursuits, and Sabine was as much alone in the world as Andre.

The days now fled rapidly by. Buried in this secluded country house, they were as free as the breeze that played through the trees of the forest, for the old lady rarely disturbed them. After the morning meal, she would beg Andre to read the newspaper to her, and fell into a doze before he had been five minutes at the task. Then the young people would slip quietly away, as merry as truants from school. They wandered beneath the shade of the giant oaks, or climbed the rocks that stood by the river bank. Sometimes, seated in a dilapidated boat, they would drift down the stream with its flower-bedecked banks. The water was often almost covered with rushes and water lilies. Two months of enchantment thus fled past, two months of the intoxications of love, though the mention of the tender passion never rose to their lips from their hearts, where it was deeply imbedded. Andre had cast all reflections regarding the perils of the future to the winds, and only thanked heaven for the happiness that he was experiencing.

"Am I not too happy?" he would say to himself. "I fear this cannot last." And he was right. Anxious to justify his remaining at Mussidan after his task was completed, Andre determined to add to what he had already done a masterpiece of modern art, by carving a garland of fruit and flowers over the old balcony, and every morning he rose with the sun to proceed with his task.

One morning the valet came to him, saying that the old lady was desirous of seeing him, and begged him to lose no time, as the business was urgent. A presentiment of evil came like a chilly blast upon the young man's heart. He felt that his brief dream of happiness was at an end, and he followed the valet as a criminal follows his executioner to the scaffold.

As he opened the door in which Sabine's aunt was awaiting him, the old man whispered,—

"Have a care, sir, have a care. *Madame* is in a terrible state; I have not seen her like this since her husband died."

The old lady was in a terrible state of excitement, and in spite of rheumatic pains was walking up and down the room, gesticulating wildly, and striking her crutch-handled stick on the floor.

"And so," cried she in that haughty tone adopted by women of aristocratic lineage when addressing a supposed inferior, "you have, I hear, had the impudence to make love to my niece?"

Andre's pale face grew crimson as he stammered out,—

"*Madame*—"

"Gracious powers, fellow!" cried the angry woman, "do you dare to deny this when your very face betrays you? Do you know that you are an insolent rogue even to venture to look on Sabine de Mussidan? How dare you! Perhaps you thought that if you compromised her, we should be forced to submit to this ignoble alliance."

"On my honour, *madame*, I assure you—"

"On your honour! To hear you speak, one would suppose that you were a gentleman. If my poor husband were alive, he would break every bone in your body; but I am satisfied with ordering you out of the house. Pick up your tools, and be off at once."

Andre stood as though petrified into stone. He took no notice of her imperious manner, but only realized the fact that he should never see Sabine again, and, turning deadly pale, staggered to a chair. The old lady was so surprised at the manner in which Andre received her communication, that for a time she too was bewildered, and could not utter a word.

"I am unfortunately of a violent temper," said she, speaking in more gentle accents, "and perhaps I have spoken too severely, for I am much to blame in this matter, as the priest of Berron said when he came to inform me of what was going on. I am so old that I forgot what happens when young people are thrown together, and I was the only one who did not know what was going on when you were affording subject of gossip for the whole countryside; my niece—"

But here Andre started to his feet with a threatening look upon his face.

"I could strangle them all," cried he.

"That is right," returned the old lady, secretly pleased at his vigour and energy, "but you cannot silence every idle tongue. Fortunately, matters have not gone too far. Go away, and forget my niece."

She might as well have told the young man to go away and die.

"*Madame!*" cried he in accents of despair, "pray listen to me. I am young, and full of hope and courage."

The old lady was so touched by his evident sorrow, that the tears rolled down her wrinkled cheeks.

"What is the good of saying this to me?" asked she. "Sabine is not my daughter. All that I can do is never to say a word to her father and mother. Great heavens, if Mussidan should ever learn what has occurred! There, do go away. You have upset me so that I do not believe

I shall eat a mouthful for the next two days."

Andre staggered out of the room. It seemed to him as if the flooring heaved and rolled beneath his feet. He could see nothing, but he felt someone take him by the hand. It was Sabine, pallid and cold as a marble statue.

"I have heard everything, Andre," murmured she.

"Yes," stammered he. "All is over, and I am dismissed."

"Where are you going to?"

"Heaven only knows, and when once I leave this place I care not."

"Do not be desperate," urged Sabine, laying her hand upon his arm.

His fixed glance terrified her as he muttered,—

"I cannot help it; I am driven to despair."

Never had Sabine appeared so lovely; her eyes gleamed with some generous impulse, and her face glowed.

"Suppose," said she, "I could give you a ray of future hope, what would you do then?"

"What would I *not* do then? All that a man could. I would fight my way through all opposition. Give me the hardest task, and I will fulfil it. If money is wanted, I will gain it; if a name, I will win it."

"There is one thing that you have forgotten, and that is patience."

"And that, *Mademoiselle*, I possess also. Do you not understand that with one word of hope from you I can live on?"

Sabine raised her head heavenwards. "Work!" she exclaimed. "Work and hope, for I swear that I will never wed other than you."

Here the voice of the old lady interrupted the lovers.

"Still lingering here!" she cried, in a voice like a trumpet call. Andre fled away with hope in his heart, and felt that he had now something to live for. No one knew exactly what happened after his departure. No doubt Sabine brought round her aunt to her way of thinking, for at her death, which happened two months afterward, she left the whole of her immense fortune directly to her niece, giving her the income while she remained single, and the capital on her marriage, whether with or without the consent of her parents. Madame de Mussidan declared that the old lady had gone crazy, but both Andre and Sabine knew what she had intended, and sincerely mourned for the excellent woman, whose last act had been to smooth away the difficulties from their path. Andre worked harder than ever, and Sabine encouraged him by fresh promises. Sabine was even more free in Paris than at Mussidan, and her attached maid, Modeste, would have committed almost any crime to promote the happiness of her beloved mistress. The lovers now corresponded regularly, and Sabine, accompanied by Modeste, frequently visited the artist's studio, and never was a saint treated with greater respect and adoration than was Sabine by Andre.

Chapter 9: Rose's Promotion

As soon as Andre had released her hand, Sabine took off her hat, and, handing it to Modeste, remarked,—

"How am I looking today, Andre?"

The young painter hastened to reassure her on this point, and she continued in joyous tones,—

"No, I do not want compliments; I want to know if I look the right thing for sitting for my portrait."

Sabine was very beautiful, but hers was a different style of beauty from that of Rose, whose ripe, sensuous charms were fitted to captivate the admiration of the voluptuary, while Sabine was of the most refined and ethereal character. Rose fettered the body with earthly trammels, while Sabine drew the soul heavenward. Her beauty was not of the kind that dazzles, for the air of proud reserve which she threw over it, in some slight measure obscured its brilliancy.

She might have passed unnoticed, like the work of a great master's brush hanging neglected over the altar of a village church; but when the eye had once fathomed that hidden beauty, it never ceased to gaze on it with admiration. She had a broad forehead, covered with a wealth of chestnut hair, soft, lustrous eyes, and an exquisitely chiselled mouth.

"Alas!" said Andre, "when I gaze upon you, I have to confess how impossible it is to do you justice. Before you came I had fancied that the portrait was completed, but now I see that I have only made a failure."

As he spoke, he drew aside the curtain, and the young girl's portrait was revealed. It was by no means a work of extraordinary merit. The artist was only twenty-four years of age, and had been compelled to interrupt his studies to toil for his daily bread, but it was full of originality and genius. Sabine gazed at it for a few moments in silence, and then murmured the words,—

"It is lovely!"

But Andre was too discouraged to notice her praise.

"It is like," remarked he, "but a photograph also has that merit.

I have only got your features, but not your expression; it is an utter failure. Shall I try again?"

Sabine stopped him with a gesture of denial.

"You shall not try again," said she decidedly.

"And why not?" asked he in astonishment.

"Because this visit will be my last, Andre."

"The last?" stammered the painter. "In what way have I so offended you, that you should inflict so terrible a punishment on me?"

"I do not wish to punish you. You asked for my portrait, and I yielded to your request; but let us talk reasonably. Do you not know that I am risking my reputation by coming here day after day?"

Andre made no reply, for this unexpected blow had almost stunned him.

"Besides," continued Mademoiselle de Mussidan, "what is to be done with the portrait? It must be hidden away, as if it were something we were ashamed of. Remember, on your success hangs our marriage."

"I do not forget that."

"Hasten then to gain all honour and distinction, for the world must agree with me in saying that my choice has been a wise one."

"I will do so."

"I fully believe you, dear Andre, and remember what I said to you a year ago. Achieve a name, then go to my father and ask for my hand. If he refuses, if my supplications do not move him, I will quit his roof forever."

"You are right," answered Andre. "I should indeed by a fool if I sacrificed a future happy life for a few hours of present enjoyment, and I will implicitly—"

"And now," said Sabine, "that we have agreed on this point, let us discuss our mutual interests, of which it seems that we have been a little negligent up till now."

Andre at once began to tell her of all that had befallen him since they had last met, his defeats and successes.

"I am in an awkward plight," said he. "Yesterday, that well known collector, Prince Crescenzi, came to my studio. One of my pictures took his fancy, and he ordered another from me, for which he would pay six thousand *francs*."

"That was quite a stroke of luck."

"Just so, but unfortunately he wants it directly. Then Jean Lamou, who has more in his hand than he can manage, has offered me the decoration of a palatial edifice that he is building for a great speculator, M. Gandelu. I am to engage all the workmen, and shall receive some seven or eight hundred *francs* a month."

"But how does this trouble you?"

"I will tell you. I have twice seen M. Gandelu, and he wants me to begin work at once; but I cannot accept both, and must choose between them."

Sabine reflected.

"I should execute the prince's commission," said she.

"So should I, only——"

The girl easily found the cause of his hesitation.

"Will you never forget that I am wealthy?" replied she.

"The one would bring in the most money," he returned, "and the other most credit."

"Then accept the offer of M. Gandelu."

The old cuckoo-clock in the corner struck five.

"Before we part, dear Andre," resumed she, "I must tell you of a fresh trouble which threatens us; there is a project for marrying me to M. de Breulh-Faverlay."

"What, that very wealthy gentleman?"

"Just so."

"Well, if I oppose my father's wishes, an explanation must ensue, and this just now I do not desire. I therefore intend to speak openly to M. de Breulh-Faverlay, who is an honourable, straightforward man; and when I tell him the real state of the case, he will withdraw his pretensions."

"But," replied Andre, "should he do so, another will come forward."

"That is very possible, and in his turn the successor will be dismissed."

"Ah!" murmured the unhappy man, "how terrible will be your life,—a scene of daily strife with your father and mother."

After a tender farewell, Sabine and Modeste left. Andre had wished to be permitted to go out and procure a vehicle, but this the young girl negatived, and took her leave, saying.—

"I shall see M. de Breulh-Faverlay tomorrow."

For a moment after he was left alone Andre felt very sad, but a happy thought flashed across his brain.

"Sabine," said he, "went away on foot, and I may follow her without injury to her reputation."

In another moment he was in the street, and caught a glimpse of

Sabine and her maid under a lamp at the next corner. He crossed to the other side of the way and followed them cautiously.

"Perhaps," murmured he, "the time is not far distant when I shall have the right to be with her in her walks, and feel her arm pressed against mine."

By this time Sabine and her companion had reached the Rue Blanche, and hailing a cab, were rapidly driven away. Andre gazed after it, and as soon as it was out of sight, decided to return to his work. As he passed a brilliantly lighted shop, a fresh young voice saluted him.

"M. Andre, M. Andre."

He looked up in extreme surprise, and saw a young woman, dressed in the most extravagant style, standing by the door of a brougham, which glittered with fresh paint and varnish. In vain he tried to think who she could be, but at length his memory served him.

"Mademoiselle Rose," said he, "or I am much mistaken."

A shrill, squeaky voice replied, "Madame Zora Chantemille, if you please."

Andre turned sharply round and found himself face to face with a young man who had completed an order he was giving to the coachman.

"Ah, is that you?" said he.

"Yes, Chantemille is the name of the estate that I intend to settle on *madame.*"

The painter examined the personage who had just addressed him with much curiosity. He was dressed in the height or rather the burlesque of fashion, wore an eyeglass, and an enormous locket on his chain. The face which surmounted all this grandeur was almost that of a monkey, and Toto Chupin had not exaggerated its ugliness when he likened it to that animal.

"Pooh," cried Rose, "what matters a name? All you have to do is to ask this gentleman, who is an old friend of mine, to dinner." And without waiting for a reply, she took Andre by the hand and led him into a brilliantly lighted hall. "You must dine with us," she exclaimed; "I will take no denial. Come, let me introduce you, M. Andre, M. Gaston de Gandelu. There, that is all settled."

The man bowed.

"Andre, Andre," repeated Gandelu; "why, the name is familiar to me,—and so is the face. Have I not met you at my father's house? Come in; we intend to have a jovial evening."

"I really cannot," pleaded Andre. "I have an engagement."

"Throw it over then; we intend to keep you, now that we have got you."

Andre hesitated for a moment, but he felt dispirited, and that he required rousing. "After all," thought he, "why should I refuse? If this young man's friends are like himself, the evening will be an amusing one."

"Come up," cried Rose, placing her foot upon the stairs. Andre was about to follow her, but was held back by Gandelu, whose face was radiant with delight.

"Was there ever such a girl?" whispered he; "but there, don't jump at conclusions. I have only had her in hand for a short time, but I am a real dab at starting a woman grandly, and it would be hard to find my equal in Paris, you may bet."

"That can be seen at a glance," answered Andre, concealing a smile.

"Well, look here, I began at once. Zora is a quaint name, is it not? It was my invention. She isn't a right down swell today, but I have ordered six dresses for her from Van Klopen; such swell gets up! You know Van Klopen, don't you, the best man-milliner in Paris. Such taste! such ideas! you never saw the like."

Rose had by this time reached her drawing-room. "Andre," said she, impatiently, "are you never coming up?"

"Quick, quick," said Gandelu, "let us go at once; if she gets into a temper she is sure to have a nervous attack, so let us hurry up."

Rose did all she could to dazzle Andre, and as a commencement exhibited to him her domestics, a cook and a maid; then he was shown every article of furniture, and not one was spared him. He was forced to admire the drawing-room suite covered with old gold silk, trimmed blue, and to test the thickness of the curtains. Bearing aloft a large candelabra, and covering himself with wax, Gandelu led the way, telling them the price of everything like an energetic tradesman.

"That clock," said he, "cost me a hundred *louis*, and dirt cheap at the price. How funny that you should have known my father! Has he not a wonderful intellect? That flower stand was three hundred *francs*, absolutely given away. Take care of the governor, he is as sharp as a needle. He wanted me to have a profession, but no, thank you. Yes, that occasional table was a bargain at twenty *louis*. Six months ago I thought that the old man would have dropped off, but now the doctors say—" He stopped suddenly, for a loud noise was heard in the vestibule. "Here come the fellows I invited," cried he, and placing the candelabra on the table, he hurried from the room.

Andre was delighted at so grand an opportunity of studying the *genus* masher. Rose felt flattered by the admiration her fine rooms evidently caused.

"You see," cried she, "I have left Paul; he bothered me awfully, and ended by half starving me."

"Why, you are joking; he came here today, and said he was earning twelve thousand *francs* a year."

"Twelve thousand humbugs. A fellow that will take five hundred *francs* from an old scarecrow he never met before is—"

Rose broke off abruptly, for at that moment young Gandelu brought in his friends, and introduced them; they were all of the same type as their host, and Andre was about to study them more intently, when a white-waistcoated waiter threw open the door, exclaiming pompously, "*Madame*, the dinner is on the table."

Chapter 10: You Are a Thief

When Mascarin was asked what was the best way to achieve certain results, his invariable reply was, "Keep moving, keep moving." He had one great advantage over other men, he put in practice the doctrines he preached, and at seven o'clock the morning after his interview with the Count de Mussidan he was hard at work in his room. A thick fog hung over the city, even penetrating into the office, which had begun to fill with clients. This crowd had but little interest for the head of the establishment, as it consisted chiefly of waiters from small eating houses, and cooks who knew little or nothing of what was going on in the houses where they were in service. Finding this to be the case, Mascarin handed them all over to Beaumarchef, and only occasionally nodded to the serviteur of some great family, who chanced to stroll in.

He was busily engaged in arranging those pieces of cardboard which had so much puzzled Paul in his first visit, and was so much occupied with his task, that all he could do was to mutter broken exclamations: "What a stupendous undertaking! but I have to work single-handed, and hold in my hands all these threads, which for twenty years, with the patience of a spider, I have been weaving into a web. No one, seeing me here, would believe this. People who pass me by in the street say, 'That is Mascarin, who keeps a servants' registry office;' that is the way in which they look upon me. Let them laugh if they like; they little know the mighty power I wield in secret. No one suspects me, no, not one. I may seem too sanguine, it is true," he continued, still glancing over his papers, "or the net may break and some of the fishes slip out. That idiot, Mussidan, asked me if I was acquainted with the Penal code. I should think I was, for no one has studied them more deeply than I have, and there is a clause in volume 3, chapter 2, which is always before me. Penal servitude for a term of years; and if I am convicted under Article 306, then it means a life sentence."

He shuddered, but soon a smile of triumph shone over his face as he resumed, "Ah, but to send a man like Mascarin for change of air to Toulon, he must be caught, and that is not such an easy task. The day he scents danger he disappears, and leaves no trace behind him. I fear that I cannot look for too much from my companions, Catenac and Hortebise; I have up to now kept them back. Croisenois would never betray me, and as for Beaumarchef, La Candele, Toto Chupin, and a few other poor devils, they would be a fine haul for the police. They couldn't split, simply because they know nothing." Mascarin chuckled, and then adjusting his spectacles with his favourite gesture, said, "I shall go on in the course I have commenced, straight as the flight of an arrow. I ought to make four millions through Croisenois. Paul shall marry Flavia, that is all arranged, and Flavia will make a grand duchess with her magnificent income."

He had by this time arranged his pasteboard squares, then he took a small notebook, alphabetically arranged, from a drawer, wrote a name or two in it, and then closing it said with a deadly smile, "There, my friends, you are all registered, though you little suspect it. You are all rich, and think that you are free, but you are wrong, for there is one man who owns you, soul and body, and that man is Baptiste Mascarin; and at his bidding, high as you hold your heads now, you will crawl to his feet in humble abasement." His musings were interrupted by a knock at the door. He struck the bell on his writing table, and the last sound of it was hardly died away, when Beaumarchef stood on the threshold.

"You desired me, sir," said he, with the utmost deference, "to complete my report regarding young M. Gandelu, and it so happens that the cook whom he has taken into his service in the new establishment he has started is on our list. She has just come in to pay us eleven *francs* that she owed us, and is waiting outside. Is not this lucky?"

Mascarin made a little grimace. "You are an idiot, Beaumarchef," said he, "to be pleased at so trivial a matter. I have often told you that there is no such thing as luck or chance, and that all comes to those who work methodically."

Beaumarchef listened to his master's wisdom in silent surprise.

"And pray, who is this woman?" asked Mascarin.

"You will know her when you see her, sir. She is registered under class D, that is, for employment in rather fast establishments."

"Go and fetch her," observed Mascarin, and as the man left the room, he muttered, "Experience has taught me that it is madness to neglect the smallest precaution."

In another moment the woman appeared, and Mascarin at once addressed her with that air of friendly courtesy which made him so popular among such women. "Well, my good girl," said he, "and so you have got the sort of place you wanted, eh?"

"I hope so, sir, but you see I have only been with Madame Zora de Chantemille since yesterday."

"Ah, Zora de Chantemille, that is a fine name, indeed."

"It is only a fancy name, and she had an awful row over it with master. She wanted to be called Raphaela, but he stood out for Zora."

"Zora is a very pretty name," observed Mascarin solemnly.

"Yes, sir, just what the maid and I told her. She is a splendid woman, and doesn't she just squander the shiners? Thirty thousand *francs* have gone since yesterday."

"I can hardly credit it."

"Not cash, you understand, but tick. M. de Gandelu has not a *sou* of his own in the world, so a waiter at Potier's told me, and he knew what was what; but the governor is rolling in money. Yesterday they had a house-warming—the dinner, with wine, cost over a thousand *francs*."

Not seeing how to utilize any of this gossip, Mascarin made a gesture of dismissal, when the woman exclaimed,—

"Stop, sir, I have something to tell you."

"Well," said Mascarin, throwing himself back in his chair with an air of affected impatience, "let us have it."

"We had eight gents to dinner, all howling swells, but my master was the biggest masher of the lot. *Madame* was the only woman at table. Well, by ten o'clock, they had all had their whack of drink, and then they told the porter to keep the courtyard clear. What do you think they did then? Why, they threw plates, glasses, knives, forks, and dishes bang out of the window. That is a regular swell fashion, so the waiter at Potier's told me, and was introduced into Paris by a Russian."

Mascarin closed his eyes and answered languidly, "Go on."

"Well, sir, there was one gent who was a blot on the whole affair.

He was tall, shabbily dressed, and with no manners at all. He seemed all the time to be sneering at the rest. But didn't *Madame* make up to him just. She kept heaping up his plate and filling his glass. When the others got to cards, he sat down by my mistress, and began to talk."

"Could you hear what they said?"

"I should think so. I was in the bedroom, and they were near the door."

"Dear me," remarked Mascarin, appearing much shocked, "surely that was not right?"

"I don't care a rap whether it was right or not. I like to hear all about the people whom I engage with. They were talking about a M. Paul, who had been *Madame's* friend before, and whom the gentleman also knew. *Madame* said that this Paul was no great shakes, and that he had stolen twelve thousand *francs*."

Mascarin pricked up his ears, feeling that his patience was about to meet its reward.

"Can you tell me the gentleman's name, to whom *Madame* said all this?" asked he.

"Not I. The others called him 'The painter.'"

This explanation did not satisfy Mascarin.

"Look here, my good girl," said he, "try and find out the fellow's name. I think he is an artist who owes me money."

"All right! Rely on me; and now I must be off, for I have breakfast to get ready, but I'll call again tomorrow;" and with a curtsy she left the room.

Mascarin struck his hand heavily on the table.

"Hortebise has a wonderful nose for sniffing out danger," said he. "This Rose and the young fool who is ruining himself for her must both be suppressed."

Beaumarchef again made a motion of executing a thrust with the rapier.

"Pooh, pooh!" answered his master; "don't be childish. I can do better than that. Rose calls herself nineteen, but she is more, she is of age, while Gandelu is still a minor. If old Gandelu had any pluck, he would put Article 354 in motion."

"Eh, sir?" said Beaumarchef, much mystified.

"Look here. Before twenty-four hours have elapsed I must know everything as to the habits and disposition of Gandelu senior. I want to know on what terms he is with his son."

"Good. I will set La Candele to work."

"And as the young fellow will doubtless need money, contrive to let him know of our friend Verminet, the chairman of the Mutual Loan Society."

"But that is M. Tantaine's business."

Mascarin paid no heed to this, so occupied was he by his own thoughts.

"This young artist seems to have more brains than the rest of the set, but woe to him if he crosses my path. Go back to the outer office, Beaumarchef, I hear some clients coming in."

The man, however, did not obey.

"Pardon me, sir," said he, "but La Candele, who is outside, will see them. I have my report to make."

"Very good. Sit down and go on."

Enchanted at this mark of condescension, Beaumarchef went on. "Yesterday there was nothing of importance, but this morning Toto Chupin came."

"He had not lost Caroline Schimmel, I trust?"

"No, sir; he had even got into conversation with her."

"That is good. He is a cunning little devil; a pity that he is not a trifle more honest."

"He is sure," continued Beaumarchef, "that the woman drinks, for she is always talking of persons following her about who menace her, and she is so afraid of being murdered that she never ventures out alone. She lives with a respectable workingman and his wife, and pays well for her board, for she seems to have plenty of money."

"That is a nuisance," remarked Mascarin, evidently much annoyed. "Where does she live?"

"At Montmartre, beyond the Château Rouge."

"Good. Tantaine will inquire and see if Toto has made no mistake, and does not let the woman slip through his fingers."

"He won't do that, for he told me that he was on the right road to find out who she was, and where she got her money from. But I ought to warn you against the young scamp, for I have found out that he robs us and sells our goods far below their value."

"What do you mean?"

"I have long had my suspicions, and yesterday I wormed it all out from a disreputable looking fellow, who came here to ask for his friend Chupin."

Men accustomed to danger are over prompt in their decisions. "Very well," returned Mascarin, "if this is the case, Master Chupin shall have a taste of prison fare."

Beaumarchef withdrew, but almost immediately reappeared.

"Sir," said he, "a servant from M. de Croisenois is here with a note."

"Send the man in," said Mascarin.

The domestic was irreproachably dressed, and looked what he was, the servant of a nobleman.

He had something the appearance of an Englishman, with a high collar, reaching almost to his ears. His face was clean shaved, and of a ruddy hue. His coat was evidently the work of a London tailor, and his appearance was as stiff as though carved out of wood. Indeed, he looked like a very perfect piece of mechanism.

"My master," said he, "desired me to give this note into your own hands."

Under cover of breaking the seal, Mascarin viewed this model servant attentively. He was a stranger to him, for he had never supplied Croisenois with a domestic.

"It seems, my good fellow," said he, "that your master was up earlier than usual this morning?"

The man frowned a little at this familiar address, and then slowly replied,—

"When I took service with the *marquis*, he agreed to give me fifteen *louis* over my wages for the privilege of calling me 'a good fellow,' but I permit no one to do so *gratis*. I think that my master is still asleep," continued the man solemnly. "He wrote the note on his return from the club."

"Is there any reply."

"Yes, sir."

"Good; then wait a little."

And Mascarin, opening the note, read the following:

My Dear Friend,—
Baccarat has served me an ugly turn, and in addition to all my ready cash I have given an I.O.U. for three thousand *francs*. To save my credit I must have this by twelve tomorrow.

"His credit," said Mascarin. "His credit! That is a fine joke indeed." The servant stood up stiffly erect, as one seeming to take no notice, and the agent continued reading the letter.

Am I wrong in looking to you for this trifle? I do not think so. Indeed, I have an idea that you will send me a hundred and fifty *louis* over and above, so that I may not be left without a coin in my pocket. How goes the great affair? I await your decision on the brink of a precipice.

Yours devotedly,

Henry De Croisenois.

"And so," growled Mascarin, "he has flung away five thousand *francs*, and asks me to find it for him in my coffers. Ah, you fool, if I did not want the grand name that you have inherited from your ancestors, a name that you daily bespatter and soil, you might whistle for your five thousand *francs*."

However, as Croisenois was absolutely necessary to him, Mascarin slowly took from his safe five notes of a thousand *francs* each, and handed them to the man.

"Do you want a receipt?" asked the man.

"No; this letter is sufficient, but wait a bit;" and Mascarin, with an eye to the future, drew a twenty *franc* piece from his pocket, and placing it on the table, said in his most honeyed accents,—

"There, my friend, is something for yourself."

"No, sir," returned the man; "I always ask wages enough to prevent the necessity of accepting presents." And with this dignified reply he bowed with the stiff air of a Quaker, and walked rigidly out of the room.

The agent was absolutely thunderstruck. In all his thirty years' experience he had never come across anything like this.

"I can hardly believe my senses," muttered he; "where on earth did the *marquis* pick this fellow up? Can it be that he is sharper than I fancied?"

Suddenly a new and terrifying idea flashed across his mind. "Can it be," said he, "that the fellow is not a real servant, after all? I have so many enemies that one day they may strive to crush me, and however skilfully I may play my cards, someone may hold a better hand." This idea alarmed him greatly, for he was in a position in which he had nothing to fear; for when a great work is approaching completion, the anxiety of the promoter becomes stronger and stronger. "No, no," he continued; "I am getting too full of suspicions;" and with these words he endeavoured to put aside the vague terrors which were creeping into his soul.

Suddenly Beaumarchef, evidently much excited, appeared upon the threshold.

"What, you here again!" cried Mascarin, angrily; "am I to have no

94

peace today?"

"Sir, the young man is here."

"What young man? Paul Violaine?"

"Yes, sir."

"Why, I told him not to come until twelve; something must have gone wrong." He broke off his speech, for at the half-open door stood Paul. He was very pale, and his eyes had the expression of some hunted creature. His attire was in disorder and betokened a night spent in aimless wanderings to and fro.

"Ah, sir!" said he, as he caught sight of Mascarin.

"Leave us, Beaumarchef," said the latter, with an imperious wave of his hand; "and now, my dear boy, what is it?"

Paul sank into a chair.

"My life is ended," said he; "I am lost, dishonoured for ever."

Mascarin put on a face of the most utter bewilderment, though he well knew the cause of Paul's utter prostration; but it was with the air of a ready sympathizer that he drew his chair nearer to that of Paul, and said,—

"Come, tell me all about it; what can possibly have happened to affect you thus?"

In deeply tragic tones, Paul replied,—

"Rose has deserted me."

Mascarin raised his hands to heaven.

"And is this the reason that you say you are dishonoured? Do you not see that the future is full of promise?"

"I loved Rose," returned Paul, and his voice was so full of pathos that Mascarin could hardly repress a smile. "But this is not all," continued the unhappy boy, making a vain effort to restrain his tears; "I am accused of theft."

"Impossible!" exclaimed Mascarin.

"Yes, sir; and you who know everything are the only person in the world who can save me. You were so kind to me yesterday that I ventured to come here before the time appointed, in order to entreat your help."

"But what do you think I can do?"

"Everything, sir; but let me tell you the whole hideous complication."

Mascarin's face assumed an air of the deepest interest, as he answered, "Go on."

"After our interview," began Paul, "I went back to the Hotel de

Perou, and on the mantelpiece in my garret found this note from Rose."

He held it out as he spoke, but Mascarin made no effort to take it.

"In it," resumed Paul, "Rose tells me she no longer loves me, and begs me not to seek to see her again; and also that, wearied out of poverty, she has accepted the offer of unlimited supplies of money, a carriage, and diamonds."

"Are you surprised at this?" asked Mascarin, with a sneer.

"How could I anticipate such an infidelity, when only the evening before she swore by all she held most sacred that she loved me only? Why did she lie to me? Did she write to make the blow fall heavier? When I ascended the staircase, I was picturing to myself her joy when I told her of your kind promises to me. For more than an hour I remained in my garret, overwhelmed with the terrible thought that I should never see her again."

Mascarin watched Paul attentively, and came to the conclusion that his words were too fine for his grief to be sincere.

"But what about the accusation of theft?"

"I am coming to that," returned the young man. "I then determined to obey your injunctions and leave the Hotel de Perou, with which I was more than ever disgusted. I went downstairs to settle with Madame Loupins, when ah! hideous disgrace! As I handed her the two weeks' rent, she asked me with a contemptuous sneer, where I had stolen the money from?" Mascarin secretly chuckled over the success of his plans thus announced by Paul.

"What did you say?" asked he.

"Nothing, sir; I was too horror-stricken; the man Loupins came up, and both he and his wife scowled at me threateningly. After a short pause, they asserted that they were perfectly sure that Rose and I had robbed M. Tantaine."

"But did you not deny this monstrous charge?"

"I was utterly bewildered, for I saw that every circumstance was against me. The evening before, Rose, in reply to Madame Loupin's importunities, had told her that she had no money, and did not know where to get any. But, as you perceive, on the very next day I appeared in a suit of new clothes, and was prepared to pay my debts, while Rose had left the house some hours before. Does not all this form a chain of strange coincidences? Rose changed the five hundred *franc* note that Tantaine had lent me at the shop of a grocer, named Melusin, and this suspicious fool was the first to raise a cry against us, and dared to assert

96

that a detective had been ordered to watch us."

Mascarin knew all this story better than Paul, but here he interrupted his young friend.

"I do not understand you," said he, "nor whether your grief arises from indignation or remorse. Has there been a robbery?"

"How can I tell? I have never seen M. Tantaine from that day. There is a rumour that he has been plundered and important papers taken from him, and that he has consequently been arrested."

"Why did you not explain the facts?"

"It would have been of no use. It would clearly prove that Tantaine was no friend of mine, not even an acquaintance, and they would have laughed me to scorn had I declared that the evening before he came into my room and made me a present of five hundred *francs*."

"I think that I can solve the riddle," remarked Mascarin. "I know the old fellow so well."

Paul listened with breathless eagerness.

"Tantaine," resumed Mascarin, "is the best and kindest fellow in the world, but he is not quite right in the upper story. He was a wealthy man once, but his liberality was his ruin. He is as poor as a church-mouse now, but he is as anxious as ever to be charitable. Unfortunately in the place I procured for him he had a certain amount of petty cash at his disposal, and moved to pity at the sight of your sufferings, he gave you the money that really belonged to others. Then he sent in his accounts, and the deficiency was discovered. He lost his head, and declared that he had been robbed. You lived in the next room; you were known to be in abject poverty on the one day and in ample funds on the next; hence these suspicions."

All was too clear to Paul, and a cold shiver ran through his frame as he saw himself arrested, tried, and condemned.

"But," stammered he, "M. Tantaine holds my note of hand, which is a proof that I acted honestly."

"My poor boy, do you think that if he hoped to save himself at your expense he would produce it?"

"Luckily, sir, you know the real state of the case."

Mascarin shook is head.

"Would my story be credited?" asked he. "Justice is not infallible, and I must confess that appearances are against you."

Paul was crushed down beneath this weight of argument. "There is no resource for me then but death," murmured he, "for I will not live a dishonoured man."

The conduct of Paul was precisely what Mascarin had expected, and he felt that the moment had arrived to strike a final blow.

"You must not give way to despair, my boy," said he.

But Paul made no reply; he had lost the power of hearing. Mascarin, however, had no time to lose, and taking him by the arm, shook him roughly. "Rouse yourself. A man in your position must help himself, and bring forward proofs of his innocence."

"There is no use in fighting," replied Paul. "Have you not just shown me that it is hopeless to endeavour to prove my innocence?"

Mascarin grew impatient at this unnecessary exhibition of cowardice, but he concealed his feelings as best he could.

"No, no," answered he; "I only wished to show you the worst side of the affair."

"There is only one side."

"Not so, for it is only a supposition that Tantaine had made away with money entrusted to him, and we are not certain of it. And we only surmise that he has been arrested, and thrown the blame on you. Before giving up the game, would it not be best to be satisfied on these points?"

Paul felt a little reassured.

"I say nothing," continued Mascarin, "of the influence I exercise over Tantaine, and which may enable me to compel him to confess the truth."

Weak natures like Paul's are raised in a moment from the lowest depths of depression to the highest pitch of exultation, and he already considered that he was saved.

"Shall I ever be able to prove my gratitude to you?" said he impulsively.

Mascarin's face assumed a paternal expression.

"Perhaps you may," answered he; "and as a commencement you must entirely forget the past. Daylight dispels the hideous visions of the night. I offer you a fresh lease of life; will you become a new man?"

Paul heaved a deep sigh. "Rose," he murmured; "I cannot forget her."

Mascarin frowned. "What," said he, "do you still let your thoughts dwell on that woman? There are people who cringe to the hand that strikes them, and the more they are duped and deceived, the more they love. If you are made of this kind of stuff, we shall never get on. Go and find your faithless mistress, and beg her to come back and share your poverty, and see what she will say."

These sarcasms roused Paul. "I will be even with her some day," muttered he.

"Forget her; that is the easiest thing for you to do."

Even now Paul seemed to hesitate. "What," said his patron reproachfully, "have you no pride?"

"I have, sir."

"You have not, or you would never wish to hamper yourself with a woman like Rose. You should keep your hands free, if you want to fight your way through the battle of life."

"I will follow your advice, sir," said Paul hurriedly.

"Very soon you will thank Rose deeply for having left you. You will climb high, I can tell you, if you will work as I bid you."

"Then," stammered Paul, "this situation at twelve thousand *francs* a year—"

"There never has been such a situation."

A ghastly pallor overspread Paul's countenance, as he saw himself again reduced to beggary.

"But, sir," he murmured, "will you not permit me to hope—"

"For twelve thousand *francs*! Be at ease, you shall have that and much more. I am getting old. I have no ties in the world—you shall be my adopted son."

A cloud settled on Paul's brow, for the idea that his life was to be passed in this office was most displeasing to him. Mascarin divined his inmost thoughts with perfect ease. "And the young fool does not know where to go for a crust of bread," thought he. "Ah, if there were no Flavia, no Champdoce;" then, speaking aloud, he resumed, "don't fancy, my dear boy, that I wish to condemn you to the treadmill that I am compelled to pass my life in. I have other views for you, far more worthy of your merits. I have taken a great liking to you, and I will do all I can to further your ambitious views.

"I was thinking a great deal of you, and in my head I raised the scaffolding of your future greatness. 'He is poor,' said I, 'and at his age, and with his tastes, this is a cruel thing. Why, pray, should I not find a wife for him among those heiresses who have a million or two to give the man they marry? When I talk like this, it is because I know of an heiress, and my friend, Dr. Hortebise, shall introduce her to you. She is nearly, if not quite, as pretty as Rose, and has the advantage of her in being well-born, well-educated, and wealthy. She has influential relatives, and if her husband should happen to be a poet, or a composer, she could assist him in becoming famous."

A flush came over Paul's face, This seemed like the realization of some of his former dreams.

"With regard to your birth," continued Mascarin, "I have devised a wonderful plan. Before '93, you know, every bastard was treated as a gentleman, as he might have been the son of some high and mighty personage. Who can say that your father may not have been of the noblest blood of France, and that he has not lands and wealth? He may even now be looking for you, in order to acknowledge you and make you his heir. Would you like to be a duke?"

"Ah, sir," stammered the young man.

Mascarin burst into a fit of laughter. "Up to now," said he, "we are only in the region of suppositions."

"Well, sir, what do you wish me to do?" asked Paul, after a short pause.

Mascarin put on a serious face. "I want absolute obedience from you," said he; "a blind and undeviating obedience, one that makes no objections and asks no questions."

"I will obey you, sir; but, oh! do not desert me."

Without making any reply, Mascarin rang for Beaumarchef, and as soon as the latter appeared, said, "I am going to Van Klopen's, and shall leave you in charge here." Then, turning to Paul, he added, "I always mean what I say; we will go and breakfast at a neighbouring restaurant. I want to have a talk with you, and afterward—afterward, my boy, I will show you the girl I intend to be your wife. I am curious to know how you like her looks."

Chapter 11: The Man-Milliner

Gaston de Gandelu was much surprised at finding that Andre should be ignorant of the existence of Van Klopen, the best-known man in Paris. To assure oneself of this, it was only necessary to glance at his circulars, which were ornamented with the representations of medals won at all sorts of exhibitions in different quarters of the world, together with various decorations received from foreign potentates. One had been presented to him by the Queen of Spain, while he had a diploma appointing him the supplier to the Court of the Czar. The great Van Klopen was not an Alsatian, as was generally supposed, but a stout, handsome Dutchman, who, in the year 1850, had been a tailor in his small native town, and manufactured in cloth, purchased on credit, the long waistcoats and miraculous coats worn by the wealthy citizens of Rotterdam. Van Klopen, however, was not successful in his business, and was compelled to close his shop and abscond from his creditors. He took refuge in Paris, where he seemed likely to die of hunger. One day over a magnificent establishment in the Rue de Grammont appeared a signboard with the name of Van Klopen, dressmaker, and in the thousands of handbills distributed with the utmost profusion, he called himself the "Regenerator of Fashion." This was an idea that would have never originated in the brain of the phlegmatic Dutchman, and whence came the funds to carry on the business? On this point he was discreetly silent. The enterprise was at first far from a success, for during nearly a month Paris almost split its sides laughing at the absurd pretensions of the self-dubbed "Regenerator of Fashion."

Van Klopen bent before the storm he had aroused, and in due time his advertisements brought him two customers, who were the first to blow the trumpet of his fame. One was the Duchess de Suirmeuse, a very great lady indeed, and renowned for her eccentricities and extravagant manner, while the other was an example of another class being no less than the celebrated Jennie Fancy, who was at that time under the protection of the Count de Tremouselle; and for these two Van Klopen invented such dresses as had never been seen before. From this moment his success was certain; indeed, it was stupendous, and Paris resounded with his praises. Now he has achieved a world-wide reputation, and has nothing to fear from the attacks of his rivals. He would not execute orders for everyone, saying that he must pick and choose his customers, and he did so, excising the names of such as he did not think would add to his reputation.

Rank and wealth disputed the honour of being his customers. The haughtiest dames did not shrink from entrusting to him secrets of form and figure, which they even hid from their husbands. They endured without shrinking the touch of his coarse hands as he measured them. He was the rage, and his showrooms were a species of neutral ground, where women of all circles of society met and examined each other. The Duchess of — did not shrink from being in the same room with the celebrated woman for whom the Baron de — had blown out the few brains he possessed. Perhaps the duchess thought that by employing the same costumier, she might also gain some of the venal beauteous attractions. Mademoiselle D—, of the Gymnase Theatre, who was well known to earn just one thousand *francs* per annum, took a delight in astonishing the haughty ladies of fashion by the reckless extravagance of her orders. Van Klopen, who was a born diplomatist, distributed his favours between his different customers; consequently he was termed the most charming and angelic of men. Many a time had he heard the most aristocratic lips let fall the words, "I shall die, Van Klopen, if my dress is not ready." On the evenings of the most aristocratic balls a long line of carriages blocked up the road in front of his establishment, and the finest women in Paris crowded the show-rooms for a word of approval from him.

He gave credit to approved customers, and also, it was whispered, lent money to them. But woe to the woman who permitted herself to be entrapped in the snare of credit that he laid for her; for the woman who owed him a bill was practically lost, never knowing to what depths she might be degraded to obtain the money to settle her account. It was not surprising that such sudden prosperity should have turned Van Klopen's head. He was stout and ruddy, impudent, vain, and cynical. His admirers said that he was witty.

It was to this man's establishment that Mascarin conducted Paul after a sumptuous breakfast at Philipe's.

It is necessary to give a slight description of Van Klopen's establish-ment. Carpets of the most expensive description covered the stairs to his door on the first floor, at which stood the liveried menials resplendent in gold lace and scarlet. As soon as Mascarin made his ap-pearance, one of these gorgeous creatures hastened to him and said, "M. Van Klopen is just now engaged with the Princess Korasoff, but as soon as he hears of your arrival he will manage to get rid of her. Will you wait for him in his private room?"

But Mascarin answered,—

"We are in no hurry, and may as well wait in the public room with the other customers. Are there many of them?"

"There are about a dozen ladies, sir."

"Good; I am sure that they will amuse me."

And, without wasting any more words, Mascarin opened a door which led into a magnificent drawing-room, decorated in very florid style. The paper on the walls almost disappeared beneath a variety of watercolour sketches, representing ladies in every possible style of costume. Each picture had an explanatory note beneath it, such as "Costume of Mde. de C— for a dinner at the Russian Ambassador's," "Ball costume of the Marchioness de V— for a ball at the Hotel de Ville," etc.

Paul, who was a little nervous at finding himself among such splen-dour, hesitated in the doorway; but Mascarin seized his young friend by the arm, and, as he drew him to a settee, whispered in his ear,—

"Keep your eyes about you; the heiress is here."

The ladies were at first a little surprised at this invasion of the room by the male element, but Paul's extreme beauty soon attracted their attention. The hum of conversation ceased, and Paul's embarrassment increased as he found a battery of twelve pairs of eyes directed full upon him.

Mascarin, however, was quite at his ease, and upon his entrance had made a graceful though rather old-fashioned bow to the fair inmates of the room. His coolness was partly due to the contempt he felt for the human race in general, and also to his coloured glasses, which hid the expression of his countenance. When he saw that Paul still kept his eyes on the ground, he tapped him gently on the arm.

"Is this the first time you ever saw well-dressed women? Surely you are not afraid of them. Look to the right," continued Mascarin, "and you will see the heiress."

A young girl, not more than eighteen, was seated near one of the windows. She was not perhaps so beautiful as Mascarin had described, but her face was a very striking one nevertheless. She was slight and good-looking, with the clear complexion of a brunette. Her features were not perhaps very regular, but her glossy black hair was a beauty in itself. She had a pair of dark, melting eyes, and her wide, high forehead showed that she was gifted with great intelligence. There was an air of restrained voluptuousness about her, and she seemed the very embodiment of passion.

Paul felt insensibly attracted toward her. Their eyes met, and both started at the same moment. Paul was fascinated in an instant, and the girl's emotion was so evident that she turned aside her head to conceal it.

The babble had now commenced again, and general attention was being paid to a lady who was enthusiastically describing the last new costume which had made its appearance in the Bois de Boulogue.

"It was simply miraculous," said she; "a real triumph of Van Klopen's art. The ladies of a certain class are furious, and Henry de Croisenois tells me that Jenny Fancy absolutely shed tears of rage. Imagine three green skirts of different shades, each draped—"

Mascarin, however, only paid attention to Paul and the young girl, and a sarcastic smile curled his lips.

"What do you think of her?" asked he.

"She is adorable!" answered Paul, enthusiastically.

103

"And immensely wealthy."

"I should fall at her feet if she had not a *sou.*"

Mascarin gave a little cough, and adjusted his glasses.

"Should you, my lad?" said he to himself; "whether your admiration is for the girl or her money, you are in my grip."

Then he added, aloud,—

"Would you not like to know her name?"

"Tell me, I entreat you."

"Flavia."

Paul was in the seventh heaven, and now boldly turned his eyes on the girl, forgetting that owing to the numerous mirrors, she could see his every movement.

The door was at this moment opened quietly, and Van Klopen appeared on the threshold. He was about forty-four, and too stout for his height. His red, pimply face had an expression upon it of extreme insolence, and his accent was thoroughly Dutch. He was dressed in a ruby velvet dressing-gown, with a cravat with lace ends. A huge cluster-diamond ring blazed on his coarse, red hand.

"Who is the next one?" asked he, rudely.

The lady who had been talking so volubly rose to her feet, but the tailor cut her short, for catching sight of Mascarin, he crossed the room, and greeted him with the utmost cordiality.

"What!" said he; "is it you that I have been keeping waiting? Pray pardon me. Pray go into my private room; and this gentleman is with you? Do me the favour, sir, to come with us."

He was about to follow his guests, when one of the ladies started forward.

"One word with you, sir, for goodness sake!" cried she.

Van Klopen turned sharply upon her.

"What is the matter?" asked he.

"My bill for three thousand *francs* falls due tomorrow."

"Very likely."

"But I can't meet it."

"That is not my affair."

"I have come to beg you will renew it for two months, or say one month, on whatever terms you like."

"In two months," answered the man brutally, "you will be no more able to pay than you are today. If you can't pay it, it will be noted."

"Merciful powers! then my husband will learn all."

"Just so; that will be what I want; for he will then have to pay me."

The wretched woman grew deadly pale.

"My husband will pay you," said she; "but I shall be lost."

"That is not my lookout. I have partners whose interests I have to consult."

"Do not say that, sir! He has paid my debts once, and if he should be angry and take my children from me—Dear M. Van Klopen, be merciful!"

She wrung her hands, and the tears coursed down her cheeks; but the tailor was perfectly unmoved.

"When a woman has a family of children, one ought to have in a needlewoman by the hour."

She did not desist from her efforts to soften him, and, seizing his hand, strove to carry it to her lips.

"Ah! I shall never dare to go home," wailed she; "never have the courage to tell my husband."

"If you are afraid of your own husband, go to someone else's," said he roughly; and tearing himself from her, he followed Mascarin and Paul.

"Did you hear that?" asked he, as soon as he had closed the door of his room with an angry slam. "These things occasionally occur, and are not particularly pleasant."

Paul looked on in disgust. If he had possessed three thousand *francs*, he would have given them to this unhappy woman, whose sobs he could still hear in the passage.

"It is most painful," remarked he.

"My dear sir," said the tailor, "you attach too much importance to these hysterical outbursts. If you were in my place, you would soon have to put their right value on them. As I said before, I have to look after my own and my partners' interests. These dear creatures care for nothing but dress; father, husband, and children are as nothing in comparison. You cannot imagine what a woman will do in order to get a new dress, in which to outshine her rival. They only talk of their families when they are called on to pay up."

Paul still continued to plead for some money for the poor lady, and the discussion was getting so warm that Mascarin felt bound to interfere.

"Perhaps," said he, "you have been a little hard."

"Pooh," returned the tailor; "I know my customer; and tomorrow my account will be settled, and I know very well where the money will come from. Then she will give me another order, and we shall have the whole comedy over again. I know what I am about." And taking Mascarin into the window, he made some confidential communication, at which they both laughed heartily.

Paul, not wishing to appear to listen, examined the consulting-room, as Van Klopen termed it. He saw a great number of large scissors, yard measures, and patterns of material, and heaps of fashion plates.

By this time the two men had finished their conversation.

"I had," said Mascarin, as they returned to the fireplace, "I had meant to glance through the books; but you have so many customers waiting, that I had better defer doing so."

"Is that all that hinders you?" returned Van Klopen, carelessly. "Wait a moment."

He left the room, and in another moment his voice was heard.

"I am sorry, ladies, very sorry, on my word; but I am busy with my silk mercer. I shall not be very long."

"We will wait," returned the ladies in chorus.

"That is the way," remarked Van Klopen, as he returned to the consulting-room. "Be civil to women, and they turn their backs on you; try and keep them off, and they run after you. If I was to put up 'no admittance' over my door, the street would be blocked up with women. Business has never been better," continued the tailor, producing a large ledger. "Within the last ten days we have had in orders amounting to eighty-seven thousand *francs*."

"Good!" answered Mascarin; "but let us have a look at the column headed 'Doubtful.'"

"Here you are," returned the arbiter of fashion, as he turned over the leaves. "Mademoiselle Virginie Cluhe has ordered five theatrical costumes, two dinner, and three morning dresses."

"That is a heavy order."

"I wanted for that reason to consult you. She doesn't owe us much—perhaps a thousand *francs* or so."

"That is too much, for I hear that her friend has come to grief. Do not decline the order, but avoid taking fresh ones."

Van Klopen made a few mysterious signs in the margin of his ledger.

"On the 6th of this month the Countess de Mussidan gave us an order—a perfectly plain dress for her daughter. Her account is a very heavy one, and the count has warned us that he will not pay it."

"Never mind that. Go on with the order, put press for payment."

"On the 7th a new customer came—Mademoiselle Flavia, the daughter of Martin Rigal, the banker."

When Paul heard this name, he could not repress a start, of which, however, Mascarin affected to take no notice.

"My good friend," said he, turning to Van Klopen, "I confide this young lady to you; give her your whole stock if she asks for it."

By the look of surprise which appeared upon the tailor's face, Paul could see that Mascarin was not prodigal of such recommendations.

"You shall be obeyed," said Van Klopen, with a bow.

"On the 8th a young gentleman of the name of Gaston de Gandelu was introduced by Lupeaux, the jeweller. His father is, I hear, very wealthy, and he will come into money on attaining his majority, which is near at hand. He brought with him a lady," continued the tailor, "and said her name was Zora de Chantemille, a tremendously pretty girl."

"That young man is always in my way," said Mascarin. "I would give something to get him out of Paris."

Van Klopen reflected for a moment. "I don't think that would be difficult," remarked he; "that young fellow is capable of any act of folly for that fair girl."

"I think so too."

"Then the matter is easy. I will open an account with him; then, after a little, I will affect doubts as to his solvency, and ask for a bill; and we shall then place our young friend in the hands of the Mutual Loan Society, and M. Verminet will easily persuade him to write his name across the bottom of a piece of stamped paper. He will bring it to me; I will accept it, and then we shall have him hard and fast."

"I should have proposed another course."

"I see no other way, however," He suddenly stopped, for a loud noise was heard in the ante-room, and the sound of voices in loud contention.

"I should like to know," said Van Klopen, rising to his feet, "who the impudent scoundrel is, who comes here kicking up a row. I expect that it is some fool of a husband."

"Go and see what it is," suggested Mascarin.

"Not I! My servants are paid to spare me such annoyances."

Presently the noise ceased.

"And now," resumed Mascarin, "let us return to our own affairs. Under the circumstances, your proposal appears to be a good one. How about writing in another name? A little forgery would make our hands stronger." He rose, and taking the tailor into the window recess, again whispered to him.

During this conversation Paul's cheek had grown paler and paler, for, occupied as he was, he could not fail to comprehend something of what was going on. During the breakfast Mascarin had partially disclosed many strange secrets, and since then he had been even more enlightened. It was but too evident to him that his protector was engaged in some dark and insidious plot, and Paul felt that he was standing over a mine which might explode at any moment. He now began to fancy that there was some mysterious link between the woman Schimmel, who was so carefully watched, and the Marquis de Croisenois, so haughty, and yet on such intimate terms with the proprietor of the registry office.

Then there was the Countess de Mussidan, Flavia, the rich heiress, and Gaston de Gandelu, who was to be led into a crime the result of which would be penal servitude,—all jumbled and mixed up together in one strange phantasmagoria. Was he, Paul, to be a mere tool in such hands? Toward what a precipice was he being impelled! Mascarin and Van Klopen were not friends, as he had at first supposed, but confederates in villainy. Too late did he begin to see collusion between Mascarin and Tantaine, which had resulted in his being accused of theft during his absence. But the web had been woven too securely, and should he struggle to break through it, he might find himself exposed to even more terrible dangers.

He felt horrified at his position, but with this there was mingled no horror of the criminality of his associates, for the skilful hand of Mascarin had unwound and mastered all the bad materials of his nature. He was dazzled at the glorious future held out before him, and said to himself that a man like Mascarin, unfettered by law, either human or Divine, would be most likely to achieve his ends. "I should be in no danger," mused he to himself, "if I yield myself up to the impetuous stream which is already carrying me along, for Mascarin is practised swimmer enough to keep both my head and his own above water."

Little did Paul think that every fleeting expression in his countenance was caught up and treasured by the wily Mascarin; and it was intentionally that he had permitted Paul to listen to this compromising conversation. He had decided that very morning, that if Paul was to be a useful tool, he must be at once set face to face with the grim realities of the position.

"Now," said he, "for the really serious reason for my visit. How do we stand now with regard to the Viscountess Bois Arden?"

Van Klopen gave his shoulders a shrug as he answered, "She is all right. I have just sent her several most expensive costumes."

"How much does she owe you?"

"Say twenty-five thousand *francs*. She has owed us more than that before."

"Really?" remarked Mascarin, "that woman has been grossly libelled; she is vain, frivolous, and fond of admiration, but nothing more. For a whole fortnight I have been prying into her life, but I can't hit upon anything in it to give us a pull over her. The debt may help us, however. Does her husband know that she has an account with us?"

"Of course he does not; he is most liberal to her, and if he inquired—"

"Then we are all right; we will send in the bill to him."

"But, my good sir," urged Van Klopen, "it was only last week that she paid us a heavy sum on account."

"The more reason to press her, for she must be hard up."

Van Klopen would have argued further, but an imperious sign from Mascarin reduced him to silence.

"Listen to me," said Mascarin, "and please do not interrupt me. Are you known to the domestics at the house of the viscountess?"

"Not at all."

"Well, then, at three o'clock sharp, the day after tomorrow, call on her. Her footman will say that *Madame* has a visitor with her."

"I will say I will wait."

"Not at all. You must almost force your way in, and you will find the viscountess talking to the Marquis de Croisenois. You know him, I suppose?"

"By sight—nothing more."

"That is sufficient. Take no notice of him; but at once present your bill, and violently insist upon immediate payment."

"What can you be thinking of? She will have me kicked out of doors."

"Quite likely; but you must threaten to take the bill to her husband. She will command you to leave the house, but you will sit down doggedly and declare that you will not move until you get the money."

"But that is most unbusinesslike behaviour."

"I quite agree with you; but the Marquis de Croisenois will interfere; he will throw a pocketbook in your face, exclaiming, 'There is your money, you impudent scoundrel!'"

"Then I am to slink away?"

"Yes, but before doing so, you will give a receipt in this form—'Received from the Marquis de Croisenois, the sum of so many *francs*, in settlement of the account of the Viscountess Bois Arden.'"

"If I could only understand the game," muttered the puzzled Van Klopen.

"There is no necessity for that now; only act up to your instructions."

"I will obey, but remember that we shall not only lose her custom, but that of all her acquaintance."

Again the same angry sounds were heard in the corridor.

"It is scandalous," cried a voice. "I have been waiting an hour; my sword and armour. What, ho, lackeys; hither, I say. Van Klopen is engaged, is he? Hie to him and say I must see him at once."

The two accomplices exchanged looks, as though they recognised the shrill, squeaky voice.

"That is our man," whispered Mascarin, as the door was violently flung open, and Gaston de Gandelu burst in. He was dressed even more extravagantly than usual, and his face was inflamed with rage.

"Here am I," cried he; "and an awful rage I am in. Why, I have been waiting twenty minutes. I don't care a curse for your rules and regulations."

The tailor was furious at this intrusion; but as Mascarin was present, and he felt that he must respect his orders, he by a great effort controlled himself.

"Had I known, sir," said he sulkily, "that you were here—"

These few words mollified the gorgeous youth, who at once broke in.

"I accept your apologies," cried he; "the lackeys remove our arms, the joust is over. My horses have been standing all this time, and may have taken cold. Of course you have seen my horses. Splendid animals, are they not? Zora is in the other room. Quick, fetch her here."

With these words he rushed into the passage and shouted out, "Zora, Mademoiselle de Chantemille, my dear one, come hither."

The renowned tailor was exquisitely uncomfortable at so terrible a scene in his establishment. He cast an appealing glance at Mascarin, but the face of the agent seemed carved in marble. As to Paul, he was quite prepared to accept this young gentleman as a perfect type of the glass of fashion and the mould of form, and could not forbear pitying him in his heart. He went across the room to Mascarin.

110

"Is there no way," whispered he, "of saving this poor young fellow?"

Mascarin smiled one of those livid smiles which chilled the hearts of those who knew him thoroughly.

"In fifteen minutes," said he, "I will put the same question to you, leaving you to reply to it. Hush, this is the first real test that you have been subjected to; if you are not strong enough to go through it, then we had better say farewell. Be firm, for a thunderbolt is about to fall!"

The manner in which these apparently trivial words were spoken startled Paul, who, by a strong effort, recovered his self-possession; but, prepared as he was, it was with the utmost difficulty that he stifled the expression of rage and surprise that rose to his lips at the sight of the woman who entered the room. The Madame de Chantemille, the Zora of the youthful Gandelu, was there, attired in what to his eyes seemed a most dazzling costume. Rose seemed a little timid as Gandelu almost dragged her into the room.

"How silly you are!" said he. "What is there to be frightened at? He is only in a rage with his flunkies for having kept us waiting."

Zora sank negligently into an easy chair, and the gorgeously attired youth addressed the all-powerful Van Klopen.

"Well, have you invented a costume that will be worthy of *Madame's* charms?"

For a few moments Van Klopen appeared to be buried in profound meditation.

"Ah," said he, raising his hand with a grandiloquent gesture, "I have it; I can see it all in my mind's eye."

"What a man!" murmured Gaston in deep admiration.

"Listen," resumed the tailor, his eye flashing with the fire of genius. "First, a walking costume with a polonaise and a cape *a la pensionnaire*; bodice, sleeves, and underskirt of a brilliant chestnut—"

He might have continued in this strain for a long time, and Zora would not have heard a word, for she had caught sight of Paul, and in spite of all her audacity, she nearly fainted. She was so ill at ease, that young Gandelu at last perceived it; but not knowing the effect that the appearance of Paul would necessarily cause, and being also rather dull of comprehension he could not understand the reason for it.

"Hold hard, Van Klopen, hold hard! the joy has been too much for her, and I will lay you ten to one that she is going into hysterics."

Mascarin saw that Paul's temper might blaze forth at any moment, and so hastened to put an end to a scene which was as absurd as it was dangerous.

111

"Well, Van Klopen, I will say farewell," said he. "Good morning, *madame*; good morning, sir;" and taking Paul by the arm, he led him away by a private exit which did not necessitate their passing through the great reception-room.

It was time for him to do so, and not until they were in the street did the wily Mascarin breathe freely.

"Well, what do you say, now?" asked he.

Paul's vanity had been so deeply wounded, and the effort that he had made to restrain himself so powerful, that he could only reply by a gasp.

"He felt it more than I thought he would," said Mascarin to himself. "The fresh air will revive him."

Paul's legs bent under him, and he staggered so that Mascarin led him into a little *café* hard by, and ordered a glass of cognac, and in a short time Paul was himself once again.

"You are better now," observed Mascarin; and then, believing it would be best to finish his work, he added, "A quarter of an hour ago I promised that I would ask you to settle what our intentions were to be regarding M. de Gandelu."

"That is enough," broke in Paul, violently.

Mascarin put on his most benevolent smile.

"You see," remarked he, "how circumstances change ideas. Now you are getting quite reasonable."

"Yes, I am reasonable enough now; that is, that I mean to be wealthy. You have no need to urge me on any more. I am willing to do whatever you desire, for I will never again endure degradation like that I have gone through today."

"You have let temper get the better of you," returned Mascarin, with a shrug of his shoulders.

"My anger may pass over, but my determination will remain as strong as ever."

"Do not decide without thinking the matter well over," answered the agent. "Today you are your own master; but if you give yourself up to me, you must resign your dearly loved liberty."

"I am prepared for all."

Victory had inclined to the side of Mascarin, and he was proportionally jubilant.

"Good," said he. "Then Dr. Hortebise shall introduce you to Martin Rigal, the father of Mademoiselle Flavia, and one week after your marriage I will give you a duke's coronet to put on the panels of your carriage."

Chapter 12: A Startling Revelation

When Sabine de Mussidan told her lover that she would appeal to the generosity of M. de Breulh-Faverlay, she had not calculated on the necessity she would have for endurance, but had rather listened to the dictates of her heart; and this fact came the more strongly before her, when in the solitude of her own chamber, she inquired of herself how she was to carry out her promise. It seemed to her very terrible to have to lay bare the secrets of her soul to anyone, but the more so to M. de Breulh-Faverlay, who had asked for her hand in marriage. She uttered no word on her way home, where she arrived just in time to take her place at the dinner table, and never was a more dismal company assembled for the evening meal.

Her own miseries occupied Sabine, and her father and mother were suffering from their interviews with Mascarin and Dr. Hortebise. What did the liveried servants, who waited at table with such an affectation of interest, care for the sorrows of their master or mistress? They were well lodged and well fed, and nothing save their wages did they care for. By nine o'clock Sabine was in her own room trying to grow accustomed to the thoughts of an interview with M. de Breulh-Faverlay. She hardly closed her eyes all night, and felt worn out and dispirited by musing; but she never thought of evading the promise she had made to Andre, or of putting it off for a time.

She had vowed to lose no time, and her lover was eagerly awaiting a letter from her, telling him of the result. In the perplexity in which she found herself, she could not confide in either father or mother, for she felt that a cloud hung over both their lives, though she knew not what it was. When she left the convent where she had been educated, and returned home, she felt that she was in the way, and that the day of her marriage would be one of liberation to her parents from their cares and responsibilities. All this prayed terribly upon her mind, and might have driven a less pure-minded girl to desperate measures. It seemed to her that it would be less painful to fly from her father's house than to have this interview with M. de Breulh-Faverlay. Luckily for her, frail as she looked, she possessed an indomitable will, and this carried her through most of her difficulties.

For Andre's sake, as well as her own, she did not wish to violate any of the unwritten canons of society, but she longed for the hour to come when she could acknowledge her love openly to the world.

At one moment she thought of writing a letter, but dismissed the thought as the height of folly. As the time passed Sabine began to reproach herself for her cowardice. All at once she heard the clang of the opening of the main gates. Peeping from her window, she saw a carriage drive up, and, to her inexpressible delight, M. de Breulh-Faverlay alighted from it.

"Heaven has heard my prayer, and sent him to me," murmured she.

"What do you intend to do, *Mademoiselle?*" asked the devoted Modeste; "will you speak to him now?"

"Yes, I will. My mother is still in her dressing-room, and no one will venture to disturb my father in the library. If I meet M. de Breulh-Faverlay in the hall and take him into the drawing-room, I shall have time for a quarter of an hour's talk, and that will be sufficient."

Calling up all her courage, she left her room on her errand. Had Andre seen the man selected by the Count de Mussidan for his daughter's husband, he might well have been proud of her preference for him. M. de Breulh-Faverlay was one of the best known men in Paris, and fortune had showered all her blessings on his head. He was not forty, of an extremely aristocratic appearance, highly educated, and witty; and, in addition, one of the largest landholders in the country. He had always refused to enter public life. "For," he would say to those who spoke to him on the matter, "I have enough to spend my money on without making myself ridiculous."

He was a perfect type of what a French gentleman should be—courteous, of unblemished reputation, and full of chivalrous devotion and generosity. He was, it is said, a great favourite with the fair sex; but, if report spoke truly, his discretion was as great as his success. He had not always been wealthy, and there was a mysterious romance in his life. When he was only twenty, he had sailed for South America, where he remained twelve years, and returned no richer than he was before; but shortly afterward his aged uncle, the Marquis de Faverlay, died bequeathing his immense fortune to his nephew on the condition that he should add the name of Faverlay to that of De Breulh. De Breulh was passionately fond of horses; but he was really a lover of them, and not a mere turfite, and this was all that the world knew of the man who held in his hands the fates of Sabine de Mussidan and Andre. As soon as he caught sight of Sabine he made a profound inclination.

The girl came straight up to him.

"Sir," said she, in a voice broken by conflicting emotions, "may I request the pleasure of a short private conversation with you?"

"*Mademoiselle*," answered De Breulh, concealing his surprise beneath another bow, "I am at your disposal."

One of the footmen, at a word from Sabine, threw open the door of the drawing-room in which the countess had thrown down her arms in her duel with Dr. Hortebise. Sabine did not ask her visitor to be seated, but leaning her elbow on the marble mantel-piece, she said, after a silence equally trying to both,—

"This strange conduct on my part, sir, will show you, more than any explanation, my sincerity, and the perfect confidence with which you have inspired me."

She paused, but De Breulh made no reply, for he was perfectly mystified.

"You are," she continued, "my parents' intimate friend, and must have seen the discomforts of our domestic hearth, and that though both my father and mother are living, I am as desolate as the veriest orphan."

Fearing that M. de Breulh might not understand her reason for speaking thus, she threw a shade of haughtiness into her manner as she resumed,—

"My reason, sir, for seeing you today is to ask,—nay, to entreat you, to release me from my engagement to you, and to take the whole responsibility of the rupture on yourself."

Man of the world as he was, M. de Breulh could not conceal his surprise, in which a certain amount of wounded self-love was mingled.

"*Mademoiselle!*" commenced he—

Sabine interrupted him.

"I am asking a great favour, and your granting it will spare me many hours of grief and sadness, and," she added, as a faint smile flickered across her pallid features, "I am aware that I am asking but a trifling sacrifice on your part. You know scarcely anything of me, and therefore you can only feel indifference toward me."

"You are mistaken," replied the young man gravely; "and you do not judge me rightly. I am not a mere boy, and always consider a step before I take it; and if I asked for your hand, it was because I had learned to appreciate the greatness both of your heart and intellect; and I believe that if you would condescend to accept me, we could be very happy together."

The girl seemed about to speak, but De Breulh continued,—

"It seems, however, that I have in some way displeased you,—I do not know how; but, believe me, it will be a source of sorrow to me for the rest of my life."

De Breulh's sincerity was so evident, that Mademoiselle de Mussidan was deeply affected.

"You have not displeased me in any way," answered she softly, "and are far too good for me. To have become your wife would have made me a proud and happy woman."

Here she stopped, almost choked by her tears, but M. de Breulh wished to fathom this mystery.

"Why then this resolve?" asked he.

"Because," replied Sabine faintly, as she hid her face,—"because I have given all my love to another."

The young man uttered an exclamation so full of angry surprise, that Sabine turned upon him at once.

"Yes, sir," answered she, "to another; one utterly unknown to my parents, yet one who is inexpressibly dear to me. This ought not to irritate you, for I gave him my love long before I met you. Besides, you have every advantage over him. He is at the foot, while you are at the summit, of the social ladder. You are of aristocratic lineage,—he is one of the people. You have a noble name,—he does not even know his own. Your wealth is enormous,—while he works hard for his daily bread. He has all the fire of genius, but the cruel cares of life drag and fetter him to the earth. He carries on a workman's trade to supply funds to study his beloved art."

Incautiously, Sabine had chosen the very means to wound this noble gentleman most cruelly, for her whole beauty blazed out as, inflamed by her passion, she spoke so eloquently of Andre and drew such a parallel between the two young men.

"Now, sir," said she, "do you comprehend me? I know the terrible social abyss which divides me from the man I love, and the future may hold in store some terrible punishment for my fidelity to him, but no one shall ever hear a word of complaint from my lips, for—" she hesitated, and then uttered these simple words—"for I love him."

M. de Breulh listened with an outwardly impassible face, but the venomed tooth of jealousy was gnawing at his heart. He had not told Sabine the entire truth, for he had studied her for a long time, and his love had grown firm and strong. Without an unkind thought the girl had shattered the edifice which he had built up with such care and pain. He would have given his name, rank, and title to have been in this unknown lover's place, who, though he worked for his bread, and

116

had no grand ancestral name, was yet so fondly loved. Many a man in his position would have shrugged his shoulders and coldly sneered at the words, "I love him," but he did not, for his nature was sufficiently noble to sympathize with hers. He admired her courage and frankness, which disdaining all subterfuges, went straight and unhesitatingly to the point she desired to reach. She might be imprudent and reckless, but in his eyes these seemed hardly to be faults, for it is seldom that convent-bred young ladies err in this way.

"But this man," said he, after a long pause,—"how do you manage ever to see him?"

"I meet him out walking," replied she, "and I sometimes go to his studio."

"To his studio?"

"Yes, I have sat to him several times for my portrait; but I have never done anything that I need blush to own. You know all now, sir," continued Sabine; "and it has been very hard for a young girl like me to say all this to you. It is a thing that ought to be confided to my mother."

Only those who have heard a woman that they are ardently attached to say, "I do not love you," can picture M. de Breulh's frame of mind. Had anyone else than Sabine made this communication he would not have withdrawn, but would have contested the prize with his more fortunate rival. But now that Mademoiselle de Mussidan had, as it were, thrown herself upon his mercy, he could not bring himself to take advantage of her confidence.

"It shall be as you desire," said he, with a faint tinge of bitterness in his tone. "Tonight I will write to your father, and withdraw my demand for your hand. It is the first time that I have ever gone back from my word; and I am sure that your father will be highly indignant."

Sabine's strength and firmness had now entirely deserted her. "From the depth of my soul, sir," said she, "I thank you; for by this act of generosity I shall avoid a contest that I dreaded."

"Unfortunately," broke in De Breulh, "you do not see how useless to you will be the sacrifice that you exact from me. Listen! you have not appeared much in society; and when you did, it was in the character of my betrothed; as soon as I withdraw hosts of aspirants for your hand will spring up."

Sabine heaved a deep sigh, for Andre had foreseen the same result.

"Then," continued De Breulh, "your situation will become even a more trying one; for if your noble qualities are not enough to excite admiration in the bosoms of the other sex, your immense wealth will arouse the cupidity of the fortune-hunters."

When De Breulh referred to fortune-hunters, was this a side blow at Andre? With this thought rushing through her brain, she gazed upon him eagerly, but read no meaning in his eyes.

"Yes," answered she dreamily, "it is true that I am very wealthy."

"And what will be your reply to the next suitor, and to the one after that?" asked De Breulh.

"I know not; but I shall find some loophole of escape when the time comes; for if I act in obedience to the dictates of my heart and conscience, I cannot do wrong, for Heaven will come to my aid."

The phrase sounded like a dismissal; but De Breulh, man of the world as he was, did not accept it.

"May I permit myself to offer you a word of advice?"

"Do so, sir."

"Very well, then; why not permit matters to remain as they now are? So long as our rupture is not public property, so long will you be left in peace. It would be the simplest thing in the world to postpone all decisive steps for a twelvemonth, and I would withdraw as soon as you notified me that it was time."

Sabine put every confidence in this proposal, believing that everything was in good faith. "But," said she, "such a subterfuge would be unworthy of us all."

M. de Breulh did not urge this point; a feeling of deep sympathy had succeeded to his wounded pride; and, with all the chivalrous instinct of his race, he determined to do his best to assist these lovers.

"Might I be permitted," asked he, "now that you have placed so much confidence in me, to make the acquaintance of the man whom you have honoured with your love?"

Sabine coloured deeply. "I have no reason to conceal anything from you: his name is Andre, he is a painter, and lives in the Rue de la Tour d'Auvergne."

De Breulh made a mental note of the name, and continued,—

"Do not think that I ask this question from mere idle curiosity; my only desire is to aid you. I should be glad to be a something in your life. I have influential friends and connections—"

Sabine was deeply wounded. Did this man propose patronizing Andre, and thus place his position and wealth in contrast with that of the obscure painter? In his eagerness de Breulh had made a false move.

"I thank you," answered she coldly; "but Andre is very proud, and any offer of assistance would wound him deeply. Forgive my scruples, which are perhaps exaggerated and absurd. All he has of his own are his self-respect and his natural pride."

As she spoke, Sabine rang the bell, to show her visitor that the conversation was at an end.

"Have you informed my mother of M. de Breulh-Faverlay's arrival?" asked she, as the footman appeared at the door.

"I have not, *mademoiselle*; for both the count and countess gave the strictest order that they were not to be disturbed on any pretext whatsoever."

"Why did you not tell me that before?" demanded M. de Breulh; and, without waiting for any explanation, he bowed gravely to Sabine, and quitted the room, after apologizing for his involuntary intrusion, and by his manner permitted all the domestics to see that he was much put out.

"Ah!" sighed Sabine, "that man is worthy of some good and true woman's affection."

As she was about to leave the room, she heard someone insisting upon seeing the Count de Mussidan. Not being desirous of meeting strangers, she remained where she was. The servant persisted in saying that his master could receive no one.

"What do I care for your orders?" cried the visitor; "your master would never refuse to see his friend the Baron de Clinchain;" and, thrusting the lackey on one side, he entered the drawing-room; and his agitation was so great that he hardly noticed the presence of the young girl.

M. de Clinchain was a thoroughly commonplace looking personage in face, figure, and dress, neither tall nor short, handsome nor ill-looking. The only noticeable point in his attire was that he wore a coral hand on his watch chain; for the baron was a firm believer in the evil eye. When a young man, he was most methodical in his habits; and, as he grew older, this became an absolute mania with him. When he was twenty, he recorded in his diary the pulsations of his heart, and at forty he added remarks regarding his digestion and general health.

"What a fearful blow!" murmured he; "and to fall at such a moment when I had indulged in a more hearty dinner than usual. I shall feel it for the next six months, even if it does not kill me outright."

Just then M. de Mussidan entered the room, and the excited man ran up to him, exclaiming,—

"For Heaven's sake, Octave, save us both, by cancelling your daughter's engagement with M. de—"

The count laid his hand upon his friend's lips.

"Are you mad?" said he; "my daughter is here."

In obedience to a warning gesture, Sabine left the room; but she had heard enough to fill her heart with agitation and terror. What engagement was to be cancelled, and how could such a rupture affect her father or his friend? That there was some mystery, was proved by the question with which the count had prevented his friend from saying any more. She was sure that it was the name of M. de Breulh-Faverlay with which the baron was about to close his sentence, and felt that the destiny of her life was to be decided in the conversation about to take place between her father and his visitor. It was deep anxiety that she felt, not mere curiosity; and while these thoughts passed through her brain, she remembered that she could hear all from the card-room, the doorway of which was only separated from the drawing-room by a curtain. With a soft, gliding step she gained her hiding-place and listened intently. The baron was still pouring out his lamentations.

"What a fearful day this has been!" groaned the unhappy man. "I ate much too heavy a breakfast, I have been terribly excited, and came here a great deal too fast. A fit of passion caused by a servant's insolence, joy at seeing you, then a sudden interruption to what I was going to say, are a great deal more than sufficient to cause a serious illness at my age."

But the count, who was usually most considerate of his friend's foibles, was not in a humour to listen to him.

"Come, let us talk sense," said he sharply; "tell me what has occurred."

"Occurred!" groaned De Clinchain; "oh, nothing, except that the whole truth is known regarding what took place in the little wood so many years back. I had an anonymous letter this morning, threatening me with all sorts of terrible consequences if I do not hinder you from marrying your daughter to De Breulh. The rogues say that they can prove everything."

"Have you the letter with you?"

De Clinchain drew the missive from his pocket. It was to the full as threatening as he had said; but M. de Mussidan knew all its contents beforehand.

"Have you examined your diary, and are the three leaves really missing?"

"They are."

"How were they stolen? Are you sure of your servants?"

"Certainly; my valet has been sixteen years in my service. You know Lorin? The volumes of my diary are always locked up in the escritoire, the key of which never leaves me. And none of the other servants ever enter my room."

"Someone must have done so, however."

Clinchain struck his forehead, as though an idea had suddenly flashed across his brain.

"I can partly guess," said he. "Some time ago Lorin went for a holiday, and got drunk with some fellows he picked up in the train. Drink brought on fighting, and he was so knocked about that he was laid up for some weeks. He had a severe knife wound in the shoulder and was much bruised."

"Who took his place?"

"A young fellow that my groom got at a servants' registry office."

M. de Mussidan felt that he was on the right track, for he remembered that the man who had called on him had had the audacity to leave a card, on which was marked:

B. Mascarin,
Servants' Registry Office, "Rue Montorgueil.

"Do you know where this place is?" asked he.

"Certainly; in the Rue du Dauphin nearly opposite to my house."

The count swore a deep oath. "The rogues are very wily; but, my dear fellow if you are ready, we will defy the storm together."

De Clinchain felt a cold tremor pass through his whole frame at this proposal.

"Not I," said he; "do not try and persuade me. If you have come to this decision, let me know at once, and I will go home and finish it all with a pistol bullet."

He was just the sort of nervous, timorous man to do exactly as he said, and would sooner have killed himself than endure all kinds of annoyance, which might impair his digestion.

"Very well," answered his friend, with sullen resignation, "then I will give in."

De Clinchain heaved a deep sigh of relief, for he, not knowing what had passed before, had expected to have had a much more difficult task in persuading his friend.

"You are acting like a reasonable man for once in your life," said he.

"You think so, because I give ear to your timorous advice. A thousand curses on that idiotic habit of yours of putting on paper not only your own secrets, but those of others."

But at this remark Clinchain mounted his hobby.

"Do not talk like that," said he. "Had you not committed the act, it would not have appeared in my diary."

Chilled to the very bone, and quivering like an aspen leaf, Sabine had listened to every word. The reality was even more dreadful than she had dreamed of. There was a hidden sorrow, a crime in her father's past life.

Again the count spoke. "There is no use in recrimination. We cannot wipe out the past, and must, therefore, submit. I promise you, on my honour, that this day I will write to De Breulh, and tell him this marriage must be given up."

These words threw the balm of peace and safety into De Clinchain's soul, but the excess of joy was too much for him, and murmuring, "Too much breakfast, and the shock of too violent an emotion," he sank back, fainting, on a couch.

The Count de Mussidan was terrified, he pulled the bell furiously, and the domestics rushed in, followed by the countess. Restoratives were applied, and in ten minutes the baron opened one eye, and raised himself on his elbow.

"I am better now," said he, with a faint smile. "It is weakness and dizziness. I know what I ought to take—two spoonfuls of *eau des carmes* in a glass of sugar and water, with perfect repose of both mind and body. Fortunately, my carriage is here. Pray, be prudent, Mussidan." And, leaning upon the arm of one of the lackeys, he staggered feebly out, leaving the count and countess alone, and Sabine still listening from her post of espial in the card-room.

Chapter 13: Husband and Wife

Ever since Mascarin's visit, the Count de Mussidan had been in a deplorable state of mind. Forgetting the injury to his foot, he passed the night pacing up and down the library, cudgelling his brains for some means of breaking the meshes of the net in which he was entangled. He knew the necessity for immediate action, for he felt sure that this demand would only be the forerunner of numerous others of a similar character. He thought over and dismissed many schemes. Sometimes he had almost decided to go to the police authorities and make a clean breast; then the idea of placing the affair in the hands of a private detective occurred to him; but the more he deliberated, the more he realized the strength of the cord that bound him, and the scandal which exposure would cause. This long course of thought had in some measure softened the bitterness of his wrath, and he was able to receive his old friend M. de Clinchain with some degree of calmness. He was not at all surprised at the receipt of the anonymous letter,—indeed, he had expected that a blow would be struck in that direction. Still immersed in thought, M. de Mussidan hardly took heed of his wife's presence, and he still paced the room, uttering a string of broken phrases. This excited the attention of the countess, for her own threatened position caused her to be on the alert.

"What is annoying you, Octave?" asked she. "Surely, not M. de Clinchain's attack of indigestion?"

For many years the count had been accustomed to that taunting and sarcastic voice, but this feeble joke at such a moment was more than he could endure.

"Don't address me in that manner," said he angrily.

"What is the matter—are you not well?"

"*Madame!*"

"Will you have the kindness to tell me what has taken place?"

The colour suffused the count's face, and his rage burst forth the more furiously from his having had to suppress it so long; and coming to a halt before the chair in which the countess was lounging, his eyes blazing with hate and anger, he exclaimed,—

"All I wish to tell you is, that De Breulh-Faverlay shall not marry our daughter."

Madame de Mussidan was secretly delighted at this reply, for it showed her that half the task required of her by Dr. Hortebise had been accomplished without her interference; but in order to act cautiously, she began at once to object, for a woman's way is always at first to oppose what she most desires.

"You are laughing at me, count!" said she. "Where can we hope to find so good a match again?"

"You need not be afraid," returned the count, with a sneer; "you shall have another son-in-law."

These words sent a pang through the heart of the countess. Was it an allusion to the past? or had the phrase dropped from her husband's lips accidentally? or had he any suspicion of the influence that had been brought to bear upon her? She, however, had plenty of courage, and would rather meet misfortune fact to face than await its coming in dread.

"Of what other son-in-law are you speaking?" asked she negligently. "Has any other suitor presented himself? May I ask his name? Do you intend to settle my child's future without consulting me?"

"I do, *madame.*"

A contemptuous smile crossed the face of the countess, which goaded the count to fury.

"Am I not the master here?" exclaimed he in accents of intense rage. "Am I not driven to the exercise of my power by the menaces of a pack of villains who have wormed out the hidden secrets which have overshadowed my life from my youth upward? They can, if they desire, drag my name through the mire of infamy."

Madame de Mussidan bounded to her feet, asking herself whether her husband's intellect had not given way.

"You commit a crime!" gasped she.

"I, *madame*, I myself! Does that surprise you? Have you never had any suspicion? Perhaps you have not forgotten a fatal accident which took place out shooting, and darkened the earlier years of our married life? Well, the thing was not an accident, but a deliberate murder committed by me. Yes, I murdered him, and this fact is known, and can be proved."

The countess grew deadly pale, and extended her hand, as though to guard herself from some coming danger.

"You are horrified, are you?" continued the count, with a sneer. "Perhaps I inspire you with horror; but do not fear; the blood is no longer on my hands, but it is here, and is choking me." And as he spoke he pressed his fingers upon his heart. "For twenty-three years I have endured this hideous recollection and even now when I wake in the night I am bathed in cold sweat, for I fancy I can hear the last gasps of the unhappy man."

"This is horrible, too horrible!" murmured Madame de Mussidan faintly.

"Ah, but you do not know why I killed him,—it was because the dead man had dared to tell me that the wife I adored with all the passion of my soul was unfaithful to me."

Words of eager denial rose to the lips of the countess; but her husband went on coldly, "And it was all true, for I heard all later on.

"Poor Montlouis! *he* was really loved. There was a little shop-girl, who toiled hard for daily bread, but she was a thousand times more honourable than the haughty woman of noble race that I had just married."

"Have mercy, Octave."

"Yes, and she fell a victim to her love for Montlouis. Had he lived, he would have made her his wife. After his death, she could no longer conceal her fault. In small towns the people are without mercy; and when she left the hospital with her baby at her breast, the women pelted her with mud. But for me," continued the count, "she would have died of hunger. Poor girl! I did not allow her much, but with it she managed to give her son a decent education. He has now grown up, and whatever happens, his future is safe."

Had M. de Mussidan and his wife been less deeply engaged in this hideous recital, they would have heard the stifled sobs that came from the adjoining room.

The count felt a certain kind of savage pleasure in venting the rage, that had for years been suppressed, upon the shrinking woman before him. "Would it not be a cruel injustice, *madame*, to draw a comparison between you and this unhappy girl? Have you always been deaf to the whisperings of conscience? and have you never thought of the future punishment which most certainly awaits you? for you have failed in the duties of daughter, wife, and mother."

Generally the countess cared little for her husband's reproaches, well deserved as they might be, but today she quailed before him.

"With your entrance into my life," continued the count, "came shame and misfortune. When people saw you so gay and careless under the oak-trees of your ancestral home, who could have suspected that your heart contained a dark secret? When my only wish was to win you for my wife, how did I know that you were weaving a hideous conspiracy against me? Even when so young, you were a monster of dissimulation and hypocrisy. Guilt never overshadowed your brow, nor did falsehood dim the frankness of your eyes. On the day of our marriage I mentally reproached myself for any unworthiness. Wretched fool that I was, I was happy beyond all power of expression, when you, *madame*, completed the measure of your guilt by adding infidelity to it."

"It is false," murmured the countess. "You have been deceived."

M. de Mussidan laughed a grim and terrible laugh.

"Not so," answered he; "I have every proof. This seems strange to you, does it? You have always looked upon me as one of those foolish husbands that may be duped without suspicion on their parts. You thought that you had placed a veil over my eyes, but I could see through it when you little suspected that I could do so. Why did I not tell you this before? Because I had not ceased to love you, and this fatal love was stronger than all honour, pride, and even self-respect." He poured out this tirade with inconceivable rapidity, and the countess listened to it in awe-struck silence. "I kept silence," continued the count, "because I knew that on the day I uttered the truth you would be entirely lost to me. I might have killed you; I had every right to do so, but I could not live apart from you. You will never know how near the shadow of death has been to you. When I have kissed you, I have fancied that your lips were soiled with the kisses of others, and I could hardly keep my hands from clutching your ivory neck until life was extinct, and failed utterly to decide whether I loved you or hated you the most."

"Have mercy, Octave! have mercy!" pleaded the unhappy woman.

"You are surprised, I can see," answered he, with a dark smile; "yet I could give you further food for wonder if I pleased, but I have said enough now."

A tremor passed over the frame of the countess. Was her husband acquainted with the existence of the letters? All hinged upon this. He could not have read them, or he would have spoken in very different terms, had he known the mystery contained in them.

"Let me speak," began she.

"Not a word," replied her husband.

"On my honour—"

"All is ended; but I must not forget to tell you of one of my youthful follies. You may laugh at it, but that signifies nothing. I actually believed that I could gain your affection. I said to myself that one day you would be moved by my deep passion for you. I was a fool. As if love or affection could ever penetrate the icy barriers that guarded your heart."

"You have no pity," wailed she.

He gazed upon her with eyes in which the pent-up anger of twenty years blazed and consumed slowly. "And you, what are you? I drained to the bottom the poisoned cup held out to a deceived husband by an unfaithful wife. Each day widened the breach between us, until at last we sank into this miserable existence which is wearing out my life. I kept no watch on you; I was not made for a jailer. What I wanted was your soul and heart. To imprison the body was easy, but your soul would still have been free to wander in imagination to the meeting-place where your lover expected you. I know not how I had the courage to remain by your side. It was not to save an honour that had already gone, but merely to keep up appearances; for as long as we were nominally together the tongue of scandal was forced to remain silent."

Again the unhappy woman attempted to protest her innocence, and again the count paid no heed to her. "I wished too," resumed he, "to save some portion of our property, for your insatiable extravagance swallowed up all like a bottomless abyss. At last your trades-people, believing me to be ruined, refused you credit, and this saved me. I had my daughter to think of, and have gathered together a rich dowry for her, and yet—" he hesitated, and ceased speaking for a moment.

"And yet," repeated Madame de Mussidan.

"I have never kissed her," he burst forth with a fresh and terrible explosion of wrath, "without feeling a hideous doubt as to whether she was really my child."

This was more than the countess could endure.

"Enough," she cried, "enough! I have been guilty, Octave; but not so guilty as you imagine."

"Why do you venture to defend yourself?"

"Because it is my duty to guard Sabine."

"You should have thought of this earlier," answered the count with a sneer. "You should have moulded her mind—have taught her what was noble and good, and have perused the unsullied pages of the book of her young heart."

In the deepest agitation the countess answered,—

"Ah, Octave, why did you not speak of this sooner, if you knew all; but I will now tell you everything."

By an inconceivable error of judgment the count corrected her speech. "Spare us both," said he. "If I have broken through the silence that I have maintained for many a year, it is because I knew that no word you could utter would touch my heart."

Feeling that all hope had fled, Madame de Mussidan fell backward upon the couch, while Sabine, unable to listen to any more terrible revelations, had crept into her own chamber. The count was about to leave the drawing-room, when a servant entered, bearing a letter on a silver salver. De Mussidan tore it open; it was from M. de Breulh-Faverlay, asking to be released from his engagement to Sabine de Mussidan. This last stroke was almost too much for the count's nerves, for in this act he saw the hand of the man who had come to him with such deadly threats, and terror filled his soul as he thought of the far-stretching arm of him whose bond-slave he found himself to be; but before he could collect his thoughts, his daughter's maid went into the room crying with all her might, "Help, help; my poor mistress is dying!"

Chapter 14: Father and Daughter

Van Klopen, the man-milliner, knew Paris and its people thoroughly like all tradesmen who are in the habit of giving large credit. He knew all about the business of his customers, and never forgot an item of information when he received one. Thus, when Mascarin spoke to him about the father of the lovely Flavia, whose charms had set the susceptible heart of Paul Violaine in a blaze, the arbiter of fashion had replied,—

"Martin Rigal; yes, I know him; he is a banker." And a banker, indeed, Martin Rigal was, dwelling in a magnificent house in the Rue Montmartre. The bank was on the ground floor, while his private rooms were in the story above. Though he did not do business in a very large way, yet he was a most respectable man, and his connection was chiefly with the smaller trades-people, who seem to live a strange kind of hand-to-mouth existence, and who might be happy were it not for the constant reappearance of that grim phantom—bills to be met. Nearly all these persons were in the banker's hands entirely. Martin Rigal used his power despotically and permitted no arguments, and speedily quelled rebellion on the part of any new customer who ventured to object to his arbitrary rules. In the morning the banker was never to be seen, being engaged in his private office, and not a clerk would venture to knock at his door. Even had one done so, no reply would have been returned; for the experiment had been tried, and it was believed that nothing short of an alarm of fire would have brought him out.

The banker was a big man, quite bald, his face was clean shaved, and his little gray eyes twinkled incessantly. His manner was charmingly courteous, and he said the most cruel things in the most honeyed accents, and invariably escorted to the door the man whom he would sell up the next day. In his dress he affected a fashionable style, much used by the modern school of Shylocks. When not in business, he was a pleasant, and, as some say, a witty companion. He was not looked on as an ascetic, and did not despise those little pleasures which enable us to sustain life's tortuous journey. He liked a good dinner, and had always a smile ready for a young and attractive face. He was a widower, and all his love was concentrated on his daughter.

He did not keep a very extravagant establishment, but the report in the neighbourhood was that Mademoiselle Flavia, the daughter of the eminent banker, would one day come into millions. The banker always did his business on foot, for the sake of his health, as he said; but Flavia had a sweet little Victoria, drawn by two thoroughbred horses, to drive in the Bois de Boulogne, under the protection of an old woman, half companion and half servant, who was driven half mad by her charge's caprices. As yet her father has never denied her anything. He worked harder than all his clerks put together, for, after having spent the morning in his counting house over his papers, he received all business clients.

On the day after Flavia and Paul Violaine had met at Van Klopen's, M. Martin Rigal was, at about half-past five, closeted with one of his female clients. She was young, very pretty, and dressed with simple elegance, but the expression of her face was profoundly melancholy. Her eyes were overflowing with tears, which she made vain efforts to restrain.

"If you refuse to renew our bill, sir, we are ruined," said she. "I could meet it in January. I have sold all my trinkets, and we are existing on credit."

"Poor little thing!" interrupted the banker.

Her hopes grew under these words of pity.

"And yet," continued she, "business has never been so brisk. New customers are constantly coming in, and though our profits are small, the returns are rapid."

As Martin Rigal heard her exposition of the state of affairs, he nodded gravely.

"That is all very well," said he at last, "but this does not make the security you offer me of any more value. I have more confidence in you."

"But remember, sir, that we have thirty thousand *francs'* worth of stock."

"That is not what I was alluding to," and the banker accompanied these words with so meaning a look, that the poor woman blushed scarlet and almost lost her nerve. "Your stock," said he, "is of no more value in my eyes than the bill you offer me. Suppose, for instance, you were to become bankrupt, the landlord might come down upon everything, for he has great power."

He broke off abruptly, for Flavia's maid, as a privileged person, entered the room without knocking.

"Sir," said she, "my mistress wishes to see you at once."

The banker got up directly. "I am coming," said he; then, taking the hand of his client, he led her to the door, repeating: "Do not worry yourself; all the difficulties shall be got through. Come again, and we will talk them over;" and before she could thank him he was half way to his daughter's apartment. Flavia had summoned her father to show him a new costume which had just been sent home by Van Klopen, and which pleased her greatly. Flavia's costume was a masterpiece of fashionable bad taste, which makes women look all alike and destroys all appearance of individuality. It was a mass of frills, furbelows, fringes, and flutings of rare hue and form, making a series of wonderful contrasts. Standing in the middle of the room, with every available candle alight, for the day was fading away, she was so dainty and pretty that even the bizarre dress of Van Klopen's was unable to spoil her appearance. As she turned round, she caught sight of her father in a mirror, panting with the haste he had made in running upstairs.

"What a time you have been!" said she pettishly.

"I was with a client," returned he apologetically.

"You ought to have got rid of him at once. But never mind that; look at me and tell me plainly what you think of me."

She had no need to put the question, for the most intense admiration beamed in his face.

"Exquisite, delicious, heavenly!" answered he.

Flavia, accustomed as she was to her father's compliments, was highly delighted. "Then you think that he will like me?" asked she.

She alluded to Paul Violaine, and the banker heaved a deep sigh as he replied,—

"Is it possible that any human being exists that you cannot please?"

"Ah!" mused she, "if it were anyone but he, I should have no doubts or misgivings."

Martin Rigal took a seat near the fire, and, drawing his daughter to him, pressed a fond kiss upon her brow, while she with the grace and activity of a cat, nestled upon his knee. "Suppose, after all, that he should not like me," murmured she; "I should die of grief."

The banker turned away his face to hide the gloom that overspread it. "Do you love him, then, even now?" asked he.

She paused for a moment, and he added, "More than you do me?"

Flavia pressed her father's hand between both her palms and answered with a musical laugh, "How silly you are, papa! Why, of course I love you. Are you not my father? I love you too because you are kind and do all I wish, and because you are always telling me that you love me. Because you are like the cupids in the fairy stories—dear old people who give their children all their heart's desire; I love you for my carriage, my horses, and my lovely dresses; for my purse filled with gold, for my beautiful jewellery, and for all the lovely presents you make me."

Every word she spoke betrayed the utter selfishness of her soul, and yet her father listened with a fixed smile of delight on his face.

"And why do you love him?" asked he.

"Because—because," stammered the girl, "first, because he is himself; and then,—well, I can't say, but I *do* love him."

Her accents betrayed such depth of passion that the father uttered a groan of anguish.

Flavia caught the expression of his features, and burst into a fit of laughter.

"I really believe that you are jealous," said she, as if she were speaking to a spoiled child. "That is very naughty of you; you ought to be ashamed of yourself. I tell you that the first time I set eyes upon him at Van Klopen's, I felt a thrill of love pierce through my heart, such love as I never felt for a human being before. Since then, I have known no rest. I cannot sleep, and instead of blood, liquid fire seems to come through my veins."

Martin Rigal raised his eyes to the ceiling in mute surprise at this outburst of feeling.

"You do not understand me," went on Flavia. "You are the best of fathers, but, after all, you are but a man. Had I a mother, she would comprehend me better."

"What could your mother have done for you more than I? Have I neglected anything for your happiness?" asked the banker, with a sigh.

"Perhaps nothing; for there are times when I hardly understand my own feelings."

In gloomy silence the banker listened to the narrative of his daughter's state of mind; then he said,—

"All shall be as you desire, and the man you love shall be your husband."

The girl was almost beside herself with joy, and, throwing her arms around his neck, pressed kiss upon kiss on his cheeks and forehead.

"Darling," said she, "I love you for this more than for anything that you have given me in my life."

The banker sighed again; and Flavia, shaking her pretty little fist at him, exclaimed, "What is the meaning of that sigh, sir? Do you by any chance regret your promise? But never mind that. How do you mean to bring him here without causing any suspicion?"

A benevolent smile passed over her father's face, as he answered,—

"That, my pet, is my secret."

"Very well, keep it; I do not care what means you use, as long as I see him soon, very soon,—tonight perhaps, in an hour, or even in a few minutes. You say Dr. Hortebise will bring him here; he will sit at our table. I can look at him without trouble, I shall hear his voice—"

"Silly little puss!" broke in the banker; "or, rather, I should say, unhappy child."

"Silly, perhaps; but why should you say unhappy?"

"You love him too fondly, and he will take advantage of your feeling for him."

"Never; I do not believe it," answered the girl.

"I hope to heaven, darling, that my fears may never be realized. But he is not the sort of husband that I intended for you; he is a composer."

"And is that anything against him!" exclaimed Flavia in angry tones; "one would think from your sneers that this was a crime. Not only is he a composer, but he is a genius. I can read that in his face. He may be poor, but I am rich enough for both, and he will owe all to me; so much the better, for then he will not be compelled to give lessons for his livelihood, and he will have leisure to compose an opera more beautiful than any that Gounod has ever written, and I shall share all his glory. Why, perhaps, he may even sing his own songs to me alone."

Her father noticed her state of feverish excitement and gazed upon her sadly. Flavia's mother had been removed from this world at the early age of twenty-four by that insidious malady, consumption, which defies modern medical science, and in a brief space changes a beautiful girl into a livid corpse, and the father viewed her excited manner, flushed cheeks, and sparkling eyes with tears and dismay.

"By heavens!" cried he, bursting into a sudden fit of passion; "if ever he ill treats you, he is a dead man."

The girl was startled at the sudden ferocity of his manner.

"What have I done to make you angry?" asked she; "and why do you have such evil thoughts of him?"

"I tremble for you, in whom my whole soul is wrapped up," answered the banker. "This man has robbed me of my child's heart, and you will be happier with him than you are with your poor old father. I tremble because of your inexperience and his weakness, which may prove a source of trouble to you."

"If he is weak, all the better; my will can guide him."

"You are wrong," replied her father, "as many other women have been before you. You believe that weak and vacillating dispositions are easily controlled, but I tell you that this is an error. Only determined characters can be influenced, and it is on substantial foundations that we find support."

Flavia made no reply, and her father drew her closer to him.

"Listen to me, my child," said he. "You will never have a better friend than I am. You know that I would shed every drop of blood in my veins for you. He is coming, so search your heart to discover if this is not some mere passing fancy."

"Father!" cried she.

"Remember that your happiness is in your own hands now, so be careful and conceal your feelings, and do not let him discover how deep your love is for him. Men's minds are so formed that while they blame a woman for duplicity, they complain far more if she acts openly and allows her feelings to be seen——"

He paused, for the door-bell rang. Flavia's heart gave a bound of intense joy.

"He has come!" gasped she, and, with a strong effort to retain her composure, she added, "I will obey you, my dear father; I will not come here again until I have entirely regained my composure. Do not fear, and I will show you that your daughter can act a part as well as any other woman."

She fled from the room as the door opened, but it was not Paul who made his appearance, but some other guests—a stout manufacturer and his wife, the latter gorgeously dressed, but with scarcely a word to say for herself. For this evening the banker had issued invitations to twenty of his friends, and among this number Paul would scarcely be noticed. He in due time made his appearance with Dr. Hortebise, who had volunteered to introduce him into good society. Paul felt ill at ease; he had just come from the hands of a fashionable tailor, who, thanks to Mascarin's influence, had in forty-eight hours prepared an evening suit of such superior cut that the young man hardly knew himself in it. Paul had suffered a good deal from conflicting emotions after the visit to Van Klopen's, and more than once regretted the adhesion that he had given to Mascarin's scheme; but a visit the next day from Hortebise, and the knowledge that the fashionable physician was one of the confederates, had reconciled him to the position he had promised to assume.

He was moreover struck with Flavia's charms, and dazzled with the accounts of her vast prospective fortune. To him, Hortebise, gay, rich, and careless, seemed the incarnation of happiness, and contributed greatly to stifle the voice of Paul's conscience. He would, however, perhaps have hesitated had he known what the locket contained that dangled so ostentatiously from the doctor's chain.

Before they reached the banker's door, driven in the doctor's elegant brougham, a similar one to which Paul mentally declared he would have, as soon as circumstances would permit, the young man's mentor spoke.

"Let me say a few words to you. You have before you a chance which is seldom afforded to any young man, whatever his rank and social standing. Mind that you profit by it."

"You may be sure I will," said Paul, with a smile of self-complacency.

"Good, dear boy; but let me fortify your courage with a little of my experience. Do you know what an heiress really is?"

"Well, really—"

"Permit me to continue. An heiress and more so if she is an only child, is generally a very disagreeable person, headstrong, capricious, and puffed up with her own importance. She is utterly spoiled by the flattery to which she has been accustomed from her earliest years, and thinks that all the world is made to bend before her."

"Ah!" answered Paul, a little discomfited. "I hope it is not Mademoiselle Flavia's portrait that you have been sketching?"

"Not exactly," answered the doctor, with a laugh. "But I must warn you that even she has certain whims and fancies. For instance, I am quite sure that she would give a suitor every encouragement, and then repulse him without rhyme or reason."

Paul, who up to this time had only seen the bright side of affairs, was a good deal disconcerted.

"Buy why should you introduce me to her then?"

"In order that you may win her. Have you not everything to insure success? She will most likely receive you with the utmost cordiality; but beware of being too sanguine. Even if she makes desperate love to you, I say, take care; it may be only a trap; for, between ourselves, a girl who has a million stitched to her petticoats is to be excused if she endeavours to find out whether the suitor is after her or her money."

Just then the brougham stopped, and Dr. Hortebise and his young friend entered the house in the Rue Montmartre, where they were cordially greeted by the banker.

Paul glanced round, but there were no signs of Flavia, nor did she make her appearance until five minutes before the dinner hour, when the guests flocked round her. She had subdued all her emotions, and not a quiver of the eyelids disclosed the excitement under which she was labouring. Her eye rested on Paul, and he bowed ceremoniously. The banker was delighted, for he had not believed much in her self-command. But Flavia had taken his advice to heart, and when seated at table abstained from casting a glance in Paul's direction. When dinner was over and many of the guests had sat down to whist, Flavia ventured to approach Paul, and in a low voice, which shook a little in spite of her efforts, said,—

"Will you not play me one of your own compositions, M. Violaine?"

Paul was but a medium performer, but Flavia seemed in the seventh heaven, while her father and Dr. Hortebise, who had taken their seats not far away, watched the young couple with much anxiety.

"How she adores him!" whispered the banker. "And yet I cannot judge of the effect that she has produced upon him."

"Surely Mascarin will worm it all out of him tomorrow," returned the doctor. "Tomorrow the poor fellow will have his hands full, for there is to be a general meeting, when we shall hear all about Catenac's ideas, and I shall be glad to know what Croisenois's conduct will be when he knows what he is wanted for."

It was growing late, and the guests began to drop off. Dr. Hortebise signalled to Paul, and they left the house together. According to the promise to her father, Flavia had acted her part so well, that Paul did not know whether he had made an impression or not.

Chapter 15: Master Chupin

Beaumarchef, when Mascarin called a general meeting of his associates, was in the habit of assuming his very best attire; for as he was often called into the inner office to answer questions, he was much impressed with the importance of the occasion. This time, however, the subordinate, although he had received due notice of the meeting, was still in his every-day dress. This discomposed him a good deal, though he kept muttering to himself that he meant no disrespect by it. Early in the morning he had been compelled to make up the accounts of two cooks, who, having obtained situations, were leaving the servants' lodging-house. When this matter was completed, he had hoped for half an hour's leisure. As he was crossing the courtyard, however, he fell in with Toto Chupin bringing in his daily report, which Beaumarchef thought would be what it usually was—a mere matter of form. He was, however, much mistaken; for though outwardly Toto was the same, yet his ideas had taken an entirely new direction; and when Beaumarchef urged him to look sharp, the request was received with a great deal of sullenness.

"I ain't lost no time," said he, "and have fished up a thing or two fresh; but before saying a word—"

He stopped, and seemed a little confused.

"Well, go on."

"I want a fresh arrangement."

Beaumarchef was staggered.

"Arrangement!" he echoed.

"Of course you can lump it if yer don't like it," said the boy. "Do you think as how I'm going to work like a horse, and not get a wink of sleep, just for a 'thank ye, Chupin?' No fear. I'm worth a sight more nor that."

Beaumarchef flew into a rage.

"Then you are not worth a pinch of salt," said he.

"All right, my cove."

"And you are an ungrateful young villain to talk like this after all the kindness your master has shown you."

Chupin gave a sarcastic laugh.

"Goodness!" cried he. "To hear you go on, one would think that the boss had ruined himself for my sake."

"He took you out of the streets, and has given you a room ever since."

"A room, do you say? I call it a dog kennel."

"You have your breakfast and dinner every day regularly."

"I know that, and half a bottle of wine at each meal, which has so much water in it that it cannot even stain the tablecloth."

"You are an ungrateful young hound," exclaimed Beaumarchef, "and forget that, in addition to this, he has set you up in business as a hot chestnut seller."

"Good old business! I am allowed to stand all day under the gateway, roasted on one side, and frozen on the other, and gain, perhaps twenty *sous*."

"You know that in summer he has promised to set you up in the fried potato line."

"Thank ye for nothing; I don't like the smell of grease."

"What is it you want, then?"

"Nothing. I feels that I ought to be a gentleman at large."

Beaumarchef cast a furious glance at the shameless youth, and told him that he would report everything to his master. The boy, however, did not seem to care a pin.

"I intends to see Master Mascarin myself presently," remarked Chupin.

"You are an idiot."

"Why so? Do you think I didn't live better before I had anything to do with this blooming old cove? I never worked then. I used to sing in front of the pubs, and easily made my three *francs* a day. My pal and I soon check 'em though, and then off we went to the theatre. Sometimes we'd make tracks for Ivry, and take our doss in a deserted factory, into which the crushers never put their noses. In the winter we used to go to the glass houses and sleep in the warm ashes. All these were good times, while now—"

"Well, what have you to grumble at now? Don't I hand you a five-*franc* piece every day that you are at work?"

"But that ain't good enough. Come, don't get shirty; all I asks is a rise of salary. Only say either Yes or No; and if you say No, why, I sends in my resignation."

Beaumarchef would have given a five-*franc* piece out of his own pocket for Mascarin to have heard the boy's impertinence.

"You are a young rascal!" said he, "and keep the worst of company. There is no use in denying it, for a hang-dog fellow, calling himself Polyte, has been here asking after you."

"My company ain't any business of yours."

"Well, I give you warning, you will come to grief."

"How?" returned Toto Chupin sulkily. "How can I come to grief? If old Mascarin interferes, I'll shut up his mouth pretty sharp. I wish you and your master wouldn't poke their noses into my affairs. I'm sick of you both. Don't you think I'm up to you? When you make me follow someone for a week at a time, it isn't to do 'em a kindness, I reckon. If things turn out badly, I've only to go before a beak and speak up; I should get off easily enough then; and if I do so, you will be sorry for not having given me more than my five *francs* a day."

Beaumarchef was an old soldier and a bold man, but he was easily upset, for the lad's insolence made him believe that he was uttering words that had been put in his mouth by some wily adviser; and not knowing how to act, the ex-soldier thought it best to adopt a more conciliating demeanour.

"How much do you want?" asked he.

"Well, seven *francs* to start with."

"The deuce you do! Seven *francs* a day is a sum. Well, I'll give it you myself today and will speak about you to the master."

"You won't get me to loosen my tongue for that amount today; you may bet your boots on that," answered the lad insolently. "I wants one hundred *francs* down on the nail."

"One hundred *francs*," echoed Beaumarchef, scandalized at such a demand.

"Yes, my cove, that and no less."

"And what will you give in return? No, no, my lad; your demand is a preposterous one; besides, you wouldn't know how to spend such a sum."

"Don't you flurry yourself about that; but of one thing you may be sure, I sha'n't spend my wages as you do—in wax for your moustache."

Beaumarchef could not endure an insult to his moustache, and Chupin was about to receive the kick he had so richly earned, when Daddy Tantaine suddenly made his appearance, looking exactly as he did when he visited Paul in his garret.

"Tut, tut; never quarrel with the door open."

Beaumarchef thanked Providence for sending this sudden reinforcement to his aid, and began in a tone of indignation,—

"Toto Chupin—"

"Stop! I have heard every word," broke in Tantaine.

On hearing this, Toto felt that he had better make himself scarce; for though he hardly knew Mascarin, and utterly despised Beaumarchef, he trembled before the oily Tantaine, for in him he recognised a being who would stand no nonsense. He therefore began in an apologetic tone,—

"Just let me speak, sir; I only wanted—"

"Money, of course, and very natural too. Come, Beaumarchef, hand this worthy lad the hundred *francs* that he has so politely asked for."

Beaumarchef was utterly stupefied, and was about to make some objection when he was struck by a signal which Toto did not perceive, and, drawing out his pocketbook, extracted a note which he offered to the lad. Toto glanced at the note, then at the faces of the two men, but was evidently afraid to take the money.

"Take the money," said Tantaine. "If your information is not worth the money, I will have it back from you; come into the office, where we shall not be disturbed."

Tantaine took a chair, and glancing at Toto, who stood before him twirling his cap leisurely, said,—

"I heard you."

The lad had by this time recovered his customary audacity.

"Five days ago," he began, "I was put on to Caroline Schimmel; I have found out all about her by this time. She is as regular as clockwork in her duties at least. She wakes at ten and takes her *absinthe*. Then she goes to a little restaurant she knows, and has her breakfast and a game at cards with anyone that will play with her. At six in the evening she goes to the Grand Turk, a restaurant and dancing-shop in the Rue des Poisonnieres. Ain't it a swell ken just! You can eat; drink, dance, or sing, just as you like; but you must have decent togs on, or they won't let you in."

"Wouldn't they let you through then?"

Toto pointed significantly to his rags as he replied,—

"This rig out wouldn't pass muster, but I have a scheme in hand."

Tantaine took down the address of the dancing-saloon, and then, addressing Toto with the utmost severity,—

"Do you think," said he, "that this report is worth a hundred *francs*?"

Toto made a quaint grimace.

"Do you think," asked he, "that Caroline can lead the life she does without money? No fear. Well, I have found out where the coin comes from."

The dim light in the office enabled Tantaine to hide the pleasure he felt on hearing these words.

"Ah," answered he carelessly, as if it was a matter of but little moment, "and so you have found out all that, have you?

"Yes, and a heap besides. Just you listen. After her breakfast, my sweet Carry began to play cards with some chaps who had been grubbing at the next table. 'Regular right down card sharpers and macemen,' said I to myself, as I watched the way in which they faked the pasteboards. 'They'll get everything out of you, old gal.' I was in the right, for in less than an hour she had to go up to the counter and leave one of her rings as security for the breakfast. He said he knew her, and would give her credit. 'You are a trump,' said she. 'I'll just trot off to my own crib and get the money.'"

"Did she go home?"

"Not she; she went to a real swell house in a bang up part of Paris, the Rue de Varennes. She knocked at the door, and in she went, while I lounged about outside."

"Do you know who lives there?"

"Of course I do. The grocer round the corner told me that it was inhabited by the duke—what was his blessed name? Oh, the duke—"

"Was it the Duke de Champdoce?"

"That is the right one, a chap they say as has his cellars chock full of gold and silver."

"You are rather slow, my lad," said Tantaine, with his assumed air of indifference. "Get on a bit, do."

Toto was much put out; for he had expected that his intelligence would have created an immense sensation.

"Give a cove time to breathe in. Well, in half an hour out comes my Carry as lively as a flea. She got into a passing cab and away she went. Fortunately I can run a bit, and reached the Palais Royal in time to see Caroline change two notes of two hundred *francs* each at the money-changers."

"How did you find out that?"

"By looking at 'em. The paper was yellow."

Tantaine smiled kindly. "You know a banknote then?"

"Yes, but I have precious few chances of handling them. Once I went into a money-changer's shop and asked them just to let me feel one, and they said, 'Get out sharp.'"

"Is that all?" demanded Tantaine.

"No; I have kept the best bit for a finish. I want to tell you that there are others on the lookout after Caroline."

Toto had no reason this time to grumble at the effect he had produced, for the old man gave such a jump that his hat fell off.

"What are you saying?" said he.

"Simply that for the last three days a big chap with a harp on his back has been keeping her in view. I twigged him at once, and he too saw her go into the swell crib that you say belongs to that duke."

Tantaine pondered a little.

"A street musician," muttered he. "I must find out all about this. Now, Toto, listen to me; chuck Caroline over, and stick to the fellow with the harp; be off with you, for you have earned your money well."

As Chupin went off, the old man shook his head.

"Too sharp by a good bit," said he; "he won't have a long lease of life."

Beaumarchef was about to ask Tantaine to remain in the office while he went off to put on his best clothes, but the old man stopped this request by saying,—

"As M. Mascarin does not like to be disturbed, I will just go in without knocking. When the other gentlemen arrive, show them in; for look you here, my good friend, the pear is so ripe that if it is not plucked, it will fall to the ground."

Chapter 16: A Turn of the Screw

Dr. Hortebise was the first to arrive. It was a terrible thing for him to get up so early; but for Mascarin's sake he consented even to this inconvenience. When he passed through the office, the room was full of clients; but this did not prevent the doctor from noticing the negligence of Beaumarchef's costume.

"Aha!" remarked the doctor, "on the drunk again, I am afraid."

"M. Mascarin is within," answered the badgered clerk, endeavouring to put on an air of dignity; "and M. Tantaine is with him."

A brilliant idea flashed across the doctor's mind, but it was with an air of gravity that he said,—

"I shall be charmed to meet that most worthy old gentleman."

When, however, he entered the inner sanctum, he found Mascarin alone, occupied in sorting the eternal pieces of pasteboard.

"Well, what news?" asked he.

"There is none that I know of."

"What, have you not seen Paul?"

"No."

"Will he be here?"

"Certainly."

Mascarin was often laconic, but he seldom gave such short answers as this.

"What is the matter?" asked the doctor. "Your greeting is quite funereal. Are you not well?"

"I am merely preoccupied, and that is excusable on the eve of the battle we are about to fight," returned Mascarin.

He only, however, told a portion of the truth; for there was more in the background, which he did not wish to confide to his friend. Toto Chupin's revolt had disquieted him. Let there be but a single flaw in the axletree, and one day it will snap in twain; and Mascarin wanted to eliminate this flaw.

"Pooh!" remarked the doctor, playing with his locket, "we shall succeed. What have we to fear, after all,—opposition on Paul's part?"

"Paul may resent a little," answered Mascarin disdainfully; "but I have decided that he shall be present at our meeting of today. It will be a stormy one, so be prepared. We might give him his medicine in minims, but I prefer the whole dose at once."

"The deuce you do! Suppose he should be frightened, and make off with our secret."

"He won't make off," replied Mascarin in a tone which froze his listener's blood. "He can't escape from us any more than the cock-chafer can from the string that a child has fastened to it. Do you not understand weak natures like his? He is the glove, I the strong hand beneath it."

The doctor did not argue this point, but merely murmured,—

"Let us hope that it is so."

"Should we have any opposition," resumed Mascarin, "it will come from Catenac. I may be able to force him into co-operation with us, but his heart will not be in the enterprise."

"Do you propose to bring Catenac into this affair?" asked Hortebise in great surprise.

"Assuredly."

"Why have you changed your plan?"

"Simply because I have recognised the fact that, if we dispensed with his services, we should be entirely at the mercy of a shrewd man of business, because—"

He broke off, listened for a moment, and then said,—

"Hush! I can hear his footstep."

A dry cough was heard outside, and in another moment Catenac entered the room.

Nature, or profound dissimulation, had gifted Catenac with an exterior which made everyone, when first introduced to him, exclaim, "This is an honest and trustworthy man." Catenac always looked his clients boldly in the face. His voice was pleasant, and had a certain ring of joviality in it, and his manner was one of those easy ones which always insure popularity. He was looked upon as a shrewd lawyer; but yet he did not shine in court. He must therefore, to make those thirty thousand *francs* a year which he was credited with doing, have some special line of business. He assayed rather risky matters, which might bring both parties into the clutches of the criminal law, or, at any rate, leave them with a taint upon both their names. A sensational lawsuit is begun, and the public eagerly await the result; suddenly the whole thing collapses, for Catenac has acted as mediator. He has even settled the disputes of murderers quarrelling over their booty. But he has even gone farther than this. More than once he has said of himself, "I have passed through the vilest masses of corruption." In his office in the Rue Jacob he has heard whispered conferences which were enough to bring down the roof above his head. Of course this was the most lucrative business that passed into Catenac's hands. The client conceals nothing from his attorney, and he belongs to him as absolutely as the sick man belongs to his physician or the penitent to his confessor.

"Well, my dear Baptiste," said he, "here I am; you summoned me, and I am obedient to the call."

"Sit down," replied Mascarin gravely.

"Thanks, my friend, many thanks, a thousand thanks; but I am much hurried; indeed I have not a moment to spare. I have matters on my hands of life and death."

"But for all that," remarked Hortebise, "you can sit down for a moment. Baptiste has something to say to you which is as important as any of your matters can be."

With a frank and genial smile Catenac obeyed; but in his heart were anger and an abject feeling of alarm.

"What is it that is so important?" asked he.

Mascarin had risen and locked the door. When he had resumed his seat he said,—

"The facts are very simple. Hortebise and I have decided to put our great plan into execution, which we have as yet only discussed generally with you. We have the Marquis de Croisenois with us."

"My dear sir," broke in the lawyer.

"Wait a little; we must have your assistance, and—"

Catenac rose from his seat. "That is enough," said he. "You have made a very great mistake if it is on this matter that you have sent for me; I told you this before."

He was turning away, and looking for his hat, proposed to beat a retreat; but Dr. Hortebise stood between him and the door, gazing upon him with no friendly expression of countenance. Catenac was not a man to be easily alarmed, but the doctor's appearance was so threatening, and the smile upon Mascarin's lips was of so deadly a character, that he stood still, positively frightened into immobility.

"What do you mean?" stammered he; "what is it you say now?"

"First," replied the doctor, speaking slowly and distinctly,—"first, we wish that you should listen to us when we speak to you."

"I am listening."

"Then sit down again, and hear what Baptiste has to say."

The command Catenac had over his countenance was so great that it was impossible to see to what conclusion he had arrived from the words and manner of his confederates.

"Then let Baptiste explain himself," said he.

"Before entering into matters completely," said he coolly, "I first want to ask our dear friend and associate if he is prepared to act with us?"

"Why should there be any doubt on that point?" asked the lawyer. "Do all my repeated assurances count as nothing?"

"We do not want promises now; what we do want is good faith and real co-operation."

"Can it be that you——"

"I ought to inform you," continued Mascarin, unheeding the interruption, "that we have every prospect of success; and, if we carry the matter through, we shall certainly have a million apiece."

Hortebise had not the calm patience of his confederate, and exclaimed,—

"You understand it well enough. Say Yes or No."

Catenac was in the agonies of indecision, and for fully a minute made no reply.

"*No*, then!" he broke out in a manner which betrayed his intense agitation. "After due consideration, and having carefully weighed the chances for and against, I answer you decidedly, No."

Mascarin and Hortebise evidently expected this reply, and exchanged glances.

"Permit me to explain," said Catenac, "what you consider as a cowardly withdrawal upon my part——"

"Call it treachery."

"I will not quibble about words. I wish to be perfectly straightforward with you."

"I am glad to hear it," sneered the doctor, "though that is not your usual form."

"And yet I do not think that I have ever concealed my real opinion from you. It is fully ten years ago since I spoke to you of the necessity of breaking up this association. Can you recall what I said? I said only our extreme need and griping poverty justified our acts. They are now inexcusable."

"You talked very freely of your scruples," observed Mascarin.

"You remember my words then?"

"Yes, and I remember too that those inner scruples never hindered you from drawing your share of the profits."

"That is to say," burst in the doctor, "you repudiated the work, but shared the booty. You wished to play the game without staking anything."

Catenac was in no way disconcerted at this trenchant argument.

"Quite true," said he, "I always received my share; but I have done quite as much as you in putting the agency in its present prosperous condition. Does it not work smoothly like a perfect piece of mechanism? Have we not succeeded in nearly all our schemes? The income comes in monthly with extreme regularity, and I, according to my rights, have received one-third. If you desire to throw up this perilous means of livelihood, say so, and I will not oppose it."

"You are really too good," sneered the doctor, with a look of menace in his glance.

"Nor," continued Catenac, "will I oppose you if you prefer to let matters stand as they are; but if you start on fresh enterprises, and embark on the tempestuous sea of danger, then I put down my foot and very boldly 'halt.' I will not take another step with you. I can see by the looks of both of you that you think me a fool and a coward. Heaven grant that the future may not show you only too plainly that I have been in the right. Think over this. For twenty years fortune has favoured us, but, believe me, it is never wise to tempt her too far, for it is well known that at some time or other she always turns."

"Your imagery is really charming," remarked Hortebise sarcastically.

"Good, I have nothing else to say but to repeat my warning: *reflect*. Grand as your hopes and expectations may be, they are as nothing to the perils that you will encounter."

This cold flood of eloquence was more than the doctor could bear.

"It is all very well for you," exclaimed he, "to reason like this, for you are a rich man."

"I have enough to live on, I allow; for in addition to the income derived from my profession, I have saved two hundred thousand *francs*; and if you can be induced to renounce your projects, I will divide this sum with you. You have only to think."

Mascarin, who had taken no part in the dispute, now judged it time to interfere.

"And so," said he, turning to Catenac, "you have only two hundred thousand *francs?*"

"That or thereabouts."

"And you offer to divide this sum with us. Really we ought to be deeply grateful to you, but—"

Mascarin paused for a moment; then settling his spectacles more firmly, he went on,—

"But even if you were to give us what you propose, you would still have eleven hundred thousand *francs* remaining!"

Catenac burst into a pleasant laugh. "You are jesting," said he.

"I can prove the correctness of my assertion;" and as he spoke, Mascarin unlocked a drawer, and taking a small notebook from it, turned over the pages, and leaving it open at a certain place, handed it to the lawyer.

"There," said he, "that is made up to December last, and shows precisely how you stand financially. Twice, then, you have increased your funds. These deposits you will find in an addenda at the end of the book."

Catenac started to his feet; all his calmness had now disappeared.

"Yes," he said, "I have just the sum you name; and I, for that very reason, refuse to have anything further to do with your schemes. I have an income of sixty thousand *francs*; that is to say, sixty thousand good reasons for receiving no further risks. You envy me my good fortune, but did we not all start penniless? I have taken care of my money, while you have squandered yours. Hortebise has lost his patients, while I have increased the number of my clients; and now you want me to tread the dangerous road again. Not I; go your way, and leave me to go home."

Again he took up his hat, but a wave of the hand from Mascarin detained him.

"Suppose," said he coldly, "that I told you that your assistance was necessary to me."

"I should say so much the worse for you."

"But suppose I insist?"

"And how can you insist? We are both in the same boat, and sink or swim together."

"Are you certain of that?"

"So certain that I repeat from this day I wash my hands of you."

"I am afraid you are in error."

"How so?"

"Because for twelve months past; I have given food and shelter to a girl of the name of Clarisse. Do you by any chance know her?"

At the mention of this name, the lawyer started, as a man starts who, walking peacefully along, suddenly sees a deadly serpent coiled across his path.

"Clarisse," stammered he, "how did you know of her? who told you?"

But the sarcastic sneer upon the lips of his two confederates wounded his pride so deeply, that in an instant he recovered his self-possession.

"I am getting foolish," said he, "to ask these men how they learned my secret. Do they not always work by infamous and underhand means?"

"You see I know all," remarked Mascarin, "for I foresaw the day would come when you would wish to sever our connection, and even give us up to justice, if you could do so with safety to yourself. I therefore took my precautions. One thing, however, I was not prepared for, and that was, that a man of your intelligence should have played so paltry a game, and even twelve months back thought of betraying us. It is almost incredible. Do you ever read the *Gazette des Tribunaux*? I saw in its pages yesterday a story nearly similar to your own. Shall I tell it to you? A lawyer who concealed his vices beneath a mantle of joviality and candour, brought up from the country a pretty, innocent girl to act as servant in his house. This lawyer occupied his leisure time in leading the poor child astray, and the moment at last came when the consequences of her weakness were too apparent. The lawyer was half beside himself at the approaching scandal. What would the neighbours say? Well, to cut the story short, the infant was suppressed,—you understand, suppressed, and the mother turned into the street."

"Baptiste, have mercy!"

"It was a most imprudent act, for such things always leak out somehow. You have a gardener at your house at Champigny, and suppose the idea seized upon this worthy man to dig up the ground round the wall at the end of the garden."

"That is enough," said Catenac, piteously. "I give in."

Mascarin adjusted his spectacles, as he always did in important moments.

"You give in, do you? Not a bit. Even now you are endeavouring to find a means of parrying my home thrusts."

"But I declare to you—"

"Do not be alarmed; dig as deeply as he might, your gardener would discover nothing."

The lawyer uttered a stifled exclamation of rage as he perceived the pit into which he had fallen.

"He would find nothing," resumed Mascarin, "and yet the story is all true. Last January, on a bitterly cold night, you dug a hole, and in it deposited the body of a new-born infant wrapped in a shawl. And what shawl? Why the very one that you purchased at the Bon Marche, when you were making yourself agreeable to Clarisse. The shopman who sold it to you has identified it, and is ready to give evidence when called upon. You may look for that shawl, Catenac, but you will not find it."

"Have you got that shawl?" asked Catenac hoarsely.

"Am I a fool?" asked Mascarin contemptuously. "Tantaine has it; but *I* know where the body is, and will keep the information to myself. Do not be alarmed; act fairly, and you are safe; but make one treacherous move, and you will read in the next day's papers a paragraph something to this effect: 'Yesterday some workmen, engaged in excavations near so-and-so, discovered the body of a new-born infant. Every effort is being made to discover the author of the crime.' You know me, and that I work promptly. To the shawl I have added a handkerchief and a few other articles belonging to Clarisse, which will render it an easy matter to fix the guilt on you."

Catenac was absolutely stunned, and had lost all power of defending himself. The few incoherent words that he uttered showed his state of utter despair.

"You have killed me," gasped he, "just as the prize, that I have been looking for for twenty years, was in my grasp."

"Work does a man no harm," remarked the doctor sententiously.

There was, however, little time to lose; the Marquis de Croisenois and Paul might be expected to arrive at any moment, and Mascarin hastened to restore a certain amount of calmness to his prostrate antagonist.

"You make as much noise as if we were going to hand you over to the executioner on the spot. Do you think that we are such a pair of fools as to risk all these hazards without some almost certain chance of success? Hortebise was as much startled as yourself when I first spoke to him of this affair, but I explained everything fully to him, and now he is quite enthusiastic in the matter. Of course you can lay aside all fear, and, as a man of the world, will bear no malice against those who have simply played a better game than yourself."

"Go on," said Catenac, forcing a smile, "I am listening."

Mascarin made a short pause.

"What we want of you," answered he, "will not compromise you in the slightest degree. I wish you to draw up a document, the particulars of which I will give you presently, and you will outwardly have no connection with the matter."

"Very good."

"But there is more yet. The Duke de Champdoce has placed a difficult task in your hands. You are engaged in a secret on his behalf."

"You know that also?"

"I know everything that may be made subservient to our ends. I also know that instead of coming direct to me you went to the very man that we have every reason to dread, that fellow Perpignan, who is nearly as sharp as we are."

"Go on," returned Catenac impatiently. "What do you expect from me on this point?"

"Not much; you must only come to me first, and report any discovery you may have made, and never give any information to the duke without first consulting us."

"I agree."

The contending parties seemed to have arrived at an amicable termination, and Dr. Hortebise smiled complacently.

"Now," said he, "shall we not confess, after all, that there was no use in making such a fuss?"

"I allow that I was in the wrong," answered Catenac meekly; and, extending his hands to his two associates with an oily smile, he said: "Let us forget and forgive."

Was he to be trusted? Mascarin and the doctor exchanged glances of suspicion. A moment afterward a knock came to the door, and Paul entered, making a timid bow to his two patrons.

"My dear boy," said Mascarin, "let me present you to one of my oldest and best friends." Then, turning to Catenac, he added: "I wish to ask you to help and assist my young friend here. Paul Violaine is a good fellow, who has neither father nor mother, and whom we are trying to help on in his journey through life."

The lawyer started as he caught the strange, meaning smile which accompanied these words.

"Great heavens!" said he, "why did you not speak sooner?"

Catenac at once divined Mascarin's project, and understood the allusion to the Duke de Champdoce.

Chapter 17: Some Scraps of Paper

The Marquis de Croisenois was never punctual. He had received a note asking him to call on Mascarin at eleven o'clock, and twelve had struck some time before he made his appearance. Faultlessly gloved, his glass firmly fixed in his eye, and a light walking cane in his hand, and with that air of half-veiled insolence that is sometimes affected by certain persons who wish the world to believe that they are of great importance, the Marquis de Croisenois entered the room.

At the age of twenty-five Henry de Croisenois affected the airs and manners of a lad of twenty, and so found many who looked upon his escapades with lenient eyes, ascribing them to the follies of youth. Under this youthful mask, however he concealed a most astute and cunning intellect, and had more than once got the better of the women with whom he had had dealings. His fortune was terribly involved, because he had insisted on living at the same rate as men who had ten times his income. Forming one of the recklessly extravagant band of which the Duke de Saumeine was the head, Croisenois, too, kept his racehorses, which was certainly the quickest way to wreck the most princely fortune. The *marquis* had found out this, and was utterly involved, when Mascarin extended a helping hand to him, to which he clung with all the energy of a drowning man.

Whatever Henry de Croisenois' anxieties may have been on the day in question, he did not allow a symptom of them to appear, and on his entrance negligently drawled, "I have kept you waiting, I fear; but really my time is not my own. I am quite at your service now, and will wait until these gentlemen have finished their business with you." And as he concluded, he again placed the cigar which he had removed while saying these words, to his lips.

His manner was very insolent, and yet the amiable Mascarin did not seem offended, although he loathed the scent of tobacco.

"We had begun to despair of seeing you, *marquis*," answered he politely. "I say so, because these gentlemen are here to meet you. Permit me to introduce to you, Dr. Hortebise, M. Catenac of the Parisian bar, and our secretary," pointing as he spoke, to Paul.

As soon as Croisenois had taken his seat, Mascarin went straight to the point, as a bullet to the target. "I do not intend," began he, "to leave you in doubt for a moment. Beatings about the bush would be absurd among persons like ourselves."

At finding himself thus classed with the other persons present, the *marquis* gave a little start, and then drawled out, "You flatter me, really."

"I may tell you, *marquis*," resumed Mascarin, "that your marriage has been definitely arranged by myself and my associates. All you have to do is to get the young lady's consent; for that of the count and countess has already been secured."

"There will be no difficulty in that," lisped the *marquis*. "I will promise her the best horsed carriage in the Bois, a box at the opera, unlimited credit at Van Klopen's, and perfect freedom. There will be no difficulty, I assure you. Of course, however, I must be presented by someone who holds a good position in society."

"Would the Viscountess de Bois Arden suit you?"

"No one better; she is a relation of the Count de Mussidan."

"Good; then when you wish, Madame de Bois Arden will introduce you as a suitor for the young lady's hand, and praise you up to the skies."

The *marquis* looked very jubilant at hearing this. "All right," cried he; "then that decides the matter."

Paul wondered whether he was awake or dreaming. He too had been promised a rich wife, and here was another man who was being provided for in the same manner. "These people," muttered he, "seem to keep a matrimonial agency as well as a servants' registry office!"

"All that is left, then," said the *marquis*, "is to arrange the—shall I call it the commission?"

"I was about to come to that," returned Mascarin.

"Well, I will give you a fourth of the dowry, and on the day of my marriage will hand you a cheque for that amount."

Paul now imagined that he saw how matters worked. "If I marry Flavia," thought he, "I shall have to share her dowry with these highly respectable gentlemen."

The offer made by the *marquis* did not, however, seem to please Mascarin. "That is not what we want," said he.

"No,—well, must I give you more? Say how much."

Mascarin shook his head.

"Well then, I will give you a third; it is not worth while to give you more."

"No, no; I would not take half, nor even the whole of the dowry. You may keep that as well as what you owe us."

"Well, but tell me what you *do* want."

"I will do so," answered Mascarin, adjusting his spectacles carefully; "but before doing so, I feel that I must give you a short account of the rise and progress of this association."

At this statement Hortebise and Catenac sprang to their feet in surprise and terror. "Are you mad?" said they at length, with one voice.

Mascarin shrugged his shoulders.

"Not yet," answered he gently, "and I beg that you will permit me to go on."

"But surely we have some voice in the matter," faltered Catenac.

"That is enough," exclaimed Mascarin angrily, "Am not I the head of this association? Do you think," he continued in tones of deep sarcasm, "that we cannot speak openly before the *marquis*?"

Hortebise and the lawyer resignedly resumed their seats. Croisenois thought that a word from him might reassure them.

"Among honest men—" began he.

"We are not honest men," interrupted Mascarin. "Sir," added he in a severe tone, "nor are you either."

This plain speaking brought a bright flush to the face of the *marquis*, who had half a mind to be angry, but policy restrained him, and he affected to look on the matter as a joke. "Your joke is a little personal," said he.

But Mascarin took no heed of his remark. "Listen to me," said he, "for we have no time to waste, and do you," he added, turning to Paul, "pay the greatest attention."

A moment of perfect silence ensued, broken only by the hum of voices in the outer office.

"*Marquis*," said Mascarin, whose whole face blazed with a gleam of conscious power, "twenty-five years ago I and my associates were young and in a very different position. We were honest then, and all the illusions of youth were in full force; we had faith and hope. We all then tenanted a wretched garret in the Rue de la Harpe, and loved each other like brothers."

"That was long, long ago," murmured Hortebise.

"Yes," rejoined Mascarin; "and yet the effluxion of times does not hinder me from seeing things as they then were, and my heart aches as I compare the hopes of those days with the realities of the present. Then, *marquis*, we were poor, miserably poor, and yet we all had vague hopes of future greatness."

Croisenois endeavoured to conceal a sneer; the story was not a very interesting one.

"As I said before, each one of us anticipated a brilliant career. Catenac had gained a prize by his *Treatise on the Transfer of Real Estate*, and

Hortebise had written a pamphlet regarding which the great Orfila had testified approval. Nor was I without my successes. Hortebise had unluckily quarrelled with his family. Catenac's relatives were poor, and I, well, I had no family. I stood alone. We were literally starving, and I was the only one earning money. I prepared pupils for the military colleges, but as I only earned twenty-five *sous* a day by cramming a dull boy's brain with algebra and geometry, that was not enough to feed us all.

"Well, to cut a long story short, the day came when we had not a coin among us. I forgot to tell you that I was devotedly attached to a young girl who was dying of consumption, and who had neither food nor fuel. What could I do? I knew not. Half mad, I rushed from the house, asking myself if I had better plead for charity or take the money I required by force from the first passer-by. I wandered along the quays, half inclined to confide my sorrow to the Seine, when suddenly I remembered it was a holiday at the Polytechnic School, and that if I went to the Café Semblon or the Palais Royal, I should most likely meet with some of my old pupils, who could perhaps lend me a few *sous*. Five *francs* perhaps, *marquis*,—that is a very small sum, but in that day it meant the life of my dear Marie and of my two friends. Have you ever been hungry, M. de Croisenois?"

De Croisenois started; he had never suffered from hunger, but how could he tell what the future might bring? for his resources were so nearly exhausted, that even tomorrow he might be compelled to discard his fictitious splendour and sink into the abyss of poverty.

"When I reached the Café Semblon," continued Mascarin, "I could not see a single pupil, and the waiter to whom I addressed my inquiries looked at me with the utmost contempt, for my clothes were in tatters; but at length he condescended to inform me that the young gentlemen had been and gone, but that they would return. I said that I would wait for them. The man asked me if I would take anything, and when I replied in the negative, contemptuously pointed to a chair in a distant corner, where I patiently took my seat.

"I had sat for some time, when suddenly a young man entered the *café*, whose face, were I to live for a century, I shall never forget. He was perfectly livid, his features rigid, and his eyes wild and full of anguish. He was evidently in intense agony of mind or body. Evidently, however, it was not poverty that was oppressing him, for as he cast himself upon a sofa, all the waiters rushed forward to receive his orders. In a voice that was almost unintelligible, he asked for a bottle of brandy, and pen, ink, and paper. In some mysterious manner, the sight of this suffering brought balm to my aching heart. The order of the young man was soon executed, and pouring out a tumbler of brandy, he took a deep draught. The effect was instantaneous, he turned crimson, and for a moment almost fell back insensible. I kept my eyes on him, for a voice within me kept crying out that there was some mysterious link connecting this man and myself, and that his life was in some manner interwoven with mine, and that the influence he would exercise over me would be for evil.

"So strongly did this idea become rooted, that I should have left the *café*, had not my curiosity been so great. In the meantime the stranger had recovered himself, and seizing a pen, scrawled a few lines on a sheet of paper. Evidently he was not satisfied with his composition, for after reading it over, he lit a match and burnt the paper. He drank more brandy, and wrote a second letter, which, too, proved a failure, for he tore it to fragments, which he thrust into his waistcoat pocket. Again he commenced, using greater care. It was plain that he had forgotten where he was, for he gesticulated, uttered a broken sentence or two and evidently believed that he was in his own house. His last letter seemed to satisfy him, and he recopied it with care.

"He closed and directed it; then, tearing the original into pieces, he flung it under the table; then calling the waiter, he said, 'Here are twenty *francs*; take this letter to the address on the envelope. Bring the answer to my house; here is my card.' The man ran out of the room, and the nobleman, only waiting to pay his bill, followed almost immediately. The morsels of white paper beneath the table had a strange fascination for me; I longed to gather them up, to put them together, and to learn the secret of the strange drama that had been acted before me. But, as I have told you, then I was honest and virtuous, and the meanness of such an act revolted all my instincts; and I should have overcome this temptation, had it not been for one of those trifling incidents which too often form the turning-point of a life.

"A draught from a suddenly opened door caught one of these morsels of paper, and wafted it to my feet. I stooped and picked it up, and read on it the ominous words, 'blow out my brains!' I had not been mistaken, then, and was face to face with some coming tragedy. Having once yielded, I made no further efforts at self-control. The waiters were running about; no one paid any attention to me; and creeping to the place that the unknown had occupied, I obtained possession of two more scraps of paper. Upon one I read, 'shame and horror!' upon the other, 'one hundred thousand *francs* by tonight.' The meaning of these few words were as clear as daylight to me; but for all that, I managed to collect every atom of the torn paper, and piecing them together, read this:—

Charles,—I must have one hundred thousand *francs* tonight, and you are the only one to whom I can apply. The shame and horror of my position are too much for me. Can you send it me in two hours? As you act, so I regulate my conduct. I am either saved, or I blow out my brains.

"You are probably surprised, *marquis*, at the accuracy of my memory, and even now I can see this scrawl as distinctly as if it were before me. At the end of this scrawl was a signature, one of the best known commercial names, which, in common with other financial houses, was struggling against a panic on the Bourse. My discovery disturbed me very much. I forgot all my miseries, and thought only of his. Were not our positions entirely similar? But by degrees a hideous temptation began to creep into my heart, and, as the minutes passed by, assume more vivid colour and more tangible reality. Why should I not profit by this stolen secret? I went to the desk and asked for some wafers and a Directory.

"Then, returning, I fastened the torn fragments upon a clean sheet of paper, discovered the address of the writer, and then left the *café*. The house was situated in the Rue Chaussee d'Autin. For fully half an hour I paced up and down before his magnificent dwelling-place. Was he alive? Had the reply of Charles been in the affirmative? I decided at last to venture, and rang the bell. A liveried domestic appeared at my summons, and said that his master did not receive visitors at that hour; besides, he was at dinner. I was exasperated at the man's insolence, and replied hotly, 'If you want to save your master from a terrible misfortune, go and tell him that a man has brought him the rough draft of the letter he wrote a little time back at the Café Semblon.'

"The man obeyed me without a word, no doubt impressed by the earnestness of my manner. My message must have caused intense consternation, for in a moment the footman reappeared, and, in an obsequious manner, said, 'Follow at once, sir; my master is waiting for you.' He led me into a large room, magnificently furnished as a library, and in the centre of this room stood the man of the Café Semblon. His face was deadly pale, and his eyes blazed with fury. I was so agitated that I could hardly speak.

155

"'You have picked up the scraps of paper I threw away?' exclaimed he.

"I nodded, and showed him the fragments fastened on to the sheet of note-paper.

"'How much do you want for that?' asked he. 'I will give you a thousand *francs.*'

"I declare to you, gentlemen, that up to this time I had no intention of making money by the secret. My intention in going had been simply to say, 'I bring you this paper, of which someone else might have taken an undue advantage. I have done you a service; lend me a hundred *francs.*' This is what I meant to say, but his behaviour irritated me, and I answered,—

"'No, I want two thousand *francs.*'

"He opened a drawer, drew out a bundle of banknotes, and threw them in my face.

"'Pay yourself, you villain!' said he.

"I can, I fear, never make you understand what I felt at this undeserved insult. I was not myself, and Heaven knows that I was not responsible for any crime that I might have committed in the frenzy of the moment, and I was nearly doing so. That man will, perhaps, never see death so near him, save at his last hour. On his writing table lay one of those Catalan daggers, which he evidently used as a paper-cutter. I snatched it up, and was about to strike, when the recollection of Marie dying of cold and starvation occurred to me. I dashed the knife to the ground, and rushed from the house in a state bordering on insanity. I went into that house an honest man, and left it a degraded scoundrel. But I must finish.

"When I reached the street, the two banknotes which I had taken from the packet seemed to burn me like coals of fire. I hastened to a money-changer, and got coin for them. I think, from my demeanour, he must have thought that I was insane. With my plunder weighing me down, I regained our wretched garret in the Rue de la Harpe. Catenac and Hortebise were waiting for me with the utmost anxiety. You remember that day, my friends. *Marquis*, my story is especially intended for you. As soon as I entered the room, my friends ran up to me, delighted at seeing me return in safety, but I thrust them aside.

"'Let me alone!' cried I; 'I am no longer fit to take an honest man's hand; but we have money, money!' And I threw the bags upon the table. One of them burst, and a flood of silver coins rolled to every part of the room.

"Marie started from her chair with upraised hands. 'Money!' she repeated, 'money! we shall have food, and I won't die.'

"My friends, *marquis*, were not as they are now, and they started back in horror, fearing that I had committed some crime.

"'No,' said I, 'I have committed no crime, not one, at least, that will bring me within the reach of the strong arm of the law. This money is the price of our honour, but no one will know that fact but ourselves.'

"*Marquis*, there was no sleeping in the garret all that night; but when daylight peered through the broken windows, it beamed on a table covered with empty bottles, and round it were seated three men, who, having cast aside all honourable scruples, had sworn that they would arrive at wealth and prosperity by any means, no matter how foul and treacherous they might be. That is all."

Chapter 18: An Infamous Trade

Mascarin, who was anxious to make as deep an impression as possible upon Croisenois and Paul, broke off his story abruptly, and paced up and down the room. Had his intention been to startle his audience, he had most certainly succeeded. Paul was breathless with interest, and Croisenois broke down in attempting to make one of his usual trivial remarks. He was not particularly intelligent, except as regarded his self-interests, and though, of course, he knew that there must be some connection between his interests and the recital that Mascarin had just made, he could not for the life of him make out what it was.

Mascarin seemed utterly careless of the effect that he had produced. But the next time that his walk brought him to his desk he stopped, and, adjusting his glasses, said, "I trust, *marquis*, that you will forgive this long preliminary address, which would really make a good sensational novel; but we have now arrived at the really practical part of the business." As he said these words, he took up an imposing attitude, with his elbow resting on the mantelpiece.

"On the night of which I have spoken, I and my friends released ourselves from all the bonds of virtue and honour, and freed ourselves from all the fetters of duty to our fellow-men. The plan emanated from my brain complete in all its details in the will I made twenty years ago to my friends. *Marquis*, as the summer goes on, you know that the ripest and reddest cherries are the fullest flavoured, just so, in the noblest and wealthiest of families in Paris there is not one that has not some terrible and ghostly secret which is sedulously concealed. Now, suppose that one man should gain possession of all of them, would he not be sole and absolute master? Would he not be more powerful than a despot on his throne? Would he not be able to sway society in any manner he might think fit? Well, I said to myself, I will be that man!"

Ever since the *marquis* had been in relation with Mascarin, he had shrewdly suspected that his business was not conducted on really fair principles.

"What you mention," said he, "is nothing but an elaborate and extended system of blackmail."

Mascarin bowed low, with an ironical smile on his face. "Just so, *marquis*, just so; you have hit on the very name. The word is modern, but the operation doubtless dates from the earliest ages. The day upon which one man began to trade upon the guilty secret of another was the date of the institution of this line of business. If antiquity makes a thing respectable, then blackmailing is worthy of great respect."

"But, sir," said the *marquis*, with a flush upon his face, "but, sir—"

"Pshaw!" broke in Mascarin, "does a mere word frighten you? Who has not done some of it in his time? Why, look at yourself. Do you not recollect this winter that you detected a young man cheating at cards? You said nothing to him at the time, but you found out that he was rich, and, calling upon him the next day, borrowed ten thousand *francs*. When do you intend to repay that loan?"

Croisenois sank back in his chair, overcome with surprise at this display of knowledge on Mascarin's part. "This is too terrible," muttered he, but Mascarin went on,—

"I know, at least, two thousand persons in Paris who only exist by the exercise of this profession; for I have studied them all, from the convict who screws money out of his former companions, in penal servitude, to the titled villain, who, having discovered the frailty of some unhappy woman, forces her to give him her daughter as his wife. I know a mere messenger in the Rue Douai, who in five years amassed a comfortable fortune. Can you guess how? When he was entrusted with a letter, he invariably opened it, and made himself master of its contents, and if there was a compromising word in it, he pounced down upon either the writer or the person to whom it was addressed.

"I also know of one large limited company which pays an annual income to a scoundrel with half a dozen foreign orders, who has found out that they have broken their statues of association, and holds proofs of their having done so. But the police are on the alert, and our courts deal very severely with blackmailers."

Mascarin went on: "The English, however, are our masters, for in London a compromising servant is as easily negotiable as a sound bill of exchange. There is in the city a respectable jeweller, who will advance money on any compromising letter with a good name at the foot. His shop is a regular pawnshop of infamy. In the States it has been elevated to the dignity of a profession, and the citizen at New York dreads the blackmailers more than the police, if he is meditating some dishonourable action. Our first operations did not bring in any quick returns, and the harvest promised to be a late one; but you have come upon us just as we are about to reap our harvest.

"The professions of Hortebise and Catenac—the one a doctor and the other a lawyer—facilitated our operations greatly. One administered to the diseases of the body, and the other to that of the purse, and, of course, thus they became professors of many secrets. As for me, the head and chief, it would not do to remain an idle looker-on. Our funds had dwindled down a good deal, and, after mature consideration, I decided to hire this house, and open a Servants' Registry Office. Such an occupation would not attract any attention, and in the end it turned out a perfect success, as my friends can testify."

Catenac and Hortebise both nodded assent.

"By the system which I have adopted," resumed Mascarin, "the wealthy and respectable man is as strictly watched in his own house as is the condemned wretch in his cell; for no act of his escapes the eyes of the servants whom we have placed around him. He can hardly even conceal his thoughts from us. Even the very secret that he has murmured to his wife with closed doors reaches our ears."

The *marquis* gave a supercilious smile.

"You must have had some inkling of this," observed Mascarin, "for you have never taken a servant from our establishment; but for all that, I am as well posted up in your affairs as yourself. You have even now about you a valet of whom you know nothing."

"Morel was recommended to me by one of my most intimate friends—Sir Richard Wakefield."

"But for all that I have had my suspicions of him; but we will talk of this later, and we will now return to the subject upon which we have met. As I told you, I conceal the immense power I had attained through our agency, and use it as occasion presents itself, and after twenty years' patient labour, I am about to reap a stupendous harvest. The police pay enormous sums to their secret agents, while I, without opening my purse, have an army of devoted adherents. I see perhaps

159

fifty servants of both sexes daily; calculate what this will amount to in a year."

There was an air of complacency about the man as he explained the working of his system, and a ring of triumph in his voice.

"You must not think that all my agents are in my secrets, for the greater part of them are quite unaware of what they are doing, and in this lies my strength. Each of them brings me a slender thread, which I twine into the mighty cord by which I hold my slaves. These unsuspecting agents remind me of those strange Brazilian birds, whose presence is a sure sign that water is to be found near at hand. When one of them utters a note, I dig, and I find. And now, *marquis*, do you understand the aim and end of our association?"

"It has," remarked Hortebise quietly, "brought us in some years two hundred and fifty thousand *francs* apiece."

If M. de Croisenois disliked prosy tales, he by no means underrated the eloquence of figures. He knew quite enough of Paris to understand that if Mascarin threw his net regularly, he would infallibly catch many fish. With this conviction firmly implanted in his mind, he did not require much urging to look with favour on the scheme, and, putting on a gracious smile, he now asked, "And what must I do to deserve admission into this association?"

Paul had listened in wonder and terror, but by degrees all feelings of disgust at the criminality of these men faded away before the power that they unquestionably possessed.

"If," resumed Mascarin, "we have up to this met with no serious obstacles, it is because, though apparently acting rashly, we are in reality most prudent and cautious. We have managed our slaves well, and have not driven anyone to desperation. But we are beginning to weary of our profession; we are getting old, and we have need of repose. We intend, therefore, to retire, but before that we wish to have all matters securely settled. I have an immense mass of documentary evidence, but it is not always easy to realize the value they represent, and I wait upon your assistance to enable me to do so."

Croisenois' face fell. Was he to take compromising letters round to his acquaintances and boldly say, "Your purse or your honour?" He had no objection to share the profits of this ignoble trade, but he objected strongly to showing his connection with it openly. "No, no," cried he hastily, "you must not depend upon me."

He seemed so much in earnest that Hortebise and Catenac exchanged glances of dismay.

"Let us have no nonsense," returned Mascarin sternly, "and wait a little before you display so much fierceness. I told you that my documentary evidence was of a peculiar kind. We very often had among our fish married people who cannot deal with their personal property. A husband, for instance, will say, 'I can't take ten thousand *francs* without my wife, knowing of it.' Women say, 'Why, I get all my money through my husband,' and both are telling the truth. They kneel at my feet and entreat me to have mercy, saying, 'Find me some excuse for using a portion of my funds and you shall have more than you ask.' For a long time I have sought for this means, and at last I have found it in the Limited Company, which you, *marquis*, will float next month."

"Really!" returned the *marquis*. "I do not see—"

"I beg your pardon; you see it all clearly. A husband who cannot, without fear of disturbing his domestic peace, put in five thousand *francs*, can put in ten thousand if he tells his wife, 'It is an investment;' and many a wife who has not any money of her own will persuade her husband to bring in the money we require by the proposal to take shares. Now, what do you say to the idea?"

"I think that it is an excellent one, but what part am I to play in it?"

"In taking the part of Chairman of the Company. I could not do so, being merely the proprietor of a Servant's Registry Office. Hortebise, as a doctor, and more than all a homeopath, would inspire no confidence, and Catenac's legal profession prevents him appearing in the matter openly. He will act as our legal adviser."

"But really I do not see anything about me that would induce people to invest," remarked De Croisenois.

"You are too modest; you have your name and rank, which, however we may look upon them, have a great effect upon the general public. There are many Companies who pay directors of rank and credible connection very largely. Before starting this enterprise you can settle all your debts, and the world will then conclude that you are possessed of great wealth, while, at the same time, the news of your approaching marriage with Mademoiselle du Mussidan will be the general talk of society. What better position could you be in?"

"But I have the reputation of being a reckless spendthrift."

"All the better. The day the prospectus comes out with your name at the head of it, there will be a universal burst of laughter. Men will say, 'Do you see what Croisenois is at now? What on earth possessed him to go into Company work?' But as this proceeding on your part will have paid your debts and given you Mademoiselle Sabine's dowry,

I think that the laugh will be on your side."

The prospect dazzled Des Croisenois.

"And suppose I accept," asked he, "what will be the end of the farce?"

"Very simple. When all the shares are taken up, you will close the office and let the Company look after itself."

Croisenois started to his feet angrily. "Why," cried he, "you intend to make a catspaw of me! Such a proceeding would send me to penal servitude."

"What an ungrateful man he is!" said Mascarin, appealing to his audience, "when I am doing all I can to prevent his going there."

"Sir!"

But Catenac now felt it time to interfere. "You do not understand," remarked he, addressing Croisenois. "You will start a Company for the development of some native product, let us say Pyrenean marble, for instance, issue a prospectus, and the shares will be at once taken up by Mascarin's clients."

"Well, what happens then?"

"Why, out of the funds thus obtained we will take care when the crash comes to reimburse any outsiders who may have taken shares in the concern, telling them that the thing has been a failure, and that we are ruined; while Mascarin will take care to obtain from all his clients a discharge in full, so the Company will quietly collapse."

"But," objected the *marquis*, "all the shareholders will know that I am a rogue."

"Naturally."

"They would hold me in utter contempt." "Perhaps so, but they would never venture to let you see it. I never thought that you would make objections; and whose character, however deep, will bear investigation?"

"Are you sure that you hold your people securely?" asked he; "and that none of them will turn surly?"

Mascarin was waiting for this question, and taking from his desk the pieces of cardboard which he took so much pains to arrange, he replied, "I have here the names of three hundred and fifty people who will each invest ten thousand *francs* in the Company. Listen to me, and judge for yourself."

He put all three pieces of cardboard together, and then drawing out one he read,—

162

N——, civil engineer. Five letters written by him to the gentleman who procured his appointment for him: worth fifteen thousand *francs*.

P——, merchant. Absolute proof that his last bankruptcy was a fraudulent one, and that he kept back from his creditors two hundred thousand *francs*. Good for twenty thousand *francs*.

Madame V——. A photograph taken in very light and airy costume. Poor, but can pay three thousand *francs*.

M. H——. Three letters from her mother, proving that the daughter had compromised herself before marriage. Letter from a monthly nurse appended. Can be made to pay ten thousand *francs*.

X——, a portion of his correspondence with L——in 1848. Three thousand *francs*.

Madame M. de M——. A true history of her adventure with M. J——.

This sample was quite sufficient to satisfy M. de Croisenois. "Enough," cried he, "I yield. I bow before your gigantic power, which utterly surpasses that of the police. Give me your orders."

Before this Mascarin had conquered Hortebise and Paul Violaine, and now he had the *marquis* at his feet. Many times during this conversation the *marquis* had more than once endeavoured to make up his mind to withdraw entirely from the business, but he had been unable to resist the strange fascination of that mysterious person who had been laying bare his scheme with such extraordinary audacity. The few vestiges of honesty that were still left in his corrupted soul revolted at the thought of the shameful compact into which he was about to enter, but the dazzling prospect held out before his eyes silenced his scruples, and he felt a certain pride in being the associate of men who possessed such seemingly illimitable power.

Mascarin saw that there was no longer any necessity for the extreme firmness with which he had before spoken, and it was with the most studied courtesy that he replied: "I have no orders to give you, *marquis*, our interests are identical, and we must all have a voice in the deliberations as to the best means of carrying them out."

This change from *hauteur* to suavity gratified Croisenois' pride immensely.

"Now," continued Mascarin, "let us speak of your own circumstances. You wrote to me recently that you had nothing, and I am aware that you have no expectations for the future."

"Excuse me, but there is the fortune of my poor brother George, who disappeared so mysteriously."

"Let me assure you," answered Mascarin, "that we had better be perfectly frank with each other."

"And am I not so?" answered the *marquis*.

"Why, in talking of this imaginary fortune?"

"It is not imaginary; it is real, and a very large one, too, about twelve or fourteen hundred thousand *francs*, and I can obtain it, for, by Articles 127 and 129 of the Code Napoleon—"

He interrupted himself, as he saw an expression of hardly-restrained laughter upon the features of Dr. Hortebise.

"Do not talk nonsense," answered Mascarin. "You could at first have filed an affidavit regarding your brother's disappearance, and applied to the Court to appoint you trustee, but this is now exactly what you wish to avoid."

"Why not, pray? Do you think—"

"Pooh, pooh, but you have raised so much money on this inheritance that there is nothing of it left hardly, certainly not sufficient to pay your debts. It is the bait you used to allure your tradespeople into giving you credit."

At finding himself so easily fathomed, Croisenois burst into a peel of laughter. Mascarin had by this time thrown himself into an armchair, as though utterly worn out by fatigue.

"There is no necessity, *marquis*," said he, "to detain you here longer. We shall meet again shortly, and settle matters. Meanwhile Catenac will draw up the prospectus and Articles of Association of the proposed Company, and post you up in the financial slang of which you must occasionally make use."

The *marquis* and the lawyer at once rose and took their leave. As soon as the door had closed behind them, Mascarin seemed to recover his energy.

"Well, Paul," said he, "what do you think of all this?"

Like all men with weak and ductile natures, Paul, after being almost prostrated by the first discovery of his master's villainy, had now succeeded in smothering the dictates of his conscience, and adopted a cynical tone quite worthy of his companions.

"I see," said he, "that you have need of me. Well, I am not a *marquis*, but you will find me quite as trustworthy and obedient."

Paul's reply did not seem to surprise Mascarin, but it is doubtful whether he was pleased by it, for his countenance showed traces of a struggle between extreme satisfaction and intense annoyance, while the doctor was surprised at the cool audacity of the young man whose mind he had undertaken to form.

Paul was a little disturbed by the long and continued silence of his patron, and at last he ventured to say timidly,—"Well, sir, I am anxious to know under what conditions I am to be shown the way to make my fortune and marry Mademoiselle Flavia Rigal, whom I love."

Mascarin gave a diabolical smile.

"Whose dowry you love," he observed. "Let us speak plainly."

"Pardon me, sir, I said just what I meant."

The doctor, who had not Mascarin's reasons for gravity, now burst into a jovial laugh.

"And that pretty Rose," said he, "what of her?"

"Rose is a creature of the past," answered Paul. "I can now see what an idiot I was, and I have entirely effaced her from my memory, and I am half inclined to deplore that Mademoiselle Rigal is an heiress, the more so if it is to form a barrier between us."

This declaration seemed to make Mascarin more easy.

"Reassure yourself, my boy," said he, "we will remove that barrier; but I will not conceal from you that the part you have to play is much more difficult than that assigned to the Marquis de Croisenois; but if it is harder and more perilous, the reward will be proportionately greater."

"With your aid and advice I feel capable of doing everything necessary," returned Paul.

"You will need great self-confidence, the utmost self-possession, and as a commencement you must utterly destroy your present identity."

"That I will do with the utmost willingness."

"You must become another person entirely; you must adopt his name, his gait, his behaviour, his virtues, and even his failings. You must forget all that you have either said or done. You must always think that you are in reality the person you represent yourself to be, for this is the only way in which you can lead others into a similar belief. Your task will be a heavy one."

"Ah, sir," cried the young man, enthusiastically, "can you doubt me?"

"The glorious beam of success that shines ahead of you will take your attention from the difficulties and dangers of the road that you are treading."

The genial Dr. Hortebise rubbed his hands.

"You are right," cried he, "quite right."

"When you have done this," resumed Mascarin, "we shall not hesitate to acquaint you with the secret of the lofty destiny that awaits you. Do you understand me fully?"

Here the speaker was interrupted by the entrance of Beaumarchef, who had signified his desire to come in by three distinct raps upon the door. He was now gorgeous to look upon, for having taken advantage of a spare half hour, he had donned his best clothes.

"What is it?" demanded Mascarin.

"Here are two letters, sir."

"Thank you; hand them to me, and leave us."

As soon as they were once more alone, Mascarin examined the letters.

"Ah," cried he, "one from Van Klopen, and the other from the Hotel de Mussidan. Let us first see what our friend the man-milliner has to say."

Dear Sir,—

You may be at ease. Our mutual friend Verminet has executed your orders most adroitly. At his instigation Gaston de Gandelu has forged the banker Martin Rigal's signature on five different bills. I hold them, and awaiting your further orders regarding them, and also with respect to Madame de Bois Arden,

I remain your obedient servant,

Van Klopen

Tossing it on the table, Mascarin opened the other letter, which he also read aloud.

Sir,—

I have to report to you the breaking off of the marriage between Mademoiselle Sabine and M. de Breulh-Faverlay. *Mademoiselle* is very ill, and I heard the medical man say that she might not survive the next twenty-four hours.

Florestan

Mascarin was so filled with rage on learning this piece of news, which seemed likely to interfere with his plans, that he struck his hand down heavily on the table.

"Damnation!" cried he. "If this little fool should die now, all our work will have to be recommenced."

He thrust aside his chair, and paced hurriedly up and down the room.

"Florestan is right," said he; "this illness of the girl comes on at the date of the rupture of the engagement. There is some secret that we must learn, for we dare not work in the dark."

"Shall I go to the Hotel de Mussidan?" asked Hortebise.

"Not a bad idea. Your carriage is waiting, is it not? You can go in your capacity as a medical man."

The doctor was preparing to go, when Mascarin arrested his progress.

"No," said he, "I have changed my mind. We must neither of us be seen near the place. I expect that one of our mines has exploded; that the count and countess have exchanged confidences, and that between the two the daughter has been struck down."

"How shall we find this out?"

"I will see Florestan and try and find out."

In an instant he vanished into his inner room, and as he changed his dress, continued to converse with the doctor.

"This blow would be comparatively trifling, if I had not so much on hand, but I have Paul to look after. The Champdoce affair must be pressed on, for Catenac, the traitor, has put the duke and Perpignan into communication. I must see Perpignan and discover how much has been told him, and how much he has guessed. I will also see Caroline Schimmel, and extract something from her. I wish to heaven that there were thirty-six hours in the day instead of only twenty-four."

By this time he had completed his change of costume and called the doctor into his room.

"I am off, now," whispered he; "do not lose sight of Paul for a single instant, for we are not sufficiently sure of him to let him go about alone with our secret in his possession. Take him to dine at Martin Rigal's, and then make some excuse for keeping him all night at your rooms. See me tomorrow."

And he went out so hurriedly that he did not hear the cheery voice of the doctor calling after him,—

"Good luck; I wish you all good luck."

Chapter 19: A Friendly Rival

On leaving the Hotel de Mussidan, M. de Breulh-Faverlay dismissed his carriage, for he felt as a man often does after experiencing some violent emotion, the absolute necessity for exercise, and to be alone with his thoughts, and by so doing recover his self-possession. His friends would have been surprised if they had seen him pacing hurriedly along the Champs Elysees. The usual calm of his manner had vanished, and the generally calm expression of his features was entirely absent. As he walked, he talked to himself, and gesticulated.

"And this is what we call being a man of the world. We think ourselves true philosophers, and a look from a pair of beautiful, pleading eyes scatters all our theories to the winds."

He had loved Sabine upon the day on which he had asked for her hand, but not so fondly as upon this day when he had learned that she could no longer be his wife, for, from the moment he had made this discovery, she seemed to him more gifted and fascinating than ever. No one could have believed that he, the idol of society, the petted darling of the women, and the successful rival of the men, could have been refused by the young girl to whom he had offered his hand.

"Yes," murmured he with a sigh, "for she is just the companion for life that I longed for. Where could I find so intelligent an intellect and so pure a mind, united with such radiant beauty, so different from the women of society, who live but for dress and gossip. Has Sabine anything in common with those giddy girls who look upon life as a perpetual value, and who take a husband as they do a partner, because they cannot dance without one? How her face lighted up as she spoke of him, and how thoroughly she puts faith in him! The end of it all is that I shall die a bachelor. In my old age I will take to the pleasures of the table, for an excellent authority declares that a man can enjoy his four meals a day with comfort. Well, that is something to look forward to certainly, and it will not impair my digestion if my heirs and expectants come and squabble round my armchair. Ah," he added, with a deep sigh, "my life has been a failure."

M. de Breulh-Faverlay was a very different type of man to that which both his friends and his enemies popularly supposed him to be. Upon the death of his uncle, he had plunged into the frivolous vortex of Parisian dissipation, but of this he had soon wearied.

All that he had cared for was to see the doings of his racehorse chronicled in the sporting journals, and occasionally to expend a few thousand *francs* in presents of jewellery to some fashionable actress. But he had secretly longed for some more honourable manner of fulfilling his duties in life, and he had determined that before his marriage he would sell his stud and break with his old associates entirely;

and now this wished-for marriage would never take place.

When he entered his club, the traces of his agitation were so visible upon his face, that some of the card-players stopped their game to inquire if Chambertin, the favourite for the Chantilly cup, had broken down.

"No, no," replied he, as he hurriedly made his way to the writing-room, "Chambertin is as sound as a bell."

"What the deuce has happened to De Breulh?" asked one of the members.

"Goodness gracious!" remarked the man to whom the question was addressed, "he seems in a hurry to write a letter."

The gentleman was right. M. de Breulh was writing a withdrawal from his demand for Sabine's hand to M. de Mussidan, and he found the task by no means an easy one, for on reading it over he found that there was a valid strain of bitterness throughout it, which would surely attract attention and perhaps cause embarrassing questions to be put to him.

"No," murmured he, "this letter is quite unworthy of me." And tearing it up, he began another, in which he strung together several conventional excuses, alleging the difficulty of breaking off his former habits and of an awkward entanglement which he had been unable to break with, as he had anticipated. When this little masterpiece of diplomacy was completed, he rang the bell, and, handing it to one of the club servants, told him to take it to the Count de Mussidan's house. When this unpleasant duty was over, M. de Breulh had hoped to experience some feeling of relief, but in this he was mistaken. He tried cards, but rose from the table in a quarter of an hour; he ordered dinner, but appetite was wanting; he went to the opera, but then he did nothing but yawn, and the music grated on his nerves.

At length he returned home. The day had seemed interminable, and he could not sleep, for Sabine's face was ever before him. Who could this man be whom she so fondly loved and preferred before all others? He respected her too much not to feel assured that her choice was a worthy one, but his experience had taught him that when so many men of the world fell into strange entanglements, a poor girl without knowledge of the dangers around her might easily be entrapped. "If he is worthy of her," thought he, "I will do my best to aid her; but if not, I will open her eyes."

At four o'clock in the morning he was still seated musing before the expiring embers of his fire; he had made up his mind to see Andre—there was no difficulty in this, for a man of taste and wealth can find a ready excuse for visiting the studio of a struggling artist. He had no fixed plan as to what he would say or do, he left all to chance, and with this decision he went to bed, and by two in the afternoon he drove straight to the Rue de la Tour d'Auvergne.

Andre's discreet portress was as usual leaning on her broom in the gallery as M. de Breulh's magnificent equipage drew up.

"Gracious me!" exclaimed the worthy woman, dazzled by the gorgeousness of the whole turnout; "he can't be coming here, he must have mistaken the house."

But her amazement reached its height when M. de Breulh, on alighting, asked for Andre.

"Fourth story, first door to the right," answered the woman; "but I will show you the way."

"Don't trouble yourself;" and with these words M. de Breulh ascended the staircase that led to the painter's studio and knocked on the door. As he did so, he heard a quick, light step upon the stairs, and a young and very dark man, dressed in a weaver's blouse and carrying a tin pail which he had evidently just filled with water from the cistern, came up.

"Are you M. Andre?" asked De Breulh.

"That is my name, sir."

"I wish to say a few words to you."

"Pray come in," replied the young artist, opening the door of his studio and ushering his visitor in. Andre's voice and expression had made a favourable impression upon his visitor; but he was, in spite of his having thrown aside nearly all foolish prejudices, a little startled at his costume. He did not, however, allow his surprise to be visible.

"I ought to apologize for receiving you like this," remarked Andre quickly, "but a poor man must wait upon himself." As he spoke, he threw off his blouse and set down the pail in a corner of the room.

"I rather should offer my excuse for my intrusion," returned M. de Breulh. "I came here by the advice of one of my friends;" he stopped for an instant, endeavouring to think of a name.

"By Prince Crescensi, perhaps," suggested Andre.

"Yes, yes," continued M. de Breulh, eagerly snatching at the rope the artist held out to him. "The prince sings your praises everywhere, and speaks of your talents with the utmost enthusiasm. I am, on his recommendation, desirous of commissioning you to paint a picture for me, and I can assure you that in my gallery it will have no need to be ashamed of its companions."

Andre bowed, colouring deeply at the compliment.

"I am obliged to you," said he, "and I trust that you will not be disappointed in taking the prince's opinion of my talent."

"Why should I be so?"

"Because, for the last four months I have been so busy that I have really nothing to show you."

"That is of no importance. I have every confidence in you."

"Then," returned Andre, "all that we have to do is to choose a subject."

Andre's manner had by this time so captivated De Breulh that he muttered to himself, "I really ought to hate this fellow, but on my word I like him better than anyone I have met for a long time."

Andre had by this time placed a large portfolio on the table. "Here," said he, "are some twenty or thirty sketches; if any of them took your fancy, you could make your choice."

"Let me see them," returned De Breulh politely, for having made an estimate of the young man's character, he now wished to see what his artistic talents were like. With this object in view he examined all the sketches in the portfolio minutely, and then turned to those on the walls. Andre said nothing, but he somehow felt that this visit would prove the turning-point of his misfortunes. But for all that the young man's heart was very sad, for it was two days since Sabine had left him, promising to write to him the next morning regarding M. de Breulh-Faverlay, but as yet he had received no communication, and he was on the tenterhooks of expectation, not because he had any doubt of Sabine, but for the reason that he had no means of obtaining any information of what went on in the interior of the Hotel de Mussidan.

"M. de Breulh had now finished his survey, and had come to the conclusion that though many of Andre's productions were crude and lacking in finish, yet that he had the true artistic metal in him. He extended his hand to the young man and said forcibly, "I am no longer influenced by the opinion of a friend. I have seen and judged for myself, and am more desirous than ever of possessing one of your pictures. I have made my choice of a subject, and now let us discuss the details."

As he spoke he handed a little sketch to Andre. It was a view of everyday life, which the painter had entitled, "Outside the Barrier." Two men with torn garments and wine-flushed faces were struggling in tipsy combat, while on the right hand side of the picture lay a woman, bleeding profusely from a cut on the forehead, and two of her terrified companions were bending over her, endeavouring to restore her to consciousness. In the background were some flying figures, who were hastening up to separate the combatants. The sketch was one of real life, denuded of any sham element of romance, and this was the one that M. de Breulh had chosen. The two men discussed the size of the picture, and not a single detail was omitted.

"I am sure that you will do all that is right," remarked De Breulh. "Let your own inspiration guide you, and all will be well." In reality he was dying to get away, for he felt in what a false position he was, and with a violent effort he approached the money part of the matter.

"*Monsieur,*" said Andre, "it is impossible to fix a price; when completed, a picture may only be worth the canvas that it is painted on, or else beyond all price. Let us wait."

"Well," broke in M. de Breulh, "what do you say to ten thousand *francs*?"

"Too much," returned Andre with a deprecatory wave of his hand; "far too much. If I succeed in it, as I hope to do, I will ask six thousand *francs* for it."

"Agreed!" answered De Breulh, taking from his pocket an elegant note-case with his crest and monogram upon it and extracting from it three thousand *francs*. "I will, as is usual, deposit half the price in advance."

Andre blushed scarlet. "You are joking," said he.

"Not at all," answered De Breulh quietly; "I have my own way of doing business, from which I never deviate."

In spite of this answer Andre's pride was hurt.

"But," remarked he, "this picture will not be ready for perhaps six or seven months. I have entered into a contract with a wealthy builder, named Candele, to execute the outside decorations of his house."

"Never mind that," answered M. de Breulh; "take as long as you like."

Of course, after this, Andre could offer no further opposition; he therefore took the money without another word.

"And now," said De Breulh, as he paused for a moment at the open doorway, "let me wish you my good luck, and if you will come and breakfast with me one day, I think I can show you some pictures which you will really appreciate." And handing his card to the artist, he went downstairs.

At first Andre did not glance at the card, but when he did so, the letters seemed to sear his eyeballs like a red-hot iron. For a moment he could hardly breathe, and then a feeling of intense anger took possession of him, for he felt that he had been trifled with and deceived.

Hardly knowing what he was doing, he rushed out on the landing, and, leaning over the banister, called out loudly, "Sir, stop a moment!"

De Breulh, who had by this time reached the bottom of the staircase, turned round.

"Come back, if you please," said Andre.

After a moment's hesitation, De Breulh obeyed; and when he was again in the studio, Andre addressed him in a voice that quivered with indignation.

"Take back these notes, sir; I will not accept them."

"What do you mean?"

"Only that I have thought the matter over, and that I will not accept your commission."

"And why this sudden change?"

"You know perfectly well, M. de Breulh-Faverlay."

The gentleman at once saw that Sabine had mentioned his name to the young artist, and with a slight lacking of generous feeling said,—

"Let me hear your reasons, sir."

"Because, because—" stammered the young man.

"Because is not an answer."

Andre's confusion became greater. He would not tell the whole truth, for he would have died sooner than bring Sabine's name into the discussion; and he could only see one way out of his difficulty.

"Suppose I say that I do not like your manner or appearance," returned he disdainfully.

"Is it your wish to insult me, M. Andre?"

"As you choose to take it."

M. de Breulh was not gifted with an immense stock of patience. He turned livid, and made a step forward; but his generous impulses restrained him, and it was in a voice broken by agitation that he said,—

"Accept my apologies, M. Andre; I fear that I have played a part unworthy of you and of myself. I ought to have given you my name at once. I know everything."

"I do not comprehend you," answered Andre in a glacial voice.

"Why doubt, then, if you do not understand? However, I have given you cause to do so. But, let me reassure you, Mademoiselle Sabine has spoken to me with the utmost frankness; and, if you still distrust me, let me tell you that this veiled picture is her portrait. I will say more," continued De Breulh gravely, as the artist still kept silent; "yesterday, at Mademoiselle de Mussidan's request, I withdrew from my position as a suitor for her hand."

Andre had already been touched by De Breulh's frank and open manner, and these last words entirely conquered him.

"I can never thank you enough," began he.

But De Breulh interrupted him.

"A man should not be thanked for performing his duty. I should lie to you if I said that I am not painfully surprised at her communication; but tell me, had you been in my place, would you not have acted in the same manner?"

"I think that I should."

"And now we are friends, are we not?" and again De Breulh held out his hand, which Andre clasped with enthusiasm.

"Yes, yes," faltered he.

"And now," continued De Breulh, with a forced smile, "let us say no more about the picture, which was, after all, merely a pretext. As I came here I said to myself, 'If the man to whom Mademoiselle de Mussidan has given her heart is worthy of her, I will do all I can to advance his suit with her family!' I came here to see what you were like; and now I say to you, do me a great honour, and permit me to place myself, my fortune, and the influence of my friends, at your disposal."

The offer was made in perfect good faith, but Andre shook his head.

"I shall never forget your kindness in making this offer, but—"; he paused for a moment, and then went on: "I will be as open as you have been, and will tell you the whole truth. You may think me foolish; but remember, though I am poor, I have still my self-respect to maintain. I love Sabine, and would give my life for her. Do not be offended at what I am about to say. I would, however, sooner give up her hand than be indebted for it to you."

"But this is mere madness."

"No, sir, it is the purest wisdom; for were I to accede to your wishes, I should feel deeply humiliated by the thought of your self-denial; for I should be madly jealous of the part you were playing. You are of high birth and princely fortune, while I am utterly friendless and unknown; all that I am deficient in you possess."

"But I have been poor myself," interposed De Breulh, "and perhaps endured even greater miseries than ever you have done. Do you know what I was doing at your age? I was slowly starving to death at

174

Sonora, and had to take the humblest position in a cattle ranch. Do you think that those days taught me nothing?"

"You will be able to judge me all the more clearly then," returned Andre. "If I raise myself up to Sabine's level, as she begged me to, then I shall feel that I am your equal; but if I accept your aid, I am your dependent; and I will obey her wishes or perish in the effort."

Up to this moment the passion which stirred Andre's inmost soul had breathed in every word he uttered; but, checking himself by a mighty effort, he resumed in a tone of greater calmness,—

"But I ought to remember how much we already owe you, and I hope that you will allow me to call myself your friend?"

M. de Breulh's noble nature enabled him to understand Andre's scruples; his feelings, however, would not for the instant enable him to speak. He slowly put the notes back in their receptacle, and then said in a low voice,—

"Your conduct is that of an honourable man; and remember this, at all times and seasons you may rely upon De Breulh-Faverlay. Farewell!"

As soon as he was alone, Andre threw himself into an armchair, and mused over this unexpected interview, which had proved a source of such solace to his feelings. All that he now longed for was a letter from Sabine. At this moment the portress entered with a letter. Andre was so occupied with his thoughts that he hardly noticed this act of condescension on the part of the worthy woman.

"A letter!" exclaimed he; and, tearing it open, he glanced at the signature. But Sabine's name was not there; it was signed Modeste. What could Sabine's maid have to say to him? He felt that some great misfortune was impending, and, trembling with excitement, he read the letter.

Sir,—
I write to tell you that my mistress has succeeded in the matter she spoke of to you; but I am sorry to say that I have bad news to give you, for she is seriously ill.

"Ill!" exclaimed Andre, crushing up the letter in his hands, and dashing it upon the floor. "Ill! ill!" he repeated, not heeding the presence of the portress; "why, she may be dead;" and, snatching up his hat, he dashed downstairs into the street.

As soon as the portress was left alone, she picked up the letter, smoothed it out, and read it.

"And so," murmured she, "the little lady's name was Sabine—a pretty name; and she is ill, is she? I expect that the old gent who called this morning, and asked so many questions about M. Andre, would give a good deal for this note; but no, that would not be fair."

Chapter 20: A Council of War

Mad with his terrible forebodings, Andre hurried through the streets in the direction of the Hotel de Mussidan, caring little for the attention that his excited looks and gestures caused. He had no fixed plan as to what to do when he arrived there, and it was only on reaching the Rue de Matignon that he recovered sufficient coolness to deliberate and reflect.

He had arrived at the desired spot; how should he set to work to obtain the information that he required? The evening was a dark one, and the gas-lamps showed a feeble light through the dull February fog. There were no signs of life in the Rue de Matignon, and the silence was only broken by the continuous surge of carriage wheels in the Faubourg Saint Honore. This gloom, and the inclemency of the weather, added to the young painter's depression. He saw his utter helplessness, and felt that he could not move a step without compromising the woman he so madly adored. He walked to the gate of the house, hoping to gain some information even from the exterior aspect of the house; for it seemed to him that if Sabine were dying, the very stones in the street would utter sounds of woe and lamentation; but the fog had closely enwrapped the house, and he could hardly see which of the windows were lighted. His reasoning faculties told him that there was no use in waiting, but an inner voice warned him to stay. Would Modeste, who had written to him, divine, by some means that he was there, in an agony of suspense, and come out to give him information and solace? All at once a thought darted across his mind, vivid as a flash of lightning.

"M. de Breulh will help me," cried he; "for though I cannot go to the house, he will have no difficulty in doing so."

By good luck, he had M. de Breulh's card in his pocket, and hurried off to his address. M. de Breulh had a fine house in the Avenue de l'Imperatrice, which he had taken more for the commodiousness of the stables than for his own convenience.

"I wish to see M. de Breulh," said Andre, as he stopped breathless at the door, where a couple of footmen were chatting.

The men looked at him with supreme contempt. "He is out," one of them at last condescended to reply.

Andre had by this time recovered his coolness, and taking out De Breulh's card, wrote these words on it in pencil:

One moment's interview. Andre.

"Give this to your master as soon as he comes in," said he.

Then he descended the steps slowly. He was certain that M. de Breulh was in the house, and that he would send out after the person who had left the card almost at once. His conclusion proved right; in five minutes he was overtaken by the panting lackey, who, conducting him back to the house, showed him into a magnificently furnished library. De Breulh feared that some terrible event had taken place.

"What has happened?" said he.

"Sabine is dying;" and Andre at once proceeded to inform De Breulh of what had happened since his departure.

"But how can I help you?"

"You can go and make inquiries at the house."

"Reflect; yesterday I wrote to the count, and broke off a marriage, the preliminaries of which had been completely settled; and within twenty-four hours to send and inquire after his daughter's health would be to be guilty of an act of inexcusable insolence; for it would look as if I fancied that Mademoiselle de Mussidan had been struck down by my rupture of the engagement."

"You are right," murmured Andre dejectedly.

"But," continued De Breulh, after a moment's reflection, "I have a distant relative, a lady who is also a connection of the Mussidan family, the Viscountess de Bois Arden, and she will be glad to be of service to me. She is young and giddy, but as true as steel. Come with me to her; my carriage is ready."

The footman were surprised at seeing their master on such terms of intimacy with the shabbily dressed young man, but ventured, of course, on no remarks.

Not a word was exchanged during the brief drive to Madame de Bois Arden's house.

"Wait for me," exclaimed De Breulh, springing from the vehicle as soon as it drew up; "I will be back directly."

Madame de Bois Arden is justly called one of the handsomest women in Paris. Very fair, with masses of black hair, and a complexion to which art has united itself to the gifts of nature, she is a woman who has been everywhere, knows everything, talks incessantly, and generally very well. She spends forty thousand *francs* per annum on dress. She is always committing all sorts of imprudent acts, and scandal is ever busy with her name. Half a dozen of the opposite sex have been talked of in connection with her, while in reality she is a true and faithful wife, for, in spite of all her frivolity, she adores her husband, and is in great awe of him. Such was the character of the lady into whose apartment M. de Breulh was introduced.

Madame de Bois Arden was engaged in admiring a very pretty fancy costume of the reign of Louis XV., one of Van Klopen's master-pieces, when M. de Breulh was announced, which she was going to wear, on her return from the opera, at a masquerade ball at the Austrian Ambassador's. Madame de Bois Arden greeted her visitor with effusion, for they had been acquaintances from childhood, and always addressed each other by their Christian names.

"What, you here at this hour, Gontran!" said the lady. "Is it a vision, or only a miracle?" But the smile died away upon her lips, as she caught a glimpse of her visitor's pale and harassed face. "Is there anything the matter?" asked she.

"Not yet," answered he, "but there may be, for I hear that Mademoiselle de Mussidan is dangerously ill."

"Is she really? Poor Sabine! what is the matter with her?"

"I do not know; and I want you, Clotilde, to send one of your people to inquire into the truth of what we have heard."

Madame de Bois Arden opened her eyes very wide.

"Are you joking?" said she. "Why do you not send yourself?"

"It is impossible for me to do so; and if you have any kindness of heart, you do as I ask you; and I want you also to promise me not to say a word of this to anyone."

Excited as she was by this mystery, Madame de Bois Arden did not ask another question.

"I will do exactly what you want," replied she, "and respect your secret. I would go at once, were it not that Bois Arden will never sit down to dinner without me; but the moment we have finished I will go."

"Thanks, a thousand times; and now I will go home and wait for news from you."

"Not at all,—you will remain here to dinner."

"I must,—I have a friend waiting for me."

"Do as you please, then," returned the viscountess, laughing. "I will send round a note this evening."

De Breulh pressed her hand, and hurried down, and was met by Andre at the door, for he had been unable to sit still in the carriage.

"Keep up your courage. Madame de Bois Arden had not heard of Mademoiselle Sabine's illness, and this looks as if it was not a very serious matter. We shall have the real facts in three hours."

"Three hours!" groaned Andre, "what a lapse of time!"

"It is rather long, I admit; but we will talk of her while we wait, for you must stay and dine with me."

Andre yielded, for he had no longer the energy to contest anything. The dinner was exquisite, but the two men were not in a condition of mind to enjoy it, and scarcely consumed anything. Vainly did they endeavour to speak on indifferent subjects, and when the coffee had been served in the library, they relapsed into utter silence. As the clock struck ten, however, a knock was heard at the door, then whisperings, and the rustle of female attire, and lastly Madame de Bois Arden burst upon them like a tornado.

"Here I am," cried she.

It was certainly rather a hazardous step to pay such a late visit to a bachelor's house, but then the Viscountess de Bois Arden did exactly as she pleased.

"I have come here, Gontran," exclaimed she, with extreme vehemence, "to tell you that I think your conduct is abominable and ungentlemanly."

"Clotilde!"

"Hold your tongue! you are a wretch! Ah! now I can see why you did not wish to write and inquire about poor Sabine. You well knew the effect that your message would have on her."

M. de Breulh smiled as he turned to Andre and said,—

"You see that I was right in what I told you."

This remark for the first time attracted Madame de Bois Arden's attention to the fact that a stranger was present, and she trembled lest she had committed some grave indiscretion.

"Gracious heavens!" exclaimed she, with a start, "why, I thought that we were alone!"

"This gentleman has all my confidence," replied M. de Breulh seriously; and as he spoke he laid his hand upon Andre's shoulder. "Permit me to introduce M. Andre to you, my dear Clotilde; he may not be known today, but in a short time his reputation will be European."

Andre bowed, but for once in her life the viscountess felt embarrassed, for she was surprised at the extremely shabby attire of this confidential friend, and then there seemed something wanting to the name.

"Then," resumed De Breulh, "Mademoiselle de Mussidan is really ill, and our information is correct."

"She is."

"Did you see her?"

"I did, Gontran; and had you seen her, your heart would have been filled with pity, and you would have repented your conduct toward her. The poor girl did not even know me. She lay in her bed, whiter than the very sheets, cold and inanimate as a figure of marble. Her large black eyes were staring wildly, and the only sign of life she exhibited was when the great tears coursed down her cheeks."

Andre had determined to restrain every token of emotion in the presence of the viscountess, but her recital was too much for him.

"Ah!" said he, "she will die; I know it."

There was such intense anguish in his tone that even the practised woman of the world was softened.

"I assure you, sir," said she, "that you go too far; there is no present danger; the doctors say it is catalepsy, which often attacks persons of a nervous temperament upon the receipt of a sudden mental shock."

"But what shock has she received?" asked Andre.

"No one told me," answered she after a short pause, "that Sabine's illness was caused by the breaking off of her engagement; but, of course, I supposed that it was."

"That was not the reason, Clotilde; but you have told us nothing; pray, go on," interposed De Breulh.

The extreme calmness of her cousin, and a glance which she observed passing between him and Andre, enlightened the viscountess somewhat.

"I asked as much as I dared," she replied, "but I could only get the vaguest answers. Sabine looked as if she were dead, and her father and mother hovered around her couch like two spectres. Had they slain her with their own hands, they could not have looked more guilty; their faces frightened me."

"Tell me precisely what answers were given to your questions," broke in he impatiently.

"Sabine had seemed so agitated all day, that her mother asked her if she was suffering any pain."

"We know that already."

"Indeed!" replied the viscountess, with a look of surprise. "It seems, cousin, that you saw Sabine that afternoon, but what became of her afterward no one appears to know; but there is positive proof that she did not leave the house, and received no letters. At all events, it was more than an hour after her maid saw her enter her own room. Sabine said a few unintelligible words to the girl, who, seeing the pallor upon her mistress's face, ran up to her. Just as she did so, Sabine uttered a wild shriek, and fell to the ground. She was raised up and laid upon the bed, but since then she has neither moved nor spoken."

"That is not all," said De Breulh, who had watched his cousin keenly.

The viscountess started, and avoided meeting her cousin's eye.

"I do not understand," she faltered. "Why do you look at me like that?"

De Breulh, who had been pacing up and down the room, suddenly halted in front of the viscountess.

"My dear Clotilde," said he, "I am sure when I tell you that the tongue of scandal has often been busy with your name, I am telling you nothing new."

"Pooh!" answered the viscountess. "What do I care for that?"

"But I always defended you. You are indiscreet—your presence here tonight shows this; but you are, after all, a true woman,—brave and true as steel."

"What do you mean by this exordium, Gontran?"

"This, Clotilde,—I want to know if I dare venture to entrust to you a secret which involves the honour of two persons, and, perhaps, the lives of more."

"Thank you, Gontran," answered she calmly. "You have formed a correct judgment of me."

But here Andre felt that he must interpose, and, taking a step forward, said, "Have you the right to speak?"

"My dear Andre," said De Breulh, "this is a matter in which my honour is as much concerned as yours. Will you not trust me?" Then turning to the viscountess, he added, "Tell us all you heard."

"It is only something I heard from Modeste. You had hardly left the house, when the Baron de Clinchain made his appearance."

"An eccentric old fellow, a friend of the Count de Mussidan's. I know him."

"Just so; well, they had a stormy interview, and at the end of it, the baron was taken ill, and it was with difficulty that he regained his carriage."

"That seems curious."

"Wait a bit. After that Octave and his wife had a terrible scene together, and Modeste thinks that her mistress must have heard something, for the count's voice rang through the house like thunder."

Every word that the viscountess uttered strengthened De Breulh's suspicions. "There is something mysterious in all this, Clotilde," said he, "as you will say when you know the whole truth," and, without omitting a single detail, he related the whole of Sabine and Andre's love story.

Madame de Bois Arden listened attentively, sometimes thrilled with horror, and at others pleased with this tale of innocent love.

"Forgive me," said she, when her cousin had concluded; "my reproaches and accusations were equally unfounded."

"Yes, yes; never mind that; but I am afraid that there is some hidden mystery which will place a fresh stumbling-block in our friend Andre's path."

"Do not say that," cried Andre, in terror. "What is it?"

"That I cannot tell; for Mademoiselle de Mussidan's sake, I have withdrawn all my pretensions to her hand,—not to leave the field open to any other intruder, but in order that she may be your wife."

"How are we to learn what has really happened?" asked the viscountess.

"In some way or other we shall find out, if you will be our ally."

Most women are pleased to busy themselves about a marriage, and the viscountess was cheered to find herself mixed up in so romantic a drama.

"I am entirely at your beck and call," answered she. "Have you any plan?"

"Not yet, but I will soon. As far as Mademoiselle de Mussidan is concerned, we must act quite openly. Andre will write to her, asking for an explanation, and you shall see her tomorrow, and if she is well enough, give her his note."

The proposal was a startling one, and the viscountess did not entertain it favourably.

"No," said she, "I think that would not do at all."

"Why not? However, let us leave it to Andre."

Andre, thus addressed, stepped forward, and said,—

"I do not think that it would be delicate to let Mademoiselle de Mussidan know that her secret is known to anyone else than ourselves."

The viscountess nodded assent.

"If," continued Andre, "the viscountess will be good enough to ask Modeste to meet me at the corner of the Avenue de Matignon; I shall be there."

"A capital idea, sir," said the lady, "and I will give your message to Modeste." She broke off her speech suddenly, and uttered a pretty little shriek, as she noticed that the hands of the clock on the mantelpiece pointed to twenty to twelve. "Great heavens!" cried she, "and I am going to a ball at the Austrian Embassy, and now not even dressed." And, with a *coquettish* gesture, she drew her shawl around her, and ran out of the room, exclaiming as she descended the stairs, "I will call here tomorrow, Gontran, on my way to the Bois," and disappeared like lightning.

Andre and his host sat over the fire, and conversed for a long time. It seemed strange that two men who had met that morning for the first time should now be on such intimate terms of friendship; but such was the case, for a mutual feeling of admiration and respect had sprung up in their hearts.

M. de Breulh wished to send Andre home in his carriage, but this the young man declined, and merely borrowed an overcoat to protect him from the inclemency of the weather.

"Tomorrow," said he, as he made his way home, "Modeste shall tell all she knows, provided always that that charming society dame does not forget all about our existence before then."

Madame de Bois Arden, however, could sometimes be really in earnest. Upon her return from the ball she would not even go to bed, lest she should oversleep herself, and the next day Andre found Modeste waiting at the appointed spot, and learnt, to his great grief, that Sabine had not yet regained consciousness.

The family doctor betrayed no uneasiness, but expressed a wish for a consultation with another medical man. Meanwhile, the girl promised to meet Andre morning and evening in the same place, and give him such scraps of information as she had been able to pick up. For two whole days Mademoiselle de Mussidan's condition remained unchanged, and Andre spent his whole time between his own studio, the Avenue de Matignon, and M. de Breulh's, where he frequently met Madame de Bois Arden.

But on the third day Modest informed him, with tears in her eyes, that though the cataleptic fit had passed away, Sabine was struggling with a severe attack of fever. Modeste and Andre were so interested in

183

their conversation, that they did not perceive Florestan, who had gone out to post a letter to Mascarin.

"Listen, Modeste," whispered Andre, "you tell me that she is in danger,—very great danger."

"The doctor said that the crisis would take place today; be here at five this evening."

Andre staggered like a madman to De Breulh's house; and so excited was he that his friend insisted upon his taking some repose, and would not, when five o'clock arrived, permit Andre to go to the appointment alone. As they turned the corner, they saw Modeste hurrying toward them.

"She is saved, she is saved!" said she, "for she has fallen into a tranquil sleep, and the doctor says that she will recover."

Andre and De Breulh were transported by this news; but they did not know that they were watched by two men, Mascarin and Florestan, who did not let one of their movements escape them. Warned by a brief note from Florestan, Mascarin had driven swiftly to Father Canon's public-house, where he thought he was certain to find the domestic, but the man was not there, and Mascarin, unable to endure further suspense, sent for him to the Hotel de Mussidan. When the servant informed Mascarin that the crisis was safely passed, he drew a deep breath of relief; for he no longer feared that the frail structure that he had built up with such patient care for twenty long years would be shattered at a blow by the chill hand of death. He bent his brow, however, when he heard of Modeste's daily interviews with the young man whom Florestan termed "*Mademoiselle's* lover."

"Ah," muttered he, "if I could only be present at one of those interviews!"

"And, as you say," returned Florestan, drawing out, as he spoke, a neat-looking watch, "it is just the hour of their meeting; and as the place is always the same, you—"

"Come, then," broke in his patron. They went out accordingly, and reached the Champs Elysees by a circuitous route. The place was admirably suited to their purpose, for close by were several of those little wooden huts, occupied in summer by the vendors of cakes and playthings.

"Let us get behind one of these," said Florestan. Night was drawing in, but objects could still be distinguished, and in about five minutes Florestan whispered, "Look, there comes Modeste, and there is the lover, but he has a pal with him tonight. Why, what can she be telling him? He seems quite overcome."

Mascarin divined the truth at once, and found that it would be a difficult task to interfere with the love of a man who displayed so much intensity of feeling.

"Then," remarked Mascarin, savagely, "that great booby, staggering about on his friend's arm, is your young lady's lover?"

"Just so, sir."

"Then we must find out who he is."

Florestan put on a crafty air, and replied in gentle accents.

"The day before yesterday, as I was smoking my pipe outside, I saw this young bantam swaggering down the street—not but what he seemed rather crestfallen; but I knew the reason for that, and should look just as much in the dumps if my young woman was laid up. I thought, as I had nothing to do, I might as well see who he was and where he lived; so, sticking my hands in my pockets, after him I sloped. He walked such a long way, that I got precious sick of my job, but at last I ran him to earth in a house. I went straight up to the lodge, and showed the portress my tobacco pouch, and said, 'I picked up this; I think that the gentleman who has just gone in dropped it. Do you know him?' 'Of course I do,' said she. 'He is a painter; lives on the fourth floor; and his name is M. Andre.'"

"Was the house in the Rue de la Tour d'Auvergne?" broke in Mascarin.

"You are right, sir," returned the man, taken a little aback. "It seems, sir, that you are better informed than I am."

Mascarin did not notice the man's surprise, but he was struck with the strange persistency with which this young man seemed to cross his plans, for he found that the acquaintance of Rose and the lover of Mademoiselle de Mussidan were one and the same person, and he had a presentiment that he would in some way prove a hindrance to his plans.

The astute Mascarin concentrated all his attention upon Andre.

The latter said something to Modeste, which caused that young woman to raise her hands to heaven, as though in alarm.

"But who is the other?" asked he,—"the fellow that looks like an Englishman?"

"Do you not know?" returned the lackey. "Why, that is M. de Breulh-Faverlay."

"What, the man who was to marry Sabine?"

"Certainly."

Mascarin was not easily disconcerted, but this time a blasphemous oath burst from his lips.

"Do you mean," said he, "that De Breulh and this painter are friends?"

"That is more than I can tell. You seem to want to know a lot," answered Florestan, sulkily.

Modeste had now left the young men, who walked arm in arm in the direction of the Avenue de l'Imperatrice.

"M. de Breulh takes his dismissal easily enough," observed Mascarin.

"He was not dismissed; it was he that wrote and broke off the engagement."

This time Mascarin contrived to conceal the terrible blow that this information caused to him, and even made some jesting remark as he took leave of Florestan; but he was in truth completely staggered, for after thoroughly believing that the game was won, he saw that, though perhaps not lost, his victory was postponed for an indefinite period.

"What!" said he, as he clenched his hand firmly, "shall the head-strong passion of this foolish boy mar my plans? Let him take care of himself; for if he walks in my path, he will find it a road that leads to his own destruction."

Chapter 21: An Academy of Music

Dr. Hortebise had for some time back given up arguing with Mascarin as to the advice the latter gave him. He had been ordered not to let Paul out of his sight, and he obeyed this command literally. He had taken him to dine at M. Martin Rigal's, though the host himself was absent; from there he took Paul to his club, and finally wound up by forcing the young man to accept a bed at his house. They both slept late, and were sitting down to a luxurious breakfast, when the servant announced M. Tantaine, and that worthy man made his appearance with the same smile upon his face which Paul remembered so well in the Hotel de Perou. The sight of him threw the young man into a state of fury. "At last we meet," cried he. "I have an account to settle with you."

"You have an account to settle with me?" asked Daddy Tantaine with a puzzled smile.

"Yes; was it not through you that I was accused of theft by that old hag, Madame Loupins?"

Tantaine shrugged his shoulders.

"Dear me," said he; "I thought that M. Mascarin had explained everything, and that you were anxious to marry Mademoiselle Flavia, and that, above all, you were a young man of intelligence and tact."

Hortebise roared with laughter, and Paul, seeing his folly, blushed deeply and remained silent.

"I regret having disturbed you, doctor," resumed Tantaine, "but I had strict orders to see you."

"Is there anything new then?"

"Yes; Mademoiselle de Mussidan is out of danger, and M. de Croisenois can commence proceedings at once."

The doctor drank off a glass of wine. "To the speedy marriage of our dear friend the Marquis and Mademoiselle Sabine," said he gaily.

"So be it," said Tantaine; "I am also directed to beg M. Paul not to leave this house, but to send for his luggage and remain here."

Hortebise looked so much annoyed that Tantaine hastened to add: "Only as a temporary measure, for I am on the lookout for rooms for him now."

Paul looked delighted at the idea of having a home of his own.

"Good!" exclaimed the doctor merrily. "And now, my dear Tantaine, as you have executed all your commissions, you can stay and breakfast with us."

"Thanks for the honour; but I am very busy with affairs of the Duke de Champdoce and must see Perpignan at once." As he spoke he rose, making a little sign which Paul did not catch, and Hortebise accompanied him to the door of the vestibule. "Don't leave that lad alone," said Tantaine; "I will see about him tomorrow; meanwhile prepare him a little."

"I comprehend," answered Hortebise; "my kind regards to that dear fellow, Perpignan."

This Perpignan was well known—some people said too well known—in Paris. His real name was Isidore Crocheteau, and he had started life as a cook in a Palais Royal restaurant. Unfortunately a breach of the Eighth Commandment had caused him to suffer incarceration for a period of three years, and on his release he bloomed out into a private inquiry agent. His chief customers were jealous husbands, but as surely as one of these placed an affair in his hands, he would go to the erring wife and obtain a handsome price from her for his silence.

Mascarin and Perpignan had met in an affair of this kind; and as they mutually feared each other, they had tacitly agreed not to cross each other's path in that great wilderness of crime—Paris. But while Perpignan knew nothing of Mascarin's schemes and operations, the former was very well acquainted with the ex-cook's doings. He knew, for instance, that the income from the Inquiry Office would not cover Perpignan's expenses, who dressed extravagantly, kept a carriage, affected artistic tastes, played cards, betted on races, and liked good dinners at the most expensive restaurants. "Where can he get his money from?" asked Mascarin of himself; and, after a long search, he succeeded in solving the riddle.

Daddy Tantaine, after leaving the doctor's, soon arrived at the residence of M. Perpignan, and rang the bell.

A fat woman answered the door. "M. Perpignan is out," said she.

"When will he be back?"

"Some time this evening."

"Can you tell me where I can find him, as it is of the utmost importance to both of us that I should see him at once?"

"He did not say where he was going to."

"Perhaps he is at the factory," said Tantaine blandly.

The fat woman was utterly taken aback by this suggestion. "What do you know about that?" faltered she.

"You see I *do* know, and that is sufficient for you. Come, is he there?"

"I think so."

"Thank you, I will call on him then. An awfully long journey," muttered Tantaine, as he turned away; "but, perhaps, if I catch the worthy man in the midst of all his little business affairs, he will be more free in his language, and not so guarded in his actual admissions."

The old man went to his task with a will. He passed down the Rue Toumenon, skirted the Luxemburg, and made his way into the Rue Guy Lussac; from thence he walked down the Rue Mouffetard, and thence direct into one of those crooked lanes which run between the Gobelins Factory and the Hopital de l'Oursine. This is a portion of the city utterly unknown to the greater number of Parisians. The streets are narrow and hardly afford room for vehicles.

A valley forms the centre of the place, down which runs a muddy, sluggish stream, the banks of which are densely crowded with tan yards and iron works. On the one side of this valley is the busy Rue Mouffetard, and on the other one of the outer boulevards, while a long line of sickly-looking poplars mark the course of the semi-stagnant stream. Tantaine seemed to know the quarter well, and went on until

188

he reached the Champs des Alouettes. Then, with a sigh of satisfaction, he halted before a large, three-storied house, standing on a piece of ground surrounded by a mouldering wooden fence. The aspect of the house had something sinister and gloomy about it, and for a moment Tantaine paused as if he could not make up his mind to enter it; but at last he did so. The interior was as dingy and dilapidated as the outside. There were two rooms on the ground floor, one of which was strewn with straw, with a few filthy-looking quilts and blankets spread over it. The next room was fitted up as a kitchen; in the centre was a long table composed of boards placed on trestles, and a dirty-looking woman with her head enveloped in a coarse red handkerchief, and grasping a big wooden spoon, was stirring the contents of a large pot in which some terrible-looking ingredients were cooking. On a small bed in a corner lay a little boy. Every now and then a shiver convulsed his frame, his face was deadly pale, and his hands almost transparent, while his great black eyes glittered with the wild delirium of fever. Sometimes he would give a deep groan, and then the old *beldame* would turn angrily and threaten to strike him with her wooden spoon.

"But I am so ill," pleaded the boy.

"If you had brought home what you were told, you would not have been beaten, and then you would have had no fever," returned the woman harshly.

"Ah, me! I am sick and cold, and want to go away," wailed the child; "I want to see mammy."

Even Tantaine felt uneasy at this scene, and gave a gentle cough to announce his presence. The old woman turned round on him with an angry snarl. "Who do you want here?" growled she.

"Your master."

"He has not yet arrived, and may not come at all, for it is not his day; but you can see Poluche."

"And who may he be?"

"He is the professor," answered the hag contemptuously. "And where is he?"

"In the music-room."

Tantaine went to the stairs, which were so dingy and dilapidated as to make an ascent a work of danger and difficulty. As he ascended higher, he became aware of a strange sound, something between the grinding of scissors and the snarling of cats. Then a moment's silence, a loud execration, and a cry of pain. Tantaine passed on, and coming to a rickety door, he opened it, and in another moment found himself in what the old hag downstairs had called the music-room. The partitions of all the rooms on the floor had been roughly torn down to form this apartment; hardly a pane of glass remained intact in the windows; the dingy, whitewashed walls were covered with scrawls and drawings in charcoal. A suffocating, nauseous odour rose up, absolutely overpowering the smell from the neighbouring tan yards.

There was no furniture except a broken chair, upon which lay a dog whip with plaited leather lash. Round the room, against the wall, stood some twenty children, dirty, and in tattered clothes. Some had violins in their hands, and others stood behind harps as tall as themselves. Upon the violins Tantaine noticed there were chalk marks at various distances. In the middle of the room was a man, tall and erect as a dart, with flat, ugly features and lank, greasy hair hanging down on his shoulders. He, too, had a violin, and was evidently giving the children a lesson. Tantaine at once guessed that this was Professor Poluche.

"Listen," said he; "here, you Ascanie, play the chorus from the *Château de Marguerite*." As he spoke he drew his bow across his instrument, while the little Savoyard did his best to imitate him, and in a squeaking voice, in nasal tone, he sang:

"Ah! great heavens, how fine and grand Is the palace!"

"You young rascal!" cried Poluche. "Have I not bid you fifty times that at the word 'palace' you are to place your bow on the fourth chalk mark and draw it across? Begin again."

Once again the boy commenced, but Poluche stopped him.

"I believe, you young villain, that you are doing it on purpose. Now, go through the whole chorus again; and if you do not do it right, look out for squalls."

Poor Ascanie was so muddled that he forgot all his instructions. Without any appearance of anger, the professor took up the whip and administered half a dozen severe cuts across the bare legs of the child, whose shouts soon filled the room.

"When you are done howling," remarked Poluche, "you can try again; and if you do not succeed, no supper for you tonight, my lad. Now, Giuseppe, it is your turn."

Giuseppe, though younger than Ascanie, was a greater proficient on the instrument, and went through his task without a single mistake.

"Good!" said Poluche; "if you get on like that, you will soon be fit to go out. You would like that, I suppose?"

"Yes," replied the delighted boy, "and I should like to bring in a few coppers too."

But the professor did not waste too much time in idle converse.

"It is your turn now, Fabio," said he.

Fabio, a little mite of seven, with eyes black and sparkling as those of a dormouse, had just seen Tantaine in the doorway and pointed him out to the professor.

Poluche turned quickly round and found himself face to face with Tantaine, who had come quickly forward, his hat in his hand.

Had the professor seen an apparition, he could not have started more violently, for he did not like strangers.

"What do you want?" asked he.

"Reassure yourself, sir," said Tantaine, after having for a few seconds enjoyed his evident terror; "I am the intimate friend of the gentleman who employs you, and have come here to discuss an important matter of business with him."

Poluche breathed more freely.

"Take a chair, sir," said he, offering the only one in the room. "My master will soon be here."

But Daddy Tantaine refused the offer, saying that he did not wish to intrude, but would wait until the lesson was over.

"I have nearly finished," remarked Poluche; "it is almost time to let these scamps have their soup."

Then turning to his pupils, who had not dared to stir a limb, he said,—

"There, that is enough for today; you can go."

The children did not hesitate for a moment, but tumbled over each other in their eagerness to get away, hoping, perhaps, that he might omit to execute certain threats that he had held out during the lesson. The hope was a vain one, for the equitable Poluche went to the head of the stairs and called out in a loud voice,—

"Mother Butor, you will give no soup to Monte and put Ravillet on half allowance."

Tantaine was much interested, for the scene was an entirely new one.

The professor raised his eyes to heaven.

"Would," said he, "that I might teach them the divine science as I would wish; but the master would not allow me; indeed, he would dismiss me if I attempted to do so."

"I do not understand you."

"Let me explain to you. You know that there are certain old women who, for a consideration, will train a linnet or a bullfinch to whistle any air?"

Tantaine, with all humility, confessed his ignorance of these matters.

"Well," said the professor, "the only difference between those old women and myself is, that they teach birds and I boys; and I know which I had rather do."

Tantaine pointed to the whip.

"And how about this?" asked he.

Poluche shrugged his shoulders.

"Put yourself in my place for a little while," remarked he. "You see my master brings me all sorts of boys, and I have to cram music into them in the briefest period possible. Of course the child revolts, and I thrash him; but do not think he cares for this; the young imps thrive on blows. The only way that I can touch them is through their stomachs. I stop a quarter, a half, and sometimes the whole of their dinner. That fetches them, and you have no idea how a little starvation brings them on in music."

Daddy Tantaine felt a cold shiver creep over him as he listened to this frank exposition of the professor's mode of action.

"You can now understand," remarked the professor, "how some airs become popular in Paris. I have forty pupils all trying the same thing. I am drilling them now in the *Marguerite*, and in a little time you will have nothing else in the streets."

Poluche was proceeding to give Tantaine some further information, when a step was heard upon the stairs, and the professor remarked,—

"Here is the master; he never comes up here, because he is afraid of the stairs. You had better go down to him."

Chapter 22: Diamond Cut Diamond

The ex-cook appeared before Tantaine in all his appalling vulgarity as the latter descended the stairs. The proprietor of the musical academy was a stout, red-faced man, with an insolent mouth and a cynical eye. He was gorgeously dressed, and wore a profusion of jewellery. He was much startled at seeing Tantaine, whom he knew to be the redoubtable Mascarin's right-hand man. "A thousand thunders!" muttered he. "If these people have sent him here for me, I must take care what I am about," and with a friendly smile he extended his hand to Tantaine.

"Glad to see you," said he. "Now, what can I do for you, for I hope you have come to ask me to do something?"

"The veriest trifle," returned Tantaine.

"I am sorry that it is not something of importance, for I have the greatest respect for M. Mascarin."

This conversation had taken place in the window, and was interrupted every moment by the shouts and laughter of the children; but beneath these sounds of merriment came an occasional bitter wail of lamentation.

"What is that?" inquired Perpignan, in a voice of thunder. "Who presumes to be unhappy in this establishment?"

"It is two of the lads that I have put on half rations," returned Poluche. "I'll make them learn somehow or—"

A dark frown on the master's face arrested his further speech. "What do I hear?" roared Perpignan. "Do you dare, under my roof, to deprive those poor children of an ounce of food? It is scandalous, I may say, infamous on your part, M. Poluche."

"But, sir," faltered the professor, "have you not told me hundreds of times—"

"That you were an idiot, and would never be anything better. Go and tell Mother Butor to give these poor children their dinner."

Repressing further manifestations of rage, Perpignan took Tantaine by the arm and led him into a little side-room, which he dignified by the name of his office. There was nothing in it but three chairs, a common deal table, and a few shelves containing ledgers. "You have come on business, I presume," remarked Perpignan.

Tantaine nodded, and the two men seated themselves at the table, gazing keenly into each other's eyes, as though to read the thoughts that moved in the busy brain.

"How did you find out my little establishment down here?" asked Perpignan.

"By a mere chance," remarked Tantaine carelessly. "I go about a good deal, and hear many things. For instance, you have taken every precaution here, and though you are really the proprietor, yet the husband of your cook and housekeeper, Butor, is supposed to be the owner of the house—at least it stands in his name. Now, if anything untoward happened, you would vanish, and only Butor would remain a prey for the police."

Tantaine paused for a moment, and then slowly added, "Such tactics usually succeed unless a man has some secret enemy, who would take advantage of his knowledge, to do him an injury by obtaining irrefragable proofs of his complicity."

The ex-cook easily perceived the threat that was hidden under these words. "They know something," muttered he, "and I must find out what it is."

"If a man has a clear conscience," said he aloud, "he is all right. I have nothing to conceal, and therefore nothing to fear. You have now seen my establishment; what do you think of it?"

"It seems to me a very well-conducted one."

"It may have occurred to you that a factory at Roubaix might have been a better investment, but I had not the capital to begin with."

Tantaine nodded. "It is not half a bad trade," said he.

"I agree with you. In the Rue St. Marguerite you will find more than one similar establishment; but I never cared for the situation of the Faubourg St. Antoine. My little angels find this spot more salubrious."

"Yes, yes," answered Tantaine amicably, "and if they howl too much when they are corrected, there are not too many neighbours to hear them."

Perpignan thought it best to take no notice of this observation. "The papers are always pitching into us," continued he. "They had much better stick to politics. The fact is, that the profits of our business are tremendously exaggerated."

"Well, you manage to make a living out of it?"

"I don't lose, I confess, but I have six little cherubs in hospital, besides the one in the kitchen, and these, of course, are a dead loss to me."

"That is a sad thing for you," answered Tantaine gravely.

Perpignan began to be amazed at his visitor's coolness.

"Damn it all," said he, "if you and Mascarin think the business such a profitable one, why don't you go in for it. You may perhaps think it easy to procure the kids; just try it. You have to go to Italy for most of them, then you have to smuggle them across the frontier like bales of contraband goods."

Perpignan paused to take a breath, and Tantaine asked,—

"What sum do you make each of the lads bring in daily?"

"That depends," answered Perpignan hesitatingly.

"Well, you can give an average?"

"Say three *francs* then."

"Three *francs*!" repeated Tantaine with a genial smile, "and you have forty little cherubs, so that makes one hundred and twenty *francs* per day."

"Absurd!" retorted Perpignan; "do you think each of the lads bring in such a sum as that?"

"Ah! you know the way to make them do so."

"I don't understand you," answered Perpignan, in whose voice a shade of anxiety now began to appear.

"No offence, no offence," answered Tantaine; "but the fact is, the newspapers are doing you a great deal of harm, by retailing some of the means adopted by your colleague to make the boys do a good day's work. Do you recollect the sentence on that master who tied one of his lads down on a bed, and left him without food for two days at a stretch?"

"I don't care about such matters; no one can bring a charge of cruelty against me," retorted Perpignan angrily.

"A man with the kindest heart in the world may be the victim of circumstances."

Perpignan felt that the decisive moment was at hand.

"What do you mean?" asked he.

"Well, suppose, to punish one of your refractory lads, you were to shut him in the cellar. A storm comes on during the night, the gutter gets choked up, the cellar fills with water, and next morning you find the little cherub drowned like a rat in his hole?"

Perpignan's face was livid.

"Well, and what then?" asked he.

"Ah! now the awkward part of the matter comes. You would not care to send for the police, that might excite suspicion; the easiest thing is to dig a hole and shove the body into it."

Perpignan got up and placed his back against the door.

"You know too much, M. Tantaine,—a great deal too much," said he.

Perpignan's manner was most threatening; but Tantaine still smiled pleasantly, like a child who had just committed some simply mischievous act, the results of which it cannot foresee.

"The sentence isn't heavy," he continued; "five years' penal servitude, if evidence of previous good conduct could be put in; but if former antecedents were disclosed, such as a journey to Nancy—"

This was the last straw, and Perpignan broke out,—

"What do you mean?" said he; "and what do you want me to do?"

"Only a trifling service, as I told you before. My dear sir, do not put yourself in a rage," he added, as Perpignan seemed disposed to speak again. "Was it not you who first began to talk of your, 'em—

well, let us say business?"

"Then you wanted to make yourself agreeable by talking all this rot to me. Well, shall I tell you in my turn what I think?"

"By all means, if it will not be giving you too much trouble."

"Then I tell you that you have come here on an errand which no man should venture to do alone. You are not of the age and build for business like this. It is a misfortune—a fatal one perhaps—to put yourself in my power, in such a house as this."

"But, my dear sir, what is likely to happen to me?"

The features of the ex-cook were convulsed with fury; he was in that mad state of rage in which a man has no control over himself. Mechanically his hand slipped into his pocket; but before he could draw it out again, Tantaine who had not lost one of his movements, sprang upon him and grasped him so tightly by the throat that he was powerless to adopt any offensive measures, in spite of his great strength and robust build. The struggle was not a long one; the old man hurled his adversary to the ground, and placed his foot on his chest, and held him down, his whole face and figure seemingly transfigured with the glories of strength and success.

"And so you wished to stab me,—to murder a poor and inoffensive old man. Do you think that I was fool enough to enter your cut-throat door without taking proper precautions?" And as he spoke he drew a revolver from his bosom. "Throw away your knife," added he sternly.

In obedience to this mandate, Perpignan, who was now entirely demoralized, threw the sharp-pointed weapon which he had contrived to open in his pocket into a corner of the room.

"Good," said Tantaine. "You are growing more reasonable now. Of course I came alone, but do you think that plenty of people did not know where I was going to? Had I not returned tonight, do you think that my master, M. Mascarin, would have been satisfied? and how long do you think it would have been before he and the police would have been here. If you do not do all that I wish for the rest of your life, you will be the most ungrateful fellow in the world."

Perpignan was deeply mortified; he had been worsted in single combat, and now he was being found out, and these things had never happened to him before.

"Well, I suppose that I must give in," answered he sulkily.

"Quite so; it is a pity that you did not think of that before."

"You vexed me and made me angry."

"Just so; well, now, get up, take that chair, and let us talk reasonably."

Perpignan obeyed without a word.

"Now," said Tantaine, "I came here with a really magnificent proposal. But I adopted the course I pursued because I wished to prove to you that *you* belonged more absolutely to Mascarin than did your wretched foreign slaves to you. You are absolutely at his mercy, and he can crush you to powder whenever he likes."

"Your Mascarin is Satan himself," muttered the discomfited man. "Who can resist him?"

"Come, as you think thus, we can talk sensibly at last."

"Well," answered Perpignan ruefully, as he adjusted his disordered necktie, "say what you like, I have no answer to make."

"Let us begin at the commencement," said Tantaine. "For some days past your people have been following a certain Caroline Schimmel. A fellow of sixteen called Ambrose, a lad with a harp, was told off for this duty. He is not to be trusted. Only a night or two ago one of my men made him drunk; and fearing lest his absence might create surprise, drove him here in a cab, and left him at the corner."

The ex-cook uttered an oath.

"Then you too are watching Caroline," said he. "I knew well that there was someone else in the field, but that was no matter of mine."

"Well, tell me why you are watching her?"

"How can you ask me? You know that my motto is silence and discretion, and that this is a secret entrusted to my honour."

Tantaine shrugged his shoulders.

"Why do you talk like that, when you know very well that you are following Ambrose on your own account, hoping by that means to penetrate a secret, only a small portion of which has been entrusted to you?" remarked he.

"Are you certain of this statement?" asked the man, with a cunning look.

"So sure that I can tell you that the matter was placed in your hands by a certain M. Catenac."

The expression in Perpignan's face changed from astonishment to fear.

"Why, this Mascarin knows everything," muttered he.

"No," replied Tantaine, "my master does not know everything, and the proof of this is, that I have come to ask you what occurred between Catenac's client and yourself, and this is the service that we expect from you."

"Well, if I must, I must. About three weeks ago, one morning, I had just finished with half a dozen clients at my office in the Rue de Fame, when my servant brought me Catenac's card. After some talk, he asked me if I could find out a person that he had utterly lost sight of. Of course I said, yes, I could. Upon this he asked me to make an appointment for ten the next morning, when someone would call on me regarding the affair. At the appointed time a shabbily dressed man was shown in. I looked at him up and down, and saw that, in spite of his greasy hat and threadbare coat, his linen was of the finest kind, and that his shoes were the work of one of our best bootmakers. 'Aha,' said I to myself, 'you thought to take me in, did you!' I handed him a chair, and he at once proceeded to let me into his reasons for coming.

"'Sir,' said he, 'my life has not been a very happy one, and once I was compelled to take to the Foundling Asylum a child that I loved very dearly, the son of a woman whom I adored. She is dead now, and I am old and solitary. I have a small property, and would give half of it to recover the child. Tell me, is there any chance of my doing so?' You must imagine, my dear sir," continued he, after a slight pause, "that I was much interested in this story, for I said to myself, that the man's fortune must be a very small one if half of it would not amply repay me for making a journey to the Foundling Hospital. So I agreed to undertake the business, but the old fellow was too sharp for me. 'Stop a bit, and let me finish,' said he, 'and you will see that your task will not be so easy as you seem to think it.' I, of course, bragged of my enormous sources of information, and the probability of ultimate success."

"Keep to your story," said Tantaine impatiently, "I know all about that."

"I will leave you, then, to imagine all I said to the old man, who listened to me with great satisfaction. 'I only hope that you are as skilful as M. Catenac says you are, and have as much influence and power as you assert, for no man has a finer chance than you now have. I have tried all means up to this, but I have failed.' I went first to the hospital where the child had been placed, and they showed me the register containing the date of his admission, but no one knew what had become of him, for at twelve years of age he had left the place, and no one had heard of him since; and in spite of every effort, I have been unable to discover whether he is alive or dead."

"A pretty riddle to guess," remarked Tantaine.

"An enigma that it is impossible to solve," returned Perpignan. "How is one to get hold of a boy who vanished ten years ago, and who must now be a grown-up man?"

"We could do it."

Tantaine's tone was so decided, that the other man looked sharply at him with a vague suspicion rising in his breast that the affair had also been placed in Mascarin's hands; and if so, whether he had worked it with more success than himself.

"You might, for all I know; but I felt that the clue was absolutely wanting," answered Perpignan sulkily. "I put on a bold face, however, and asked for the boy's description. The man told me that he could provide me with an accurate one, for that many people, notably the lady superior, remembered the lad. He could also give other details which might be useful."

"And these you obtained, of course?"

"Not yet."

"Are you joking?"

"Not a bit. I do not know whether the old man was sharp enough to read in the expression of my features that I had not the smallest hope of success; be that as it may, he could give me no further information that day, declaring that he came in only to consult me, and that everything must be done in a most confidential way. I hastened to assure him that my office was a perfect tomb of secrets. He told me that he took that for granted. Then telling me that he wished me to draw up a *precis* of my intended course, he took out a note for five hundred *francs*, which he handed to me for my time. I refused to take it, though it cost me a struggle to do so, for I thought that I should make more out of him later on. But he insisted on my taking it, saying that he would see me again soon, and that Catenac would communicate with me. He left me less interested in the search than in who this old man could possibly be."

Tantaine felt that Perpignan was telling the truth.

"Did you not try and find out that?" asked he.

Perpignan hesitated; but feeling convinced that there was no loophole for escape, he answered, "Hardly had my visitor left than, slipping on a cap and a workman's blouse, I followed him in his track, and saw him enter one of the finest houses in the Rue de Varennes."

"He lived there then?"

"He did, and he was a very well-known man—the Duke de Champdoce."

"Yes, I know all that," answered Tantaine, placidly, "but I can't, for the life of me, imagine the connection between the duke and Caroline Schimmel."

Perpignan raised his eyebrows.

"Why did you put a man to watch her?" asked Tantaine.

"My reasons for doing so were most simple. I made every inquiry regarding the duke; learned that he was very wealthy, and lived a very steady life. He is married, and loves his wife dearly. They had one son, whom they lost a year ago, and have never recovered from the shock. I imagine that this duke, having lost his legitimate heir, wished me to find his other son. Do you not think that I am right?"

"There is something in it; but, after all, you have not explained your reasons for watching Caroline."

Perpignan was no match for Mascarin's right-hand man, but he was keen enough to discern that Tantaine was putting a string of questions to him which had been prepared in advance. This he, however, was powerless to resent.

"As you may believe," said he, "I made every inquiry into the past as well as the present of the duke, and also tried to discover who was the mother of the child, but in this I entirely failed."

"What! not with all your means?" cried Tantaine, with a sneer.

"Laugh at me as much as you like; but out of the thirty servants in the Champdoce establishment, not one has been there more than ten years. Nor could I anywhere lay my hands upon one who had been in the duke's service in his youth. Once, however, as I was in the wine shop in the Rue de Varennes, I quite by chance heard allusion made to a woman who had been in the service of the duke twenty-five years ago, and who was now in receipt of a small allowance from him. This woman was Caroline Schimmel. I easily found out her address, and set a watch on her."

"And of what use will she be to you?" "Very little, I fear. And yet the allowance looks as if she had at one time done something out of the way for her employers. Can it be that she has any knowledge of the birth of this natural child?"

"I don't think much of your idea," returned Tantaine carelessly.

"Since then," continued Perpignan, "the duke has never put in an appearance in my office."

"But how about Catenac?"

"I have seen him three times."

"Has he told you nothing more? Do you not even know in which hospital the child was placed?"

"No; and on my last visit I plainly told him that I was getting sick of all this mystery; and he said that he himself was tired, and was sorry that he had ever meddled in the affair."

Tantaine was not surprised at hearing this, and accounted for Catenac's change of front by the threats of Mascarin.

"Well, what do you draw from this?" asked he.

"That Catenac has no more information than I have. The duke most likely proposes to drop the affair; but, were I in his place, I should be afraid to find the boy, however much I might at one time have desired to do so. He may be in prison—the most likely thing for a lad who, at twelve years of age, ran away from a place where he was well treated. I have, however, planned a mode of operation, for, with patience, money, and skill, much might be done."

"I agree with you."

"Then let me tell you. I have drawn an imaginary circle round Paris. I said to myself, 'I will visit every house and inn in the villages round within this radius; I will enter every isolated dwelling, and will say to the inhabitants, "Do any of you remember at any time sheltering and feeding a child, dressed in such and such a manner?"' giving at the same time a description of him. I am sure that I should find someone who would answer in the affirmative. Then I should gain a clue which I would follow up to the end."

This plan appeared so ingenious to Tantaine, that he involuntarily exclaimed,—

"Good! excellent!"

Perpignan hardly knew whether Tantaine was praising or blaming him. His manner might have meant either.

"You are very fast," returned he dismally. "Perhaps presently you will be good enough to allow that I am not an absolute fool. Do you really think that I am an idiot? At any rate, I sometimes hit upon a judicious combination. For example, with regard to this boy, I have a notion which, if properly worked might lead to something."

"Might I ask what it is?"

"I speak confidentially. If it is impossible to lay our hands upon the real boy, why should we not substitute another?"

At this suggestion, Tantaine started violently.

"It would be most dangerous, most hazardous," gasped he.

"You are afraid, then?" said Perpignan, delighted at the effect his proposal had made.

"It seems it is you who were afraid," retorted Tantaine.

"You do not know me when you say that," said Perpignan.

"If you were not afraid," asked Tantaine, in his most oily voice, "why did you not carry out your plan?"

"Because there was one obstacle that could not be got over."

"Well, I can't see it myself," returned Tantaine, desirous of hearing every detail.

"Ah, there is one thing that I omitted in my narrative. The duke informed me that he could prove the identity of the boy by certain scars."

"Scars? And of what kind, pray?"

"Now you are asking me too much. I do not know."

On receiving this reply, Tantaine rose hastily from his chair, and thus concealed his agitation from his companion.

"I have a hundred apologies to make for taking up so much of your valuable time. My master has got it into his head that you were after the same game as ourselves. He was mistaken, and now we leave the field clear to you."

Before Perpignan could make any reply, the old man had passed through the doorway. On the threshold he paused, and said,—

"Were I in your place, I would stick to my first plan. You will never find the boy, but you will get several thousand *francs* out of the duke, which I am sure will come in handy."

"There are scars now, then," muttered Tantaine, as he moved away from the house, "and that Master Catenac never said a word about them!"

Chapter 23: Father and Son

Two hours after Andre had left the Avenue de Matignon, one of Mascarin's most trusty emissaries was at his heels, who could watch his actions with the tenacity of a bloodhound. Andre, however, now that he had heard of Sabine's convalescence, had entirely recovered the elasticity of his spirits, and would never have noticed that he was being followed. His heart, too, was much rejoiced at the friendship of M. de Breulh and the promise of assistance from the Viscountess de Bois Arden; and with the assistance of these two, he felt that he could end his difficulties.

"I must get to work again," muttered he, as he left M. de Breulh's hospitable house. "I have already lost too much time. Tomorrow, if you look up at the scaffolding of a splendid house in the Champs Elysees, you will see me at work."

Andre was busy all night with his plans for the rich contractor, M.

Gandelu, who wanted as much ornamental work on the outside of his house as he had florid decorations within. He rose with the lark, and having gazed for a moment on Sabine's portrait, started for the abode of M. Gandelu, the proud father of young Gaston. This celebrated contractor lived in a splendid house in the Rue Chasse d'Antin, until his more palatial residence should be completed.

When Andre presented himself at the door, an old servant, who knew him well, strongly urged him not to go up.

"Never," said he, "in all the time that I have been with master, have I seen him in such a towering rage. Only just listen!"

It was easy to hear the noise alluded to, mingled with the breaking of glass and the smashing of furniture.

"The master has been at this game for over an hour," remarked the servant, "ever since his lawyer, M. Catenac, has left him."

Andre, however, decided not to postpone his visit. "I must see him in spite of everything; show me up," said he.

With evident reluctance the domestic obeyed, and threw open the door of a room superbly furnished and decorated, in the centre of which stood M. Gandelu waving the leg of a chair frantically in his hand. He was a man of sixty years of age, but did not look fifty, built like a Hercules, with huge hands and muscular limbs which seemed to fret under the restraint of his fashionable garments. He had made his enormous fortune, of which he was considerably proud, by honest labour, and no one could say that he had not acted fairly throughout his whole career. He was coarse and violent in his manner, but he had a generous heart and never refused aid to the deserving and needy. He swore like a trooper, and his grammar was faulty; but for all that, his heart was in the right place, and he was a better man than many who boast of high birth and expensive education.

"What idiot is coming here to annoy me?" roared he, as soon as the door was opened.

"I have come by appointment," answered Andre, and the contractor's brow cleared as he saw who his visitor was.

"Ah, it is you, is it? Take a seat; that is, if there is a sound chair left in the room. I like you, for you have an honest face and don't shirk hard work. You needn't colour up, though; modesty is no fault. Yes, there is something in you, and when you want a hundred thousand *francs* to go into business with, here it is ready for you; and had I a daughter, you should marry her, and I would build your house for you."

"I thank you much," said Andre; "but I have learned to depend entirely on myself."

"True," returned Gandelu, "you never knew your parents; you never knew what a kind father would do for his child. Do you know my son?" asked he, suddenly turning upon Andre.

This question at once gave Andre the solution of the scene before him. M. Gandelu was irritated at some folly that his son had committed. For a moment Andre hesitated; he did not care to say anything that might revive the old man's feeling of anger, and therefore merely replied that he had only met his son Gaston two or three times.

"Gaston," cried the old man, with a bitter oath; "do not call him that. Do you think it likely that old Nicholas Gandelu would ever have been ass enough to call his son Gaston? He was called Peter, after his grandfather, but it wasn't a good enough one for the young fool; he wanted a swell name, and Peter had too much the savour of hard work in it for my fine gentleman. But that isn't all; I could let that pass," continued the old man. "Pray have you seen his cards? Over the name of Gaston de Gandelu is a count's coronet. He a count indeed! the son of a man who has carried a hod for years!"

"Young people will be young people," Andre ventured to observe; but the old man's wrath would not be assuaged by a platitude like this.

"You can find no excuse for him, only the fellow is absolutely ashamed of his father. He consorts with titled fools and is in the seventh heaven if a waiter addresses him as 'count,' not seeing that it is not he that is treated with respect, but the gold pieces of his old father, the working man."

Andre's position was now a most painful one, and he would have given a good deal not to be the recipient of a confidence which was the result of anger.

"He is only twenty, and yet see what a wreck he is," resumed Gandelu. "His eyes are dim, and he is getting bald; he stoops, and spends his nights in drink and bad company. I have, however, only myself to blame, for I have been far too lenient; and if he had asked me for my head, I believe that I should have given it to him. He had only to ask and have. After my wife's death, I had only the boy. Do you know what he has in this house? Why, rooms fit for a prince, two servants and four horses. I allow him monthly, fifteen hundred *francs*, and he goes about calling me a niggard, and has already squandered every bit of his poor mother's fortune." He stopped, and turned pale, for at that moment the door opened, and young Gaston, or rather Peter, slouched into the room.

"It is the common fate of fathers to be disappointed in their off-spring, and to see the sons who ought to have been their honour and glory the scourge to punish their worldly aspirations," exclaimed the old man.

"Good! that is really a very telling speech," murmured Gaston approvingly, "considering that you have not made a special study of elocution."

Fortunately his father did not catch these words, and continued in a voice broken by emotion, "That, M. Andre, is my son, who for twenty years has been my sole care. Well, believe it or not, as you like, he has been speculating on my death, as you might speculate on a race-horse at Vincennes."

"No, no," put in Gaston, but his father stopped him with a disdainful gesture.

"Have at least the courage to acknowledge your fault. You thought me blind because I said nothing, but your past conduct has opened my eyes."

"But, father!"

"Do not attempt to deny it. This very morning my man of business, M. Catenac, wrote to me, and with that real courage which only true friends possess, told me all. I must tell you, M. Andre," resumed the contractor, "I was ill. I had a severe attack of the gout, such as a man seldom recovers from, and my son was constant in his attendance at my sick couch. This consoled me. 'He loves me after all,' said I. But it was only my testamentary arrangements that he wanted to discover, and he went straight to a money-lender called Clergot and raised a hundred thousand *francs* assuring the blood-sucker that I had not many hours to live."

"It is a lie!" cried Gaston, his face crimsoning with shame.

The old man raised the leg of the chair in his hand, and made so threatening a movement that Andre flung himself between father and son. "Great heavens!" cried he, "think what you are doing, sir, and forbear."

The old man paused, passed his hand round his brow, and flung the weapon into a remote corner of the room. "I thank you," said he, grasping Andre's hand; "you have saved me from a great crime. In another moment I should have murdered him."

Gaston was no coward, and he still retained the position he had been in before.

"This is quite romantic," muttered he. "The governor seems to be going in for infanticide."

Andre did not allow him to finish the sentence, for, grasping the young man's wrist, he whispered fiercely, "Not another word; silence!"

"But I want to know what it all means?" answered the irrepressible youth.

"I had in my hands," said the old man, addressing Andre, and ignoring the presence of his son, "the important paper he had copied. Yes; not more than an hour ago I read it. These were the terms: if I died within eight days from the date of signature, my son agreed to pay a bonus of thirty thousand *francs*; but if I lived for one month, he would take up the bill by paying one hundred and fifty thousand. If, however, by any unforeseen chance, I should recover entirely, he bound himself to pay Clergot the hundred thousand *francs*."

The old man tore the cravat from his swelling throat, and wiped the beads of cold sweat that bedewed his brow.

"When this man recovers his self-command," thought Andre, "he will never forgive me for having been the involuntary listener to this terrible tale." But in this Andre was mistaken, for unsophisticated nature requires sympathy, and Nichols Gandelu would have said the same to the first comer.

"Before, however, delivering the hundred thousand *francs*, the usurer wished to make himself more secure, and asked for a certificate from someone who had seen me. This person was his friend. He spoke to me of a medical man, a specialist, who would understand my case at once. Would I not see him? Never had I seen my son so tender and affectionate. I yielded to his entreaties at last, and one evening I said to him, 'Bring in this wonderful physician, if you really think he can do anything for me,' and he did bring him.

"Yes, M. Andre, he found a medical man base and vile enough to become the tool of my son, and a money-lender; and if I choose, I can expose him to the loathing of the world, and the contempt of his brethren.

"The fellow came, and his visit lasted nearly an hour. I can see him now, asking questions and feeling my pulse. He went away at last, and my son followed him. They both met Clergot, who was waiting in the street. 'You can pay him the cash; the old man won't last twenty-four hours longer,' said the doctor; and then my son came back happy and radiant, and assured me that I should soon be well again. And strange as it may seem, a change for the better took place that very night. Clergot had asked for forty-eight hours in which to raise the sum required. He heard of my convalescence, and my son lost the money.

"Was it courage you lacked?" asked the old man, turning for the first time to his son. "Did you not know that ten drops instead of one of the medicine I was taking would have freed you from me for ever?"

Gaston did not seem at all overwhelmed. Indeed, he was wondering how the matter had reached his father's ears, and how Catenac had discovered the rough draft of the agreement.

The contractor had imagined that his son would implore forgiveness; but seeing that he remained obdurate, his violence burst forth again. "And do you know what use my son would make of my fortune? He would squander it on a creature he picked up out of the streets,—a woman he called Madame de Chantemille,—a fit companion for a noble count!"

The shaft had penetrated the impassability which Gaston had up to this displayed. "You should not insult Zora," said he.

"I shall not," returned his father with a grim laugh, "take the trouble to do that; you are not of age, and I shall clap your friend Madame de Chantemille into prison."

"You would not do that!"

"Would I not? You are a minor; but your Zora, whose real name is Rose, is much older; the law is wholly on my side."

"But father—"

"There is no use in crying; my lawyer has the matter in hand, and by nightfall your Zora will be securely caged."

This blow was so cruel and unexpected, that the young man could only repeat,—

"Zora in prison!"

"Yes, in the House of Correction, and from thence to Saint Lazare. Catenac told me the very things to be done."

"Shameful!" exclaimed Gaston, "Zora in prison! Why, I and my friends will lay siege to the place. I will go to the Court, stand by her side, and depose that this all comes from your devilish malignity. I will say that I love and esteem her, and that as soon as I am of age I will marry her; the papers will write about us. Go on, go on; I rather like the idea."

However great a man's self-control may be, it has its limits. M. Gandelu had restrained himself even while he told his son of his villainous conduct; but these revolting threats were more than he could endure, and Andre seeing this, stepped forward, opened the door, and thrust the foolish youth into the corridor.

"What have you done" cried the contractor; "do you not see that he will go and warn that vile creature, and that she will escape from justice?"

And as Andre, fearing he knew not what, tried to restrain him, the old man, exerting all his muscular strength, thrust him on one side with perfect ease, and rushed from the room, calling loudly to his servants.

Andre was horrified at the scene at which, in spite of himself, he had been compelled to assist as a witness. He was not a fool, and had lived too much in the world of art not to have witnessed many strange scenes and met with many dissolute characters; but, as a rule, the follies of the world had amused rather than disgusted him. But this display of want of feeling on the part of a son toward a father absolutely chilled his blood. In a few minutes M. Gandelu appeared with a calmer expression upon his face.

"I will tell you how matters now stand," said he, in a voice that quivered in spite of his efforts. "My son is locked up in his room, and a trustworthy servant whom he cannot corrupt has mounted guard over him."

"Do you not fear, sir, that in his excitement and anger he may—?"

The contractor shrugged his shoulders.

"You do not know him," answered he, "if you imagine that he resembles me in any way. What do you think that he is doing now? Lying on his bed, face downward, yelling for his Zora. Zora, indeed! As if that was a name fit for a Christian. How is it that these creatures are enabled to drug our boys and lead them anywhere? Had his mother not been a saint on earth, I should scarcely believe that he was my son."

The contractor sank into a chair and buried his face in his hands.

"You are in pain, sir?" said Andre.

"Yes; my heart is deeply wounded. Up to this time I have only felt as a father; now I feel as a man. Tomorrow I send for my family and consult with them; and I shall advertise that for the future I will not be responsible for any debts that my son may contract. He shall not have a penny, and will soon learn how society treats a man with empty pockets. As to the girl, she will disappear in double quick time. I have thoroughly weighed the consequences of sending this girl to gaol, and they are very terrible. My son will do as he has threatened, I am sure of that; and I can picture him tied to that infamous creature for life, looking into her face, and telling her that he adores her, and glorying in his dishonour, which will be repeated by every Parisian newspaper."

"But is there no other way of proceeding?" asked Andre.

"No, none whatever. If all modern fathers had my courage, we should not have so many profligate sons. It is impossible that this conferring with the doctor and the money-lender could have originated in my son's weak brain. He is a mere child, and someone must have put him up to it."

The poor father was already seeking for some excuse for the son's conduct.

"I must not dwell on this longer," continued Gandelu, "or I shall get as mad as I was before. I will look at your plans another day. Now, let us get out of the house. Come and look at the new building in the Champs Elysees."

The mansion in question was situated at the corner of the Rue de Chantilly, near the Avenue des Champs Elysees, and the frontage of it was still marked by scaffolding, so that but little of it could be seen. A dozen workmen, engaged by Andre, were lounging about. They had expected to see him early, and were surprised at his non-appearance, as he was usually punctuality itself. Andre greeted them in a friendly manner, but M. Gandelu, though he was always on friendly terms with his workmen, passed by them as if he did not even notice their existence. He walked through the different rooms and examined them carelessly, without seeming to take any interest in them, for his thoughts were with his son,—his only son. After a short time he returned to Andre.

"I cannot stay longer," said he; "I am not feeling well; I will be here tomorrow;" and he went away with his head bent down on his chest.

The workmen noticed his strange and unusual manner.

"He does not look very bright," remarked one to his comrade. "Since his illness he has not been the same man. I think he must have had some terrible shock."

Chapter 24: An Artful Trick

Andre had removed his coat and donned his blouse, the sleeves of which were rolled up to his shoulders. "I must get to business," murmured he, "to make up for lost time." He set to work with great vigour, but had hardly got into the swing, when a lad came actively up the ladder and told him that a gentleman wished to see him, "and a real swell, too," added the boy. Andre was a good deal put out at being disturbed, but when he reached the street and saw that it was M. de

Breulh-Faverlay who was waiting for him, his ill-humour disappeared like chaff before the wind.

"Ah, this is really kind of you," cried he; for he could never forget the debt of gratitude he owed to the gentleman. "A thousand thanks for remembering me. Excuse my not shaking hands, but see;" and he exhibited his palms all white with plaster. As he did so the smile died away on his lips, for he caught sight of his friend's face.

"What is the matter?" exclaimed he, anxiously. "Is Sabine worse? Has she had a relapse?"

De Breulh shook his head, but the expression of his face clearly said,—"Would to heavens it were only that!"

But the news that Sabine was not worse relieved Andre at once, and he patiently waited for his friend to explain.

"I have seen her twice for you," answered De Breulh; "but it is absolutely necessary that you should come to a prompt decision on an important affair."

"I am quite at your service," returned Andre a good deal surprised and troubled.

"Then come with me at once, I did not drive here, but we shall not be more than a quarter of an hour in reaching my house."

"I will follow you almost immediately. I only ask five minutes' grace to go up to the scaffold again."

"Have you any orders to give?"

"No, I have none."

"Why should you go, then?"

"To make myself a little more presentable."

"Is it an annoyance or inconvenience for you to go out in that dress?"

"Not a bit, I am thoroughly used to it; but it was for your sake."

"If that is all, come along."

"But people will stare at seeing you in company with a common workman."

"Let them stare." And drawing Andre's arm through his, M. de Breulh set off.

Andre was right; many persons did turn round to look at the fashionably dressed gentleman walking arm in arm with a mason in his working attire, but De Breulh took but little heed, and to all Andre's questions simply said, "Wait till we reach my house."

At length they arrived, without having exchanged twenty words, and entering the library closed the door. M. de Breulh did not inflict the torture of suspense upon his young friend a moment longer than was necessary.

"This morning, about twelve o'clock, as I was crossing the Avenue de Matignon, I saw Modeste, who had been waiting for you more than an hour."

"I could not help it."

"I know that. As soon as she saw me, she ran up to me at once. She was terribly disappointed at not having seen you; but knowing our intimacy, she entrusted me with a letter for you from Mademoiselle de Mussidan."

Andre shuddered; he felt that the note contained evil tidings, with which De Breulh was already acquainted. "Give it to me," said he, and with trembling hands he tore open the letter and perused its contents.

Dearest Andre,—

I love you, and shall ever continue to do so, but I have duties—most holy ones—which I must fulfil; duties which my name and position demand of me, even should the act cost me my life. We shall never meet again in this world, and this letter is the last one you will ever receive from me. Before long you will see the announcement of my marriage. Pity me, for great as your wretchedness will be, it will be as nothing compared to mine. Heaven have mercy upon us both! Andre, try and tear me out of your heart. I have not even the right to die, and oh, my darling, this—this is the last word you will ever receive from your poor unhappy

Sabine.

If M. de Breulh had insisted upon taking Andre home with him before he handed him the letter, it was because Modeste had given him some inkling of its contents. He feared that the effect would be tremendous upon nerves so highly strung and sensitive as those of Andre. But he need not have been alarmed on this point. As the young painter mastered the contents of the letter his features became ghastly pale, and a shudder convulsed every nerve and muscle of his frame. With a mechanical gesture he extended the paper to M. de Breulh, uttering the one word, "Read."

His friend obeyed him, more alarmed by Andre's laconism than he could have been by some sudden explosion of passion.

"Do not lose heart," exclaimed he.

But Andre interrupted him. "Lose heart!" said he; "you do not know me. When Sabine was ill, perhaps dying, far away from me, I did feel cast down; but now that she tells me that she loves me, my feelings are of an entirely different nature."

M. de Breulh was about to speak, but Andre went on.

"What is this marriage contract which my poor Sabine announces to me, as if it was her death-warrant? Her parents must all along have intended to break with you, but you were beforehand with them. Can they have received a more advantageous offer of marriage already? It is scarcely likely. When she confided the secret of her life to you, she certainly knew nothing of this. What terrible event has happened since then? My brave Sabine would never have submitted unless some coercion had been used that she could not struggle against; she would rather have quitted her father's house for ever."

As Andre uttered these words De Breulh's mind was busy with similar reflections, for Modeste had given him some hint of the approaching marriage, and had begged him to be most careful how he communicated the facts to Andre.

"You must have noticed," continued the young painter, "the strange coincidence between Sabine's illness and this note. You left her happy and full of hope, and an hour afterward she falls senseless, as though struck by lightning; as soon as she recovers a little she sends me this terrible letter. Do you remember that Madame de Bois Arden told us that during Sabine's illness her father and mother never left her bedside? Was not this for fear lest some guilty secret of theirs might escape her lips in a crisis of delirium?"

"Yes, I remember that, and I have long had reason to imagine that there is some terrible family secret in the Mussidans' family, such as we too often find among the descendants of noble houses."

"What can it be?"

"That I have no means of ascertaining, but that there is one I am sure."

Andre turned away and paced rapidly up and down the room. "Yes," said he, suddenly, "there is a mystery; but you and I will leave no stone unturned until we penetrate it." He drew a chair close to the side of his friend, who was reclining on a couch. "Listen," said he, "and correct me if you fancy that I am not right in what I am saying. Do you believe that the most terrible necessity alone has compelled Sabine to write this letter?"

"Most certainly."

"Both the count and countess were willing to accept you as their son-in-law?"

"Exactly so."

"Could M. de Mussidan have found a more brilliant match for his daughter, one who could unite so many advantages of experience and education to so enormous a fortune?"

De Breulh could hardly repress a smile.

"I am not wishing to pay you a compliment," said Andre impatiently. "Reply to my question."

"Very well then, I admit that according to the opinion of the world, I was a most eligible suitor, and that M. de Mussidan would find it hard to replace me."

"Then tell me how it comes about that neither the count nor the countess has made any effort to prevent this rupture?"

"Their pride, perhaps, has been wounded."

"Not so, for Modeste tells us that on the very day you sent the letter the count was going to call on you to break off the engagement."

"Yes, that is so, if we are to believe Modeste."

As if to give more emphasis to his words, Andre started to his feet. "This," cried he, "this man, who has so suddenly appeared upon the scene, will marry Sabine, not only against her own will, but against that of her parents, and for what reason? Who is this man, and what is the mysterious power that he possesses? His power is too great to spring from an honourable source. Sabine is sacrificing herself to this man for some reason or other, and he, like a dastardly cur, is ready to take advantage of the nobleness of her heart."

"I admit the correctness of your supposition," said he; "and now, how do you propose to act?"

"I shall do nothing as yet," answered the young man, with a fierce gleam in his eyes. "Sabine asks me to tear her from my heart. I will affect to do so for the time. Modeste believes in me, and will help me. I have patience. The villain who has wrecked my life does not know me, and I will only reveal myself upon the day that I hold him helpless in my hand."

"Take care, Andre," urged De Breulh; "a false step would ruin your hopes for ever."

"I will make none; as soon as I have this man's name, I will insult him; there will be a duel, and I shall kill him—or he me."

"A duel will be the height of madness, and would ruin all your hopes of marriage with Sabine."

"The only thing that holds me back is that I do not wish that there should be a corpse between Sabine and myself. Blood on a bridal dress, they say, brings misery; and if this man is what I suspect him to be, I should be doing him too much honour if I crossed swords with him. No, I must have a deeper vengeance than this, for I can never forget that he nearly caused Sabine's death."

He paused for a few seconds, and once again broke the silence which reigned in the room.

"To abuse the power that he must possess shows what a miserable wretch he must be; and men do not attain such a height of infamy by a single bound. The course of his life must be full of similar crimes, growing deeper and deadlier as he moves on. I will make it my business to unmask him and to hold him up to the scorn and contempt of his fellow-men."

"Yes; that is the plan to pursue."

"And we will do so, sir. Ah! heaven help me! I say 'we,' for I have relied on you. The generous offer that you made to me I refused, and I was in the right in doing so; but I should now be a mere madman if I did not entreat you to grant me your aid and advice. We have both known hardship and are capable of going without food or sleep, if necessity requires it of us. We have both graduated in the school of poverty and sorrow. We can keep our plans to ourselves and act."

Andre paused, as if waiting for a reply, but his friend remained silent.

"My plan is most simple," resumed the young painter. "As soon as we know the fellow's name we shall be able to act. He will never suspect us, and we can follow him like his very shadow. There are professional detectives who, for a comparatively small sum, will lay bare a man's entire life. Are we not as clever as this fine fellow? We can work well together in our different circles; you, in the world of fashion, can pick up intelligence that I could not hope to gain; while I, from my lowly position, will study the hidden side of his life, for I can talk to the servants lounging at the front doors or the grooms at the public-houses without suspicion."

M. de Breulh was delighted at finding that he could have some occupation which would fill up the dreary monotony of his life.

"I am yours!" cried he; "and will work with you heart and soul!"

Before the artist could reply a loud blow was struck upon the library door, and a woman's voice exclaimed,—

"Let me in, Gontran, at once."

"It is Madame de Bois Arden," remarked De Breulh, drawing the bolt back; and the viscountess rushed hastily into the room and threw herself into a low chair.

Her beautiful face was bedewed with tears, and she was in a terrible state of excitement.

"What is the matter, Clotilde?" asked De Breulh kindly, as he took her hand.

"Something terrible," answered she with a sob; "but you may be able to help me. Can you lend me twenty thousand *francs*?"

De Breulh smiled; a heavy weight had been lifted from his heart.

"If that is all you require, do not shed any more tears."

"But I want them at once."

"Can you give me half an hour?"

"Yes; but lose no time."

De Breulh drew a check and despatched his valet for the money.

"A thousand thanks!" said the viscountess; "but money is not all that I require, I want your advice."

Andre was about to leave the cousins together, but the lady stopped him.

"Pray remain, M. Andre," said she; "you are not at all in the way; besides, I shall have to speak of someone in whom you take a very deep interest—of Mademoiselle de Mussidan, in short.

"I never knew such a strange occurrence," continued the viscountess, recovering her spirits rapidly, "as that to which, my dear Gontran, you owe my visit. Well, I was just going up to dress, for I had been detained by visitor after visitor, when at two o'clock another came before I could give my order, 'Not at home.' This was the Marquis de Croisenois, the brother of the man who twenty years ago disappeared in so mysterious a manner. I hardly knew him at all, though of course we have met in society, and he bows to me in the Bois, but that is all."

"And yet he called on you today?" remarked De Breulh.

"Don't interrupt me," said the viscountess. "Yes, he called, and that is enough. He is good-looking, faultlessly dressed, and talks well. He brought a letter from an old friend of my grandmother's, the Marchioness d'Arlanges. She is a dear old thing, she uses awful language, and some of her stories are quite too—you know what I mean. In the letter the old lady said that the *marquis* was one of her friends, and begged me for her sake to do him the service he required. Of course I asked him to be seated, and assured him that I would do anything that lay in my power. Then he began talking about M. de Clinchain, and told me a funny story about that eccentric man and a little actress, when I heard a great noise in the anteroom. I was about to ring and inquire the cause, when the door flew open and in came Van Klopen, the ladies' tailor, with a very inflamed countenance. I thought that he had come in a hurry because he had hit on something extremely fetching and wished me to be the first to see it. But do you know what the impudent fellow wanted?"

A smile shone in De Breulh's eyes, as he answered,—

"Money, perhaps!"

"You are right," returned the viscountess, gravely; "he brought my bill into my very drawing-room, and handed it in before a stranger. I never thought that a man who supplies the most aristocratic portion of society could have been guilty of such a piece of impertinence. I ordered him to leave the room, taking it for granted that he would do so with an apology, but I was wrong. He flew into a rage and threatened me, and swore that if I did not settle the bill on the spot, he would go to my husband. The bill was nearly twenty thousand *francs*; imagine my horror! I was so thunderstruck at the amount that I absolutely entreated him to give me time. But my humility added to his annoyance, and taking a seat in an armchair, he declared that he would not move from it until he received his money, or had seen my husband."

"What was Croisenois doing all this time?" asked M. de Breulh.

"He did nothing at first, but at this last piece of audacity he took out his pocketbook, and throwing it in Van Klopen's face, said: 'Pay yourself, you insolent scoundrel, and get out of this.'"

"And the tailor went off?"

"No. 'I must give you a receipt,' said he, and taking writing materials from his pocket, he wrote at the foot of the bill, 'Received from the Marquis de Croisenois, on account of money owing by the Viscountess de Bois Arden, the sum of twenty thousand *francs*.'"

"Well," said De Breulh, looking very grave, "and after Van Klopen's departure, I suppose Croisenois remained to ask the favour regarding which he had called?"

"You are mistaken," answered his cousin. "I had great difficulty in making him speak; but at last he confessed that he was deeply in love with Mademoiselle de Mussidan, and entreated me to present him to her parents and exert all my influence in his behalf."

Both the young men started.

"That is the man!" cried they.

"What do you mean?" asked the viscountess, looking from one to

216

the other.

"That your Marquis de Croisenois is a despicable scoundrel, who had imposed upon the Marchioness d'Arlanges. Just you listen to our reasons for coming to this conclusion." And with the most perfect clearness De Breulh had the whole state of the case before the viscountess.

The lady listened attentively, and then said,—

"Your premises are wrong; just let me say a word on the matter. You say that there is some man who by means of the influence that he exercises over the count and countess, can coerce them into granting him Sabine's hand. But, my dear Gontran, an utter stranger to the family could not exercise this power. Now M. de Croisenois has never entered the doors of the house, and came to me to ask for an introduction."

The justness of this remark silenced De Breulh, but Andre took another view of the matter.

"This seems all right at a first glance, but still, after the extraordinary scene that the viscountess has described, I should like to ask a few questions. Was not Van Klopen's behaviour very unexpected?"

"It was brutal and infamous."

"Are you not one of his best customers?"

"I am, and I have spent an enormous sum with him."

"But Van Klopen is nasty sometimes; did he not sue Mademoiselle de Riversac?" asked De Breulh.

"But he did not, I expect, force his way into her drawing-room and behave outrageously before a perfect stranger. Do you know M. de Croisenois?" returned Andre.

"Very slightly; he is of good family, and his brother George was much esteemed by all who knew him."

"Has he plenty of money?"

"I do not think so, but in time he will inherit a large fortune; very likely he is over head and ears in debt."

"And yet he had twenty thousand *francs* in his pocketbook; is not that rather a large sum to carry when you are simply making a morning call? and it is curious, too, that it should have been the exact sum wanted. Then there is another point; the pocketbook was hurled into Van Klopen's face. Did he submit without a word to such treatment?"

"He certainly said nothing," replied Madame de Bois Arden.

"One question more, if you please. Did Van Klopen open the book and count the notes before he gave the receipt?"

The viscountess thought for a moment.

"I was a good deal excited," said she at length, "but I am almost sure that I saw no notes in Van Klopen's hands."

Andre's face grew radiant.

"Good, very good; he was told to pay himself, and yet he never looked to see if the money was there, but gave a receipt at once. Of course, as Van Klopen kept the pocketbook, the *marquis* could have had nothing in it besides the exact sum that was required."

"It does seem odd," muttered De Breulh.

"But," said Andre, "your bill was not exactly twenty thousand *francs*, was it?"

"No," answered the viscountess. "I ought to have had change to the amount of a hundred or a hundred and twenty *francs*, but I suppose he was too much excited to give it me."

"But for all that he could remember that he had writing materials with him, and give you a receipt?"

The viscountess was utterly bewildered.

"And," continued Andre, "how is it that Van Klopen knew De Croisenois' name? And now, lastly, where is the receipt?"

Madame de Bois Arden turned very pale and trembled violently.

"Ah," said she, "I felt sure that something was going to happen, and it was on this very point that I wanted your advice. Well, I have not got the receipt. M. de Croisenois crumpled it up in his hand and threw it on the table. After a while, however, he took it up and put it in his pocket."

"It is all perfectly clear," said Andre in jubilant tones; "M. de Croisenois had need of your aid, he saw that he could not easily obtain it, and so sought to bind you by the means of a loan made to you at a time of great need."

"You are right," said De Breulh.

The viscountess' giddy mode of action had brought her into many scrapes, but never into so terrible a one as this.

"Great heavens!" cried she, "what do you think that M. de Croisenois will do with this receipt?"

"He will do nothing," answered M. de Breulh, "if you do everything to advance his suit; but pause for an instant, and he will show the hand of steel which has up to now been covered by the velvet glove."

"I am not alarmed at a new slander?" returned the viscountess.

"And why not?" answered De Breulh. "You know very well that in these days of lavish expenditure and unbridled luxury there are many women in society who are so basely vile that they ruin their lovers with as little compunction as their frailer sisters. Tomorrow even De Croisenois may say at the club, 'On my word that little Bois Arden costs me a tremendous lot,' and hands about this receipt for twenty thousand *francs*. What do you imagine that people will think then?"

"The world knows me too well to think so ill of me."

"No, no, Clotilde, there is no charity in society; they will simply say that you are his mistress, and finding that the allowance from your husband is not enough for your needs, you are ruining your lover. There will be a significant laugh among the members, and in time, a very short time, the scandal in a highly sensational form will come to the ears of your husband."

The viscountess wrung her hands.

"It is too horrible," wailed she. "And do you know that Bois Arden would put the worst construction on the whole affair, for he declares that a woman will sacrifice anything in order to outshine her sex in dress. Ah, I will never run up another bill anywhere; tell me, Gontran, what I had better do. Can you not get the receipt from De Croisenois?"

M. de Breulh paused for a moment and then replied, "Of course I could do so, but such a step would be very damaging to your reputation. I have no proof; and if I went to him, he would deny everything of course, and it would make him your enemy for life."

"Besides," added Andre, "you would put him on his guard, and he would escape us."

The unhappy woman glanced from one to the other in utter despair.

"Then I am lost," she exclaimed. "Am I to remain for the rest of my days in this villain's power?"

"Not so," returned Andre, "for I hope soon to put it out of M. de Croisenois' power to injure anyone. What did he say when he asked you to introduce him to the Mussidans?"

"Nothing pointed."

"Then, *madame*, do not disturb yourself tonight. So long as he hopes you will be useful, so long he will stay his hand. Do as he wishes; never allude to the receipt; introduce him and speak well of him, while I, aided by M. de Breulh, will do my utmost to unmask this scoundrel; and as long as he believes himself to be in perfect security, our task will be an easy one."

Just then the servant returned from the bank, and as soon as the man had left the room De Breulh took the notes and placed them in his cousin's hand.

"Here is the money for De Croisenois," said he. "Take my advice, and give it to him this evening with a polite letter of thanks."

"A thousand thanks, Gontran; I will act as you advise."

"Remember you must not allude in your letter to his introduction to the Mussidans. What do you think, Andre?"

"I think a receipt for the money would be a great thing," answered he.

"But such a demand would arouse his suspicions."

"I think not, *madame*, and I see a way of doing it; have you a maid upon whom you could rely?"

"Yes, I have one."

"Good, then give the girl a letter and the notes done up in a separate parcel, and tell her exactly what she is to do. When she sees the *marquis*, let her pretend to be alarmed at the great responsibility that she is incurring in carrying this large sum, and insist upon a receipt for her own protection."

"There is sound sense in that," said De Breulh.

"Yes, yes," said the viscountess, "Josephine will do—as sharp a girl as you could find in a day's journey—and will manage the thing admirably. Trust to me," she continued, as a smile of hope spread over her face; "I will keep De Croisenois in a good humour; he will confide in me, and I will tell you everything. But, oh dear! what shall I do without Van Klopen? Why, there is not another man in Paris fit to stand in his shoes."

With these words the viscountess rose to leave.

"I am completely worn out," remarked she; "and I have a dinner-party tonight. Goodbye then, until we meet again;" and with her spirits evidently as joyous as ever, she tripped into her carriage.

"Now," said Andre, as soon as they were once more alone, "we are on the track of De Croisenois. He evidently holds Madame de Mussidan as he holds Madame de Bois Arden. His is a really honourable mode of action; he surprises a secret, and then turns extortioner."

Chapter 25: A New Skin

Dr. Hortebise's private arrangements were sadly upset by his being compelled to accede to the desire of Tantaine and Mascarin, and in granting hospitality to Paul Violaine; and in spite of the brilliant visions of the future, he often devoutly wished that Mascarin and his young friend were at the other side of the world; but for all that he never thought of attempting to evade the order he had received. He therefore set himself steadily to his task, endeavouring to form Paul's mind, blunt his conscience, and prepare him for the inevitable part that he would soon have to play.

Paul found in him a most affable companion, pleasant, witty, and gifted with great conversational powers. Five days were thus spent breakfasting at well-known restaurants, driving in the Bois, and dining at clubs of which the doctor was a member, while the evenings were passed at the banker's. The doctor played cards with his host, while Paul and Flavia conversed together in low whispers, or else hung over the piano together. But every kind of agreeable existence comes to an end, and one day Daddy Tantaine entered the room, his face radiant with delight.

"I have secured you the sweetest little nest in the world," cried he merrily. "It is not so fine as this, but more in accordance with your position."

"Where is it?" asked Paul.

Tantaine waited. "You won't wear out much shoe leather," said he, "in walking to a certain banker's, for your lodgings are close to his house."

That Tantaine had a splendid talent for arrangement Paul realized as soon as he entered his new place of abode, which was in the Rue Montmartre, and consisted of some neat, quiet rooms, just such as an artist who had conquered his first difficulties would inhabit. The apartments were on the third floor, and comprised a tiny entrance hall, sitting-room, bed and dressing room. A piano stood near the window in the sitting-room. The furniture and curtains were tasteful and in good order, but nothing was new. One thing surprised Paul very much; he had been told that the apartments had been taken and furnished three days ago, and yet it seemed as if they had been inhabited for years, and that the owner had merely stepped out a few minutes before. The unmade bed, and the half-burnt candles in the sleeping-room added to this impression, while on the rug lay a pair of worn slippers. The fire had not gone out entirely, and a half-smoked cigar lay on the mantelpiece.

On the table in the sitting-room was a sheet of music paper, with a few bars jotted down upon it. Paul felt so convinced that he was in another person's rooms, that he could not help exclaiming, "But surely someone has been living in these chambers."

"We are in your own home, my dear boy," said Tantaine.

"But you took over everything, I suppose, and the original proprietor simply walked out?"

Tantaine smiled, as though an unequivocal compliment had been paid him.

"Why, do you not know your own home?" asked he; "you have been living here for the last twelve months."

"I can't understand you," answered Paul, opening his eyes in astonishment; "you must be jesting."

"I am entirely in earnest; for more than a year you have been established here. If you want a proof of the correctness of my assertion, call up the porter." He ran to the head of the staircase and called out, "Come up, Mother Brigaut."

In a few moments a stout old woman came panting into the room.

"And how are you, Mother Brigaut?" said Tantaine gaily. "I have a word or two to say to you. You know that gentleman, do you not?"

"What a question? as if I did not know one of the gentlemen lodging here?"

"What is his name?"

"M. Paul."

"What, plain M. Paul, and nothing else?"

"Well, sir, it is not his fault if he did not know his father or mother."

"What does he do?"

"He is a musician; he gives lessons on the piano, and composes music."

"Does he do a good business?"

"I can't say, sir, but I should guess about two or three hundred *francs* a month; and he makes that do, for he is economical and quiet, and as modest as a young girl."

Tantaine's face shone all over with satisfaction.

"You must have known M. Paul for some time, as you seem so thoroughly acquainted with his habits?" said he.

"Well, I ought to, for he has been here nearly fifteen months, and all that time I have looked after his room."

"Do you know where he lived before he came here?"

"Of course I do, for I went to inquire about him in the Rue Jacob. The people there were quite cut up at his leaving, but you see this was more handy for the music publisher in the Rue Richelieu, for whom he works."

"Good, Mother Brigaut; that will do; you can leave us now."

As Paul listened to this brief conversation, he wondered if he was awake or asleep. Tantaine stood at the door and watched the woman down stairs; then he closed it carefully, and coming up to Paul, said,—

"Well, what do you think of all this?"

At first Paul was so astounded that he could hardly find words in which to express himself; but he remembered the words that Dr. Hortebise had so often dinned into his ears during the last five days,—

"Let nothing astonish you."

"I suppose," said he at last, "that you had taught this old woman her lesson beforehand."

"Merciful powers!" exclaimed Tantaine in tones of extreme disgust. "If these are all the ideas you have gained from what you have heard, our task will not be by any means an easy one."

Paul was wounded by Tantaine's contemptuous manner.

"I understand well enough, sir," answered he sulkily, "that this is merely a prologue to a romantic drama."

"You are right, my lad," cried he, in a more satisfied voice; "and it is one that is quite indispensable. The plot of the drama will be revealed to you later on, and also the reward you will receive if you play your part well."

"But why cannot you tell me everything now?"

Tantaine shook his head.

"Have patience, you rash boy!" said he. "Rome was not built in a day. Be guided by me, and follow blindly the orders of those interested in you. This is your first lesson; think it over seriously."

"My first lesson! What do you mean?"

"Call it a rehearsal if you like. All that the good woman told you," continued Tantaine, "you must look upon as true; nay, it is true, and when you believe this thoroughly, you are quite prepared for the fray, but until then you must remain quiescent. Remember this, you cannot impress others unless you firmly believe yourself. The greatest impostors of all ages have ever been their own dupes."

At the word impostor, Paul seemed about to speak, but a wave of Tantaine's hand silenced him.

"You must cast aside your old skin, and enter that of another. Paul Violaine, the natural son of a woman who kept a small drapery shop at Poitiers, Paul Violaine, the youthful lover of Rose, no longer exists. He died of cold and hunger in a garret in the Hotel de Perou, as M. de Loupins will testify when necessary."

The tone in which Tantaine spoke showed his intense earnestness, and with emphatic gestures he drove each successive idea into Paul's brain.

"You will rid yourself of your former recollections as you do of an old coat, which you throw aside, and forget the very existence of. And not only that, but you must lose your memory, and that so entirely, that if anyone in the street calls out Violaine, you will never even dream of turning round."

Paul's brain seemed to tremble beneath the crime that his companion was teaching him.

"Who am I then?" asked he.

A sardonic smile crossed Tantaine's face.

"You are just what the portress told you, Paul, and nothing more. Your first recollections are of a Foundling Hospital, and you never knew your parents. You have lived here fifteen months, and before that you resided in the Rue Jacob. The portress knows no more; but if you will come with me to the Rue Jacob, the people there can tell you more about your life when you were a lodger in the house. Perhaps, if you are careful, we may take you back to your more childish days, and even find you a father."

"But," said Paul, "I might be questioned regarding my past life: what then? M. Rigal or Mademoiselle Flavia might interrogate me at any moment?"

"I see; but do not disquiet yourself. You will be furnished with all necessary papers, so that you can account for all your life during the twenty-five years you spent in this world."

"Then I presume that the person into whose shoes I have crept was a composer and a musician like myself?"

Again Tantaine's patience gave way, and it was with an oath that he exclaimed,—

"Are you acting the part of a fool, or are you one in reality? No one has ever been here except you. Did you not hear what the old woman said? She told you that you are a musician, a self-made one, and while waiting until your talents are appreciated, you give lessons in music."

"And to whom do I *give* them?"

Tantaine took three visiting cards from a china ornament on the mantelshelf.

"Here are three pupils of yours," said he, "who can pay you one hundred *francs* per month for two lessons a week, and two of them will assure you that you have taught them for some time. The third,

Madame Grandorge, a widow, will vow that she owes all her success, which is very great, to your lessons. You will go and give these pupils their lessons at the hours noted on their cards, and you will be received as if you had often been to the house before; and remember to be perfectly at your ease."

"I will do my best to follow your instructions."

"One last piece of information. In addition to your lessons, you are in the habit of copying for certain wealthy amateurs the fragments of old and almost obsolete operas, and on the piano lies the work that you are engaged on for the Marquis de Croisenois, a charming composition by Valserra. You see," continued Tantaine, taking Paul by the arm, and showing him round the room, "that nothing has been forgotten, and that you have lived here for years past. You have always been a steady young man, and have saved up a little money. In this drawer you will find eight certificates of scrip from the Bank of France."

Paul would have put many more questions, but the visitor was already on the threshold, and only paused to add these words,—

"I will call here tomorrow with Dr. Hortebise." Then, with a strange smile playing on his lips, he added, as Mascarin had before, "You will be a duke yet."

The old portress was waiting for Tantaine, and as soon as she saw him coming down the stairs immersed in deep thought, out she ran toward him with as much alacrity as her corpulency would admit.

"Did I do it all right?" asked she.

"Hush!" answered he, pushing her quickly into her lodge, the door of which stood open. "Hush! are you mad or drunk, to talk like this, when you do not know who is listening?"

"I hope you were pleased with my success," continued the woman, aghast at his sudden anger.

"You did well—very well; you piled up the evidence perfectly. I shall have an excellent report to make of you to M. Mascarin."

"I am so glad; and now my husband and I are quite safe?"

The old man shook his head with an air of doubt.

"Well, I can hardly say that yet; the master's arm is long and strong; but you have numerous enemies. All the servants in the house hate you, and would be glad to see you come to grief."

"Is that really so, sir? How can that be, for both I and my husband have been very kind to all of them?"

"Yes, perhaps you have been lately, but how about the times before? You and your husband both acted very foolishly. Article 386 cannot be got now, and two women can swear that they saw you and your husband, with a bunch of keys in your hand, on the second floor."

The fat woman's face turned a sickly yellow, she clasped her hands, and whined in tones of piteous entreaty,—

"Don't speak so loud, sir, I beg of you."

"You made a terrible mistake in not coming to my master earlier, for there had been then so much talk that the matter had reached the ears of the police."

"But for all that, if M. Mascarin pleased—"

"He does please, my good woman, and is quite willing to serve you. I am sure that he will manage to break the inquiry; or if it must go on, he has several witnesses who will depose in your favour; but, you know, he gives nothing for nothing, and must have implicit obedience."

"Good, kind man that he is, my husband and I would go through fire and water for him, while my daughter, Euphenice, would do anything in the world for him."

Tantaine recoiled uneasily, for the old woman's gratitude was so demonstrative that he feared she was about to embrace him.

"All you have to do is to stick firmly to what you have said about Paul," continued he, when he found himself at a safe distance; "and if ever you breathe a word of what you have been doing, he will hand you over to the law, and then take care of Article 386."

It was evident that this portion of the Code, that had reference to the robbery of masters by servants, struck terror into the woman's soul.

"If I stood on the scaffold," said she, "I would tell the story about M. Paul exactly as I have been taught."

Her tone was so sincere, that Tantaine addressed her in a kindlier voice.

"Stick to that," said he, "and I can say to you, 'Hope.' Upon the day on which the young man's business is settled you will get a paper from me, which will prove your complete innocence, and enable you to say, 'I have been grossly maligned.'"

"May the dear young man's business be settled sharp," said she.

"It will not be long before it is so; but, remember, in the meantime you must keep an eye upon him."

"I will do so."

"And, remember, report to me whoever comes to see him, no mat-

226

ter who it may be."

"Not a soul can go upstairs without my seeing or hearing him."

"Well, if anyone, save the master, Dr. Hortebise, or myself comes, do not lose a moment, but come and report."

"You shall know in five minutes."

"I wonder if that is all I have to say?" mused Tantaine. "Ah! I remember: note exactly the hour at which this young man comes and goes. Do not have any conversation with him; answer all questions he addresses you with a simple 'Yes,' or 'No,' and, as I said before, watch his every movement."

And Tantaine turned to go away, paying no attention to the woman's eager protestations.

"Keep a strict watch," were his last words, "and, above all, see that the lad gets into no scrape."

In Tantaine's presence Paul had endeavoured to assume an air of bravado, but as soon as he was left alone he was seized with such mortal terror, that he sank in a half fainting condition into an easy-chair. He felt that he was not going to put on a disguise for a brief period, but for life, and that now, though he rose in life, wealth, title, even a wife would all have been obtained by a shameful and skilfully planned deception, and this deception he must keep up until the day of his death. He shuddered as he recalled Tantaine's words, "Paul Violaine is dead." He recalled the incidents in the life of the escaped galley-slave Coignard, who, under the name of Pontis de St. Helene, absolutely assumed the rank of a general officer, and took command of a domain. Coignard was recognised and betrayed by an old fellow-prisoner, and this was exactly the risk that Paul knew he must run, for any of his old companions might recognise and denounce him. Had he on such an occasion sufficient presence of mind to turn laughingly to his accuser, and say, "Really, my good fellow, you are in error, for I never set eyes on you before?"

He felt that he could not do it, and had he any means of existence, he would have solved the difficulty by taking to flight. But he knew that men like Mascarin, Hortebise, and Tantaine were not easily eluded, and his heart sank within him as he remembered the various crumbs of information that each of these men had dropped before him. To agree to their sordid proposals, and to remain in the position in which he was, was certainly to incur a risk, but it was one that was a long way off, and might never eventually come to pass; while to change his mind would be as sure to bring down swift and condign punishment upon his head; and the weak young man naturally chose the more remote contingency, and with this determination the last qualms of his conscience expired.

The first night he slept badly in his new abode, for it seemed to him as if the spectre of the man whose place he was to usurp was hovering over his couch. But with the dawn of day, and especially when the hour arrived for him to go out and give his lessons, he felt his courage return to him, though rashness perhaps would be the more correct word. And with a mien of perfect confidence he repaired to the house of Mademoiselle Grandorge, the oldest of his pupils. Impelled by the same feeling of curiosity as to how Paul would comport himself, both Dr. Hortebise and Father Tantaine had been hanging about the Rue Montmartre, and taking advantage of a heavy dray that was passing, caught a good glimpse of the young man.

"Aha," chuckled Tantaine, delighted at seeing Paul look so brisk and joyous, "our young cock is in full feather; last night he was decidedly rather nervous."

"Yes," answered the doctor, "he is on the right road, and I think that we shall have no further trouble with him."

They then thought it would be as well to see Mother Brigaut, and were received by the old woman with slavish deference.

"No one has been near the dear young gentleman," said she, in reply to their questions. "Last night he came down about seven o'clock, and asked where the nearest eating-house was. I directed him to Du Val's, and he was back by eight, and by eleven I saw that he had put out his light."

"How about today?"

"I went up stairs at nine, and he had just finished dressing. He told me to get his breakfast ready, which I did. He ate well, and I said to myself, 'Good; the bird is getting used to its cage.'"

"And then?"

"Then he commenced singing like a very bird, the dear fellow. His voice is as sweet as his face; any woman would fall in love with him. I'm precious glad that my girl, Euphenice is nowhere near."

"And after that he went out?" continued Tantaine. "Did he say how long he would be away?"

"Only to give his lessons. I suppose he expected that you would call."

"Very good," remarked the old man; then, addressing Dr. Hortebise, he said, "Perhaps, sir, you are going to the Registry Office?"

228

"Yes; I want to see Mascarin."

"He is not there; but if you want to see him on any special matter, you had better come to our young friend's apartment, and await his arrival."

"Very well, I will do so," answered the doctor.

Hortebise was much more impressed than Paul with the skill of the hand which had imparted such a look of long occupation to the rooms.

"On my word, the quiet simplicity of these rooms would induce any father to give his daughter to this young fellow."

The old man's silence surprised him, and turning sharply round, he was struck by the gloomy look upon his features.

"What is the matter?" asked Hortebise, with some anxiety. "What is troubling you?"

Tantaine had thrown himself into a chair, and for a moment made no reply; then, springing to his feet, he gave the expiring embers a furious kick, and faced the doctor with folded arms.

"I see much trouble before us," said he at last.

The doctor's face grew as gloomy as that of his companion.

"Is it Perpignan who interferes?" asked he.

"No, Perpignan is only a fool; but he will do what I tell him."

"Then I really do not see—"

"Do not see," exclaimed Tantaine; "but luckily for us all, I am not so blind. Have you forgotten this marriage of De Croisenois? There lies the danger. All had gone so smoothly, every combination had been arranged, and every difficulty foreseen, and now—"

"Well, you had made too sure, that was all; and you were unprepared for the slightest check."

"Not so, but I had made no attempt to guard against the impossible."

"Of course, there are limits to all human intelligence, but pray explain yourself."

"This is it, then, doctor. The most adroit energy could never have put in our way such an obstacle as now threatens us. Have you in your experience of society ever come across a wealthy heiress who is indifferent to all the allurements of luxury, and is capable of disinterested love?"

The doctor smiled an expressive denial.

"But such an heiress does exist," said Tantaine, "and her name is Sabine de Mussidan. She loves—and whom do you think?—why a mere painter, who has crossed my path three times already. He is full, too, of energy and perseverance, and for these qualities I have never met his equal."

"What, a man without friends, money, or position, what can—"

A rapid gesture of Tantaine's checked his companion's speech.

"Unfortunately he is not without friends," remarked the genial Tantaine. "He has one friend at least; can you guess who it is? No less a personage than the man who was to have married Sabine, M. de Breulh-Faverlay."

At this unexpected news Hortebise remained silent and aghast.

"How on earth those two met I cannot imagine. It must have been Sabine that brought them together, but the facts remain the same. They are close friends anyhow. And these two men have in their interests the very woman that I had selected to push De Croisenois' suit."

"Is it possible?"

"That is my present belief. At any rate, these three had a long interview last night, and doubtless came to a decision hostile to the interests of the *marquis*."

"What do you mean?" asked Hortebise, his lips tightly compressed with anxiety. "Do you mean that they are aware of the manner by which De Croisenois hopes to succeed?"

"Look here?" answered Tantaine. "A general, on the eve of a battle, takes every precaution, but among his subordinates there are always fools, if not traitors. I had arranged a pretty little scene between Croisenois and Van Klopen, by which the viscountess would be securely trapped. Unfortunately, though the rehearsal was excellent, the representation was simply idiotic. Neither of the actors took the least trouble to enter into the spirit of his part. I had arranged a scene full of delicacy and *finesse*, and they simply made a low, coarse exhibition of it and themselves. Fools! they thought it was the easiest thing in the world to deceive a woman; and finally the *marquis*, to whom I had recommended the most perfect discretion, opened fire, and actually spoke of Sabine and his desire to press his suit. The viscountess found, with a woman's keen perceptions, that there was something arranged between Van Klopen and her visitor, and hurried off to her cousin, M. de Breulh-Faverlay for advice and assistance."

The doctor listened to this recital, pallid and trembling.

"Who told you all this?" gasped he.

"No one; I discovered it; and it was easy to do so. When we have a result, it is easy to trace it back to the cause. Yes, this is what took place."

"Why don't you say at once that the whole scheme is knocked on the head?" asked the doctor.

"Because I do not think that it is; I know that we have sustained a very severe check; but when you are playing *ecarte* and your adversary has made five points to your one, you do not necessarily throw down the cards and give up the game? Not a bit; you hold on and strive to better your luck."

The worthy Dr. Hortebise did not know whether the most to admire the perseverance or deplore the obstinacy of the old man, and exclaimed,—

"Why, this is utter madness; it is like plunging headlong into a deep pit, which you can easily see in your path."

Tantaine gave a long, low whistle.

"My friend," said he, "what in your opinion would be the best course to pursue?"

"I should say, without a moment's hesitation, turn up the whole scheme, and look out for another one, which, if less lucrative, would not be so full of danger. You had hoped to win the game, and with good reason too. Now throw aside all feelings of wounded vanity, and accept your defeat. After all, it does not matter to us who Mademoiselle de Mussidan marries. The great enterprise fortunately does not lie in this alliance. We have still the idea of the Company to which all old people must subscribe remaining to us, and we can work it up at once."

He stopped short, abashed by the look on Tantaine's face.

"It strikes me," resumed the doctor, a little mortified, "that my proposal is not utterly ridiculous, and certainly deserves some consideration."

"Perhaps so; but is it a practical one?"

"I see no reason why it should not be."

"Indeed, then, you look at the thing in a very different manner to myself. We are too far advanced, my dear doctor, to be our own masters. We must go on, and have no option to do otherwise. To beat a retreat would simply be to invite our enemies to fall upon our disorganized battalions. We must give battle; and as the first to strike has always the best chance of victory, we must strive to take the initiative."

"The idea is good, but these are mere words."

"Was the secret that we confided to De Croisenois only words?"

This thrust went home.

"Do you mean that you think he would betray us?" said he.

"Why should he not if it were to his interests to do so? Reflect, Croisenois is almost at the end of his tether. We have dangled the line of a princely fortune before his eyes. Do you think he would do nothing if we were to say, 'Excuse us, but we made a mistake; poor as you are, so you must remain, for we do not intend to help you?'"

"But is it necessary to say that at all?"

"Well, at any rate, whatever we choose to say, what limit do you think he will place upon his extortions now that he holds our secret? We have taught him his music, and he will make us do our part in the chorus, and can blackmail us as well as we can others."

"We played a foolish game," answered Dr. Hortebise moodily.

"No; we had to confide in someone. Besides, the two affairs, that of Madame de Mussidan and the Duke de Champdoce, ran so well together. They were the simultaneous emanations of my brain. I worked them up together, and together they must stand or fall."

"Then you are determined to go on?"

"Yes; more determined than ever."

The doctor had been playing with his locket for some time, and the contact of the cold metal seemed to have affected his nerves; for it was in a trembling voice that he replied,—

"I vowed long ago that we should sink or swim together." He paused, and then, with a melancholy smile upon his face, continued,— "I have no intention of breaking my oath, you see; but I repeat, that your road seems to be a most perilous one, and I will add that I consider you headstrong and self-opinionated; but for all that I will follow you, even though the path you have chosen leads to the grave. I have at this moment a something between my fingers that will save me from shame and disgrace—a little pill to be swallowed, a gasp, a little dizziness, and all is over."

Tantaine did not seem to care for the doctor's explanation.

"There, that will do," said he. "If things come to the worst, you can use the contents of your locket as much as you like, but in the meantime leave it alone, and do not keep jingling it in that distracting manner. For people of our stamp a danger well known is a comparatively slight peril, for threats furnish us with means of defence. Woe, I say, woe to the man who crosses my path, for I will hold my hand from nothing!" He stopped for a little, opened every door, and assured himself that there were no eavesdroppers, and then, in a low whisper, he said to Hortebise, "Do you not see that there is but one obstacle

232

to our success, and that is Andre? Remove him, and the whole of our machinery will work as smoothly as ever."

Hortebise winced, as if suffering from a sudden pain.

"Do you mean—?" asked he.

But Tantaine interrupted him with a low laugh, terrible to listen to.

"And why not?" said he. "Is it not better to kill than to be killed?"

Hortebise trembled from head to foot. He had no objection to extorting money by the basest threats, but he drew the line at murder.

"And suppose we were found out?" muttered he.

"Nonsense! How could we be discovered? Justice always looks for a motive; how, then could they bring it home to us? They could only find out that a young lady adored by De Breulh had thrown him over in order to marry Andre."

"Horrible!" murmured the doctor, much shocked.

"I daresay that it is horrible, and I have no wish to proceed to extremities. I only wish to speak of it as a remote possibility, and one that we may be compelled to adopt. I hate violence just as much as you do, and trust that it may not be necessary."

Just then the door opened, and Paul entered, a letter in his hand. He seemed in excellent spirits, and shook hands with both his visitors.

Tantaine smiled sarcastically as he contrasted Paul's high spirits with the state of depression in which he had left him not many hours ago.

"Things are evidently going well with you," remarked the doctor, forcing a smile.

"Yes; I cannot find any reason for complaint."

"Have you given your lesson?"

"Yes; what a delightful woman Madame Grandorge is! she has treated me so kindly."

"That is a good reason for your being so happy," remarked the doctor, with a tinge of irony in his voice.

"Ah, that is not the only reason," returned Paul.

"Shall I be indiscreet if I ask the real cause, then?"

"I am not quite sure whether I ought to speak on this matter," said he fatuously.

"What! a love adventure already?" laughed the doctor.

The vanity of Paul's nature beamed out in a smile.

"Keep your secret, my boy," said Tantaine, in louder accents.

This, of course, was enough to loosen Paul's tongue.

"Do you think, sir," said he, "that I would keep anything from you?" He opened the letter he held in his hand, continuing: "The portress handed this to me as I came in; she said it was left by a bank messenger. Can you guess where it came from? Let me tell you—it is from Mademoiselle Flavia Rigal, and leaves no room to doubt of her sentiments toward me."

"Is that a fact?"

"It is so; and whenever I choose, Mademoiselle Flavia will be only too ready to become Madame Paul."

For an instant a bright flush crimsoned old Tantaine's wrinkled face, but it faded away almost as soon as it appeared.

"Then you feel happy?" asked he, with a slight quiver in his voice.

Paul threw back his coat, and, placing his fingers in the armholes of his waistcoat, remarked carelessly,—

"Yes, of course, I am happy, as you may suppose; but the news is not particularly startling to me. On my third visit to M. Rigal's, the girl let me know that I need not sigh in vain."

Tantaine covered his face with his hands as Paul passed his fingers through his hair, and, striking what he considered an imposing attitude, read as follows:—

My Dear Paul,—

I was very naughty, and I repent of it. I could not sleep all night, for I was haunted by the look of sorrow I saw in your face when you took leave of me. Paul, I did it to try you. Can you forgive me? You might, for I suffered much more than you could have done. Someone who loves me—perhaps more than you do—has told me that when a girl shows all the depths of her heart to a man she runs the risk of his despising her. Can this be true? I hope not, Paul, for never—no, never—can I conceal my feelings; and the proof of my faith in you is that I am going now to tell you all. I am sure that if your good friend and mine, Dr. Hortebise, came to my father with a certain request from you, it would not be rejected.

Your own

Flavia.

"Did not this letter go straight to your heart?" asked Tantaine.

"Of course it did. Why, she will have a million for her wedding portion!"

On hearing these words, Tantaine started up with so threatening an aspect that Paul recoiled a step, but a warning look from the doctor restrained the old man's indignation.

"He is a perfect sham!" muttered he; "even his vices are mere pretence."

"He is our pupil, and is what we have made him," whispered Tantaine.

Meanwhile Tantaine had gone up to Paul, and, placing his hand caressingly on his shoulder, said,—

"My boy, you will never know how much you owe to Mademoiselle Flavia."

Paul could not understand the meaning of this scene. These men had done their best to pervert his morals, and to deaden the voice of his conscience, and now that he had hoped to earn their praise by an affectation of cynicism they were displeased with him. Before, however, he could ask a question, Tantaine had completely recovered his self-command.

"My dear boy," said he, "I am quite satisfied with you. I came here today expecting to find you still undecided, and I am pleased with the change."

"But, sir—" said Paul.

"On the contrary, you are firm and strong."

"Yes, he has got on so well," said the doctor, "that we should now treat him as one of ourselves, and confide more in him. Tonight, my young friend, M. Mascarin will get from Caroline Schimmel the solution of the riddle that has for so long perplexed us. Be at the office tomorrow at ten o'clock, and you shall be told everything."

Paul would have asked more questions, but Tantaine cut him short with a brief good-morning, and went off hurriedly, taking the doctor with him, and seemingly wishing to avoid a hazardous and unpleasant explanation.

"Let us get out of this," whispered he. "In another moment I should have knocked the conceited ass down. Oh, my Flavia! my poor Flavia! your weakness of today will yet cost you very dear!"

Paul remained rooted to the ground, with an expression of surprise and confusion upon every line of his face. All his pride and vanity had gone. "I wonder," muttered he, "what these disagreeable persons are saying about me? Perhaps laughing at my inexperience and ridiculing my aspirations." The idea made him grind his teeth with rage; but he was mistaken, for neither Tantaine nor the doctor mentioned his name after they had left his apartment. As they walked up the Rue Montmartre, all their ideas were turning upon how it would be easiest to checkmate Andre.

"I have not yet got sufficient information to act on," remarked Tantaine meditatively. "My present plan is to remain perfectly quiescent, and I have told Croisenois not to make a move of any kind. I have an eye and ear watching and listening when they think themselves in perfect privacy. Very soon I shall fathom their plans, and then—, but in the meantime have faith in me, and do not let the matter worry you."

On the boulevard Tantaine took leave of his friend.

"I shall very likely not see you tonight, for I have an appointment at the Grand Turk with that precious young rascal, Toto Chupin. I *must* find Caroline, for I am sure that with her lies the Champdoce secret. She is very cunning, but has a weakness for drink, and, with Satan's help, I hope to find out the special liquor which will make her open her lips freely."

Chapter 26: At the Grand Turk

Tantaine took a cab, and, promising the cabman a handsome gratuity if he would drive fast, stopped at the spot where the Rue Blanche intersects the Rue de Douai, and told the coachman to wait for him, and entered the house where the younger Gandelu had installed the fair Madame de Chantemille. It was some time before his ring at the door was answered, but at last the door was opened by a stout, red-faced girl, with an untidy cap. Upon seeing Tantaine, she uttered an exclamation of delight, for it was the cook that had been placed in Zora's employment by M. Mascarin's agency.

"Ah, Daddy Tantaine," said she, "you are as welcome as the sun in winter."

"Hush, hush," returned the old man, gazing cautiously round him.

"Don't be frightened," returned the girl. "*Madame* has gone to a place from when there is no return ticket, at least, for some time. You know the greater the value of an article the closer we keep it under lock and key."

Tantaine gathered from this that Rose had been arrested, and his astonishment appeared to be unmeasured.

"Surely you don't mean that she has gone to quod?" said he.

"It is as I tell you," answered she; "but come in, and have a glass of wine, while you hear all about it."

She led the old man into the dining-room, round the table in which a half dozen guests were seated, just concluding a late breakfast. Tantaine at once recognised four of the several guests as servants whom he knew from their having applied for situations at the office, and there were two men of a very unprepossessing exterior.

"We are having a regular spree today," observed the cook, handing a bottle to Tantaine; "but yesterday there was not much of a jollification here, for just as I was setting about getting the dinner two fellows came in and asked for my mistress, and as soon as they saw her they clapped their hands on her and said that she must come to the stone jug. When *madame* heard this she shrieked so loud as to have been heard in the next street. She would not go a foot with them, clung to the furniture and banisters, so they just took her up by the head and feet, and carried her down to a cab that was standing at the door. I seem to bring ill luck wherever I go, for this is the fourth mistress I have seen taken off in this way; but come, you are taking nothing at all."

But Tantaine had had enough, and making an excuse, retired from a debauch which he saw would continue as long as the wine held out.

"All is going well," muttered he, as he climbed into the cab; "and now for the next one."

He drove straight to the house that the elder Gandelu was building in the Champs Elysees, and putting his head out of the window, he accosted a light, active young fellow who was warning the foot passengers not to pass under the scaffolding.

"Anything new, La Cordille?" enquired the old man.

"No, nothing; but tell the master I am keeping a good watch."

From there Tantaine visited a footman in De Breulh's employment, and a woman in the service of Madame de Bois Arden. Then, paying his fare, he started on foot for Father Canon's wine shop, in the Rue St. Honore, where he met Florestan, who was as saucy and supercilious to Tantaine as he was obsequious to Mascarin. But although he paid for Florestan's dinner, all that he could extort from him was, that Sabine was terribly depressed. It was fully eight o'clock before Tantaine had got rid of Florestan, and hailing another cab, he ordered the driver to take him to the Grand Turk, in the Rue des Poissonniers.

The magnificent sign of the Grand Turk dances in the breeze, and invites such youths as Toto Chupin and his companions. The whole aspect of the exterior seemed to invite the passers-by to step in and try the good cheer provided within,—a good *table d'hote* at six p.m., coffee, tea, liquors, and a grand ball to complete the work of digestion. A long corridor leads to this earthly Eden, and the two doors at the end of it open, the one into the dining, and the other into the ball-room. A motley crew collected there for the evening meal, and on Sundays it is next to impossible to procure a seat. But the dining-room is the Grand Turk's greatest attraction, for as soon as the dessert is over the head waiter makes a sign, and dishes and tablecloths are cleared away in a moment. The dining-room becomes a *café*, and the click of dominoes gives way to the rattle of forks, while beer flows freely. This, however, is nothing, for, at a second signal, huge folding doors are thrown open, and the strains of an orchestra ring out as an invitation to the ball, to which all diners are allowed free entrance. Nothing is danced but round dances, polkas, mazurkas, and waltzes.

The German element was very strong at the Grand Turk, and if a gentleman wished to make himself agreeable to his fair partners, it was necessary for him, at any rate, to be well up in the Alsatian dialect. The master of the ceremonies had already called upon the votaries of Terpsichore to take their places for the waltz as Daddy Tantaine entered the hall. The scene was a most animated one, and the air heavy with the scent of beer and tobacco, and would have asphyxiated anyone not used to venture into such places.

It was the first time that he had ever visited the Grand Turk, and yet anyone observing would have sworn that he was one of the regular frequenters as he marched idly through the rooms, making constant pauses at the bar. But glance around him as he might, he could see neither Toto Chupin nor Caroline Schimmel.

"Have I come here for nothing," muttered he, "or is the hour too early?"

It was hard to waste time thus, but at last he sat down and ordered some beer. His eyes wandered to a large picture on the wall, representing a fat, eastern-looking man, with a white turban and loose, blue garments, seated in a crimson chair, with his feet resting upon a yellow carpet. One hand was caressing his protuberant paunch, while the other was extended toward a glass of beer. Evidently this is the Grand Turk. And finally by an odalisque, who fills his goblet with the foaming infusion of malt and hops. This odalisque is very fair and stout, and some fair Alsatian damsel has evidently sat as the model. As Tantaine was gazing upon this wondrous work of art he heard a squeaking voice just behind him.

"That is certainly that young rogue Chupin," muttered he.

He turned sharply round, and two tables off, in a dark corner, he discovered the young gentleman that he had been looking for. As he gazed on the lad, he was not surprised that he had not recognised him at first, for Toto had been strangely transmogrified, and in no degree resembled the boy who had shivered in a tattered blouse in the archway near the Servants' Registry Office. He was now gorgeous to behold. From the moment that he had got his hundred *francs* he had chalked out a new line of life for himself, and was busy pursuing it. He had found that he could make all his friends merry, and he had succeeded. He had made a selection from the most astounding wares that the Parisian tailor keeps on hand. He had sneered at young Gaston de Gandelu, and called him an ape; but he had aped the ape.

He wore a very short, light coat, a waistcoat that was hideous from its cut and brilliancy, and trousers strapped tightly under his feet. His collar was so tall and stiff, that he had the greatest difficulty in turning his head. He had gone to a barber, and his lank hair had been artistically curled. The table in front of him was covered with glasses and bottles. Two shocking looking scamps of the true barrier bully type, with loose cravats and shiny-peaked caps, were seated by him, and were evidently his guests. Tantaine's first impulse was to catch the debauched youth by the ear, but he hesitated for an instant and reflection conquered the impulse. With the utmost caution so that he might not attract Toto's attention, he crept down to him, concealing himself as best he could behind one of the pillars that supported the gallery, and by this manoeuvre found himself so close to the lad that he could catch every word he said.

Chupin was talking volubly.

"Don't you call me a swell, nor yet say that I brag," said he. "I shall always make this kind of appearance, for to work in the manner I propose, a man must pay some attention to dress."

At this his companions roared with laughter.

"All right," returned Toto. "I'm precious sharp, though you may not think so, and shall go in for all kinds of elegant accomplishments, and come out a regular masher."

"Wonders will never cease," answered one of the men. "When you go on your trip for action in the Bois among the toffs, will you take me with you?"

"Anyone can go to the Bois who has money: and just tell me who are those who make money. Why, those who have plenty of cheek and a good sound business. Well, I have learned my business from some real downy cards, who made it pay well. Why should I not do the same?"

With a sickening feeling of terror, Tantaine saw that the lad was half drunk. What could he be going to say? and how much did he know? Toto's guests evidently saw that he had taken too much; but as he seemed ready to let them into a secret, they paid great attention, and exchanged a look of intelligence. The young rogue's new clothes and his liberality all proved that he had found a means of gaining money; the only question was what the plan could be. To induce him to talk they passed the bottle rapidly and flattered him up. The younger man of the two shook his head with a smile.

"I don't believe you have any business at all," said he.

"Nor have I, if by business you mean some low handicraft. It is brain work I mean, my boy; and that's what I do."

"I don't doubt that a bit," answered the elder guest coaxingly.

"Come on! Tell us what it is," broke in the other. "You don't expect us to take your word."

"It is as easy as lying," replied Toto. "Listen a bit, and you shall have the whole bag of tricks. Suppose I saw Polyte steal a couple of pairs of boots from a trotter-case seller's stall—"

Polyte interrupted the narrator, protesting so strongly that he would not commit such an act, that Tantaine perceived at once that some such trifling act of larceny weighed heavily on his conscience.

"You needn't kick up such a row," returned Toto. "I am only just putting it as a thing that might happen. We will say you had done the trick, and that I had twigged you. Do you know what I should go? Well, I would hunt up Polyte, and say quietly, 'Halves, old man, or I will split.'"

"And I should give you a crack in the jaw," returned Polyte angrily.

Forgetting his fine dress, Toto playfully put his thumb to his nose and extended his fingers.

"You would not be such an ass," said he. "You would say to yourself, 'If I punch this chap, he will kick up no end of a row, and I shall be taken up, and perhaps sent to the mill.' No; you would be beastly civil, and would end by doing just as I wished."

"And this is what you call your business, is it?"

"Isn't it a good one—the mugs stand the racket, and the downy cards profit by it?"

"But there is no novelty in this; it is only blackmail after all."

"I never said it wasn't; but it is blackmailing perfected into a system."

As Toto made this reply he hammered on the table, calling for more drink. "But," remarked Polyte, with an air of disappointment, "you don't get chances every day, and the business is often a precious poor one. You can't always be seeing chaps prigging boots."

"Pooh! pooh!" answered Toto, "if you want to make money in this business, you must keep your eyes about you. Our customers don't come to you, but there is nothing to prevent you going to them. You can hunt until you find them."

"And where are you to hunt, if you please?"

"Ah, that's tellings."

A long silence ensued, during which Tantaine was half tempted to come forward. By doing so he would assuredly nip all explanations in the bud; but, on the other hand, he wanted to hear all the young rascal had to say. He therefore only moved a little nearer, and listened more intently.

Forgetting his curls, Toto was abstractedly passing his fingers through his hair, and reflecting with all the wisdom of a muddled brain. Finally, he came to the conclusion that he might speak, and, leaning forward, he whispered,—

"You won't peach if I tell you the dodge?"

His companions assured him that he might have every confidence in them.

"Very well; I make my money in the Champs Elysees, and sometimes get a harvest twice a day."

"But there are no shoemakers' shops there."

"You are a fool," answered Toto contemptuously. "Do you think I blackmail thieves? That wouldn't be half good enough. Honest people, or at least people who call themselves honest, are my game. These are the ones who can be made to pay up."

Tantaine shuddered; he remembered that Mascarin had made use of the same expression, and at once surmised that Toto must have had an occasional ear to the keyhole.

"But," objected Polyte, "honest people have no occasion to pay up."

Toto struck his glass so heavily on the table that it flew to shivers.

"Will you let me speak?" said he.

"Go on, go on, my boy," returned his friend.

"Well, when I'm hard up for cash, I go into the Champs Elysees, and take a seat on one of the benches. From there I keep an eye on the cabs and see who gets out of them. If a respectable woman does so, I am sure of my bird."

"Do you think you know a respectable woman when you see her?"

"I should think that I did. Well, when a respectable woman gets

241

out of a cab where she ought not to have been, she looks about her on all sides, first to the right and then to the left, settles her veil, and, as soon as she is sure that no one is watching her, sets off as if old Nick was behind her."

"Well, what do you do then?"

"Why, I take the number of the cab, and follow the lady home. Then I wait until she has had time to get to her own rooms, and go to the porter and say, 'Will you give me the name of the lady who has just come in?'"

"And do you think the porter is fool enough to do so?"

"Not a bit; I always take the precaution of having a delicate little purse in my pocket; and when the man says, as he always does, 'I don't know,' I pull out the purse, and say, 'I am sorry for that, for she dropped this as she came in, and I wanted to return it to her.' The porter at once becomes awfully civil; he gives the name and number, and up I go. The first time I content myself with finding out if she is married or single. If she is single, it is no go; but if the reverse, I go on with the job."

"Why, what do you do next?"

"Next morning I go there, and hang about until I see the husband go out. Then I go upstairs, and ask for the wife. It is ticklish work then, my lads; but I say, 'Yesterday, *madame*, I was unlucky enough to leave my pocketbook in cab number so-and-so. Now, as I saw you hail the vehicle immediately after I had left it, I have come to ask you if you saw my pocketbook.' The lady flies into a rage, denies all knowledge of the book, and threatens to have me turned out. Then, with the utmost politeness, I say, 'I see, *madame*, that there is nothing to be done but to communicate the matter to your husband.' Then she gets alarmed, and—she pays."

"And you don't see any more of her?"

"Not that day; but when the funds are low, I call and say, 'It is I again, *madame*; I am the poor young man who lost his money in such and such a cab on a certain day of the month.' And so the game goes on. A dozen such clients give a fellow a very fair income. Now, perhaps, you understand why I am always so well dressed, and always have money in my pocket. When I was shabbily attired, they offered me a five-*franc* piece, but now they come down with a flimsy."

The young wretch spoke the truth; for to many women, who in a mad moment of passion may have forgotten themselves, and been tracked to their homes by some prowling blackmailer, life has been an

242

endless journey of agony. Every knock at the door makes them start, and every footfall on the staircase causes a tremor as they think that the villain has come to betray their guilty secret.

"That is all talk," said Polyte; "such things are never done."

"They *are* done," returned Toto sulkily.

"Have you ever tried the dodge yourself, then?" sneered Polyte.

At another time Chupin would have lied, but the fumes of the drink he had taken, added to his natural self-conceit, had deprived him of all judgment.

"Well," muttered he, "if I have not done it myself exactly, I have seen others practise it often enough—on a much larger scale, it is true; but one can always do things in a more miniature fashion with perhaps a better chance of success."

"What! *you* have seen this done?"

"Of course I have."

"And had you a share in the swag?"

"To a certain extent. I have followed the cabs times without number, and have watched the goings on of these fine ladies and gentlemen; only I was working for others, like the dog that catches the hare, and never has a bit of it to eat. No, all I got was dry bread, with a kick or a cuff for dessert. I sha'n't put up with it any longer, and have made up my mind to open on my own account."

"And who has been employing you?"

A flash of sense passed through Chupin's muddled brain. He had never wished to injure Mascarin, but merely to increase his own importance by extolling the greatness of his employer.

"I worked for people who have no equal in Paris," said he proudly. "They don't mince matters either, I can tell you; and they have more money than you could count in six months. There is not a thing they cannot do if they desire; and if I were to tell you—"

He stopped short, his mouth wide open, and his eyes dilated with terror, for before him stood old Daddy Tantaine.

Tantaine's face had a most benign expression upon it, and in a most paternal voice he exclaimed,—

"And so here you are at last, my lad; and, bless me, how fine! why, you look like a real swell."

But Toto was terribly disconcerted. The mere appearance of Tantaine dissipated the fumes of liquor which had hitherto clouded the boy's brain, and by degrees he recollected all that he had said, and, becoming conscious of his folly, had a vague idea of some swift-coming retribution. Toto was a sharp lad, and he was by no means deceived by Tantaine's outward semblance of friendliness, and he almost felt as if his life depended on the promptness of his decision. The question was, had the old man heard anything of the preceding conversation?

"If the old rogue has been listening," said he to himself, "I am in a hole, and no mistake."

It was, therefore, with a simulated air of ease that he answered,—

"I was waiting for you, sir, and it was out of respect to you that I put on my very best togs."

"That was very nice of you; I ought to thank you very much. And now, will you—"

Toto's courage was coming back to him rapidly.

"Will you take a glass of beer, or a liquor of brandy, sir?" said he.

But Daddy Tantaine excused himself on the plea that he had just been drinking.

"That is all the more reason for being thirsty," remarked Toto. "My friends and I have drunk the contents of all these bottles since dinner."

Tantaine raised his shabby hat at this semi-introduction, and the two roughs bowed smoothly. They were not entirely satisfied with the appearance of the new-comer, and thought that this would be a good moment for taking leave of their host. The waltz had just concluded, and the master of the ceremonies was repeating his eternal refrain of—"Take your places, ladies and gentlemen;" and taking advantage of the noise, Toto's friends shook hands with their host and adroitly mixed with the crowd.

"Good fellows! jolly fellows;" muttered Toto, striving to catch a last glimpse of them.

Tantaine gave a low, derisive whistle. "My lad," said he, "you keep execrable company, and one day you will repent it."

"I can look after myself, sir."

"Do as you like, my lad; it is no business of mine. But, take my word for it, you will come to grief some day. I have told you that often enough."

"If the old rascal suspected anything," thought Toto, "he would not talk in this way."

Wretched Toto! he did not know that when his spirits were rising the danger was terribly near, for Tantaine was just then saying to himself,—

"Ah! this lad is much too clever—too clever by half. If I were going on with the business, and could make it worth his while, how useful he would be to me! but just now it would be most imprudent to allow him to wander about and jabber when he gets drunk."

Meanwhile Toto had called a waiter, and, flinging a ten-*franc* piece on the table, said haughtily: "Take your bill out of that." But Tantaine pushed the money back toward the lad, and, drawing another ten-*franc* piece from his pocket, gave it to the waiter.

This unexpected act of generosity put the lad in the best possible humour. "All the better for me," exclaimed he; "and now let us hunt up Caroline Schimmel."

"Is she here? I could not find her."

"Because you did not know where to look for her. She is at cards in the coffee-room. Come along, sir."

But Tantaine laid his hand upon the boy's arm.

"One moment," said he. "Did you tell the woman just what I ordered you to say?"

"I did not omit a single word."

"Tell me what you said, then."

"For five days," began the lad solemnly, "your Toto has been your Caroline's shadow. We have played cards until all sorts of hours, and I took care that she should always win. I confided to her that I had a jolly old uncle,—a man not without means, a widower, and crazy to be married again,—who had seen her and had fallen in love with her."

"Good! my lad, good! and what did she say?"

"Why, she grinned like half a dozen cats; only she is a bit artful, and I saw at once that she thought I was after her cards, but the mention of my uncle's property soon chucked her off that idea."

"Did you give my name?"

"Yes, at the end, I did. I knew that she had seen you, and so I kept it back as long as I could; but as soon as I mentioned it she looked rather confused, and cried out: 'I know him quite well.' So you see, sir, all you have now is to settle a day for the marriage. Come on; she expects you."

Toto was right. The late domestic of the Duke de Champdoce was playing cards; but as soon as she caught sight of Toto and his pretended uncle, in spite of her holding an excellent hand, she threw up her cards, and received him with the utmost civility. Toto looked on with delight. Never had he seen the old rascal (as he inwardly called him in his heart) so polite, agreeable, and talkative. It was easy to see that Caroline Schimmel was yielding to his fascinations, for she had never had such extravagant compliments whispered in her ear in so persuasive a tone. But Tantaine did not confine his attentions to wine only: he first ordered a bowl of punch, and then followed that up by a bottle of the best brandy. All the old man's lost youth seemed to have come back to him: he sang, he drank, and he danced. Toto watched them in utter surprise, as the old man whirled the clumsy figure of the woman round the room.

And he was rewarded for this tremendous exertion, for by ten o'clock she had consented, and Caroline left the Grand Turk on the arm of her future husband, having promised to take supper with him.

Next morning, when the scavengers came down from Montmartre to ply their matutinal avocations, they found the body of a woman lying on her face on the pavement. They raised her up and carried her to an hospital. She was not dead, as had been at first supposed; and when the unhappy creature came to her senses, she said that her name was Caroline Schimmel, that she had been to supper at a restaurant with her betrothed, and that from that instant she remembered nothing. At her request, the surgeon had her conveyed to her home in the Rue Mercadet.

Chapter 27: The Last Link

For some days M. Mascarin had not shown himself at the office, and Beaumarchef was terribly harassed with inquiries regarding his absent master. Mascarin, on the day after the evening on which Tantaine had met Caroline Schimmel at the Grand Turk, was carefully shut up in his private room; his face and eyes were red and inflamed, and he occasionally sipped a glass of some cooling beverage which stood before him, and his compressed lips and corrugated brow showed how deeply he was meditating. Suddenly the door opened, and Dr. Hortebise entered the room.

"Well!" exclaimed Mascarin, "have you seen the Mussidans, as I told you to do."

"Certainly," answered Hortebise briskly; "I saw the countess, and told her how pressing the holders of her letters were growing, and urged on her the necessity for immediate action. She told me that both she and her husband had determined to yield, and that Sabine, though evidently broken-hearted, would not oppose the marriage."

"Good," said Mascarin; "and now, if Croisenois only follows out the orders that I have given him, the marriage will take place without the knowledge of either De Breulh or Andre. Then we need fear them no longer. The prospectus of the new Company is ready, and can be issued almost immediately; but we meet today to discuss not that matter, but the more important one of the heir to the Champdoce title."

A timid knock at the door announced the arrival of Paul who came in hesitatingly, as if doubtful what sort of a reception he might receive; but Mascarin gave him the warmest possible welcome.

"Permit me," said he, "to offer you my congratulations on having won the affections of so estimable and wealthy a young lady as Mademoiselle Flavia. I may tell you that a friend of mine has informed me of the very flattering terms in which her father, M. Rigal, spoke of you, and I can assure you that if our mutual friend Dr. Hortebise were to go to the banker with an offer of marriage on your part, you have no cause to dread a refusal."

Paul blushed with pleasure, and as he was stammering out a few words, the door opened for the third time, and Catenac made his appearance. To cover the lateness of his arrival, he had clothed his face in smiles, and advanced with outstretched hands toward his confederates; but Mascarin's look and manner were so menacing, that he recoiled a few steps and gazed on him with an expression of the utmost wonder and surprise.

"What is the meaning of this reception?" asked he.

"Can you not guess?" returned Mascarin, his manner growing more and more threatening. "I have sounded the lowest depths of your infamy. I was sure the other day that you meant to turn traitor, but you swore to the contrary, and you—"

"On my honour—"

"It is useless. One word from Perpignan set us on the right track. Were you or were you not ignorant that the Duke de Champdoce had a certain way of recognising his son, and that was by a certain ineffaceable scar?"

"It had escaped my memory—"

The words faded from his lips, for even his great self-command failed him under Mascarin's disdainful glance.

"Let me tell you what I think of you," said the latter. "I knew that you were a coward and a traitor. Even convicts keep faith with each other, and I had not thought you so utterly infamous."

"Then why have you forced me to act contrary to my wishes?"

This reply exasperated Mascarin so much that he grasped Catenac by the throat, and shook him violently.

"I made use of you, you viper," said he, "because I had placed you in such a position that you could not harm us. And now you will serve me because I will show you that I can take everything from you—name, money, liberty, and *life*. All depends upon our success. If we fail, you fall into an abyss of the depth and horrors of which you can have no conception. I knew with whom I had to deal, and took my measures accordingly. The most crushing proofs of your crime are in the hands of a person who has precise orders how to act. When I give the signal, he moves; and when he moves, you are utterly lost."

There was something so threatening in the silence that followed this speech that Paul grew faint with apprehension.

"And," went on Mascarin, "it would be an evil day for you if anything were to happen to Hortebise, Paul, or myself; for if one of us were to die suddenly, your fate would be sealed. You cannot say that you have not been warned."

Catenac stood with his head bent upon his breast, rooted to the ground with terror. He felt that he was bound, and gagged, and fettered hand and foot. Mascarin swallowed some of the cooling draught that stood before him, and tranquilly commenced,—

"Suppose, Catenac, that I were to tell you that I know far more of the Champdoce matter than you do; for, after all, your knowledge is only derived from what the duke has told you. You think that you have hit upon the truth; you were never more mistaken in your life. I, perhaps you are unaware, have been many years engaged in this matter. Perhaps you would like to know how I first thought of the affair. Do you remember that solicitor who had an office near the Law Courts, and did a great deal of blackmail business? If you do, you must remember that he got two years' hard labour."

"Yes, I remember the man," returned Catenac in a humble voice.

"He used," continued Mascarin, "to buy up waste paper, and search through the piles he had collected for any matters that might be concealed in the heterogeneous mass. And many things he must have found. In what sensational case have not letters played a prominent part? What man is there who has not at one time or other regretted that he has had pen and ink ready to his hand? If men were wise, they would use those patent inks, which fade from the paper in a few days. I followed his example, and, among other strange discoveries, I made this one."

He took from his desk a piece of paper—ragged, dirty, and creased—and, handing it to Hortebise and Paul, said,—

"Read!"

They did so, and read the following strange word:

248

TNAFNEERTONIOMZEDNEREITIPZEYAETNECON-
NISIUSEJECARG

While underneath was written in another hand the word, *Never.*

"It was evident that I had in my hands a letter written in cipher, and I concluded that the paper contained some important secret."

Catenac listened to this narrative with an air of contempt, for he was one of those foolish men who never know when it is best for them to yield.

"I daresay you are right," answered he with a slight sneer.

"Thank you," returned Mascarin coolly. "At any rate, I was deeply interested in solving this riddle, the more as I belonged to an association which owes its being and position to its skill in penetrating the secrets of others. I shut myself up in my room, and vowed that I would not leave it until I had worked out the cipher."

Paul, Hortebise, and Catenac examined the letter curiously, but could make nothing of it.

"I can't make head or tail of it," said the doctor impatiently.

Mascarin smiled as he took back the paper, and remarked,—

"At first I was as much puzzled as you were, and more than once was tempted to throw the document into the waste-paper basket, but a secret feeling that it opened a way to all our fortunes restrained me. Of course there was the chance that I might only decipher some foolish jest, and no secret at all, but still I went on. If the commencement of the word was written in a woman's hand, the last word had evidently been added by a man. But why should a cryptogram have been used? Was it because the demand was of so dangerous and compromising a character that it was impossible to put it in plain language? If so, why was the last word not in cipher? Simply because the mere rejection of what was certainly a demand would in no manner compromise the writer.

"You will ask how it happens that demand and rejection are both on the same sheet of paper. I thought this over, and came to the conclusion that the letter had once been meant for the post, but had been sent by hand. Perhaps the writers may have occupied rooms in the same house. The woman, in the anguish of her soul, may have sent the letter by a servant to her husband, and he, transported by rage, may have hurriedly scrawled this word across it, and returned it again: 'Take this to your mistress.' Having settled this point, I attacked the cipher, and, after fourteen hours' hard work, hit upon its meaning.

"Accidentally I held the piece of paper between myself and the light, with the side on which the writing was turned from me, and read it at once. It was a cryptogram of the simplest kind, as the letters forming the words were simply reversed. I divided the letters into words, and made out this sentence: '*Grace, je suis innocente. Ayez pitie; rendez-moi notre enfant* (Mercy, I am innocent. Give me back our son).'"

Hortebise snatched up the paper and glanced at it.

"You are right," said he; "it is the art of cipher writing in its infancy."

"I had succeeded in reading it,—but how to make use of it! The mass of waste paper in which I found it had been purchased from a servant in a country house near Vendome. A friend of mine, who was accustomed to drawing plans and maps, came to my aid, and discovered some faint signs of a crest in one corner of the paper. With the aid of a powerful magnifying glass, I discovered it to be the cognizance of the ducal house of Champdoce. The light that guided me was faint and uncertain, and many another man would have given up the quest. But the thought was with me in my waking hours, and was the companion of my pillow during the dark hours of the night. Six months later I knew that it was the duchess who had addressed this missive to her husband, and why she had done so. By degrees I learned all the secret to which this scrap of paper gave me the clue; and if I have been a long while over it, it is because one link was wanting which I only discovered yesterday."

"Ah," said the doctor, "then Caroline Schimmel has spoken."

"Yes; drink was the magician that disclosed the secret that for twenty years she had guarded with unswerving fidelity."

As Mascarin uttered these words he opened a drawer, and drew from it a large pile of manuscript, which he waved over his head with an air of triumph.

"This is the greatest work that I have ever done," exclaimed he. "Listen to it, Hortebise, and you shall see how it is that I hold firmly, at the same time, both the Duke and Duchess de Champdoce, and Diana the Countess de Mussidan. Listen to me, Catenac,—you who distrusted me, and were ready to play the traitor, and tell me if I do not grasp success in my strong right hand." Then, holding out the roll of papers to Paul, he cried, "And do you, my dear boy, take this and read it carefully. Let nothing escape you, for there is not one item, however trivial it may seem to you, that has not its importance. It is the history of a great and noble house, and one in which you are more interested

250

than you may think."

Paul opened the manuscript, and, in a voice which quivered with emotion, he read the facts announced by Mascarin, which he had entitled *The Mystery of Champdoce*.

★★★★★★★

The conclusion of this exciting narrative will be found in the following chapters'

Chapter 28: A Ducal Monomaniac

The traveller who wishes to go from Poitiers to London by the shortest route will find that the simplest way is to take a seat in the stage-coach which runs to Saumur; and when you book your place, the polite clerk tells you that you must take your seat punctually at six o'clock. The next morning, therefore, the traveller has to rise from his bed at a very early hour, and make a hurried and incomplete toilet, and on arriving, flushed and panting, at the office, discover that there was no occasion for such extreme haste.

In the hotel from whence the coach starts everyone seems to be asleep, and a waiter, whose eyes are scarcely open, wanders languidly about. There is not the slightest good in losing your temper, or in pouring out a string of violent remonstrances. In a small restaurant opposite a cup of hot coffee can be procured, and it is there that the disappointed travellers congregate, to await the hour when the coach really makes a start.

At length, however, all is ready, the conductor utters a tremendous execration, the coachman cracks his whip, the horses spring forward, the wheels rattle, and the coach is off at last. Whilst the conductor smokes his pipe tranquilly, the passengers gaze out of the windows and admire the beautiful aspect of the surrounding country. On each side stretch the woods and fields of Bevron. The covers are full of game, which has increased enormously, as the owner of the property has never allowed a shot to be fired since he had the misfortune, some twenty years ago, to kill one of his dependents whilst out shooting.

On the right hand side some distance off rise the tower and battlements of the Château de Mussidan. It is two years ago since the Dowager Countess of Chevanche died, leaving all her fortune to her niece, Mademoiselle Sabine de Mussidan. She was a kind-hearted woman, rough and ready in her manner, but very popular amongst the peasantry. Farther off, on the top of some rising ground, appears an imposing structure, of an ancient style of architecture; this is the ancient residence of the Dukes de Champdoce. The left wing is a picturesque mass of ruins; the roof has fallen in, and the mullions of the windows are dotted with a thick growth of clustering ivy. Rain, storm, and sunshine have all done their work, and painted the mouldering walls with a hundred varied tints. In 1840 the inheritor of one of the noblest names of France resided here with his only son.

The name of the present proprietor was Caesar Guillaume Duepair de Champdoce. He was looked upon both by the gentry and peasantry of the country side as a most eccentric individual. He could be seen any day wandering about, dressed in the most shabby manner, and wearing a coat that was frequently in urgent need of repair, a leathern cap on his head, wooden shoes, and a stout oaken cudgel in his hand. In winter he supplemented to these an ancient sheepskin coat. He was sixty years of age, very powerfully built, and possessing enormous strength. The expression upon his face showed that his will was as strong as his thews and sinews. Beneath his shaggy eyebrows twinkled a pair of light-gray eyes, which darkened when a fit of passion overtook him, and this was no unusual occurrence.

During his military career in the army of the Conde, he had received a sabre cut across his cheek, and the *cicatrice* imparted a strange and unpleasant expression to his face. He was not a bad-hearted man, but headstrong, violent, and tyrannical to a degree. The peasants saluted him with a mixture of respect and dread as he walked to the chapel, to which he was a regular attendant on Sundays, with his son. During the Mass he made the responses in an audible voice, and at its conclusion invariably put a five-*franc* piece into the plate. This, his subscription to the newspaper, and the sum he paid for being shaved twice each week, constituted the whole of his outlay upon himself. He kept an excellent table, however; plump fowls, vegetables of all kinds, and the most delicious fruit were never absent from it.

Everything, however, that appeared upon his well-plenished board was the produce of his fields, gardens, or woods. The nobility and gentry of the neighbourhood frequently invited him to their hospitable tables, for they looked upon him as the head and chief of the nobility of the county; but he always refused their invitations, saying plainly, "No man who has the slightest respect for himself will accept hospitalities which he is not in a position to return." It was not the grinding clutch of poverty that drove the duke to this exercise of severe economy, for his income from his estates brought him in fifty thousand *francs per annum*; and it was reported that his investments brought him in as much more. As a matter of course, therefore, he was looked upon as a miser, and a victim to the sordid vice of avarice.

His past life might, in some degree, offer an explanation of this conduct. Born in 1780, the Duke de Champdoce had joined the band of emigrants which swelled the ranks of Conde's army. An implacable opposer of the Revolution, he resided, during the glorious days of the Empire, in London, where dire poverty compelled him to gain a livelihood as a fencing master at the Restoration. He came back with the Bourbons to his native land, and, by an almost miraculous chance, was put again in possession of his ancestral domains. But in his opinion he was living in a state of utter destitution as compared to the enormous revenues enjoyed by the dead-and-gone members of the Champdoce family; and what pained him more was to see rise up by the side of the old aristocracy a new race which had attached itself to commerce and entered into business transactions.

As he gazed upon the new order of things, the man whose pride of birth and position almost amounted to insanity, conceived the project to which he determined to devote the remainder of his life. He imagined that he had discovered a means by which he could restore the ancient house of Champdoce to all its former splendour and position. "I can," said he, "by living like a peasant and resorting to no unnecessary expense, treble my capital in twenty years; and if my son and my grandson will only follow my example, the race of Champdoce will again recover the proud position that it formerly held."

Faithful to this idea, he wedded, in 1820, although his heart was entirely untouched, a young girl of noble birth but utterly devoid of beauty, though possessed of a magnificent dowry. Their union was an extremely unhappy one, and many persons did not hesitate to accuse the duke of treating with harshness and severity a young girl, who, having brought her husband five hundred thousand *francs*, could not understand why she should be refused a new dress when she urgently needed it. After twelve months of inconceivable unhappiness, she gave birth to a son who was baptized Louis Norbert, and six months afterwards she sank into an untimely grave.

The duke did not seem to regret his loss very deeply. The boy appeared to be of a strong and robust constitution, and his mother's dowry would go to swell the revenues of the Champdoce family. He made his recent loss, too, the pretext for further retrenchments and economies.

Norbert was brought up exactly as a farmer's son would have been.

Every morning he started off to work, carrying his day's provisions in a basket slung upon his back. As he grew older, he was taught to sow and reap, to estimate the value of a standing crop at a glance, and, last but not least, to drive a hard bargain. For a long time the duke debated the expediency of permitting his son to be taught to read or write; and if he did so at last, it was owing to some severe remarks by the parish priest upon the day on which Norbert took the sacrament for the first time.

All went on well and smoothly until the day when Norbert, on his sixteenth birthday, accompanied his father to Poitiers for the first time.

At sixteen years of age, Louis Norbert de Champdoce looked fully twenty, and was as handsome a youth as could be seen for miles round. The sun had given a bronzed tint to his features which was exceedingly becoming. He had black hair, with a slight curl running through it, and large melancholy blue eyes, which he inherited from his mother. Poor girl! it was the sole beauty that she had possessed. He was utterly uncultured, and had been ruled with such a rod of iron by his father that he had never been a league from the *château*. His ideas were barred by the little town of Bevron, with its sixty houses, its town hall, its small chapel, and principal river; and to him it seemed a spot full of noise and confusion. In the whole course of his life he had never spoken to three persons who did not belong to the district. Bred up in this secluded manner, it was almost impossible for him to understand that anyone could lead a different existence to that of his own. His only pleasure was in procuring an abundant harvest, and his sole idea of excitement was High Mass on Sunday.

For more than a year the village girls had cast sly glances at him, but he was far too simple and innocent to notice this. When Mass was over, he generally walked over the farm with his father to inspect the work of the past week, or to set snares for the birds. His father at last determined to give him a wider experience, and one day said that he was to accompany him to Poitiers.

At a very early hour in the morning they started in one of the low country carts of the district, and under the seat were small sacks, containing over forty thousand *francs* in silver money. Norbert had long wished to visit Poitiers, but had never done so, though it was but fifteen miles off. Poitiers is a quaint old town, with dilapidated pavements and tall, gloomy houses, the architecture of which dates from the tenth century; but Norbert thought that it must be one of the most magnificent cities in the world. It was market day when they drove in, and he was absolutely stupefied with surprise and excitement. He had never believed there could be so many people in one place, and hardly noticed that the cart had pulled up opposite a lawyer's office. His father shook him roughly by the shoulder.

"Come, Norbert, lad, we are there," said he.

The young man jumped to the ground, and assisted mechanically to remove the sacks. The servile manner of the lawyer did not strike him, nor did he listen to the conversation between him and his father. Finally, the business being concluded, they took their departure, and, driving to the Market Place, put up the horse and cart at an old-fashioned, dingy inn, where they took their breakfast in the public room at a table where the wagoners were having a violent quarrel over their meal. The duke, however, had other business to transact than the investment of his money, for he wanted to find the whereabouts of a miller who was somewhat in his debt. Norbert waited for him in front of the inn, and could not help feeling rather uncomfortable at finding himself alone. All at once someone came up and touched him lightly on the shoulder. He turned round sharply, and found himself face to face with a young man, who, seeing his look of surprise, said,—

"What! have you entirely forgotten your old friend Montlouis?"

Montlouis was the son of one of the duke's farmers, and he and Norbert had often played together in past years. They had driven their cows to the meadows together, and had spent long days together fishing or searching for birds' nests. The dress now worn by Montlouis had at first prevented Norbert from recognising him, for he was attired in the uniform of the college at which his father had placed him, being desirous of making something more than a mere farmer of his son.

"What are you doing here?" asked Norbert.

"I am waiting for my father."

"So am I. Let us have a cup of coffee together."

Montlouis led his playmate into a small wine shop near at hand. He seemed a little disposed to presume upon the superior knowledge of the world which he had recently acquired.

"If there was a billiard-table here," said he, "we could pass away the time with a game, though, to be sure, it runs into money."

Norbert never had had more than a few pence in his pocket at one time, and at this remark the colour rose to his face, and he felt much humiliated.

"My father," added the young collegian, "gives me all I ask for. I am certain of getting one, if not two prizes at the next examination;

and when I have taken my degree, the Count de Mussidan has promised to make me his steward. What do you think that you will do?"

"I—I don't know," stammered Norbert.

"You will, I suppose, dig and toil in the fields, as your father has done before you. You are the son of the noblest and the richest man for miles round, and yet you are not so happy as I am."

Upon the return of the Duke de Champdoce some little time after this conversation, he did not detect any change in his son's manner; but the words spoken by Montlouis had fallen into Norbert's brain like a subtle poison, and a few careless sentences uttered by an inconsiderate lad had annihilated the education of sixteen years, and a complete change had taken place in Norbert's mind, a change which was utterly unsuspected by those around him, for his manner of bringing up had taught him to keep his own counsel.

The fixed smile on his features entirely masked the angry feelings that were working in his breast. He went through his daily tasks, which had once been a pleasure to him, with utter disgust and loathing. His eyes had been suddenly opened, and he now understood a host of things which he had never before even endeavoured to comprehend. He saw now that his proper position was among the nobles, whom he never saw except when they attended Mass at the little chapel in Bevron. The Count de Mussidan, so haughty and imposing, with his snow-white hair; the aristocratic-looking Marquis de Laurebourg, of whom the peasants stood in the greatest awe, were always courteous and even cordial in their salutations, while the noble dames smiled graciously upon him.

Proud and haughty as they were, they evidently looked upon his father and himself as their equals, in spite of the coarse garments that they wore. The realization of these facts effected a great change in Norbert. He was the equal of all these people, and yet how great a gulf separated him from them. While he and his father tramped to Mass in heavy shoes, the others drove up in their carriages with powdered footmen to open the doors. Why was this extraordinary difference? He knew enough of the value of crops and land to know that his father was as wealthy as any of these gentlemen. The labourers on the farm said that his father was a miser, and the villagers asserted that he got up at night and gazed with rapture upon the treasure that was hidden away from men's eyes.

"Norbert is an unhappy lad," they would say. "He who ought to be able to command all the pleasures of life is worse off than our own children."

He also recollected that one day, as his father was talking to the Marquis de Laurebourg, an old lady, who was doubtless the *marchioness*, had said, "Poor boy! he was so early deprived of a mother's care!" What did that mean unless it was a reflection upon the arbitrary behaviour of his father? Norbert saw that these people always had their children with them, and the sight of this filled him with jealousy, and brought tears of anguish to his eyes. Sometimes, as he trudged wearily behind his yoke of oxen, goad in hand, he would see some of these young scions of the aristocracy canter by on horseback, and the friendly wave of the hand with which they greeted him almost appeared to his jaundiced mind a premeditated insult. What could they find to do in Paris, to which they all took wing at the first breath of winter? This was a question which he found himself utterly unable to solve. To drink to intoxication offered no charms to him, and yet this was the only pleasure which the villagers seemed to enjoy. Those young men must have some higher class of entertainment, but in what could it consist? Norbert could hardly read a line without spelling every word; but these new thoughts running through his mind caused him to study, so as to improve his education. His father had often told him that he did not like lads who where always poring over books; and so Norbert did not discontinue his studies, but simply avoided bringing them under his father's notice. He knew that there was a large collection of books in one of the upstairs rooms of the *château*. He managed to force the lock of the door, and he found some thousands of volumes, of which at least two hundred were novels, which had been the solace of his mother's unhappy life. With all the eagerness of a man who is at the point of starvation and finds an unexpected store of provisions, Norbert seized upon them. At first he had great difficulty in dividing fact from fiction.

He arrived at two conclusions from perusing this heterogeneous mass of literature—one was, that he was most unhappy; and the other was, that he hated his father with a cold and determined loathing. Had he dared, he would have shown this feeling openly, but the Duke de Champdoce inspired him with an unconquerable feeling of terror. This state of affairs continued for some months, and at the end of that time the duke felt that he ought to make his son acquainted with his projects. One Sunday, after supper, he commenced this task. Norbert had never seen his father so animated as he was at this moment, when all his ancestral pride blazed in his eyes. He explained at length the acts and deeds of those heroes who had been the ornament of their house, and enumerated the influential marriages which had been made by them in the days when their very name was a power in the land. And what remained of all their power and rank, save their Parisian domicile, their old *château*, and some two hundred thousand *francs* of income?

Norbert could hardly credit what he heard; he had never believed that his father possessed such enormous wealth. "Why, it is inconceivable!" he muttered. And yet, as he looked round, he saw that the surroundings were those of a peasant's cottage. How could he endure so many discomforts and wounds to his pride? In his anger he absolutely started to his feet with the intention of reproaching his father, but his courage failed him, and he fell back into a chair, quivering with emotion.

The Duke de Champdoce was pacing up and down the room.

"Do you think it so little?" asked he angrily.

Norbert knew that not one of the neighbouring nobility who had the reputation of being wealthy possessed half this annual income, and it was with a feeling of bitter anger in his heart that he listened to the broken words which fell from his father's lips. All at once the duke halted in front of his son's chair.

"What fortune I have now," said he in a hoarse voice, "is little or nothing in times like these, when the tradesman contrives to make an almost unlimited income, and, setting up as a gentleman, imitates, not our virtues, but our vices; while the nobles, not understanding the present hour, are in poverty and want. Without money, nothing can be done. To hold his own against these mushroom fortunes, a Champdoce should possess millions. Neither you nor I, my son, will see our coffers overflowing with millions, but our descendants will reap the benefit of our toil. Our ancestors gained their name and glory by their determination; let us show that we are their worthy offspring."

As he approached the subject which had occupied his mind entirely for years, the old noble's voice quivered and shook.

"I have done my duty," said he, calming himself by a mighty effort, "and it is now your turn to do yours. You shall marry some wealthy heiress, and you shall bring up your son as I have reared and nurtured you. You will be able to leave him fifteen millions; and if he will only follow in our footsteps, he will be able to bequeath to his heir a fortune that a monarch might envy. And this shall and will come to pass, because it is my fixed determination."

The strange outburst of confidence petrified Norbert.

"The task is heavy and painful," continued the duke, "but it is one that several scores of illustrious houses have accomplished. He who wishes to revive the fallen fortunes of some mighty house must live only in the future, and have no thought but for the prosperity of his descendants. More than once I have faltered and hesitated, but I have conquered my weakness, and now only live to make the line of Champdoce the most wealthy in France. You have seen me haggle for an hour over a wretched *louis*, but it was for the reason that at a future day one of our descendants might fling it to a beggar from the window of his magnificent equipage. Next year I will take you to Paris and show you our house there. You will see in it the most wonderful tapestry, pictures by the best masters, for I have ornamented and embellished it as a lover adorns a house for a beloved mistress, and that house, Norbert, is the home that your grandchildren will dwell in."

The duke uttered these words in a tone of jubilant triumph.

"I have spoken to you thus," resumed he, after a short pause, "because you are now of an age to listen to the truth, and because I wished you to understand the rules by which you are to regulate your life. You have now arrived at years of discretion, and must do of your own free will what you have up to this time done at my bidding. This is all that I have to say. Tomorrow you will take twenty-five sacks of wheat to the miller at Bevron."

Like all tyrannical despots, the duke never contemplated for a moment the possibility of anyone disobeying his commands; yet at this very moment Norbert was registering a solemn mental oath that he would never carry out his father's wishes. His anger, which his fears had so long restrained, now burst all bounds, and it was in the broad chestnut tree avenue, behind the *château*, far from any listening ear, that he gave way to his despair. So long as he had only looked upon his father as a mere miser, he had permitted himself to indulge in hope; but now he understood him better, and saw that life-long plans, such as the duke had framed, were not to be easily overruled.

"My father is mad," said he; "yes; decidedly mad."

He had made up his mind that for the present he would yield to his despotism, but afterwards, in the future, what was he to do?

It is an easy thing to find persons to give you bad advice, and the very next day Norbert found one at Bevron in the shape of a certain man called Daumon, a bitter enemy of the duke.

Chapter 29: A Dangerous Acquaintance

Daumon was not a native of this part of the country, and no one knew from whence he came. He said that he had been an attorney's clerk, and had certainly resided for a long time in Paris. He was a little man of fifty years of age, clean shaved, and with a sharp and cunning expression of countenance. His long nose, sharp, restless eyes, and thin lips, attracted attention at first sight. His whole aspect aroused a feeling of distrust. He had come to Bevron, some fifteen years before, with all his provisions in a cotton handkerchief slung over his shoulder. He was willing to make money in any way, and he prospered and rose. He owned fields, vineyards, and a cottage, which is at the juncture of the highway to Poitiers and the cross road that leads to Bevron. His aim and object were to be seen everywhere, to know everybody, and to have a finger in every pie in the neighbourhood around. If any of the farmers or the labourers wanted small advances, they went to him, and he granted them loans at exorbitant rates of interest.

He gave most disputants counsel, and had every point of law at his fingers' ends. He could teach people how to sail as close to the wind as possible, and yet to be beyond the reach of the law. He affected to be only too anxious to ameliorate the lot of the peasant class, and yet he was drawing heavy sums from them by way of interest. He endeavoured by every means in his power to rouse their feelings of animosity against both the priesthood and the gentry. His artful way of talking, and the long black coat which he wore, had given him the nickname of the "Counsellor" in the district.

The reason why he disliked the duke was because the latter had more than once shown himself hostile to him, and had taken him before the court of justice, from which Daumon only escaped by means of bribery of suborned witnesses. He vowed that he would be revenged for this, and for five years had been watching his opportunity, and this was the man whom Norbert met when he went to deliver his corn to the miller. As he was coming back with his empty wagon, Daumon asked for a lift back as far as the cross road that led to his cottage.

"I trust, sir," said he with the most servile courtesy, "that you will excuse the liberty I take, but I am so utterly crippled with rheumatism that I can hardly walk, *marquis*." Daumon had read somewhere that the eldest son of a duke was entitled to be styled *marquis*, and it was the first time that Norbert had been thus addressed. Before this he would have laughed at the appellation, but now his wounded vanity, and his exasperation at the unhappy condition in which he found himself, tempted him to accept the title without remonstrance.

"All right, I can give you a lift," said he, and the counsellor clambered into the cart.

All the time that he was showering thanks upon Norbert for his courtesy he was watching the young man's face carefully.

"Evidently," thought the counsellor to himself, "something unusual has taken place at the Château de Champdoce. Was not the opportunity for revenge here?"

Long since he had decided that through the son he could strike the father. But he must be cautious.

"You must have been up very early, *marquis*," said he.

The young man made no reply.

"The duke," resumed Daumon, "is most fortunate in having such a son as you. I know more than one father who says to his children, 'See what an excellent example the young Marquis de Champdoce sets to you all. He is not afraid of hard work, though he is noble by birth, and should not soil his hands by labour.'"

A sudden lurch brought the counsellor's eloquence to a sudden close, but he speedily resumed again.

"I was watching you as you hefted the sacks. Heavens! what muscles! what a pair of shoulders!"

At any other moment Norbert would have gloried in such laudation, but now he felt displeased and annoyed, and vented his anger by a sharp cut at his team.

"When people say that you are as innocent as a girl," continued Daumon, "I always say that you are a sensible young fellow after all, and that if you choose to lead a regular life, it is far better than wasting your future fortune in wine, billiards, cards, or women."

"I don't know that I might not do something of the kind," returned Norbert.

"What did you say?" answered his wily companion.

"I said that if I were my own master, I would live as other young men."

The lad paused abruptly, and Daumon's eyes gleamed with joy.

"Aha," murmured he to himself; "I have the game in my own hands. I will teach his Grace to interfere with me."

Then, in a voice which could reach Norbert's ears, he continued,—

"Of course some parents are far too strict."

An impatient gesture from Norbert showed him that he had wounded him deeply.

"Yes, yes," put in the wily counsellor, "as the head grows bald, and the blood begins to stagnate, they forget,—they forget the days when all was so different. They forget the time when they were young, and when they sowed their wild oats with so lavish a hand. When your father was twenty-five, he was precious wild. Ask your father, if you do not believe me."

At this moment the wagon passed the cross road, and Norbert pulled up.

"I cannot thank you enough, *marquis*," said the counsellor as he alighted with difficulty; "but if you would condescend to come and taste my brandy, I would esteem it a great honour."

Norbert hesitated for an instant: his reasoning powers urged him to decline the offer, but he refused to listen to them, and, fastening his horses to a tree, he followed Daumon down the by-road. The cottage was an excellent one, and extremely well furnished. A woman, who acted as Daumon's housekeeper, served the refreshments. The office—for he called his room an office, just as if he was a professional man—was a strange-looking place. On one side was a desk covered with account books, and against the wall were sacks of seed. A number of books on legal matters crowded the shelves, and from the ceiling hung a quantity of dried herbs. The counsellor welcomed the heir to the dukedom of Champdoce with the greatest deference, seated him in his own capacious leathern armchair, and pressed the brandy which he had refused upon him.

"I got this brandy from a man down Arcachon way in return for a kindness that I did him; for, without boasting, I may say that I have done kindnesses for many people in my time." He raised his glass to his lips as he spoke. "It is good, is it not?" said he. "You can't get stuff with an aroma like that hereabouts."

The extreme deference of the man, coupled with the excellence of the spirit, opened Norbert's heart in a very short space of time. Up to the present the conduct of poor Norbert had been blameless, but now, without knowing anything of the counsellor's character or reputation, he poured out all the secret sorrows of his heart, while Daumon chuckled secretly, preserving all the time the imperturbable face of a physician called in to visit a patient.

"Dear me! dear me!" said he; "this is really too bad. Poor fellow!

I really pity you. Were it not for the deep respect that I have for the duke, your father, I should feel inclined to say that he was not quite in his right senses."

"Yes," continued Norbert, the tears starting to his eyes, "this is just how I am situated. My destiny has been marked out for me, and I am helpless to alter it. I had better a thousand times be lying under the cold greensward, than vegetate thus above ground."

The peculiar smile on Daumon's lips caused him to pause in his complaint.

"Perhaps," he went on, "you think that I am childish in talking thus?"

"Not at all, *marquis*, you have suffered too deeply; but forgive me if I say that you are foolish to despond so much over the future that lies before you."

"Future!" repeated Norbert angrily, "what is the use of speaking to me of the future, when I may be kept in this horrible servitude for the next thirty years? My father is still hale and hearty."

"What of that? You will be of age soon, and then you will have full right to claim your mother's fortune."

The extreme surprise displayed by Norbert at this intelligence convinced the counsellor that he was much more unsophisticated than he had supposed him to be.

"A man," continued he, "can, when he attains his majority, dispose of his inheritance as he thinks fit, and your mother's fortune will render you independent of your father."

"But I should never dare to claim it; how could I venture to do so?"

"You need not make the application personally; your solicitor would manage all that for you; but, of course, you must wait until you are of age."

"But I cannot wait until then," said Norbert; "I must at once free myself from this tyranny."

"Luckily there are ways."

"Do you really think so, Daumon?"

"Yes, and I will show you what is done every day. Nothing is more common in noble families. Would you like to be a soldier?"

"No, I do not care for that, and yet—"

"That is your last resource, *marquis*. First, then, we could lay a plaint before the court."

"A plaint?"

"Certainly. Do you suppose that our laws do not provide for such a case as a father exceeding the proper bounds of parental authority? Tell me, has the duke, your father, ever struck you?"

"Never once."

"Well, that is almost a pity. We will say that your father's property is worth two millions, and yet you derive so slight a benefit from this that you are known everywhere as the 'Young Savage of Champdoce'!"

Norbert started to his feet.

"Who dares speak of me like that?" said he furiously. "Tell me his name."

This outburst of passion did not in the smallest degree discompose Daumon.

"Your father has many enemies, *marquis*," he resumed, "for his manners are overbearing and exacting; but you have many friends, and among them all you will find none more devoted than myself, humble though my position may be. Many ladies of high rank take a great interest in you. Only a day or two ago some persons were speaking of you in the presence of Mademoiselle de Laurebourg, and she blushed crimson at your name. Do you know Mademoiselle Diana?"

Norbert coloured.

"Ah, I understand," replied Daumon. "And when you have broken the fetters that now bind you, we shall see something one of these days. And now—"

But at this moment Norbert's eyes caught a glimpse of the old-fashioned cuckoo clock that hung on the wall in one corner of the room. He started to his feet.

"Why, it is dinner-time!" said he. "What upon earth will my father say?"

"What, does he keep you in such order as that?"

But, never heeding the sarcastic question of the counsellor, Norbert had regained his cart, and was driving off at full speed.

Chapter 30: A Bold Adventure

Daumon had in no way exaggerated when he said that Norbert was spoken of as the "Young Savage of Champdoce," though no one used this appellation in an insulting form. Public opinion had changed considerably regarding the Duke de Champdoce. The first time that he had made his appearance, wearing wooden shoes and a leathern jacket, everyone had laughed, but this did not affect him at all, and in the end people began to term his dogged obstinacy indomitable perseverance. The gleam that shone from his hoarded millions imparted a brilliant lustre to his shabby garments. Why should they waste their pity upon a man who would eventually come into a gigantic fortune, and have the means of gratifying all his desires?

Mothers, with daughters especially, took a great interest in the young man, for to get a girl married to the "Young Savage of Champdoce" would be a feat to be proud of; but unluckily his father watched him with all the vigilance of a Spanish *duenna*. But there was a young girl who had long since secretly formed a design of her own, and this bold-hearted beauty was Diana de Laurebourg. It was with perfect justice that she had received the name of the "Belle of Poitiers." She was tall and very fair, with a dazzling complexion and masses of lustrous hair; but her eyes gleamed with a suppressed fire, which plainly showed the constitution of her nature. She had been brought up in a convent, and her parents, who had wished her to take the veil, had only been induced to remove her owing to her obstinate refusal to pronounce the vows, coupled with the earnest entreaties of the lady superior, who was kept in a constant state of ferment owing to the mutinous conduct of her pupil. Her father was wealthy, but all the property went over to her brother, ten years older than herself; and so Diana was portionless, with the exception of a paltry sum of forty thousand *francs*.

"My child!" said her father to her the first day of her return, "you have come back to us once more, and now all you have to do is to fascinate some gentleman who is your equal in position and who has plenty of money. If you fail in that, back you go to the convent."

"Time enough to talk about that some years hence," answered the girl with a smile; "at present I am quite contented with being at home with you."

M. de Laurebourg had commented with some severity upon the conduct of the Duke de Champdoce towards his son, but he was perfectly willing to sacrifice his daughter's heart for a suitable marriage.

"I shall gain my end," murmured the girl, "I am sure of it."

She had heard a friend of her father's speaking of Norbert and his colossal expectations.

"Why should I not marry him?" she asked of her own heart; and, with the utmost skill, she applied herself to the execution of her design; for the idea of being a duchess, with an income of two hundred thousand *francs*, was a most fascinating one. But how was she to meet

Norbert? And how bring over the money-raking duke to her side? Before, however, she could decide on any plan, she felt that she must see Norbert. He was pointed out to her one day at Mass, and she was struck by his beauty and by an ease of manner which even his shabby dress could not conceal. By the quick perception which many women possess, she dived into Norbert's inmost soul; she felt that he had suffered, and her sympathy for him brought with it the dawn of love, and by the time she had left the chapel she had registered a solemn vow that she would one day be Norbert's wife. But she did not acquaint her parents with this determination on her part, preferring to carry out her plans without any aid or advice. Mademoiselle Diana was shrewd and practical, and not likely to err from want of judgment.

The frank and open expression of her features concealed a mind of superior calibre, and one which well knew how to weigh the advantages of social rank and position. She affected a sudden sympathy with the poor, and visited them constantly, and might be frequently met in the lanes carrying soup and other comforts to them. Her father declared, with a laugh, that she ought to have been a Sister of Charity, and did not notice the fact that all Diana's pensioners resided in the vicinity of Champdoce. But it was in vain that she wandered about, continually changing the hour of her visits. The "Savage of Champdoce" was not to be seen, nor was he even a regular attendant at Mass. At last a mere trifle changed the whole current of the young man's existence; for, a week after the conversation in which the duke had laid bare his scheme to his son, he again referred to it, after their dinner, which they had partaken of at the same table with forty labourers, who had been hired to get in the harvest.

"You need not, my son," began the old gentleman, "go back with the labourers today."

"But, sir—"

"Allow me to continue, if you please. My confidential conversation with you the other night was merely a preliminary to my telling you that for the future I did not expect you to toil as hard as you had hitherto done, for I wish you to perform a duty less laborious, but more responsible; you will for the future act as farm-bailiff."

Norbert looked up suddenly into his father's face.

"For I wish you to become accustomed to independent action, so that at my death your sudden liberty may not intoxicate you."

The duke then rose from his seat, and took a highly finished gun from a cupboard.

"I have been very much pleased with you for some time past," said he, "and this is a sign of my satisfaction. The gamekeeper has brought in a thoroughly trained dog, which will also be yours. Shoot as much as you like, and, as you cannot go about without money in your pocket, take this, but be careful of it; for remember that extravagance on your part will procrastinate the day upon which our descendants will resume their proper station in the world."

The duke spoke for some time longer, but his son paid no heed to his words, and was too much astonished to accept the six five-*franc* pieces which his father tendered to him.

"I suppose," said the duke at last in angry accents, "that you will have the grace to thank me."

"You will find that I am not ungrateful," stammered Norbert, aroused by this reproach.

The duke turned away impatiently.

"What has the boy got into his head now?" muttered he.

It was owing to the advice of the priest of Bevron that the duke had acted as he had done; but this indulgence came too late, for Norbert's detestation of his tyrant was too deeply buried in his heart to be easily eradicated.

A gun was not such a wonderful present after all—a matter of a few *francs*, perhaps. Had the duke offered him the means of a better education, it would be a different matter; but as it was, he would still remain the "Young Savage of Champdoce."

However, Norbert took advantage of the permission accorded to him, and rambled daily over the estate with his gun and his dog Bruno, to which he had become very much attached. His thoughts often wandered to Daumon; but he had made inquiries, and had heard that the counsellor was a most dangerous man, who would stick at nothing; but for all that, he had made up his mind to go back to him again for further advice, though his better nature warned him of the precipice on the brink of which he was standing.

Chapter 31: A Financial Transaction

Daumon was expecting a visit from the young man, and had been waiting for him with the cool complacency of a bird-catcher, who, having arranged all his lines and snares, stands with folded arms until his feathered victims fall into his net. The line that he had displayed before the young man's eyes was the sight of liberty. Daumon had emissaries everywhere, and knew perfectly well what was going on at the Château de Champdoce, and could have repeated the exact words made use of by the duke in his last conversation with his son, and was aware of the leave of liberty that had been granted to Norbert, and was as certain as possible that this small concession would only hasten the rebellion of the young *marquis*.

He often took his evening stroll in the direction of Champdoce, and, pipe in mouth, would meditate over his schemes. Pausing on the brow of a hill that overlooked the *château*, he would shake his fist, and mutter,—

"He will come; ah, yes, he must come to me!"

And he was in the right, for, after a week spent in indecision, Norbert knocked at the door of his father's bitterest enemy. Daumon, concealed behind the window curtain, had watched his approach, and it was with the same air of deference that he had welcomed the *marquis*, as he took care to call him; but he affected to be so overcome by the honour of this visit that he could only falter out,—

"*Marquis*, I am your most humble servant."

And Norbert, who had expected a very warm greeting, was much disconcerted. For a moment he thought of going away again, but his pride would not permit him to do so, for he had said to himself that it would be an act of a fool to go away this time without having accomplished anything.

"I want to have a bit of advice from you, counsellor," said he; "for as I have but little experience in a certain matter, I should like to avail myself of your knowledge."

"You do me too much honour, *marquis*," murmured the counsellor with a low bow.

"But surely," said the young man, "you must feel that you are bound to assist me after all you told me a day or two back. You mentioned two means by which I could regain my freedom, and hinted that there was a third one. I have come to you today to ask you what it was."

Never did any man more successfully assume an air of astonishment than did Daumon at this moment.

"What," said he, "do you absolutely remember those idle words I made use of then?"

"I do most decidedly."

The villain's heart of Daumon was filled with delight, but he replied,—

"Oh, *marquis*! you must remember that we say many things that really have no special meaning, for between act and intention there is a tremendous difference. I often speak too freely, and that has more than once got me into trouble."

Norbert was no fool, in spite of his want of education, and the hot blood of his ancestors coursed freely through his veins. He now struck the butt-end of his gun heavily upon the floor.

"You treated me like a simpleton, then, it appears?" remarked he angrily.

"My dear *marquis*—"

"And imagined that you could trifle with me. You managed to learn my real feelings for your own amusement; but, take care; this may cost you more than you think."

"Ah, *marquis*, can you believe that I would act so basely?"

"What else can I think?"

Daumon paused for a moment, and then said,—

"You will be angry when you hear what I have to say, but I cannot help speaking the truth."

"I shall not be angry, and you can speak freely."

"I am but a very poor and humble man. What have I to gain by securing any note, and by encouraging you to brave your father's anger? Just think what must happen if I opposed the all-powerful Duke de Champdoce; why, I might find myself in prison in next to no time."

"And for what reason, if you please?" asked Norbert.

"Have you never studied law in the slightest degree, *marquis*? Dear me, how neglectful some parents are! You are not of age, and there is a certain article, 354 in the code, that could be so worked that a poor humble creature like me could be locked up for perhaps five years. The law deals very hardly when anyone has dealings with a minor, the more especially when the father is a man of untold wealth. If the duke should ever discover—"

"But how could he ever do so?"

Daumon made no reply, and his silence so plainly showed Norbert that the counsellor did not trust him, that he repeated the question in an angry voice.

"Your blind subservience to your father is too well known."

"You believe that I should confess everything to him?"

"You yourself told me that when his eyes were fixed on yours you could not avoid yielding to his will."

Norbert's anger gradually died away, as he replied in accents of intense bitterness,—

"I may be a savage, but I am not likely to become a traitor. If I once promised to keep a secret, no measures or tortures would tear it from me. I may fear my father, but I am a Champdoce, and fear no other mortal man. Do you understand me?"

"But, *marquis*—"

"No other mortal man," interrupted Norbert sternly, "will ever know from me that we have ever exchanged words together."

An expression passed over the features of the counsellor which cast a ray of hope upon the young man's heart.

"Upon my word," said he, "anyone would judge from my hesitation that I had some wrong motive in acting as I am doing, but I never give bad advice, and anyone will tell you the same about me, and this is the breviary by which I regulate all my actions."

As he spoke, he took a book from his desk, and waved it aloft.

Norbert looked puzzled and angry.

"What do you mean?" asked he.

"Nothing, *marquis*, nothing; have patience; your majority is not far off, and you have only a few years to wait. Remember that your father is an old man; let him carry out his plan for a few years longer, and—"

Norbert struck his fist savagely upon the table, crying out furiously. "It was not worth my coming here if this was all that you had to say;" and, whistling to Bruno, the young man prepared to quit the room.

"Ah, *marquis*! you are far too hasty," said the counsellor humbly.

Norbert paused. "Speak then," answered he roughly.

In a low, impressive voice, Daumon went on.

"Remember, *marquis*, that though I should like to see you have a better understanding with your father, yet, at the same time, I should like to work for the happiness of you both. I am like a judge in court, who endeavours to bring about a compromise between the litigants. Can you not, while affecting perfect submission, live in a manner more suited to you? There are many young men of your age in a precisely similar position."

Norbert took a step forward and began to listen earnestly.

"You have more liberty now," continued Daumon. "Pray, does your father know how you employ your time?"

"He knows that I can do nothing but shoot."

"Well, I know what I would do if I were your age."

"And what would that be?"

"First of all, I would stay at home sufficiently often not to arouse papa's suspicions, and the rest of my leisure I would spend in Poitiers, which is a very pleasant town. I could take nice rooms in which I could be my own master. At Champdoce I could keep to my peasant's clothes, but in Poitiers I would be dressed by the best tailor. I should pick up a few boon companions amongst the jolly students, and have plenty of friends, ladies as well as gentlemen. I would dance, sing, and drink, and would dip into every kind of life, so that—"

He paused for a second and then said, "There ought to be a fast horse or so in your father's stables, eh? Well then, if there are, why not take one for your own riding? Then at night, when you are supposed to be snug between the sheets, creep down to the stable, clap a bridle on the horse, and, hey, presto! you are in Poitiers. Put on the clothes suitable to the handsome young noble you are, and have a joyous carouse with your many companions; and if you do, next day, not choose to go back until the morning, the servants will only tell your father that you are out shooting."

Norbert was a thoroughly strong, honest youth, and the idea of meanness and duplicity were most repugnant to his feelings in general; and yet he listened eagerly to this proposition, for oppression had utterly changed his nature. The career of dissipation and pleasure proposed so adroitly by Daumon dazzled his imagination and his eyes began to sparkle.

"Well," asked the counsellor invidiously, "and, pray, what is there to prevent you doing all this?"

"Want of funds," returned Norbert, with a deep sigh; "I should want a great deal, and I have hardly any; if I were to ask my father for any, he would refuse me, and wonder—"

"Have you no friends who would find you such a sum as you would require until you came of age?"

"None at all;" and, overwhelmed with the sense of his utter helplessness, Norbert sank back upon a chair.

After a brief period of reflection, Daumon spoke with apparent reluctance,—

"No, *marquis*, I cannot see you so miserably unhappy without doing my best to help you. A man is a fool who puts out his hand to interfere between father and son, but I will find money to lend you what you want."

"Will you do so, counsellor?"

"Unluckily I cannot, I am only a poor fellow, but some of the neighbouring farmers entrust me with their savings for investment. Why should I not use them to make you comfortable and happy?"

Norbert was almost choked with emotion. "Can this be done?"

asked he eagerly.

"Yes, *marquis*; but you understand that you will have to pay very heavy interest on account of the risk incurred in lending money to a minor. For the law does not recognise such transactions, and I myself do not like them. If I were in your place, I would not borrow money on these terms, but wait until some friend could help me."

"I have no friends," again answered the young man.

Daumon shrugged his shoulders with the air of a man who says: "Well, I suppose I must give in, but at any rate I have done my duty." Then he began aloud, "I am perfectly aware, *marquis*, that, considering the wealth that must one day be yours, this transaction is a most paltry one."

He then went on to enumerate the conditions of the loan, and at each clause he would stop and say, "Do you understand this?"

Norbert understood him so well that at the end of the conversation, in exchange for the thousand *francs*, he handed to the counsellor the promissory notes for four thousand *francs* each, which were made payable to two farmers, who were entirely in Daumon's clutches. The young man, in addition, pledged his solemn word of honour that he would never disclose that the counsellor had anything to do with the transaction.

"Remember, *marquis*, prudence must be strictly observed. Come here to me only after the night has set in."

This was the last piece of advice that Daumon gave his client; and when he was again left alone, he perused with feelings of intense gratification, the two notes that Norbert had signed. They were entirely correct and binding, and drawn up in proper legal form. He had made up his mind to let the young man have all his savings, amounting to some forty thousand *francs*, and not to press for payment until the young man come into his fortune.

All this, however, hinged upon Norbert's silence and discretion, for, at the first inkling of the matter, the duke would scatter all the edifice to the winds; but of this happening Daumon had no fear.

As Norbert walked along, followed by his dog, he could not resist putting his hands into his pockets and fingering the tempting, crisp banknotes which lurked there, and making sure that it was a reality and not a dream. That night seemed interminable; and the next morning, with his gun on his shoulder and his dog at his heels, he walked briskly along the road to Poitiers. He had determined to follow Daumon's advice,—to have suitable rooms, and to make the acquaintance of some of the students. On his arrival at Poitiers, which he had only once before visited, Norbert felt like a half-fledged bird who knows not how to use its wings. He wandered about the streets, not knowing how to commence what he wanted. Finally, after a sojourn in the town of a very brief duration, he went to the inn where he had breakfasted with his father on his former visit, and, after an unsatisfactory meal, returned to Champdoce, as wretched as he had been joyful and hopeful at his early start in the morning. But later on he went to Daumon, who put him in communication with a friend who, for a commission, took the unsophisticated lad about, hired some furnished rooms, and finally introduced him to the best ladies in the town, while Norbert ordered clothes to the tune of five hundred *francs*. He now thought himself on the high road to the full gratification of his desires; but, alas! the reality, compared with what his imagination had pictured, appeared rank and chilling. His timidity and shyness arrested all his progress; he required an intimate friend, and where could he hit upon one?

One evening he entered the Café Castille. He found a large number of students collected there, and was a little disgusted at their turbulent gayety, and, hastily withdrawing, he spent the rest of the weary evening in his own rooms with Bruno, who, for his part, would have much preferred the open country. He had really only enjoyed the four evenings on which he had visited the Martre; but these limited hours of happiness did not make up for the web of falsehood in which he had enmeshed himself, or the daily dread of detection in which he lived.

The duke had noticed his son's absence, but his suspicions were very wide of the truth. One morning he laughed at Norbert on the continued non-success of his shooting.

"Do your best today, my boy," said he, "and try and bring home some game, for we shall have a guest to dinner."

"To dinner, here?"

"Yes," answered the duke suppressing a smile. "Yes, actually here; M. Puymandour is coming, and the dining-room must be opened and put into proper order."

"I will try and kill some game," answered Norbert to himself as he started on his errand.

This, however, was more easily resolved on than executed. At last he caught sight of an impudent rabbit near a hedge; he raised his gun and fired. A shriek of anguish followed the report, and Bruno dashed into the hedge, barking furiously.

Chapter 32: A Bad Start

Diana de Laurebourg was a strange compound; under an appearance of the most artless simplicity she concealed an iron will, and had hidden from every one of her family, and even from her most intimate friends, her firm resolve to become the Duchess of Champdoce. All her rambles in the neighbourhood had turned out of no avail; and as the weather was now very uncertain, it seemed as if her long strolls in the country roads and fields would soon come to an end. "The day must eventually come," murmured she, "when this invisible prince must make his appearance." And at last the long-expected day arrived.

It was in the middle of the month of November, and the weather was exceedingly soft and balmy for the time of year. The sky was blue, the few remaining leaves rustled on the trees, and an occasional bird whistled in the hedgerows. Diana de Laurebourg was walking slowly along the path leading to Mussidan, when all at once she heard a rustling of branches. She turned round sharply, and all the blood in her body seemed to rush suddenly to her heart, for through an opening in the hedge she caught sight of the man who for the past two months had occupied all her waking thoughts. Norbert was waiting for something with all the eagerness of a sportsman, his finger on the trigger of his gun.

Here was the opportunity for which she had waited so long, and with such ill-concealed impatience; and yet she could derive no advantage from it, for what would happen? Simply this: Norbert would bow to her, and she would reply with a slight inclination of her head, and perhaps two months might pass away before she met him again. Just as she was about to take some bold and decisive step she saw Norbert raise his gun and point it in her direction. She endeavoured to call out to him, but her voice failed her, and in another moment the report rang out, and she felt a sharp pang, like the touch of a red-hot iron upon her ankle. With a wild shriek she threw up her arms and fell upon the pathway. She did not lose her senses, for she heard a cry in response to her own, and the crashing of something forcing its way through the hedge. Then she felt a hot breath upon her face, and then something cold and wet touched her cheek. She opened her eyes languidly, and saw Bruno licking her face and hands.

At the same moment Norbert dashed through the hedge and stood before her. At once she realized the advantage of her position and closed her eyes once more. Norbert, as he hung over the seemingly unconscious form of this fair young creature, felt that his senses were deserting him, for he greatly feared that he had killed Mademoiselle de Laurebourg. His first impulse was to fly precipitately, and his second to give what aid he could to his victim. He knelt down by her, and, to his infinite relief, found that life was not extinct. He raised her beautiful head.

"Speak to me, *mademoiselle*, I entreat you," cried he.

All this time Diana was returning thanks to kind Providence for the fulfilment of her wishes. After a time she made a slight move, and Norbert uttered an exclamation of joy. Then, opening her beautiful eyes, she gazed upon the young man with the air of a person just awaking from a dream.

"It is I," faltered the distracted young man. "Norbert de Champdoce. But forgive me, and tell me if you are in pain?"

Pity came over the wounded girl. She gently drew herself away from the arm that encircled her, and said softly,—

"It is I who ought to apologize for my foolish weakness; for I am really more frightened than hurt."

Norbert felt that heaven had opened before his very eyes. "Let me go for help," exclaimed he.

"No, no; it was a mere scratch." And, raising her skirt, she displayed a foot that might have turned a steadier head than Norbert's. "See," said she, "it is there that I am in pain."

And she pointed to a spot of blood upon the delicate white stocking. At the sight of this the young man's terror increased, and he started to his feet.

"Let me run to the *château*," said he, "and in less than an hour—"

"Do nothing of the kind," interrupted the girl; "it is a mere nothing. Look, I can move my foot with ease."

"But let me entreat you—"

"Hush! we shall soon see what it is that has happened." And she inspected what she laughingly termed his terrible wound.

It was, as she had supposed, a mere nothing. One pellet had grazed the skin, another had lodged in the flesh, but it was quite on the surface.

"A surgeon must see to this," said Norbert.

"No, no." And with the point of a penknife she pulled out the little leaden shot. The young man remained still, holding his breath, as a child does when he is putting the topmost story on a house of cards. He had never heard so soft a voice, never gazed on so perfectly lovely a face. In the meantime Diana had torn up her handkerchief and bandaged the wound. "Now that is over," exclaimed she, with a light laugh, as she extended her slender fingers to Norbert, so that he might assist her to rise.

As soon as she was on her feet, she took a few steps with the prettiest limp imaginable.

"Are you in pain?" said he anxiously.

"No, I am not indeed; and by this evening I shall have forgotten all about it. But confess, *marquis*," she added, with a *coquettish* laugh, "that this is a droll way of making an acquaintance."

Norbert started at the word *marquis*, for no one but Daumon had ever addressed him thus.

"She does not despise me," thought he.

"This little incident will be a lesson to me," continued she. "Mamma always has told me to keep to the highroad; but I preferred the by-paths because of the lovely scenery."

Norbert, for the first time in his life, realized that the view was a beautiful one.

"I am this way nearly every day," pursued Diana, "though I am very wicked to disobey my mother. I go to see poor La Berven. She is dying of consumption, poor thing, and I take her a little soup and wine every now and then."

She spoke like a real Sister of Mercy, and, in Norbert's opinion, wings only were lacking to transform her into a perfect angel.

"The poor woman has three children, and their father does nothing for them, for he drinks what he earns," the young girl went on.

Berven was one of the identical men to whom Norbert had given his promissory note for four thousand *francs*, for he was one of the two men who had entrusted Daumon with their savings for investment; but the young man was not in a condition to notice this. Diana had meantime slung her basket on her arm.

"Before I leave you today," said she, "I should so much like to ask a favour of you."

"A favour of me, *mademoiselle*?"

"Yes; oblige me by saying nothing of what has occurred today to anyone; for should it come to my parents' ears, they would undoubtedly deprive me of the little liberty that they now grant me."

"*Mademoiselle*," answered Norbert, "be sure that I will never mention the terrible accident that my awkwardness has caused."

"Thank you, *marquis*," answered the girl, with a half-mocking courtesy. "Another time let me advise you, before you shoot, to look that no one is behind a hedge."

With these words she tripped away, without her tiny feet showing any signs of lameness. She had read Norbert's heart like the pages of a book, and felt that there was every chance of her winning the game. "I am sure of it now," said she; "I shall be the Duchess of Champdoce." How grateful she felt for that untimely shot! And she felt sure that Norbert had understood what she meant when she had said that she went along that path. She felt certain that the young man had not lost one word. She believed that the only opposition would come from his father. As she looked round for a moment, she saw Norbert standing fixed and motionless as the trees around him.

After Diana had departed, the unhappy lad felt as if she had taken half his life with her. Was it all a dream? He knelt down, and, after a slight search, discovered the little pellet, the cause of all the mischief; and, taking it up carefully, returned home. To his extreme surprise, he found the main gateway wide open, and from a window he heard his father's voice calling out in kindly accents,—

"Come up quickly, my boy, for our guest has arrived."

Chapter 33: The Count De Puymandour

Since the death of the Duchess of Champdoce the greater portion of the *château* had been closed, but the reception rooms were always ready to be used at a very short notice.

The dining-room was a really magnificent apartment. There were massive buffets of carved oak, black with age, ornamented with brass mountings. The shelves groaned beneath their load of goblets and salvers of the brightest silver, engraved with the haughty armorial bearings of the house of Champdoce.

Standing near one of the windows, Norbert saw a man, stout, robust, bald and red-faced, wearing a moustache and slight beard. His clothes were evidently made by a first-rate tailor, but his appearance was utterly commonplace.

"This is my son," said the duke, "the Marquis de Champdoce. *Marquis*, let me introduce you to the Count de Puymandour."

This was the first time that his father had ever addressed Norbert by his title, and he was greatly surprised. The great clock in the outer hall, which had not been going for fifteen years, now struck, and instantly a butler appeared, bearing a massive silver soup tureen, which he placed on the table, announcing solemnly that his Grace was served, and the little party at once seated themselves. A dinner in such a vast chamber would have been rather dull had it not been enlivened by the amusing tales and witty anecdotes of the Count de Puymandour, which he narrated in a jovial but rather vulgar manner, seasoned with bursts of laughter. He ate with an excellent appetite, and praised the quality of the wine, which the duke himself had chosen from the cellar, which he had filled with an immense stock for the benefit of his descendants. The duke, who was generally so silent and morose, smiled buoyantly, and appeared to enjoy the pleasantries of his guest. Was this only the duty of the host, or did his geniality conceal some hidden scheme? Norbert was utterly unable to settle this question, for though not gifted with much penetration, he had studied his father's every look as a slave studies his master, and knew exactly what annoyed and what pleased him.

The Count de Puymandour lived in a magnificent house, with his daughter Marie, about three miles from Champdoce, and he was exceedingly fond of entertaining; but the gentry, who did not for a moment decline to accept his grand dinners, did not hesitate to say that Puymandour was a thief and a rogue. Had he been convicted of larceny, he could not have been spoken of with more disdainful contempt. But he was very wealthy, and possessed at least five millions of *francs*. Of course this was an excellent reason for hating him, but the fact was, that Puymandour was a very worthy man, and had made his money by speculation in wool on the Spanish frontier.

For a long period he had lived happy and respected in his native town of Orthez, when all at once he was tempted by the thought of titular rank, and from that time his life was one long misery. He took the name of one of his estates, he bought his title in Italy, and ordered his coat-of-arms from a heraldic agent in Paris, and now his ambition was to be treated as a real nobleman. The mere fact of dining with the eccentric Duke de Champdoce, who never invited anyone to his table, was to him, as it were, a real patent of nobility.

At ten o'clock he rose and declared he must leave, and the duke escorted him the length of the avenue to the great gates opening on the main road, and Norbert, who walked a few paces in the rear, caught now and then a few words of their conversation.

"Yes," remarked Puymandour, "I will give a million down."

Then came a few words from the duke, of which Norbert could only catch the words, "thousands and millions."

He paid, however, but little attention, for his mind was many miles away. Since the unlooked-for meeting with that fair young face, he had thought of nothing else, and he mechanically shook hands with, and bade his guest "Goodnight" when his father did.

When the duke was sure that M. de Puymandour could not hear his voice, he took his son by the arm, and the bitterness of feeling which he had so long repressed burst forth in words.

"This," said he, "is a specimen of the mushroom aristocracy that has sprung up, and not a bad sample either; for though he is puffed up by ridiculous vanity, the man is shrewd and intelligent enough, and his descendants, who will have the advantages of a better education than their progenitors, will form a new class, with more wealth and as much influence as the old one."

For more than an hour the Duke de Champdoce enlarged on his favourite topic; but he might as well have been alone, for his son paid no attention to what he said, for his mind was still dwelling upon his adventures of the morning. Again that sweet, soft laugh, and that modulated voice rang in his ears. How foolish he must have seemed to her! and what a ridiculous figure he must have cut in her eyes! He had by no means omitted to engrave on the tablet of his memory the fact that Diana passed daily down the little path on her errand of bounty, and that there he had the chance of again seeing her. He fancied that he had so much to say to her; but as he found that his bashfulness would deprive him of the power of utterance, he determined to commit his sentiments to paper.

That night he composed and destroyed some fifty letters. He did not dare to say openly, "I love you," and yet that was exactly what he wanted to express, and he strove, but in vain, to find words which would veil its abruptness and yet disclose the whole strength of his feelings. At last, however, one of his efforts satisfied him. Rising early, he snatched up his gun, and whistling to Bruno, made his way to the spot where he had the day before seen Diana stretched upon the ground. But he waited in vain, and hour after hour passed away, as he paced up and down in an agony of suspense. Diana did not come. The young lady had considered her plans thoroughly and kept away. The next day he might have been again disappointed but for a lucky circumstance. Norbert was seated on the turf, awaiting with fond expectation the young girl's approach and as Diana passed the opening to the pathway Bruno scented her, and rushed forward with a joyous bark. She had then no option but to walk up to the spot where Norbert was seated. Both the young people were for the moment equally embarrassed, and Norbert stood silent, holding in his hand the letter which had caused him so much labour to indite.

"I have ventured to wait for you here, *mademoiselle*," said he in a voice which trembled with suppressed emotion, "because I was full of anxiety to know how you have been. How did you contrive to return home with your wounded foot?"

He paused, awaiting a word of encouragement, but the girl made no reply, and he continued,—

"I was tempted to call and make inquiries at your father's house, but you had forbidden me to speak of the accident, and I did not dare to disobey you."

"I thank you sincerely," faltered Diana.

"Yesterday," the young man went on, "I passed the whole day here. Are you angry with me for my stupidity? I had thought that perhaps you had noticed my anxiety, and might have deigned to—"

He stopped short, terrified at his own audacity.

"Yesterday," returned Diana with the most ingenuous air in the world, and not appearing to perceive the young man's embarrassment, "I was detained at home by my mother."

"Yes," replied he, "for the past two days your form, lying senseless and bleeding on the ground, has ever been before my eyes, for I felt as if I were a murderer. I shall always see your pale, white face, and how, when I raised up your head it rested on my arm for a moment, and all the rapture—"

"You must not talk like that, *marquis*," interrupted Diana, but she spoke in such a low tone that Norbert did not hear her and went on,—

"When I saw you yesterday my feelings so overpowered me that I could not put them into words; but as soon as you had left me, it appeared as if all grew dark around me, and throwing myself on my knees, I searched for the tiny leaden pellet that might have caused your death. I at last found it, and no treasure upon earth will ever be more prized by me."

To avoid showing the gleam of joy that flashed from her eyes, Diana was compelled to turn her head on one side.

"Forgive me, *mademoiselle*," said Norbert, in despair, as he noticed this movement; "forgive me if I have offended you. Could you but know how dreary my past life has been, you would pardon me. It seemed to me, the very moment that I saw you, I had found a woman who would feel some slight interest in me, and that for her sweet compassion I would devote my whole life to her. But now I see how mad and foolish I have been, and I am plunged into the depths 'of despair.'"

She accompanied these words with a glance sufficiently tender to restore all Norbert's courage.

"Ah, *mademoiselle*," said he; "do not trifle with me, for that would be too cruel."

She let her head droop on her bosom, and, falling upon his knees, he poured a stream of impassioned kisses upon her hands. Diana felt herself swept away by this stream of passion; she gasped, and her fingers trembled, as she found that she was trapped in the same snare that she had set for another. Her reason warned her that she must bring this dangerous interview to a conclusion.

"I am forgetting all about my poor pensioners," said she.

"Ah, if I might but accompany you!"

"And so you may, but you must walk fast."

It is quite true that great events spring from very trivial sources; and had Diana gone to visit La Besson, Norbert might have heard something concerning Daumon that would have put him on his guard; but, unfortunately, today Diana was bound on a visit to an old woman in another part of the parish.

Norbert looked on whilst this fair young creature busied herself in her work of charity, and then he silently placed two *louis* from the money he had borrowed, on the table, and left the cottage. Diana followed him, and, laying her finger upon her lips with the significant word "tomorrow," turned down the path that led to her father's house. Norbert could hardly believe his senses when he found himself again alone. Yes, this lovely girl had almost confessed her affection for him, and he was ready to pour out his life blood for her. He tore up the letter which had cost him so much trouble to compose, for he felt that he could make no use of it. He had now no anxieties regarding the future, and he thanked Providence for having caused him to meet Diana de Laurebourg. It never entered his brain that this apparently frank and open-hearted girl had materially furthered the acts of Providence. At supper that night he was so gay, and in such excellent spirits, that even his father's attention was at last attracted.

"I would lay a wager, my boy," remarked the duke, "that you have had a good day's sport."

"You would win your wager," answered the young man boldly.

His father did not pursue the subject; but as Norbert felt that he must give some colour to his assertion, he stopped the next day, and purchased some quails and a hare. He waited fully half an hour for Diana; and when she did appear, her pale face and the dark marks under her eyes showed that anxiety had caused her to pass a sleepless night.

No sooner had she parted from Norbert than she saw the risk that she was running by her imprudent conduct. She was endangering her whole future and her reputation,—all indeed that is most precious to a young girl. For an instant the thought of confiding all to her parents entered her brain; but she rejected the idea almost as soon as she had conceived it, for she felt that her father would believe that the parsimonious Duke de Champdoce would never consent to such a marriage, and that her entire liberty would be taken from her, and that she might even be sent back to the convent.

"I cannot stop now," she murmured, "and must be content to run all risks to effect an object in which I am now doubly interested."

Diana and Norbert had a long conversation together on this day in a spot which had become so dear to them both, and it was only the approach of a peasant that recalled the girl to the sense of her rash imprudence, and she insisted on going on her ostensible errand of charity. Norbert, as before, escorted her, and even went so far as to offer his arm, upon which she pressed when the road was steep or uneven.

These meetings took place daily, and after a few short minutes spent in conversation, the young lovers would set off on a ramble. More than once they were met by the villagers, and a little scandal began to arise. This was very imprudent on Diana's side; but it had been a part of her plan to permit her actions to be talked of by the tongue of scandal. Unfortunately the end of November was approaching, and the weather growing extremely cold. One morning, as Norbert arose from his couch, he found that a sharp icy blast was swaying the bare branches of the trees, and that the rain was descending in torrents. On such a day as this he knew that it was vain to expect Diana, and, with his heart full of sadness, he took up a book and sat himself down by the huge fire that blazed in the great hall.

Mademoiselle de Laurebourg had, however, gone out, but it was in a carriage, and she had driven to a cottage to see a poor woman who had broken her leg, and who had nothing but the scanty earnings of her daughter Francoise upon which to exist. As soon as Diana entered the cottage she saw that something had gone wrong.

"What is the matter?" asked she.

The poor creature, with garrulous volubility, exhibited a summons which she had just received, and said that she owed three hundred *francs*, and that as she could no longer pay the interest, she had been summoned, and that her little property would be seized, and so a finishing stroke would be put to her troubles.

"It is the counsellor," said she, "that rogue Daumon, who has done all this."

The poor woman went on to say that when she went to her creditor to implore a little delay, he had scoffingly told her to send her pretty daughter to him to plead her cause.

Mademoiselle de Laurebourg was disgusted at this narrative, and her eyes gleamed with anger.

"I will see this wicked man," said she, "and will come back to you at once."

She drove straight to the counsellor's house. Daumon was engaged in writing when the housekeeper ushered Diana into the office. He rose to his feet, and, taking off his velvet skull cap, made a profound bow, advancing at the same time a chair for his visitor's accommodation.

Though Diana knew nothing of this man, she was not so unsophisticated as Norbert, and was not imposed upon by the air of servile obsequiousness that he assumed. With a gesture of contempt, she declined the proffered seat, and this act made Daumon her bitter enemy.

"I have come," said she in the cold, disdainful words in which young girls of high birth address their inferiors,—"I have come to you from Widow Rouleau."

"Ah! you know the poor creature then?"

"Yes, and I take a great interest in her."

"You are a very kind young lady," answered the counsellor with a sinister smile.

"The poor woman is in the most terrible distress both of mind and body. She is confined to her bed with a fractured limb, and without any means of support."

"Yes, I heard of her accident."

"And yet you sent her a summons, and are ready to seize all she possesses in the world."

Daumon put on an air of sympathy.

"Poor thing!" said he. "How true it is that misfortunes never come singly!"

Diana was disgusted at the man's cool effrontery.

283

"It seems to me," answered she, "that her last trouble is of your making."

"Is it possible?"

"Why, who is it but you who are the persecutor of this poor lone creature?"

"I!" answered he in extreme astonishment; "do you really think that it is I? Ah! *mademoiselle*, why do you listen to the cruel tongues of scandal-mongers? To make a long story short, this poor woman bought barley, corn, potatoes, and three sheep from a man in the neighbourhood, who gave her credit to the extent of I daresay three hundred *francs*. Well, in time, the man asked—most naturally—for his money, and failing to get it, came to me. I urged him to wait, but he would not listen to me, and vowed that if I did not do as he wished he would go to someone else. What was I to do? He had the law on his side too. Ah!" continued he, as though speaking to himself, "if I could only see a way of getting this poor creature out of her trouble! But that cannot be done without money."

He opened a drawer and pulled out about fifty *francs*.

"This is all my worldly wealth," said he sadly. "But how foolish I am! For, of course, when poor Widow Rouleau has a wealthy young lady to take an interest in her, she must have no further fear."

"I will speak to my father on the matter," answered Diana in a voice which showed that she had but little hope of interesting him in the widow's misfortunes.

Daumon's face fell.

"You will go to the Marquis de Laurebourg?" asked he. "Now, if you would take my advice, I should say, go to some intimate friend,—to the Marquis de Champdoce, for instance. I know," he went on, "that the duke does not make his son a very handsome allowance; but the young gentleman will find no difficulty in raising whatever he may desire—as it will not be long before he is of age—without counting his marriage, which will put an enormous sum at his disposal even before that."

Diana fell in an instant into the trap the wily Daumon had laid for her.

"A marriage!" exclaimed she.

"I know very little about it; only I know that if the young man wishes to marry without his father's consent, he will have to wait at least five years."

"Five years?"

"Yes; the law requires that a young man who marries against his father's desire should be twenty-five years of age."

This last stroke was so totally unexpected, that the girl lost her head.

"Impossible!" cried she. "Are you not making a mistake?"

The counsellor gave a quiet smile of triumph.

"I am not mistaken," said he, and calmly pointed out in the code the provision to which he had alluded. As Diana read the passage to which his finger pointed, he watched her as a cat watches a mouse.

"After all, what does it matter to me?" remarked Diana, making an effort to recover herself. "I will speak about this poor woman's case to my father;" and, with her limbs bending under her, she left the room.

As Daumon returned from accompanying her to the door, the counsellor rubbed his hands.

"Things are getting decidedly warm," muttered he.

He felt that he must gain some further information, and this he could not get from Norbert. It would be also as well, he thought, to tell the sheriff to stay proceedings relative to the Widow Rouleau. By this means he might secure another interview with Mademoiselle de Laurebourg, and perhaps win the poor girl's confidence.

As Diana rode home, she abandoned herself to the grief which the intelligence that she had just heard had caused her, for the foresight of the framers of the law had rendered all her deeply laid plans of no avail.

"The Duke de Champdoce," murmured she to herself, "will never consent to his son's marriage with so scantily a dowered woman as I am; but as soon as Norbert is of age he can marry me, in spite of all his father's opposition; but, oh! 'tis a dreary time to wait."

For a moment she dared to think of the possible death of the old man; but she shuddered as she remembered how strong and healthy he was, and felt that the frail edifice of her hope had been crushed into ten thousand atoms. For all this, however, she did not lose courage. She was not one of those women who, at the first check, beat a retreat. She had not yet decided upon a fresh point of departure, but she had fully made up her mind that she would gain the victory. The first thing was to see Norbert with as little delay as possible. Just then the carriage pulled up at the widow's cottage, which she entered hastily.

"I have seen Daumon," said she. "Do not be alarmed; all matters will be arranged shortly."

Then, without listening to the thanks and blessings which the poor woman showered upon her, she said,—

"Give me a piece of paper to write on," and, standing near the casement, she wrote in pencil on a soiled scrap of paper the following words:—

"Diana would, perhaps, have been at the usual meeting place today, in spite of the weather, had she not been compelled to visit a poor woman in a contrary direction. Upon the same business, she will have to call tomorrow at the house of a man called Daumon." She folded the note and said,—

"This letter must be taken at once to M. Norbert de Champdoce. Who will carry it?"

Francoise had made a smock frock for one of the farm servants at Champdoce, and the delivery of it formed a good excuse for going up to the *château*, and she willingly undertook the errand.

The next day, in the midst of a heavy shower of rain, Norbert made his appearance at Daumon's office, saying, as a pretext for his visit, that he had exhausted his stock of money, and required a fresh supply. He too was feeling very unhappy, for he feared that this father might entertain matrimonial designs for him which would be utterly opposed to his passion for Mademoiselle de Laurebourg.

Had not the inexorable old man once said, "You will marry a woman of wealth?" But in the event of this matter being brought up, Norbert swore that he would no longer be obedient, but would resist to the last; and he calculated on receiving assistance from Daumon. He was on the point of referring to this matter, when a carriage drew up at the door of the cottage, and Mademoiselle de Laurebourg descended from it. Daumon at once saw how matters stood, and wasted no time in addressing Diana.

"The sheriff will stop proceedings," said he. "I can show you his letter to that effect."

He turned away, and searched as diligently for the letter as if it had existed anywhere except in his own imagination.

"Dear me," said he at length. "I cannot find it. I must have left it in the other room. I have so much to do, that really there are times when I forget everything. I must find it, however. Excuse me, I will be back immediately."

His sudden departure from the room had been a mere matter of calculation; for, guessing that an assignation had been planned, he thought that he might know what took place at it by a little eavesdropping. He therefore applied first his ear and then his eye to the keyhole, and by these means acquired all the information he desired.

A moment of privacy with the object of his affections seemed to Norbert an inestimable boon. When Diana had first entered, he was horrified at the terrible alteration that had taken place in the expression of her face. He seized her hand, which she made no effort to withdraw, and gazed fixedly into her eyes.

"Tell me," murmured he in accents of love and tenderness, "what it is that has gone wrong."

Diana sighed, then a tear coursed slowly down her cheek. Norbert was in the deepest despair at these signs of grief.

"Great heavens!" cried he. "Will you not trust me? Am not I your truest and most devoted friend?"

At first she refused to answer him, but at length she yielded to his entreaties, and confessed that the evening before her father had informed her that a young man had sought her hand in marriage, and one who was a perfectly eligible suitor.

Norbert listened to this avowal, trembling from head to foot, with a sudden access of jealousy.

"And did you make no objections?" asked he.

"How could I?" retorted she. "What can a girl do in opposition to the will of all her family, when she has to choose between the alternative that she loathes, or a life-long seclusion in a convent?"

Daumon shook with laughter, as he kept his ear closely to the keyhole.

"Good business," muttered he. "Not so bad. Here's a little girl from a convent. She has a clever brain and a glib tongue, and under my tuition would be a perfect wonder. If this country booby does not make an open declaration at once, I wonder what her next move will be?"

"And you hesitated," said Norbert reproachfully. "Remember you may escape from the walls of the convent, but not from the bonds of an ill-assorted marriage."

Diana, who looked more beautiful than ever in her despair, wrung her hands.

"What reason can I give to my father for declining this offer?" said she. "Everyone knows that I am almost portionless, and that I am sacrificed to my brother, immolated upon the altar erected before the cruel idol of family pride; and how dare I refuse a suitable offer when one is made for my hand?"

"Have you forgotten me?" cried Norbert. "Have you no love for me?

"Ah, my poor friend, you are no more free than I am."

"Then you look on me as a mere weak boy?" asked he, biting his lips. "Your father is very powerful," answered she in tones of the deepest resignation; "his determination is inflexible, and his will inexorable. You are completely in his power."

"What do I care for my father?" cried the young man fiercely. "Am not I a Champdoce too? Woe be to anyone, father or stranger, who comes between me and the woman I love devotedly; for I do love you, Diana, and no mortal man shall take you from me."

He clasped Diana to his breast, and pressed a loving kiss upon her lips. "Aha," muttered Daumon, who had lost nothing from his post of espial, "this is worth fifty thousand *francs* at least to me."

For a moment Diana remained clasped in her lover's embrace, and then, with a faint cry, released herself from him. She then felt that she loved him, and his kiss and caresses sent a thrill like liquid fire through her veins. She was half pleased and half terrified. She feared him, but she feared herself more.

"What, Diana! Would you refuse me?" asked he, after a moment's pause. "Do you refuse me, when I implore you to be my wife, and to share my name with me? Will you not be the Duchess of Champdoce?"

Diana only replied with a glance; but if her eyes spoke plainly, that look said "Yes."

"Why, then," returned Norbert, "should we alarm ourselves with empty phantoms? Do you not trust me? My father may certainly oppose my plans, but before long I shall escape from his tyrannical sway, for I shall be of age."

"Ah, Norbert," returned she sadly, "you are feeding upon vain hopes. You must be twenty-five years of age before you can marry and give the shelter of your name to the woman whom you have chosen for your wife."

This was exactly the explanation for which Daumon had been waiting.

"Good again, my young lady," cried he. "And so this is why she came here. There is some credit in giving a lesson to so apt a pupil."

"It is impossible," cried Norbert, violently agitated; "such an iniquitous thing cannot be."

"You are mistaken," answered Diana calmly. "Unfortunately I am telling you exactly how matters stand. The law clearly fixes the age at twenty-five. During all this time will you remember that a broken-hearted girl—"

"Why talk to me of law? When I am of age, I shall have plenty of money," broke in Norbert; "and do you think that I will tamely submit to my father's oppression? No, I will wrest his consent from him."

During this conversation the counsellor was carefully removing the dust from the knees of his trousers.

"I will pop in suddenly," thought he, "and catch a word or two which will do away with the necessity of all lengthy explanations."

He suited the action to the word, and appeared suddenly before the lovers. He was not at all disconcerted at the effect his entrance produced upon them, and remarked placidly, "I could not find the sheriff's letter, but I assure you that Widow Rouleau's matter shall be speedily and satisfactorily arranged."

Diana and Norbert exchanged glances of annoyance at finding their secret at the mercy of such a man. This evident distrust appeared to wound Daumon deeply.

"You have a perfect right," remarked he dejectedly, "to say, 'Mind your own business;' but the fact is, that I hate all kinds of injustice so much that I always take the side of the weakest, and so, when I come in and find you deploring your troubles, I say to myself, 'Doubtless here are two young people made for each other.'"

"You forget yourself," broke in Diana haughtily.

"I beg your pardon," stammered Daumon. "I am but a poor peasant, and sometimes I speak out too plainly. I meant no harm, and I only hope that you will forgive me."

Daumon looked at Diana; and as she made no reply, he went on: "'Well,' says I to myself, 'here are two young folks that have fallen in love, and have every right to do so, and yet they are kept apart by unreasonable and cruel-minded parents. They are young and know nothing of the law, and without help they would most certainly get into a muddle. Now, suppose I take their matter in hand, knowing the law thoroughly as I do, and being up to its weak as well as its strong points.'"

He spoke on in this strain for some minutes, and did not notice that they had withdrawn a little apart, and were whispering to each other.

"Why should we not trust him?" asked Norbert. "He has plenty of experience."

"He would betray us; he would do anything for money."

"That is all the better for us then; for if we promise him a handsome sum, he will not say a word of what has passed today."

"Do as you think best, Norbert."

Having thus gained Diana's assent, the young man turned to Daumon. "I put every faith in you, and so does Mademoiselle de Laurebourg. You know our exact situation. What do you advise?"

"Wait and hope," answered the counsellor. "The slightest step taken before you are of age will be fatal to your prospects, but the day you are twenty-one I will undertake to show you several methods of bringing the duke on his knees."

Nothing could make this speech more explicit; but he was so cheerful and confident, that when Diana left the office, she felt a fountain of fresh hope well up in her heart.

This was nearly their last interview that year, for the winter came on rapidly and with increased severity, so that it was impossible for the lovers to meet out of doors, and the fear of spying eyes prevented them from taking advantage of Daumon's hospitality. Each day, however, the widow's daughter, Francoise, carried a letter to Laurebourg, and brought back a reply to Champdoce. The inhabitants of the various country houses had fled to more genial climates, and only the Marquis de Laurebourg, who was an inveterate sportsman, still lingered; but at the first heavy fall of snow he too determined to take refuge in the magnificent house that he owned in the town of Poitiers. Norbert had foreseen this, and had taken his measures accordingly.

Two or three times in the week he mounted his horse and rode to the town. After changing his dress, he made haste to a certain garden wall in which there was a small door. At an agreed hour this door would gently open, and as Norbert slipped through he would find Diana ready to welcome him, looking more bewitching than ever. This great passion, which now enthralled his whole life, and the certainty that his love was returned, had done away with a great deal of his bashfulness and timidity. He had resumed his acquaintanceship with Montlouis, and had often been with him to the Café Castille. Montlouis was only for a short time at Poitiers, for as soon as spring began he was to join the young Count de Mussidan, who had promised to find some employment for him. The approaching departure was not at all to Montlouis' taste, as he was madly in love with a young girl who resided in the town. He told all to Norbert; and as confidence begets confidence, he more than once accompanied the young *marquis* to the door in the garden wall of the Count de Laurebourg's town house.

April came at last. The gentry returned to their country houses, and in time the happy day arrived when Diana de Laurebourg was to return to her father's country mansion. The lovers had now every opportunity to meet, and would exhort each other to have patience, and a week after Diana's return they spent a long day together in the woods. After this delicious day, Norbert, happy and light-hearted, returned to his father's house.

"*Marquis*," said the duke, plunging at once into the topic nearest his heart, "I have found a wife for you, and in two months you will marry her."

Chapter 34: An Unlucky Blow

The falling of a thunderbolt at his feet would have startled Norbert less than these words did. The duke took, or affected to take, no notice of his son's extreme agitation, and in a careless manner he continued,—

"I suppose, my son, that it is hardly necessary for me to tell you the young lady's name. Mademoiselle Marie de Puymandour cannot fail to please you. She is excessively pretty, tall, dark, and with a fine figure. You saw her at Mass one day. What do you think of her?"

"Think!" stammered Norbert. "Really I—"

"Pshaw," replied the old gentleman; "I thought that you had begun to use your eyes. And look here, *marquis*, you must adopt a different style of dress. You can go over with me to Poitiers tomorrow, and one of the tailors there will make you some clothes suitable to your rank, for I don't suppose that you wish to alarm your future wife by the uncouthness of your appearance."

"But, father—"

"Wait a moment, if you please. I shall have a suite of apartments reserved for you and your bride, and you can pass your honeymoon here. Take care you do not prolong it for too lengthened a period; and when it is all over, we can break the young woman into all our ways."

"But," interrupted Norbert hastily, "suppose I do not fancy this young lady?"

"Well, what then?"

"Suppose I should beg you to save me from a marriage which will render me most unhappy?"

The duke shrugged his shoulders. "Why this is mere childishness," said he. "The marriage is a most suitable one, and it is my desire that it should take place."

"But, father," again commenced Norbert.

"What! Are you opposing my will?" asked his father angrily. "Pray, do you hesitate?"

"No," answered his son coldly, "I do not hesitate."

"Very good, then. A man of no position can consult the dictates of his heart when he takes a wife, but with a nobleman of rank and station it is certainly a different matter, for with the latter, marriage should be looked upon as a mere business transaction. I have made excellent arrangements. Let me repeat to you the conditions. The count will give two-thirds of his fortune, which is estimated at five millions—just think of that!—and when we get that, we shall be able to screw and save with better heart. Think of the restoration of our house, and the colossal fortune that our descendants will one day inherit, and realize all the beauties of a life of self-denial."

While the duke was uttering this string of incoherent sentences, he was pacing up and down the room, and now he halted immediately in front of his son. "You understand," said he; "tomorrow you will go to Poitiers, and on Sunday we will dine at the house of your future father-in-law."

In this fearful crisis Norbert did not know what to say or how to act.

"Father," he once more commenced, "I have no wish to go to Poitiers tomorrow."

"What are you saying? What in heaven's name do you mean?"

"I mean that as I shall never love Mademoiselle de Puymandour, she will never be my wife."

The duke had never foreseen the chance of rebellion on the part of his son, and he could not bring his mind to receive such an unlooked-for event.

"You are mad," said he at last, "and do not know what you are saying."

"I know very well."

"Think of what you are doing."

"I have reflected."

The duke was making a violent effort to compose his ordinarily violent temper.

"Do you imagine," answered he disdainfully, "that I shall be satisfied with an answer of this kind? I hope that you will submit to my wishes, for I think that, as the head of the family, I have conceived a splendid plan for its future aggrandizement; and do you think that, for the mere whim of a boy, I will be turned aside from my fixed determination?"

"No, father," answered Norbert, "it is no boyish whim that makes me oppose your wishes. Tell me, have I not ever been a dutiful son to you? Have I ever refused to do what I was ordered? No; I have obeyed you implicitly. I am the son of the wealthiest man in Poitiers, and I have lived like a labourer's child. Whatever your mandates were, I have never complained or murmured at them."

"Well, and now I order you to marry Mademoiselle de Puymandour."

"Anything but that; I do not love her, and I shall never do so. Do you wish my whole life to be blighted? I entreat you to spare me this sacrifice!"

"My orders are given, and you must comply with them."

"No," answered Norbert quietly, "I will not comply with them."

A purple flush passed across the duke's face, then it faded away, leaving every feature of a livid whiteness.

"Great heavens!" said he in a voice before which Norbert, at one time, would have quailed. "Whence comes the audacity that makes you venture to dispute my orders?"

"From the feeling that I am acting rightly."

"How long is it that it has been right for children to disobey their parents' commands?"

"Ever since parents began to issue unjust commands."

This speech put the finishing stroke to the duke's rage. He made a step across the room, towards his son, raising the stick that he usually carried high in the air. For a moment he stood thus, and then, casting it aside, he exclaimed,—

"No, I cannot strike a Champdoce."

Perhaps it was Norbert's intrepid attitude that restrained the duke's frenzy, for he had not moved a muscle, but stood still, with his arms folded, and his head thrown haughtily back.

"No, this is an act of disobedience that I will not put up with," exclaimed the old man in a voice of thunder, and, springing upon his son, he grasped him by the collar and dragged him up to a room on the second floor, and thrust him violently through the doorway.

"You have twenty-four hours in which to reflect whether you will be willing to accept the wife that I have chosen for you," said he.

"I have already decided on that point," answered Norbert quietly.

The duke made no reply, but slammed the door, which was of massive oak, and secured by a lock of enormous proportions.

Norbert gazed round; the only other exit from the room was by means of a window some forty feet from the ground. The young man, however, imagined that someone would surely come to make up his bed for the night; that would give him two sheets; these he could knot together and thus secure a means of escape. He might not be able to see Diana at once, but he could easily send her a message by Daumon, warning her of what had taken place. Having arranged his plans, he threw himself into an armchair with a more easy mind than he had experienced for many months past. The decisive step had been taken, and the relations between his father and himself clearly defined, and thus he naturally considered great progress had been made, and the task before him seemed as nothing to what he had already performed.

"My father," thought he, "must be half mad with passion."

And Norbert was not wrong in his opinion. When the duke, as usual, took his place at the table, at which the farm labourers ate their meals, not one of them had the courage to make a single observation. Everyone knew what a serious altercation had taken place between father and son, and each one was devoured by the pangs of ungratified curiosity.

As soon as the meal was concluded, the duke called an old and trustworthy servant, who had been in his employment for over thirty years.

"Jean," said he, "your young master is locked in the yellow room. Here is the key. Take him something to eat."

"Very good, your Grace."

"Wait a little. You will spend the night in his room and keep a strict watch upon him. He may design to make his escape. If he attempts it, restrain him, if necessary, by physical force. Should he prove too strong for you, call to me; I shall be near, and will come to your aid."

This unexpected precaution upon the duke's part upset all Norbert's plans of escape. He endeavoured to persuade Jean to allow him to go out for a couple of hours, giving his word of honour that he would return at the expiration of that time. Prayers and menaces, however, had no effect. Had the young man gazed from the window, he would have seen his father striding moodily up and down the courtyard, with the thought gnawing at his heart that perhaps after all these many years of waiting his plans might yet be frustrated.

"There is a woman at the bottom of all this," said he to himself. "It is only woman's wiles that in this brief space of time would effect so complete a change in a young man's disposition. Besides, he would not have so obstinately declined to listen to the proposal I made him had not his affections been engaged elsewhere. Who can she be? and by what means shall I find her out?"

It would be absurd to question Norbert, and the duke was excessively unwilling to institute any regular inquiry into the matter. He passed the whole night in gloomy indecision, but towards morning an inspiration came to him which he looked upon as a special interposition of Providence.

"Bruno," he exclaimed with a mighty oath. "The dog will show me the place that his master frequents and perhaps lead me to the very woman who had bewitched him."

The brilliant idea soothed him a great deal, and at one o'clock he took his seat as usual at the head of the table, and ordered food to be taken up to Norbert, but that none of the measures for his safe custody were to be relaxed.

When he thought the moment was a favourable one, he whistled to Bruno, and, though the dog rarely followed him, yet in the absence of his master, he condescended to accompany the duke down the avenue to the front gates. Three roads branched off from here, but the dog did not hesitate for a moment, and took the one to the left, like an animal who knew his destination perfectly well. Bruno went ahead for nearly half an hour, until he reached the exact spot where Diana had met with her accident. He made a cast round, but finding nothing, sat down, clearly saying,—

"Let us wait."

"This, then," muttered the duke, "is the place where the lovers have been in the habit of meeting each other."

The place was a very lonely one, and, standing on the rising ground, commanded a view of the country for a long way round.

The duke noticed this, and took up a position where the trunk of a giant oak almost concealed him from observation. He was delighted at his sagacity, and was almost in a good humour; for now that he had reflected, the danger did not seem by any means so great, for to whom could Norbert have lost his heart? To some little peasant girl, perhaps, who, thinking that the lad was an easy dupe, had tried to induce him to marry her. As these thoughts passed through the duke's brain, Bruno gave a joyous bark.

"Here she is," muttered he, as he emerged from his hiding place, and at that moment Diana de Laurebourg made her appearance; but as soon as she saw the duke she uttered a faint cry of alarm. She was inclined to turn and fly, but her strength failed her, and, extending her hands, she grasped the boughs of a slender birch tree that grew close by, to prevent herself from falling. The duke was quite as much astonished as the young lady. He had expected to see a peasant girl, and here was the daughter of the Marquis de Laurebourg. But anger soon succeeded to surprise; for though he might have had nothing to fear from the peasant, the daughter of the Marquis de Laurebourg was an utterly different antagonist. He could not rely upon aid from her family, as, for all he knew, they might be aiding and abetting her.

"Well, my child," began he, "you do not seem very glad to see me."

"Your Grace."

"Yes, when you come out to meet the son, it is annoying to meet the father; but do not blame poor Norbert, for I assure you he is not in fault."

Though Mademoiselle de Laurebourg had been startled at first, she was possessed of too strong a will to give in, and soon recovered her self-possession.

She never thought to screen herself by a denial of her reasons for being on the spot, for such a course she would have looked on as an act of treacherous cowardice.

"You are quite right," answered she. "I came here to meet your son, and therefore you will pardon me if I take my leave of you."

With a deep courtesy she was about to move away, when the duke laid a restraining grip upon her arm.

"Permit me, my child," said he, endeavouring to put on a kind and paternal tone,—"let me say a few words to you. Do you know why Norbert did not come to meet you?"

"He has doubtless some very good reason."

"My son is locked up in a room, and my servants have my orders to prevent his making his escape by force, if necessary."

"Poor fellow! He deserves the deepest commiseration."

The duke was much surprised at this piece of impertinence, as he considered it.

"I will tell you," returned he in tones of rising anger, "how it comes that I treat my son, the heir to my rank and fortune, in this manner."

He looked savagely angry as he spoke, but Diana answered negligently, "Pray go on; you quite interest me."

"Well then, listen to me. I have chosen a wife for Norbert; she is as young as you are—beautiful, clever, and wealthy."

"And of noble birth, of course."

The sarcasm conveyed in this reply roused the duke to fury.

"Fifteen hundred thousand *francs* as a marriage portion will outweigh a coat of arms, even though it should be a tower argent on a field azure." The duke paused as he made this allusion to the Laurebourg arms, and then continued, "In addition to this, she has great expectations; and yet my son is mad enough to refuse the hand of this wealthy heiress."

"If you think that this marriage will cause your son's happiness, you are quite right in acting as you have done."

"Happiness! What has that to do with the matter, as long as it adds to the aggrandizement of our house and name? I have made up my mind that Norbert shall marry this girl; I have sworn it, and I never break my oath. I told him this myself."

Diana suffered acutely, but her pride supported her, whilst her confidence in Norbert was so great that she had the boldness to inquire, "And what did he say to that?"

"Norbert will become a dutiful son once more when he is removed from the malignant influence which has been so injurious to him," returned the duke fiercely.

"Indeed."

"He will obey me, when I show him that though he may not value his name and position, there are others who do so; and that many a woman would fight a brave battle for the honour of being the Duchess of Champdoce. Young lady, my son is a mere boy; but I have known the world, and when I prove to the poor fool that it was only grasping ambition which assumed the garb of love, he will renounce his folly and resume his allegiance to me. I will tell him what I think of the poverty-stricken adventuresses of high birth, whose only weapons are their youth and beauty, and with which they think that they can win a wealthy husband in the battle of life."

"Continue, sir," broke in Diana haughtily. "Insult a defenceless girl with her poverty! It is a noble act, and one worthy of a high-born gentleman like yourself!"

"I believed," said the duke, "that I was addressing the woman whose advice had led my son to break into open rebellion against my authority. Am I right or wrong? You can prove me to be mistaken by urging upon Norbert the necessity for submission."

She made no reply, but bent her head upon her bosom.

"You see," continued the duke, "that I am correct, and that if you continue to act as you have done, I shall be justified in retaliating in any manner that I may deem fit. You have now been warned. Carry on this intrigue at your peril."

He placed such an insulting emphasis upon the word "intrigue" that Diana's anger rose to boiling point. At that instant, for the sake of vengeance, she would have risked her honour, her ambition, her very life itself.

Forgetting all prudence, she cast aside her mask of affected indifference, and, with her eyes flashing angry gleams of fire, and her cheeks burning, she said,—

"Listen to me. I, too, have sworn an oath, and it is that Norbert shall be my husband; and I tell you that he shall be so! Shut him up in prison, subject him to every indignity at the hands of your menials, but you will never break his spirit, or make him go back from his plighted word. If I bid him, he will resist your will even unto the bitter end. He and I will never yield. Believe me when I tell you, that before you attack a young girl's honour, you had better pause; for one day she will be a member of your family. Farewell."

Before the duke could recover his senses, Diana was far down the path on her way homewards; and then he burst into a wild storm of menaces, oaths, and insults. He fancied that he was alone, but he was mistaken; for the whole of that strange scene had a hidden witness, and that witness was Daumon. He had heard of the treatment of the young *marquis* from one of his servants at the *château*, and his first thought had been to acquaint Diana with it. Unfortunately he saw no means of doing this. He dared not go to Laurebourg, and he would have died sooner than put pen to paper. He was in a position of the deepest embarrassment when the idea struck him of going to the lovers' trysting place. The little cry that Diana had uttered upon perceiving the duke had put him upon his guard.

Bruno had found him out; but, as he knew him, merely fawned upon him. He was delighted at the fury of the duke, whom he hated with cold and steady malignity; but the courage of Diana filled him with admiration. Her sublime audacity won his warmest praises, and he longed for her as an ally to aid him in his scheme of revenge. He knew that the girl would find herself in a terribly embarrassing position, and thus she would be sure to call upon him for advice before returning home.

"Now," thought he, "if I wish to profit by her anger, I ought to strike while the iron is hot; and to do so, I should be at home to meet her."

Without a moment's delay, he dashed through the woods, striving to get home without the young girl's perceiving him. His movements in the underwood caught the duke's eye.

"Who is there?" exclaimed he, moving towards the spot from whence the rustling came. There was no reply. Surely he had not been mistaken. Calling to Bruno, he strove to put him on the scent, but the dog showed no signs of eagerness. He sniffed about for a time, and seemed to linger near one special spot. The duke moved towards it, and distinctly saw the impression of two knees upon the grass.

"Someone has been eavesdropping," muttered he, much enraged at his discovery. "Who can it be? Has Norbert escaped from his prison?"

As he returned through the courtyard, he called one of the grooms to him.

"Where is my son?" asked he.

"Upstairs, your Grace," was the answer.

The duke breathed more freely. Norbert was still in security, and therefore could not have been the person who had been listening.

"But," added the lad, "the young master is half frantic."

"What do you mean?"

"Well, he declared that he would not remain in his room an instant longer; so old Jean called for help. He is awfully strong, and it took six of us to hold him. He said that if we would let him go, he would return in two hours, and that his honour and life were involved."

The duke listened with a sarcastic smile. He cared nothing about the frantic struggles of his son, for his heart had grown cold and hard from the presence of the fixed idea which had actuated his conduct for so many years, and it was with the solemn face of a man who was fulfilling a sacred duty that he ascended to the room in which his son was imprisoned. Jean threw open the door, and the duke paused for a moment on the threshold. The furniture had been overturned, some of it broken, and there were evident signs of a furious struggle having taken place.

A powerful labourer stood near the window, and Norbert was lying on the bed, with his face turned to the wall.

"Leave us," said the duke, and the man withdrew at once.

"Get up, Norbert," he added; "I wish to speak to you."

His son obeyed him. Anyone but the duke would have been alarmed by the expression of the young man's face.

"What is the meaning of all this?" asked the old nobleman in his most severe voice. "Are not my orders sufficient to insure obedience? I hear that absolute force has had to be used towards you during my absence. Tell me, my son, what plans you have devised during these hours of solitude, and what hopes you still venture to cherish."

"I intend to be free, and I will be so."

The duke affected not to hear the reply, uttered as it was in a tone of derision.

"It was very easy for me to discover, from your obstinacy, that some woman had endeavoured to entrap you, and by her insidious counsels inducing you to disobey your best friend."

He paused, but there was no reply.

"This woman—this dangerous woman—I have been in search of, and as you can conceive, I easily found her. I went to the Forest of Bevron, and there I need not tell you I found Mademoiselle de Laurebourg."

"Did you speak to her?"

"I did so, certainly. I told her my opinion of those manoeuvring women who fascinate the dupes they intend to take advantage of—"

"Father!"

"Can it be possible that you, simple boy even as you are, could have been deceived by the pretended love of this wily young woman? It is not you, *marquis*, that she loves, but our name and fortune; but *I* know if *she* does not that the law will imprison women who contrive to entrap young men who are under age."

Norbert turned deadly pale.

"Did you really say that to her?" asked he, in a low, hoarse voice, utterly unlike his own. "You dare to insult the woman I love, when you knew that I was far away and unable to protect her! Take care, or I shall forget that you are my father."

"He actually threatens me," said the duke, "my son threatens me;" and, raising the heavy stick he held in his hand, he struck Norbert a violent blow. By a fortunate movement the unhappy boy drew back, and so avoided the full force of the stroke, but the end of the stick struck him across the temple, inflicting a long though not a serious wound. In his blind rage Norbert was about to throw himself upon his father, when his eyes caught sight of the open door. Liberty and safety lay before him, and, with a bound, he was on the stairs, and before the duke could shout for aid from the window, his son was tearing across the park with all the appearance and gesture of a madman.

Chapter 35: The Little Glass Bottle

In order to avoid being seen by Mademoiselle de Laurebourg, Daumon had to take a much longer route to regain his home than the one that Diana had followed. This, however, he could not help. As soon as he arrived at his home he ran hastily upstairs and took from a cleverly concealed hiding-place in the wainscoting of his bedroom a small bottle of dark green glass, which he hastily slipped into his pocket. When he had once more descended to his office, he again took it out and examined it carefully to see that it had in no way been tampered with; then, with a hard, cruel smile, he placed it upon his desk among his ledgers and account books. Diana de Laurebourg might pay him a visit as soon as she liked, for he was quite prepared for her, for he had slipped on his dressing-gown and placed his velvet skull cap upon his head, as if he had not quitted the house that day.

"Why on earth does she not come?" muttered he.

He began to be uneasy. He went to the window and glanced eagerly down the road; then he drew out his watch and examined the face of it, when all at once his ears detected a gentle tapping at the door of the office.

"Come in," said he.

The door opened, and Diana entered slowly, without uttering a word, and took no notice of the servile obsequiousness of the counsellor; indeed, she hardly seemed to notice his presence, and with a deep sigh she threw herself into a chair.

In his inmost heart Daumon was filled with the utmost delight; he now understood why Diana had taken so long in reaching his house; it was because her interview with the duke had almost overcome her.

She soon, however, recovered her energy, and shook off the languor that seemed to cling to her limbs, and turning towards her host, said abruptly,—

"Counsellor, I have come to you for advice, which I sorely need. About an hour ago—"

With a gesture of sympathy Daumon interrupted her,—

"Alas!" said he; "spare me the recital, I know all."

"You know—"

"Yes, I know that M. Norbert is a prisoner at the *château*. Yes, *mademoiselle*, I know this, and I know, too, that you have just met the Duke de Champdoce in the Forest of Bevron. I know, moreover, all that you said to the old nobleman, for I have heard every word from a person who has just left."

In spite of her strong nerves, Diana was unable to restrain a movement of dismay and terror.

"But who told you of this?" murmured she.

"A man who was out cutting wood. Ah! my dear young lady, the forest is not a safe place to tell secrets in, for you never know whether watchful eyes and listening ears are not concealed behind every tree. This man, and I am afraid some of his companions, heard every word that was spoken, and as soon as you left the duke the man scampered off to tell the story. I made him promise not to say a word, but he is a married man and is sure to tell it to his wife. Then there are his companions; dear me! it is most annoying."

"Then all is lost, and I am ruined," murmured she.

But her despair did not last long, for she was by no means the woman to throw down her arms and sue for mercy. She grasped the arm of the counsellor.

"The end has not come yet, surely? Speak! What is to be done? You must have some plan. I am ready for anything, now that I have nothing to lose. No one shall ever say that that cowardly villain, the Duke de Champdoce, insulted me with impunity. Tell me, will you help me?"

"In the name of heaven!" cried he, "do not speak so loud. You do not know the adversary that you have to contend with."

"Are you afraid of him?"

"Yes, I do fear him; and what is more, I fear him very much. He is a determined man, and will gain his object at any cost or risk. Do you know that he did his best to crush me because I summoned him to court on behalf of one of my clients? So that now, when anyone comes to me and wishes to proceed against the duke, I am glad to decline to take up the matter."

"And so," returned the young girl in a tone of cold contempt, "after leading us to this compromising position, you are ready to abandon us at the most critical moment?"

"Can you think such a thing, *mademoiselle*?"

"You can act as you please, counsellor; Norbert is still left to me; he will protect me."

Daumon shook his head with an air of deep sorrow.

"How can we be sure that at this very moment the *marquis* has not given in to all his father's wishes?"

"No," exclaimed the girl; "such a supposition is an insult to Norbert. He would sooner die than give in. He may be timid, but he is not a coward; the thoughts of me will give him the power to resist his father's tyranny."

Daumon allowed himself to fall into his great armchair as though overcome by the excitement of this interview.

302

"We can talk coolly enough here and with no one to threaten us; but the *marquis*, on the other hand, is exposed to all his father's violence and ill treatment, moral as well as physical, without any defence for aid from a soul in the world, and in such times as these the strongest will may give way."

"Yes, I see it all; Norbert may give in, he may marry another woman, and I shall be left alone, with my reputation gone, and the scorn and scoff of all the neighbourhood."

"But, *mademoiselle*, you still have——"

"All I have left is life, and that life I would gladly give for vengeance."

There was something so terribly determined in the young girl's voice that again Daumon started, and this time his start was sincere and not simulated.

"Yes, you are right," said he, "and there are many besides myself who have vowed to have revenge on the duke, and their time will come, have no fear. A quiet shot in the woods in the dusk of the evening would settle many a long account. It has been tried, but the old man seems to have the luck of the evil one; and if the gun did not miss fire, the bullets flew wide of the mark. A judge might take a very serious view of such a matter, and term a crime what was merely an act of justice. Who can say whether the death of the Duke de Champdoce might not save him from the commission of many acts of tyranny and oppression and render many deserving persons happy?"

The face of Diana de Laurebourg turned deadly pale as she listened to these specious arguments.

"As things go," continued Daumon, "the duke may go on living to a hundred; he is wealthy and influential, and to a certain degree looked up to. He will die peacefully in his bed, there will be a magnificent funeral, and masses will be sung for the repose of his soul."

While he spoke the counsellor had taken the little bottle from beside his account books and was turning it over and over between his fingers.

"Yes," murmured he, thoughtfully; "the duke is quite likely to outlive us all, unless, indeed——"

He took the cork from the bottle, and poured a little of the contents into the palm of his hand. A few grains of fine white powder, glittering like crystal, appeared on the brown skin of the counsellor.

"And yet," he went on, in cold, sinister accents, "let him take but a small pinch of this, and no one need fear his tyranny again in this world. No one is much afraid of a man who lies some six feet under ground, shut up in a strong oak coffin, with a finely carved gravestone over his head."

He stopped short, and fixed his keen eyes upon the agitated girl, who stood in front of him. For at least two minutes the man and the girl stood face to face, motionless, and without exchanging a word. Through the dead, weird silence, the pulsations of their hearts were plainly audible. It seemed as if before speaking again each wished to fathom the depths of guilt that lay in the other's heart. It was a compact entered into by look and not by speech; and Daumon so well understood this, that at length, when he did speak, his voice sank to a hoarse whisper, as though he himself feared to listen to the utterance of his own thoughts.

"A man taking this feels no pain. It is like a heavy, stunning blow on the forehead—in ten seconds all is over, no gasp, no cry, but the heart ceases to beat forever; and, best of all, it leaves no trace behind it. A little of this, such a little, in wine or coffee, would be enough. It is tasteless, colourless, and scentless, its presence is impossible to be detected."

"But in the event of a *post-mortem* examination?"

"By skilful analysts in Paris or the larger towns, there would be a chance; but in a place like this, never! Never, in fact, anywhere, unless there had been previous grounds for suspicion. Otherwise only apoplectic symptoms would be observed; and even if it was traced there comes the question, By whom was it administered?"

He stopped short, for a word rose to his lips which he did not dare utter; he raised his hands to his mouth, coughed slightly, and went on,—

"This substance is not sold by chemists; it is very rarely met with, difficult to prepare, and terribly expensive. The smallest quantity might be met with in the first-class laboratories for scientific purposes, but it is most unlikely for anyone in these parts to possess any of this drug, or even to know of its existence."

"And yet you—"

"That is quite another matter. Years ago, when I was far away from here, it was in my power to render a great service to a distinguished chemist, and he made me a present of this combination of his skill. It would be impossible to trace this bottle; I have had it ten years, and the man who gave it to me is dead. Ten years? No, I am wrong, it is now twelve."

"And in all these years has not this substance lost any of its destructive powers?"

"I tried it only a month ago. I threw a pinch of it into a basin of milk and gave it to a powerful mastiff. He drank the milk and in ten seconds fell stark and dead."

"Horrible!" exclaimed Diana, covering her face with her hand, and recoiling from the tempter.

A sinister smile quivered upon the thin lips of the counsellor.

"Why do you say horrible?" asked he; "the dog had shown symptoms of rabies, and had he bitten me, I might have expired in frightful torture. Was it not fair self-defence? Sometimes, however, a man is more dangerous than a dog. A man blights the whole of my life; I strike him down openly, and the law convicts me and puts me to death; but I do not contemplate doing so, for I would suppress such a man secretly."

Diana placed her hands on the man's mouth and stopped a further exposition of his ideas.

"Listen to me," said she. But at this moment a heavy step was heard outside. "It is Norbert," gasped she.

"Impossible! It is more likely his father."

"It is Norbert," cried Mademoiselle de Laurebourg, and snatching the little bottle from the counsellor's hands, she thrust it into her bosom. The door flew open, and Norbert appeared on the threshold. Diana and the counsellor both uttered a shriek of terror. His livid countenance seemed to indicate that he had passed through some terrible scene; his gait was unsteady, his clothes torn and disordered, and his face stained with blood, which had flowed from a cut over his temple. Daumon imagined that some outrage had taken place.

"You have been wounded, *marquis*?" said he.

"Yes, my father struck me."

"Can it be possible?"

"Yes, he struck me."

Mademoiselle Diana had feared this, and she trembled with the terror of her vague conjectures as she made a step towards her lover.

"Permit me to examine your wound," said she.

She placed both her hands at the side of his head and stood on tiptoe, the better to inspect the cut. As she did so, she shuddered; an inch lower, and the consequences might have been fatal.

"Quick," she said, "give me some rags and water."

Norbert gently disengaged himself. "It is a mere nothing," said he, "and can be looked after later on. Fortunately I did not receive the whole weight of the blow, which would otherwise have brought me senseless to the ground, and perhaps I should have been slain by my father's hand."

"By the duke? and for what reason did he strike you?"

"Diana, he had grossly insulted you, and he dared to tell me of it. Had he forgotten that the blood of the race of Champdoce ran in my veins as well as in his?"

Mademoiselle de Laurebourg burst into a passion of tears.

"I," sobbed she, "I have brought all this upon you."

"You? Why, it is to you that he owes his life. He dared to strike me as if I had been a lackey, but the thoughts of you stayed my hand. I turned and fled, and never again will I enter that accursed house. I renounce the Duke de Champdoce, he is no longer my father, and I will never look upon his face again. Would that I could forget that such a man existed; but, no, I would rather that I remembered him for the sake of revenge."

Again the heart of Daumon overflowed with joy. All his deeply malignant spirit thrilled pleasantly as he heard these words.

"*Marquis,*" said he, "perhaps you will now believe with me that in all misfortunes there is an element of luck, for your father has committed an act of imprudence which will yet cost him dear. It is very strange that so astute a man as the Duke de Champdoce should have allowed his passion to carry him away."

"What do you mean?"

"Simply that you can be freed from the tyranny of your father whenever you like now. We now have all that is necessary for lodging a formal plaint in court. We have sequestration of the person, threats and bodily violence by the aid of third parties, and words and blows which have endangered life; our case is entirely complete. A surgeon will examine your wound, and give a written deposition. We can produce plenty of evidence, and the wound on the head will tell its own story. As a commencement we will petition that we may not be ordered back to our father's custody, and it will further be set forth that our reason for this is that a father has assaulted a son with undue and unnecessary violence. We shall be sure to gain the day, and—"

"Enough," broke in Norbert; "will the decision give me the right to marry whom I please without my father's consent?"

Daumon hesitated. Under the circumstances, it seemed to him very likely that the court would grant Norbert the liberty he desired;

he, however, thought it advisable not to say so, and answered boldly, "No, *marquis*, it will not do so."

"Well, then, the Champdoce family have never exposed their differences to the public, nor will I begin to do so," said Norbert decisively.

The counsellor seemed surprised at this determination.

"If, *marquis*," he began, "I might venture to advise you—"

"No advice is necessary, my mind is entirely made up, but I need some help, and in twenty-four hours I require a large sum of money—twenty thousand *francs*."

"You can have them, *marquis*, but I warn you that you will have to pay heavily for the accommodation."

"That I care nothing for."

Mademoiselle de Laurebourg was about to speak, but with a gesture of his hand Norbert arrested her.

"Do you not comprehend me, Diana?" said he; "we must fly, and that at once. We can find some safe retreat where we can live happily, where no one will harm us."

"But this is mere madness!" cried Diana.

"You will be pursued," remarked the counsellor; "and most likely overtaken."

"Can you not trust your life to me?" asked Norbert reproachfully. "I swear that I will devote everything to you, life, thought, and will. On my knees I entreat you to fly with me."

"I cannot," murmured she; "it is impossible."

"Then you do not love me," said he in desponding accents. "I have been a thrice-besotted fool to believe that your heart was mine, for you can never have loved me."

"Hear him, merciful powers! he says that I, who am all his, do not love him."

"Then why cast aside our only chance of safety?"

"Norbert, dearest Norbert!"

"I understand you too well; you are alarmed at the idea of the world's censure, and—"

He paused, checked by the gleam of reproach that shone in Diana's eyes.

"Must it be so?" said she; "must I condescend to justify myself? You talk to me of the world's censure? Have I not already defied it, and has it not sat in judgment upon me? And what have I done, after all? Every act and word that has passed between us I can repeat to my mother without a blush rising to my cheek; but would anyone credit my words? No, not a living soul. Most likely the world has come to a decision. My reputation is gone, is utterly lost, and yet I am spotless as the driven snow."

Norbert was half-mad with anger.

"Who would dare to treat you with anything save the most profound respect?" said he.

"Alas! my dear Norbert," replied she, "tomorrow the scandal will be even greater. While your father was talking to me with such brutal violence and contempt, he was overheard by a woodcutter and perhaps by some of his companions."

"It cannot be."

"No, it is quite true," returned Daumon. "I had it from the man myself."

Mademoiselle de Laurebourg shot one glance at the counsellor; it was only a glance, but he comprehended at once that she wished to be left alone with her lover.

"Pardon me," said he, "but I think I have a visitor, and I must hinder anyone from coming in here."

He left the room as he spoke, closing the door noisily behind him.

"And so," resumed Norbert when alone, "it seems that the Duke de Champdoce did not even take the ordinary precaution of assuring himself that you were in privacy before he spoke as he did, and was so carried away by his fury that he never thought that in casting dishonour upon you, he was heaping infamy on me. Does he think by these means to compel me to marry the heiress whom he has chose for me, the Mademoiselle de Puymandour?"

For the first time Diana learned the name of her rival.

"Ah!" moaned she between her sobs, "so it is Mademoiselle de Puymandour that he wants you to marry?"

"Yes, the same, or rather her enormous wealth; but may my hand wither before it clasps hers. Do you hear me, Diana?"

She gave a sad smile and murmured, "Poor Norbert!"

The heart of the young man sank; so melancholy was the tone of her voice.

"You are very cruel," said he. "What have I done to deserve this want of confidence?"

Diana made no reply, and Norbert, believing that he understood the reason why she refused to fly with him, said, "Is it because you have no faith in me, that you will not accompany me in my flight?"

"No; I have perfect faith in you."

"What is it, then? Do I not offer you fortune and happiness? Tell me what it is then."

She drew herself up, and said proudly, "Up to this time, my conscience has enabled me to hold my own against all the scandalous gossip that has been flying about, but now it says, 'Halt, Diana de Laurebourg! You have gone far enough.' My burden is heavy, my heart is breaking, but I must draw back now. No, Norbert; I cannot fly with you."

She paused for a moment, as though unable to proceed, and then went on with more firmness, "Were I alone and solitary in the world, I might act differently; but I have a family, whose honour I must guard as I would my own."

"A family indeed, which sacrifices you to your elder brother."

"It may be so, and therefore my task is all the greater. Who ever head of virtue as something easy to practise?"

Norbert never remembered what an example of rebellion she had set.

"My heart and my conscience dictate the same course to me. The result must ever be fatal, when a young girl sets at defiance the rules and laws of society; and you would never care to look with respect on one upon whom others gazed with the eye of contempt."

"What sort of an opinion have you of me, then?"

"I believe you to be a man, Norbert. Let us suppose that I fly with you, and that the next day I should hear that my father has been killed in a duel fought on my account; what then? Believe me, that when I tell you to fly by yourself, I give you the best advice in my power. You will forget me, I know; but what else can I hope for?"

"Forget you!" said Norbert angrily. "Can you forget me?"

His face was so close to hers that she felt the hot breath upon her cheek.

"Yes," stammered she, with a violent effort, "I can."

Norbert drew a pace back, that he might read her meaning more fully in her eyes.

"And if I go away," asked he, "what will become of you?"

A sob burst from the young girl's breast, and her strength seemed to desert her limbs.

"I," answered she, in the calm, resigned voice of a Christian virgin about to be cast to the lions that roared in the arena, "I have my destiny. Today is the last time that we shall ever meet. I shall return to my home, where everything will shortly be known. I shall find my father angry and menacing. He will place me in a carriage, and the next day I shall find myself within the walls of the hated convent."

"But that life would be one long, slow agony to you. You have told me this before."

"Yes," answered she, "it would be an agony, but it would also be an expiation; and when the burden grows too heavy, I have this."

And as she spoke, she drew the little bottle from its hiding-place in her bosom, and Norbert too well understood her meaning. The young man endeavoured to take it from her, but she resisted. This contest seemed to exhaust her little strength, her beautiful eyes closed, and she sank senseless into Norbert's arms. In an agony of despair, the young man asked himself if she was dying; and yet there was sufficient life in her to enable her to whisper, soft and low, these words, "My only friend—let me have it back, dear Norbert." And then, with perfect clearness, she repeated all the deadly properties of the drug, and the directions for its use that the counsellor had given to her.

On hearing the woman whom he loved with such intense passion confess that she would sooner die than live apart from him, Norbert's brain reeled.

"Diana, my own Diana!" repeated he, as he hung over her.

But she went on, as though speaking through the promptings of delirium.

"The very day after such a fair prospect! Ah, Duke de Champdoce! You are a hard and pitiless man. You have robbed me of all I held dear in the world, blackened my reputation, and tarnished my honour, and now you want my life."

Norbert uttered such a cry of anger, that even Daumon in the passage was startled by it. He placed Diana tenderly in the counsellor's armchair, saying,—

"No, you shall not kill yourself, nor shall you leave me."

She smiled faintly, and held out her arms to him. Her magic spells were deftly woven.

"No," cried he; "the poison which you had intended to use on yourself shall become my weapon of vengeance, and the instrument of punishment of the one who has wronged you."

And with the gait of a man walking in his sleep, he left the counsellor's office.

Hardly had the young man's footsteps died away, than Daumon entered the room. He had not lost a word or action in the foregoing scene, and he was terribly agitated; and he could scarcely believe his eyes when he saw Diana, whom he had supposed to be lying half-sensible in the armchair, standing at the window, gazing after Norbert, as he walked along the road leading from the counsellor's cottage.

"Ah! what a woman!" muttered he. "Gracious powers, what a wonderful woman!"

When Diana had lost sight of her lover, she turned round to Daumon. Her face was pale, and her eyelids swollen, but her eyes flashed with the conviction of success.

"Tomorrow, counsellor," said she, "tomorrow I shall be the Duchess de Champdoce."

Daumon was so overwhelmed that, accustomed as he was to startling events and underhand trickery, he could find no words to express his feelings.

"That is to say," added Diana thoughtfully, "if all goes as it should tonight."

Daumon felt a cold shiver creep over him, but summoning up all his self-possession, he said, "I do not understand you. What is this that you hope will be accomplished tonight?"

She turned so contemptuous and sarcastic a look on him, that the words died away in his mouth, and he at once saw his mistake in thinking that he could sport with the girl's feelings as a cat plays with a mouse; for it was she who was playing with him, and she, a simple girl, had made this wily man of the world her dupe.

"Success is, of course, a certainty," answered she coldly; "but Norbert is impetuous, and impetuous people are often awkward. But I must return home at once. Ah, me!" she added, as her self-control gave way for a moment, "will this cruel night never pass away, and give way to the gentle light of dawn? Farewell, counsellor. When we meet again, all matters will be settled, one way or other."

The Parthian dart which Mademoiselle de Laurebourg had cast behind her went true to the mark; the allusion to Norbert's impetuosity and awkwardness rendered the counsellor very unhappy. He sat down in his arm-chair, and, resting his head on his hands, and his elbows on his desk, he strove to review the position thoroughly. Perhaps by now all might be over. Where was Norbert, and what was he doing? he asked himself.

At the time that Daumon was reflecting, Norbert was on the road leading to Champdoce. He had entirely lost his head, but he found that his reason was clear and distinct. Those who have been accus-

311

tomed to the treatment of maniacs know with what startling rapidity they form a chain of action, and the cloud that veiled Norbert's brain appeared to throw out into stronger relief the murderous determination he had formed. He had already decided how the deed was to be done. The common wine of the country was always served to the labourers at the table, but the duke kept a better quality for his own drinking, and the bottle containing this was after meals placed on a shelf in a cupboard in the dining-room. It was thus within everyone's reach, but not a soul in the household would have ventured to lay a finger upon it. Norbert's thoughts fell upon this bottle, and in his mind's eye he could see it standing in its accustomed place. He crossed the courtyard, and the labourers, engaged in their tasks, gazed at him curiously. He passed them, and entered the dining-room, which was untenanted. With a caution that was not to be expected from the agitation of his mind, he opened each door successively, in order to be certain that no eyes were gazing upon him. Then, with the greatest rapidity, he took down the bottle, drew the cork with his teeth, and dropped into the wine, not one, but two or three pinches of the contents of the little vial. He shook the bottle gently, to facilitate the dissolution of the powder. A few particles of the poison clung to the lip of the bottle; he wiped off these, not with a napkin, a pile of which lay on the shelf beside him, but with his own handkerchief. He replaced the bottle in its accustomed place, and seating himself by the fire, awaited the course of events.

At this moment the Duke de Champdoce was coming up the avenue at a rapid pace. For the first time, perhaps, in his life, this man perceived that one of his last acts had been insensate and foolish in the extreme. All the possibilities of the law to which Daumon had alluded struck the duke with over-whelming force, and he at once saw that his violent conduct had given ample grounds upon which to base a plaint, with results which he greatly feared. If the court entertained the matter, his son would most likely be removed from his control. He knew that such an idea would never cross Norbert's brain, but there were plenty of persons to suggest it to him. The danger of his position occurred to him, and at the same time he felt that he must frame his future conduct with extreme prudence. He had not given up his views regarding his son's marriage with Mademoiselle de Puymandour. No; he would sooner have resigned life itself, but he felt that he must renounce violence, and gain his ends by diplomacy. The first thing to be done was to get Norbert to return home, and the father greatly doubted whether the son would do so. While thinking over these things, with a settled gloom upon his face, one of the servants came running up to him with the news of Norbert's return.

"I hold him at last," muttered he, and hastened on to the *château*.

When the duke entered the dining-room, Norbert did not rise from his seat, and the duke was disagreeably impressed by this breach of the rules of domestic etiquette.

"On my word," thought he, "it would appear that the young booby thinks that he owes me no kind of duty whatever."

He did not, however, allow his anger to be manifest in his features; besides, the sight of the blood, with which his son's face was still smeared, caused him to feel excessively uncomfortable.

"Norbert, my son," said he, "are you suffering? Why have you not had that cut attended to?"

The young man made no reply, and the duke continued,—

"Why have you not washed the blood away? Is it left there as a reproach to me? There is no need for that, I assure you; for deeply do I deplore my violence."

Norbert still made no answer, and the duke became more and more embarrassed. To give himself time for reflection, more than because he was thirsty, he took a glass, and filled it from his own special bottle.

Norbert trembled from head to foot as he saw this act.

"Come, my son," continued the duke, "just try if you cannot find some palliation for what your old father has done. I am ready to ask your forgiveness, and to apologize, for a man of honour is never ashamed to acknowledge when he has been in the wrong."

He raised his glass, and raised it up to the light half mechanically. Norbert held his breath; the whole world seemed turning round. "It is hard, very hard," continued the duke, "for a father thus to humiliate himself in vain before his son."

It was useless for Norbert to turn away his head; he saw the duke place the glass to his lips. He was about to drink, but the young man could endure it no longer, and with a bound he sprang forward, snatched the glass from his father's hand, and hurled it from the window, shouting in a voice utterly unlike his own,—

"Do not drink."

The duke read the whole hideous truth in the face and manner of his son. His features quivered, his face grew purple, and his eyes filled with blood. He strove to speak, but only an inarticulate rattle could be heard; he then clasped his hands convulsively, swayed backwards and forwards, and then fell helplessly backwards, striking his head against an oaken sideboard that stood near. Norbert tore open the door.

"Quick, help!" cried he. "I have killed my father."

Chapter 36: The Honour of the Name

The account that the Duke de Champdoce had given of M. de Puymandour's mad longing for rank and title was true, and afforded a melancholy instance of that peculiar kind of foolish vanity. He was a much happier man in his younger days, when he was known simply as Palouzet, which was his father's name, whose only wish for distinction was to be looked upon as an honest man. In those days he was much looked up to and respected, as a man who had possessed brains enough to amass a very large fortune by strictly honest means. All this vanished, however, when the unhappy idea occurred to him to affix the title of count to the name of an estate that he had recently purchased.

From that moment, all his tribulations in life may have been said to have commenced. The nobility laughed at his assumption of hereditary rank, while the middle classes frowned at his pretensions to be superior to them, so that he passed the existence of a shuttlecock, continually suspended in the air, and struck at and dismissed from either side.

It may, therefore, be easily imagined how excessively anxious he was to bring about the marriage between his daughter Marie and the son of that mighty nobleman, the Duke de Champdoce. He had offered to sacrifice one-third of his fortune for the honour of forming this connection, and would have given up the whole of it, could he but have seen a child in whose veins ran the united blood of Palouzet and the Champdoce seated upon his knee. A marriage of this kind would have given him a real position; for to have a Champdoce for a son-in-law would compel all scoffers to bridle their tongues.

The day after he had received a favourable reply from the duke, M. de Puymandour thought that it was time to inform his daughter of his intentions. He never thought that she would make any opposition, and, of course, supposed that she would be as delighted as he was at the honour that awaited her. He was seated in a magnificently furnished room which he called his library when he arrived at this conclusion, and ringing the bell, ordered the servant to inquire of *mademoiselle's* maid if her mistress could grant him an interview. He gave this curious message, which did not appear to surprise the servant in the least, with an air of the utmost importance. The communication between the father and daughter was always carried on upon this basis; and scoffers wickedly asserted that M. de Puymandour had modelled it upon a book of etiquette, for the guidance of her household, written by a venerable arch-duchess.

Shortly after the man had departed on his errand, a little tap came to the door.

"Come in," exclaimed M. de Puymandour.

And Mademoiselle Marie ran in and gave her father a kiss upon each cheek. He frowned slightly, and extricated himself from her embrace.

"I thought it better to come to you, my dear father," said she, "than to give you the trouble of coming all the way to me."

"You always forget that there are certain forms and ceremonies necessary for a young lady of your position."

Marie gave a little gentle smile, for she was no stranger to her father's absurd whims; but she never thwarted them, for she was very fond of him. She was a very charming young lady, and in the description that the duke had given of her to his son, he had not flattered her at all. Though she differed greatly in appearance from Mademoiselle de Laurebourg, Marie's beauty was perfect in a style of its own. She was tall and well proportioned, and had all that easy grace of movement, characteristic of women of Southern parentage. Her large soft dark eyes offered a vivid contrast to her creamy complexion; her hair, in utter disregard of the fashionable mode of dressing, was loosely knotted at the back of her head. Her nature was soft and affectionate, capable of the deepest devotion, while she had the most equable temper that can be imagined.

"Come, my dear papa," said she; "do not scold me any more. You know that the Marchioness of Arlanges has promised to teach me how to behave myself according to all the rules of fashionable society next winter, and I declare to you that I will so practise them up in secret, that you will be astonished when you behold them."

"How woman-like!" muttered her father. "She only scoffs at matters of the most vital importance."

He rose from his seat, and, placing his back to the fireplace, took up an imposing position, one hand buried in his waistcoat, and the other ready to gesticulate as occasion required.

"Oblige me with your deepest attention," commenced he. "You

were eighteen years of age last month, and I have an important piece of intelligence to convey to you. I have had an offer of marriage for you."

Marie looked down, and endeavoured to hide her confusion at these tidings.

"Before coming to a conclusion upon a matter of such importance," continued he, "it was, of course, necessary for me to go into the question most thoroughly. I spared no means of obtaining information, and I am quite certain that the proposed connection would be conducive to your future happiness. The suitor for your hand is but little older than yourself; he is very handsome, very wealthy, and is a *marquis* by hereditary right."

"Has he spoken to you then?" inquired Marie in tones of extreme agitation.

"He! Whom do you mean by he?" asked M. de Puymandour; and as his daughter did not reply, he repeated his question.

"Who? Why, George de Croisenois."

"Pray, what have you to do with Croisenois? Who is he, pray? Not that dandy with a moustache, that I have seen hanging about you this winter?"

"Yes," faltered Marie; "that is he."

"And why should you presume that he had asked me for your hand? Did he tell you that he was going to do so?"

"Father, I declare——"

"What, the daughter of a Puymandour has listened to a declaration of love unknown to her father? Ten thousand furies! Has he written to you? Where are those letters?"

"My dear father——"

"Silence; have you those letters? Let me see them. Come, no delay; I will have those bits of paper, if I turn the whole house upside down."

With a sigh Marie gave the much prized missives to her father; there were four only, fastened together with a morsel of blue ribbon.

He took one out at random, and read it aloud, with a running fire of oaths and invectives as a commentary upon its contents.

Mademoiselle,——
Though there is nothing upon earth that I dread so much as your anger, I dare, in spite of your commands to the contrary, to write to you once again. I have learned that you are about to quit Paris for several months. I am twenty-four years of age. I

have neither father nor mother, and am entirely my own master. I belong to an ancient and honourable family. My fortune is a large one, and my love for you is of the most honourable and devoted kind. My uncle, M. de Saumeuse, knows your father well; and will convey my proposals to him upon his return from Italy, in about two or three weeks' time. Once more entreating you to forgive me,

I remain,

Yours respectfully,

George De Croisenois

"Very pretty indeed," said M. de Puymandour, as he replaced the letter in its envelope. "This is sufficient, and I need not read the others; but pray, what answer did you give?"

"That I must refer him to you, my dear father."

"Indeed, on my word, you do me too much honour; and did you really think that I would listen to such proposals? Perhaps you love him?"

She turned her lovely face towards her father, with the great tears rolling down her cheeks for her sole reply.

This mute confession, for as such he regarded it, put the finishing touch to M. de Puymandour's exasperation.

"You absolutely love him, and have the impudence to tell me so?"

Marie glanced at her father, and answered,—

"The Marquis de Croisenois is of good family."

"Pooh! you know nothing about it. Why, the first Croisenois was one of Richelieu's minions, and Louis XIII. conferred the title for some shady piece of business which he carried out for him. Has this fine *marquis* any means of livelihood?"

"Certainly; about sixty thousand *francs* a year."

"Humbug! What did he mean by addressing you secretly? Only to compromise your name, and so to secure your fortune, and perhaps to break off your marriage with another."

"But why suppose this?"

"I suppose nothing; I am merely going upon facts. What does a man of honour do when he falls in love?"

"My dear father—"

"He goes to his solicitor, acquaints him with his intentions, and explains what his means are; the solicitor goes to the family solicitor of the young lady, and when these men of the law have found out that all is satisfactory, then love is permitted to make his appearance upon the scene. And now you may as well attend to me. Forget De Croisenois as soon as you can, for I have chosen a husband for you, and, having pledged my word of honour, I will abide by it. On Sunday the eligible suitor will be introduced to you, and on Monday we will visit the Bishop, asking him to be good enough to perform the ceremony. On Tuesday you will show yourself in public with him, in order to announce the betrothal. Wednesday the marriage contract will be read. Thursday a grand dinner-party. Friday an exhibition of the marriage presents; Saturday a day of rest; Sunday the publication of the banns, and at the end of the following week the marriage will take place."

Mademoiselle Marie listened to her father's determination with intense horror.

"For pity's sake, my dear father, be serious," cried she.

M. de Puymandour paid no attention to her entreaty, but added, as an afterthought:

"Perhaps you would wish to know the name of the gentleman I have selected as a husband for you. He is the Marquis Norbert, the son and heir of the Duke de Champdoce."

Marie turned deadly pale.

"But I do not know him; I have never seen him," faltered she.

"*I* know him, and that is quite sufficient. I have often told you that you should be a duchess, and I mean to keep my word."

Marie's affection for George de Croisenois was much deeper than she had told her father, much deeper even than she had dared to confess to herself, and she resented this disposal of her with more obstinacy than anyone knowing her gentle nature would have supposed her capable of; but M. de Puymandour was not the man to give up for an instant the object which he had sworn to attain. He never gave his daughter an instant's peace, he argued, insisted, and bullied until, after three days' contest, Marie gave her assent with a flood of tears. The word had scarcely passed her lips, before her father, without even thanking her for her terrible sacrifice, exclaimed in a voice of triumph:

"I must take these tidings to Champdoce without a moment's delay."

He started at once, and as he passed through the doorway said:

"Goodbye, my little duchess, goodbye."

He was most desirous of seeing the duke, for, on taking leave of him, the old nobleman had said, "You shall hear from me tomorrow;"

but no letter had as yet reached him from Champdoce. This delay however, had suited M. de Puymandour's plans, for it had enabled him to wring the consent from his daughter; but now that this had been done, he began to feel very anxious, and to fear that there might be some unforeseen hitch in the affair.

When he reached Bevron, he saw Daumon talking earnestly with Francoise, the daughter of the Widow Rouleau. M. de Puymandour bowed graciously, and stopped to talk with the man, for he was just now seeking for popularity, as he was a candidate, and the elections would shortly take place; and, besides, he never failed to talk to persons who exercised any degree of influence, and he knew that Daumon was a most useful man in electioneering.

"Good morning, counsellor," said he gaily. "What is the news to-day?"

Daumon bowed profoundly.

"Bad news, count," answered he. "I hear that the Duke de Champdoce is seriously indisposed."

"The duke ill—impossible!"

"This girl has just given me the information. Tell us all about it, Francoise."

"I heard today at the *château* that the doctors had quite given him over."

"But what is the matter with him?"

"I did not hear."

M. de Puymandour stood perfectly aghast.

"It is always the way in this world," Daumon philosophically said. "In the midst of life we are in death!"

"Good morning, counsellor," said De Puymandour; "I must try and find out something more about this."

Breathless, and with his mind filled with anxiety, he hurried on.

All the servants and labourers on the Champdoce estate were gathered together in a group, talking eagerly to each other, and as soon as M. de Puymandour appeared, one of the servants, disengaging himself from his fellows, came towards him. This was the duke's old, trustworthy servant.

"Well?" exclaimed M. de Puymandour.

"Oh, sir," cried the old man, "this is too horrible; my poor master will certainly die."

"But I do not know what is the matter with him; no one has told me anything, in fact."

"It was terribly sudden," answered the man. "It was about this time the day before yesterday that the duke was alone with M. Norbert in the dining-room. All at once we heard a great outcry. We ran in and saw my poor master lying senseless on the ground, his face purple and distorted."

"He must have had a fit of apoplexy."

"Not exactly; the doctor called it a rush of blood to the brain; at least, I think that is what he said, and he added that the reason he did not die on the spot was because in falling he had cut open his head against the oaken sideboard, and the wound bled profusely. We carried him up to his bed; he showed no signs of life, and now—"

"Well, how is he now?"

"No one dare give an opinion; my poor master is quite unconscious, and should he recover—and I do not think for a moment that he will—the doctor says his mind will have entirely gone."

"Horrible! Too horrible! And a man of such intellectual power, too. I shall not ask you to let me look at him, for I could do no good, and the sight would upset me. But can I not see M. Norbert?"

"Pray, do not attempt to do so, sir."

"I was his father's intimate friend, and if the condolences of such a one could assuage the affliction under which—"

"Impossible!" answered the man in a quick, eager manner. "M. Norbert was with his father at the time of his seizure, and has given strict orders that he is not to be disturbed on any account; but I must go to him at once, for we are expecting the physicians who are coming from Poitiers."

"Very well, then I will go now, but tonight I will send up one of my people for news."

With these words, M. de Puymandour walked slowly away, absorbed in thought. The manner and expression of the servant had struck him as extremely strange. He noted the fact that Norbert was alone with his father at the time of the seizure, and, recalling to mind the opposition he had met with from his daughter, he began to imagine that the duke had found his son rebellious, and that the apoplectic fit had been brought on by a sudden access of passion. Interest and ambition working together brought him singularly near the truth.

"If the duke dies, or becomes a maniac," thought he to himself, "the end as regards us will be the same for Norbert will break off the match to a certainty."

He felt that such a proceeding would cause him to be more jeered at and ridiculed than ever, and that the only path of escape left open to him was to marry his daughter to the Marquis de Croisenois, which was a most desirable alliance, in spite of all he had said against it. A voice close to his ear aroused him from his reflections: it was that of Daumon, who had come up unperceived.

"Was the girl's information correct, count?" asked he. "How are the duke and M. Norbert, for of course you have seen them both?"

"M. Norbert is too much agitated by the sad event to see anyone."

"Of course that was to be looked for," returned the wily counsellor; "for the seizure was terribly sudden."

M. de Puymandour was too much occupied with his own thoughts to spare much pity for Norbert. He would have given a great deal to have known what the young man was doing, and especially what he was thinking of at the present moment.

The poor lad was standing by the bedside of his dying father, watching eagerly for some indication, however slight, of returning life or reason. The hours of horror and self-reproach had entirely changed his feelings and ideas; for it was only at the instant when he saw his father raise the poisoned wine to his lips that he saw his crime in all its hideous enormity. His soul rose up in rebellion against his crime, and the words, "Parricide! murderer!" seemed to ring in his ears like a trumpet call. When his father fell to the ground, his instinct made him shout for aid; but an instant afterwards terror took possession of him, and, rushing from the house, he sought the open country, as though striving to escape from himself.

Jean, the old servant, who had noticed Norbert's strange look, was seized with a terrible fear. Trusted as he was by both the duke and his son, he had many means of knowing all that was going on in the household, and was no stranger to the differences that had arisen recently between father and son. He knew how violent the tempers of both were, and he also knew that some woman was urging on Norbert to a course of open rebellion. He had seen the cruel blow dealt by the duke, and had wondered greatly when he saw Norbert return to the *château*. Why had he done so? He had been in the courtyard when Norbert threw the glass from the window.

Putting all these circumstances together, as soon as the inanimate body of the duke had been laid upon a bed, Jean went into the dining-room, feeling sure that he should make some discovery which would confirm his suspicions. The bottle from which the duke had filled his glass stood half emptied upon the table. With the greatest care, he poured a few drops of its contents into the hollow of his hand, and tasted it with the utmost caution. The wine still retained its customary taste and scent. Not trusting, however, to this, Jean, after making sure that he was not observed, carried the bottle to his own room, and concealed it. After taking this precaution, he ordered one of the other servants to remain by the side of the duke until the arrival of the doctor, and then went in search of Norbert.

For two hours his efforts were fruitless. Giving up his search in despair, he turned once more to regain the *château*, and, taking the path through the wood, suddenly perceived a human form stretched on the turf beneath a tree. He moved cautiously towards the figure, and at once recognised Norbert. The faithful servant bent over his young master, and shook him by the arm to arouse him from his state of stupor. At the first touch, Norbert started to his feet with a shriek of terror. With mingled fear and pity, Jean noticed the look that shone in the young man's eyes, more like that of some hunted animal than a human being.

"Do not be alarmed, M. Norbert; it is only I," said he.

"And what do you want?"

"I came to look for you, and to entreat you to come back with me to Champdoce."

"Back to Champdoce?" repeated Norbert hoarsely; "no, never!"

"You must, Master Norbert; for your absence now would cause a terrible scandal. Your place at this critical time is by the bedside of your father."

"Never! never!" repeated the poor boy; but he yielded passively when Jean passed his arm through his, and led him away towards the *château*. Supported thus by the old man's arm, he crossed the courtyard, and ascended the staircase; but at his father's door he withdrew his hand, and struggled to get away.

"I will not; no, no, I cannot," gasped he.

"You must and you shall," returned the old man firmly. "Whatever your feelings may be, no stain shall rest on the family honour."

These words roused Norbert; he stepped across the room, and dropped on his knees by the bed, placing his forehead upon his father's icy hand. He burst into a passion of tears and sobs, and the simple peasants, who surrounded the couch of the insensible nobleman, breathed a sigh; for, from his pallid face and burning eyes, they believed he must be mad. They were not far out in this surmise; but the tears relieved his over-wrought brain, and with this relief came the sense of intense suffering. When the physician arrived, he was able to appear before him merely as a deeply anxious son.

"There is no hope for the duke, I regret to say," said the medical man, who felt that it was useless to keep Norbert in suspense. "There is a feeble chance of saving his life; but even should we succeed in doing so, his intellect will be irretrievably gone. This is a sad truth, but I feel it my duty to inform you of it. I will come again tomorrow."

As the doctor left the room, Norbert threw himself into a chair, and clasped his hands round his head, which throbbed until it seemed as if it would burst. For more than half an hour he sat motionless, and then started to his feet with a stifled cry; for he remembered the bottle into which he had poured the poison, and which had been left on the table. Had anyone drunk from it? What had become of it? The agony of his mind gave him the necessary strength to descend to the dining-room; but the bottle was not on the table, nor was it in its customary place in the cupboard. The unhappy boy was looking for it everywhere, when the door silently opened, and Jean appeared on the threshold. The expression upon his young master's face so startled the faithful old man that he nearly dropped the lighted candle that he carried in his hand.

"Why are you here, Master Norbert?" asked he in a voice that trembled with emotion.

"I was looking for—I wanted to find—," faltered Norbert.

Jean's suspicions at once became certainties; he walked up to his young master, and whispered in his ear,—

"You are looking for the duke's bottle of wine, are you not? It is quite safe; for I have taken it to my room. Tomorrow the contents shall be emptied away, and there will be no proof existing."

Jean spoke in such a low voice that Norbert guessed rather than heard his words, and yet it seemed that the accusing whisper resounded like thunder through the *château*, filling the old house from cellar to roof-tree.

"Be quiet," said he, laying his hand on the old man's lips, and gazing around him with wild and affrighted glances.

A more complete confession could hardly have been made.

"Fear nothing, Master Norbert," answered Jean; "we are quite alone. I know that there are words which should never be even breathed; and if I have ventured to speak, it was because it was my duty to warn you, and to inculcate on you the necessity of caution."

Norbert was filled with horror when he saw that the old man believed him to be really guilty.

"Jean," cried he, "you are wrong in your suspicions. I tell you that my father never tasted that wine. I snatched the glass from him before his lips had touched it. I flung it out into the courtyard, and, if you search, you will find its scattered fragments there still."

"I am not sitting in judgment upon you; what you tell me to believe I am ready to accept."

"Ah!" cried Norbert passionately, "he does not believe me; he thinks that I am guilty. I swear to you by all that I hold most sacred in this world, that I am innocent of this deed."

The attached servant shook his head with a melancholy air.

"Of course, of course," said he; "but it is for us two to save the honour of the house of Champdoce. Should it happen that any suspicions should be aroused, put all the guilt upon my shoulders. I will defend myself in a manner which will only fix the crime more firmly upon me. I will not throw away the bottle, but will retain it in my room, so that it may be found there, and its contents will be a damnatory evidence against me. What matters it how a poor man like me is sent out of the world? but with you it is different. You—"

Norbert wrung his hands in abject despair; the sublime devotion of the old servant showed how firmly Jean believed in his criminality. He was about to assert his innocence further, when the loud sound of a closing door was heard above stairs.

"Hush!" said the old man; "someone approaches; we must not be seen whispering together like two plotters, for their suspicions would be certainly awakened; and I fear that my face or your eyes will reveal the secret. Quick, go upstairs, and endeavour, as soon as possible, to resume your calmness. I beg you not to compromise the honour of your name, which is in deadly peril."

Without another word Norbert obeyed. His father was alone, and only the man to whom Jean had delegated the task of watcher remained by his bedside. At the sight of his young master he rose.

"The prescription which the doctor ordered to be made up has arrived," said he. "I have administered a dose to the duke, and it seems to me that the result has been favourable."

Norbert drew up a heavy arm-chair to the foot of the bed, and took his seat upon it. From this position he could see his father's face. His brain was dazed, and it was with the utmost difficulty that he could recall the chain of events which had drawn him towards the abyss into which he had so nearly been precipitated.

The veil had been taken from his eyes, and he now saw with perfect clearness and seemed again to hear his father's voice as it roughly warned him that the woman he loved was a mere plotter, who cared not for him, but was scheming for his fortune and his name. Then he had been furiously indignant and looked upon the words as almost blasphemous, but now he saw that his father was right. How was it that he had not before seen that Diana was flinging herself in his way, and that all her affected openness and simplicity were merely the perfections of art, and that step by step she had led him to the brink of the terrible precipice which yawned before him? The whole hideous part as played by Daumon was no longer a sealed book to him. She whom he had looked on as a pure and innocent girl was merely the accomplice of a scheming villain like the counsellor, and after exciting his hatred and anger almost to madness, had placed the poison which was to take his father's life in his hands. A cold shiver ran through him as he realized this, and all his ardent love for Diana de Laurebourg was changed into a feeling of loathing and disgust.

At last the first pale rays of dawn broke through the casement, but before that Norbert, worn out with conflicting emotions, had fallen into a restless and uneasy sleep, and when he awoke the doctor was standing by the bedside of the sick man. At the first sound made by Norbert as he stirred in the chair, the doctor came towards him, saying, "We shall preserve his life."

This prognostication was complete, for that very evening the Duke de Champdoce was able to move in his bed, the next day he uttered some incoherent words, and later on asked for food; but the will of iron had passed away, the features had lost their expression of determination, and the eye the glitter of pride and power. Never again would the duke be able to exert that keen, stern intellect which had enabled him to influence all those around him; and in this terrible state of imbecility the haughty nobleman would ever remain, fed and looked after like a child, with no thought beyond his desires and his warm fire, and without a care for anything that was going on in the world around him.

After the enormity of his crime had been brought before him, the greatness of the punishment that he must endure now came across Norbert's mind. It was only now that Jean had ventured to tell him of M. de Puymandour's visit; and such a change had taken place in Norbert that he looked upon this visit as a special arrangement made by Providence.

325

"My father's will shall be carried out in every respect," said he to himself, and without an hour's delay he wrote to M. de Puymandour, begging him to call, and hoping that the grief which had fallen upon him had in no way altered the plan which had already been arranged.

Chapter 37: A Thunderbolt

As the miner, who sets fire to the fuse and seeks shelter from the coming explosion, so did Diana de Laurebourg return to her father's house after her visit to Daumon. During dinner it was impossible for her to utter a word, and it was with the greatest difficulty that she succeeded in swallowing a mouthful. Fortunately neither her father nor mother took any notice of her. They had that day received a letter announcing the news that their son, for whose future prosperity they had sacrificed Diana, was lying dangerously ill in Paris, where he was living in great style. They were in terrible affliction, and spoke of starting at once, so as to be with him. They therefore expressed no surprise when, on leaving the table, Diana pleaded a severe headache as an excuse for retiring to her own room. When once she was alone, having dismissed her maid, she heaved a deep sigh of relief. She never thought of retiring to bed, but throwing open her window, leaned out with her elbow on the window-sill.

It seemed to her that Norbert would certainly make some effort to see her, or at any rate by some means to let her know whether he had succeeded or failed.

"But I must be patient," murmured she, "for I can't hear anything until the afternoon of tomorrow."

In spite, however, of her resolutions, patience fled from her mind, and as soon as the servants had begun moving about, she went out into the garden and took up a position which commanded a view of the highroad, but no one appeared. The bell rang for breakfast. Again she had to seat herself at table with her parents, and the terrible penance of the past evening had to be repeated. At three o'clock she could endure the suspense no longer, and making her escape from the *château*, she went over to Daumon, who, she felt, must have obtained some intelligence. Even if she found that he knew nothing, it would be a relief to speak to him and to ask him when he thought that this terrible delay would come to an end. But she got no comfort at Daumon's, for he had passed as miserable a night as herself, and was nearly dead with affright. He had remained in his office all the morning, starting at the slightest sound, and though he was as anxious as

326

Diana for information, he had only gone out a little before her arrival. He met Mademoiselle Laurebourg on his return at the door of his cottage, and taking her inside, he informed her that at a late hour the night before the doctor had been sent for to Champdoce to attend the duke, who was supposed to be dying. Then he reproved her bitterly for her imprudence in visiting him.

"Do you wish," said he, "to show all Bevron that you and I are Norbert's accomplices?"

"What do you mean?" asked she.

"I mean that if the duke does not die, we are lost. When I say we, I mean myself, for you, as the daughter of a noble family, will be sure to escape scot free, and I shall be left to pay for all."

"You said that the effect was immediate."

"I did say so, and I thought so too. Ah, if I had but reflected a little! You will however see that I do not intend to give in without a fight. I will defend myself by accusing you. I am an honest man, and have been your dupe. You have thought to make me a mere tool; your fine Norbert is a fool, but he will pay for his doings with his head all the same."

At these gross insults Mademoiselle de Laurebourg rose to her feet and attempted to speak, but he cut her short.

"I can't stop to pick and choose my words, for I feel at the present moment as if the axe of the guillotine were suspended over my head. Now just oblige me by getting out of this, and never show your face here again."

"As you like. I will communicate with Champdoce."

"You shall not," exclaimed Daumon with a gesture of menace. "You might as well go and ask how the duke enjoyed the taste of the poison."

His words, however, did not deter Diana, for any risk seemed preferable to her than the present state of suspense.

With a glance of contempt at the counsellor she left the cottage, determined to act as she thought fit.

After Diana's departure, Daumon felt too that he must learn how matters were going on, and going over to the Widow Rouleau's, he despatched her daughter Francoise to the Château de Champdoce, under the pretext that he wanted some money which he had lent to one of the duke's servants. He had instructed the girl so cunningly that she had no suspicion of the real end and object of her mission, and set out on it with the most implicit confidence. He had not long to wait for her return, for in about half an hour his messenger returned.

"Well," said he anxiously, "has the scamp sent my money?"

"No, sir, I am sorry to say that I could not even get to speak to him."

"How was that? Was he not at Champdoce?"

"I cannot even tell you that. Ever since the duke has been ill, the great gates of the *château* have been bolted, for it seems that the poor old gentleman is at his last gasp."

"Did you not hear what was the matter with him?"

"No, sir, the little I have told you I got from a stable boy, who spoke to me through a grating in the gate, but before he could say ten words Jean came up and sent him off."

"Do you mean Jean, the duke's confidential man?"

"Just so," returned the girl, "and very angry he was. He abused the lad and told him to be off to the stables, and then asked, 'Well, my girl, and pray what do you want?' I told him that I had come with a message to the man Mechenit; but before I could say any more he broke in with, 'Well, he isn't here, you can call again in a month.'"

"You silly little fool, was that all you said?"

"Not quite, for I said that I must see Mechenit. Then, looking at me very suspiciously, he said, 'And who sent you here, you little spy?'"

The counsellor started.

"Indeed! and what did you say in return?" asked he.

"Why, of course I said that you had sent me."

"Yes, yes, that was right."

"And then Jean rubbed his hand over his chin, and looking at me very curiously, said sternly,—

"'So you have come from the counsellor, have you? Ah, I see it all, and so shall he one of these days.'"

At these words Daumon felt his knees give way under him; but all further questioning was stopped by the appearance of M. de Puymandour on his way to Champdoce. He therefore dismissed Francoise, and awaited the return of this gentleman, from whom he hoped to gain the fullest information regarding the duke's malady. The intelligence which he received calmed him a little, and repenting of his treatment of Diana, he went and hung about the gates of the Château de Laurebourg, until he was lucky enough to catch sight of the girl in the garden, for her anxiety would not permit her to remain in the house. He beckoned to her, and then said,—

"M. Norbert did not make the dose strong enough. The duke is as strong as a horse; but it is all right, for should he live, he will be an idiot, and so our end is as much gained as if he had died."

"But why does not Norbert write to me?" asked Diana seriously.

"Why, because he has some faint glimmerings of common sense. How do you know that he may not have half a dozen spies about him? You must wait."

Diana and the counsellor waited for a week, but Norbert made no sign. Diana suffered agonies, and the days seemed to pass with leaden feet. Sunday came at last. The Marchioness de Laurebourg had attended early Mass, and had given orders that her daughter should go to high Mass under the escort of her maid. Diana was highly pleased with this arrangement, for she hoped to have a chance of seeing Norbert, but she was disappointed. The Mass had commenced when she entered, but the spot occupied by the duke and his son was vacant. She followed the service in a purely mechanical manner, and at last noticed that the priest had taken his place in the pulpit.

This was generally an exciting moment for the inhabitants of Bevron, for it was immediately before the sermon that the banns of marriage were published. The priest gazed blandly down upon the expectant crowd, coughed slightly, used his handkerchief, and finally took from his breviary a sheet of paper.

"I have," said he, "to publish the banns of marriage between—" here he made a little pause, and all the congregation were on the tenterhooks of expectation; "between," he continued, "Monsieur Louis Norbert, Marquis de Champdoce, a minor, and only legitimate son of Guillaume Caesar, Duke de Champdoce, and of his wife Isabella de Barnaville, now deceased, but who both formerly resided in this parish, and Desiree Anne Marie Palouzet, minor, and legitimate daughter of Rene Augustus Palouzet, Count de Puymandour, and of Zoe Staplet, his wife, but now deceased, also residents of this parish."

This was the thunderbolt launched from the pulpit, which seemed to crush Diana into the earth, and her heart almost ceased to beat.

"Let anyone," continued the priest, "who knows of any impediment to this marriage, take warning that he or she must acquaint us with it, under the penalty of excommunication. At the same time let him be warned under the same penalty to bring forward nothing in malice or without some foundation."

An impediment! What irony lay veiled beneath that word. Mademoiselle de Laurebourg knew of more than one. A wild desire filled her heart to start from her seat and cry out,—

"It is impossible for this marriage to take place, for that Norbert was her affianced husband in the sight of Heaven, and that he was bound to her by the strongest of all links, that of crime."

But by a gigantic effort she controlled herself, and remained motionless, pallid as a spectre, but with a forced smile on her lips, and with unparalleled audacity made a little sign to one of her female friends, which plainly meant, "This is, indeed, something unexpected." All her mind was concentrated to preserve a calm and unmoved aspect. The singing of the choir seemed to die away, the strong odour of the incense almost overpowered her, and she felt that unless the service soon came to an end, she must fall insensible from her chair. At last the priest turned again to the congregation and droned out the *Ita missa est*, and all was over. Diana grasped the arm of her maid and forced her away, without saying a word. As she reached home, a servant ran up to her with a face upon which agitation was strongly painted.

"Ah, *mademoiselle*," gasped he, "such a frightful calamity. Your father and mother are expecting you; it is really too terrible." Diana hastened to obey the summons. Her father and mother were seated near each other, evidently in deep distress. She went towards them, and the *marquis*, drawing her to him, pressed her against his heart.

"Poor child! My dear daughter!" murmured he, "you are all that is left to us now."

Their son had died, and the sad news had been brought to the *château* while Diana was at Mass. By her brother's death she had succeeded to a princely fortune, and would now be one of the richest heiresses for many a mile round. Had this event happened but a week before, her marriage to Norbert would have met with no opposition from his father, and she would never have plunged into this abyss of crime. It was more than the irony of fate; it was the manifest punishment of an angry Divinity. She shed no tear for her brother's death. Her thoughts were all firmly fixed on Norbert, and that fearful announcement made in the house of God rang still in her ears. What could be the meaning of this sudden arrangement, and why had the marriage been so suddenly decided on?

She felt that some mystery lay beneath it all, and vowed that she would fathom it to its nethermost depths. What was it that had taken place at Champdoce? Had the duke, contrary to Daumon's prognostications, recovered? Had he discovered his son' insidious attack upon his life, and only pardoned it upon a blind compliance being given to his will? She passed away the whole day in these vain suppositions, and tried to think of every plan to stay the celebration of this union, for she had not given up her hopes, nor did she yet despair of ultimate success. Her new and unlooked-for fortune placed a fresh weapon at her disposal, and she felt that the victory would yet be hers if she could but see Norbert again, were it but for a single instant. Was she not certain of the absolute power that she exercised over him, for had she not by a few words induced him to enter upon the terrible path of crime? She must see him, and that without a moment's delay, for the danger was imminent. A day now would be worth a year hereafter. She determined that, upon that very night, she would visit Champdoce. A little after midnight, when the inhabitants of the *château* were wrapped in slumber, she crept on tiptoe down the grand staircase, and made her exit by a side door. She had arranged her plan as to how she would find Norbert, for he had often described the interior arrangements of the *château* to her. She knew that his room was on the ground floor, with two windows looking on to the courtyard. When, however, she reached the old *château*, she hesitated. Suppose that she should go to the wrong window. But she had gone too far to recede, and determined that if anyone else than Norbert should open the window, she would turn and fly. She tapped at the window softly, and then more loudly. She had made no mistake. Norbert threw open the window, with the words,—

"Who is there?"

"It is I, Norbert; I, Diana."

"What do you want?" asked Norbert in an agitated tone of voice. "What do you want to do here?"

She looked at him anxiously and hardly recognised his face, so great was the change that had come over it. It absolutely terrified her.

"Are you going to marry Mademoiselle de Puymandour?" asked she.

"Yes I am."

"And yet you pretended to love me?"

"Yes, I loved you ardently, devotedly, with a love that drove me to crime; but you had no love; you cared but for rank and fortune."

Diana raised her hands to heaven in an agony of despair.

"Should I be here at this hour if what you say is true?" asked she wildly. "My brother is dead, and I am as wealthy as you are, Norbert, and yet I am here. You accuse me of being mercenary, and for what reason? Was it because I refused to fly with you from my father's house? Oh, Norbert, it was but the happiness of our future life that I strove to protect. It was—"

331

Her speech failed her, and her eyes dilated with horror, for the door behind Norbert opened, and the Duke de Champdoce entered the room, uttering a string of meaningless words, and laughing with that mirthless laugh which is so sure a sign of idiocy.

"Can you understand now," exclaimed Norbert, pointing to his father, "why the remembrance of my love for you has become a hateful reminiscence? Do you dare to talk of happiness to me, when this spectre of a meditated crime will ever rise between us?" and with a meaning gesture he pointed to the open gate of the courtyard.

She turned; but before passing away, she cast a glance upon him full of the deepest fury and jealousy. She could not forgive Norbert for his share in the crime that she herself prompted,—for the crime which had blighted all her hopes of happiness. Her farewell was a menace.

"Norbert," she said, as she glided through the gate like a spectre of the night, "I will have revenge, and that right soon."

Chapter 38: Marriage Bells, Funeral Knells

Three days of hard work had completed all the arrangements necessary for the marriage of Norbert and Mademoiselle de Puymandour. He had been presented to the lady, and neither had received a favourable impression of the other. At the very first glance each one felt that inevitable repugnance which the lapse of years can never efface. While dreading the anger of her obdurate father, Marie had at one time thought of confiding the secret of her attachment to George de Croisenois to Norbert, for she had the idea that if she told him that her heart was another's, he might withdraw his pretensions to her hand; but several times, when the opportunity occurred, fear restrained her tongue, and she let the propitious moment pass away. Had she done so, Norbert would at once have eagerly grasped at a pretext for absolving himself from a promise which he had made mentally of obeying in all things a father who now, alas! had no means of enforcing his commands.

Each day he paid his visit to Puymandour as an accepted suitor, bearing a large bouquet with him, which he regularly presented to his betrothed upon his entrance into the drawing-room, which she accepted with a painful flush rising to her cheek. The pair conversed upon indifferent topics, while an aged female connection sat in the room to play propriety. For many hours they would remain thus, the girl bending over her fancy work, and he vainly striving to find topics of conversation, and, consequently, saying hardly anything, in spite of Marie's feeble efforts to assist in the conversation. It was a slight relief when M. de Puymandour proposed a walk; but this was a rare occurrence, for that gentleman usually declared that he never had a moment's leisure. Never had he seemed so gay and busy since the approaching marriage of his daughter had been the theme of every tongue. He took all the preparations for the ceremony into his own hands, for he had determined that everything should be conducted on a scale of unparalleled magnificence. The *château* was refurnished, and all the carriages repainted and varnished, while the Champdoce and the Puymandour arms were quartered together on their panels. This coat of arms was to be seen everywhere—over the doors, on the walls, and engraved on the silver, and it was believed that M. de Puymandour would have made no objection to their being branded on his breast.

In the midst of all this turmoil and bustle Norbert and Marie grew sadder and sadder as each day passed on. One day M. de Puymandour heard so astounding a piece of intelligence that he hurried into the drawing-room, where he knew that he should find the lovers (as he styled them) together.

"Well, my children," exclaimed he, "you have set such an excellent example, that everybody seems disposed to copy you, and the mayor and the priest will be kept to their work rather tightly this year."

His daughter tried to put on an appearance of interest at this speech.

"Yes," continued M. de Puymandour, "I have just heard of a marriage that will come off almost directly after yours has been celebrated, and will make a stir, I can assure you."

"And whose is that, pray?"

"You are acquainted, I presume," returned the father, addressing himself to Norbert, "with the son of the Count de Mussidan?"

"What, the Viscount Octave?"

"The same."

"He lives in Paris, does he not?"

"Yes, generally; but he has been staying at Mussidan, and in the short space of a week has managed to lose his heart here; and to whom do you think? Come, give a guess."

"We cannot think who it can be, my dear father," said Marie, "and we are devoured with curiosity."

"It is reported that the Viscount de Mussidan has proposed for the hand of Mademoiselle de Laurebourg."

"Why," remarked Marie, "it is only three weeks since her brother died!"

Norbert flushed scarlet, and then turned a livid white; so great was his agitation at hearing this news, that he nearly dropped the album which he held in his hand.

"I like the viscount," continued M. de Puymandour, "while Mademoiselle Diana is a charming girl. She is very handsome, and, I believe, has many talents; and she is a good model for you to copy, Marie, as you are so soon to become a duchess."

When he got upon his favourite hobby, it was very difficult to check M. de Puymandour. His daughter, therefore, waited until he had concluded, and then left the room, under the pretext of giving an order to the servants. The count hardly noticed her absence, as he had still Norbert at his mercy.

"Reverting again to Mademoiselle Diana," said he: "she looks charming in black, for women should look upon a death in the family as a most fortunate occurrence; but I ought not to be praising her to you, who are so well acquainted with her."

"I?" exclaimed Norbert.

"Yes, you. I do not suppose that you intend to deny that you have had a little flirtation with her?"

"I do not understand you."

"Well, *I* do then, my boy; I heard all about your making love to her. Why, you are really blushing! What is up now?"

"I can assure you—"

De Puymandour burst into a loud laugh.

"I have heard a good deal of your little country walks, and all the pretty things that you used to say to each other."

In vain did Norbert deny the whole thing, for his intended father-in-law would not believe him; and at last he got so annoyed that he refused to remain and dine with the count, alleging anxiety for his father as an excuse. He returned home as soon as he possibly could, much agitated by what he had heard; and as he was walking rapidly on, he heard his name called by someone who was running after him: Norbert turned round, and found himself face to face with Montlouis.

"I have been here a week," said the young man. "I am here with my patron, for I have one now. I am now with the Viscount de Mussidan, as his private secretary. M. Octave is not the most agreeable man in the world to get on with, as he gets into the most violent passions on very trivial occasions; but he has a good heart, after all, and I am very pleased with the position I have gained."

"I am very glad to hear it, Montlouis, very much pleased indeed."

"And you, *marquis*, I hear, are to marry Mademoiselle de Puymandour; I could scarcely credit the news."

"And why, pray?"

"Because I remembered when we used to wait outside a certain garden wall, until we saw a certain door open discreetly."

"But you must efface all this from your memory, Montlouis."

"Do not be alarmed; save to you, my lips would never utter a word of this. No one else would ever make me speak."

"Stop!" said Norbert, with an angry gesture. "Do you venture to say—"

"To say what?"

"I wish you to understand that Mademoiselle Diana is as free from blame today as she was when first I met her. She has been indiscreet, but nothing more, I swear it before heaven!"

"I believe you perfectly."

In reality Montlouis did not believe one word of Norbert's assertion, and the young *marquis* could read this in his companion's face.

"The more so," continued the secretary, "as the young lady is about to be married to my friend and patron."

"But where," asked Norbert, "did the viscount meet with Mademoiselle de Laurebourg?"

"In Paris; the viscount and her brother were very intimate, and nursed him during his last illness, and as soon as the scheming parents heard of the viscount being in the neighbourhood they asked him to call on them. Of course he did so, and saw Mademoiselle Diana, and returned home in a perfect frenzy of love."

Norbert seemed so incensed at this that Montlouis broke off his recital, feeling confident that the *marquis* still loved Diana, and was consumed with the flame of jealousy.

"But, of course," he added carelessly, "nothing is yet settled."

Norbert, however, was too agitated to listen to the idle gossip of Montlouis any longer, so he pressed his hand and left him rather abruptly, walking away at the top of his speed, leaving his friend silent with astonishment. It seemed to Norbert as if he was imprisoned in one of those iron dungeons he had read of, which slowly contracted day by day, and at last crushed their victims to atoms. He saw Diana married to the Viscount de Mussidan, and compelled to meet daily the man who knew all about her illicit meetings with her former lover, and who had more than once, when Norbert was unable to leave Champdoce, been entrusted with a letter or a message for her. And how would Montlouis behave under the circumstances? Would he possess the necessary tact and coolness to carry him through so difficult a position? What would be the end of this cruel concatenation of circumstances? Would Diana be able to endure the compromising witness of her youthful error? She would eagerly seek out some pretext for his dismissal; he could easily detect this, and in his anger at the loss of a position which he had long desired, would turn on her and repeat the whole story. Should Montlouis let loose his tongue, the viscount, indignant at the imposition that had been practised upon him, would separate from his wife. What would be Diana's conduct when she found herself left thus alone, and despised by the society of which she had hoped to be a queen? Would she not, in her turn, seek to revenge herself on Norbert? He had just asked himself whether at this juncture death would not be a blessing to him, when he caught sight of Francoise, the daughter of the Widow Rouleau, close by him. For two hours she had been awaiting his coming, concealed behind a hedge.

"I have something to give you, my lord *marquis*," said she.

He took the letter that she held out to him, and, opening it, he read,—

"You said that I did not love you—perhaps this was but a test to prove my love. I am ready to fly with you tonight. I shall lose all, but it will be for your sake. Reflect, Norbert; there is yet time, but tomorrow it will be too late."

These were the words that Mademoiselle de Laurebourg had had the courage to pen, which to the former lover were full of the most thrilling eloquence. The usually bold, firm writing of Diana was, in the letter before him, confused and almost illegible, showing the writer's frame of mind. There were blurs and blisters upon the paper as though tears had fallen upon it, perhaps because the writing had been made purposely irregular and drops of water are an excellent substitute for tears.

"Does she really love me?" murmured he.

He hesitated; yes, he absolutely hesitated, impressed by the idea that for him she was ready to sacrifice position and honour, that he had but to raise his finger and she was his, and that in the space of a couple of hours she might be the companion of his flight to some far-distant land. His pulse throbbed madly, and he could scarcely draw his breath, when some fifty paces down the road he caught sight of the figure of a man; it was his father. This was the second time that the duke by his mere presence had spread the web of Diana's temptations and allurements.

"Never!" exclaimed Norbert, with such fire and energy that the girl fell back a pace. "Never! no, never!" and crushing up the letter, he dashed it upon the ground, from whence Francoise picked it up as he ran forward to meet his father. The duke had recovered from his attack as far as the mere fact of his life not having been sacrificed; he could walk, sleep, eat and drink as he had formerly done. He could look at the labourers in the fields or the horses in the stables, but five minutes afterwards he had no recollection of what he heard or saw. The sudden loss of his father's aid would have caused Norbert much embarrassment had it not been for the shrewdness and sagacity of M. de Puymandour, who had assisted him greatly. But all these arrangements which had to be made had necessarily delayed the wedding. But it came at last; M. de Puymandour took absolute possession of him, and after the unhappy young man had passed a sleepless night, he was allowed no time for reflection. At eleven o'clock he entered the carriage, and was driven fast to the Mayor's office, and from thence to the chapel, and by twelve o'clock all was finished and he fettered for life. A little before dinner the Viscount de Mussidan came to offer his congratulations, and gained them at the same time for himself by announcing his speedy union with Mademoiselle Diana de Laurebourg.

Five days later the newly married pair took possession of their mansion at Champdoce. Hampered with a wife whom he had never affected to love, and whose tearful face was a constant reproach to him, and with a father who was an utter imbecile, the thoughts of suicide more than once crossed Norbert's brain. One day a servant informed Norbert that his father refused to get up. A doctor was sent for, and he declared that the duke was in a highly critical condition. A violent reaction had taken place, and all day the invalid was in a state of intense excitement.

The power of speech, which he had almost entirely lost, seemed to have returned to him in a miraculous manner; at length, however, he became delirious, and Norbert dismissed the servants who had been watching by his father's bed, lest in the incoherent ravings of the invalid, the words "Parricide" or "Poison" should break forth. At eleven o'clock he grew calmer, and slept a little, when all at once he started up in bed, exclaiming: "Come here, Norbert," and Jean, who had remained by his old master's side, ran up to the bed and was much startled at the sight. The duke had entirely recovered his former appearance. His eyes flashed, and his lips trembled, as they always did when he was greatly excited.

"Pardon, father; pardon," cried Norbert, falling upon his knees.

The duke softly stretched out his hand. "I was mad with family pride," said he; "and God punished me. My son, I forgive you."

Norbert's sobs broke the stillness of the chamber.

"My son, I renounce my ideas," continued the duke. "I do not desire you to wed Mademoiselle de Puymandour if you feel that you cannot love her."

"Father," answered Norbert, "I have obeyed your wishes, and she is now my wife."

A gleam of terrible anguish passed over the duke's countenance; he raised his hands as though to shield his eyes from some grizzly spectre, and in tones of heartrending agony exclaimed: "Too late! Too late!"

He fell back in terrible convulsions, and in a moment was dead. If, as has been often asserted, the veil of the hereafter is torn asunder, then the Duke de Champdoce had a glimpse into a terrible future.

Chapter 39: Rash Word, Rash Deed

After her repulse by Norbert, Diana, with the cold chill of death in her heart, made her way back to the *château* of the De Laurebourgs, over the same road which but a short time before she had travelled full of expectation and hope. The sudden appearance of the Duke de Champdoce had filled her with alarm, but her imagination was not of that kind upon which unpleasant impressions remain for any long period; for after she had regained her room, and thrown aside her out-door attire, and removed all signs of mud-stains, she once more became herself, and even laughed a little rippling laugh at all her own past alarms. Overwhelmed with the shame of her repulse, she had threatened Norbert; but as she reasoned calmly, she felt that it was not he for whom she felt the most violent animosity. All her hatred was reserved for that woman who had come between her and her lover—for Marie de Puymandour. Some hidden feeling warned her that she must look into Marie's past life for some reason for the rupture of her engagement with Norbert, though the banns had already been published. This was the frame of mind in which Diana was when the Viscount de Mussidan was introduced to her, the friend of the brother whose untimely death had left her such a wealthy heiress. He was tall and well made, with handsomely chiselled features; and, endowed with physical strength and health, Octave de Mussidan had the additional advantages of noble descent and princely fortune. Two women, both renowned for their wit and beauty, his aunt and his mother, had been entrusted with the education which would but enable him to shine in society.

Dispatched to Paris, with an ample allowance, at the age of twenty, he found himself, thanks to his birth and connections, in the very centre of the world of fashion. At the sight of Mademoiselle de Laurebourg his heart was touched for the first time. Diana had never been more charmingly fascinating than she was at this period. Octave de Mussidan did not suit her fancy; there was too great a difference between him and Norbert, and nothing would ever efface from her memory the recollection of the young *marquis* as he had appeared before her on the first day of their meeting in the Forest of Bevron, clad in his rustic garb, with the game he had shot dangling from his hand. She delighted to feast her recollection, and thought fondly of his shyness and diffidence when he hardly ventured to raise his eyes to hers.

Octave, however, fell a victim at the first glance he caught of Diana, and permitted himself to be swept away by the tide of his private emotions, which upon every visit that he paid to Laurebourg became more powerful and resistless. Like a true knight, who wishes that he himself should gain the love of his lady fair, Octave addressed himself directly to Diana, and after many attempts succeeded in finding himself alone with her, and then he asked her if she could permit him to crave of her father, the Marquis de Laurebourg, the honour of her hand. This appeal surprised her, for she had been so much absorbed in her own troubles that she had not even suspected his love for her. She was not even frightened at his declaration, as is the patient when the surgeon informs him that he must use the knife.

She glanced at De Mussidan strangely as he put this question to her, and after a moment's hesitation, replied that she would give him a reply the next day. After thinking the matter over, she wrote and dispatched the letter which Francoise had carried to Norbert. The prisoner in the dock as he anxiously awaits the sentence of his judge, can alone appreciate Diana's state of agonized suspense as she stood at the end of the park at Laurebourg awaiting the return of the girl. Her anxiety of mind lasted nearly three hours, when Francoise hurried up breathless.

"What did the *marquis* say?" asked Diana.

"He said nothing; that is, he cried out very angrily, 'Never! no, never!'"

In order to prevent any suspicions arising in the girl's mind, Mademoiselle de Laurebourg contrived to force a laugh, exclaiming: "Ah! indeed, that is just what I expected."

Francoise seemed as if she had something to say on the tip of her tongue, but Diana hurriedly dismissed her, pressing a coin into her hand. All anxiety was now at an end; for her there was no longer any suspense or anguish; all her struggles were now futile, and she felt grateful to Octave for having given her his love. "Once married," thought she, "I shall be free, and shall be able to follow the duke and duchess to Paris."

Upon her return to the *château*, she found Octave awaiting her. His eyes put the question that his lips did not dare to utter; and, placing her hand in his with a gentle inclination of her head, she assented to his prayer.

This act on her part would, she believed, free her from the past; but she was in error. Upon hearing that his dastardly attempt at murder had failed, the counsellor was for the time utterly overwhelmed with terror, but the news that he had gained from M. de Puymandour calmed his mind in a great measure. He was not, however, completely reassured until he heard for certain that the duke had become a helpless maniac, and that the doctor, having given up all hopes of his patient's recovery, had discontinued his visits to the *château*. As soon as he had heard that Norbert's marriage had been so soon followed by his father's death, he imagined that every cloud had disappeared from the sky.

All danger now seemed at an end, and he recalled with glee that he had in his strong box the promissory notes, signed by Norbert, to the amount of twenty thousand *francs*, which he could demand at any moment, now that Norbert was the reigning lord of Champdoce. The first step he took was to hang about the neighbourhood of Laurebourg, for he thought that some lucky chance would surely favour him with an opportunity for a little conversation with Mademoiselle Diana. For several days in succession he was unsuccessful, but at last he was delighted at seeing her alone, walking in the direction of Bevron. Without her suspecting it, he followed her until the road passed through a small plantation, when he came up and addressed her.

"What do you want with me?" asked she angrily.

He made no direct reply; but after apologising for his boldness, he began to offer his congratulations upon her approaching marriage, which was now the talk of the whole neighbourhood, and which pleased him much, as M. de Mussidan was in every way superior to—

"Is that all you have to say to me?" asked Diana, interrupting his string of words.

As she turned from him, he had the audacity to lay his hand upon the edge of her jacket.

"I have more to say," said he, "if you will honour me with your attention. Something about—you can guess what."

"About whom or what?" asked she, making no effort to hide her supreme contempt.

He smiled, glanced around to see that no one was within hearing, and then said in a low voice,—

"It is about the bottle of poison."

She recoiled, as though some venomous reptile had started up in front of her.

"What do you mean?" cried she. "How dare you speak to me thus?"

All his servile manner had now returned to him, and he uttered a string of complaints in a whining tone of voice. She had played him a most unfair trick, and had stolen a certain little glass bottle from his office; and if anything had leaked out, his head would have paid the penalty of a crime in which he had no hand. He was quite ill, owing to the suspense and anxiety he had endured; sleep would not come to his bed, and the pangs of remorse tortured him continually.

"Enough," cried Diana, stamping her foot angrily on the ground. "Enough, I say."

"Well, *mademoiselle*, I can no longer remain here. I am far too nervous, and I wish to go to some foreign country."

"Come, let me hear the real meaning of this long preface."

Thus adjured, Daumon spoke. He only wished for some little memento to cheer his days and nights of exile, some little recognition of his services; in fact, such a sum as would bring him in an income of three thousand *francs*.

"I understand you," replied Diana. "You wish to be paid for what you call your kindness."

"Ah, *mademoiselle!*"

"And you put a value of sixty thousand *francs* upon it; that is rather a high price, is it not?"

"Alas! it is not half what this unhappy business has cost me."

"Nonsense; your demand is preposterous."

"Demand!" returned he; "I make no demand. I come to you respectfully and with a little charity. If I were to demand, I should come to you in quite a different manner. I should say, 'Pay me such and such a sum, or I tell everything.' What have I to lose if the whole story comes to light? A mere nothing. I am a poor man, and am growing old. You and M. Norbert are the ones that have something to fear. You are noble, rich, and young, and a happy future lies before you."

Diana paused and thought for an instant.

"You are speaking," answered she at last, "in a most foolish manner. When charges are made against people, proofs must be forthcoming."

"Quite right, *mademoiselle*; but can you say that these proofs are not in my hands? Should you, however, desire to buy them, you are at liberty to do so. I give you the first option, and yet you grumble."

As he spoke, he drew a battered leather pocket-book from his breast, and took from it a paper, which, after having been crumpled, had been carefully smoothed out again. Diana glanced at it, and then uttered a stifled cry of rage and fear, for she at once recognised her last letter to Norbert.

"That wretch, Francoise, has betrayed me," exclaimed she, "and I saved her mother from a death by hunger and cold."

The counsellor held out the letter to her. She thought that he had no suspicion of her, and made an attempt to snatch it from him; but he was on his guard, and drew back with a sarcastic smile on his face.

"No, *mademoiselle*," said he; "this is not the little bottle of poison; however, I will give it to you, together with another one, when I have obtained what I ask. Nothing for nothing, however; and if I must go to the scaffold, I will do so in good company."

Mademoiselle de Laurebourg was in utter despair.

"But I have no money," said she. "Where is a girl to find such a sum?"

"M. Norbert can find it."

"Go to him, then."

Daumon made a negative sign with his head.

"I am not quite such a fool," answered he; "I know M. Norbert too well. He is the very image of his father. But you can manage him, *mademoiselle*; besides, you have much interest in having the matter settled."

"Counsellor!"

"There is no use in beating about the bush. I come to you humbly enough, and you treat me like so much dirt. I will not submit to this, as you will find to your cost. *I* never poisoned anyone; but enough of this kind of thing. Today is Tuesday; if on Friday, by six o'clock, I do not have what I have asked for, your father and the count Octave will have a letter from me, and perhaps your fine marriage may come to nothing after all."

This insolence absolutely struck Diana dumb, and Daumon had disappeared round a turning of the road before she could find words to crush him for his vile attempt at extortion. She felt that he was capable of keeping his word, even if by so doing he seriously injured himself without gaining any advantage.

A nature like Diana's always looks danger boldly in the face. She had, however, but little choice how she would act—for to apply to Norbert was the only resource left to her—for she knew that he would do all in his power to ward off the danger which threatened both of them so nearly. The idea, however, of applying to him for aid was repugnant to her pride. To what depths of meanness and infamy had she descended! and to what avail had been all her aspirations of ambition and grandeur?

She was at the mercy of a wretch—of Daumon, in fact. She was forced to go as a suppliant to a man whom she had loved so well that she now hated him with a deadly hatred. But she did not hesitate for a moment. She went straight to the cottage of Widow Rouleau, and despatched Francoise in quest of Norbert.

She ordered the girl to tell him that he must without fail be at the wicket gate in the park wall at Laurebourg on the coming night, where she would meet him, and that the matter was one of life and death.

As Diana gave these orders to Francoise, the woman's nervous air and flushed features plainly showed that she was a mere creature of Daumon's; but Mademoiselle de Laurebourg felt it would be unwise to take any notice of her discovery, but to abstain from employing her in confidential communications for the future.

As the hour of the meeting drew near a host of doubts assailed her. Would Norbert come to the meeting? Had Francoise contrived to see him? Might he not be absent from home? It was now growing dark, and the servants brought candles into the dining-room, and Diana, contriving to slip away, gained the appointed spot. Norbert was waiting, and when he caught sight of her, rushed forward, but stopped as though restrained by a sudden thought, and remained still, as if rooted to the ground.

"You sent for me, *mademoiselle?*" said he.

"I did."

After a pause, in which she succeeded in mastering her emotion, Diana began with the utmost volubility to explain the extortion that Daumon was endeavouring to practise upon her, magnifying, though there was but little need to do so, all the threats and menaces that he had made use of. She had imagined that this last piece of roguery on the part of Daumon would drive Norbert into a furious passion, but to her surprise it had no such effect. He had suffered so much and so deeply, that his heart was almost dead against any further emotion.

"Do not let this trouble you," answered he apathetically; "I will see Daumon and settle with him."

"Can you leave me thus, at our last meeting, without even a word?" asked she.

"What have I to say? My father forgave me on his death-bed, and I pardon you."

"Farewell, Norbert; we shall see no more of each other. I am going to marry, as you have doubtless been informed. Can I oppose my parent's will? Besides, what does it signify? Farewell; remember no one wishes more sincerely for your future happiness than I do."

"Happy!" exclaimed Norbert. "How can I ever be happy again? If you know the secret, for pity's sake break it to me. Tell me how to forget and how to annihilate thought. Do you not know that I had planned a life of perfect happiness with you by my side? I had visions; and now plans and visions are alike hateful to me. And as they ever and *anon* recur to my memory, they will fill me with terror and despair."

As Diana heard these words of agony, a wild gleam of triumph shot from her eyes, but it faded away quickly, and left her cold and emotionless as a marble statue; and when she reappeared in the drawing-room, after taking leave of Norbert, her face wore so satisfied an expression, that the viscount complimented her upon her apparent happiness.

She made some jesting retort, but there was a shade of earnestness mixed with her playfulness, for to her future husband she only wished to show the amiable side of her character; but all the time she was thinking. Will Norbert see Daumon in time?

The duke kept his word, and the next day the faithful Jean discreetly handed her a packet. She opened it and found that besides the two letters of which the counsellor had spoken, it contained all her correspondence with Norbert—more than a hundred letters in

344

all, some of great length, and all of them compromising to a certain extent. Her first thought was to destroy them, but on reflection she decided not to do so, and hid the packet in the same place as she had concealed the letters written by Norbert to her.

Norbert had given Daumon sixty thousand *francs*, and in addition owed him twenty thousand on his promissory notes. This sum, in addition to what he had already saved, would form such a snug little fortune that it would enable the counsellor to quit Bevron, and take up his abode in Paris, where his peculiar talents would have more scope for development. And eight days later the village was thrown into a state of intense excitement by the fact becoming known that Daumon had shut up his house and departed for Paris, taking Francoise, the Widow Rouleau's daughter, with him. The Widow Rouleau was furious, and openly accused Mademoiselle de Laurebourg of having aided in the committal of the act which had deprived her of her daughter's services in her declining years; and the old woman who had acted as housekeeper, who on Daumon's departure had thrown open the place, did not hesitate to assert that all her late master's legal lore had been acquired in prison, where he had undergone a sentence of ten years' penal servitude.

In spite of all this, however, Mademoiselle de Laurebourg was secretly delighted at the departure of Daumon and Francoise; for she experienced an intense feeling of relief at knowing that she no longer was in any risk of meeting her accomplice in her daily walks. Norbert, too, was going to Paris with his wife; and M. de Puymandour was going about saying that his daughter, the Duchess of Champdoce, would not return to this part of the country for some time to come.

Diana drew a long breath of relief, for it seemed to her as if all the threatening clouds, which had darkened the horizon, were fast breaking up and drifting away. Her future seemed clear, and she could continue the preparations for her marriage, which was to be celebrated in a fortnight's time; and the friend of Octave who had been asked to act as his best man had answered in the affirmative.

Diana had taken accurate measurement of the love that Octave lavished upon her, and did her utmost to increase it. She had another cruel idea, and that was that the bewitching manner which she had assumed towards her betrothed was excellent practice, and by it she might judge of her future success in society when she resided in Paris. Octave was utterly conquered, as any other man would have been under similar circumstances.

Upon the day of her wedding she was dazzling in her beauty, and her face was radiant with happiness; but it was a mere mask, which she had put on to conceal her real feelings. She knew that many curious eyes were fixed on her as she left the chapel; and the crowd formed a line for her to pass through. She saw many a glance of dislike cast upon her; but a more severe blow awaited her, for on her arrival at the Château de Mussidan, to which she was driven directly after the ceremony, the first person she met was Montlouis, who came forward to welcome her. Bold and self-possessed as she was, the slight of this man startled her, and a bright flush passed across her face. Fortunately Montlouis had had time to prepare himself for this meeting, and his face showed no token of recognition. But though his salutation was of the most respectful description, Madame de Mussidan thought she saw in his eyes that ironical expression of contempt which she had more than once seen in Daumon's face.

"That man must not, shall not, stay here," she murmured to herself.

It was easy enough for her to ask her husband to dismiss Montlouis from his employ, but it was a dangerous step to take; and her easiest course was to defer the dismissal of the secretary until some really good pretext offered itself. Nor was this pretext long in presenting itself; for Octave was by no means satisfied with the young man's conduct. Montlouis who had been full of zeal while in Paris, had renewed his liaison, on his return to Mussidan, with the girl with whom he had been formerly entangled at Poitiers. This, of course, could not be permitted to go on, and an explosion was clearly to be expected; but what Diana dreaded most was the accidental development of some unseen chance.

After she had been married some two weeks, when Octave proposed in the afternoon that they should go for a walk, she agreed. Her preparations were soon completed, and they started off, blithe and lively as children on a holiday ramble. As they loitered in a wooded path, they heard a dog barking in the cover. It was Bruno, who rushed out, and, standing on his hind legs, endeavoured to lick Diana's face.

"Help, help, Octave!" she exclaimed, and her husband, springing to her side, drove away the animal.

"Were you very much alarmed, dearest?" asked he.

"Yes," answered she faintly; "I was almost frightened to death."

"I do not think that he would do you any harm," remarked Octave.

"No matter; make him go away;" and as she spoke she struck at him with her parasol. But the dog never for a moment supposed that

Diana was in earnest, and, supposing that she intended to play with him, as she had often done before, began to gambol round her, barking joyously the whole time.

"But this dog evidently knows you, Diana," observed the viscount.

"Know me? Impossible!" and as she spoke Bruno ran up and licked her hand. "If he does, his memory is better than mine; at any rate, I am half afraid of him. Come, Octave, let us go."

They turned away, and Octave would have forgotten all about the occurrence had not Bruno, delighted at having found an old acquaintance, persisted in following them.

"This is strange," exclaimed the viscount, "very strange indeed. Look here, my man," said he, addressing a peasant, who was engaged in clipping a hedge by the roadside, "do you know whose dog this is?"

"Yes, my lord, it belongs to the young Duke de Champdoce."

"Of course," answered Diana, "I have often seen the dog at the Widow Rouleau's, and have occasionally given it a piece of bread. He was always with Francoise, who ran off with that man Daumon. Oh, yes, I know him now; here, Bruno, here!"

The dog rushed to her, and, stooping down, she caressed him, thus hoping to conceal her tell-tale face.

Octave drew his wife's arm within his without another word. A strange feeling of doubt had arisen in his mind. Diana, too, was much disturbed, and abused herself mentally for having been so weak and cowardly. Why had she not at once confessed that she knew the dog? Had she said at once, "Why, that is Bruno, the Duke de Champdoce's dog," her husband would have thought no more about the matter; but her own folly had made much of a merely trivial incident.

Ever since that fatal walk the viscount's manner appeared to have changed, and more than once Diana fancied that she caught a look of suspicion in his eyes. How could she best manage to make him forget this unlucky event? She saw that for the rest of her life she must affect a terror of dogs; and, for the future, whenever she saw one, she uttered a little cry of alarm, and insisted upon all Octave's being chained up. But for all this she lived in a perfect atmosphere of suspicion and anxiety, while the very ground upon which she walked seemed to have been mined beneath her feet. Her sole wish now was to fly from Mussidan, and leave Bevron and its environs, she cared not for what spot. It has been first arranged that immediately after the marriage they should make a short tour; but in spite of this, they still lingered at Mussidan; and all that Diana could do was to keep this previous determination before her husband, without making any direct attack.

The blow came at last, and was more unexpected and terrible than she had anticipated. On the afternoon of the 26th of October, as Diana was gazing from her window, an excited crowd rushed into the courtyard of the *château*, followed by four men bearing a litter covered with a sheet, under which could be distinguished the rigid limbs of a dead body, while a cruel crimson stain upon one side of the white covering too plainly showed that someone had met with a violent death.

The hideous sight froze Diana with terror, and it was impossible for her to leave the window or quit the object on the litter, which seemed to have a terrible fascination for her. That very morning her husband, accompanied by his friend the Baron de Clinchain, Montlouis, and a servant named Ludovic, had gone out for a day's shooting. It was evident that something had happened to one of the party; which of them could it be? The doubt was not of very long duration; for at that moment her husband entered the courtyard, supported by M. de Clinchain and Ludovic. His face was deadly pale, and he seemed scarcely able to drag one leg after the other. The dead man therefore must be Montlouis. She need no longer plot and scheme for the dismissal of the secretary, for his tongue had been silenced for ever.

A ray of comfort dawned in Diana's heart at this idea, and gave her the strength to descend the staircase. Halfway down she met M. de Clinchain, who was ascending. He seized her by the arm, and said hoarsely,—

"Go back, *madame*, go back!"

"But tell me what has happened."

"A terrible calamity. Go back to your room, I beg of you. Your husband will be here presently;" and, as Octave appeared, he absolutely pushed her into her own room.

Octave followed, and, extending his arms, pressed his wife closely to his breast, bursting as he did so into a passion of sobs.

"Ah!" cried M. de Clinchain joyously, "he is saved. See, he weeps; I had feared for his reason."

After many questions and incoherent answers, Madame de Mussidan at last arrived at the fact that her husband had shot Montlouis by accident. Diana believed this story, but it was far from the truth. Montlouis had met his death at her hands quite as much as the Duke de Champdoce had done. He had died because he was the possessor of a fatal secret.

This was what had really occurred. After lunch, Octave, who had drunk rather freely, began to rally Montlouis regarding his mysterious movements, and to assert that some woman must be at the bottom of them. At first Montlouis joined in the laugh; but at length M. de Mussidan became too personal in remarks regarding the woman his secretary loved, and Montlouis responded angrily.

This influenced his master's temper, and he went on to say that he could no longer permit such doings, and he reproached his secretary for risking his present and future for a woman who was worthy neither of love nor respect, and who was notoriously unfaithful to him. Montlouis heard this last taunt with compressed lips and a deep cloud upon his brow.

"Do not utter a word more, count," said he; "I forbid you to do so."

He spoke so disrespectfully that Octave was about to strike him, but Montlouis drew back and avoided the blow; but he was so intoxicated with fury that this last insult roused him beyond all bounds.

"By what right do you speak thus," said he, "who have married another man's mistress? It well becomes you to talk of woman's virtue, when your wife is a—"

He had no time to finish his sentence, for Octave, levelling his gun, shot him through the heart.

M. de Mussidan kept these facts from his wife because he really loved her, and true love is capable of any extreme; and he felt that, however strong the cause might be, he should never have the courage to separate from Diana; that whatever she might do in the future, or had already done in the past, he could not choose but forgive her.

Acquitted of all blame, thanks to Clinchain's and Ludovic's evidence—for they had mutually agreed that the tragical occurrence should be represented to have been the result of an accident—the conscience of M. de Mussidan left him but little peace. The girl whom Montlouis had loved had been driven from her home in disgrace, owing to having given birth to a son. Octave sought her out, and, without giving any reason for his generosity, told her that her son, whom she had named Paul, after his father, Montlouis, should never come to want.

Shortly after this sad occurrence, M. de Mussidan and his wife quitted Poitiers, for Diana had more than once determined that she would make Paris her residence for the future. She had taken into her service a woman who had been in the service of Marie de Puymandour, and through her had discovered that, previous to her marriage with Norbert, Marie had loved George de Croisenois; and she intended to use this knowledge at some future date as a weapon with which to deal the Duke de Champdoce a deadly blow.

Chapter 40: A Scheme of Vengeance

The marriage between Norbert and Mademoiselle de Puymandour was entirely deficient in that brief, ephemeral light that shines over the honeymoon. The icy wall that stood between them became each day stronger and taller. There was no one to smooth away inequalities, no one to exercise a kindly influence over two characters, both haughty and determined. After his father's death, when Norbert announced his intention of residing in Paris, M. de Puymandour highly approved of this resolution, for he fancied that if he were to remain alone in the country, he could to a certain extent take the place and position of the late duke, and, with the permission of his son-in-law, at once take up his residence at Champdoce.

Almost as soon as the young duchess arrived in Paris she realized the fact that she was the most unfortunate woman in the world. As Champdoce was almost like her own home, her eyes lighted on familiar scenes; and if she went out, she was sure of being greeted by kindly words and friendly features; but in Paris she only found solitude, for everything there was strange and hostile. The late duke, pinching and parsimonious as he had been towards himself and his son, launched out into the wildest extravagances when he imagined he was working for his coming race, and the home which he had prepared for his great-grandchildren was the incarnation of splendour and luxury.

Upon the arrival of Norbert and his wife, they could almost fancy that they had only quitted their town house a few days before, so perfect were all the arrangements. Had Norbert been left to act for himself, he might have felt a little embarrassed, but his trusty servant Jean aided him with his advice, and the establishment was kept on a footing to do honour to the traditions of the house of Champdoce. Everything can be procured in Paris for money, and Jean had filled the ante-rooms with lackeys, the kitchens and offices with cooks and scullions, and the stables with grooms, coachmen, and horses, while every description of carriage stood in the place appointed for their reception.

But all this bustle and excitement did not seem in the eyes of the young duchess to impart life to the house. It appeared to her dead and empty as a sepulchre. It seemed as if she were living beneath the weight of some vague and indefinable terror, some hideous and hidden spectre which might at any moment start from its hiding place and drive her mad with the alarm it excited. She had not a soul in whom she could confide. She had been forbidden by Norbert to renew her acquaintance with her old Parisian friends, for Norbert did not consider them of sufficiently good family, and in addition he had used the pretext of the deep mourning they were in to put off receiving visitors for a twelvemonth at least. She felt herself alone and solitary, and, in this frame of mind, how was it possible for her not to let her thoughts wander once again to George de Croisenois. Had her father been willing, she might have been his wife now, and have been wandering hand in hand in some sequestered spot beneath the clear blue sky of Italy. *He* had loved her, while Norbert——.

Norbert was leading one of those mad, headstrong lives which have but two conclusions—ruin or suicide. His name had been put up for election at a fashionable club by his uncle, the Chevalier de Septraor, as soon as he arrived in Paris. He had been elected at once, being looked on as a decided acquisition to the list of members. He bore one of the oldest names to be found among the French nobility, while his fortune—gigantic as it was—had been magnified threefold by the tongue of common report. He was received with open arms everywhere, and lived in a perfect atmosphere of flattery. Not being able to shine by means of cultivation or polish, he sought to gain a position in his club by a certain roughness of demeanour and a cynical mode of speech. He flung away his money in every direction, kept racers, and was uniformly fortunate in his betting transactions. He frequented the world of gallantry, and was constantly to be seen in the company of women whose reputations were exceedingly equivocal. His days were spent on horseback, or in the fencing room, and his nights in drinking, gambling, and all kinds of debauchery. His wife scarcely ever saw him, for when he returned home it was usually with the first beams of day, either half intoxicated or savage from having lost large sums at the gambling table. Jean, the old and trusty retainer of the house of Champdoce, was deeply grieved, not so much at seeing his master so rapidly pursuing the path to ruin as at the fact that he was ever surrounded by dissolute and disreputable acquaintances.

"Think of your name," he would urge; "of the honour of your name."

"And what does that matter," sneered Norbert, "provided that I live a jolly life, and shuffle out of the world rapidly?"

There was one fixed star in all the dark clouds that surrounded him, which now seemed to blaze brightly, and this star was Diana de Mussidan. Do what he would, it was impossible to efface her image from his memory. Even amidst the fumes of wine and the debauched revelry of the supper table he could see the form that he had once so passionately loved standing out like a pillar of light, clear and distinct against the darkness. He had led this demoralizing existence for fully six months, when one day, as he was riding down the Avenue des Champs Elysees, he saw a lady give him a friendly bow. She was seated in a magnificent open carriage, wrapped in the richest and most costly furs.

Thinking that she might be one of the many actresses with whom he was acquainted, Norbert turned his horse's head towards the carriage; but as he got nearer he saw, to his extreme amazement and almost terror, that it was Diana de Mussidan who was seated in it. He did not turn back, however; and as the carriage had just drawn up, he reined in his horse alongside of it. Diana was as much agitated as he was, and for a moment neither of them spoke, but their eyes were firmly fixed upon each other, and they sat pale and breathless, as if each had some sad presentiment which fate was preparing for them both. At last Norbert felt that he must break the silence, for the servants were beginning to gaze upon them with eyes full of curiosity.

"What, *madame*, you here, in Paris?" said he with an effort.

She had drawn out a slender hand from the mass of furs in which she was enveloped, and extended it to him, as she replied in a tone which had a ring of tenderness beneath its commonplace tone,—

"Yes, we are established here, and I hope that we shall be as good friends as we were once before. Farewell, until we meet again."

As if her words had been a signal, the coachman struck his horses lightly with his whip, and the magnificent equipage rolled swiftly away. Norbert had not accepted Diana's proffered hand, but presently he realized the whole scene, and plunging his spurs into his horse dashed furiously up the Avenue in the direction of the Arc de Triomphe.

"Ah!" said he, as a bitter pang of despair shot through his heart, "I still love her, and can never care for anyone else; but I will see her again. She has not forgotten me. I could read it in her eyes, and detect it all in the tones of her voice." Here a momentary gleam of reason crossed his brain. "But will a woman like Diana ever forgive an offence like mine? and when she seems most friendly the danger is the more near."

Unfortunately he thrust aside this idea, and refused to listen to the voice of reason. That evening he went down to his club with the intention of asking a few questions regarding the Mussidans. He heard enough to satisfy himself, and the next day he met Madame de Mussidan in the Champs Elysees, and for many days afterwards in rapid succession. Each day they exchanged a few words, and at last Diana, with much simulated hesitation, promised to alight from her carriage when next they met in the Bois, and talk to Norbert unhampered by the presence of the domestics.

Madame de Mussidan had made the appointment for three o'clock, but before two Norbert was on the spot, in a fever of expectation and doubt.

"Is it I," asked he of himself, "waiting once more for Diana, as I have so often waited for her at Bevron?"

Ah, how many changes had taken place since then! He was now no longer waiting for Diana de Laurebourg, but for the Countess de Mussidan, another man's wife, while he also was a married man. It was no longer the whim of a monomaniac that kept them apart, but the dictates of law, honour, and the world.

"Why," said he, in a mad burst of passion, "why should we not set at defiance all the cold social rules framed by an artificial state of society; why should not the woman leave her husband and the man his wife?" Norbert had consulted his watch times without number before the appointed hour came. "Ah," sighed he, "suppose that she should not come after all."

As he said these words a cab stopped, and the Countess de Mussidan alighted from it. She came rapidly along towards him, crossing an open space without heeding the irregularities of the ground, as that diminished the distance which separated her from Norbert. He advanced to meet her, and taking his arm, they plunged into the recesses of the Bois. There had been heavy rain on the day previous, and the pathway was wet and muddy, but Madame de Mussidan did not seem to notice this.

"Let us go on," said she, "until we are certain of not being seen from the road. I have taken every precaution. My carriage and servants are waiting for me in front of St. Philippe du Roule; but for all that I may have been watched."

"You were not so timid in bygone days."

"Then I was my own mistress; and if I lost my reputation, the loss affected me only; but on my wedding day I had a sacred trust confided to me—the honour of the man who has given me his name, and that

I must guard with jealous care."

"Then you love me no longer."

She stopped suddenly, and overwhelming Norbert with one of those glacial glances which she knew so well how to assume, answered in measured accents,—

"Your memory fails you; all that has remained to me of the past is the rejection of a proposal conveyed in a certain letter that I wrote."

Norbert interrupted her by a piteous gesture of entreaty.

"Mercy!" said he. "You would pardon me if you knew all the horrors of the punishment that I am enduring. I was mad, blind, besotted, nor did I love you as I do at this moment."

A smile played round Diana's beautiful mouth, for Norbert had told her nothing that she did not know before, but she wished to hear it from his own lips.

"Alas!" murmured she; "I can only frame my reply with the fatal words, '*Too late!*'"

"Diana!"

He endeavoured to seize her hand, but she drew it away with a rapid movement.

"Do not use that name," said she; "you have no right to do so. Is it not sufficient to have blighted the young girl's life? and yet you seek to compromise the honour of the wife. You must forget me; do you understand? It is to tell you this that I am here. The other day, when I saw you again, I lost my self-command. My heart leapt up at the sight of you, and, fool that I was, I permitted you to see this; but base no hopes on my weakness. I said to you, Let us be friends. It was a mere act of madness. We can never be friends, and had better, therefore, treat each other as strangers. Do you forget that lying tongues at Bevron accused me of being your mistress? Do you think that this falsehood has not reached my husband's ears? One day, when your name was mentioned in his presence, I saw a gleam of hatred and jealousy in his eye. Great heavens! should he, on my return, suspect that my hand had rested in yours, he would expel me from his house like some guilty wretch! The door of our house must remain for ever closed to you. I am miserable indeed. Be a man; and if your heart still holds one atom of the love you once bore for me, prove it by never seeking me again."

As she concluded she hurried away, leaving in Norbert's heart a more deadly poison than the one she had endeavoured to persuade the son to administer to his father, the Duke de Champdoce. She knew each chord that vibrated in his heart, and could play on it at will.

She felt sure that in a month he would again be her slave, and that she could exercise over him a sway more despotic than she had yet done, and, in addition to this, that he would assist her in executing a cruel scheme of revenge, which she had long been plotting.

After having followed Diana about like her very shadow for several days, Norbert at last ventured to approach her in the Champs Elysees. She was angry, but not to such an extent that he feared to repeat his offence. Then she wept, but her tears could not force him to avoid her. At first her system of defence was very strong, then it gradually grew weaker. She granted him another interview, and then two others followed. But what were these meetings worth to him? They took place in a church or a public gallery, in places where they could scarcely exchange a grasp of the hand. At length she told him that she had thought of a place which would render their interviews less perilous, but that she hardly dared tell him where it was. He pressed her to tell him, and, by degrees, she permitted herself to be persuaded. Her idea was to become the friend of the Duchess of Champdoce.

Norbert now felt that she was more an angel than a woman, and it was agreed that on the next day he himself would introduce her to his wife.

Chapter 41: False Friend, Old Lover

It was on a Wednesday morning that the Duke de Champdoce, instead of, as usual, going to his own or one of his friends' clubs to breakfast, took his seat at the table where his wife was partaking of her morning meal. He was in excellent spirits, gay, and full of pleasant talk, a mood in which his wife had never seen him since their ill-fated marriage. The duchess could not understand this sudden change in her husband; it terrified and alarmed her, for she felt that it was the forerunner of some serious event, which would change the current of her life entirely.

Norbert waited until the domestics had completed their duty and retired, and as soon as he was alone with his wife he took her hand and kissed it with an air of gallantry.

"It has been a long time, my dear Marie, since I had resolved to open my heart to you entirely, and now a full and open explanation has become absolutely necessary."

"An explanation!" faltered Marie.

"Yes, certainly; but do not let the word alarm you. I fear that I must have appeared in your eyes the most morose and disagreeable of husbands. Permit me to explain. Since we came here, I have gone about my own affairs, I have gone out early and returned extremely late, and sometimes three days have elapsed without our even setting eyes on each other."

The young duchess listened to him like a woman who could not believe her ears. Could this be her husband who was heaping reproaches upon himself in this manner?

"I have made no complaint," stammered she.

"I know that, Marie; you have a noble and forgiving nature; but, however, it is impossible, as a woman, that you should not have condemned me."

"Indeed, but I have not done so."

"So much the better for me. On this I shall not have to find either defence or excuse for my conduct; you must know, however, that you are ever foremost in my thoughts, even when I am away from you."

He was evidently doing his best to put on an air of tenderness and affection, but he failed; for though his words were kind, the tone of his voice was neither tender nor sympathetic.

"I hope I know my duty," said the duchess.

"Pray, Marie," broke in he, "do not let the word duty be uttered between us. You know that you have been much alone, because it was impossible for the friends of Mademoiselle de Puymandour to be those of the Duchess de Champdoce!"

"Have I made any opposition to your orders?"

"Then, too, our mourning prevents us going out into the world for five months longer at least."

"Have I asked to go out?"

"All the more reason that I should endeavour to make your home less dull for you. I should like you to have with you some person in whose society you could find pleasure and distraction. Not one of those foolish girls who have no thought save for balls and dress, but a sensible woman of the world, and, above all, one of your own age and rank,—a woman, in short, of whom you could make a friend. But where can such a one be found? It is a perilous quest to venture on, and upon such a friend often depends the happiness and misery of a home.

"But," continued he, after a brief pause, "I think that I have discovered the very one that will suit you. I met her at the house of Madame d'Ailange, who spoke eloquently of her charms of mind and body, and I hope to have the pleasure of presenting her to you today."

"Here, at our house?"

"Certainly; there is nothing odd in this. Besides, the lady is no stranger to us; she comes from our own part of the country, and you know her."

A flush came over his face, and he busied himself with the fire to conceal it as he added,—

"You recollect Mademoiselle de Laurebourg?"

"Do you mean Diana de Laurebourg?"

"Exactly so."

"I saw very little of her, for my father and hers did not get on very well together. The Marquis de Laurebourg looked on us as too insignificant to—"

"Ah, well," interrupted he, "I trust that the daughter will make up for the father's shortcomings. She married just after our wedding had been celebrated, and her husband is the Count de Mussidan. She will call on you today, and I have told your servants to say that you are at home."

The silence that followed this speech lasted for nearly a couple of minutes, and became exceedingly embarrassing, when suddenly the sound of wheels was heard on the gravel of the courtyard, and in a moment afterwards a servant came and announced that the Countess de Mussidan was in the drawing-room. Norbert rose, and, taking his wife's arm, led her away.

"Come, Marie, come," said he; "she has arrived."

Diana had reflected deeply before she had taken this extraordinarily bold step. In paying a visit so contrary to all the usual rules of etiquette, she exposed herself to the chance of receiving a severe rebuff. The few seconds that elapsed while she was still alone in the drawing-room seemed like so many centuries; but the door was opened, and Norbert and his wife appeared. Then, with a charming smile, Madame de Mussidan rose and bowed gracefully to the Duchess de Champdoce, making a series of half-jesting apologies for her intrusion. She had been utterly unable, she said, to resist the pleasure she should experience in seeing an old country neighbour, the more so as they were now separated by so short a distance. She had, therefore, disregarded all the rules of etiquette so that they might have a cosy chat about Poitiers, Bevron, Champdoce, and all the country where she had been born, and which she so dearly loved.

The duchess listened in silence to this torrent of words, and the expression of her face showed how surprised she was at this unexpected visit. A less perfectly self-possessed woman than Diana de Mussidan might have felt abashed, but the slight annoyance was not to be compared to the prospective advantages that she hoped to gain, and she brought all the mettle of her talent and diplomacy into play.

Norbert was moving about the room, half ashamed of the ignoble part that he was playing. As soon as he thought that the welcome between the two ladies had been partially got over, and imagined that they were conversing more amicably together, he slipped out of the room, not knowing whether to be pleased or angry at the success of the trick.

The trick was rather a more difficult one than Diana had, from Norbert's account, anticipated, as she had thought that she would have been received by the duchess like some ministering angel sent down to earth to console an unhappy captive. She had expected to find a simple, guileless woman, who, upon her first visit, would throw her arms round her visitor's neck and yield herself entirely to her influence. Far, however, from being dismayed, Diana was rather pleased at this unexpected difficulty, and so fully exerted all her powers of fascination, that when she took her leave, she believed that she had made a little progress.

On that very evening the duchess remarked to her husband,—

"I think that I shall like Madame de Mussidan; she seems an excellent kind of woman."

"Excellent is just the proper word," returned Norbert. "All Bevron was in tears when she was married and had to leave, for she was a real angel among the poor."

Norbert was intensely gratified by Diana's success; for was it not for him that she had displayed all her skill, and was not this a proof that she still cherished a passion for him?

He was not, however, quite so much pleased when he met Madame de Mussidan the next day in the Champs Elysees. She looked sad and thoughtful.

"What has gone wrong?" asked he.

"I am very angry with myself for having listened to the voice of my own heart and to your entreaties," answered she, "and I think that both of us have committed a grave error."

"Indeed, and what have we done?"

"Norbert, your wife suspects something."

"Impossible! Why, she was praising you after you had left."

"If that is the case, then she is indeed a much more clever woman than I had imagined, for she knows how to conceal her suspicions until she is in a position to prove them."

Diana spoke with such a serious air of conviction, that Norbert became quite alarmed.

"What shall we do?" asked he.

"The best thing would be to give up meeting each other, I think."

"Never; I tell you, never!"

"Let me reflect; in the meantime be prudent; for both our sakes, be prudent."

To further his ends, Norbert entirely changed his mode of life. He gave up going to his clubs, refused invitations to fast suppers, and no longer spent his nights in gambling and drinking. He drove out with his wife, and frequently spent his evenings with her, and at the club began to be looked on as quite a model husband. This great change, however, was not effected without many a severe inward struggle. He felt deeply humiliated at the life of deception that he was forced to lead, but Diana's hand, apparently so slight and frail, held him with a grip of steel.

"We must live in this way," said she, in answer to his expostulations, "first, because it must be so; and, secondly, because it is my will. On our present mode of conduct depends all our future safety, and I wish the duchess to believe that with me happiness and content must have come to her fireside."

Norbert could not gainsay this very reasonable proposition on the part of Madame de Mussidan, for he was more in love than ever, and the terrible fear that if he went in any way contrary to her wishes that she would refuse to see him any more, stayed the words of objection that rose to his lips.

After hesitating for a little longer, the duchess made up her mind to accept the offer of friendship which Diana had so ingenuously offered to her, and finished by giving herself up to the bitterest enemy that she had in the world. By degrees she had no secrets from her new friend, and one day, after a long and confidential conversation, she acknowledged to Diana the whole secret of the early love of her girlish days, the memory of which had never faded from the inmost recesses of her heart, and was rash enough to mention George de Croisenois by name. Madame de Mussidan was overjoyed at what she considered so signal a victory.

"Now I have her," thought she, "and vengeance is within my grasp."

Marie and Diana were now like two sisters, and were almost constantly together; but this intimacy had not given to Norbert the facile means of meeting Diana which he had so ardently hoped for. Though Madame de Mussidan visited his house nearly every day, he absolutely saw less of her than he had done before, and sometimes weeks elapsed without his catching a glimpse of her face. She played her game with such consummate skill, that Marie was always placed as a barrier between Norbert and herself, as in the farce, when the lover wishes to embrace his mistress, he finds the wrinkled visage of the *duenna* offered to his lips. Sometimes he grew angry, but Diana always had some excellent reason with which to close his mouth. Sometimes she held up his pretensions to ridicule, and at others assumed a haughty air, which always quelled incipient rebellion upon his part.

"What did you expect of me?" she would say, "and of what base act did you do me the honour to consider me capable?"

He was treated exactly like a child, or more cruel still, like a person deficient in intellect, and this he was thoroughly aware of. He could not meet Madame de Mussidan as he had formerly done, for now in the Bois, at Longchamps, or at any place of public amusement she was invariably surrounded by a band of fashionable admirers, among whom George de Croisenois was always to be found. Norbert disliked all these men, but he had a special antipathy to George de Croisenois, whom he regarded as a supercilious fool; but in this opinion he was entirely wrong, for the Marquis de Croisenois was looked upon as one of the most talented and witty men in Parisian society, and in this case the opinion of the world was a well-founded one. Many men envied him, but he had no enemies, and his honest and straightforward conduct was beyond all doubt. He had the noble instincts of a knight of the days of chivalry.

"Pray," asked Norbert, "what is it that you can see in this sneering dandy who is always hanging about you?"

But Diana, with a meaning smile, always made the same reply,—

"You ask too much; but some time you will learn all."

Every day she contrived, when with the duchess, to turn the conversation skilfully upon George de Croisenois, and she had in a manner accustomed Marie to look certain possibilities straight in the face, from the very idea of which she would a few months back have recoiled with horror. This point once gained, Madame de Mussidan believed that the moment had arrived to bring the former lovers together again, and fancied that one sudden and unexpected encounter would advance matters much more quickly than all her half-veiled insinuations. One day, therefore, when the duchess had called on her friend, on entering the drawing-room, she found it only tenanted by George de Croisenois. An exclamation of astonishment fell from the lips of both as their eyes met; the cheek of each grew pale. The duchess, overcome by her feelings, sank half-fainting into a chair near the door.

"Ah," murmured he, scarcely knowing the meaning of the words he uttered, "I had every confidence in you, and you have forgotten me."

"You do not believe the words you have just spoken," returned the duchess haughtily; "but," she added in softer accents, "what could I do? I may have been weak in obeying my father, but for all that I have never forgotten the past."

Madame de Mussidan, who had stationed herself behind the closed door, caught every word, and a gleam of diabolical triumph flashed from her eyes. She felt sure that an interview which began in this manner would be certain to be repeated, and she was not in error. She soon saw that by some tacit understanding the duchess and George contrived to meet constantly at her house, and this she carefully abstained from noticing. Things were working exactly as she desired and she waited, for she could well afford to do so, knowing that the impending crash could not long be delayed.

Chapter 42: A Stab in the Dark

September had now arrived; and though the weather was very bad, the Duke de Champdoce, accompanied by his faithful old servant, Jean, left Paris on a visit to his training stables. Having had a serious difference with Diana, he had made up his mind to try whether a long absence on his part would not have the effect of reducing her to submission, and at the same time remembering the proverb, that "absence makes the heart grow fonder."

He had already been away two whole days, and was growing extremely anxious at not having heard from Madame de Mussidan, when one evening, as he was returning from a late inspection of his stud, he was informed that there was a man waiting to see him. The man was a poor old fellow belonging to the place, who eked out a wretched subsistence by begging, and executing occasional commissions.

"Do you want me?" asked the duke.

With a sly look, the man drew from his pocket a letter.

"This is for you," muttered he.

"All right; give it to me, then."

"I was told to give it to you only in private."

"Never mind that; hand it over."

"Well, if I must, I must."

Norbert's sole thought was that this letter must have come from Diana, and throwing the man a coin, hurried to a spot where it was light enough to read the missive. He did not, however, recognise Diana's firm, bold hand on the envelope.

"Who the devil can this be from?" thought Norbert, as he tore open the outer covering. The paper within was soiled and greasy, and the handwriting was of the vilest description, it was full of bad spelling, and ran thus:—

Sir,—

I hardly dare tell you the truth, and yet my conscience will give me no relief until I do so. I can no longer bear to see a gentleman such as you are deceived by a woman who has no heart or honourable feeling. Your wife is unfaithful to you, and will soon make you a laughing stock to all. You may trust to this being true, for I am a respectable woman, and you can easily find out if I am lying to you. Hide yourself this evening, so that you may command a view of the side-door in the wall of your garden, and between half-past ten and eleven you will see your wife's lover enter. It is a long time since he has been furnished with a key. The hour for the meeting has been judiciously fixed, for all the servants will be out; but I implore you not to be violent, for I would not do your wife any harm, but I feel that you ought to be warned.

From one
Who Knows.

Norbert ran through the contents of this infamous anonymous letter in an instant. The blood surged madly through his brain, and he uttered a howl of fury. His servants ran in to see what was the matter.

"Where is the fellow who brought this letter?" said he. "Run after him and bring him back to me."

In a few minutes the sturdy grooms made their appearance, pushing in the messenger, who seemed over-powered with tears.

"I am not a thief," exclaimed he. "It was given to me, but I will give it back."

He was alluding to the *louis* given to him by Norbert, for the largeness of the sum made him think that the donor had made a mistake.

"Keep the money," said the duke; "I meant it for you; but tell me who gave this letter to you."

"I can't tell you," answered the man. "If I ever saw him before, may my next glass of wine choke me. He got out of a cab just as I was passing near the bridge, and calling to me, said, 'Look at this letter; at half-past seven take it to the Duke de Champdoce, who lives by his stables in the road to the forest. Do you know the place?' 'Yes,' I says, and then he slips the letter and a five-*franc* piece into my hand, got back into the cab, and off he went."

"What was the man like?" asked he.

"Well, I can hardly say. He wasn't young or old, or short or tall. I recollect he had a gold watch-chain on, but that was about all I noticed."

"Very well; you can be off."

At this moment Norbert's anger was turned against the writer of the letter only, for he did not place the smallest credence in the accusations against his wife. If he did not love her, he at any rate respected her. "My wife," said he to himself, "is an honourable and virtuous woman, and it is some discharged menial who has taken this cowardly mode of revenge." A closer inspection of the letter seemed to show him that the faults in calligraphy were intentional. The concluding portion of the letter excited his attention, and, calling Jean, he asked him if it was true that all the servants would be absent from the house today.

"There will be none there this evening; not until late at night," answered the old man.

"And why, pray?"

"Have you forgotten, your Grace, that the first coachman is going to be married, and the duchess was good enough to say that all might go to the wedding dinner and ball, as long as someone remained at the porter's lodge?"

After the first outburst, Norbert affected an air of calmness, and laughed at the idea of having permitted himself to be disturbed for so trivial a cause. But this was mere pretence, for doubt and suspicion had entered his soul, and no power on earth could expel them. "Why should not my wife be unfaithful to me?" thought Norbert. "I give her credit for being honourable and right-minded, but then all deceived husbands have the same idea. Why should I not take advantage of this information, and judge for myself? But no. I will not stoop to such an act of baseness. I should be as infamous as the writer of this letter if I was to play the spy, as she recommends me to do." He glanced round, and perceived that his servants were looking at him with undisguised curiosity.

"Go to your work," said he. "Extinguish the lights, and see that all the doors and windows are carefully closed."

He had made up his mind now, and taking out his watch, saw that it was just eight o'clock. "I have time to reach Paris," muttered he, "by the appointed time." Then he called Jean to him again. There was no need to conceal anything from this trusty adherent of the house of Champdoce. "I must start for Paris," said the duke, "without an instant's delay."

"On account of that letter?" asked the old man with an expression of the deepest sorrow upon his features.

"Yes, for that reason only."

"Someone has been making false charges against the duchess."

"How do you know that?"

"It was easy enough to guess."

"Have the carriage got ready, and tell the coachman to wait for me in front of the club. I myself will go on foot."

"You must not do that," answered Jean gravely. "The servants may have conceived the same suspicions as I have. You ought to creep away without anyone being a bit the wiser. The other domestics need not even suppose that you have left the house. I can get you a horse out of the little stables without anyone being the wiser. I will wait for you on the other side of the bridge."

"Good; but remember that I have not a moment to lose."

Jean left the room, and as he reached the passage Norbert heard him say to one of the servants, "Put some cold supper on the table; the duke says that he is starving."

Norbert went into his bedroom, put on a great coat and a pair of high boots, and slipped into his pocket a revolver, the charges of which he had examined with the greatest care. The night was exceedingly dark, a fine, icy rain was falling, and the roads were very heavy. Norbert found Jean with the horse at the appointed spot, and as he leaped into the saddle the duke exclaimed, "Not a soul saw me leave the house."

"Nor I either," returned the attached domestic. "I shall go back and act as if you were at supper. At three in the morning I will be in the wine-shop on the left-hand side of the road. When you return,

give a gentle tap on the window-pane with the handle of your whip."
Norbert sprang into the saddle, and sped away through the darkness
like a phantom of the night. Jean had made an excellent choice in
the horse he had brought for his master's use, and the animal made its
way rapidly through the mud and rain; but Norbert by this time was
half mad with excitement, and spurred him madly on. As he neared
home a new idea crossed his brain. Suppose it was a practical joke
on the part of some of the members of the club? In that case, they
would doubtless be watching for his arrival, and, after talking to him
on indifferent subjects, would, when he betrayed any symptoms of
impatience, overwhelm him with ridicule. The fear of this made him
cautious. What should he do with the horse he was riding? The wine-
shops were open, and perhaps he might pick up some man there who
would take charge of it for him. As he was debating this point, his eyes
fell upon a soldier, probably on his way to barracks.

"My man," asked the duke, "would you like to earn twenty *francs*?"

"I should think so, if it is nothing contrary to the rules and regulations of the army."

"It is only to take my horse and walk him up and down while I
pay a visit close by."

"I can stay out of the barracks a couple of hours longer, but no
more," returned the soldier.

Norbert told the soldier where he was to wait for him, and then
went on rapidly to his own house, and reached the side street along
which ran the garden belonging to his magnificent residence. On the
opposite side of the street the houses all had porticoes, and Norbert
took up his position in one of these, and peered out carefully. He had
studied the whole street, which was not a long one, from beginning
to end, and was convinced that he was the only person in it. He made
up his mind that he would wait until midnight; and if by that time no
one appeared, he would feel confident that the duchess was innocent,
and return without anyone but Jean having known of his expedition.

From his position he could see that three windows on the second floor of his house were lighted up, and those windows were in
his wife's sleeping apartment. "She is the last woman in the world to
permit a lover to visit her," thought he. "No, no; the whole thing is a
hoax." He began to think of the way in which he had treated his wife.
Had he nothing to reproach himself with? Ten days after their marriage he had deserted her entirely; and if during the last few weeks he
had paid her any attention, it was because he was acting in obedience

to the whims of another woman. Suppose a lover was with her now, what right had he to interfere? The law gave him leave, but what did his conscience say? He leaned against the chill stone until he almost became as cold as it was. It seemed to him at that moment that life and hope were rapidly drifting away from him. He had lost all count of how long he had been on guard. He pulled out his watch, but it was too dark to distinguish the hands or the figures on the dial-plate.

A neighbouring clock struck the half-hour, but this gave him no clue as to the time. He had almost made up his mind to leave, when he heard the sound of a quick step coming down the street. It was the light, quick step of a sportsman,—of a man more accustomed to the woods and fields than the pavement and asphalt of Paris. Then a shadow fell upon the opposite wall, and almost immediately disappeared. Then Norbert knew that the door had opened and closed, and that the man had entered the garden. There could be no doubt upon this point, and yet the duke would have given worlds to be able to disbelieve the evidence of his senses. It might be a burglar, but burglars seldom work alone; or it might be a visitor to one of the servants, but all the servants were absent.

He again raised his eyes to the windows of his wife's room. All of a sudden the light grew brighter; either the lamp had been turned up, or fresh candles lighted. Yes, it was a candle, for he saw it borne across the room in the direction of the great staircase, and now he saw that the anonymous letter had spoken the truth, and that he was on the brink of a discovery. A lover had entered the garden, and the lighted candle was a signal to him. Norbert shuddered; the blood seemed to course through his veins like streams of molten fire, and the misty atmosphere that surrounded him appeared to stifle him. He ran across the street, forced the lock, and rushed wildly into the garden.

Chapter 43: Husband and Lover

The writer of the anonymous communication had only known the secret too well, for the Duchess de Champdoce was awaiting a visit that evening from George de Croisenois; this was, however, the first time. Step by step she had yielded, and at length had fallen into the snare laid for her by the treacherous woman whom she believed to be her truest friend. The evening before this eventful night she had been alone in Madame de Mussidan's drawing-room with George de Croisenois. She had been impressed by his ardent passion, and had listened with pleasure to his loving entreaties.

"I yield," said she. "Come tomorrow night, at half-past ten, to the little door in the garden wall; it will only be kept closed by a stone being placed against it inside; push it, and it will open; and when you have entered the garden, acquaint me with your presence by clapping yours hands gently once or twice."

Diana had, from a secure hiding-place, overheard these words, and feeling certain that the duchess would repent her rash promise, she kept close to her side until George's departure, to give her no chance of retracting her promise. The next day she was constantly with her victim, and made an excuse for dining with her, so as not to quit her until the hour for the meeting had almost arrived.

It was not until she was left alone that the duchess saw the full extent of her folly and rashness. She was terrified at the promise that she had given in a weak moment, and would have given worlds had she been able to retract.

There was yet, however, one means of safety left her—she could hurry downstairs and secure the garden gate. She started to her feet, determined to execute her project; but she was too late for the appointed signal was heard through the chill gloom of the night. Unhappy woman! The light sound of George de Croisenois' palms striking one upon the other resounded in her ears like the dismal tolling of the funereal bell. She stooped to light a candle at the fire, but her hand trembled so that she could scarcely effect her object. She felt sure that George was still in the garden, though she had made no answer to his signal. She had never thought that he would have had the audacity to open a door that led into the house from the garden, but this is what he had done.

In the most innocent manner imaginable, and so that her listener in no way suspected the special reason that she had for making this communication, Diana de Mussidan had informed George de Croisenois that upon this night all the domestics of the Champdoce household would be attending the coachman's wedding, and that consequently the mansion would be deserted. George knew also that the duke was away at his training establishment, and he therefore opened the door, and walked boldly up the main staircase, so that when the duchess, with the lighted candle in her hand, came to the top steps she found herself face to face with George de Croisenois, pallid with emotion and quivering with excitement.

At the sight of the man she loved she started backwards with a low cry of anguish and despair.

"Fly!" she said "fly, or we are lost!"

He did not, however, seem to hear her, and the duchess recoiled slowly, step by step, through the open door of her chamber, across the carpeted floor, until she reached the opposite wall of her room, and could go no farther.

George followed her, and pushed to the door of the room as he entered it. This brief delay, however, had sufficed to restore Marie to the full possession of her senses. "If I permit him to speak," thought she,—"if he once suspects that my love for him is still as strong as ever, I am lost."

Then she said aloud,—

"You must leave this house, and that instantly. I was mad when I said what I did yesterday. You are too noble and too generous not to listen to me when I tell you that the moment of infatuation is over, and that all my reason has returned to me, and my openness will convince you of the truth of what I say—George de Croisenois, I love you."

The young man uttered an exclamation of delight upon hearing this news.

"Yes," continued Marie, "I would give half the years of my remaining life to be your wife. Yes, George, I love you; but the voice of duty speaks louder than the whispers of the heart. I may die of grief, but there will be no stain upon my marriage robe, no remorse eating out my heart. Farewell!"

But the *marquis* would not consent to this immediate dismissal, and appeared to be about to speak.

"Go!" said the duchess, with an air of command. "Leave me at once!" Then, as he made no effort to obey her, she went on, "If you really love me, let my honour be as dear to you as your own, and never try to see me again. The peril we are now in shows how necessary this last determination of mine is. I am the Duchess de Champdoce, and I will keep the name that has been entrusted to me pure and unsullied, nor will I stoop to treachery or deception."

"Why do you use the word deception?" asked he. "I do, it is true, despise the woman who smiles upon the husband she is betraying, but I respect and honour the woman who risks all to follow the fortunes of the man she loves. Lay aside, Marie, name, title, fortune, and fly with me."

"I love you too much, George," answered she gently, "to ruin your future, for the day would surely come when you would regret all your self-denial, for a woman weighed down with a sense of her dishonour is a heavy burden for a man to bear."

George de Croisenois did not understand her thoroughly.

"You do not trust me," said he. "You would be dishonoured. Shall I not share a portion of the world's censure? And, if you wish me, I will be a dishonoured man also. Tonight I will cheat at play at the club, be detected, and leave the room an outcast from the society of all honourable men for the future. Fly with me to some distant land, and we will live happily under whatever name you may choose."

"I must not listen to you," cried she wildly. "It is impossible now."

"Impossible!—and why? Tell me, I entreat you."

"Ah, George," sobbed she, "if you only knew—"

He placed his arm around her waist, and was about to press his lips on that fair brow, when all at once he felt Marie shiver in his clasp, and, raising one of her arms, point towards the door, which had opened silently during their conversation, and upon the threshold of which stood Norbert de Champdoce, gloomy and threatening.

The *marquis* saw in an instant the terrible position in which his insensate folly had placed the woman he loved.

"Do not come any nearer," said he, addressing Norbert; "remain where you are."

A bitter laugh from the duke made him realize the folly of his command. He supported the duchess to a couch, and seated her upon it. She recovered consciousness almost immediately, and, as she opened her eyes, George read in them the most perfect forgiveness for the man who had ruined her life and hopes.

This look, and the fond assurance conveyed in it, restored all George's coolness and self-possession, and he turned towards Norbert.

"However compromising appearances may seem, I am the only one deserving punishment; the duchess has nothing to reproach herself with in any way; it was without her knowledge, and without any encouragement from her, that I dared to enter this house, knowing as I did that the servants were all absent."

Norbert, however, still maintained the same gloomy silence. He too had need to collect his thoughts. As he ascended the stairs he knew that he should find the duchess with a lover, but he had not calculated upon that lover being George de Croisenois, a man whom he loathed and detested more than anyone that he was in the habit of meeting in society. When he recognised George, it was with the utmost difficulty that he restrained himself from springing upon him

369

and endeavouring to strangle him. He had suspected this man of having gained Diana's affections, and now he found him in the character of the lover of his wife, and he was silent simply because he had not yet made up his mind what he would say. If his face was outwardly calm and rigid as marble, while the flames of hell were raging in his heart, it was because his limbs for the moment refused to obey his will; but, in spite of this, Norbert was, for the time, literally insane.

Croisenois folded his arms, and continued,—

"I had only just come here at the moment of your arrival. Why were you not here to listen to all that passed between us? Would to heaven that you had been! Then you would have understood all the grandeur and nobility of your wife's soul. I admit the magnitude of my fault, but I am at your service, and am prepared to give you the satisfaction that you will doubtless demand."

"From your words," answered Norbert slowly, "I presume that you allude to a duel; that is to say, that having effected my dishonour tonight, you purpose to kill me tomorrow morning. In the game that you have been playing a man stakes his life, and you, I think, have lost."

Croisenois bowed. "I am a dead man," thought he as he glanced towards the duchess, "and not for your sake, but on account of quite another woman."

The sound of his own voice excited Norbert, and he went on more rapidly: "What need have I to risk my life in a duel? I come to my own home, I find you with my wife, I blow out your brains, and the law will exonerate me." As he said these last words, he drew a revolver from his pocket and levelled it at George. The moment was an intensely exciting one, but Croisenois did not show any sign of emotion, Norbert did not press the trigger, and the suspense became more than could be borne.

"Fire!" cried George, "fire!"

"No," returned Norbert coldly; "on reflection I have come to the conclusion that your dead body would be a source of extreme inconvenience to me."

"You try my forbearance too far. What are your intentions?"

"I mean to kill you," answered Norbert in such a voice of concentrated ferocity that George shuddered in spite of all his courage, "but it shall not be with a pistol shot. It is said that blood will wash out any stain, but it is false; for even if all yours is shed, it will not remove the stain from my escutcheon. One of us must vanish from the face of the earth in such a manner that no trace of him may remain."

"I agree. Show me how this is to be done."

"I know a method," answered Norbert. "If I was certain that no human being was aware of your presence here tonight—"

"No one can possibly know it."

"Then," answered the duke, "instead of taking advantage of the rights that the law gives me and shooting you down on the spot, I will consent to risk my life against yours."

George de Croisenois breathed a sigh of relief. "I am ready," replied he, "as I before told you."

"I heard you; but remember that this will be no ordinary duel, in the light of day, with seconds to regulate the manner of our conduct."

"We will fight exactly as you wish."

"In that case, I name swords as the weapons, the garden as the spot, and this instant as the hour."

The *marquis* cast a glance at the window.

"You think," observed Norbert, comprehending his look, "that the night is so dark that we cannot see the blades of our swords?"

"Quite so."

"You need not fear; there will be light enough for this death struggle of the one who remains in the garden, for you understand that one *will* remain."

"I understand you; shall we go down at once?"

Norbert shook his head in the negative.

"You are in too great a hurry," said he, "and have not given me time to fix my conditions."

"I am listening."

"At the end of the garden there is a small plot of ground, so damp that nothing will grow there, and consequently is almost unfrequented; but for all that it is thither that you must follow me. We will each take spade and pick-axe, and in a very brief period we can hollow out a receptacle for the body of the one who falls. When this work is completed, we will take to our swords and fight to the death, and the one who can keep his feet shall finish his fallen adversary, drag his body to the hole, and shovel the earth over his remains."

"Never!" exclaimed Croisenois. "Never will I agree to such barbarous terms."

"Have a care then," returned Norbert; "for I shall use my rights. That clock points to five minutes to eleven. If, when it strikes, you have not decided to accept my terms, I shall fire."

The barrel of the revolver was but a few inches from George de

Croisenois' heart, and the finger of his most inveterate enemy was curved round the trigger; but his feelings had been so highly wrought up that he thought not of this danger. He only remembered that he had four minutes in which to make up his mind. The events of the last thirty minutes had pressed upon each other's heels with such surprising alacrity that he could hardly believe that they had really occurred, and it seemed to him as if it might not, after all, be only a hideous vision of the night.

"You have only two minutes more," remarked the duke.

Croisenois started; his soul was far away from the terrible present. He glanced at the clock, then at his enemy, and lastly at Marie, who lay upon the couch, and from her ashen complexion might have been regarded as dead, save for the hysterical sobs which convulsed her frame. He felt that it was impossible to leave her in such a condition without aid of any kind, but he saw well that any show of pity on his part would only aggravate his offence. "Heaven have mercy on us!" muttered he. "We are at the mercy of a maniac," and with a feeling of deadly fear he asked himself what would be the fate of this woman, whom he loved so devotedly, were he to die. "For her sake," he thought, "I must slay this man, or her life will be one endless existence of torture—and slay him I will."

"I accept your terms," said he aloud.

He spoke just in time, for as the words were uttered came the whirr of the machinery and then the first clear stroke of the bell.

"I thank you," answered Norbert coldly as he lowered the muzzle of his revolver.

The icy frigidity of manner in a period of extreme danger, which is the marked characteristic of a certain type of education, had now vanished from the *marquis*'s tone and behaviour.

"But that is not all," he continued; "I, too, have certain conditions to propose."

"But we agreed—"

"Let me explain; we are going to fight in the dark in your garden without seconds. We are to dig a grave and the survivor is to bury his dead antagonist. Tell me, am I right?"

Norbert bowed.

"But," went on the *marquis*, "how can you be certain that all will end here, and that the earth will be content to retain our secret? You do not know, and you do not seem to care, that if one day the secret will be disclosed and the survivor accused of being the murderer of the other, arrested, dragged before a tribunal, condemned, and sent to a life-long prison——"

"There is a chance of that, of course."

"And do you think that I will consent to run such a risk as that?"

"There is such a risk, of course," answered Norbert phlegmatically; "but that will be an incentive for you to conceal my death as I should conceal yours."

"That will not be sufficient for me," returned De Croisenois.

"Ah! take care," sneered Norbert, "or I shall begin to think that you are afraid."

"I *am* afraid; that is, afraid of being called a murderer."

"That is a danger to which I am equally liable with yourself."

Croisenois, however, was fully determined to carry his point. "You say," continued he, "that our chances are equal; but if I fall, who would dream of searching here for my remains? You are in your own house and can take every precaution; but suppose, on the other hand, I kill you. Shall I look to the duchess to assist me? Will not the finger of suspicion be pointed at her? Shall she say to her gardener when all Paris is hunting for you, 'Mind that you do not meddle with the piece of land at the end of the garden.'"

The thought of the anonymous letter crossed Norbert's mind, and he remembered that the writer of it must be acquainted with the coming of George de Croisenois. "What do you propose then?" asked he.

"Merely that each of us, without stating the grounds of our quarrel, write down the conditions and sign our names as having accepted them."

"I agree; but use dispatch."

The two men, after the conditions had been described, wrote two letters, dated from a foreign country, and the survivor of the combat was to post his dead adversary's letter, which would not fail to stop any search after the vanished man. When this talk was concluded, Norbert rose to his feet.

"One word in conclusion," said he: "a soldier is leading the horse on which I rode here up and down in the Place des Invalides. If you kill me, go and take the horse from the man, giving him the twenty *francs* I promised him."

"I will."

"Now let us go down."

They left the room together. Norbert was stepping aside to permit Croisenois to descend the stairs first, when he felt his coat gently pulled, and, turning round, saw that the duchess, too weak to rise to her feet, had crawled to him on her knees. The unhappy woman had heard everything, and in an almost inaudible voice she uttered an agonized prayer:

"Mercy, Norbert! Have mercy! I swear to you that I am guiltless. You never loved me, why should you fight for me. Have pity! Tomorrow, by all that I hold sacred, I swear to you that I will enter a convent, and you shall never see my face again. Have pity!"

"Pray heaven, *madame*, that it may be your lover's sword that pierces my heart. It is your only hope, for then you will be free."

He tore his coat from her fingers with brutal violence, and the unhappy woman fell to the floor with a shriek as he closed the door upon her, and followed his antagonist downstairs.

Chapter 44: Blade to Blade

Several times in the course of this interview Norbert de Champdoce had been on the point of bursting into a furious passion, but he restrained himself from a motive of self-pride; but now that his wife was no longer present, he showed a savage intensity of purpose and a deadly earnestness that was absolutely appalling. As he followed Croisenois down the great staircase, he kept repeating the words, "Quick! quick! we have lost too much time already;" for he saw that a mere trifle might upset all his plans—such as a servant returning home before the others. When they reached the ground-floor, he led George into a by-room which looked like an armoury, so filled was it with arms of all kinds and nations.

"Here," said he, with a bitter sneer, "we can find, I think, what we want;" and placing the candle he carried on the mantelpiece, he leaped upon the cushioned seat that ran round the room, and took down from the wall several pairs of duelling swords, and, throwing them upon the floor, exclaimed, "Choose your own weapon."

George was an anxious as Norbert to bring this painful scene to a close, for anything was preferable to this hideous state of suspense. The last despairing glance of the duchess had pierced his heart like a dagger thrust, and when he saw Norbert thrust aside his trembling wife with such brutality, it was all he could do to refrain from striking him down. He made no choice of weapons, but grasped the nearest, saying,—

"One will do as well as another."

"We cannot fight in this darkness," said Norbert, "but I have a means to remedy that. Come with me this way, so that we may avoid the observation of the porter."

They went into the stables, where he took up a large lantern, which he lighted.

"This," said he, "will afford ample light for our work."

"Ah, but the neighbours will see it, too; and at this hour a light in the garden is sure to attract attention," observed George.

"Don't be afraid; my grounds are not overlooked."

They entered the garden, and soon reached the spot to which the duke had alluded. Norbert hung the lantern on the bough of a tree, and it gave the same amount of light as an ordinary street lamp.

"We will dig the grave in that corner," observed he; "and when it is filled in, we can cover it with that heap of stones over there."

He threw off his great coat, and, handing a spade to Croisenois, took another himself, repeating firmly the words,—

"To work! To work!"

Croisenois would have toiled all night before he could have completed the task, but the muscles of the duke were hardened by his former laborious life, and in forty minutes all was ready.

"That will do," said Norbert, exchanging his spade for a sword. "Take your guard."

Croisenois, however, did not immediately obey. Impressible by nature, he felt a cold shiver run through his frame; the dark night, the flickering lantern, and all these preparations, made in so cold-blooded a manner, affected his nerves. The grave, with its yawning mouth, fascinated him.

"Well," said Norbert impatiently, "are you not ready?"

"I will speak," exclaimed De Croisenois, driven to desperation. "In a few minutes one of us will be lying dead on this spot. In the presence of death a man's words are to be relied on. Listen to me. I swear to you, on my honour and by all my hopes of future salvation, that the Duchess de Champdoce is entirely free from guilt."

"You have said that before; why repeat it again?"

"Because it is my duty; because I am thinking that, if I die, it will be my insane passions that have caused the ruin of one of the best and purest women in the world. I entreat you to believe that she has nothing to repent of. See, I am not ashamed to descend to entreaty. Let my death, if you kill me, be an expiation for everything. Be gentle with your wife; and if you survive me, do not make her life one prolonged existence of agony."

"Silence, or I shall look upon you as a dastard," returned Norbert fiercely.

"Miserable fool!" said De Croisenois. "On guard, then, and may heaven decide the issue!"

There was a sharp clash as their swords crossed, and the combat began with intense vigour.

The space upon which the rays of the lantern cast a glimmering and uncertain light was but a small one; and while one of the combatants was in complete shade the other was in the light, and exposed to thrusts which he could not see. This was fatal to Croisenois, and, as he took a step forward, Norbert made a fierce lunge which pierced him to the heart.

The unfortunate man threw up his arms above his head; his sword escaping from his nerveless fingers and his knees bending under him, he fell heavily backwards without a word escaping from his lips. Thrice he endeavoured to regain his feet, and thrice he failed in his attempts. He strove to speak, but he could only utter a few unintelligible words, for his life blood was suffocating him. A violent convulsion shook every limb, then arose a long, deep-drawn sigh, and then silence— George de Croisenois was dead.

Yes, he was dead, and Norbert de Champdoce stood over him with a wild look of terror in his eyes, and his hair bristling upon his head, as a shudder of horror convulsed his body. Then, for the first time, he realized the horror of seeing a man slain by his own hand; and yet what affected Norbert most was not that he had killed George de Croisenois—for he believed that justice was on his side and that he could not have acted otherwise—but the perspiration stood in thick beads upon his forehead, as he thought that he must raise up that still warm and quivering body, and place it in its unhallowed grave.

He hesitated and reasoned with himself for some time, going over all the reasons that made dispatch so absolutely necessary—the risk of detection, and the honour of his name.

He stooped and prepared to raise it, but recoiled again before his hands had touched the body. His heart failed him, and once more he assumed an erect position. At last he nerved himself, grasped the body, and, with an immense exertion of strength, hurled it into the gaping grave. It fell with a dull, heavy sound which seemed to Norbert like the roar of an earthquake. The violent emotions which he had endured had ended by acting on his brain, and, snatching up the spade which his late antagonist had used with so unpractised a hand, shovelled the earth upon the body, flattened down the ground, and finally covered it with straw and dead leaves.

"And this is the end of a man who wronged a Champdoce; yes, his life has paid the penalty of his deed."

All at once, a few paces off, in the deep shadow of the trees, he thought that he detected the outline of a human head with a pair of glittering eyes fixed upon him. The shock was so terrible that for an instant he stopped and nearly fell, but he quickly recovered himself, and, snatching up his blood-stained sword, he dashed to the spot where he fancied he had seen this terrible witness of his deed.

At this rapid movement on the part of the duke, a figure started up with a faint cry for mercy. It was a woman.

She fled with inconceivable swiftness towards the house, but he caught her just as she had gained the steps.

"Have mercy on me!" cried she. "Do not murder me!"

He dragged her back to where the lantern was hanging. She was a girl of about eighteen years of age, ugly, badly clothed, and dirty looking. Norbert looked earnestly at her, but could not say who she was, though he was certain that he had seen her face somewhere.

"Who are you?" asked he.

She burst into a flood of tears, but made no other reply.

"Come," resumed he, in more soothing accents; "you shall not be hurt. Tell me who you are."

"Caroline Schimmel."

"Caroline?" repeated he.

"Yes. I have been in your service as scullery maid for the last three months."

"How is it that you did not go to the wedding with the rest of them?"

"It was not my fault. I was asked, and I did so long to go, but I was too shabby; I had no finery to put on. I am very poor now, for I have only fifteen *francs* a month, and none of the other maids would lend me anything to wear."

"How did you come into the garden?" asked Norbert.

"I was very miserable, and was sitting in the garden crying, when I suddenly saw a light down there. I thought it was theirs, and crept down the back stairs."

"And what did you see?"

"I saw it all."

"All what?"

"When I got down here, you and the other were digging. I thought you were looking for money! but ah, dear me! I was wrong. Then the other began to say something, but I couldn't catch a word; then you fought. Oh, it was awful! I was so frightened, I could not take my eyes off you. Then the other fell down on his back."

"And then?"

"Then," she faltered, "you buried him, and then—"

"Could you recognise this—this other?"

"Yes, my lord duke, I did."

"Had you ever seen him before? Do you know who he was?"

"No."

"Listen to me, my girl. If you know how to hold your tongue, if you can forget all you have seen tonight, it will be the greatest piece of luck for you in the world that you did not go to this wedding."

"I won't open my lips to a soul, my lord duke. Hear me swear, I won't. Oh, do believe me!"

"Very well; keep your oath, and your fortune is made. Tomorrow I will give you a fine, large sum of money, and you can go back to your village and marry some honest fellow to whom you have taken a fancy."

"Are you not making game of me?"

"No; go to your room and go to bed, as if nothing had happened. Jean will tell you what to do tomorrow, and you must obey him as you would me."

"Oh, my lord! Oh, my lord duke!"

Unable to contain her delight, she mingled her laughter and her tears.

And Norbert knew that his name, his honour, and perhaps his life were in the hands of a wretched girl like this. All the peace and happiness of his life were gone, and he felt like some unhappy prisoner who through the bars of his dungeon sees his jailer's children sporting with lighted matches and a barrel of gunpowder. He was at her mercy, for well he knew that it would resolve into this—that the smallest wish of this girl would become an imperative command that he dared not disobey. However absurd might be her whims and caprices, she had but to express them, and he dared not resist. What means could he adopt to free himself from this odious state of servitude? He knew but of one—the dead tell no tales. There were four persons who were the sharer of Norbert's secret. First, the writer of the anonymous letter; then the duchess; then Caroline Schimmel; and, finally, Jean, to whom he must confide all. With these thoughts ringing through his brain, Norbert carefully effaced the last traces of the duel, and then bent his steps towards his wife's chamber.

He had expected to find her still unconscious on the spot where he had left her lying. Marie was seated in an armchair by the side of the fire; her face was terribly pale, and her eyes sparkling with the inward flame that consumed her.

"My honour has been vindicated; the Marquis de Croisenois is no more; I have slain your lover, *madame*."

Marie did not start; she had evidently prepared herself for this blow. Her face assumed a more proud and disdainful expression, and the light in her dark eyes grew brighter and brighter.

"You are wrong," said she, "M. de Croisenois was not my lover."

"You need no longer take the pains to lie; I ask nothing now."

Marie's utter calmness jarred inexpressibly upon Norbert's exasperated frame of mind. He would have given much to change this mood of hers, which he could not at all understand. But in vain did he say the most cutting things, and coupled them with bitter taunts, for she had reached a pitch of exaltation far above his sarcasms and abuse.

"I am not lying," answered she frigidly. "What should I gain by it? What more have I to gain in this world? You desire to learn the truth; here it is then: It was with my knowledge and permission that George was here tonight. He came because I had asked him to do so, and I left the gate in the garden wall open, so as to facilitate his entrance. He had not been more than five minutes in the room, when you arrived, and he had never been there before. It would have been easy for me to have left you; but as I bear your name, I could not dishonour it. As you entered, he was entreating me to fly with him; both his life and his honour were in my hands. Ah, why did I pause for an instant? Had I consented, he would still have been alive, and in some far distant country he and I might have learned that this world has something more to offer than unhappiness and misery. Yes, as you will have it, you shall have all. I loved him ere I knew that you even existed. I have only my own folly to blame, only my own unhappy weakness to deplore. Why did I not steadily refuse to become your wife? You say that you have slain George. Not so, for in my heart his memory will ever remain bright and ineffaceable."

"Beware!" said Norbert furiously, "beware if—"

"Ah, would you kill me too? Do not fear resistance; my life is a blank without him. He is dead; let death come to me; it would be a welcome visitant. The only kindness that you could now bestow upon me would be my death-blow. Strike then, and end it all! In death we should be united, George and I; and as my limbs grew stiff and my breath passed away, my whitening lips would murmur words of thanks."

Norbert listened to her, overwhelmed by the intensity of her passion, and marvelling that he had any power to feel after the terrible event which had fallen upon his devoted head.

Could this be Marie, the soft and gentle woman, who spoke with such passionate vehemence and boldly braved his anger? How could he have so misunderstood her? He forgot all his anger in his admiration. She seemed to him to have undergone a complete change. There was an unearthly style of beauty around her—her eyes blazed and shone with the lurid light of a far-distant planet, while her wealth of raven hair fell in disordered masses on her shoulders. It was passion, real passion, that he beheld tonight, not that mere empty delusion which he had so long followed blindly. Marie was really capable of a deep-rooted feeling of adoration for the man she loved, while with Diana de Mussidan, the woman with her fair hair and the steel-blue eyes, love was but the lust of conquest, or the desire to jeer at a suitor's earnestness. Ah, what a revelation had been made to him now! And what would he not have given to have wiped out the past! He advanced towards her with outstretched arms.

"Marie!" said he, "Marie!"

"I forbid you to call me Marie!" shrieked she wildly.

He made no reply, but still advanced towards her, when, with a terrible cry, she recoiled from him.

"Blood!" she screamed, "ah, heavens! he has blood upon his hands!"

Norbert glanced downwards; upon the wristband of his shirt there was a tell-tale crimson stain.

The duchess raised her hand, and pointed towards the door.

"Leave me," said she, with an extraordinary assumption of energy, "leave me; the secret of your crime is safe; I will not betray you or hand you over to justice. But remember that a murdered man stands between us, and that I loathe and execrate you."

Rage and jealousy tortured Norbert's soul. Though George de Croisenois was no more, he was still his successful rival in Marie's love.

"You forget," said he in a voice hoarse with passion, "that you are mine, and that, as your husband, I can make your existence one long scene of agony and misery. Keep this fact in your memory. Tomorrow, at six o'clock, I shall be here."

The clock was striking two as he left the house and hastened to the spot where he had left his horse.

The soldier was still pacing backwards and forwards, leading the duke's horse.

"My faith!" said the man, as soon as he perceived Norbert, "you pay precious long visits. I had only leave to go to the theatre, and I shall get into trouble over this."

"Pshaw! I promised you twenty *francs*. Here are two *louis*."

The soldier pocketed the money with an air of delighted surprise, and Norbert sprang into the saddle.

An hour later he gave the appointed signal upon the window pane, behind which the trusty Jean was waiting.

"Take care that no one sees you as you take the horse to the stable," said the duke hastily, "and then come to me, for I want your assistance and advice."

Chapter 45: The Heir of Champdoce

As long as she was in Norbert's presence, anger and indignation gave the Duchess de Champdoce strength; but as soon as she was left alone her energy gave way, and with an outburst of tears she sank, half fainting, upon a couch. Her despair was augmented from the fact that she felt that had it not been for her, George de Croisenois would never have met with his death.

"Had I not made that fatal appointment," she sobbed, "he would be alive and well now; my love has slain him as surely as if my hand had held the steel that has pierced his heart!"

She at first thought of seeking refuge with her father, but abandoned the idea almost immediately, for she felt that he would refuse to enter into her grievance, or would say, "You are a duchess; you have an enormous fortune. You must be happy; and if you are not, it must be your own fault."

In terrible anguish the night passed away; and when her maids entered the room, they found her lying on the floor, dressed as she had been the night before. No one knew what to do, and messengers were dispatched in all directions to summon medical advice.

Norbert's return was eagerly welcomed by the terrified domestics, and a general feeling of relief pervaded the establishment.

The duke had grown very uneasy as to what might have happened during his absence. He questioned the servants as diplomatically as he could; and while he was thus engaged, the doctors who had been summoned arrived.

After seeing their patient, they did not for a moment conceal their opinion that the case was a very serious one, and that it was possible that she might not survive this mysterious seizure. They impressed upon Norbert the necessity of the duchess being kept perfectly quiet and never left alone, and then departed, promising to call again in the afternoon.

Their injunctions were unnecessary, for Norbert had established himself by his wife's bedside, resolved not to quit her until her health was re-established or death had intervened to release her from suffering. Fever had claimed her for its own, and in her delusion she uttered many incoherent ravings, the key to which Norbert alone held, and which filled his soul with dread and terror.

This was the second time that Norbert had been compelled to watch over a sick-bed, guarding within his heart a terrible secret. At Champdoce he had sat by his father's side, who could have revealed the terrible attempt against his life; and now it was his wife that he was keeping a watch on, lest her lips should utter the horrible secret of the death of George de Croisenois.

Compelled to remain by his wife's side, the thoughts of his past life forced themselves upon him, and he shuddered to think that, at the age of twenty-five he had only to look back upon scenes of misery and crime, which cast a cloud of gloom and horror over the rest of his days. What a terrible future to come after so hideous a past!

He had another source of anxiety, and frequently rang the bell to inquire for Jean.

"Send him to me as soon as he comes," was his order.

At last Jean made his appearance, and his master led him into a deeply-recessed window.

"Well?" asked he.

"All is settled, my lord; be easy."

"And Caroline?"

"Has left. I gave her twenty thousand *francs*, and saw her into the train myself. She is going to the States, where she hopes to find a cousin who will marry her; at least, that is her intention."

Norbert heaved a deep sigh of relief, for the thought of Caroline Schimmel had laid like a heavy burden upon his heart.

"And how about the other matter?" asked he.

The old man shook his head.

"What has been done?"

"I have got hold of a young fellow who believes that I wish to send him to Egypt, to purchase cotton. He will start tomorrow, and will post the two letters written by the Marquis de Croisenois, one at Marseilles, and the other at Cairo."

"Do you not think that these letters will insure my perfect security?"

"I see that any indiscretion on our agent's part, or a mere act of carelessness, may ruin us."

"And yet it must be done."

After consulting together, the doctors had given some slight hope, but the position of the patient was still very precarious. It was suggested that her intellect might be permanently affected; and during all these long and anxious hours Norbert did not even dare to close his eyes, and it was with feelings of secret terror that he permitted the maids to perform their duties around their invalid mistress.

Upon the fourth day the fever took a favourable turn, and Marie slept, giving Norbert time to review his position.

How was it that Madame de Mussidan, who was a daily visitor, had not appeared at the house since that eventful night? He was so much surprised at this that he ventured to dispatch a short note, acquainting her of the sudden illness of his wife.

In an hour he received a reply, merely containing these words:—

"Can you account for M. de Mussidan's sudden determination to spend the winter in Italy? We leave this evening. Farewell.—D."

And so she, too, had abandoned him, taking with her all the hopes he had in the world. Still, however, his infatuation held its sway over him, and he forced himself to believe that she felt this separation as keenly as he did.

Some five days afterwards, when the Duchess de Champdoce had been pronounced out of immediate danger, one of the doctors took him mysteriously aside. He said that he wanted to inform the duke of a startling, but he hoped a welcome piece of intelligence—that the Duchess de Champdoce was in the way to present the duke with an heir to his title and estates.

It was the knowledge of this that had decided her not to leave her husband's roof, and had steeled her heart against George's entreaties. She had hesitated, and had almost yielded to the feelings of her heart, when this thought troubled her.

Unfortunately for herself, she had not disclosed her condition to her husband, and, at the news, all Norbert's former suspicions revived, and his wrath rose once more to an extraordinary height. His lips grew pale, and his eyes blazed with fury.

"Thank you, doctor!" exclaimed he. "Of course, the news is very welcome. Goodbye. I must go to the duchess at once."

Instead of going to his wife, Norbert went and locked himself up in his own private apartment. He had need to be alone, in order to look this fresh complication more fully in the face, and the more he reflected, the more convinced was he that he had been the dupe of a guilty woman. He had begun by doubting, and he ended by being convinced that the child was not his. Was he to accept this degraded position, and rear up as his own the child of George de Croisenois? The child would grow up under his own roof-tree, bear his name, and finally inherit his title and gigantic fortune. "Never," muttered he. "No, never; for sooner than that, I will crush the life out of it with my own hands!"

The more he thought how he should have to deceive the world by feigning love and lavishing caresses upon this interloping child, the more he felt that it would be impossible to perform his task. He had, however, much to do at present. The sudden and mysterious disappearance of George de Croisenois had created much stir and excitement in Paris, and the letter which had been posed by the agent dispatched by Jean, instead of explaining matters, had only deepened the mystery and caused fresh grounds of surprise to arise in the minds of the friends of the *marquis* and the police authorities. But the disappearance of the *marquis* was only a nine days' wonder after all. Some other strange event excited the attention of the fickle public, and George de Croisenois' name was no longer in everyone's mouth.

Norbert breathed freely once more, for he felt his secret was safe.

Diana de Mussidan had now been absent for three months and had not vouchsafed him a single line. A river of blood flowed between him and his wife. Among all his acquaintances he had not one friend on whom he could rely, and his reckless life of debauchery and dissipation began to weary him. His thoughts were always fixed upon this coming child. How could he ever bear to bring it up as if it were his own? He had thought over many plans, but always trusted to the first one he had conceived. This was to procure an infant, it mattered not where or by what means, and substitute it for the new-born child of his wife. As time rolled on, he became more imbued with this idea, and at length he summoned Jean to him, that faithful old man, who served his master so truly out of affection to the house of Champdoce.

For the first time Jean raised an objection to his master's proposal, declaring that such an act would bring shame and misery upon all concerned in it; but when he found that Norbert was determined, and that, if he refused, his master would employ some less scrupulous agent, he, with tears in his eyes and a tremor in his voice, promised obedience.

About a month later, Jean came to his master and suggested that it would be best the *accouchement* of the duchess should take place at a *château* belonging to the Champdoce family near Montroire, and that this once done, he, Jean would arrange everything. The removal was effected almost at once, and the duchess, who was a mere shadow of her former self, made no opposition. She and Norbert lived together as perfect strangers. Sometimes a week would elapse without their meeting; and if they had occasion to communicate, it was done by letter.

The estate to which Norbert had conducted the duchess was admirably adapted for his purpose. The unhappy woman was entirely alone in the world, and had no one to whom she could apply for protection or advice. Her father, the Count de Puymandour, had died suddenly a month before, owing to chagrin caused by his defeat when a candidate for a seat in the Chamber. The brief note from the despairing mother, in which followed the words, "Have mercy! Give me back my child!" hardly describes the terrible events that occurred in the lonely *château* to which Norbert had conducted his innocent victim.

The child of the Duchess de Champdoce had been placed by Jean in the Foundling Hospital at Vendome, while the infant that was baptized with the grandiloquent names of Anne Rene, Gontran de Duepair, Marquis de Champdoce, was the bastard child of a girl living near Montroire, who was known in the neighbourhood as "The Witch."

Chapter 46: Mascarin Speaks

This was the conclusion of the manuscript handed by Mascarin to Paul Violaine, and the young man laid down the roll of paper with the remark, "And that is all."

He had consumed six hours in reading this sad account of the follies and crimes of the owners of illustrious names.

Mascarin had listened with the complacency of an author who hears his own work read aloud to him, but all the while he was keenly watching him beneath his spectacles and the faces of his companions. The effect that was produced was immense, and exactly what he had anticipated. Paul, Hortebise, and Catenac gazed upon each other with faces in which astonishment at the strange recital, and then at the power of the man who had collected these facts together, were mingled, and Catenac was the first who spoke. The sound of his own voice seemed gradually to dispel the vague sense of apprehension that hung about the office.

"Aha!" cried he, "I always said that our old friend Mascarin would make his mark in literature. As soon as his pen touches the paper the business man vanishes; we have no longer a collection of dry facts and proofs, but the stirring pages of a sensational novel."

"Do you really consider that as a mere romance?" asked Hortebise.

"It reads like one certainly; you must allow that."

"Catenac," remarked Mascarin in his bitterly sarcastic tone, "is best able to pronounce upon the truth or falsehood of this narrative, as he is the professional adviser of this same Duke de Champdoce, the very Norbert whose life has just been read to you."

"I do not deny that there is some slight foundation to it," returned the lawyer.

"Then what is it that you do deny?"

"Nothing, nothing; I merely objected, more in jest than otherwise, to the sentimental manner in which you have set forward your case."

"Catenac," remarked Mascarin, addressing the others, "has received many confidential communications from his noble client, which he has not thought fit to communicate to us; and though he fancied that we were drifting into quicksands and among breakers, he displayed no signal of warning to save us from our danger, hoping, like a true friend, that, by this means, he might get rid of us."

Catenac began to utter protestations and denials, but Mascarin cut him short with an imperative gesture, and, after a long pause, he again commenced,—

"You must understand that my inquisitors have had but little to do in this affair, for my work has chiefly consisted in putting fragments together. It is not to me that you are indebted for the sensational (I think that that was the term used) part of my story, but rather to Madame de Mussidan and Norbert de Champdoce. I am sure that some of the phrases must have struck you considerably."

"It seems to me," objected Catenac—

"Perhaps," broke in Mascarin, "you have forgotten the correspondence which the Countess de Mussidan preserved so carefully—both his letters and her own, which Norbert returned to her."

"And we have those?"

"Of course we have, only there is a perfect romance contained in these letters. What I have read is a mere bald extract from them; and this is not all. The man who assisted me in the unravelling of this dark intrigue was the original promoter—Daumon."

"What, is the counsellor still alive?"

"Certainly, and you know him. He is not quite in his first youth, and has aged somewhat, but his intellect is as brilliant as ever."

Catenac grew serious. "You tell me a great deal," said he.

"I can tell you even more. I can tell you that the account of the deed was written under the dictation of Caroline Schimmel," broke in Mascarin. "This unlucky woman started for Havre, intending to sail for the United States, but she got no further than that seaport town, for the good looks and the persuasive tongue of a sailor induced her to alter her plans. As long as her money lasted he remained an ardent lover, but vanished with the disappearance of her last thousand-*franc* note. Starving and poverty-stricken, Caroline returned to Paris and to the Duke de Champdoce, who accepted her constant demands for money as a penitent expiation of his crime. But she remained faithful to her oath; and had it not been for her terrible propensity for drink, Tantaine would never have succeeded in extracting her secret from her. If, on her recovery from her fit of drunk coma, she recollects what has taken place, she will, if I read her character right, go straight to the Duke de Champdoce and tell him that his secret has passed into better hands."

At this idea being promulgated, Catenac started from his chair with a loud oath.

"Did you think," asked Mascarin, "that I should feel so much at my ease if I found that there was the slightest risk? Let us consider what it is that Caroline can say. Who is it that she can accuse of having stolen her secret from her? Why, only a poor old wretch named Tantaine. How can the duke possibly trace any connection between this miserable writer and Catenac?"

"Yes, I think that it would be a difficult task."

"Besides," pursued Mascarin, "what have we to fear from the Duke de Champdoce? Nothing, as far as I can see. Is he not as much in our power as the woman he formerly loved—Diana de Mussidan? Do we not hold the letters of both of them, and do we not know in what corner of his garden to dig to discover a damning piece of evidence? Remember that there will be no difficulty in identifying the skeleton, for at the time of his disappearance, Croisenois had about him several Spanish *doubloons*, a fact which was given to the police."

"Well," said Catenac, "I will act faithfully. Tell me your plans, and I will let you know all that I hear from the duke."

For a moment a smile hovered upon Mascarin's lips, for this time he placed firm reliance upon the good faith of the lawyer.

"Before we go further," said he, "let me conclude this narrative which Paul has just read. It is sad and simple. The united ages of the duke and duchess did not exceed fifty years; they had unlimited wealth, and bore one of the grandest historic names of France; they were surrounded with every appliance of luxury, and yet their lives were a perfect wreck. They simply dragged on an existence and had lost all hopes of happiness, but they made up their minds to conceal the skeleton of their house in the darkest cupboard, and the world knew nothing of their inner life. The duchess suffered much in health, and merely went out to visit the sick and poor. The duke worked hard to make up for the deficiencies of his early education, and made a name and reputation throughout Europe."

"And how about Madame de Mussidan?" asked Catenac.

"I am coming to that," returned Mascarin. "With that strange determination that fills the hearts of our women, she did not consider her revenge complete until Norbert learned that she was the sole instrument in heaping the crowing sorrow of his life on his head; and on her return from Italy, she sent for him and told him everything. Yes, she absolutely had the audacity to tell him that it was she who had done her best to throw his wife into De Croisenois' arms. She told him that it was she who had worked the arrangements for the meeting, and had written the anonymous letter."

"Why did he not kill her?" cried Hortebise. "Had she not all his letters, and taunted him with the production of them? Ah, my dear friends, do not let us flatter ourselves that we have the sole monopoly of blackmailing. The high-born countess plunged her hand into the duke's coffers just as if she had been a mere adventuress. It is only ten days ago that she borrowed—you will observe the entry of it as a loan—a large sum to settle an account of Van Klopen's. But let us now speak of the child who took the place of the boy whom the duchess brought into the world. You know him, doctor?"

"Yes, I have often seen him. He was a good-looking young fellow."

"He was, but he was a degraded scoundrel, after all. He was educated and brought up without regard to expense, but he always displayed low tastes, and, had he lived, would have brought discredit on the name he bore. He was a thorn in the side of the duke and duchess, and I believe that they felt great relief when he died of brain fever, brought on by a drunken debauch. His parents, or those whom he supposed to be such, were present at his death-bed, for they had learned to consider their sorrows as the just chastisement of heaven. The boy having died, the family of Champdoce seemed likely to become extinct, and then it was that Norbert decided to do what his wife had long urged upon him, to seek for and reclaim the child which he had caused to be placed in the Foundling Hospital at Vendome.

"It went against his pride to diverge from the course he had determined on as best, but doubts had arisen in his mind as to his wife's guilt, and Diana's confessions had reassured him as to the paternity of the missing boy. It was thus with hope in his heart, and furnished with every necessary document, that he started for Vendome; but there a terrible disappointment awaited him. The authorities of the hospital, on consulting the register, found that a child had been admitted on the day and hour mentioned by Norbert, and that his description of the infant's clothing tallied exactly with the entries. But the child was no longer in the hospital, and there was no clue to his whereabouts. He had, at the age of twelve, been apprenticed to a tanner, but he had run away from his master, and the most active and energetic search had failed to arrest the fugitive."

Catenac listened to all these exact details with an unpleasant feeling gnawing at his heart, for he saw that his associates knew everything, and he had relied upon again securing their confidence by furnishing them with those details which were evidently already known to them. Mascarin, however, affected not to notice his surprise, and went on with his narrative.

"This terrible disappointment will certainly kill the Duke de Champdoce. It seemed to him that after having so bitterly expiated the crimes and follies of his youth, he might hope to have his old age in peace and quiet, with a son who might cheer the loneliness of his desolate fireside. His countenance, as soon as he appeared before the duchess, who had been expecting his return in an agony of anguish and suspense, told her at once that all hope had fled. In a few days, however, the duke had perfectly recovered from the shock, and had decided that to give up the search would be an act of madness. The world is wide, and a friendless boy, without a name, difficult to trace; but, with ample funds, almost anything can be done, and he was willing to sacrifice both life and fortune to attain his object. So immense were his resources, that it was easy for him to employ the most skilful detectives; and whatever the result might be, he had come to look upon this task as a sacred duty to which he ought to devote all the remaining years of his life. He swore that he would never rest or cease from his search until he had been furnished with the indisputable proofs of the existence or the death of his son.

"He did not confide all this project to the duchess; for he feared— and he had by this time learned to have some consideration for her enfeebled frame—her health had given way so completely that any extra degree of excitement might prove fatal to her. He, therefore, as a preliminary, applied to that element which in the Rue de Jerusalem acts as the terrestrial guardians of society. But the police could do nothing for the duke. They heard what he had to say gravely, took notes, told him to call again later on, and there was an end to their proceedings. It can easily be understood that the rank and position of the duke prevented him from making his name known in his inquiries; and as he dared not divulge the whole truth, he gave such a bald version of the case, that it excited no deep feelings of interest. At last he was sent to a certain M. Lecoq."

To Paul's utter astonishment, the name produced a sudden and terrible effect upon Doctor Hortebise, who started to his feet as if propelled from his chair by the unexpected application of some hidden motive power, and, fingering the locket that hung from his chain, gazed round upon his associates with wild and excited eyes.

"Stop!" cried he. "If that fellow Lecoq is to put his nose into your case, I withdraw; I will have nothing to do with it, for it is certain to be a failure."

He appeared to be so thoroughly frightened, that Catenac condescended to smile.

"Yes, yes," said he, "I can understand your alarm; but be at ease; Lecoq has nothing to do with us."

But Hortebise was not satisfied with Catenac's assurance, and looked for confirmation from Mascarin.

"Lecoq has nothing to do with us," repeated his friend. "The fool said that his position prevented him from giving his time to any investigation of a private nature, which, by the way, is quite true. The duke offered him a heavy sum to throw up his appointment, but he refused, saying he did not work for money, but from love for his profession."

"Which is quite true," interrupted Catenac.

"However," continued Mascarin, "to cut short my narrative, the duke, on the refusal of Lecoq to act, applied to Catenac."

"Yes," answered the lawyer, "and the duke has placed the conduct of the search in my hands."

"Have you formed any plan of action?"

"Not at present. The duke said, 'Ask every living soul in the world, if you can succeed in no other way'; this is all the instruction he has given me; and," added he, with a slight shrug of his shoulders, "I am almost of Perpignan's opinion, that the search will be a fruitless one."

"Lecoq did not think so."

"He only said that he believed he should succeed if he were to take it in hand."

"Well," answered Mascarin coldly, "I have been certain of success from the very commencement."

"Have you been to Vendome?" asked Catenac.

"Never mind, I have been somewhere, and at this very moment could place my hand upon the shoulder of the heir to the dukedom of Champdoce."

"Are you in earnest?"

"I was never more in earnest in my life. I have found him; only as it is impossible for me to appear in the matter, I shall delegate to you and Perpignan the happiness of restoring the lost son to his father's arms."

Catenac glanced from Mascarin to Hortebise, and from them to Paul, and seemed to wish to be certain that he was not being made an object of ridicule.

"And why do you not wish to appear in the matter?" asked he at last, in a suspicious tone of voice. "Do you foresee some risk, and want me to bear the brunt?"

Mascarin shrugged his shoulders.

"First," said he, "I am not a traitor, as you know well enough; and then the interests of all of us depend on your safety. Can one of us be compromised without endangering his associates? You know that this is impossible. All you have to do is to point out where the traces commence; others will follow them at their own risk, and all you will have to do will be to look calmly on."

"But—"

Mascarin lost his patience, and with a deep frown, replied,—

"That is enough. We require no more argument, I am the master, and it is for you to obey."

When Mascarin adopted this tone, resistance was out of the question; and as he invariably made all yield to him, it was best to obey with a good grace, and Catenac relapsed into silence, completely subjugated and very much puzzled.

"Sit down at my desk," continued Mascarin, "and take careful notes of what I now say. Success is, as I have told you, inevitable, but I must be ably backed. All now depends upon your exactitude in obeying my orders; one false step may ruin us all. You have heard this, and cannot say that you are not fully warned."

Chapter 47: A Sudden Check

Catenac seated himself at the writing-table without a word, concealing his anger and jealousy beneath a careless smile. Mascarin was no longer the plotter consulting with his confederates; he was the master issuing his orders to his subordinates. He had now taken from a box some of those square pieces of pasteboard, which he spent his time in reading over.

"Try and not miss one word of what I am saying," remarked he, bending his keen glance upon Paul; then, turning to Catenac, he continued, "Can you persuade the Duke de Champdoce and Perpignan to start for Vendome on Saturday?"

"Perhaps I may be able to do so."

"I want a Yes or No. Can you or can you not make these people go there?"

"Well, yes, then."

"Very well. Then, on going to Vendome, you will stop at the Hotel de Porte."

"Hotel de Porte," repeated Catenac, as he made a note of the name.

"Upon the day of your arrival at Vendome," continued Mascarin, "you could do very little. Your time would be taken up in resting after your journey, and perhaps you may make a few preliminary inquiries. It will be on Sunday that you will go to the hospital together, and make the same inquires which the duke formerly made by himself. The lady superior is a woman of excellent taste and education, and she will do all that she can to be useful to you. Through her you will be able to obtain the boy's description, and the date on which he left the hospital to be apprenticed to a tanner. She will tell you that, disliking the employment, he ran away from them at the age of twelve and a half years, and that since then no trace of him has been found. You will hear from her that he was a tall, well-built lad, looking two years older than he really was, with an intelligent cast of feature, and keen, bright eyes, full of health and good looks. He had on, on the day of his disappearance, blue and white striped trousers, a gray blouse, a cap with no peak, and a spotted silk cravat. Then to assist you still further in your researches she will add that he carried in a bundle, enveloped in a red plaid cotton handkerchief, a white blouse, a pair of gray cloth trousers, and a pair of new shoes."

Catenac watched Mascarin as he was speaking with an expression of ill-concealed enmity.

"You are well informed, on my word," muttered he.

"I think I am," returned Mascarin. "After this you will go back to the hotel, and not until then—do you understand?—and you will consult as to the first steps to be taken. The plan proposed by Perpignan is an excellent one."

"What! you know it then?"

"Of course I do. He proposed to divide Vendome and its suburbs into a certain number of circles, and to make a house-to-house visitation in each of them. Let him go to work in this manner. Of course, to do so, you will require a guide."

"Of course we should require such a person."

"Here, Catenac, I must leave a little to chance, for I am not quite omnipotent. But there are nine chances out of ten that your host will advise you to avail yourself of the services of a man called Frejot, who acts as commissioner to the hotel. It may be, however, that he may designate someone else; but in that case you must, by some means or other, manage to employ the services of one other man."

"What am I to say to him?"

"He understands what he is to do completely. Well, these preliminaries being settled, you will commence on Monday morning to search the suburb called Areines, under the guidance of Frejot. Leave all the responsibility to Perpignan, but make sure that the duke comes with you. Ask the denizens a series of questions which you have prepared beforehand, such as 'My friends, we are in search of a boy. A reward of ten thousand *francs* is offered to anyone who will put us on his track. He must have left these parts in August, 1856, and some of you may have seen him.'"

Here Catenac stopped Mascarin.

"Wait a moment. Your own words are excellent; I will write them down."

"All Monday," continued Mascarin, "you will not make much progress, and for the next few days it will be the same, but on Saturday prepare yourself for a great surprise; for on that day Frejot will take you to a large, lonely farmhouse, on the shores of a lake. This farm is held by a man named Lorgelin, who cultivates it with the assistance of his wife and his two sons. You will find these worthy people at dinner. They will offer you some refreshment, and you will accept. At the next word you utter you will find that they will glance at each other in a meaning manner, and the wife will exclaim, 'Blessed Virgin! Surely the gentleman is speaking of the poor lad we have so often talked about.'"

As Mascarin went on describing his arrangements, his whole form seemed to dilate, and his face shone with the knowledge of mastery and power. His voice was so clear and his manner so full of authority and command, that it carried conviction to the minds of all those who were seated listening to him. He spoke of what would happen as if he was dealing with an absolute certainty, and went on with such wonderful lucidity and force of reasoning that they seemed to be absolutely real.

"Oh! the farmer's wife will say this, will she?" demanded Catenac, in a tone of the utmost surprise.

"Yes, this, and nothing more. Then the husband will explain that they found the poor lad half dead in a ditch by the side of the road, and that they took him home, and did what they could for him; and will add, this was in the beginning of September, 1856. You will offer to read him your description of the lad, but he will volunteer his own, which you will find exactly to tally with the one you have. Then Lorgelin will tell you what an excellent lad he was, and how the farm seemed quite another place as long as he remained there. All the family will join in singing his praises—he was so good-tempered, so obliging, and at thirteen he could write like a lawyer's clerk. And then they will produce some of his writing in an old copy book.

"But after all the old woman, with a tear in her eye, will say that she found the lad had not much gratitude in his composition, for at the end of the following September he left the farm where he had received so much kindness. Yes, he left them to go away with some strolling performers. You will be absolutely affected by the words of these worthy people, and before you leave they will show you the clothes the lad left behind him."

Catenac was waiting for the conclusion, and then exclaimed, in rather a disappointed tone,—

"But I do not see what we have gained when Lorgelin's story has been repeated to us."

Mascarin raised his hand, as though to deprecate immediate criticism, and to ask for further patience on the part of his audience.

"Permit me to go on," said he. "You would now not know what to do, but Perpignan will not hesitate for a moment. He will tell you that he holds the end of the clue, and that all that remains to be done is to follow it up carefully."

"I think that you overrate Perpignan's talents."

"Not a bit; each man to his own line of business. Besides, if he wanders off the course, you must get him back to it. In this you must act diplomatically. His first move will naturally be to take you to the office of the mayor of the township, where a register of licenses is kept. There you will find that in September, 1857, there passed through the place a troupe of travelling performers, consisting of nine persons, with the caravans, under the management of a man known as Vigoureux, nicknamed the Grasshopper."

Catenac rapidly jotted down these items. "Not so fast," said he; "I cannot follow you."

After a short pause, Mascarin continued.

"An attentive examination of the book will prove to you that no other troupe of itinerant performers passed through the place during that month; and it is clear that it must have been the Grasshopper with whom the lad went away. You will then peruse the man's description. Vigoureux, born at Bourgogne, Vosges. Age, forty-seven. Height, six feet two inches. Eyes, small and gray, rather near-sighted. Complexion dark. Third finger of left hand cut off at first joint. If you confound him, after reading this, with any other man of his profession, you must certainly be rather foolish."

"I shall now be able to find him," muttered Catenac.

"But that is Perpignan's business. You will see him put on an air of the greatest importance, and appear quite overjoyed at the news he has obtained at the office of the mayor. He will say that the inquiry at Vendome is over, and that it will be best to return to Paris at once. Of course, you will make no objection. You will permit the duke to make a handsome present to Lorgelin and Frejot; but take care not to leave him behind you. I advise you to regain Paris without a moment's delay. The wily Perpignan, on your return, will at once take you to the head police office, where Vigoureux will have left his papers, like other men of his profession. If there is any difficulty in obtaining a sight of them, the Duke de Champdoce will act as a talisman. You will then discover that in 1864, the man Vigoureux was sentenced to a term of imprisonment for disorderly conduct, and that he now keeps a wine-shop at the corner of the Rue Depleux."

"Stop a bit," said Catenac, "and let me take down the address."

"When you go there, you will recognise Vigoureux by the loss of his finger. He will at once admit that the lad followed him, and remained in the troupe for ten months. He was a good enough lad, but as grand as a peacock, and as lazy as a dormouse. He made great friends with an old Alsatian, called Fritz, who was the conductor of the orchestra, and by-and-by both were so fond of each other, that one day they went off in each other's company. Now you want to know what has become of Fritz? I know Vigoureux will get tired of this prolonged string of questions, and behave violently; then you will threaten him for having carried off a youth of tender years, and he will calm down, and become as mild as mother's milk, and will promise to gain information for you. In a week he will give the information that Fritz is to be found at the Hospital Magloire."

Absolutely dumb with surprise, the audience listened to these strange assertions, which dovetailed so exactly into each other, and seemed to have been the work of years of research.

"Fritz," continued Mascarin, "is a sly old dog. You will find an old, rickety, blue-eyed man at the hospital, and remember to tell the Duke de Champdoce that he must not put too much faith in him. This wily old Alsatian will tell you of all the sacrifices he made for the dear lad. He will tell you that he often went without his beer and tobacco in order to pay for the music lessons that he forced the boy to take. He will tell you that he wanted to get him into the Government School of Music, for that he possessed great vocal and instrumental talent, and he cherished the hope of one day seeing him a great composer, like Weber or Mozart. I expect that this flow of self-praise will melt the heart of your client, for he will see that his son had made an effort to rise out of the mire by his own exertions, and will, in this energy, recognise one of the characteristics of the Champdoce family; and on the strength of this testimony he will almost be ready to accept the young man as his son."

Catenac had for some time past been striving to decipher the meaning hidden behind the inscrutable countenance of Mascarin, but in vain.

"Let us get on," said the lawyer impatiently. "All that you have told me I shall hear later on in the course of the inquiry."

"If your sagacity requires no further explanation from me," rejoined Mascarin, "you will, I trust, permit me to continue them for the benefit of our young friend, Paul Violaine. You will feel compassion when the Alsatian tells you of his sufferings, at the boys' description of him, and his subsequent prosperity in the Rue d'Arras. You had better listen to the old man as long as he continues to grumble on, the more so as you will detect in the rancour and bitterness of his remarks all the vexation of a disappointed speculator. He will confess to you besides that he subsists entirely on the bounty of the lad, whom he had stigmatized as an ungrateful villain.

"Of course, the duke will have to leave behind him some testimonial of his pleasure, and you will hurry off to the Rue d'Arras. The proprietor of the house will tell you that some four years ago he got rid of his musician, the only one of his class who had dared to establish himself there, and a small present and a few adroit questions will obtain for you the address of one of the young man's pupils, Madame Grandorge, a widow lady, residing in the Rue St. Louis. This lady will tell you that she does not know the address of her former master, but that he used to live at 57, Rue de la Harpe. From the Rue de la Harpe you will be sent to the Rue Jacob, and from thence to the Rue Montmartre, at the corner of the Rue Joquelet."

Mascarin paused, drew a long breath, and chuckled inwardly, as though at some excellent joke.

"Be comforted, Catenac," said he. "You have nearly reached the end of your journey. The portress at the house in the Rue Montmartre is the most obliging woman in the world. She will tell you that the musician still retains his rooms in the house, but that he resides there no longer, for he has made a lucky hit, and last month he married the daughter of a wealthy banker living close by. The young lady, Mademoiselle Rigal, saw him, and fell in love with him."

A clever man like Catenac should have foreseen what was coming, but he had not, and at this conclusion he uttered a loud exclamation of surprise.

"Yes, just so," said Mascarin, with an air of bland triumph. "The Duke de Champdoce will then drag you off to our mutual friend Martin Rigal, and there you will find our young *protégé*, the happy

397

husband of the beautiful Flavia."

Mascarin drew himself up, and adjusted his glasses firmly on his nose.

"Now, my dear Catenac, show the liberality and amiability of your disposition by congratulating our friend Paul as Gontran, Marquis de Champdoce."

Hortebise, of course, knew what was coming; he knew the lines of the plot of the play as if he had been a joint author of it, and was as much excited as if he were assisting at a first rehearsal.

"Bravo!" he exclaimed, clapping his hands together. "Bravo, my dear Mascarin, you have excelled yourself today!"

Worried and perplexed as Paul had been, as Mascarin concluded he sank back in his chair, sick and giddy with emotion.

"Yes," said Mascarin in a clear and ringing voice, "I accept your praise without any affectation of false modesty. We have no reason to fear the intervention of that grain of sand which sometimes stops the working of the machine. Perpignan, poor fool though he is, will be our best friend, and will do our work quite unconsciously. Can the duke retain any atom of suspicion after these minute investigations? Impossible. But to remove the slightest element of doubt, I have another and an additional plan. I will make him retrace the path upon which he has started. He shall take Paul to all these various places, and at all of them the statements will be even more fully confirmed. Paul, the son-in-law of Martin Rigal, the husband of Flavia, will be recognised in the Rue Montmartre, the Rue Jacob, and the Rue de la Harpe. He will be joyfully welcomed in the Rue d'Arras; Fritz will embrace his ungrateful pupil; Vigoureux will remind him of his skilful feats on the trapeze; the Lorgelin family will press the lad whom they gave shelter to, to their hearts, and this will happen, Catenac, because I will it, and because all the people from the portress in the Rue Montmartre to the Lorgelins are my slaves, and dare not disobey one single command which I may issue."

Catenac rose slowly and solemnly from his seat.

"I recognise your patience and ingenuity thoroughly, only I am going with one word to crush the fabric of hope that you have so carefully erected."

Catenac might be a coward, he might also be a traitor but he was a clever and clear-sighted man too. Consequently Hortebise shivered as he heard these words, but Mascarin smiled disdainfully, basking in his dream of success.

"Go on then," said he.

"Well, then, let me tell you that you will not overreach and deceive the duke."

"And why not, pray?" asked Mascarin. "But are you sure that I wish to deceive him? You have not been open with me, why should I be frank with you? Am I in the habit of confiding in those who do not repose confidence in me? Does Perpignan for a moment suspect the part that he is to play? Why may I not have judged it best to keep from you the fact that Paul is really the child you are seeking?"

Mascarin spoke so confidently that Catenac gazed upon him, hardly knowing to what conclusion to come, for his conscience was by no means clear. His intellect quickly dived into the depths of all probabilities, and yet he could not see in all these combinations any possible peril to himself.

"I only hope," said he, "that Paul is all that you represent him to be; but why all these precautions? Only, mark my words, the duke has an infallible way of detecting, or rather of preventing, any attempt at imposition. It is ever thus, the most trivial circumstance will overset the best laid plans, and the inevitable destroy the combinations of the most astute intellect."

Mascarin interrupted his associate.

"Paul is the son of the Duke de Champdoce," said he decisively.

What was the meaning of this? Catenac felt that he was being played with, and grew angry.

"As you please; but you will, I presume, permit me to convince myself of the truth of this assertion."

Then, advancing towards Paul, the lawyer said,—

"Have the goodness to remove your coat."

Paul took it off, and threw it upon the back of a chair.

"Now," added Catenac, "roll up your right shirt sleeve to the shoulder."

Scarcely had the young man obeyed, and the lawyer cast a rapid glance at the bare flesh, than he turned to his associates and observed,—

"No, he is not the right man."

To his extreme surprise, Mascarin and Hortebise burst into a fit of unrestrained laughter.

"No," pursued the lawyer, "this is not the child who was sent to the Hospital of Vendome, and the duke will recognise this better than I can. You laugh, but it is because you do not know all."

"Enough," returned Mascarin, and then, turning to the doctor, he remarked, "Tell him, my friends, that we know more than he thinks."

"And so," said Hortebise, taking Paul's hand, "you are certain that this is not the lost child because he has not certain marks about him; but these will be seen upon the day on which Paul is introduced to the duke, and legibly enough to satisfy the most unbelieving."

"What do you mean?"

"Let me explain in my own way. If in early childhood Paul had been scalded on his shoulder by boiling water, he would have a scar whose appearance would denote its origin?"

Catenac nodded, "You are quite accurate," said he.

"Well, then listen. Paul is coming home with me. I shall take him into my consulting-room; he will lie on a couch. I shall give him chloroform, for I do not wish him to suffer any pain. Mascarin will help me. Then I shall apply, on the proper part, a piece of flannel steeped in a certain liquid which is an invention of my own. I am not a fool, as you may have discovered before this; and in a drawer at home is a piece of flannel cut so as exactly to resemble the irregular outline of a scar of the kind you describe, and a few little bits here and there will do the rest of the work artistically. When the liquid has effected its work, which will be in ten minutes, I shall remove it, and apply an ointment, another invention of my own, to the wound; then I shall restore Paul to his senses, and go to dinner."

Mascarin rubbed his hands with delight.

"But you forget that a certain space of time is required to give a scar the appearance of not having been recent," objected Catenac.

"Let me speak," broke in the doctor. "If we only needed time— six months, say, or a year—we should postpone our concluding act until then; but I, Hortebise, assure you that in two months, thanks to another discovery of my own—will show you a scar that will pass muster, not perhaps before a fellow-practitioner, but certainly before the duke."

Catenac's sunken eyes blazed as he thought of the prospective millions.

"May the devil fly away with all scruples!" cried he. "My friends, I am yours soul and body; you may rely on your devoted Catenac."

The doctor and Mascarin exchanged a look of triumph.

"Of course we share and share alike," observed the lawyer. "It is true that I come in rather late; but the part I play is a delicate and an important one, and you can do nothing without me."

"You shall have your share," answered Mascarin evasively.

"One word more," said the lawyer. "Do you think that the duke has kept nothing back? The infant was hardly seen by him or the duchess; but Jean saw it, and he, though very old and infirm, would come forward at any moment to defend the name and honour of the Champdoce family."

"Well, and what then?"

"Jean, you know, was against the substitution of another child. May he not have foreseen the chance of such a case as this arising?"

Mascarin looked grave. "I have thought of that before," returned he; "but what can be done?"

"I will find out," said Catenac. "Jean has the most implicit confidence in me, and I will question him."

The cold calmness of the lawyer had vanished, and Catenac only displayed the zealous eagerness of the man who, admitted at a late hour into an enterprise which he imagines will be lucrative, burns to do as much as he can to further it.

"But," added he, as an after-thought, "how can we be certain that there is no one to recognise Paul?"

"I can answer for that; his poverty had isolated him from all but a woman named Rose, and I took care that she should be sent to the prison of St. Lazare. At one time I was a little anxious, as I heard that Paul had a patron; but he, as I have found out, was the Count de Mussidan, the murderer of Montlouis, who, as you may have guessed, was Paul's father."

"We have nothing, then, to fear from that quarter," said the doctor.

"Nothing; and while you get on with your work, I will hurry on Paul's marriage with Rigal's daughter. But this will not prevent my busying myself in another quarter; for before a month Henri de Croisenois will have floated his Company, and become the husband of Sabine de Mussidan."

"I think that it is about time for dinner," remarked Hortebise, and, turning to the *protégé* of the association, he added, "Come, Paul."

But Paul made no movement, and then for the first time it was seen that the poor boy had fainted, and they had to sprinkle cold water upon him before he regained consciousness.

"Surely," remarked the doctor, "it is not the idea of a trifling operation that you will not feel which has so frightened you?"

Paul shook his head. "It is not that," said he.

"What, then, is it?"

"Simply that the real man exists; I know him, and know where he lives."

"What do you mean?" they cried.

"I know him, I tell you—the son of the Duke de Champdoce."

"Let us hear all!" cried Mascarin, who was the first to come to his senses. "Explain yourself."

"Simply this. I know such a young man, and it was the thought of this that made me feel so ill. He is thirty-three. He was at the Foundling Hospital; he left it at the age of twelve and a half years; and he has just such a scald on his shoulder, which he got when he was apprenticed to a tanner."

"And where," asked Mascarin quickly, "is this same young man? What is his name, and what does he do for a living?"

"He is a painter; his name is Andre, and he lives—"

A blasphemous oath from Mascarin interrupted him. "This is the third time," said he fiercely, "that this cursed fellow has crossed our path; but I swear that it shall be the last."

Hortebise and Catenac were livid with alarm.

"What do you intend to do?" asked they.

"I shall do nothing," answered he; "but you know that this Andre, in addition to being a painter, is an ornamental sculptor and house decorator, and so is often on lofty scaffolds. Have you never heard that accidents frequently happen to that class of people?"

Chapter 48: A Melancholy Masher

When Mascarin spoke of suppressing the man who stood in his way as easily as if he was alluding to extinguishing a candle, he was not aware that there was one circumstance which considerably enhanced the difficulty of his task, for Andre had been forewarned, and this note of warning had been sounded on the day on which he had received that letter from Sabine, in which she spoke in such despairing terms of her approaching marriage, which she had been compelled to agree to to save the honour of her family. This feeling was strengthened by a long conversation he had had with M. de Breulh-Faverlay and the Viscountess de Bois Arden, in which it was unanimously decided that the Count and Countess de Mussidan were victims of some plot of which Henri de Croisenois was certainly one of the promoters. He had no conception on what side to look for the danger, but he had an instinctive feeling that it was impending. He prepared, therefore, to act on the defensive. It was not only his life that was in danger, but his love and his future happiness. M. de Breulh-Faverlay had also serious apprehensions for the safety of a man for whom he entertained so great a respect and regard.

"I would lay a heavy wager," said he, "that we have to do with some villainous blackmailers, and the difficulty of the business is, that we must do the work ourselves, for we dare not invite the aid of the police. We have no proof to offer, and the police will not stir a foot on mere suppositions, and we should not earn the thanks of those we are desirous of assisting if we called the attention of the law to certain acts in their past lives; for who can say what the terrible secret is, that some vile wretch holds over the heads of M. and Madame de Mussidan? And it is quite on the cards that the count and the countess might be compelled to join the blackmailers and oppose us. We must act with the greatest prudence and caution. Remember, that if you are out at night, you must avoid dark corners, for it would be the easiest thing in the world to put a knife into your back."

The conclusion that was arrived at, at this interview, was that for the present Andre and De Breulh should cease to see each other so frequently. They felt convinced that a watch had been set on them, and that their intimacy would certainly be notified to De Croisenois; and of course they had every desire to cause him to imagine that they were not acting in any way together. The arrangement, therefore, that they entered into was that each should act from his own point of vantage against Henri de Croisenois, and that when necessary they should meet in the evening to compare notes in a small *café* in the Champs Elysees, not far from the house in which Andre was at work.

His courage was still as high as ever, but the first symptoms of rashness had vanished. He was a born diplomatist, and fully realized that cunning and treachery must be met by similar weapons. He must not break his engagement to M. Gandelu; but how could he superintend the workmen and keep an eye on Croisenois at the same time? Money was absolutely necessary, and yet he felt a strange disinclination to accept a loan from M. de Breulh. If he were to throw up his work, it would naturally create suspicion.

M. Gandelu had a shrewd head, and Andre, remembering the old man's kindness to him on all occasions, determined to confide the matter to him, and with this object he called on him the next morning as the clock was striking nine. His surprise was extreme when he saw Gaston de Gandelu in the courtyard. He was just the same looking Gaston, the lover of Madame de Chantemille, to the outward eye, but some grave calamity had evidently entirely changed the inner man. He was smoking his cigar with an air of desperation, and seemed to be utterly weary of the world and its belongings.

At the moment Andre entered the young man caught sight of him.

"Halloo!" said he; "here is my artistic friend. I lay ten to one that you have come to ask my father to do you a favour."

"You are quite right; is he at home?"

"The governor is in the sulks; he has shut himself up, and will not see me."

"You are joking."

"Not I; the old man is a regular despot, and I am sick of everything."

Noticing that one of the grooms was listening, Gaston had sufficient sense to draw Andre a little on one side.

"Do you know," asked he, "that the governor has docked my screw and vows that he will advertise himself as not responsible for the debts of yours truly; but I cannot think he will do so, for that would be a regular smash-up for me. You haven't such a trifle as ten thousand *francs* about you that you could lend me, have you? I'd give twenty thousand for the accommodation when I came of age."

"I must say——," began Andre.

"All right; never mind; I understand. If you had the ready, you wouldn't be hanging about here; but for all that, I must have the cash. Hang it all, I signed bills to that amount payable to Verminet. Do you know the fellow?"

"Not at all."

"Where were you dragged up? Why, he is the head of the Mutual Loan Society. The only nuisance is, that to make matters run a bit smooth, I wrote down the wrong name. Do you tumble, eh?"

"But, great heavens! that is forgery," said Andre, aghast.

"Not a bit, for I always intended to pay; besides, I wanted the money to square Van Klopen. You know *him*, I suppose?"

"No."

"Well, he is the chap to dress a girl. I had those costumes for Zora from him; but it is out and out the governor's fault. Why did he drive me to desperation? Yes, it is all the old man's doing. He wasn't satisfied with pitching into me, but he collared that poor, helpless lamb and shut her up. She never did him any harm, and I call it a right down cowardly and despicable act to hurt Zora."

"Zora," repeated Andre, who did not recognise the name.

"Yes, Zora; you know; you had a feed with us one day."

"Yes, yes; you mean Rose."

"That's it; but I don't like anyone to call her by that ugly, common name. Well, the governor has gone mad about her, and filed a complaint against her of decoying a minor, as if I was a fellow anyone could decoy. Well, the end of it was, that she is now in the prison of St. Lazare."

The tears started to the young man's eyes as he related this grievance.

"Poor Zora," he added; "I was never mashed on a woman like I was on her. And then what a splendid form she has! Why, the hairdresser said he had never seen such hair in his life; and she is at St. Lazare. As soon as the police came for her, her first thoughts were of me, and she shrieked out, 'Poor Gaston will kill himself when he hears of this.' The cook told me this, and added that her mistress's sufferings were terrible. And she is at St. Lazare. I tried to see her, but it was no go;" and here the boy's voice broke into a sob.

"Come," said Andre, "keep up your spirits."

"Ah! you shall see if, as soon as I am twenty-one, I don't marry her. I don't put all the blame on the old man. He has been advised by his lawyer, a beast by the name of Catenac. Do you know *him*?"

"No."

"You don't seem to know anyone. Well, I shall send him a challenge tomorrow. I have got my seconds all ready. By the way, would you like to act for me? I can easily get rid of one of the others."

"I have had no experience in such matters."

"Ah, then you would be of no use. My seconds must put him into a regular blue funk."

"In that case—"

"No; I know what you are going to say: you mean that I had best look out for a military swell; but, after all, the matter lies in a nutshell. I am the insulted party, and draw pistols at ten paces. If that frightens him, he will make the governor drop all this rubbish."

Had his mind not been so much occupied, this *rhodomontade* on Gaston's part would have amused Andre very much, but now he asked himself what would be the quickest way to escape from him.

Just at this moment a servant emerged from the house.

"Sir," said he, addressing Andre, "my master has seen you from his window, and begs that you will go up to him at once."

"I will be with him immediately," answered Andre; and, holding out his hand to Gaston, he took leave of him with a few words of encouragement.

Chapter 49: A Gentleman in Difficulties

When Andre had got rid of the young man, and had been ushered into M. Gandelu's presence, the change in the gentleman's appearance struck him with horror. His eyes were red and swollen as if he had been weeping, but as soon as he caught sight of Andre his face brightened, and he welcomed him warmly.

"Oh, it does me good to see you, and I bless the fortunate chance that has brought you here today."

"It is not a very fortunate chance," answered Andre, as he shook his head sadly.

For the first time Gandelu noticed the air of gravity which marked the young man, and the shade of sorrow upon his brow.

"What ails you, Andre?" asked he.

"A great misfortune is hanging over me."

"What do you mean?"

"The naked truth and this misfortune may bring death and despair to me."

"I am your friend, my dear boy," said the old man, "and would gladly be of service to you. Tell me if I can be of any use?"

"I come to you today to ask a favour at your hands."

"And you thought of the old man, then? I thank you for doing so. Give me your hand; I like to feel the grasp of an honest man's hand; it warms my heart."

"It is the secret of my life that I am going to confide to you," said he, with some solemnity.

M. Gandelu made no reply, but struck his clenched fist upon his breast, as though to show that any secret confided to him would be locked up in the safe security of his heart.

Then Andre hesitated no longer, and, with the exception of giving names, told the whole story of his love, his ambitions, and his hopes, and gave a clear account of how matters stood.

"How can I help you?" asked M. Gandelu.

"Allow me," said Andre, "to hand over the work with which you have entrusted me to one of my friends. I will retain the responsibility, but will merely act as one of the workmen. This, to a certain extent, will give me my liberty, while at the same time I shall be earning a little money, which is just now of vast importance to me."

"Is that what you call a favour?"

"Certainly, and a very great one, too."

Gandelu rose hastily, and, opening an iron safe which stood in one corner of the room, and taking from it a bundle of banknotes, he placed them on the table before Andre with an expressive look, which meant, "Take what you desire."

The unlooked-for kindness of this man, who forgot all his own sorrows in his anxiety to relieve the necessities of another, affected Andre deeply.

"I do not need money," began he.

With a wave of his hand Gandelu inspired silence. "Take these twenty thousand *francs*," said he, "and then I can tell you why I asked you to come upstairs."

A refusal would have wounded the old man deeply, and so Andre took the proffered loan.

Gandelu resumed his seat, and remained in gloomy silence for some time.

"My dear boy," said he, in a voice broken by emotion, "a day or two back you saw something of the trouble that I am labouring under. I have no longer any respect or esteem for that wretched fool, my son, Pierre."

Andre had already guessed that he had been incensed with reference to something connected with Gaston.

"You son has behaved very foolishly," said he; "but remember he is very young."

A sad smile passed over the old man's face.

"My son is old in vice," replied he. "I have thought the matter over only too plainly. Yesterday he declared that he would kill himself. An absurd threat. Up to this time I have been culpably weak, and it is no use now to act in an opposite direction. The unhappy boy is infatuated with a degraded woman named Rose, and I have had her locked up; but I have made up my mind to let her out again, and also to pay his debts. It is weak folly, I allow; but what am I to do? I am his father after all; and while I cannot respect her, I must love him. He has almost broken my heart, but it was his to do as he liked with."

Andre made no reply, and Gandelu went on.

"I have not deceived myself; my son is ruined. I can but stand by and wait for the end. If this Rose is not everything that is bad, her influence may be of some use to him. But I want someone to undertake these negotiations, and I had hopes, Andre, that you would have been able to do so."

Andre felt that all his efforts ought to be devoted to the interests of Sabine, but at the same time he could not leave the kind old man to the mercy of others, and by a display of absolute heroism he determined to accede to the broken-hearted father's desires and briefly told him that he was at his service. Gandelu thanked him warmly, and Andre seating himself at the table, the two men entered into a long discussion as to the best means to be adopted. It was finally decided that Andre should act with freedom and according to his own instincts, and that M. Gandelu should, to actual appearance, remain firm in the course he had entered upon, and should only be induced, by Andre's intercession, to adopt milder measures. The result justified their anticipations, for Gaston was even more crushed and downcast than Andre had imagined, and it was in an agony of suspense that he awaited the return of the young painter. As soon as he saw him descending the steps he sprang forward to greet him.

"Well," said he, in a tone of eager inquiry.

"Your father," returned Andre, "is terribly angry with you, but I hope to be able to induce him to do something for you."

"Will he set Zora at liberty?"

"Perhaps he will; but first he must have something more from you than promises—he must have stable guarantees."

At these words Gaston's face fell. "Guarantees," answered he sulkily. "Is not my word of honour enough? What sort of guarantees does he require?"

"That I cannot tell you, and you must find out for yourself; but I will do all I can for you."

Gaston gazed upon Andre in surprise.

"Do you mean to tell me," asked he, "that you can do pretty well what you like with the governor?"

"Not exactly; but surely you can see that I have a good deal of influence over him. If you want a proof of this, see, here is the money to take up these bills you told me of."

"What, Verminet's?"

"I suppose so. I am speaking of those to which you were mad enough to forge another man's name."

Foolish as the boy was, this act of his had caused him many a sleepless night, and he had reflected very often how he could possibly escape from the consequence of his act of rashness.

"Give me the money," cried he.

Andre shook his head, however. "Forgive me," said he, "but this money does not quit my hand until the bills are handed over to me. Your father's orders on this point are decided; but the sooner we settle the affair the better."

"That is too bad; the governor is as sly as a fox; but he must have his own way, I suppose, so come on. Only just wait till I slip on a coat more suitable to my position than this lounging suit."

He rushed away, and was back again in ten minutes as neat as a new pin, and full of gayety and good spirits.

"We can walk," said he, putting his arm through Andre's. "We have to go to the Rue St. Anne."

Verminet had his office in this street—the office of the Mutual Loan Society, of which he was the managing director. The house, in spite of its grandiloquent title, was of excessively shabby exterior. The Mutual Loan Society was frequented by those who, having lost their credit, wished to obtain a fresh amount, and who, having no money, wanted to borrow some.

Verminet's plan of financial operations was perfectly simple. A tradesman on the verge of bankruptcy would come to him, Verminet would look into his case and make him sign bills for the sum he required, handing him in exchange bills drawn by other tradesman in quite as serious a predicament as himself, and pocketed a commission of two *per cent.* upon both the transactions. Verminet obtained clients from the simple fact that an embarrassed tradesman is utterly reckless, cares not what he signs, and will clutch at a straw to keep his head above water. But there were many other transactions carried on at the office of the Mutual Loan Society, for its largest means of income was drawn from even less respectable sources, and it was alleged that many of these bogus bills which are occasionally cashed by some respectable bankers were manufactured there. At any rate, Verminet managed to make money somehow.

Chapter 50: Ringing the Changes

Andre, who was gifted with plenty of intelligence, at once judged of the kind of business done by the Mutual Loan Society by the dinginess of the brass plate on the door and the generally dilapidated aspect of the house.

"I don't like the look of it at all," said he.

"It does not go in for show," answered Gaston, affecting an air of wisdom, "but it is deemed handy sometimes. It does all sorts of business that you would never think of. A real downy card is Verminet."

Andre could easily believe this, for, of course, there could be but one opinion concerning the character of a man who could have induced a mere simpleton like Gaston to affix a forged signature to the bills which he had discounted. He made no remark, however, but entered the house, with the interior arrangements of which Gaston appeared to be perfectly familiar. They passed through a dirty, ill-smelling passage, went across a courtyard, cold and damp as a cell, and ascended a flight of stairs with a grimy balustrade. On the second floor Gaston made a halt before a door upon which several names were painted. They passed through into a large and lofty room. The paper on the walls of this delectable chamber was torn and spotted, and a light railing ran along it, behind which sat two or three clerks, whose chief occupation appeared to be consuming the breakfast which they had brought with them to the office. The heat of the stove, which was burning in one corner of the room, the general mouldiness of the atmosphere, and the smell of the coarse food, were sufficient to turn the stomach of anyone coming in from the fresh air.

"Where is M. Verminet?" asked Gaston authoritatively.

"Engaged," replied one of the clerks, without pausing to empty his mouth before he replied.

"Don't you talk to me like that. What do I care whether he is engaged or not? Tell him that Gaston de Gandelu desires to see him at once."

The clerk was evidently impressed by his visitor's manner, and, taking the card which was handed to him, made his exit through a door at the other end of the room.

Gaston was delighted at this first victory, and glanced at Andre with a triumphant smile.

The clerk came back almost at once. "M. Verminet," cried he, "has a client with him just now. He begs that you will excuse him for a few minutes, when he will see you;" and evidently anxious to be civil to the gorgeously attired youths before him, he added, "My master is just now engaged with M. de Croisenois."

"Aha," cried Gaston; "I will lay you ten to one that the dear *marquis* will be delighted to see me."

Andre started on hearing this name, and his cheek crimsoned. The man whom he most hated in this world; the wretch who, by his possession of some compromising secret, was forcing Sabine into a detested marriage; the villain whom he, M. de Breulh, and Madame de Bois Arden had sworn to overreach, was within a few paces of him, and that now he should see him face to face. Their eyes would meet, and he would hear the tones of the scoundrel's voice. His rage and agitation were so intense that it was with the utmost difficulty that he concealed it. Luckily for him, Gaston was not paying the slightest attention to his companion; for having, at the clerk's invitation, taken a chair, he assumed an imposing attitude, which struck the shabby young man behind the railing with the deepest admiration.

"I suppose," said he, in a loud voice, "that you know my dear friend, the *marquis*?"

Andre made some reply, which Gaston interpreted as a negative.

"Really," said he, "you know *no* one, as I told you before. Where have you lived? But you must have heard of him? Henri de Croisenois is one of my most intimate friends. He owes me over fifty *louis* that I won of him one night at baccarat."

Andre was now certain that he had estimated Verminet's character correctly, and the relations of the Marquis de Croisenois with this very equivocal personage assumed a meaning of great significance to him. He felt now that he had gained a clue, a beacon blazed out before him, and he saw his way more clearly into the difficult windings of this labyrinth of iniquity which he knew that he must penetrate before he gained the secret he longed for.

He felt like a child playing the game called "Magic Music," when, as the seeker nears the hiding place of the article of which he is in search, the strains of the piano swell higher and higher. He now found that the boy whose master he had become, knew, or said he knew, a good deal of this *marquis*. Why should he not gain some information from him?

"Are you really intimate with the Marquis de Croisenois?" asked he.

"I should rather think I was," returned Gandelu the younger. "You will see that precious sharp. I know all about him, and who the girl is that he is ruining himself for, but I mustn't talk about that; mum's the word, you know."

At that moment the door opened, and the *marquis* appeared, followed by Verminet.

Henri de Croisenois was attired in the most fashionable manner, and formed an utter contrast to the flashy dress of Gaston. He was smoking a cigar, and mechanically tapping his boots with an elegant walking cane. In a moment the features and figure of the viscount were indelibly photographed upon Andre's brain. He particularly noticed his eyes, which had in them a half-concealed look of terror, and his face bore the haunted expression of a person who expects some terrible blow to fall upon him at any moment.

At a little distance the *marquis* still seemed young, but a closer inspection showed that the man looked even older than he really was, so worn and haggard were his mouth and eyes. Nights at the gaming-table and the anxiety as to where the fresh supplies should come from to furnish the means to prolong his life of debauchery had told heavily upon him. Today, however, he seemed to be in the best temper imaginable, and in the most cheerful manner he addressed a few words to Verminet, in conclusion of the conversation that had been going on in the inner office.

"It is settled then," remarked he, "that I am to have nothing more to do with a business with which neither of us has any real concern?"

"Just so," answered Verminet.

"Very well, then; but remember that any mistake you may make in the other affair will be attended with the most serious results."

This caution seemed to suggest some new idea to Verminet, for he said something in a low voice to his client at which they both laughed.

Gaston was fidgeting about, very uneasy at the *marquis* having paid no attention to him, and he now advanced with a magnificent salutation and a friendly wave of the hand. If the *marquis* was charmed at meeting Gandelu, he concealed his delight in a most wonderful manner. He seemed surprised, but not agreeably so; he bent his head, and he extended his gloved hand with a negligent, "Ah, pleased to see you." Then without taking any more notice of Gaston, he turned on his heel and continued his conversation with Verminet.

"The worst part is over," said he, "and therefore no time is to be lost. You must see Mascarin and Martin Rigal, the banker, today."

At these words Andre started. Were these people Croisenois' accomplices? Certainly he had accomplices on the brain just now, and their names remained deeply engraved on the tablets of his memory.

"Tantaine was here this morning," observed Verminet, "and told me that his master wanted to see me at four this afternoon. Van Klopen will be there also. Shall I say a word to him about your fine friend?"

"'Pon my soul," remarked the *marquis*, shrugging his shoulders, "I had nearly forgotten her. There will be a tremendous fuss made, for she will be wanting all sorts of things. Speak to Van Klopen certainly, but do not bind yourself. Remember that I do not care a bit for the fair Sara."

"Quite so; I understand," answered Verminet; "but keep things quiet, and do not have any open disturbances."

"Of course not. Good morning," and with a bow to the managing director and a nod to Gaston, he lunged out of the office, not condescending to take the slightest notice of Andre. Verminet invited Andre and Gaston into his sanctum, and, taking a seat, motioned to them to do the same. Verminet was a decided contrast to his office, which was shabby and dirty, for his dress did his tailor credit, and he appeared to be clean. He was neither old nor young, and carried his years well. He was fresh and plump, wore his whiskers and hair cut in the English fashion, while his sunken eyes had no more expression in them than those of a fish.

Gandelu was in a hurry to begin.

"Let us get to business," said he. "Last week you lent me some money."

"Just so. Do you want any more?"

"No; I want to return my bills."

A cloud passed over Verminet's face.

"The first does not fall due until the 15th," remarked he.

"No matter; I have the money with me, and I will pay it on you handing over the bills to me."

"I can't do it."

"And why so, pray?"

"The bills have passed out of my hands."

Gaston could scarcely credit his ears, nor believe in the truth of this last statement, and was certainly upset, now knowing what to do.

"But," stammered he, "you promised, when I signed those bills, that they should never go out of your hands."

"I don't say I did not; but one can't always keep to one's promise. I was forced to part with them. I wanted money, and so had to discount them."

Andre was not at all surprised, for he had anticipated some such difficulty; and seeing that Gaston had entirely lost his head, he broke in on the conversation.

"Excuse me, sir," remarked he; "but it seems to me that there are certain circumstances in this case which should have made you keep your promise."

Verminet stared at him.

"Who have I the honour of speaking to?" asked he, instead of making a direct reply.

"I am a friend of M. de Gandelu's," returned Andre, thinking it best not to give any name.

"A confidential friend?"

"Entirely so. He had, I think, ten thousand *francs* from you."

"Pardon me, five thousand."

Andre turned toward his companion in some surprise.

Gaston grew crimson.

"What is the meaning of this?" asked the artist.

"Can't you see?" whispered Gaston. "I had ten because I wanted the other five for Zora."

"Oh, indeed," returned Andre, with a slight uplifting of his eyebrows. "Well, then, M. Verminet, it was five thousand *francs* that you lent to my young friend here. That was right enough; but what do you say to inducing him to forge a signature?"

"I! I do such a thing?" answered Verminet. "Why, I did not know that the signature was not genuine."

This insolent denial aroused the unhappy Gaston from his state of stupor.

"This is too much, a deuced deal too much," cried he. "Did you not yourself tell me that, for your own security, you must insist upon another name in addition to mine? Did you not give me a letter, and say, 'Write a signature like the one at the bottom of this, it is that of Martin Rigal, the banker in the Rue Montmartre'?"

"An utterly false accusation, without a shadow of proof; and remember that a libel uttered in the presence of a third party is punishable by law."

"And yet, sir," continued Andre, "you did not hesitate for a moment in discounting these bills. Have you calculated what terrible results may come of this breach of faith on your part?—what will happen if this forged signature is presented to M. Martin Rigal?"

"Very unlikely. Gandelu is the drawer, Rigal merely the endorser. Bills, when due, are always presented to the drawer," returned Verminet laconically.

Evidently a trap had been laid for Gaston, but the reason was still buried in obscurity.

"Then," remarked Andre, "we have but one course to pursue: we must trace those notes to the hands in which they now are, and take them up."

"Quite right."

"But to enable us to do so, you must first let us know the name of the party who discounted them."

"I don't know; I have forgotten," answered Verminet, with a careless wave of his hand.

"Then," returned Andre, in a low, deep voice of concentrated fury, "let me advise you, for your own sake, to make an immediate call upon your powers of memory."

"Do you threaten me?"

"And if you do not succeed in remembering the name or names, the consequences may be more serious than you seem to anticipate."

Verminet saw that the young painter was in dangerous earnest, and rose from his chair, but Andre was too quick for him.

"No," said he, placing his back against the door; "you will not leave this room until you have done what I require."

For fully ten minutes the men stood gazing at each other. Verminet was green with terror, while Andre's face, though pale, was firm and determined.

"If the scoundrel makes any resistance," said he to himself, "I will fling him out of the window."

"The man is a perfect athlete," thought Verminet, "and looks as if he would stick at nothing."

Seeing that he had better give in, the managing director took up a bulky ledger, and began to turn over the leaves with trembling fingers.

Andre saw that he was holding it upside-down.

"There it is," cried Verminet at last.

"Bills for five thousand *francs*. Gandelu and Rigal, booked for discount to Van Klopen, ladies' tailor."

Andre was silent.

Why was it that Verminet had suggested Rigal's signature as the one he ought to imitate? And why had he handed the bills over to Van Klopen? Was it mere chance that had arranged it all? He did not believe it, but felt sure that some secret tie united them all together, Verminet, Van Klopen, Rigal, and the Marquis de Croisenois.

"Do you want anything more?" asked the manager of the Mutual Loan Society.

"Are the bills in Van Klopen's hands?"

"I can't say."

"Never mind, he will have to tell me where they are, if he has not got them," returned Andre.

They left the house, and as soon as they were again in the street Andre took his companion's arm, and hurried him off in the direction of the Rue de Grammont.

"I don't want to give this thief, Verminet, time to warn Van Klopen of what has taken place; I had rather fall upon him with the suddenness of an earthquake. Come, let us go to his establishment at once."

Chapter 51: The Vanishing Bills

Had Andre known a little more of the man he had to deal with, he would have learned that no one could fall like an earthquake upon Van Klopen. Shut up in the sanctum where he composed the numberless costumes that were the wonder and delight of Paris, Van Klopen made as careful arrangements to secure himself from the interview as the Turk does to guard the approaches to his *seraglio*; and so Andre and Gandelu were accosted in the entrance hall by his stately footmen, clad in gorgeous liveries, glittering with gold.

"M. van Klopen is of the utmost importance," asserted Andre.

"Our master is composing."

Entreaties, threats, and even a bribe of one hundred *francs* were alike useless; and Andre, seeing that he was about to be checkmated, was half tempted to take the men by the collar and hurl them on one side, but he calmed himself, and, already repenting of his violence at Verminet's, he determined on a course of submission, and so meekly followed the footmen into the famous waiting-room, styled by Van Klopen his purgatory. The footmen, however, had spoken the truth, for several ladies of the highest rank and standing were awaiting the return of this *arbiter elegantiarum*. All of them turned as the young men entered—all save one, who was gazing out of the window, drawing with her pretty fingers on the window panes. Andre recognised her in an instant as Madame de Bois Arden.

"Is it possible?" thought he. "Can the countess have returned here after what has occurred?"

Gaston felt that five charming pairs of eyes were fixed upon him, and studied to assume his most graceful posture.

After a brief time given to arrangement, Andre grew disgusted.

"I wish that she would look round," said he to himself. "I think she would feel rather ashamed. I will say a word to her."

He rose from his chair, and, without thinking how terribly he might compromise the lady, he took up a position at her side. She was, however, intently watching something that was going on in the street, and did not turn her head.

"*Madame,*" said he.

She started, and, as she turned and recognised Andre, she uttered a little cry of surprise.

"Great heavens! is that you?"

"Yes, it is I."

"And here? I dare say that my presence in this place surprises you," she went on, "and that I have a short memory, and no feelings of pride."

Andre made no reply, and his silence was a sufficient rejoinder to the question.

"You do me a great injustice," muttered the countess. "I am here because De Breulh told me that in your interests I ought to pardon Van Klopen, and go to him again as I used to do; so you see, M. Andre, that it is never safe to judge by appearance, and a woman more than anything else."

"Will you forgive me?" asked Andre earnestly.

The lady interrupted him by a little wave of her hand, invisible to all save to him, which clearly said,—

"Take care; we are not alone."

She once more turned her eyes towards the street, and he mechanically did the same. By this means their faces were hidden from observation.

"De Breulh," went on the lady, "has heard a good deal about De Croisenois, and, as no doubt you can guess, but very little to his credit, and quite enough to justify any father in refusing him his daughter's hand; but in this case it is evident to me that De Mussidan is yielding to a secret pressure. We must ferret out some hidden crime in De Croisenois' past which will force him to withdraw his proposal."

"I shall find one," muttered Andre.

"But remember there is no time to be lost. According to our agreement, I treat him in the most charming manner, and he thinks that I am entirely devoted to his interests, and tomorrow I have arranged to introduce him to the count and countess at the Hotel de Mussidan, where the count and countess have agreed to receive him."

Andre started at this news.

"I saw," continued the lady, "that you were quite right in the opinion you had formed, for in the first place the common danger has almost reconciled the count and countess affectionately to each other, though it is notorious that they have always lived in the most unhappy manner. Their faces are careworn and full of anxiety, and they watch every movement of Sabine with eager eyes. I think that they look upon her as a means of safety, but shudder at the sacrifice she is making on their account."

"And Sabine?"

"Her conduct is perfectly sublime, and she is ready to consummate the sacrifice without a murmur. Her self-sacrificing devotion is perfectly admirable; but what is more admirable still is the way in which she conceals the suffering that she endures from her parents. Noble-hearted girl! she is calm and silent, but she has always been so. She has grown thinner, and perhaps her cheek is a trifle paler, but her forehead was burning and seemed to scorch my lips as I kissed her. With this exception, however, there was nothing else about her that would betray her tortures. Modeste, her maid, told me, moreover, that when night came she seemed utterly worn out, and the poor girl, with tears in her eyes, declared 'that her dear mistress was killing herself.'"

Andre's eyes overflowed with tears.

"What have I done to deserve such love?" asked he.

A door suddenly opened, and Andre and the viscountess turned hastily at the sound. It was Van Klopen who came in, crying, according to his usual custom,—

"Well, and whose turn is it next?"

When, however, he saw Gaston, his face grew white, and it was with a smile that he stepped towards him, motioning back the lady whose turn it was, and who protested loudly against this injustice.

"Ah, M. de Gandelu," said he, "you have come, I suppose, to bespeak some fresh toilettes for that exquisite creature, Zora de Chantemille?"

"Not today," returned Gaston. "Zora is a little indisposed."

Andre, however, who had arranged the narrative that he was about to pour into the ears of the famous Van Klopen, was in too much haste to permit of any unnecessary delay.

"We have come here," said he hurriedly, "upon a matter of some moment. My friend, M. Gaston de Gandelu, is about to leave Paris for some months, and, before doing so, is anxious to settle all outstanding accounts, and retire all his bills, which may not yet have fallen due."

"Have I any bills of M. de Gandelu?" said Van Klopen slowly. "Ah, yes, I remember that I had some now. Yes, five bills of one thousand *francs* each, drawn by Gandelu, and accepted by Martin Rigal. I received them from the Mutual Loan Society, but they are no longer in my hands."

"Is that the case?" murmured Gaston, growing sick with apprehension.

"Yes, I sent them to my cloth merchants at St. Etienne, Rollon and Company."

Van Klopen was a clever scoundrel, but he sometimes lacked the necessary perception of when he had said enough; and this was proved today, for, agitated by the steady gaze that Andre kept upon him, he added,—

"If you do not believe my word, I can show you the acknowledgment that I received from that firm."

"It is unnecessary," replied Andre. "Your statement is quite sufficient."

"I should prefer to let you see the letter."

"No, thank you," replied Andre, not for a moment duped by the game that was being played. "Pray take no more trouble. We shall, I presume, find that the bills are at St. Etienne. There is no use in taking any more trouble about them, and we will wait until they arrive at maturity. I have the honour to wish you good morning."

And with these words he dragged away Gaston, who was actually about to consult Van Klopen as to the most becoming costume for Zora to appear in on leaving the prison of St. Lazare. When they were a few doors from the man-milliner's, Andre stopped and wrote down the names of Van Klopen's cloth merchants. Gaston was now quite at his ease.

"I think," remarked he, "that Van Klopen is a sharp fellow; he knows that I am to be relied on."

"Where do you think your bills are?"

"At St. Etienne's, of course."

The perfect innocence of the boy elicited from Andre a gesture of impatient commiseration.

"Listen to me," said he, "and see if you can comprehend the awful position in which you have placed yourself."

"I am listening, my dear fellow; pray go on."

"You drew these bills through Verminet because Van Klopen would not give you credit."

"Exactly so."

"How, then, do you account for the fact that this man, who was at first disinclined to trust you, should without rhyme or reason, offer to supply you now as he did today?"

"The deuce! That never struck me. It does seem queer. Does he want to play me a nasty trick? But which of them is it—Verminet or Van Klopen?"

"It is plain to me that the pair of them have entered into a pleasant little plot to blackmail you."

Young Gandelu did not at all like this turn, and he exclaimed,—

"Blackmail me, indeed! why, I know my way about better than that. They won't get much out of me, I can tell you."

Andre shrugged his shoulders.

"Then," said he, "just tell me what you intend to say to Verminet when he comes to you upon the day your bills fall due, and says to you, 'Give me one hundred thousand *francs* for these five little bits of paper, or I go straight to your father with them'?"

"I should say, of course—ah, well, I really do not know what I should say."

"You could say nothing, except that you had been imposed on in the most infamous way. You would plead for time, and Verminet would give it to you if you would execute a deed insuring him one hundred thousand *francs* on the day you came of age."

"A hundred thousand devils are all the rogue would get from me. That's the way I do things, do you see? If people try and ride rough-shod over me, I merely hit out, and then just look out for broken bones. Pay this chap? Not I! I know the governor would make an almighty shine, but I'll choose that sooner than be had like that."

He was quite serious but could only put his feelings into the language he usually spoke.

"I think," answered Andre, "that your father would forgive this imprudence, but that it will be even harder for him to do so than it was to send a doctor to number the hours he had to live. He will forgive you because he is your father, and because he loves you; but Verminet, when he finds that the threat to go to your father does not appal you, will menace you with criminal proceedings."

"Hulloo!" said Gandelu, stopping short. "I say, that is very poor fun," gasped he.

"There is no fun in it, for such fun, when brought to the notice of a court of justice, goes by the ugly name of forgery, and forgery means a swinging heavy sentence."

Gaston turned pale, and trembled from head to foot.

"Tried and sentenced," faltered he. "No, I don't believe you, but I hold no honours and will turn up my cards." He quite forgot that he

420

was in the public street, and was talking at the top of his shrill falsetto voice, and gesticulating violently.

"The poor old governor, I might have made him so happy, and, after all, I have only been a torment to him. Ah, could I but begin once more; but then the cards are dealt, and I must go on with the game, and I have made a nice muddle of the whole thing before I am twenty years of age; but no criminal courts for me, no, the easiest way out of it is a pistol shot, for I am an honest man's son, and I will not bring more disgrace on him than I have already done."

"Do you really mean what you say?" asked Andre.

"Of course I do. I can be firm enough sometimes."

"Then we will not despair yet," answered the young painter. "I think that we shall be able to settle this ugly business, but you cannot be too cautious. Keep indoors, and remember that I may have urgent need of you at almost any time of day or night."

"I agree, but remember this, Zora is not to be forgotten."

"Don't fret over that; I will call and see her tomorrow. And now, farewell for today, as I have not an instant to lose," and with these words Andre hurried off.

Andre's reason for haste was that he had caught a few words addressed by Verminet to Croisenois—"I shall see Mascarin at four o'clock." And he determined to loiter about the Rue St. Anne, and watch the Managing Director when he came out, and so find out who this Mascarin was, who he was certain was mixed up in the plot. He darted down the Rue de Grammont like an arrow from a bow, and as the clock in a neighbouring belfry chimed half-past three, he was in the Rue St. Anne. There was a small wine-shop almost opposite to the office of the Mutual Loan Society, and there Andre ensconced himself and made a frugal meal, while he was waiting for Verminet's appearance, and just as he had finished his light refreshment he saw the man he wanted come out of the office, and crept cautiously after him like a Red Indian on the trail of his enemy.

Chapter 52: The Spy

As Verminet swaggered down the street he had the air of a successful man, of a capitalist, in short, and the Managing Director of a highly lucrative concern. Andre had no difficulty in following his man, though detective's business was quite new to him, which is no such easy matter, although everyone thinks that he can become one. Andre kept his man in sight, and was astonished at the numerous acquaintances that Verminet seemed to have. Occasionally he said to himself, "Perhaps I am mistaken after all, for fancy is a bad pair of spectacles to see through. This man may be honest, and I have let my imagination lead me astray."

Meanwhile, Verminet who had reached the Boulevard Poisonniere, assumed a totally different air, throwing off his old manner as he cast away his cigar. When he had reached the Rue Montorgueil he turned underneath a large archway. Verminet had gone into the office of M. B. Mascarin, and that person simply kept a Servants' Registry Office for domestics of both sexes. In spite of his surprise, however, he determined to wait for Verminet to come out; and, not to give himself the air of loitering about the place, he crossed the road and appeared to be interested in watching three workmen who were engaged in fixing the revolving shutters to a new shop window. Luckily for the young painter he had not to wait a very long while, for in less than a quarter of an hour Verminet came out, accompanied by two men. The one was tall and thin, and wore a pair of spectacles with coloured glasses, while the other was stout and ruddy, with the unmistakable air of a man of the world about him. Andre would have given the twenty thousand *francs* which he still had in his pocket if he could have heard a single word of their conversation. He was moving skilfully forward so as to place himself within earshot, when not two feet from him he heard a shrill whistle twice repeated. There was something so strange and curious in the sound of this whistle that Andre looked round and noticed that the three men whom he was watching had been also attracted by it.

The tall man with the coloured glasses glanced suspiciously around him, and then after a nod to his companions turned and re-entered the office, while Verminet and the other walked away arm in arm. Andre was undecided; should he try and discover who these two men were? Near the entrance he saw a lad selling hot chestnuts. "Ah!" said he, "the little chestnut seller will always be there; but I may lose the others if I stay here." He followed the two men as quickly as possible. They did not go very far, and speedily entered a fine house in the Rue Montmartre. Here Andre was for a moment puzzled, as he did not know to whom they were paying a visit, but noticing an inscription on the wall of "Cashier's Office on the first floor," he exclaimed,—

"Ah! it is to the banker's they have gone!"

He questioned a man coming downstairs and heard that M. Martin Rigal, the banker, had his offices and residence there.

"I have struck a vein of good luck today," thought he; "and now if my little friend the chestnut seller can only tell me the names of these men, I have done a good day's work. I *do* hope that he has not gone."

The boy was still there, and he had two customers standing by the chafing-dish which contained the glowing charcoal, and a working lad in cap and blouse was arguing so hotly with the lad that they did not notice Andre's appearance.

"You can stow that chat," said the boy; "I have told your father the price I would take. You want my station and stock-in-trade. Hand over two hundred and fifty *francs*, and they are yours."

"But my dad will only give two hundred," returned the other.

"Then he don't need give nothing, for he won't get 'em," answered the chestnut vender sharply. "Two hundred *francs* for a pitch like this! Why, I have sometimes taken ten *francs* and more, and that ain't a lie, on the word of Toto Chupin."

Andre was tickled with this strange designation, and addressed himself to the lad who bore it.

"My good boy," said he, "I think you were here an hour ago. Did you see anything of three gentlemen who came out of the house and stood talking together for a short time?"

The lad turned sharply round and examined his questioner from tip to toe with an air of the most supreme impertinence; and then, in a tone which matched his look, replied,—

"What does it signify to you who they are? Mind your own business, and be off!"

Andre had had some little experience of this delightful class of street Arab, of which Toto Chupin was so favourable a specimen, and knew their habits, customs, and language.

"Come, my chicken," said he, "spit it out, it won't blister your tongue, to answer a man who asks a civil question."

"Well, then, I saw 'em, sharp enough, and what then?"

"Why, that I should like to have their names if they have such an article belonging to 'em!"

Toto raised his cap and scratched his head, as if to stimulate his brains, and as he brushed up his thick head of dirty yellow hair, he eyed Andre cunningly.

"And suppose I know the blokes' names and tells 'em out to you, what will you stand?" asked he.

"Ten *sous*."

The delightful youth puffed out his cheeks, then expelled the

pent-up wind by a sudden slap, as a mark of his disgust at the meanness of the offer.

"Pull up your braces, my lord," said he sarcastically, "or you'll be
losing the contents of your breeches pockets. Ten *sous*, indeed! Perhaps
you'd like me to lend 'em to yer?"

Andre smiled pleasantly.

"Did you think, my little man, that I was going to offer you twenty
thousand shiners?" asked he.

"Won again!" cried Toto; "I laid myself a new hat that you weren't
a fool, and I have collared the stakes."

"Why do you think I am not a fool?"

"Because a fool would have begun by offering me five *francs* and
gone up slick to ten, while you began at a modest figure."

The painter smiled.

"But you were too old a bird to be caught like that," continued the
lad; and as he spoke, he stopped, and contracted his brow as if in deep
perplexity. Of course he was acquainted with the names, but ought
he to give them? Instantly he scented an enemy. Harmless people did
not usually ask questions of itinerant chestnut vendors, and to open
his mouth might be to injure Mascarin, Beaumarchef, or the guileless
Tantaine.

This last thought determined the lad.

"Keep your ten *sous*, my pippin," said the boy; "I'll tell you what
you want to know all *gratis* and for nothing, because I've taken a real
fancy to the cut of your mug. The tall chap was Mascarin, the fat un
Doctor Hortebise, and t'other—stop, let me think it out in my knowledge box; ah! I have it, he was Verminet."

Andre was so delighted that, drawing from his pocket a five-*franc*
piece, he tossed it to the boy.

"Thanks, my noble lord," said Chupin, and was about to add something more in a similar vein, when he glanced down the street. His
look changed in an instant, and he fixed his eyes upon the painter's
face with a very strange expression.

"What is the matter, my lad?" asked Andre, surprised at this sudden
change.

"Nothing," answered Chupin; "nothing at all; only as you seem a
decentish sort of chap, I should recommend you to keep your wits
about you, and to look out for squalls."

"Eh, what do you mean?"

"I mean—why—be careful, of course. Hang me if I exactly know what I do mean. It is just an idea that came to me all of a jump. But there, be off; I ain't going to say another word."

With much difficulty Andre repressed his astonishment. He saw that this young scamp was the possessor of many secrets which might be of inestimable value to him; but he also saw that he was determined to hold his tongue, and that it would at present be a waste of time to try and get anything out of him; and an empty cab passing at this moment, Andre hailed it, and told the coachman to drive fast to the Champs Elysees. In obedience to the warning that he had just received from Toto, he did not give the name of the *café* where he was to meet De Breulh, for he made up his mind to be careful, yes, extremely careful. He recollected the two odd whistles which had seemed to make Mascarin wince, and which certainly broke off the conference of the three men, and he remembered that it was after a glance down the street that Toto had become less communicative and had given him that curt warning. "By heaven," said he, as the recollection of a story he had read not long ago dawned on him, "I am being followed." He lowered the front glass of the cab, and attracted the coachman's attention by pulling him by the sleeve.

"Listen to me," said he, as the man turned, "and do not slacken your speed. Here, take your five *francs* in advance."

"But look here—"

"Listen to me. Go as sharp as you can to the Rue de Matignon; turn down it, and, as you do, go a bit slower; then drive on like lightning, and when you are in the Champs Elysees do what you like, for your cab will be empty."

The driver chuckled.

"Aha," said he; "I see you are being followed, and you want to give 'em leg bail."

"Yes, yes; you are right."

"Then listen to me. Take care when you jump, and don't do it on the pavement, for t'other is the safest."

Andre succeeded in alighting safely, and turned down a narrow court before his pursuer had entered the street; but it was vain for the young painter to lurk in a doorway, for after five minutes had elapsed there was nothing to be seen, and no spy had made his appearance.

"I have been over-cautious," muttered he.

More than a quarter of an hour had elapsed, and Andre felt that he might leave his hiding-place, and go in quest of De Breulh; and as he approached the spot chosen for their meeting-place, he saw his friend's carriage, and near it was the owner, smoking a cigar. The two men caught sight of each other almost at the same moment. De Breulh advanced to greet the young man with extended hand.

"I have been waiting for you for the last twenty minutes," said he.

Andre commenced to apologize, but his friend checked him.

"Never mind," returned he; "I know that you must have had some excellent reasons; but, to tell you the honest truth, I had become rather nervous about you."

"Nervous! and why, pray?"

"Do you not recollect what I said the other evening? De Croisenois is a double-dyed scoundrel."

Andre remained silent, and his friend, putting his arm affectionately through his, continued,—

"Let us walk," said he; "it is better than sitting down in the *café*. I believe De Croisenois capable of anything. He had the prospect before him of a large fortune,—that of his brother George; but this he has already anticipated. A man in a position like this is not to be trifled with."

"I do not fear him."

"But I do. I am, however, a little relieved by the fact that he has never seen you."

The painter shook his head.

"Not only has he seen me, but I half believe that he suspects my designs."

"Impossible!"

"But I am sure that I have been followed today. I have no actual proof, but still I am fully convinced that it was so."

And Andre recounted all that had occurred during the day.

"You are certainly being watched," answered De Breulh, "and every step that you take will be known to your enemies, and at this very moment perhaps eyes are upon us."

As he spoke he glanced uneasily around; but it was quite dark, and he could see no one.

"We will give the spies a little gentle exercise," said he, "and if we dine together they will find it hard to discover the place."

De Breulh's coachman was dozing on the driving-seat. His master aroused him, and whispered some order in his ear. The two young men then got in, and the carriage started at a quick pace.

"What do you think of this expedient?" asked De Breulh. "We shall go at this pace for the next hour. We will then alight at the corner of the Chaussee d'Autin, and be free for the rest of the night, and those who wish to follow us tonight must have good eyes and legs."

All came to pass as De Breulh had arranged; but as he jumped out he saw a dark form slip from behind the carriage and mingle with the crowd on the Boulevard.

"By heavens," said he; "that was a man. I thought that I was throwing a spy off the track, and I was in reality only treating him to a drive."

To make sure, he took off his glove and felt the springs of the carriage.

"See," said he, "they are still warm from the contact with a human body."

The young painter was silent, but all was now explained: while he jumped from the cab, his tracker had been carried away upon it. This discovery saddened the dinner, and a little after ten Andre left his friend and returned home.

Chapter 53: Mascarin Moves

The Viscountess de Bois Arden had not been wrong when she told Andre in Van Klopen's establishment that community of sorrow had brought the Count and Countess of Mussidan nearer together, and that Sabine had made up her mind to sacrifice herself for the honour of the family. Unfortunately, however, this change in the relations of husband and wife had not taken place immediately; for after her interview with Doctor Hortebise, Diana's first impulse had not been to go to her husband, but to write to Norbert, who was as much compromised by the correspondence as she herself. Her first letter did not elicit a reply. She wrote a second, and then a third, in which, though she did not go into details, she let the duke know that she was the victim of a dark intrigue, and that a deadly peril was hanging over her daughter's head. This last letter was brought back to her by the messenger, without any envelope, and across it Norbert had written,—

"The weapon which you have used against me has now been turned against yourself. Heaven is just."

These words started up in letters of fire before her eyes as the presage of coming misfortune, and telling her that the hour of retribution had now come, and that she must be prepared to suffer, as an atonement for her crimes. Then it was that she felt all was lost, and she must go to her husband for aid, unless she desired that copies of the stolen letters should be sent to him; and in a little *boudoir*, adjoining Sabine's own room, she opened her heart and told her husband all. She performed it with all the skill of a woman who, without descending to falsehood, contrives to conceal the truth. But she could not hide the share that she had taken, both in the death of the late Duke de Champdoce and the disappearance of George de Croisenois.

The count's brain reeled. He called up to his memory what Diana had been when he first saw and loved her at Laurebourg: how pure and modest she looked! what virginal candour sat upon her brow! and yet she was even then doing her best to urge on a son to murder his father.

De Mussidan had had hideous doubts concerning the relations of Norbert and Diana, both before and after marriage; but his wife firmly denied this at the moment when she was revealing the other guilty secrets of her past life. He had believed that Sabine was not his child, and now he had to reproach himself with the indifference he had displayed towards her.

He made no answer to the terrible revelation that was poured into his ears; but when the countess had concluded, he rose and left the room, stretching out his hands and grasping the walls for support, like a drunken man.

The count and countess believed that Sabine had slept through this interview, but they were mistaken, for Sabine had heard all those fatal words—"ruin, dishonour, and despair!" At first she scarcely understood. Were not these words merely the offspring of her delirium? She strove to shake it off, but too soon she knew that the whispered words were sad realities, and she lay on her bed quivering with terror. Much of the conversation escaped her, but she heard enough. Her mother's past sins were to be exposed if the daughter did not marry a man entirely unknown to her—the Marquis de Croisenois. She knew that her torments would not be of very long duration, for to part with her love for Andre would be to part with life itself. She made up her mind to live until she had saved her parents' honour by the sacrifice of herself, and then she would be free to accept the calm repose of the grave.

But the terrible revelation bore its fruits, for her fever came back, and a relapse was the result. But youth and a sound constitution gained the day, and when she was convalescent her will was as strong as ever.

Her first act was to write the letter to her lover which had driven him to the verge of distraction; and then, fearing lest her father might, in his agony and remorse, be driven to some rash act, she went to him and told him that she knew all.

"I never loved M. de Breulh," said she with a pitiful smile, "and therefore the sacrifice is not so great after all."

The count was not for a moment the dupe of the generous-souled girl, but he did not dare to brave the scandal of the death of Montlouis, and still less the exposure of his wife's conduct. Time was passing, however, and the miscreants in whose power they were made no signs of life. Hortebise did not appear any more, and there were moments when the miserable Diana actually ventured to hope. "Have they forgotten us?" thought she.

Alas! no; they were people who never forgot.

The Champdoce affair had been satisfactorily arranged, and every precaution had been taken to prevent the detection of Paul as an impostor, and engaged as he had been, Mascarin had no time to turn his attention to the marriage of Sabine and De Croisenois. The famous Limited Company, with the *marquis* as chairman, had, too, to be started, the shares of which were to be taken up by the unhappy victims of the blackmailers; but first some decided steps must be taken with the Mussidans, and Tantaine was dispatched on this errand.

This amiable individual, though he was going into such very excellent society, did not consider it necessary to make any improvement in his attire. This was the reason why the footman, upon seeing such a shabby visitor and hearing him ask for the count or countess, did not hesitate to reply, with a sneer, that his master and mistress had been out for some months, and were not likely to return for a week or two. This fact did not disconcert the wily man, for drawing one of Mascarin's cards from his pocket, he begged the kind gentleman to take it upstairs, when he was sure that he would at once be sent for.

De Mussidan, when he read the name on the card, turned ghastly pale.

"Show him into the library," said he curtly.

Florestan left the room, and the count mutely handed the card to his wife, but she had no need to read it.

"I can tell what it is," gasped she.

"The day for settling accounts has come," said the count, "and this name is the fatal sign."

The countess flung herself upon her knees, and taking the hand that hung placidly by his side, pressed her lips tenderly to it.

"Forgive me, Octave!" she muttered. "Will you not forgive me? I am a miserable wretch, and why did not Heaven punish me for the sins that I have committed, and not make others expiate my offences?"

The count put her gently aside. He suffered intensely, and yet no word of reproach escaped his lips against the woman who had ruined his whole life.

"And Sabine," she went on, "must she, a De Mussidan, marry one of these wretched scoundrels?"

Sabine was the only one in the room who preserved her calmness; she had so schooled herself that her distress of mind was not apparent to the outward eye.

"Do not make yourselves miserable," said she, with a faint smile; "how do we know that M. de Croisenois may not make me an excellent husband after all?"

The count gazed upon his daughter with a look of the fondest affection and gratitude.

"Dearest Sabine!" murmured he. Her fortitude had restored his self-command. "Let us be outwardly resigned," said he, "whatever our feelings may be. Time may do much for us, and at the very church door we may find means of escape."

Chapter 54: A Cruel Slur

Florestan had conducted Tantaine to the sumptuous library, in which the count had received Mascarin's visit; and, to pass away the time, the old man took a mental inventory of the contents of the room. He tried the texture of the curtains, looked at the handsome bindings of the books, and admired the magnificent bronzes on the mantelpiece.

"Aha," muttered he, as he tried the springs of a luxurious armchair, "everything is of the best, and when matters are settled, I half think that I should like a resting-place just like this—"

He checked himself, for the door opened, and the count made his appearance, calm and dignified, but very pale. Tantaine made a low bow, pressing his greasy hat against his breast.

"Your humble servant to command," said he.

The count had come to a sudden halt.

"Excuse me," said he, "but did you send up a card asking for an interview?"

"I am not Mascarin certainly, but I used that highly respectable gentleman's name, because I knew that my own was totally unknown to you. I am Tantaine, Adrien Tantaine."

M. de Mussidan gazed with extreme surprise upon the squalid individual before him. His mild and benevolent face inspired confidence, and yet he doubted him.

"I have come on the same business," pursued the old man. "I have been ordered to tell you that it must be hurried on."

The count hastily closed the door and locked it; the manner of this man made him feel even too plainly the ignominy of his position.

"I understand," answered he. "But how is it that you have come, and not the other one?"

"He intended to come; but at the last moment he drew back; Mascarin, you see, has a great deal to lose, while I—" He paused, and holding up the tattered tails of his coat, turned round, as though to exhibit his shabby attire. "All my property is on my back," continued he.

"Then I can treat with you?" asked the count.

Tantaine nodded his head. "Yes, count, I have the missing leaves from the Baron's journal, and also, well—I suppose you know everything, all of your wife's correspondence."

"Enough," answered the count, unable to hide his disgust. "Sit down."

"Now, count, I will go to the point—are you going to put the police on us?"

"I have said that I would do nothing of the kind."

"Then we can get to business."

"Yes, if—"

The old man shrugged his shoulders.

"There is no 'if' in the case," returned he. "We state our conditions, for acceptance or rejection."

These words were uttered in a tone of such extreme insolence that the count was strongly tempted to hurl the extortionate scoundrel from the window, but he contrived to restrain his passion.

"Let us hear the conditions then," said he impatiently.

Tantaine extracted from some hidden recess of his coat a much-worn pocketbook, and drew from it a paper.

"Here are our conditions," returned he slowly. "The Count de Mussidan promises to give the hand of his daughter to Henri Marquis de Croisenois. He will give his daughter a wedding portion of six hundred thousand *francs*, and promises that the marriage shall take place without delay. The Marquis de Croisenois will be formally introduced at your house, and he must be cordially received. Four days afterwards he must be asked to dinner. On the fifteenth day from that M. de Mussidan will give a grand ball in honour of the signing of the marriage contract. The leaves from the diary and the whole of the correspondence will be handed to M. de Mussidan as soon as the civil ceremony is completed."

With firmly compressed lips and clenched hands, the count sat listening to these conditions.

"And who can tell me," said he, "that you will keep your engagements, and that these papers will be restored to me at all?"

Tantaine looked at him with a air of pity.

"Your own good sense," answered he. "What more could we expect to get out of you than your daughter and your money?"

The count did not answer, but paced up and down the room, eyeing the ambassador keenly, and endeavouring to detect some weak point in his manner of cynicism and audacity. Then speaking in the calm tone of a man who had made up his mind, he said,—

"You hold me as in a vice, and I admit myself vanquished. Stringent as your conditions are, I accept them."

"That is the right style of way to talk in," remarked Tantaine cheerfully.

"Then," continued the count, with a ray of hope gleaming in his face, "why should I give my daughter to De Croisenois at all?—surely this is utterly unnecessary. What you want is simply six hundred thousand *francs*; well, you can have them, and leave me Sabine."

He paused and waited for the reply, believing that the day was his; but he was wrong.

"That would not be the same thing at all," answered Tantaine. "We should not gain our ends by such means."

"I can do more," said the count. "Give me six months, and I will add a million to the sum I have already offered."

Tantaine did not appear impressed by the magnitude of this offer. "I think," remarked he, "that it will be better to close this interview, which, I confess, is becoming a little annoying. You agreed to accept the conditions. Are you still in that mind?"

The count bowed. He could not trust himself to speak.

"Then," went on Tantaine, "I will take my leave. Remember, that as you fulfil your engagement, so we will keep to ours."

He had laid his hand on the handle of the door, when the count said,—

"Another word, if you please. I can answer for myself and Madame de Mussidan, but how about my daughter?"

Tantaine's face changed. "What do you mean?" asked he.

"My daughter may refuse to accept M. de Croisenois."

"Why should she? He is good-looking, pleasant, and agreeable."

"Still she may refuse him."

"If *mademoiselle* makes any objection," said the old man in peremptory accents, "you must let me see her for a few minutes, and after that you will have no further difficulty with her."

"Why, what could you have to say to my daughter?"

"I should say—"

"Well, what would you say?"

"I should say that if she loves anyone, it is not M. de Breulh." He endeavoured to pass through the half-opened door, but the count closed it violently.

"You shall not leave this room," cried he, "until you have explained this insulting remark."

"I had no intention of offending you," answered Tantaine humbly. "I only—" He paused, and then, with an air of sarcasm which sat strangely upon a person of his appearance, went on, "I am aware that the heiress of a noble family may do many things without having her reputation compromised, when girls in a lower social grade would be forever lost by the commission of anyone of them; and I am sure if the family of M. de Breulh knew that the young lady to whom he was engaged had been in the habit of passing her afternoons alone with a young man in his studio—"

He paused, and hastily drew a revolver, for it seemed to him as if the count were about to throw himself upon him. "Softly, softly, if you please," cried he. "Blows and insults are fatal mistakes. I have better information than yourself, that is all. I have more than ten times seen your daughter enter a house in the Rue Tour d'Auvergne, and asking for M. Andre, creep silently up the staircase."

The count felt that he was choking. He tore off his cravat, and cried wildly, "Proofs! Give me proofs!"

During the last five minutes Tantaine had shifted his ground so skilfully that the heavy library table now stood between himself and the count, and he was comparatively safe behind this extemporized defence.

"Proofs?" answered he. "Do you think that I carry them about with me? In a week I could give you the lovers' correspondence. That, you will say, is too long to wait; but you can set your doubts at rest at once. If you go to the address I will give you before eight tomorrow morning, and enter the rooms occupied by M. Andre, you will find the portrait of Mademoiselle Sabine carefully concealed from view behind a green curtain, and a very good portrait it is. I presume you will admit that it could not have been executed without a sitting."

"Leave this," cried the count, "without a moment's delay."

Tantaine did not wait for a repetition of these words. He passed through the doorway, and as soon as he was outside he called out in cheerful accents. "Do not forget the address, Number 45, Rue Tour d'Auvergne, name of Andre, and mind and be there before eight a.m."

The count made a rush at him on hearing this last insult, but he was too late, for Tantaine slammed the door, and was in the hall before the infuriated master of the house could open it. Tantaine had resumed all his airs of humility, and took off his hat to the footmen as he descended the steps. "Yes," muttered he, as he walked along, "the idea was a happy one. Andre knows that he is watched, and will be careful; and now that M. de Mussidan is aware that his sweet, pure daughter has had a lover, he will be only too happy to accept the Marquis de Croisenois as his son-in-law." Tantaine believed that Sabine was more culpable than she really had been, for the idea of pure and honourable love had never entered his brain.

Chapter 55: The Tempter

By this time Tantaine was in the Champs Elysees, and stared anxiously around. "If my Toto makes no mistake," muttered he, "surely my order was plain enough."

The old man got very cross as he at last perceived the missing lad conversing with the proprietor of a pie-stall, having evidently been doing a little jawing with him.

"Toto," he called, "Toto, come here."

Toto Chupin heard him, for he looked round, but he did not move, for he was certainly much interested in the conversation he was carrying on. Tantaine shouted again, and this time more angrily than before, and Toto, reluctantly leaving his companion, came slowly up to his patron.

"You have been a nice time getting here," said the lad sulkily. "I was just going to cut it. Ain't you well that you make such a row? If you ain't, I'd better go for a doctor."

"I am in a tremendous hurry, Toto."

"Yes, and so is the postman when he is behind time. I'm busy too."

"What, with the man you have just left?"

"Yes; he is a sharper chap than I am. How much do you earn every day, Daddy Tantaine? Well, that chap makes his thirty or forty *francs* every night, and does precious little for it. I should like a business like that, and I think that I shall secure one soon."

"Have patience. I thought that you were going into business with those two young men you were drinking beer with at the Grand Turk?"

Toto uttered a shrill cry of anger at these words. "Business with them?" shrieked he; "they are regular clever night thieves."

"Have they done you any harm, my poor lad?"

"Yes; they have utterly ruined me. Luckily, I saw Mascarin yesterday, and he set me up in the hot-chestnut line. He ain't a bad one, is Mascarin."

Tantaine curled his lip disdainfully. "Not a bad fellow, I dare say, as long as you don't ask him for anything."

Toto was so surprised at hearing Tantaine abuse Mascarin, that he was unable to utter a word.

"Ah, you may look surprised," continued the old man, "but when a man is rolling in riches, and leaves an old friend to starve, then he is not what I call a real good fellow. Now, Toto, you are a bright lad, and so I don't mind letting you know that I am only waiting for a good chance to drop Mascarin, and set up on my own account. Work for yourself, my boy."

"I know that; but it is a good deal easier to say than to do."

"You have tried then?"

"Yes, I have; but I came to grief over it. You know all about it as well as I do, for don't tell me you didn't hear every word I said that night you were hunting up Caroline Schimmel. However, I'll tell you. One day when I saw a lady who looked rather nervous get out of a cab, I followed her. I was decently togged out, so I rang at the door. I was so sure that I was going to make a haul that I would not have taken ninety-nine *francs* for the hundred that I expected to make. Well, I rang, a girl opened the door, and in I went. What an ass I made of myself! I found a great brute of a man there, who thrashed me within an inch of my life, and then kicked me downstairs. See, he made his mark rather more plainly than I liked." And removing his cap, the boy showed several bruises about his forehead.

During this conversation Tantaine and the lad had been walking slowly up the Champs Elysees, and had by this time arrived just opposite M. Gandelu's house, where Andre was at work. Tantaine sat down on a bench.

"Let us rest a bit," said he; "I am tired out; and now let me tell you, my lad, that your tale only shows me that it is experience you want.

Now, I have any amount of that, and I was really the prime mover in most of Mascarin's schemes. If I were to start on my own account, I should be driving in my carriage in twelve months. The only thing against my success is my age, for I am getting to be an old man. Why, even now I have a matter in my hands that is simply splendid. I have had half the money down, but I want a smart young fellow to pull it through."

"Why couldn't I be the smart young fellow?" asked Toto.

Tantaine shook his head. "You are as much too young as I am too old," answered he. "At your age you are too apt to be frightened, and would shrink back at the critical time. Besides, I have a conscience."

"And so have I," exclaimed Toto; "and it's grown like your own, old man; it can be stretched for miles and folded up into nothing."

"Well, we may be able to do something," returned Tantaine, as, drawing out a ragged check pocket-handkerchief, he wiped his glasses.

"Listen to me, my lad; I'll put what we call a supposititious case to you. You hate those two fellows who have robbed you, for I suppose that is what you meant; well, suppose you knew that they were at work all day on a high scaffold like that one opposite to us, what would you do?"

Toto scratched his head, and remarked after a pause,—

"If that crack-jawed idea you talk of was true," answered he, "those gay lads might as well make their wills, for I'd step up the scaffolding at night and just saw the planks that they are in the habit of clapping their toes on, half through, and when one of the mates stepped on it, why, there would be a bit of a smash, eh, Daddy Tantaine?"

"Not so bad, not so bad for a lad of your years," said the old man with an approving smile.

Toto's bosom swelled with pride.

"Besides," he continued, "I would arrange matters so well that not a soul would think that I had done the trick."

"The more I hear you speak, Chupin," answered Tantaine, "the more I believe you are the lad I want, and I am sure that we shall make heaps of money together."

"I am cock sure of that too."

"You can use carpenters' tools, I think you once told me?"

"Yes."

"Well," continued Tantaine, "let me tell you then that I know an old man with any amount of money, and there is a fellow whom he hates and detests, a young chap who ran off with the girl he loved."

"The old bloke must have been jolly wild."

"Well, to tell the truth, he wasn't a bit pleased. Now it so happens that this gay young dog spends ten hours a day at least on that very scaffolding opposite to us. The old fellow, who has his head screwed on the right way, had the very same idea as yours, but he is too old and too stout to do the trick for himself; and, to cut the matter short, he would give five thousand *francs* to the persons who would carry out his idea. Just think, two thousand *francs* for a few cuts of a saw!"

The boy was violently agitated, but Tantaine pretended not to notice it.

"First, my lad," said he, "I must explain to you in what measure the old gentleman's plans are different from yours. If we did not take care, some other poor devil might break his neck, but I have hit on a dodge to avoid all this."

"I ain't curious, but I should like to hear it."

Tantaine smiled blandly.

"Listen! Do you see high up; that little shed built of planks? That is used by the carvers and stone-cutters. Well, this little house, a couple of hundred feet above us, has a kind of a window; well, if this window and the planks below it were cut nearly through, anyone leaning against it would be very likely to fall into the street and perhaps to hurt himself."

Chupin nodded.

"Now, suppose," went on Tantaine, "that the enemy of our old gentleman was in that little shed, all at once he hears a woman shriek, 'Help! It is I you love; help me!' what would this young fellow do? Why, he would recognise the voice, rush to the window, lean out, and as the woodwork and supports had been cut away, he would—Well, do you see now?"

Chupin hesitated for a moment.

"I don't say I won't," muttered he; "but, look here, will the old chap pay down smart?"

"Yes, and besides, did I not tell you that he had given half down?"

The boy's eyes glistened as the old man unpinned the tattered lining of his pocket, and holding the pin between his teeth, pulled out the banknotes, each one for a thousand *francs*. Chupin's heart rose at the sight of this wealth.

"Is one of those for me?" asked he. Tantaine held the note towards the boy, who shuddered at the touch of the crisp paper and kissed the precious object in a paroxysm of pleasure. He then started from his seat, and regardless of the astonishment of the passers-by, executed a wild dance of triumph.

All was soon settled. Toto was to creep into the unfinished building by night, and not to leave it until he had completed his work. Tantaine, who had a thought for everything, told the boy what sort of a saw to employ, and gave him the address of a man who supplied the best class instruments.

"You must remember, my dear lad," said he, "not to leave behind you any traces of your work which may cause suspicion. One grain of sawdust on the floor might spoil the whole game. Take a dark lantern with you, grease your saw, and rasp out the tooth-nicks of the saw when you have finished your work."

Toto listened to the old man in surprise; he had never thought that he was of so practical a turn. He promised that he would be careful, and imagining that he had received all his directions, rose to leave; but the old man still detained him.

"Here," said he, "suppose you tell me a little about Caroline Schimmel. You told Beaumarchef that she said I had made her scream, and that when she caught me, I should have a bad time of it, eh?"

"You weren't my partner then," returned the lad with an impudent laugh; "and I wanted to give you a bit of a fright. The truth is, that you made the poor old girl so drunk that she has had to go to the hospital."

Tantaine was overjoyed at this news, and, rising from his seat, said, "Where are you living now?"

"Nowhere in particular. Yesterday I slept in a stable, but there isn't room for all my furniture there, so I must shift."

"Would you like to have my room for a day or two?" asked Tantaine, chuckling at the boy's jest. "I have moved from there, but the attic is mine for another fortnight yet."

"I'm gone; where is it?"

"You know well enough, in the Hotel de Perou, Rue de la Hachette. Then I will send a line to the landlady;" and tearing a leaf from his pocketbook, he scrawled on it a few words, saying that young relative of his, M. Chupin, was to have his room.

This letter, together with his banknote, Toto carefully tied up in the corner of his neckerchief, and as he crossed the street the old man watched him for a moment, and then stood gazing at the workmen on the scaffolding. Just then Gandelu and his son came out, and the contractor paused to give a few instructions. For a few seconds Gaston and Chupin stood side by side, and a strange smile flitted across

Tantaine's face as he noted this. "Both children of Paris," muttered he, "and both striking examples of the boasted civilization. The dandy struts along the pavement, while the street Arab plays in the gutter."

But he had no time to spend in philosophical speculations, as the omnibus that he required appeared, and entering it, in another half-hour he entered Paul Violaine's lodgings in the Rue Montmartre.

The portress, Mother Brigaut, was at her post as Tantaine entered the courtyard and asked,—

"And how is our young gentleman today?"

"Better, sir, ever so much better; I made him a lovely bowl of soup yesterday, and he drank up every drop of it. He looks like a real king this morning, and the doctor sent in a dozen of wine today, which will, I am sure, effect a perfect cure."

With a smile and a nod Tantaine was making his way to the stairs, when Mother Brigaut prevented his progress.

"Someone was here yesterday," remarked she, "asking about M. Paul."

"What sort of a looking person was it?"

"Oh, a man like any other, nothing in particular about him, but he wasn't a gentleman, for after keeping me for fully fifteen minutes talking and talking, he only gave me a five-*franc* piece."

The description was not one that would lead to a recognition of the person, and Tantaine asked in tones of extreme annoyance,—

"Did you not notice anything particular about the man?"

"Yes, he had on gold spectacles with the mountings as fine as a hair, and a watch chain as thick and heavy as I have ever seen."

"And is that all?"

"Yes," answered she. "Oh! there was one thing more—the person knows that you come here."

"Does he? Why do you think so?"

"Because all the time he was talking to me he was in a rare fidget, and always kept his eyes on the door."

"Thanks, Mother Brigaut; mind and keep a sharp lookout," returned Tantaine, as he slowly ascended the stairs.

Every now and then he paused to think. "Who upon earth can this fellow be?" asked he of himself. He reviewed the whole question— chances, probabilities, and risks, not one was neglected, but all in vain.

"A thousand devils!" growled he; "are the police at my heels?"

His nerves were terribly shaken, and he strove in vain to regain his customary audacity. By this time he had reached the door of Paul's room, and, on his ringing, the door was at once opened; but at the sight of this woman he started back, with a cry of angry surprise; for it was a female figure that stood before him, a young girl—Flavia, the daughter of Martin Rigal, the banker.

The keen eyes of Tantaine showed him that Flavia's visit had not been of long duration. She had removed her hat and jacket, and was holding in her hand a piece of fancy work.

"Whom do you wish to see, sir?" asked she.

The old man strove to speak, but his lips would not frame a single sentence. A band of steel seemed to be compressing his throat, and he appeared like a man about to be seized with an apoplectic fit.

Flavia gazed upon the shabby-looking visitor with an expression of intense disgust. It seemed to her that she had seen him somewhere; in fact, there was an inexplicable manner about him which entirely puzzled her.

"I want to speak to M. Paul," said the old man in a low, hoarse whisper; "he is expecting me."

"Then come in; but just now his doctor is with him."

She threw open the door more widely, and stepped back, so that the greasy garments of the visitor might not touch her dress. He passed her with an abject bow, and crossed the little sitting-room with the air of a man who perfectly understands his way. He did not knock at the door of the bedroom, but went straight in; there a singular spectacle at once arrested his attention. Paul, with a very pale face, was seated on the bed, while Hortebise was attentively examining his bare shoulder. The whole of Paul's right arm and shoulder was a large open wound, which seemed to have been caused by a burn or scald, and must have been extremely painful. The doctor was bending over him, applying a cooling lotion to the injured place with a small piece of sponge. He turned sharply round on Daddy Tantaine's entrance; and so accustomed were these men to read each other's faces at a glance that Hortebise saw at once what had happened; for Tantaine's expression plainly said, "Is Flavia mad to be here?" while the eyes of Hortebise answered, "She may be, but I could not help it."

Paul turned, too, and greeted the old man with an exclamation of delight.

"Come here," said he merrily, "and just see to what a wretched state I have been reduced between the doctor and M. Mascarin."

Tantaine examined the wound carefully. "Are you quite sure," asked he, "that not only will it deceive the duke, who will see but with our eyes, but also those of his wife, and perhaps of his medical man?"

"We will hoodwink the lot of them."

"And how long must we wait," asked the old man, "until the place skins over, and assumes the appearance of having been there from childhood?"

"In a month's time Paul can be introduced to the Duke de Champdoce."

"Are you speaking seriously?"

"Listen to me. The scar will not be quite natural then, but I intend to subject it to various other modes of treatment."

The dressing was now over, and Paul's shirt being readjusted, he was permitted to lie down again.

"I am quite willing to remain here forever," said he, "as long as I am allowed to retain the services of the nurse that I have in the next room, and who, I am sure, is waiting with the greatest eagerness for your departure."

Hortebise fumed, and cast a glance at Paul which seemed to say, "Be silent;" but the conceited young man paid no heed to it.

"How long has this charming nurse been with you?" asked Tantaine in an unnatural voice.

"Ever since I have been in bed," returned Paul with the air of a gay young fellow. "I wrote a note that I was unable to go over to her, so she came to me. I sent my letter at nine o'clock, and at ten minutes past she was with me."

The diplomatic doctor slipped behind Tantaine, and made violent gestures to endeavour to persuade Paul to keep silence, but all was in vain.

"M. Martin Rigal," continued the vain young fool, "passes the greater part of his life in his private office. As soon as he gets up he goes there, and is not seen for the rest of the day. Flavia can therefore do entirely as she likes. As soon as she knows that her worthy father is deep in his ledgers, she puts on her hat and runs round to me, and no one could have a kinder and a prettier visitor than she is."

The doctor was hard at work at his danger signals, but it was useless. Paul saw them, but did not comprehend their meaning; and Tantaine rubbed his glasses savagely.

"You are perhaps deceiving yourself a little," said he at last.

"And why? You know that Flavia loves me, poor girl. I ought to marry her, and of course I shall; but still, if I do not do so—well, you know, I need say no more."

"You wretched scoundrel!" exclaimed the usually placid Tantaine. His manner was so fierce and threatening that Paul shifted his position to one nearer the wall.

It was impossible for Tantaine to say another word, for Hortebise placed his hand upon his lips, and dragged him from the room.

Chapter 56: The Tafila Copper Mines, Limited

Paul could not for the life of him imagine why Tantaine had left the room in apparently so angry a mood. He had certainly spoken of Flavia in a most improper manner; for the very weakness of which she had been guilty should have caused him to treat her with tender deference and respect. He could understand the anger of Hortebise, who was Rigal's friend; but what on earth had Tantaine in common with the wealthy banker and his daughter? Forgetful of the pain which the smallest movement upon his part produced, Paul sat up in his bed, and listened with intense eagerness, hoping to catch what was going on in the next room; but he could hear nothing through the thick walls and the closed door.

"What can they be doing?" asked he. "What fresh plot are they contriving?"

Daddy Tantaine and Hortebise passed out of the room hastily, but when they reached the staircase they stood still. The doctor wore the same smiling expression of face, and he endeavoured to calm his companion, who appeared to be on the verge of desperation.

"Have courage," whispered he; "what is the use of giving way to passion? You cannot help this; it is too late now. Besides, even if you could, you would not, as you know very well, indeed!"

The old man was moving his spectacles, not to wipe his glasses, but his eyes.

"Ah!" moaned he, "now I can enter into the feelings of M. de Mussidan when I proved to him that his daughter had a lover. I have been hard and pitiless, and I am cruelly punished."

"My old friend, you must not attach too much importance to what you have heard. Paul is a mere boy, and, of course, a boaster."

"Paul is a miserably cowardly dog," answered the old man in a fierce undertone. "Paul does not love the girl as she loves him; but what he says is true, only too true, I can feel. Between her father and her lover she would not hesitate for a moment. Ah! unhappy girl, what a terrible future lies before her."

He stopped himself abruptly.

"I cannot speak to her myself," resumed he; "do you, doctor, strive and make her have reason."

Hortebise shrugged his shoulders. "I will see what my powers of oratory can do," answered he; "but you are not quite yourself today. Remember that a chance word will betray the secret of our lives."

"Go at once, and I swear to you that, happen what may, I will be calm."

The doctor went back into Paul's room, while Tantaine sat down on the topmost stair, his face buried in his hands.

Mademoiselle Flavia was just going to Paul, when the doctor again appeared.

"What, back again?" asked she petulantly. "I thought that you had been far away by this time."

"I want to say something to you," answered he, "and something of a rather serious nature. You must not elevate those charming eyebrows. I see you guess what I am going to say, and you are right. I am come to tell you that this is not the proper place for Mademoiselle Rigal."

"I know that."

This unexpected reply, made with the calmest air in the world, utterly disconcerted the smiling doctor.

"It seems to me—" began he.

"That I ought not to be here; but then, you see, I place duty before cold, worldly dictates. Paul is very ill, and has no one to take care of him except his affianced bride; for has not my father given his consent to our union?"

"Flavia, listen to the experience of a man of the world. The nature of men is such that they never forgive a woman for compromising her reputation, even though it be in their own favour. Do you know what people will say twenty-four hours after your marriage? Why, that you had been his mistress for weeks before, and that it was only the knowledge of that fact that inclined your father to consent to the alliance."

Flavia's face grew crimson. "Very well," said she, "I will obey, and never say again that I was obstinate; but let me say one word to Paul, and then I will leave him."

The doctor retired, not guessing that this obedience arose from the sudden suspicion which had arisen in Flavia's mind. "It is done," said he, as he rejoined Tantaine on the stairs; "let us hasten, for she will follow us at once."

By the time that Tantaine got into the street, he seemed to have recovered a certain amount of his self-command. "We have succeeded," said he, "but we shall have to work hard, and this marriage must be hastened by every means in our power. It can be celebrated now without any risk, for in twelve hours the only obstacle that stands between that youth there and the colossal fortune of the Champdoce will have vanished away."

Though he had expected something of the kind, the face of the doctor grew very pale.

"What, Andre?" faltered he.

"Andre is in great danger, doctor, and may not survive tomorrow, and a portion of the work necessary to this end will be done tonight by our young friend Toto Chupin."

"By that young scamp? Why, only the other day you laughed when I suggested employing him."

"I shall this time kill two birds with one stone. Once an investigation is made—let us speak plainly—into Andre's death, there will be some inquiry made as to a certain window frame that has been sawed through, and suspicion will fall upon Toto Chupin, who will have been seen lurking about the spot. It will be proved that he purchased a saw, and that he changed just before a note for one thousand *francs*; he will be found hiding in a garret in the Hotel de Perou."

The doctor looked aghast. "Are you mad?" cried he. "Toto will accuse you."

"Very likely, but by that time poor old Tantaine will be dead and buried. Then Mascarin will disappear, our faithful Beaumarchef will be in the United States, and we can afford to laugh at the police."

"It seems like a success," said the doctor, "but push on for mercy's sake; all these delays and fluctuations will make me seriously ill."

The two worthy associates held this conversation in a doorway, anxious to be sure that Flavia had kept her promise. In a brief space of time they saw her come out of the house and move in the direction of her father's bank.

"Now," said Tantaine, "I can go in peace, doctor; farewell for the present;" and without waiting for a reply he was walking rapidly away when he was stopped by Beaumarchef, who came up breathless and barred his passage.

"I was looking for you," cried he; "the Marquis de Croisenois is in the office and is swearing at me like anything."

"Go back to the office and tell the *marquis* that the master will soon be with him;" and thus speaking, Tantaine disappeared down a court by the side of Martin Rigal's house.

The *marquis* was striding up and down the office, every now and then discharging a rumbling cannonade of oaths. "Fine business people," remarked he, "to make an appointment and then not to keep it!" He checked himself; for the door of the inner office slowly opened, and Mascarin appeared on the threshold. "Punctuality," said he, "does not consist in coming *before*, but *at* the time appointed."

The *marquis* was cowed at once, and followed Mascarin into the sanctum and watched him with curious gaze as the redoubtable head of the association seemed to be searching for something among the papers on his desk. When Mascarin had found what he was in search of, he turned and addressed the *marquis*.

"I desired to see you," said he, "with reference to the great financial enterprise which you are to launch almost immediately."

"Yes; I understand that we must discuss it, fully understand it, and feel our way."

Mascarin uttered a contemptuous whistle.

"Do you think," asked he, "that I am the kind of person to stand and wait while you feel your way? Because if you do, the sooner you undeceive yourself the better. Things that I take in hand are carried out like a flash of lightning. You have been playing while I and Catenac have been working, and nothing remains to be done but to act."

"Act! What do you mean?"

"I mean that offices have been taken in the Rue Vivienne, that the articles of association have been drawn up, the directors chosen, and the Company registered. The printer brought the prospectus here yesterday; you can begin sending them out tomorrow."

"But—"

"Read it for yourself," said Mascarin, handing a printed paper to him. "Read, and then, perhaps, you will be convinced."

Croisenois, in a dazed sort of manner, accepted the paper and read it aloud.

Copper Mines of Tafila, Algeria.

Chairman: The Marquis Henri de Croisenois.

Capital: Four Million *Francs*.

This company does not appeal to that rash class of speculators who are willing to incur great risks for the sake of obtaining for a time heavy dividends.

The shareholders in the Tafila Copper Mining Company, Limited, must not look for a dividend of more than six, or at the utmost seven, *per cent.*

"Well," interrupted Mascarin, "what do you think of this for a beginning?"

"It seems fair enough," answered De Croisenois, "but suppose others than those whose names you have in your black list take shares, what do you say we are to do then?"

"We should simply decline to allot shares to them, that is all. See the Article XX. in the Articles of Association. 'The Board of Directors may decline to allot shares to applicants without giving any reason for so doing.'"

"And suppose," continued the *marquis*, "that one of our own people dispose of his share, may we not find our new shareholder a thorn in our side?"

"Article XXI. 'No transfer of stock is valid, unless passed by the Board of Directors, and recorded in the books of the Company,'" read out Mascarin.

"And how will the game be brought to a conclusion?"

"Easily enough. You will advertise one morning that two-thirds of the capital having been unsuccessfully sunk in the enterprise, you are compelled to apply for a winding-up of the Company under Article XVII. Six months afterwards you will announce that the liquidation of the Company has, after all expenses have been paid, left no balance whatsoever. Then you wash your hands of the whole thing, and the matter is at an end."

Croisenois felt that he had no ground to stand upon, but he ventured on one more objection.

"It seems rather a strange thing to launch this enterprise at the present moment. May it not interfere with my marriage prospects? and may not the Count de Mussidan decline to give me his daughter and risk her dowry in this manner? One moment, I—"

The agent sneered and cut short the tergiversations of the *marquis*.

"You mean, I suppose," said he, "that when once you are safely married and have received Mademoiselle Sabine's dowry, you will take leave of us. Not so, my dear young friend; and if this is your idea, put it aside, for it is utter nonsense. I should hold you then as I do now."

The *marquis* saw that any further struggle would be of no avail, and gave in.

★★★★★★

That evening, when M. Martin Rigal emerged from his private

office, his daughter Flavia was more than usually demonstrative in her tokens of affection. "How fondly I love you, my dearest father!" said she, as she rained kisses on his cheeks. "How good you are to me!" but on this occasion the banker was too much preoccupied to ask his daughter the reason for this extreme tenderness on her part.

Chapter 57: The Veiled Portrait

The danger with which Andre was menaced was most terrible, and the importance of the game he was playing made him feel that he had everything to fear from the boldness and audacity of his enemies. He knew this, and he also knew that spies dogged all his movements. What could be wanted but a favourable opportunity to assassinate him. But even this knowledge did not make him hesitate for an instant, and all his caution was fully exercised, for he felt that should he perish, Sabine would be inevitably lost. On her account he acted with a prudence which was certainly not one of his general characteristics. He was quite aware that he might put himself under the protection of the police, but this he knew would be to imperil the honour of the Mussidan family.

He was sure that with time and patience he should be able to unravel the plots of the villains who were at work. But he had not time to do so by degrees. No, he must make a bold dash at once. The hideous sacrifice of which Sabine was to be the victim was being hurried on, and it seemed to him as if his very existence was being carried away by the hours as they flitted by. He went over recent events carefully one by one, and he strove to piece them together as a child does the portions of a dissected map. He wanted to find out the one common interest that bound all these plotters together—Verminet, Van Klopen, Mascarin, Hortebise, and Martin Rigal. As he submitted all this strange combination of persons to the test, the thought of Gaston de Gandelu came across his mind.

"Is it not curious," thought he, "that this unhappy boy should be the victim of the cruel band of miscreants who are trying to destroy us? It is strange, very strange."

Suddenly he started to his feet, for a fresh idea had flashed across his brain—a thought that was as yet but crude and undefined, but which seemed to bear the promise of hope and deliverance. It seemed to him that the affair of young Gandelu was closely connected with his own, that they were part and parcel of the same dark plot, and that these bills with their forged acceptance had more to do with him

447

than he had ever imagined. How it was that he and Gaston could be connected he could not for a moment guess; yet now he would have cheerfully sworn that such was the case. Who was it that had informed the father of the son's conduct? Why, Catenac. Who had advised that proceedings should be taken against Rose, *alias* Zora? Why, Catenac again; and this same man, in addition to acting for Gandelu, it seems, was also the confidential solicitor of the Marquis de Croisenois and Verminet. Perhaps he had only obeyed their instructions. All this was very vague and unsatisfactory, but it might be something to go upon, and who could say what conclusion careful inquiry might not lead him to? and Andre determined to carry on his investigations, and endeavour to find the hidden links that connected this chain of rascality together. He had taken up a pencil with the view of making a few notes, when he heard a knock at his door. He glanced at the clock; it was not yet nine.

"Come in," cried he as he rose.

The door was thrown open, and the young artist started as he recognised in his early visitor the father of Sabine. It was after a sleepless night that the count had decided to take the present step. He was terribly agitated, but had had time to prepare himself for this all-important interview.

"You will, I trust, pardon me, sir," said he, "for making such an early call upon you, but I thought that I should be sure to find you at this hour, and much wanted to see you."

Andre bowed.

In the space of one brief instant a thousand suppositions, each one more unlikely than the other, coursed through his brain. Why had the count called? Who could have given him his address? And was the visit friendly or hostile?

"I am a great admirer of paintings," began the count, "and one of my friends upon whose taste I can rely has spoken to me in the warmest terms of your talent. This I trust will explain the liberty I have taken. Curiosity drove me to—"

He paused for a moment, and then added,—

"My name is the Marquis de Bevron."

The concealment of the count's real name showed Andre that the visit was not entirely a friendly one, and Andre replied,—

"I am only too pleased to receive your visit. Unfortunately just now I have nothing ready, only a few rough sketches in short. Would you like to see them?"

The count replied eagerly in the affirmative. He was terribly embarrassed under his fictitious name, and shrank before the honest, open
gaze of the young artist, and his mental disturbance was completed by
seeing in one corner of the room the picture covered with a green
cloth, which Tantaine had alluded to. It was evident that the old villain had told the truth, and that his daughter's portrait was concealed
behind this wrapper. She had evidently been here—had spent hours
here, and whose fault was it? She had but listened to the voice of her
heart, and had sought that affection abroad which she was unable to
obtain at home. As the count gazed upon the young man before him,
he was forced to admit that Mademoiselle Sabine had not fixed her
affections on an unworthy object, for at the very first glance he had
been struck with the manly beauty of the young artist, and the clear
intelligence of his face.

"Ah," thought Andre, "you come to me under a name that is not
your own, and I will respect your wish to remain unknown, but I will
take advantage of it by letting you know things which I should not
dare say to your face."

Great as was Andre's preoccupation, he could not fail to notice
that his visitor's eyes sought the veiled picture with strange persistency.
While M. de Mussidan was looking at the various sketches on the
walls, Andre had time to recover all his self-command.

"Let me congratulate you, sir," remarked the count, as he returned
to the spot where the painter was standing. "My friend's admiration
was well founded. I am sorry, however, that you have nothing finished
to show me. You say that you have nothing, I believe?"

"Nothing, *marquis*."

"Not even that picture whose frame I can distinguish through the
serge curtain that covers it?"

Andre blushed, though he had been expecting the question from
the commencement.

"Excuse me," answered he; "that picture is certainly finished, but
it is not on view."

The count was now sure that Tantaine's statement was correct.

"I suppose that it is some woman's portrait," remarked the false
marquis.

"You are quite correct."

Both men were much agitated at this moment, and avoided meeting each other's eyes.

The count, however, had made up his mind that he would go on to the end.

"Ah, you are in love, I see!" remarked he with a forced laugh. "All great artists have depicted the charms of their mistresses on canvas."

"Stop," cried Andre with an angry glance in his eyes. "The picture you refer to is the portrait of the purest and most innocent girl in the world. I shall love her all my life; but, if possible, my respect for her is greater than my love. I should consider myself a most degraded wretch, had I ever whispered in her ear a word that her mother might not have listened to."

A feeling of the most instantaneous relief thrilled through M. de Mussidan's heart.

"You will pardon me," suggested he blandly, "but when one sees a portrait in a studio, the inference is that a sitting or two has taken place?"

"You are right. She came here secretly, and without the knowledge of her family, at the risk of her honour and reputation, thus affording me the strongest proof of her love. It was cruel of me," continued the young artist, "to accept this proof of her entire devotion, and yet not only did I accept it, but I pleaded for it on my bended knee, for how else was I to hear the music of her voice, or gladden my eyes with her beauty? We love each other, but a gulf wider than the stormy sea divides us. She is an heiress, come of a proud and haughty line of nobles, while I—"

Andre paused, waiting for some words wither of encouragement or censure; but the count remained silent, and the young man continued,—

"Do you know who I am? A poor foundling, placed in the Hospital of Vendome, the illicit offspring of some poor betrayed girl. I started in the world with twenty *francs* in my pocket, and found my way to Paris; since then I have earned my bread by my daily work. You only see here the more brilliant side of my life; for an artist here—I am a common work-man elsewhere."

If M. de Mussidan remained silent, it was from extreme admiration of the noble character, which was so unexpectedly revealed to him, and he was endeavouring to conceal it.

"She knows all this," pursued Andre, "and yet she loves me. It was here, in this very room, that she vowed that she could never be the wife of another. Not a month ago, a gentleman, well born, wealthy, and fascinating, with every characteristic that a woman could love, was a suitor for her hand. She went boldly to him, told him the story of our love, and, like a noble-hearted gentleman, he withdrew at once, and today is my best and kindest friend. Now, *marquis*, would you like to see this young girl's picture?"

"Yes," answered the count, "and I shall feel deeply grateful to you for such a mark of confidence."

Andre went to the picture, but as he touched the curtain he turned quickly towards his visitor.

"No," said he, "I can no longer continue this farce; it is unworthy of me."

M. de Mussidan turned pale.

"I am about to see Sabine de Mussidan's portrait. Draw the curtain."

Andre obeyed, and for a moment the count stood entranced before the work of genius that met his eyes.

"It is she!" said the father. "Her very smile; the same soft light in her eyes. It is exquisite!"

Misfortune is a harsh teacher; some weeks ago he would have smiled superciliously at the mere idea of granting his daughter's hand to a struggling artist, for then he thought only of M. de Breulh, but now he would have esteemed it a precious boon had he been allowed to choose Andre as Sabine's husband. But Henri de Croisenois stood in the way, and as this idea flashed across the count's mind he gave a perceptible start. He was sure from the excessive calmness of the young man that he must be well acquainted with all recent events. He asked the question, and Andre, in the most open manner, told him all he knew. The generosity of M. de Breulh, the kindness of Madame Bois Arden, his suspicions, his inquiries, his projects, and his hopes. M. de Mussidan gazed once more upon his daughter's portrait, and then taking the hand of the young painter, said,—

"M. Andre, if ever we can free ourselves from those miscreants, whose daggers are pointed at our hearts, Sabine shall be your wife."

Chapter 58: Gaston's Dilemma

Yes, Sabine might yet be his, but between the lovers stood the forms of Croisenois and his associates. But now he felt strong enough to contend with them all.

"To work!" said he, "to work!"

Just then, however, he heard a sound of ringing laughter outside his door. He could distinguish a woman's voice, and also a man's, speaking in high, shrill tones. All at once his door burst open, and a hurricane of silks, velvets, feathers, and lace whirled in. With extreme surprise, the young artist recognised the beautiful features of Rose, *alias* Zora de Chantemille. Gaston de Gandelu followed her, and at once began,—

"Here we are," said he, "all right again. Did you expect to see us?"

"Not in the least."

"Ah! well, it is a little surprise of the governor's. On my word, I really will be a dutiful son for the future. Today, the good old boy came into my room, and said, 'This morning I took the necessary steps to release the person in whom you are interested. Go and meet her.' What do you think of that? So off I ran to find Zora, and here we are."

Andre did not pay much attention to Gaston, but was engaged in watching Zora, who was looking round the studio. She went up to Sabine's portrait, and was about to draw the curtain, when Andre exclaimed,—

"Excuse me," said he; "I must put this picture to dry." And as the portrait stood on a moveable easel, he wheeled it into the adjoining room.

"And now," said Gaston, "I want you to come and breakfast with us to celebrate Zora's happy release."

"I am much obliged to you, but it is impossible. I must get on with my work."

"Yes, yes; work is an excellent thing, but just now you must go and dress."

"I assure you that it is quite out of the question. I cannot leave the studio yet."

Gaston paused for a moment in deep thought.

"I have it," said he triumphantly. "You will not come to breakfast; then breakfast shall come to you. I am off to order it."

Andre ran after him, but Gaston was too quick, and he returned to the studio in anything but an amiable temper. Zora noticed his evident annoyance.

"He always goes on in this absurd way," said she, with a shrug of her pretty shoulders, "and thinks himself so clever and witty, bah!"

Her tone disclosed such contempt for Gaston that Andre looked at her in perplexed surprise.

"What do you look so astonished at? It is easy to see you do not know much of him. All his friends are just like him; if you listen to them for half an hour at a stretch, you get regularly sick. When I think of the terrible evenings that I have spent in their company, I feel ready to die with yawning;" and as she spoke, she suited the action to the word. "Ah! if he really loved me!" added she.

"Love you! Why, he adores you."

Zora made a little gesture of contempt which Toto Chupin might have envied.

"Do you think so?" said she. "Do you know what it is he loves in me? When people pass me they cry out, 'Isn't she good style?' and then the idiot is as pleased as Punch; but if I had on a cotton gown, he would think nothing of me."

Rose had evidently learned a good ideal, as her beauty had never been so radiant. She was one glow of health and strength.

"Then my name was not good enough for him," she went on. "His aristocratic lips could not bring themselves to utter such a common name as Rose, so he christened me Zora, a regular puppy dog's name. He has plenty of money, but money is not everything after all. Paul had no money, and yet I loved him a thousand times better. On my word, I have almost forgotten how to laugh, and yet I used to be as merry as the day was long."

"Why did you leave Paul then?"

"Well, you see, I wanted to experience what a woman feels when she has a Cashmere shawl on, so one fine morning I took wing. But there, who knows? Paul would very likely have left me one day. There was someone who was doing his best to separate us, an old blackguard called Tantaine, who lived in the same house."

"Ah!" answered he cautiously. "What interest could he have had in separating you?"

"I don't know," answered the girl, assuming a serious air; "but I am sure he was trying it on. A fellow doesn't hand over banknotes for nothing, and I saw him give one for five hundred *francs* to Paul; and more than that, he promised him that he should make a great fortune through a friend of his called Mascarin."

Andre started. He remembered the visit that Paul had made him, on the pretext of restoring the twenty *francs* he had borrowed, and at which he had boasted that he had an income of a thousand *francs* a month, and might make more, though he had not said how this was to be done. "I think that Paul has forgotten me. I saw him once at Van Klopen's, and he never attempted to say a word to me. He was certainly with that Mascarin at the time."

Andre could only draw one conclusion from this, either that Paul was protected by the band of conspirators, or else that he formed one of it. In that case he was useful to them; while Rose, who was in their way, was persecuted by them. Andre's mind came to this conclusion in an instant. It seemed to him that if Catenac had been desirous of imprisoning Rose, it was because she was in the way, and her presence disturbed certain combinations. Before, however, he could work out his line of deduction, Gaston's shrill voice was heard upon the stairs, and in another moment he made his appearance.

"Place for the banquet," said he; "make way for the lordly feast."

Two waiters followed him, bearing a number of covered dishes on trays. At another time Andre would have been very angry at this invasion, and at the prospect of a breakfast that would last two or three hours and utterly change everything; but now he was inclined to bless Gaston for his happy idea, and, with the assistance of Rose, he speedily cleared a large table for the reception of the viands.

Gaston did nothing, but talked continually.

"And now I must tell you the joke of the day. Henri de Croisenois, one of my dearest friends, has absolutely launched a Company."

Andre nearly let fall a bottle, which he was about to place upon the table.

"Who told you this?" asked he quickly.

"Who told me? Why, a great big flaming poster. Tafila Copper Mines; capital, four millions. And my esteemed friend, Henri, has not a five-*franc* piece to keep the devil out of his pocket."

The face of the young artist expressed such blank surprise that Gaston burst into a loud laugh.

"You look just as I did when I read it. Henri de Croisenois, the chairman of a Company! Why, if you had been elected Pope, I should not have been more surprised. Tafila Copper Mines! What a joke! The shares are five hundred *francs*."

The waiters had now retired, and Gaston urged his friends to take their places at the table, and all seemed merry as a marriage bell; but many a gay commencement has a stormy ending.

Gaston, whose shallow brain could not stand the copious draughts of wine with which he washed down his repast, began all at once to overwhelm Zora with bitter reproaches at her not being able to comprehend how a man like him, who was destined to play a serious part in society, could have been led away, as he had been, by a person like her.

Gaston had a tongue which was never at a loss either to praise or blame, and Zora was equally ready to retort, and defended herself with such acrimony that the lad, knowing himself to be in fault, entirely lost the small remnant of temper which he still possessed, and dashed out of the room, declaring that he never wished to set eyes upon Zora again, and that she might keep all the presents that he had lavished upon her for all he cared.

His departure was hailed with delight by Andre, who, now that he was left alone with Zora, hoped to derive some further information from her, and especially a distinct description of Paul, whom he felt that he must now reckon among his adversaries. But his hopes were destined to be frustrated, for Zora was so filled with anger and excitement that she refused to listen to another word; and putting on her hat and mantle, with scarcely a glance at the mirror, rushed out of the studio with the utmost speed, declaring that she would seek out Paul, and make him revenge the insults that Gaston had put on her.

All this passed so rapidly that the young painter felt as if a tornado had passed through his humble dwelling; but as peace and calm returned, he began to see that Providence had directly interposed in his favour, and had sent Rose and Gaston to his place to furnish him with fresh and important facts. All that Rose had said, incomplete as her statement was, had thrown a ray of light upon an intrigue which, up till now, had been shaded in the thickest gloom. The relations of Paul with Mascarin explained why Catenac had been so anxious to have Rose imprisoned, and also seemed to hint vaguely at the reason for the extraction of the forged signatures from the simple Gaston. What could be the meaning of the Company started by De Croisenois at the very moment when he was about to celebrate his union with Sabine?

Andre desired to see the advertisement of the Company for himself; and without stopping to change his blouse, ran downstairs to the corner of the street, where Gaston had told him that the announcement of the Company was placarded up. He found it there, in a most conspicuous position, with all its advantages most temptingly set forth. Nothing was wanting; and there was even a woodcut of Tafila, in Algiers, which represented the copper mines in full working operation; while at the top, the name of the chairman, the Marquis de Croisenois, stood out in letters some six inches in height.

Andre stood gazing at this wonderful production for fully five minutes, when all at once a gleam of prudence flashed across his mind.

"I am a fool," said he to himself. "How do I know how many watchful eyes are now fixed on me, reading on my countenance my designs regarding this matter and its leading spirit?"

Upon his return to his room, he sat for more than an hour, turning over the whole affair in his mind, and at length he flattered himself that he had hit upon an expedient. Behind the house in which he lodged was a large garden, belonging to some public institution, the front of which was in the Rue Laval. A wall of about seven feet in height divided these grounds from the premises in the Rue de la Tour d'Auvergne. Why should he not go out by the way of these ornamental grounds and so elude the vigilance of the spies who might be in waiting at the front of the house? "I can," thought he, "alter my appearance so much that I shall not be recognised. I need not return here to sleep. I can ask a bed from Vignol, who will help me in every possible way."

This Vignol was the friend to whom, at Andre's request, M. Gandelu had given the superintendence of the works at his new house in the Champs Elysees.

"I shall," continued he, "by this means escape entirely from De Croisenois and his emissaries, and can watch their game without their having any suspicion of my doing so. For the time being, of course, I must give up seeing those who have been helping me,—De Breulh, Gandelu, Madame de Bois Arden, and M. de Mussidan; that, however, cannot be avoided. I can use the post, and by it will inform them all of the step that I have taken."

It was dark before he had finished his letters, and, of course, it was too late to try anything that day; consequently he went out, posted his letters, and dined at the nearest restaurant.

On his return home, he proceeded to arrange his disguise. He had it ready, among his clothes: a blue blouse, a pair of check trousers, well-worn shoes, and a shabby cap, were all that he required, and he then applied himself to the task of altering his face. He first shaved off his beard. Then he twisted down two locks of hair, which he managed to make rest on his forehead. Then he commenced applying some colouring to his face with a paint-brush; but this he found to be an extremely difficult business, and it was not for a long while that he was satisfied with the results that he had produced. He then knotted an old handkerchief round his neck, and clapped his cap on one side, with the peak slanting over one eye. Then he took a last glance in the glass, and felt that he had rendered himself absolutely unrecognisable. He was about to impart a few finishing touches, when a knock came at his door. He was not expecting anyone at such an hour, nine o'clock; for the waiters from the restaurant had already removed the remains of the feast.

"Who is there?" cried he.

"It is I," replied a weak voice; "I, Gaston de Gandelu."

Andre decided that he had no cause to distrust the lad, and so he opened his door.

"Has M. Andre gone out?" asked the poor boy faintly. "I though I heard his voice."

Gaston had not penetrated his disguise, and this was Andre's first triumph; but he saw now that he must alter his voice, as well as his face.

"Don't you know me?" asked he.

It was evident that young Gaston had received some terrible shock; for it could not have been the quarrel in the morning that had reduced him to this abject state of prostration.

"What has gone wrong with you?" asked Andre kindly.

"I have come to bid you farewell; I am going to shoot myself in half an hour."

"Have you gone mad?"

"Not in the least," answered Gaston, passing his hand across his forehead in a distracted manner; "but those infernal bills have turned up. I was just leaving the dining-room, after having treated the governor to my company, when the butler whispered in my ear that there was a man outside who wanted to see me. I went out and found a dirty-looking old scamp, with his coat collar turned up round the nape of his neck."

"Did he say that his name was Tantaine?" exclaimed Andre.

"Ah! was that his name? Well, it doesn't matter. He told me in the most friendly manner that the holder of my bills had determined to place them in the hands of the police tomorrow at twelve o'clock, but that there was still a way for me to escape."

"And this was to take Rose out of France with you," said Andre quickly.

Gaston was overwhelmed with surprise.

"Who the deuce told you that?" asked he.

"No one; I guessed it; for it was only the conclusion of the plan which they had initiated when you were induced to forge Martin Rigal's signature. Well, what did you say?"

"That the idea was a ridiculous one, and that I would not stir a yard. They shall find out that I can be obstinate, too; besides, I can see their little game. As soon as I am out of the way they will go to the governor and bleed him."

But Andre was not listening to him. What was best to be done? To advise Gaston to go and take Rose with him was to deprive himself of a great element of success; and to permit him to kill himself was, of course, out of the question.

"Just attend to me," said he at last; "I have an idea which I will tell you as soon as we are out of this house; but for reasons which are too long to go into at present it is necessary for me to get into the street without going through the door. You will, therefore, go away, and as the clock strikes twelve you will ring at the gateway of 29, Rue de Laval. When it is opened, ask some trivial question of the porter; and when you leave, take care that you do not close the gate. I shall be in the garden of the house and will slip out and join you."

The plan succeeded admirably, and in ten minutes Gaston and Andre were walking along the boulevards.

Chapter 59: M. Lecoq

The Marquis de Croisenois lived in a fine new house on the Boulevard Malesherbes near the church of St. Augustine, and in a suite of rooms the rental of which was four thousand *francs per annum*. He had collected together sufficient relics of his former splendour to dazzle the eyes of the superficial observer. The apartment and the furniture stood in the name of his body-servant, while his horse and brougham were by the same fiction supposed to be the property of his coachman, for even in the midst of his ruin the Marquis de Croisenois could not go on foot like common people.

The *marquis* had two servants only in his modest establishment—a coachman, who did a certain amount of indoor work, and a valet, who knew enough of cookery to prepare a bachelor breakfast. This valet Mascarin had seen once, and the man had then produced so unpleasant an impression on the astute proprietor of the Servants' Registry Office that he had set every means at work to discover who he was and from whence he came. Croisenois said that he had taken him into his service on the recommendation of an English baronet of his acquaintance, a certain Sir Richard Wakefield. The man was a Frenchman, but he had resided for some time in England, for he spoke that language with tolerable fluency. Andre knew nothing of these details, but he had heard of the existence of the valet from M. de Breulh, when he had asked where the *marquis* lived.

At eight o'clock on the morning after he had surreptitiously left his home in the manner described, Andre took up his position in a small wine-shop not far from the abode of the Marquis de Croisenois. He had done this designedly, for he knew enough of the manner and customs of Parisian society to know that this was the hour usually selected by domestics in fashionable quarters to come out for a gossip while their masters were still in bed. Andre had more confidence in himself than heretofore, for he had succeeded in saving Gaston; and these were the means he had employed. After much trouble, and even by the use of threats, he had persuaded the boy to return to his father's house. He had gone with him; and though it was two in the morning, he had not hesitated to arouse M. Gandelu, senior, and tell him how his son had been led on to commit the forgery, and how he threatened to commit suicide.

The poor old man was much moved.

"Tell him to come to me at once," said he, "and let him know that we two will save him."

Andre had not far to go, for Gaston was waiting in the next room in an agony of suspense.

As soon as he came into the old man's presence he fell upon his knees, with many promises of amendment for the future.

"I do not believe," remarked old Gandelu, "that these miscreants will venture to carry their threats into execution and place the matter in the hands of the police; but for all that, my son must not remain in a state of suspense. I will file a complaint against the Mutual Loan Society before twelve today, and we will see how an association will be dealt with that lends money to minors and urges them to forge signatures as security. It will, however, be as well for my son to leave for Belgium by the first train this morning; but, as you will see, he will not remain very many days."

Andre remained for the rest of the hours of darkness at the kind old man's house, and it was in Gaston's room that he renewed his "make-up" before leaving. The future looked very bright to him as he walked gaily up the Boulevard Malesherbes. The wine-shop in which he had taken up his position was admirably adapted for keeping watch on De Croisenois, for he could not avoid seeing all who came in and went out of the house; and as there was no other wine-shop in the neighbourhood, Andre felt sure that all the servants in the vicinity, and those of the *marquis*, of course, among the number, would come there in the course of the morning; so that here he could get into conversation with them, offer them a glass of wine, and, perhaps, get some information from them. The room was large and airy, and was full of customers, most of whom were servants. Andre was racking his brain for a means of getting into conversation with the proprietor, when two new-comers entered the room. These men were in full livery, while all the other servants had on morning jackets. As soon as they entered, an old man, with a calm expression of face, who was struggling perseveringly with a tough beefsteak at the same table as that by which Andre seated, observed,—

"Ah! here comes the De Croisenois' lot."

"If they would only sit here," thought Andre, "by the side of this fellow, who evidently knows them, I could hear all they said."

By good luck they did so, begging that they might be served at once, as they were in a tremendous hurry.

"What is the haste this morning?" asked the old man who had recognised them.

"I have to drive the master to his office, for he has one now. He is chairman of a Copper Mining Company, and a fine thing it is, too. If you have any money laid by, M. Benoit, this is a grand chance for you."

Benoit shook his head gravely.

"All is not gold that glitters," said he sententiously; "nor, on the other hand, are things as bad as they are painted."

Benoit was evidently a prudent man, and was not likely to commit himself.

"But if your master is going out, you, M. Mouret, will be free, and we can have a game at cards together."

"No, sir," answered the valet.

"What! are you engaged too?"

"Yes; I have to carry a bouquet of flowers to the young lady my master is engaged to. I have seen the young lady; she seems to be rather haughty."

The man, who wore an enormously high and stiff collar, was absolutely speaking of Sabine, and Andre could have twisted his neck with pleasure.

"Let us hope," remarked the coachman, as he hastily swallowed his breakfast, "that the *marquis* does not intend to invest his wife's dowry in this new venture of his."

The men then ceased to speak of their master, and began to busy themselves with their own affairs, and went out again without alluding to him any further, leaving Andre to reflect what a difficult business the detective line was.

The customers looked upon him with distrustful eyes, for it must be confessed that his appearance was decidedly against him, and he had not yet acquired the necessary art of seeing and hearing while affecting to be doing neither; and it was easy for the dullest observer to be certain that it was not for the sake of obtaining a breakfast that he had entered the establishment. Andre had penetration enough to see the effect he had produced, and he became more and more embarrassed.

He had finished his meal now and had lighted a cigar, and had ordered a small glass of brandy. Nearly all the customers had withdrawn, leaving only five or six, who were playing cards at a table near the door. Andre was anxious to see Croisenois enter his carriage, and so he lingered, ordering another glass of brandy as an excuse.

He had just been served, when a man, whose dress very much resembled his own, lounged into the wine-shop. He was a tall, clumsily built fellow, with an insolent expression upon his beardless face. His coat and cap were in an equally dilapidated condition; and in the squeaky voice of the rough, he ordered a plate of beef and half a bottle of wine, and, as he brushed past Andre, upset his glass of brandy. The artist made no remark, though he felt quite sure that this act was intentional, as the fellow laughed impudently when he saw the damage that he had done. When his breakfast was served, he carelessly spit upon Andre's boots. The insult was so apparent that Andre began to reflect.

"Had he not succeeded in eluding his spies, as he thought that he had done? And was it not quite possible that this man had been sent to pick a quarrel with him, and deal him a disabling, or even a fatal blow?"

Prudence counselled him to leave the place at once, but he felt that he could not go until he had found out the real truth. There seemed to be but little doubt on the matter, however; for as the fellow cut up his meat, he jerked every bit of skin and gristle into his neighbour's lap; then, after finishing up his wine, he managed to upset the few drops remaining on to Andre's arm and shoulder. This was the finishing stroke.

"Please, remember," remarked Andre calmly, "that there is someone at the table besides yourself."

"Do you think I'm blind, mate?" returned the fellow brutally. "Mind your own business, or—" And to conclude the sentence, he shook his fist threateningly in the young man's face.

Andre started to his feet, and, with a well-directed blow in the chest, sent the fellow rolling under the table.

At the sound of the scuffle, the card-players turned round, and saw Andre standing erect, with quivering lips and eyes flashing with rage, while his antagonist was lying on the floor among the overturned chairs.

"Come, come! No squabbling here!" remarked one of the players.

The fellow scrambled to his feet, and made a savage rush at the young man, who, using his right foot skilfully, tripped his antagonist up, and sent him again rolling on the ground. It was most adroitly done, and secured the applause of the lookers-on, who now complained no longer, and were evidently interested in the scene.

Again the rough came up, but Andre contented himself with standing on the defensive. Some tables, a stool, and a glass were injured, and at last the proprietor came upon the scene of action.

"Get out of this," cried he, "and take care that I don't see your faces here again."

At these words, the rough burst out into a torrent of foul language.

"Don't put up with his cheek," said one of the customers; "give him in charge at once."

Hardly, however, had the manager started to summon the police, than, as if by magic, a body of them appeared; and Andre found himself walking down the boulevard between a couple, while his late antagonist followed in the safe custody of two more. To have attempted any resistance would have been utter folly, and the young man resigned himself to what he felt he could not help. But as he went on, he reflected on the strange scene through which he had just passed. All had gone on so rapidly that he could hardly recall the events to his memory. He was, however, quite sure that this unprovoked assault concealed some motive with which at present he was unacquainted.

The police led their prisoners through the doorway of a dingy-looking old house, and then Andre saw that he was not at the regular police-station. The whole party entered an office, where a superintendent and two clerks were at work. The ruffian who had assaulted Andre changed his manner directly he entered the office; he threw his tattered cap upon a bench, passed his fingers through his hair, and shook hands with the superintendent; he then turned to Andre.

"Permit me, sir," said he, "to compliment you on being so handy with your fists. You precious nearly did for me, I can tell you."

At that moment a door opened at the other end of the room, and a voice was heard to say, "Send them in."

Andre and his late antagonist soon found themselves in an office evidently sacred to someone high up in the police. At a desk near the window was seated a man, with a rather distinguished air, wearing a white necktie and a pair of gold glasses.

"Have the goodness to take a seat," said this gentleman, addressing Andre with the most perfect urbanity.

He took a chair, half stupefied by the strangeness of the whole affair, and waited. Could he be awake, or was he dreaming? He could hardly tell.

"Before I say anything," remarked the gentleman in the gold spectacles, "I ought to apologize for a proceeding which is—well, what shall I call it?—a little rough, perhaps; but it was necessary to make use of it to obtain this interview with you. Really, however, I had no choice. You are closely watched, and I did not wish the persons who had set spies on you to have any knowledge of this conference."

"Do you say I am watched?" stammered Andre.

"Yes, by a certain La Candele, as sharp a fellow at that kind of work as you could find in Paris. Are you surprised at this?"

"Yes, for I had thought—"

The gentleman's features softened into a benevolent smile.

"You thought," he said, "that you had succeeded in throwing them off the scent. So I had imagined this morning, when I saw you in your present disguise. But permit me, my dear M. Andre, to assure you that there is great room for improvement in it. I admit that a first attempt is always to be looked on leniently; but it did not deceive La Candele, and even at this distance I can plainly see your whole makeup; and what I can see, of course, is patent to others."

He rose from his seat, and came closer to Andre.

"Why on earth," asked he, "should you daub all this colour on your face, which makes you look like an Indian warrior in his war-paint? Only two colours are necessary to change the whole face—red and black—at the eyebrows, the nostrils, and the corners of the mouth. Look here;" and taking from his pocket a gold pencil-case, he corrected the faults in the young artist's work.

As soon as he had finished, Andre went up to the mirror over the chimney-piece, and was surprised at the result.

"Now," said the strange gentleman, "you see the futility of your attempts. La Candele knew you at once. I wished to speak to you; so I sent for Palot, one of my men, and instructed him to pick a quarrel with you. The policemen arrested you, and we have met without anyone being at all the wiser. Be kind enough to efface my little corrections, as they will be noticed in the street."

Andre obeyed, and as he rubbed away with the corner of his handkerchief, he vainly sought for some elucidation of this mystery.

The man with the gold spectacles had resumed his seat, and was refreshing himself with a pinch of snuff.

"And now," resumed he, "we will, if you please, have a little talk together. As you see, I know you. Doctor Loulleux tells me that he knows no one so high-minded and amiable as yourself. He declares that your honour is without a stain, and your courage undoubted."

"Ah! my dear sir!" interposed the painter, with a deep blush.

"Pray let me go on. M. Gandelu says that he would trust you with all he possessed, while all your comrades, with Vignol at their head, have the greatest respect and regard for you. So much for the present. As for your future, two of the greatest ornaments of the artistic world say that you will one day occupy a very high place in the profession. You gain now about fifteen *francs* a day. Am I correct?"

"Certainly," answered Andre, more bewildered than ever.

The gentleman smiled.

"Unfortunately," he went on, "my information ends here, for the means of inquiry possessed by the police are, of course, very limited. They can only act upon facts, not on intentions, and so long as these are not displayed in open acts, the hands of the police are tied. It is only forty-eight hours since I heard of you for the first time, and I have already your biography in my pocket. I hear that the day before yesterday you were dining with M. de Breulh-Faverlay, and that this morning you were walking with young Gandelu, and that La Candele was following you like a shadow. These are all facts, but—"

He paused, and cast a keen glance upon Andre, then, in a slow and measured voice, he continued,—

"But no one has been able to tell me why you dogged Verminet's footsteps, or why you went to Mascarin's house, or why, finally, you disguised yourself to keep a watch on the movements of the most honourable the Marquis de Croisenois. It is the motive that we cannot arrive at, for the facts are perfectly clear."

Andre fidgeted uneasily in his chair beneath the spell of those magnetic glasses, which seemed to draw the truth from him.

"I cannot tell you, sir," faltered he at last, "for the secret is not mine to divulge."

"You will not trust me? Well, then, I must speak. Remember, all that I have told you was the account of what I knew positively; but, in addition to this, I have drawn my own inferences. You are watching De Croisenois because he is going to marry a wealthy heiress."

Andre blushed crimson.

"We assume, therefore, that you wish to prevent this marriage; and why, pray? I have heard that Mademoiselle de Mussidan was formerly engaged to M. de Breulh-Faverlay. How comes it that the Count and Countess de Mussidan prefer a ruined spendthrift to a wealthy and strictly honourable man? It is for you to answer this question. It is perfectly plain to me that they hand over their daughter to De Croisenois under pressure of some kind, and that means that a terrible secret exists with which Croisenois threatens them."

"Your deduction is wrong, sir," exclaimed Andre eagerly, "and you are quite wrong."

"Very good," was the calm reply. "Your emphatic denial shows that I am in the right. I want no further proofs. M. de Mussidan paid you a visit yesterday, and one of my agents reported that his face was much happier on leaving you than when he was on his way to your house. I therefore infer that you promised to release him from Croisenois' persecutions, and in return he promised you his daughter's hand in marriage. This, of course, explains your present disguise, and now tell me again that I am wrong, if you dare."

Andre would not lie, and therefore kept silence.

"And now," continued the gentleman, "how about the secret? Did not the count tell it you? I do not know it; and yet I think that if I were to search for it, I could find it. I can call to my mind certain crimes which three generations of detective have striven to find out. Did you ever hear that De Croisenois had an elder brother named George, who disappeared in a most wonderful manner? What became of him? This very George, twenty-three years back, was a friend of Madame de Mussidan's. Might not his disappearance have something to do with this marriage?"

"Are you the fiend himself?" cried the young man.

"I am M. Lecoq."

Andre started back in absolute dread at the name of this celebrated detective.

"M. Lecoq!" repeated he.

The vanity of the great detective was much flattered when he saw the impression that his name had produced.

"And now, my dear M. Andre," said he blandly, "now that you know who I am, may I not hope that you will be more communicative?"

M. de Mussidan had not told his secret to the young artist, but he had said enough for him to feel that the detective was correct in his inference.

"Surely," continued Lecoq, "we ought to be able to come to a more definite understanding, and I think that my openness should elicit some frankness on your side. I saw that you were watched by the very person that I was watching. For three days my men have followed you, and today I made up my mind that you could furnish me with the clue I am seeking."

"I, sir?"

"For many years," continued Lecoq, "I have been certain that an organized association of blackmailers exists in Paris; family differences, sin, shame, and sorrow are worked by these wretches like veritable gold mines, and bring them in enormous annual revenues."

"Ah," returned Andre, "I expected something of this kind."

"Of course, when I was quite sure of these facts," continued Lecoq, "I said to myself, 'I will break up this gang;' but it was easier said than done. There is one very peculiar thing about blackmailing. Those who carry it on are almost certain of doing so with impunity, for the victims will pay and not complain. Yes, I tell you that I have often found out these unhappy pigeons, but never could get one to speak."

The detective was so indignant and acrimonious withal in his indignation, that Andre could not repress a smile.

"Very soon," continued Lecoq, "I recognised the futility of my attempts, and the impossibility of reaching these scoundrels through their victims, and then I determined to strike at the plunderers themselves, but this was a scheme that took patience and time. I have waited my chance for three years, and for eighteen months one of my men has been in the service of the Marquis de Croisenois, and up to now this band of villains has cost the government over ten thousand *francs*. That superlative scoundrel, Mascarin, has put several white threads in my hair. I believe him to be Tantaine; yes, and Martin Rigal too.

"The idea of there being a means of communication between the banker's house in the Rue Montmartre and the Servants' Registry Office in the Rue Montorgueil only came into my head this morning. But this time they have gone too far, and I have them. I know them all, from the chief, Mascarin-Tantaine-Rigal, down to their lowest agent, Toto Chupin, and Paul Violaine, the docile puppet of their will. We will get hold of the whole gang, and neither Van Klopen nor Catenac will escape. Just now the latter is travelling about with the Duke de Champdoce and a fellow named Perpignan, and two of my sweet lads are close upon them, and send in almost hourly reports of what is going on. My trap has a tempting bait, the spring is strong, and we shall catch every one of them. And now do you still hesitate to confide all you know to me? I swear on my honour that I will respect as sacred what you tell me, no matter what may occur."

Andre yielded, as did every person who came under the influence of this remarkable man and his strange and inexplicable fascination. If he hid anything from him today, would not Lecoq be acquainted with it tomorrow? And so, with the most perfect frankness, he told his story and everything that he knew.

"Now," cried Lecoq, "I see it all clearly. Aha, they want to force young Gandelu to disappear with Rose, do they?"

Beneath his gold-rimmed spectacles his eyes flashed fiercely. He seemed to be occupied in drawing out his plan of campaign.

"From this moment," said he, "be at ease. In another month Mademoiselle de Mussidan shall be your wife; this I promise you, and the promises of Lecoq are never broken."

He paused for an instant, as though to collect his thoughts, and then continued,—

"I can answer for all, except for your life. So many are interested in your disappearance from this world, that every effort will be made to get rid of you. Do not cease your caution for an instant. Never eat twice running at the same restaurant, throw away food that has the slightest strange taste. Avoid crowds in the street; do not get into a cab; never lean from a window before ascertaining that its supports are solid; in a word, fear and suspect everything."

For a moment longer Lecoq detained the young artist.

"Tell me," said he, "have you the mark of a wound on your shoulder or arm?"

"I have, sir; the scar of a very severe scald."

"I thought so; yes, I was almost certain of it," said Lecoq thoughtfully; and as he conducted the young man to the door, he took leave of him with the same words that Mascarin had often used to Paul,—

"Farewell for the present, Duke de Champdoce."

Chapter 60: Through the Air

At these last words Andre turned round, but the door closed, and he heard the key grate in the lock. He passed through the outer office, where the superintendent, his two clerks, and his late adversary all seemed to gaze upon him with a glance of admiration and esteem.

He gained the open street.

What did those last words of Lecoq mean? He was a foundling, it is true; but what foundling has not had lofty aspirations, and felt that, for all he knew, he might be the scion of some noble house.

As soon as Lecoq thought that the coast was clear, he opened the door, and called the agent, Palot.

"My lad," said the great man, "you saw that young man who went out just now? He is a noble fellow, full of good feeling and honour. I look upon him as my friend."

Palot made a gesture signifying that henceforth his late antagonist was as something sacred in his eyes.

"You will be his shadow," pursued Lecoq, "and keep near enough to him to rush to his aid at a moment of danger. That gang, of which Mascarin is the head, want his life. You are my right-hand man, and I trust him to you. I have warned him, but youth is rash; and you will scent danger where he would never dream that it lurked. If there is any peril, dash boldly forward, but endeavour to let no one find out who you are. If you must speak to him—but only do so at the last extremity—whisper my name in his ear, and he will know you have come from me. Remember, you are answerable for him; but change your face. La Candele and the others must not recognise in you the wine-shop bully; that would spoil all. What have you on under that blouse, a commissionaire's dress?

"That will do; now change the face."

Palot pulled out a small parcel from his pocket, from which he extracted a red beard and wig, and, going to the mirror, adjusted them with dexterous activity; and, in a few minutes, went up to his master, who was waiting, saying,—

"How will this do?"

"Not bad, not bad," returned Lecoq; "and now to your work."

"Where shall I find him?" asked Palot.

"Somewhere near Mascarin's den, for I advised him not to give up playing the spy too suddenly."

Palot was off like the wind, and when he reached the Rue Montmartre, he caught sight of the person who had been entrusted to his care.

Andre was walking slowly along, thinking of Lecoq's cautions, when a young man, with his arm in a sling, overtook him, going in the same direction as he was. Andre was sure that it was Paul, and as he knew that he could not be recognised, he passed him in his turn, and saw that it was indeed the Paul so much regretted by Zora.

"I will find out where he goes to," thought Andre.

He followed, and saw him enter the house of M. Rigal. Two women were gossiping near the door, and Andre heard one of them say,—

"That is the young fellow who is going to marry Flavia, the banker's daughter."

Paul, therefore, was to marry the daughter of the chief of the gang. Should he tell Lecoq this? But, of course, the detective knew it.

Time was passing, and Andre felt that he had but little space to gain the house that Gandelu was building in the Champs Elysees, if he wished to ask hospitality from his friend Vignol.

He found all the workmen there, and not one of them recognised him when he asked for Vignol.

"He is engaged up there," said one. "Take the staircase to the left."

The chief part of the ornamental work was in front, and it was there that the little hut which Tantaine had pointed out to Toto Chupin was erected. Vignol was in it, and was utterly surprised when Andre made himself known, for he did not recognise him under his strange disguise.

"It is nothing," returned the young man cautiously, as Vignol paused for an explanation; "only a little love affair."

"Do you expect to win a girl's heart by making such a guy of yourself?" asked his friend with a laugh.

"Hush! I will explain matters later on. Can you give me shelter for a night or two?"

He stopped himself, turned terribly pale, and listened intently. He fancied he had heard a woman's scream, and his own name uttered.

"Andre, it is I—your Sabine; help!"

Quick as lightning Andre rushed to the window, opened it, and leaned out to discover from whence those sounds came.

The young miscreant, Toto Chupin, had too fatally earned the note with which Tantaine had bribed him. The whole of the front of the window gave way with a loud crash, and Andre was hurled into space.

The hut was at least sixty feet from the pavement, and the fall was the more appalling because the body of Andre struck some of the intervening scaffolding first, and thence bounced off, until the unhappy young man fell with a dull thud, bleeding and senseless in the street.

Nearly three hundred persons in the Champs Elysees witnessed this hideous sight; for, at Vignol's cry, everyone had stopped, and, frozen with horror, had not missed one detail of the grim tragedy.

In an instant a crowd was collected round the poor, inert mass of humanity which lay motionless in a pool of blood. But two workmen, roused by Vignol's shrieks, were soon on the spot, and pushed their way through the crowd of persons who were gazing with a morbid curiosity on the man who had fallen from a height of sixty feet.

Andre gave no sign of life. His face was dreadfully bruised, his eyes were closed, and a stream of blood poured from his mouth, as Vignol raised his friend's head upon his knee.

"He is dead!" cried the lookers on. "No one could survive such a fall."

"Let us take him to the Hospital Beaujon!" exclaimed Vignol. "We are close by there."

An ambulance was speedily procured, and the workmen, placing their insensible friend carefully in it, asked permission to carry him to the hospital.

One curious event had excited the attention of some of the lookers on. Just as Andre fell, a *commissaire* had rushed forward and seized a woman. She was one of the class of unfortunates who frequent the Champs Elysees, and she it was who had uttered the cry that had lured Andre to destruction. The woman made an effort to escape, but Palot, for it was he, caught her arm.

"Not a word," said he sternly. The wretched creature seemed in abject terror, and obeyed him.

"Why did you cry out?" asked he.

"I do not know."

"It is a lie!"

"No, it is true; a gentleman came up to me, and said, '*Madame*, if you will cry out now, Andre, it is I—your Sabine; help! I will give you two *louis*.' Of course I agreed. He gave me the fifty *francs*, and I did as he asked me."

"What was this man like?"

"He was tall, old, and very shabby and dirty, with glasses on. I never set eyes on him before."

"Do you know," returned the *commissaire* sternly, "that the words you have uttered have caused the death of the poor fellow who has just fallen from the house?"

"Why did he not take more care?" asked she indifferently.

Palot, with an angry gesture, handed her over to a police-constable.

"Take her to the station-house," said he, "and do not lose sight of her, for she will be a most important witness at a trial that must soon come on."

"What the woman says is true," muttered Palot. "She did not know what she was doing, and it was Tantaine that gave her the two coins. He shall pay for this; but certainly, if the whole gang are collared, it won't bring the poor young fellow to life."

He had, however, not much time for reflection, for he had to gather up every link of evidence. How was it that this accident had occurred? The frame of the window had fallen out with Andre, and lay in fragments on the pavement. He picked up one of the pieces, and at once saw what had been done; the woodwork had been sawed almost in two, and the putty with which the marks of the cuts had been concealed still clung to the wood. Palot called one of the workmen, who appeared to be more intelligent than his fellows, pointed out the marks to him, and bade him gather up the fragments and put them in some place of security.

This duty being accomplished, Palot joined the crowd; but he was too late, for Andre had been taken away to the hospital. He looked around to see if there was anyone from whom he could gain information, and suddenly perceived on a bench someone whom he had often followed. It was Toto Chupin, no longer clad in the squalid rags of a day or two back. He was dressed in gorgeous array, but his face was livid, his eyes wild, and his lips kept moving convulsively, for he was a victim to a novel sensation—the pangs of remorse—and was meditating whether he should not go to the nearest police-station and give himself up, so that he might revenge himself on Tantaine, who had made him a murderer. For a moment the idea of arresting Toto passed through Palot's mind, but he, after a moment's thought, muttered,—

"No; that would never do. We should risk losing the whole gang. Besides, he can't get away. I may even have committed an error in arresting that woman. My master will say that I am not to be trusted. He placed one of his friends in my charge, and this is what has happened. I knew that the young man's life was in deadly peril, and yet I let him enter a house in the course of erection; why, I might as well have cut his throat myself."

In a terrible state of anxiety, Palot presented himself at the hospital, and asked for the young man who had just been brought in.

"You mean Number 17?" returned one of the assistant-surgeons. "He is in a most critical state; we fear internal injuries, fracture of the skull, and—in fact, we fear everything."

It was two days before Andre recovered consciousness. It was midnight when he first woke again to the realities of life. At a glance he guessed where he was. He felt pain when he endeavoured to turn over, but he could move his legs and one arm.

"How long have I been here, I wonder?" he thought.

He tried to think, but he was weak, and thoughts would not come at his command, and in a few seconds he dropped off to sleep again; and when he awoke, it was broad day; the ward was full of life and motion, for it was the hour of the house surgeon's visit. He was a young man still, with a cheerful face, followed by the band of students. He went from bed to bed, explaining cases, and cheering up the sufferers. When Andre's turn came, the surgeon told him that his shoulder was put out, his arm broken in two places, a bad cut on his head, while his body was one mass of bruises; but, for all that, he was in luck to have got off so easily.

Andre listened to him with but a vague understanding of his meaning, for, with the return of reason, the remembrance of Sabine had come, and he asked himself what would become of her while he was confined to his bed in the hospital. As this thought passed through his mind, he uttered a faint groan. One of the students, a stout person, with red whiskers, a white tie, and a rather shabby hat, who looked as if he had just arrived from the country, stepped up to his bed, and leaning over the patient, murmured, "Lecoq." Andre opened his eyes wide at the name.

"M. Lecoq," gasped he, wondering at the excellence of the disguise.

"Hush, who knows who is watching us? I come to give your mind ease, which will do you more good than all the doctor's stuff. Without in any way committing you, I have seen M. de Mussidan, and have furnished him with a valid excuse for postponing his daughter's marriage for another month. You must remain here; you could not be in a place of greater security; but even here you cannot be too cautious. Eat nothing that is not given you by someone who utters the word 'Lecoq.' M. Gandelu will certainly call to see you. If you want to see or write to me, the patient on your right will manage that; he is one of my men. You shall have news every day; but be patient and prudent."

"I can wait now," answered the young man, "because I have hope."

"Ah," murmured Lecoq, as he moved softly away, "is not hope the true secret of life and happiness?"

Chapter 61: The Day of Reckoning

M. Lecoq enjoined prudence and caution on Andre, and the utmost care on the part of his agents, because he was fully aware of the skill and cunning of the adversary with whom he had to cope.

"You should not talk or make a noise," he would say, "when you are fighting."

He could now prove that the head of this association, the man who concealed his identity under a threefold personality, was the instigator of a murder. But he did not intend to make use of this discovery at once, for he had sworn that he would take the whole gang, and his proceedings had been so carefully conducted that his victims did not for a moment suspect the net that was closing around them. The day after the accident to Andre, Mascarin sent an anonymous communication to the head of the police, giving up Toto as the author of the crime, and saying where he could be found.

"Of course," thought this wily plotter, "Toto will denounce Tantaine, but that worthy man is dead and buried, and I think that even the sharpest agents of the police will be unable to effect his resurrection."

Mascarin had carefully consumed in a large fire every particle of the tattered garments that Tantaine had been in the habit of wearing, and laughed merrily as he watched the columns of sombre smoke roll upwards.

"Look for him as much as you please," laughed he. "Old Daddy Tantaine has flown up the chimney."

The next business was to suppress Mascarin; this was a more difficult operation. Few would care to inquire about Tantaine, but Mascarin was well known as the head of a prosperous business; his disappearance would create a sensation, and the police would take up the matter. His best course would be to conduct matters openly, and sell his business on the plea of family affairs causing him to retire. He easily found a purchaser, and in twenty-four hours the matter had been arranged.

The night before handing over the business to his successor Mascarin had much to do. Assisted by Beaumarchef, he carried into Martin Rigal's private office the papers with which the Registry Office was crammed. This removal was effected by means of a door marked by a panel between Mascarin's office and the banker's private room; and when the last scrap of paper had been removed, Mascarin pointed

473

out a heap of bricks and a supply of mortar to his faithful adherent.

"Wall up this door," said he.

It was a long and wearisome task, but it was at length completed, and by rubbing soot and dust over the new work it lost its appearance of freshness. The evening before Beaumarchef had received twelve thousand *francs* on the express condition that he would start at once for America, and the leave-taking between him and the master he had so faithfully served was a most affecting one. He knew hardly anything of the diabolical plots going on around him, and was the only innocent person in that house of crime.

Mascarin was in haste to depart; he had annihilated Tantaine in order to free himself from Toto. Mascarin was about to disappear, and he contemplated retaining his third personality, and in it to pass away the remainder of his life honoured and respected; but he must first induct his successor into his business; and he went through the books with him, and explained all the practical working of the machinery. This took him nearly all day, and it was getting late when his luggage was put on a cab which he had in waiting. A new plate had already been placed on the door: *J. Robinet, late B. Mascarin.*

Knowing that he must carry out the deception completely, Mascarin drove to the western railway station, and took a ticket for Rouen. He felt rather uncomfortable, for he feared that he was being watched, and he made up his mind not to leave a single trace behind him. At Rouen he abandoned his luggage, which he had taken care should afford no clue as to ownership, he also relinquished his beard and spectacles, and returned to Paris as the well-known banker, Martin Rigal, the pretty Flavia's father, having, as he thought, obliterated Mascarin as completely as he had done Tantaine; but he had not noticed in the train with him a very dark young man with piercing eyes, who looked like the traveller of some respectable commercial firm.

As soon as he reached his home, and had tenderly embraced his daughter, he went to the private room of Martin Rigal, and opened it with the key that never left his person, and then gazed at a large rough mass of brickwork which disfigured one side of the room, and which was the remains of the wall that erewhile had been so hastily erected in the Office of the Servants' Registry.

"This won't do," muttered he; "it must be plastered, and then re-papered."

He picked up the bits of brick and plaster that lay on the floor, and threw them into the fire, and then pushed a large screen in front of the rough brickwork. He had just finished his work when Hortebise entered the room, with his perpetually smiling face.

"Now, you unbeliever," cried Mascarin gaily, "is not fortune within our grasp? Tantaine and Mascarin are dead, or rather, they never existed. Beaumarchef is on his way to America, La Candele will be in London in a week, and now we may enjoy our millions."

"Heaven grant it," said the doctor piously.

"Pooh, pooh! we have nothing more to fear, as you would have known had you gone into the case as thoroughly as I have done. Who was the enemy whom we had most need to dread? Why, Andre. He certainly is not dead, but he is laid up for some weeks, and that is enough. Besides, he has given up the game, for one of my men who managed to get into the hospital says that he has not received a visitor or dispatched a letter for the last fifteen days."

"But he had friends."

"Pshaw! friends always forget you! Why, where was M. de Breulh-Faverlay?"

"It is the racing season, and he is a fixture in his stables."

"Madame de Bois Arden?"

"The new fashions are sufficient for her giddy head."

"M. Gandelu?"

"He has his son's affairs to look after and there is no one else of any consequence."

"And how about young Gandelu?"

"Oh! he has yielded to Tantaine's winning power, and has made it up with Rose, and the turtle doves have taken wing for Florence."

But the doctor was still dissatisfied. "I am uneasy about the Mussidans," said he.

"And pray why? De Croisenois has been very well received. I don't say that Mademoiselle Sabine has exactly jumped into his arms, but she thanks him every evening for the flowers he sends in the morning, and you can't expect more than that."

"I wish the count had not put off the marriage. Why did he do so?"

"It annoys me, too; but we can't have everything; set your mind at rest."

By this time the banker had contrived to reassure the doctor.

"Besides," he added, "everything is going on well, even our Tafila mines. I have taxed our people, according to their means, from one to twenty thousand *francs*, and we are certain of a million."

The doctor rubbed his hands, and a delicious prospect of enjoyments stretched out before him.

"I have seen Catenac," continued Martin Rigal. "He has returned from Vendome, and the Duke de Champdoce is wild with hope and expectation, and is on the path which he thinks will take him to his son."

"And how about Perpignan?"

Mascarin laughed.

"Perpignan is just as much a dupe as the duke is; he thinks absolutely that he has discovered all the clues that I myself placed on his road. Before, however, they have quite concluded their investigations, Paul will be my daughter's husband and Flavia the future Duchess of Champdoce, with an income that a monarch might envy."

He paused, for there was a light tap on the door, and Flavia entered. She bowed to the doctor, and, with the graceful movement of a bird, perched herself upon her father's knee, and, throwing her arms round his neck, kissed him again and again.

"This is a very nice little preface," said the banker with a forced smile. "The favour is granted in advance, for, of course, this means that you have come to ask one."

The girl shook her head, and returned in the tone of one addressing a naughty child,—

"Oh, you bad papa! Am I in the habit of selling my kisses? I am sure that I have only to ask and to have."

"Of course not, only—"

"I came to tell you that dinner was ready, and that Paul and I are both very hungry; and I only kissed you because I loved you; and if I had to choose a father again, out of the whole it would be you."

He smiled fondly.

"But for the last six weeks," said he, "you have not loved me so well."

"No," returned she with charming simplicity, "not for so long— nearly for fifteen days perhaps."

"And yet it is more than a month since the good doctor brought a certain young man to dinner."

Flavia uttered a frank, girlish laugh.

"I love you dearly," said she, "but especially for one thing."

"And what is that, pray?"

"Ah! that is the secret; but I will tell it you for all that. It is only within the last fortnight that I have found out how really good you have been, and how much trouble you took in bringing Paul to me;

but to think that you should have to put on those ugly old clothes, that nasty beard and those spectacles."

At these words the banker started so abruptly to his feet that Flavia nearly fell to the ground.

"What do you mean by this?" said he.

"Do you suppose a daughter does not know her father? You might deceive others, but I—"

"Flavia, I do not comprehend your meaning."

"Do you mean to tell me," asked she, "that you did not come to Paul's rooms the day I was there?"

"Are you crazy? Listen to me."

"No, I will not; you must not tell me fibs. I am not a fool; and when you went out with the doctor, I listened at the door, and I heard a few words you said; and that isn't all, for when I got here, I hid myself and I saw you come into this room."

"But you said nothing to anyone, Flavia?"

"No, certainly not."

Rigal breathed a sigh of relief.

"Of course I do not count Paul," continued the girl, "for he is the same as myself."

"Unhappy child!" exclaimed the banker in so furious a voice, and with such a threatening gesture of the hand, that for the first time in her life Flavia was afraid of her father.

"What have I done?" asked she, the tears springing to her eyes. "I only said to Paul that we should be terribly ungrateful if we did not worship him; for you don't know what he does for us. Why, he even dresses up in rags, and goes to see you."

Hortebise, who up to this time had not said a word, now interfered.

"And what did Paul say?" asked he.

"Paul? Oh, nothing for a moment. Then he cried out, 'I see it all now,' and laughed as if he would have gone into a fit."

"Did you not understand, my poor child, what this laugh means? Paul thinks that you have been my accomplice, and believes that it was in obedience to your orders that I went to look for him."

"Well, and suppose he does?"

"A man like Paul never loves a woman who has run after him; and no matter how great her beauty may be, will always consider that she has thrown herself in his path. He will accept all her devotion, and make no more return than a stone or a wooden idol would do. You cannot see this, and God grant that it may be long before the bandage is removed from your eyes. Can you not read the quality of this foolish boy, who has not a manly instinct in him?"

"Enough!" she cried, "enough! I am not such a coward as to allow you to insult my husband."

He shuddered at the thought that his words might cost him his daughter's love, but Hortebise interposed by putting his arm round Flavia's waist and leading her from the room. When he returned, he observed,—

"I cannot understand your anger. It seems to me that all recrimination is most indiscreet, for you can at any moment break off this marriage."

"Do you think it is nothing for me to be at the mercy of that cowardly wretch, Paul?"

"Not more so than you are by the foolish weakness of your daughter. Is not Paul our accomplice? And are we any more compromised because he has discovered the secret of your triple personality?"

"Ah! you have not a father's feelings. Up till now Paul did not know that I was Mascarin, and believed me to be the victim of blackmailers. As a dupe he respected me, as an accomplice he will scorn me. This disastrous marriage must be hastened."

Paul and Flavia's marriage took place at the end of the next week, and Paul left his simple bachelor abode to take possession of the magnificent suite of rooms prepared for him by the banker in his house in the Rue Montmartre. The change was great, but Paul was no longer surprised at anything. He did not feel the faintest tinge of remorse; he only feared one thing, and that was that by some blunder he might compromise his future, when the eventful day arrived which would give him the social position and standing of heir to a dukedom.

When, however, the Duke de Champdoce came, accompanied by Perpignan, the young imposter rose to the level of his masters, and played his part with most consummate skill. The duke, whose life had been one long scene of misery, and who had so cruelly expiated the sins of his youth, seemed to have become suddenly lenient; and had Paul obeyed him, he would at once have established himself with his young wife at the Hotel de Champdoce, but Martin Rigal put a veto upon this, for he was not quite satisfied that his son-in-law was really the heir to the Champdoce dukedom; and finally it was agreed that the duke should come to breakfast the next morning and take away Paul. Eleven was the hour fixed, but the duke appeared at the banker's house at ten, where he, Catenac, Hortebise, and Paul were assembled together in solemn conclave.

"Now, papa," said Flavia, who kept her father on thorns by her gay and frolicsome criticisms, "you will no longer blame me for falling in love with a poor Bohemian, for you see that he is a Champdoce, and that his father possesses millions."

The duke was now seated on the sofa, holding the hand of the young man whom he believed to be his son tightly in his. The duchess, to whom he had given a hint of what was going on, had been taken seriously ill from over-excitement, but had recovered herself a little, and the duke was describing this when he was suddenly interrupted by a series of full and heavy blows struck upon the other side of the wall of the room. A pickaxe was evidently at work. The whole house was shaken by the violence of the attack, and a screen, which stood near the spot, was thrown down.

The plotters gazed upon each other with pale and terror-stricken faces, for it was evident that the fresh brick wall, the work of Mascarin and Beaumarchef, was being destroyed. The duke sat in perfect amazement, for the alarm of his host and his friends was plainly evident. He could feel Paul's hand tremble in his, but could not understand why work evidently going on in the next house could cause such feelings of alarm. Flavia was the only one who had no suspicion, and she remarked, "Dear me! I should like to know the meaning of this disturbance."

"I will send and inquire," said her father; but scarcely had he opened the door than he retreated with a wild expression of terror in his face, and his arms stretched out in front of him, as though to bar the approach of some terrible spectre. In the doorway stood an eminently respectable-looking gentleman, wearing a pair of gold-rimmed spectacles, and behind him a commissary of police, girt with his official scarf, while farther back still were half a dozen police officers.

"M. Lecoq," cried the three confederates in one breath, while through their minds flashed the same terrible idea—"We are lost."

The celebrated detective advanced slowly into the room, curiously watching the group collected there. There was an air of entire satisfaction visible on his countenance.

"Aha!" he said, "I was right, it seems. I was sure that I was making no mistake in rapping at the other side of the wall. I knew that it would be heard in here."

By this time, however, the banker had, to all outward appearance, regained his self-command.

"What do you want here?" asked he insolently. "What is the meaning of this intrusion?"

"This gentleman will explain," returned Lecoq, stepping aside to make way for the commissary of police to come forward. "But, to shorten matters, I may tell you that I have obtained a warrant for your arrest, Martin Rigal, *alias* Tantaine, *alias* Mascarin."

"I don't understand you!"

"Indeed. Do you think that Tantaine has cleaned his hands so completely that not a drop of Andre's blood clings to the fingers of Martin Rigal?"

"On my word, you are speaking in riddles."

A bland smile passed over Lecoq's face as, drawing a folded letter from his pocket, he answered,—

"Perhaps you are acquainted with the handwriting of your daughter. Well, then, listen to what she wrote not so very long ago to the very Paul who is sitting on the sofa there.

My Dearest Paul,—
We should be guilty of the deepest ingratitude if—

"Enough! Enough!" cried the banker in a hoarse voice. "Lost, lost, lost! My own child has been my ruin!"

The calmest of the conspirators was now the one who was generally the first to take alarm, and this was the genial Doctor Hortebise. When he recognised Lecoq, he had gently opened his locket and taken from it a small pellet of greyish-coloured paste, and, holding it between his fingers, had waited until his leader should declare that all hope was gone.

In the meantime Lecoq turned towards Catenac.

"And you too are included in this warrant," said he.

Catenac, perhaps owing to his legal training, made no reply to Lecoq, but addressing the commissary, observed,—

"I am the victim of a most unpleasant mistake, but my position—"

"The warrant is quite regular," returned the commissary. "You can see it if you desire."

"No, it is not necessary. I will only ask you to conduct me to the magistrate who issued it, and in five minutes all will be explained."

"Do you think so?" asked Lecoq in a quiet tone of sarcasm. "You have not heard, I can see, of what took place yesterday. A labourer, in the course of his work, discovers the remains of a newly-born infant, wrapped in a silk handkerchief and a shawl. The police soon set inquiries on foot, and have found the mother—a girl named Clarisse."

Had not Lecoq suddenly grasped Catenac's arm, the lawyer would have flown at Martin Rigal's throat.

"Villain, traitor!" panted he, "you have sold me!"

"My papers have been stolen," faltered the banker.

He now saw that the blows struck upon the other side of the wall were merely a trick, for Lecoq had thought that a little preliminary fright would render them more amenable to reason.

Hortebise still looked on calmly; he knew that the game was lost.

"I belong to a respectable family," thought he, "and I will not bring dishonour upon it. I have no time to lose."

As he spoke he placed the contents of the locket between his lips and swallowed them.

"Ah," murmured he, as he did so, "with my constitution and digestion, it is really hard to end thus."

No one had noticed the doctor's movements, for Lecoq had moved the screen, and was showing the commissary a hole which had been made in the wall large enough for the body of a man to pass through. But a sudden sound cut these investigations short, for Hortebise had fallen to the ground, and was struggling in a series of terrible convulsions.

"How stupid of me not to have foreseen this," exclaimed Lecoq. "He has poisoned himself; let someone run for a doctor. Take him into another room and lay him on a bed."

While these orders were being carried out, Catenac was removed to a cab which was in waiting, and Martin Rigal seemed to have lapsed into a state of moody imbecility. Suddenly he started to his feet, crying,—

"My daughter Flavia! yes, her name is Flavia, what is to become of her? She has no fortune, and she is married to a man who can never provide for her. My child will perhaps starve. Oh, horrible thought!"

The man's strong mind had evidently given way, and his love for his child and the hideous future that lay before her had broken down the barrier that divides reason from insanity. He was secured by the officers, raving and struggling. When Lecoq was left alone with the duke, Paul and Flavia, he cast a glimpse of pity at the young girl, who had crouched down in a corner, and evidently hardly understood the terrible scene that had just passed.

"Your Grace," said he, turning to the duke, "you have been the victim of a foul conspiracy; this young man is not your son; he is Paul

481

Violaine, and is the son of a poor woman who kept a petty haberdashery shop in the provinces."

The miserable young fool began to bluster, and attempted to deny this statement; but Lecoq opened the door, and Rose appeared in a most becoming costume. Paul now made no effort to continue his protestations, but throwing himself on his knees, in whining accents confessed the whole fraud and pleaded for mercy, promising to give evidence against his accomplices.

"Do not despair, your Grace," said Lecoq, as he conducted the duke to his carriage; "this certainly is not your son; but *I* have found him, and tomorrow, if you like, you shall be introduced to him."

Chapter 62: Every Man to His Own Place

Obedient to the wishes of M. Lecoq, Andre resigned himself to a lengthy sojourn at the Hospital de Beaujon, and had even the courage to affect that state of profound indifference that had deceived Mascarin. The pretended sick man in the next bed to his told him all that had taken place, but the days seemed to be interminable, and he was beginning to lose patience, when one morning he received a letter which caused a gleam of joy to pass through his heart.

"All is right," wrote Lecoq. "Danger is at an end. Ask the house surgeon for leave to quit the hospital. Dress yourself smartly. You will find me waiting at the doors.—L."

Andre was not quite convalescent, for he might have to wear his arm in a sling for many weeks longer; but these considerations did not deter him. He now dressed himself in a suit which he had sent for to his rooms, and about nine o'clock he left the hospital.

He stood upon the steps inhaling deep draughts of the fresh air, and then began to wonder where the strange personage was to whom he owed his life. While he was deliberating what to do, an open carriage drew up before the door of the hospital.

"You have come at last," exclaimed Andre, rushing up to the gentleman who alighted from it. "I was getting quite anxious."

"I am about five minutes late," returned Lecoq; "but I was detained," and then, as Andre began to pour out his thanks, he added, "Get into the carriage; I have a great deal to say to you."

Andre obeyed, and as he did so, he detected something strange in the expression of his companion's face.

"What!" remarked Lecoq, "do you see by my face that I have something to tell you? You are getting quite a keen observer. Well,

I have, indeed, for I have passed the night going through Mascarin's papers, and I have just gone through a painful scene—I may say, one of the most painful that I have ever witnessed. The intellect of Mascarin," said he, "has given way under the tremendous pressure put upon it. The ruling passion of the villain's life was his love for his daughter. He imagines that Flavia and Paul are without a *franc* and in want of bread; he thinks that he continually hears his daughter crying to him for help. Then, on his knees, he entreats the warder to let him out, if only for a day, swearing that he will return as soon as he has succoured his child.

"Then, when his prayer is refused, he bursts into a frenzied rage and tears at his door, howling like an infuriated animal; and this state may last to the end of his life, and every minute in it be a space of intolerable torture. Doctor Hortebise is dead; but the poison upon which he relied betrayed him, and he suffered agonies for twenty-four hours. Catenac will fight to the bitter end, but the proofs are against him, and he will be convicted of infanticide. In Rigal's papers I have found evidence against Perpignan, Verminet and Van Klopen, who will all certainly hear something about penal servitude. Nothing has been settled yet about Toto Chupin, for it must be remembered that he came and gave himself up."

"And what about Croisenois?"

"His Company will be treated like any other attempt to extort money by swindling, and the *marquis* will be sent to prison for two months, and the money paid for shares returned to the dupes, and that, I think, is all that I have to tell you, except that by tomorrow M. Gandelu will receive back the bills to which his son affixed a forged signature. And now," continued Lecoq, after a short pause, "the time has come for me to tell you why, at our first interview, I saluted you as the heir of the Duke de Champdoce. I had guessed your history, but it was only last night I heard all the details."

Then the detective gave a brief but concise account of the manuscript that Paul had read aloud. He did not tell much, however, but passed lightly over the acts of the Duke de Champdoce and Madame de Mussidan, for he did not wish Andre to cease to respect either his father or the mother of Sabine. The story was just concluded as the carriage drew up at the corner of the Rue de Matignon.

"Get down here," said Lecoq, "and mind and don't hurt your arm."

Andre obeyed mechanically.

"And now," went on Lecoq, "listen to me. The Count and Countess de Mussidan expect you to breakfast and here is the note they handed to me for you. Come back to your studio by four o'clock, and I will then introduce you to your father; but till then, remember, absolute silence."

Andre was completely bewildered with his unexpected happiness. He walked instinctively to the Hotel de Mussidan and rang the bell. The intense civility of the footmen removed any misgivings that he might have left, and, as he entered the dining-room, he darted back, for face to face with him was the portrait of Sabine which he had himself painted. At that moment the count came forward to meet him with extended hands.

"Diana," said he to his wife, "this is our daughter's future husband." He then took Sabine's hand, which he laid in Andre's.

The young artist hardly dared raise his eyes to Sabine's face; when he did so, his heart grew very sad, for the poor girl was but a shadow of her former self.

"You have suffered terribly," said he tenderly.

"Yes," answered she, "and I should have died had it lasted much longer."

Andre had the greatest difficulty in refraining from telling his secret to his beloved, and it was with even more difficulty that he tore himself away at half-past three.

He had not been five minutes in his studio when there was a knock at the door, and Lecoq entered, followed by an elderly gentleman of aristocratic and haughty appearance. It was the Duke de Champdoce.

"This gentleman," said the duke, with a gesture of his hand towards Lecoq, "will have told you that certain circumstances rendered it expedient, according to my ideas, that I should not acknowledge you as my heir, but my son. The fault that I then committed has been cruelly expiated. I am not forty-eight; look at me."

The duke looked at least sixty.

"My sins," continued the duke, "still pursue me. Today, in spite of all my desires, I cannot claim you as my legitimate son, for the law only permits me to give you my name and fortune by exercising the right of adoption."

Andre made no reply, and the duke went on with evident hesitation,—

"You can certainly institute proceedings against me for the recovery of your rights, but—"

"Ah!" interrupted the young man, "really, what sort of person do you think I am? Do you believe me capable of dishonouring your name before I assumed it?"

The duke drew a deep breath of relief. Andre's manner had checked and restrained him, for it was frigid and glacial to a degree. What a difference there was between the haughty mien of Andre and the gushing effusiveness of Paul!

"Will you permit me," asked Andre, "to address a few words to you?"

"A few words?"

"Yes. I do not like to use the word 'conditions,' but I think that you will understand what I mean. My daily toil for bread gave me neither the means nor the leisure which I required to cultivate my art, for that is a profession that I could never give up."

"You will be certainly your own master."

Andre paused, as if to reflect.

"This is not all I had to say," he continued at last. "I love and am loved by a pure and beautiful girl; our marriage is arranged, and I think—"

"I think," broke in the duke, "that you could not love anyone who was not a fit bride for a member of our family."

"But I did not belong to this family yesterday. Be at ease, however, for she is worthy of a Champdoce. I am engaged to Sabine de Mussidan."

A deadly paleness overspread the duke's face as he heard this name.

"Never," said he. "Never; I would rather see you dead at my feet."

"And I would gladly suffer ten thousand deaths than give her up."

"Suppose I refuse my consent? Suppose that I forbid—"

"You have no claim to exercise paternal authority over me; this can only be purchased by years of tender care. Duke de Champdoce, I owe you nothing. Leave me to myself, as you have hitherto done, and all will be simplified."

The duke reflected. Must he give up his son, who had been restored to him by such a series of almost miraculous chances, or must he see him married to Diana's daughter? Either alternative appeared to him to be equally disagreeable.

"I will not yield on the point," said he. "Besides, the countess would never give her consent. She hates me as much as I hate her."

M. Lecoq, who had up to this moment looked on in silence, now thought it time to interpose.

"I think," remarked he blandly, "that I shall have no difficulty in obtaining the consent of Madame de Mussidan."

The duke, at these words, threw open his arms.

"Come, my son!" said he. "All shall be as you desire."

That night, Marie, Duchess de Champdoce, experienced happiness for the first time in the affection and caresses of a son who had been so long lost to her, and seemed to throw off the heavy burden that had so heavily pressed her down beneath its own weight.

When Madame de Mussidan heard that Andre was Norbert's son, she declared that nothing could induce her to give her consent to his marriage with her daughter; but among Mascarin's papers Lecoq had discovered the packet containing the compromising correspondence between the Duke de Champdoce and herself. The detective handed this over to her, and, in her gratitude, she promised to give up all further opposition to the match.

Lecoq always denied that this act came under the head of blackmailing.

Andre and Sabine took up their residence after marriage at the Château de Mussidan, which had been magnificently restored and decorated. They seldom leave it, for they love it for its vicinity to the leafy groves, in which they first learned that they had given their hearts to each other. And Andre frequently points out the unfinished work on the balcony, which was the occasion of his first visit to the Château de Mussidan. He says that he will complete it as soon as he has time, but it is doubtful whether he will ever find leisure to do this for a long time, for before the new year comes there is every chance of there being a baptism at the little chapel at Bevron.